DISCARD

The Intriguers

PASSAGE OF ARMS → *Gold dagger award*

STATE OF SIEGE

THE SCHIRMER INHERITANCE

JUDGMENT ON DELTCHEV

The Intriguers

FOUR SUPERB

NOVELS OF SUSPENSE BY

Eric Ambler

NEW YORK: *Alfred · A · Knopf*

THIS IS A BORZOI BOOK,
PUBLISHED BY ALFRED A. KNOPF, INC.

FIRST COLLECTED EDITION

PASSAGE OF ARMS
Published March 7, 1960

STATE OF SIEGE
Published September 17, 1956
Published in Great Britain under the title *The Night Comers* by William Heinemann, Ltd.

THE SCHIRMER INHERITANCE
Published July 20, 1953

JUDGMENT ON DELTCHEV
Published March 19, 1951

Contents

PASSAGE OF ARMS

passage . . .

> 9. A mutual act or transaction; something that goes on between two persons mutually; a negotiation; an interchange or exchange of vows, endearments, or the like; an interchange or exchange of blows; encounter; altercation; a fencing, as in argument; as, a *passage* at or of arms.

> *Webster's New International Dictionary*

PASSAGE OF ARMS

CHAPTER I

ALL THAT MR. WRIGHT, the rubber-estate manager, ever knew of the business was that an army patrol had ambushed a band of terrorists within a mile of his bungalow, that five months later his Indian clerk, Girija Krishnan, had reported the theft of three tarpaulins from the curing sheds, and that three years after that someone had removed the wheels from an old scooter belonging to one of his children. As it never occurred to him to look for a possible connection between the three incidents, he remained unaware even of that knowledge. In Malaya, at that time, there were more important facts to ponder and attempt to correlate. Stolen tarpaulins and missing scooter wheels were trivial mysteries; and, although the ambush itself was not forgotten, it was remembered more for its proximity than its novelty.

Mr. and Mrs. Wright had been at breakfast when they heard the sound of firing. It began with a flurry of submachine-gun bursts and continued intermittently for about two minutes.

The truck which took the tappers out to the work areas had not yet left the compound; and, although there was a lot of shouting and excitement, there was no panic and little confusion. Almost before the firing had ceased, the barbed-wire barricades were in position and the inner defense posts manned. During the long silence that followed, Mrs. Wright, a woman of character, calmed the servants and ordered fresh toast and tea so that she and her husband could finish breakfast.

At eight-thirty the patrol appeared: fifteen Malay infantrymen under a British subaltern, and two R.A.F. radio operators. They had been in the jungle for several weeks and their success that morning would probably earn them a rest period. They were smiling and talking as they toiled up the steep track to the compound.

Shortly after they arrived, Girija was summoned to the bungalow. As he went up the veranda steps he could see the officer, a downy, blue-eyed Englishman with paratroop wings on his jungle-green bush shirt. Mrs. Wright was pouring him a cup of tea.

"All Chinese, and on their way to mine the main road, by the look of things," he was saying. "We got the lot."

"Nice work," said Mr. Wright.

"Could have been better, sir." The young officer grinned. "They were all killed outright. You can't ask them questions about their chums when they're dead."

Mr. Wright chuckled and then, seeing his clerk waiting outside, beckoned him in.

"Girija, this is Lieutenant Haynes. He's just wiped out a gang of terrorists. I said we'd let him have some men to help bury them. Will you see to it?"

"Certainly, sir." Girija turned with a slight bow to the officer.

Lieutenant Haynes nodded genially. "I left two men there on guard," he said. "They'll give your chaps a hand if you send extra spades. The ground's quite soft, I think. Shouldn't take long. If you'll speak to my sergeant, he'll detail a guide for you."

"Thank you, sir. I will make all necessary arrangements."

The officer's grin faded slightly. "Seen many dead terrorists around these parts?" he asked.

"No, sir. Have not had that pleasure."

"Well, mind you spread the good news."

"I understand, sir. Two men from each kampong?"

"That's the idea. And tell them they'll be seeing plenty more before we're done."

Girija smiled politely and withdrew to organize the burial party.

He was well aware of the reason for it. The Malay villages in the area had long been suspected by the authorities of aiding the Communist guerrillas with food and shelter. It was not that the villagers approved of the invaders, but simply that the savage reprisals that could follow any refusal of aid were more intimidating to contemplate than the possibility of having fines or other collective punishments imposed by the British. They were not warlike people; their villages were often isolated; the British forces were scattered. In the past, glib official assurances that the police and army were at last gaining the upper hand and able to protect the outlying areas from the terrorists had been given too often, and too often proved baseless. Now, the villagers believed only what they saw themselves, or what had been seen by their own people. Dead terrorists had to be shown to be dead. The burial party was in the nature of a morale-building or public-relations device.

Girija found the head tapper and explained what was wanted: two men from each of the four neighboring villages, and picks and shovels. Then he went to the Malay sergeant and secured a guide. Within twenty minutes the party was ready to move. The head tapper was obviously hoping to go with it, but Girija sent him off with the truck and the remaining men to the work areas. He had decided to take charge of the burial party himself.

The action had taken place in a deep gully carved out of the red laterite hillside by the monsoon rains, and flanked on both sides by bamboo thickets, tree ferns, and dense tangles of croton undergrowth. It was a natural route for men to use on that otherwise trackless hillside, and a perfect site for an ambush.

There were ten bodies there: four within a few feet of one another, and the rest scattered along the gully for a distance of some twenty-five yards. It was easy to see what had happened. Concealed in the undergrowth along both lips of the gully, the patrol had been able to open fire at point-blank range without fear of hitting each other or the smallest chance of missing the enemy below them. One or two of the dead men were lying in attitudes which suggested desperate split-second attempts to claw their way to cover behind the roots of a fallen tree. One had been hit in the back as he turned to run. One, the farthest away, had tried to return the patrol's fire; there were empty shells scattered on the ground by him; but he was as dead as the rest. Nobody in the patrol had been hit.

The two Malay soldiers left on guard were squatting on their heels by a Sterno fuel stove, heating cans of tea and smoking. They took no notice of the burial party. Beside them, on a ground sheet, were stacked the arms and equipment collected from the dead: machine pistols, boxes of ammunition and road mines, and canvas belts with pouches containing hand grenades.

The soldier who had guided the party from the compound joined his friends at the stove. Girija knew that they would not help with the digging unless he told them what Lieutenant Haynes had said; but he made no attempt to do so. During his brief inspection of the gully he had made two small discoveries. They had aroused his curiosity and made him wish to know more about the dead terrorists. He put the burial party to work and sat down on the ground nearby.

The first thing he had noted was the fact that, although the bodies had been searched and stripped of all arms and equipment, there had been no cooking utensils of any kind found on them. This meant almost certainly that they were within a day's marching distance of their camp; which meant, in turn, that they had probably been living off one or more of the four villages near the estate. They would be known, if only by sight, to at least two members of the burial party.

His second discovery had to do with the arms and equipment. He was sure that the machine pistols were new; not new in type necessarily, but newly acquired. His father had been a subahdar in the British army, and Girija had spent his childhood in barracks and cantonments. He knew the look of a new gun and how soon it acquired the patina of use from normal cleaning and handling. At least three of the machine pistols on the ground sheet had been so recently unpacked, and so little used and cleaned, that traces of brown preservative grease were still visible on them. The ammunition boxes, the mines, and the grenades were also new. The grenades were of an old type with cast-iron fragmentation cases; but the gray paint on them was fresh and the pins were clean and bright.

The gully was only partly shaded by the overhanging trees, and by eleven o'clock the sun was shining directly into it. The tappers were craftsmen, used to the careful work of milking rubber trees without damaging them. Digging graves on a hillside, and in ground which, despite Lieutenant Haynes' assurance, had proved to be rock hard, was not a job which they could be expected to tackle with enthusiasm. The excitement of the occasion and the sight of ten bloody corpses were novelties that had soon palled. By the time the third grave had been dug, most of the men had lost their customary good humor. Criticism began to be voiced of the soldiers squatting in the shade and drinking tea while others cleaned up the mess they had made. There was even an exchange of remarks, meant to be overheard, to the effect that the tuan's clerk might, without serious loss of face, enhance his already considerable popularity by taking a shovel and doing a bit of digging himself.

Girija was able to ignore this unworthy suggestion with equanimity. The tappers' complaints interested him for reasons other than their substance. He was almost certain now that he knew the area in which the band had made their headquarters. Only two of the burial party had remained cheerful. Malays were not good at concealing their emotions, and although these two were trying hard to conform to the mood of the others, their satisfaction with the turn of events and the task in which they were engaged kept showing through their scowls. Girija watched them dump one of the bodies into its grave with unmistakable gusto, and then glance round guiltily when they caught themselves grinning at one another.

The two men came from a village named Awang on a river three miles away to the west. Once there had been tin mining in the district, but falling yields and rising operating costs had made the mines uneconomic. The small labor force of Awang had been gradually absorbed by the rubber estates.

Girija had been to the village once or twice to pay sick benefits to the families of men in hospital, but he did not know it well. It was at the end of a secondary road which had degenerated in recent years to no more than a cycle track. Beyond the old tin workings the jungle-covered hills stretched all the way to the borders of Thailand. In that lush wilderness, small groups of disciplined men with minds and bodies adapted to the environment could remain healthy and mobile almost indefinitely. At that period it was impossible either to police the area effectively or to halt the stream of Chinese militants filtering down the peninsula from the north. Villages like Awang became staging points for the terrorist bands cautiously working their way southward toward the politically more sensitive areas of Selangor, Negri Sembilan, Malacca, and Johore. The men now being buried had probably made their camp within a mile or so of it, going in at night to receive food, gather information, browbeat the headman, and talk earnestly to potential recruits.

Girija walked over to the two tappers and stood watching them as they filled in the grave. They had fallen silent as he approached. After a moment or two he moved in closer.

"A good day's work," he remarked.

They looked at him warily.

He smiled. "The past buries itself."

That raised a sheepish grin.

"And honest men are free again," he added.

They went on working. The body was covered now.

"The tuan was pleased," Girija said thoughtfully; "pleased that these pigs were all foreigners. To him that proved the loyalty and courage of our men here."

They looked at him again. One of them mumbled: "The tuan is a father to us."

"It is unfortunate," Girija went on, "that the lieutenant tuan does not agree with him."

They stared at him in dismay.

Girija shrugged. "He said that this gang was new to the district. He said that a week was no test of loyalty."

He had them now. Dismay gave way to indignation.

The man who had spoken before spoke again. "The tuan was right," he said firmly. "The lieutenant tuan does not speak the truth."

Girija shrugged again. "It is not important."

"The lieutenant tuan is wrong," the man insisted. "It was many weeks."

Girija made sympathetic sounds.

"Many weeks," repeated the other man emphatically.

Girija spread out his hands. "It is not my business. Perhaps you should tell this to the lieutenant tuan." He saw the sudden panic in their eyes and went on smoothly: "Myself, I do not think it necessary, or wise. The pigs are dead. They are best forgotten."

"Yes, yes. It is best. We will forget."

Girija smiled benignly and moved away. He knew that they were watching him and wondering fearfully if he would betray them to the lieutenant. He had no intention of doing so; but there was no point in telling them that. They would not quite believe him; and in any case they had served their purpose. He had found out what he wanted to know.

ii

GIRIJA was born of Bengali parents at Cawnpore in the United Provinces of India. He had five sisters but no brothers. When he was six his father, the subahdar, went to London with a detachment of his regiment to march in the Coronation procession of King George the Sixth. During his stay the subahdar was taken on a conducted tour of the city, which included visits to the Tower of London, Westminster Abbey, the Houses of Parliament, the British Museum, the Law Courts, Battersea power station, and, for some obscure reason, a factory in Acton where bus bodies were made. He returned to India laden with souvenirs and fired with ambition for his only son. The Law Courts had particularly impressed him. Girija would become a lawyer or, failing that, a policeman.

Girija became neither. The subahdar was killed at the battle of Alamein, and Girija spent the next three years in a military orphanage at Benares. When the war ended, however, his mother wrote to a brother, who had a cotton-goods business in Singapore, explaining that she had only her widow's pension and asking if she might join him with the children. The prospect of securing this windfall of cheap labor appealed to the brother, and he replied sending passage money. In December 1946 the family sailed as deck passengers from Calcutta. With them went the subahdar's medals and the precious souvenirs of his visit to London: the Coronation mug, the picture postcards, the newspaper cuttings, the photographs, the ash tray from the warrant officers' mess at Chelsea Barracks, and the bus-body manufacturer's catalogue.

In his last year at the orphanage Girija had been taught bookkeeping, office organization, and the jargon of commercial letter writing. The uncle in Singapore found him useful—so useful, indeed, that after three months he got rid of the bookkeeper to whom he had been paying forty dollars (Straits) a week and replaced him with Girija, to whom he paid twenty. Girija was sixteen then. He stayed two years in Singapore. During them he learned Malay and a smattering of Cantonese and made friends with a Parsee who worked in the offices of a Chinese financial syndicate.

At that time, shortage of capital, ill health brought about by internment, and sheer hopelessness engendered by the early successes of the terrorists were persuading many British rubber planters in Malaya to sell out. The Chinese syndicate was buying. It was through his Parsee friend that Girija heard that the new manager of a recently acquired estate in the north was asking the Singapore office for a clerk.

His uncle was angered by Girija's decision to leave him, and talked darkly of getting a court order requiring Girija to repay the cost of his passage from Calcutta. To his astonishment, the bluff failed. Girija, whom he had come to regard as a pliant and somewhat timid young man, not only laughed loudly and made a disrespectful noise with his lips, but also threatened to take his mother and sisters north with him unless their wages were immediately doubled. There was a shrill Bengali family quarrel during which Girija uttered a further and more compelling threat. He had made a secret analysis of his uncle's accounts which he was prepared to send to the Inspector of Taxes. The uncle wept and spoke of ingratitude, but capitulated. Girija's mother embraced her son proudly and said that he was his father's true heir.

When the time came for Girija to leave, however, he asked her for only one thing that had belonged to his father: the bus-body manufacturer's catalogue. His sisters were relieved. They had been afraid that, as a man, he would feel himself entitled to the subahdar's medals.

The catalogue was a quarto-size book with a brown cover on which the name of the manufacturer was embossed in green. Inside there were forty-eight pages of thick, shiny paper displaying the specifications of twenty different types of buses together with color illustrations of the exterior and interior of each. There were double-deckers and single-deckers, buses designed to enable the driver to collect the fares, and buses designed to carry conductors. There were twelve-seaters, twenty-four-seaters, and sixty-seaters. There were buses for long distances and buses for local service in cities, for cold climates and for hot. The cover was dog-eared from much handling, and some of the pages were loose. There was an inkstain on the title page. It was Girija's most treasured possession.

As a small boy he had sat for hours turning the pages, studying the illustrations and rereading the text. He had, in the end, come to know it by heart. At the orphanage, when he had been separated both from his mother and from the catalogue, he had found comfort in reciting it to himself, beginning with the Foreword by the Chairman ("*In presenting to our customers all over the world this, the Eighteenth Edition of our Catalogue and Price List, we are proudly conscious that . . .*") and finishing with the specifications of a forty-seat medium-range staging coach (available on A.E.C. or Commer chassis) "*as supplied to the Argentine Government. Price £8,586, f.o.b. London.*"

One day in the streets of Benares he had seen a new bus that he thought he recognized as a modification of one of those listed in the catalogue. It had been just starting away and he had run for almost half a mile before he had caught up with it at a stopping place. Breathlessly he had searched for the body manufacturer's name plate. The bus had been moving off again before he had found it; but it had been the right plate. A wave of excitement had swept over him. From that moment he had known exactly what he wanted to do in the world. He would operate a bus service.

His first letter to the body manufacturer had been written from Singapore on his uncle's business stationery. He had been aware for some time that the original catalogue from London, precious though it was and always would be, was now very much out of date. Nevertheless, the decision to send for the latest edition had not been easily taken. For some reason that he had been unable to account for, it had seemed almost like an act of treachery.

However, the arrival of the new catalogue had given him other things to worry about. The catalogue itself had been magnificent. Unfortunately, it had been accompanied by a courteous letter from the sales manager, informing him that the company's Far Eastern representative, Mr. W. W. Belden, would shortly be visiting Singapore and would take that opportunity of meeting Mr. Krishnan and discussing his fleet requirements with him personally. For weeks Girija had gone in fear of W. W. Belden's arrival at his uncle's office and the humiliating scenes that would ensue when the truth was known. But Mr. Belden had never come, and eventually Girija had drawn the correct conclusion. Mr. Belden had investigated the financial status of this new prospective customer and decided not to waste his time.

His prudence had been understandable. The cheapest twenty-four-seater now cost over three thousand pounds—almost double the price of the cheapest bus in the 1937 catalogue. But one thing in the new edition had caught Girija's eye: a quotation from a trade journal devoted to the interests and activities of road-transport operators. Girija had found that this journal could be obtained in Singapore and had bought a subscription. From the articles it published he began to learn about the economics of public transportation. By the time he went to work for Mr. Wright, he had acquired a reasonably realistic view of his chances of achieving his life's ambition. Unless he could find a working capital of at least twenty thousand dollars (Straits), his chances of starting even the most modest country bus service were nonexistent.

iii

GIRIJA had a one-room atap house in the estate compound, and an arrangement with one of the servants at the Wrights' bungalow to keep it clean. There were Indian families of his own caste living in a village six miles away, and on Sundays he would cycle over there for tiffin. One of the families had an attractive daughter named Sumitra, whom he thought he would one day marry. However, during the week the curfew kept him at home, and there he always cooked his own food. Sometimes he would go back to the office after he had eaten his evening meal and do some more work before going to bed; at others he would listen to Radio Malaya and read and dream.

On the evening of the day of the ambush he stayed late in the office, trying to make up for the time he had lost by going with the burial party. The following morning he would have to drive in with Mr. Wright to the bank at Bukit Amphu to cash the weekly wages check, and he had not yet completed the time sheets.

The work required care and concentration, and he was glad of it, for it postponed the moment when he would have to entertain once more the dangerous thoughts which had come to him in the morning.

The things he had observed at the scene of the ambush, and learned from the two tappers, had made it possible for him to reconstruct the recent history of the dead men with reasonable certainty.

They had only recently arrived from the north and were relatively inexperienced. Of that he was sure. Their use of the easy route offered by the gully showed that. True, they had had a lot to carry, but that did not excuse carelessness. In an area where British patrols were being supplied by the R.A.F., a fact which they could scarcely help knowing, they had not even troubled to send scouts on ahead to feel the way, but had blundered straight into the ambush in a body.

The Lieutenant's opinion was that they had been on their way to mine the main road. Girija did not agree with that. The quantity of ammunition they had been carrying was out of all proportion to the needs of such an operation. And how was the absence of cooking utensils and food supplies to be explained if they were going so far from their base? To Girija there seemed only one possible explanation. What the Lieutenant's patrol had ambushed was a supply column on its way to deliver mines and ammunition to another gang operating farther south.

It had been at this point in his argument with himself that Girija's heart had begun to beat faster, and that an unpleasant sensation had come to his stomach. If his reasoning were correct, it could mean only one thing. The base camp near Awang was a guerrilla arms dump.

He finished his work, locked up the office, and walked slowly back across the courtyard to his house. It was a warm, humid night. He took off his shirt and khaki drill shorts, washed himself carefully all over, and then put on a dhoti. There was some lentil soup in an iron saucepan. He lit the oil burner under it and sat down to wait.

What had disconcerted him had been not so much the nature of his thoughts as the way in which they had presented themselves. He did not regard himself as being fundamentally honest or dishonest, idealistic or corrupt, law-abiding or delinquent. He did not think of himself as definable in such terms. His dilemmas had always been capable of resolution into simple questions of choice. Choice A would be wise (advantageous). Choice B would be stupid (disadvantageous). The discovery that his mind could explore enthusiastically the possibility of his committing a major crime, with only a belated and distasteful glance at the path of recitude, had been disturbing.

And a major crime it undoubtedly would be.

He had heard about these dumps and caches. It was known that the arms were brought in by professional smugglers operating from beyond the Thai border and employing different routes from those used by the guerrillas. A number of consignments had been intercepted, but it was generally believed that a far greater number always got through. Terrorists captured far to the south in the Kuala Lumpur area had been found to be in possession of substantial quantities of weapons, ammunition and explosives of the same pattern as those intercepted in the north. It was said that there were not enough troops in the whole of Malaya to patrol the border with Thailand effectively.

Just before the burial party had finished its work that morning the Malay Sergeant and four more soldiers had arrived with packing crates strung on bamboo poles. When the ammunition and grenades had been loaded into the crates, they were taken off to the compound. While the machine pistols were being gathered up, Girija had asked the Sergeant a question.

The Sergeant had looked down at the machine pistol in his hands and shrugged. "How should I know what they cost?"

"But don't you know how much your own cost, Sergeant? Supposing a man lost one."

"He would be court-martialed."

"But surely he would have stoppages of pay, too?"

"Oh, yes. Two hundred dollars perhaps."

"So much?"

"They do not grow on trees."

The Sergeant had gone. Girija had turned and looked at the row of graves. Each man had had a machine pistol, and ammunition was costly stuff. It was more than likely that what the ten men had been carrying between them was worth anything up to three thousand dollars. It would be interesting to know how much more there was where that had come from.

The soup began to bubble. He poured it into a bowl and, when it had cooled a little, began to eat.

The penalty for being found in the illegal possession of arms was death. Whether or not knowledge of the whereabouts of smuggled arms would constitute possession, and whether concealment of such knowledge carried the same penalty he did not know. One thing was clear: the illegal *selling* of smuggled arms would certainly be a hanging matter—at least while the emergency regulations remained in force. The best thing he could do was to go to Mr. Wright immediately and make a clean breast of the matter.

But a clean breast of *what* matter? He did not really *know* anything about an arms dump. He only believed one to be there. And where was "there"? Assuming that his deductions were correct, the dump was concealed in an area of jungle covering at least three square miles. It might prove quite impossible to find. Mr. Wright would not thank him for starting a wild-goose chase, and neither would the police. When the time came for him to apply for a local bus-service franchise, they might remember the trouble he had caused and hold it against him. No. The best thing he could do was nothing.

He finished his soup and felt better. He was an innocent man again, quietly digesting his evening meal. What did he want with smuggled arms? Could he ever have sold them? Of course not. Who would buy? And supposing others knew of the dump, if dump there were. Ten men had been killed; but supposing that other members of the guerrilla band had stayed behind. It might be highly dangerous to start searching in the area for their camp. Besides, there was always a chance that one or two of the men living at Awang already knew where it was. Not a very big chance, perhaps; the guerrillas would not have trusted their unwilling hosts to that extent; but someone might have found out by chance. Naturally, no man or woman from the village would dare to go to the police with the information—or not immediately, anyway. A decent interval would have to elapse before the dump could be discovered "accidentally." More likely it would just be forgotten. And that perhaps was what he should do: forget about it. After all, he could always remember again later, if he wanted to.

There was a metal trunk in one corner of the room. In it he kept his catalogues and trade papers and the schedule of a projected daily bus service linking ten of the principal rubber estates in the district with Bukit Amphu sixteen miles away. He took the schedule out, read it through very carefully, and then began to make one or two long-contemplated modifications.

iv

A MONTH went by before Girija made any move to locate the arms dump.

There had been no reports of any special patrol activity in the district, and guerrilla attacks in the province had been concentrated on areas nearer the coast. He had watched the men from Awang carefully without detecting anything unusual in their demeanor. But such reassurances came mingled with doubt. If no dump had been discovered, it could well be for the simple reason that none existed.

It was, in fact, the growing conviction that he must have been mistaken that gave him the courage he needed to go on. If there were nothing to find, he argued, there could be nothing incriminating in the search.

The first part of his plan called for a satisfactory cover for repeated visits to the Awang area. He might avoid going through the village itself, but he would have to use a mile or more of the road leading to it. Encounters with men who knew him, and who might gossip or ask questions, would be inevitable. The difficulty had seemed insurmountable at first; but finally he had had an idea.

The latex produced by the estate went thirty miles by road down to the port of Kuala Pangkalan and from there was shipped to Singapore.

Since the emergency, the trucks from the coast had had to be provided with armored-car escorts and, consequently, did not make the journey so often. Mr. Wright had been talking for some time, and writing to Singapore, about the need for additional storage sheds. The Singapore office had been reluctant to authorize the expenditure. Girija's idea was to make the new sheds an excuse for his trips to Awang.

Near the abandoned mine workings there were a number of derelict corrugated-iron buildings which had been used as offices, stores, and repair shops. Girija wrote to the head office of the mining company in Kota Bharu and asked permission to inspect the property with a possible view to making an offer for the material of the buildings.

He did not tell Mr. Wright. If Mr. Wright found out, no great harm would be done. Indeed, Mr. Wright would probably give him a pat on the back for his zeal and initiative in attempting to solve the problem of the new storage sheds. But Mr. Wright would also tell him something he already knew: that the mining company's rust-eaten buildings were not worth the cost of dismantling them, and that it would be a waste of time for him to go and inspect them.

The mining company replied with understandable enthusiasm that Mr. Krishnan had their full permission to inspect the buildings any time he liked. That was all he needed. No one person he might encounter there would know exactly how many visits of inspection he had made, or how many might be necessary. It would be assumed that he was acting on Mr. Wright's instructions. If he were ever challenged, he could produce the letter.

The following Sunday he cycled out to Awang. Just short of the village he turned off the road onto the overgrown track which led to the mining company's property. He met nobody on the way.

Ground sluicing had cleared some twenty acres of land in the bend of the river. No topsoil had been left for the jungle to reclaim, and the brown scars of the workings were still visible beneath a thin film of scrub and weed. Girija walked along the riverbank until he came to the shell of a building that had housed a big rotary pump, and went through the motions of inspecting it and taking notes. This was for the benefit of anyone who might have seen him and be watching from across the river. After a few minutes he moved away, circling out of sight of the riverbank until he reached the cover of some trees.

He had thought long and carefully about the problems of searching the area. The only large-scale map which covered it, and to which he might ordinarily have had access, was an ordnance survey sheet marked with the estate boundary lines. Unfortunately, a strict security regulation governed the distribution and custody of such maps at that time, and it had to be kept by Mr. Wright in his personal safe. Girija was forced to rely on his none too vivid recollection of it.

The picture in his mind was one of three parallel ridges, rather like

steps, with contour lines very close together. That meant, he knew, that
the sides of the ridges were steep and that there were deep ravines between them. It was not much to go on; but it was something. He did not
believe that even inexperienced men would choose the floor of a ravine
for a base camp, any more than they would choose to perch on the summit of a ridge. To that extent the likely areas of search were limited.
And there was another factor to be considered. Even if they had had
only small quantities of arms and ammunition to store, they would have
tried to find a place for them which gave some protection from the
weather. He thought it unlikely that there were caves there; but on the
steeper hillsides there would be sizable hollows made during the monsoons, when the heavier trees fell and tore their roots out of the ground.
Such hollows could easily be made into shelters. All in all, it seemed sensible to start the search by working along the upper slopes.

He attempted to do so; and that first Sunday expedition was very nearly
the last. It took him an hour to climb three hundred yards up the side
of the first ridge, and almost as long to get down again. He tore his
clothes, scratched his arms and legs, and ended by becoming completely
exhausted. He also became frightened. If some patrolling policeman were
to ask him to account for the tears and scratches, he would be hard put
to it to invent a convincing explanation.

He succeeded in getting back to his house unobserved, but the experience had thoroughly unnerved him and he decided to abandon the
whole project. For several days he did succeed in putting it out of his
mind. Then, as the scratches on his arms and legs began to heal, he began to think again. None of the ambushed men had had scratches on
arms or legs. That meant that they must have found an easy route to
and from their hiding place. The beauty of this deduction restored his
confidence.

The next time he made no attempt to penetrate the jungle. Instead
he worked his way around the fringes of it, looking for easy ways in. He
found several and noted them for future reference.

The following Sunday he began a systematic probe. He had learned
well from his initial mistake. When the going became too hard, he made
no attempt to force a path through, but went back and tried a different
or more circuitous way. He knew by now that he could never hope to
cover anything like the whole area, but he had become philosophical
about the search; it was a kind of game now, and although he did not
expect to win, he had not yet reached the point of conceding his defeat.

Eight weeks after he began, he received his first piece of encouragement. He had been following a dry stream bed up a fold in a hillside.
On both sides there were cane thickets of a kind he had learned to avoid.
It was useless to try to push your way through. You had to go around
them, and they often covered wide areas. Then, as the stream bed bore

away sharply to the left, he paused. There were a few pieces of dead cane lying on the ground. At first he thought that they had been broken away by some animal grubbing for food among the roots. Then he saw that they had been cut.

He stood still for a moment, staring. There was no mistaking the marks on the cane. They had been made by a metal cutting edge. He examined the border of the thicket carefully. For a distance of about two feet the cane was thinner and greener, and near the ground he could see short stumps of older cane in among the new growth. At some time in the not too distant past someone had cleared a path there.

It was getting late, and he was a mile and a half or more from the tin workings and the shed where he had left his bicycle. He decided to leave further investigation until the following Sunday. During the week, on the pretext of checking an inventory, he went to the tool store, borrowed one of the long chopping knives, called parangs, that the estate workers used for clearing underbrush, and hid it in his room. On Sunday morning he wrapped the parang in newspaper, tied it to the crossbar of his bicycle, and set off early for Awang.

He found his way back to the cane thicket without difficulty and started hacking a path through it with the parang. The new growth had not yet had time to harden, and the going was fairly easy. He had no fear of running into surviving members of the band. If this were indeed the way to their camp, it had not been used for several months.

The path was uphill. After he had gone fifteen yards, the cane thinned out and he found himself on a shallow ledge from which he could see down into the stream bed. On the ground there were some dead tree branches arranged to form a sort of chair. It looked as if the ledge had been used as a vantage point from which a sentry could cover the approach along the stream bed. A well-worn track led off to the right. He followed it, his heart pounding.

The camp was in a clearing shielded both from the sun and from air observation by the branches of a large flame-of-the-forest. The jungle apes had been there before him. Pieces of clothing had been torn apart and scattered over the clearing amid cooking pots, an earthenware chatty, and empty rice bags. The only thing that seemed to have escaped the apes' attentions was a metal box. It was full of leaflets, printed in Malay and Chinese, calling upon the people of Malaya to rise against the imperialist exploiters and establish a people's democracy.

There was another path leading down from the clearing, and Girija followed it. It ended at the hole which had been dug for use as a latrine. He walked back slowly to the clearing. In the long search for the camp site his doubts had been forgotten. Now he remembered them and faced the bitterness of defeat. Lieutenant Haynes had been right. He, Girija, had been wrong. Sunday after Sunday he had exchanged the pleasures of tiffin with his future mother-in-law, and the soft glances of Sumitra,

for senseless walks in the jungle and the pursuit of an illusion. There was
no arms dump; there never had been.

He had started to retrace his footsteps when his foot struck something
that tinkled. He looked down. Lying on the ground was a brass cartridge
case. As he bent down to pick it up, he saw another one. A minute later
he had found three more. He stared at them, puzzled. They were of
.303 caliber. He went over the ground again and found what he was
looking for: the clip which had held the five rounds.

There was no doubt about it. A .303 rifle had been fired there. But
no rifle of any kind had been found at the scene of the ambush. And
none of the weapons had been of .303 caliber. Where, then, was the
rifle?

He searched the camp site thoroughly first. He found a small fixed-
frequency radio in a teak box, but no rifle. He began to search the hillside above the camp, taking any route that looked as if it might conceivably have been used before. After about an hour he came upon a
clump of bamboo from which a number of thick stalks had been cut.
Then, about twelve yards away, he saw what he had been looking for.

Braced between the steep hillside and the trunk of a tree was a tri-
angular roof of bamboo. Cane screens had been plaited to enclose the
sides of the structure and form a shelter.

Girija scrambled toward it, slipping and sliding about on the spongy
carpet of dead leaves and slashing wildly with the parang at the undergrowth in his path. When he reached the shelter, he stood for an instant,
breathless and trying to prepare himself for the crushing disappointment
of finding it empty. Then he pulled one of the screens aside.

There was a sudden, swift rustle and his heart leaped as some small
brown animal rushed out past him. He pulled the screen back farther
and looked inside.

The hillside beneath the roof had been dug out to make the space
roughly rectangular. It was about six feet high and ten feet long and
filled from floor to roof with wood and metal packing cases.

He sat down on the ground to get his breath back and stared at the
cases. A number of them, he could see, were long and narrow and had
rope handles. One of these was near the screen and looked as if it had
been opened. He crawled over to it and prized the lid off with the parang.

Inside, carefully packed on slotted wood bearers, were six .303 rifles.
Five of them were heavily greased and wrapped in thick oiled paper with
the name of a Belgian manufacturer printed on it. One had been un-
wrapped. Girija took it out and opened the breach. It had been fired,
presumably down at the camp site, and put back without being cleaned.
The barrel was corroded.

Girija clucked disapprovingly. That was no way to treat valuable property. He returned the rifle to its case and began to examine the rest of
his find. He soon discovered that there was more there than he had at

first supposed. There were ten cases of rifles and at least thirty other boxes and cases of various sizes, in addition to ammunition containers.

He began to move some of these so as to get a look at the stenciled markings on the bigger cases, and then stopped. He would have to start back soon and there was no hope of taking an inventory that day. Besides, he had no need of an inventory.

He knew that all he had really found was hope. Of course, it would have been agreeable to dream of what was there in terms of wealth; but wealth that could only be realized, if at all, in some unmeasurable fullness of time was meaningless. It would be the hope that mattered in the days to come; and if he could draw from it the strength to go on quietly reading his transport trade journals, and turning the pages of his catalogues, and revising notional timetables, and faithfully continuing to serve Mr. Wright—if, in short, he could be patient and discreet—he might perhaps one day fulfill himself.

v

He waited, patiently and discreetly, for three years.

In the beginning it had been comparatively easy. There had been practical matters to attend to.

First, he thoroughly cleaned and greased the rifle that had been fired; then he gave some thought to the long-term problems of storage and preservation. The monsoon rains would arrive shortly, and the bamboo roof was not waterproof.

He decided to reconstruct the shelter. One Sunday he moved all the boxes out of it and laid a framework of bamboo on the ground to ensure a proper circulation of air. Over this he put a heavy tarpaulin taken from the estate compound, and then rearranged the boxes on top of it. Another tarpaulin went over the boxes and was lashed down firmly with wire rope. A third tarpaulin he incorporated in the roof. He also repaired the screens.

Thereafter, he only went to the place once a month to make sure that all was in order. He would have gone more often if he could have trusted himself, but, rather to his surprise, he had found patience easier to cultivate than discretion.

In spite of his initial resolution, it had proved hard not to take an inventory of what was in the shelter and keep it in his tin trunk. He knew that such a document was premature and pointless. He knew that if, through some mischance, Mr. Wright happened to see it and ask questions, his lies would be unconvincing. Yet the temptation had persisted. There had also been an insane desire to confide in Sumitra, to bask in her admiration and flattery, and bind her future more securely to his. He knew that she would certainly tell her mother, who would tell the father, who worked in the bank at Bukit Amphu and was a notorious chatterbox; but that temptation, too, had continued to haunt him.

During the second year he had other troubles. His mother died; and two of the cases resting on the lower tarpaulin were attacked by termites. Fortunately, he noticed the fact in good time and was able to minimize the damage. The ammunition boxes were metal, and, having given them a thick coat of bitumen paint, he moved them to the bottom of the stack. The damaged boxes he repaired with strips of teak, and sprayed all the wood containers with a powerful solution of benzine hexachloride.

The second year went by; and the third. General Templer's policy of winning the co-operation and goodwill of the people of Malaya and enlisting them in the fight against the terrorists began to succeed; and, as success snowballed into victory, curfews were lifted and road blocks removed. Areas free of terrorists were declared "white," and restrictions on unescorted civil transport movements canceled.

The day that the province in which he worked was declared "white," Girija wrote to England for a new bus-body catalogue. The following Sunday he went to the shelter and spent two of the happiest hours of his life, taking an inventory.

CHAPTER II

WHEN THE RUBBER ESTATES in the Pangkalan district had latex for shipment, they generally notified the Anglo-Malay Transport Company at the port of Kuala Pangkalan. The company would then send their trucks to collect the latex, store it temporarily in their godowns, and finally, when instructions came through from Singapore, ship it out in one of their big motor junks.

The founder, manager, and sole proprietor of this useful enterprise was a Chinese, Mr. Tan Siow Mong.

Mr. Tan had been educated at a mission school in Macao, and spoke Hokkien and Portuguese as well as Cantonese, Malay, and English. His father had owned a fishing junk, and had divided his working year between snapper fishing and carrying cargoes of rattan up the coast to Hong Kong. When he died, in the early thirties, Mr. Tan and his two brothers had taken over the junk and turned to the more lucrative business of opium smuggling. They had been caught, in the end, by a British gunboat, and their junk had been impounded. By that time they had had a substantial sum of money saved and could accept the forfeiture of the junk with equanimity. However, a family council had considered it advisable for the Tans to leave the China Coast for a while and seek their fortunes elsewhere. One brother had gone to Singapore, another to Manila. Tan Siow Mong, the eldest, had taken his mother to Kuala Pangkalan. There, with his share of the family capital, he had started to deal in copra and lend money to Malays at forty per cent. During the Japanese occupation he had accepted a disused godown in discharge of a debt. After the war he had tried to sell it. Unable to find a buyer, he had eventually decided to make it pay for itself. The Anglo-Malay Transport Company had grown from that decision.

Mr. Tan was in the late forties now, with graying hair and rimless glasses. He wore well-cut tussore suits, and was never seen without a dark tie even in the hottest weather. He had an air of well-bred dignity that was much admired in the Chinese business community of Kuala Pangkalan.

His office was so placed that he could, without moving from his desk, see the trucks in the unloading bay of number-one godown and the wooden quay at which the junks discharged and took on cargo. By turning his head he could also see, through a glass panel let into the wall beside the door, his four Chinese assistants. Mr. Tan did not believe in elaborate organization. Working sixty-five hours a week, the four assistants were well able to take care of most of the routine paper work of the business. The accounts he preferred to look after himself.

Two of the trucks were unloading bales of latex which had come down that afternoon from one of the Chiang Thye Phu Syndicate estates, and he could see the Indian clerk from the estate office checking off the weights with the godown foreman.

Mr. Tan did not like that. Mr. Wright, the estate manager, had always, and rightly, trusted the company before. Why had he suddenly felt it necessary to send his clerk to check the weighing?

The clerk and the godown foreman had evidently agreed the figures now, for, as Mr. Tan watched, the clerk smiled and turned away. Mr. Tan had made a note to ask the foreman what reason, if any, had been given for this uncomplimentary change of procedure, when he saw that the clerk was walking across the yard towards his office.

Mr. Tan looked down at the papers on his desk. It would be undignified to be seen peering out. A moment or two later, one of his assistants came in to say that Mr. Krishnan desired the pleasure of a few moments' conversation with him.

Mr. Tan disapproved of Indians. He had often found them to be disagreeably acute in business matters. He also disapproved of estate clerks, who, if they were not given occasional presents, could delay the payment of accounts and cause other inconveniences.

This one he remembered only from having seen him with Mr. Wright, the estate manager. He was lean and very dark, with bright, intelligent eyes and a predatory mouth that smiled too much. It would be interesting to discover how accurately he would estimate his nuisance value.

He greeted Girija with grave courtesy and asked him to sit down.

"It is not often," he went on in English, "that we have the pleasure of seeing you, Mr. Krishnan."

Girija smiled. "Thank you. Mr. Wright sends all compliments and best favors."

Mr. Tan congratulated himself on choosing English for the conversation. His own, he knew, was excellent. The clerk's was little better than the illiterate commercial patois that the British called "Babu." It placed him at a disadvantage, small but possibly useful.

"And are Mr. and Mrs. Wright well?"

"Both very well. We hope ditto for Mrs. Tan, self, and family."

"Thank you, yes."

Tea was brought in from the outer office and served in minute cups. Tentative moves might now be made toward a discussion of the real object of the visit.

"This must be a busy time for you at the estate," observed Mr. Tan.

What this banality was in effect asking was why Mr. Wright had thought it necessary to waste his clerk's time by sending him in to Kuala Pangkalan to supervise a normal warehousing operation.

Girija smiled and answered in Malay. "With the rubber market so firm, we are always busy now."

Mr. Tan nodded. He was wondering if by some faint flicker of expression he had revealed his amusement at the clerk's English. The Malay was fluent. Courteously, he answered in the same language.

"Let us hope the bad times are ended for good."

"Good business for one is good business for all," said Girija.

"Very true." Now, Mr. Tan decided, they were coming to the point. Reference to mutual advantage was the accepted preliminary to a squeeze.

"This tea is excellent, sir," said Girija.

Mr. Tan instantly sent for more. This again postponed pointed discussion, and further inanities were exchanged. Grudgingly, Mr. Tan had to admit to himself that the young man was handling the interview well. He found himself becoming interested.

When they were alone again, he said: "Mr. Wright is a very good manager. It must be a pleasure to work for such a man."

Girija nodded. "Indeed it is. He is, as you say, a fine manager. But he is also a man of good heart."

"I can well believe that."

"In fact," Girija went on, "when I asked him if he would allow me to come down to Kuala Pangkalan on personal business, he did not even question me before giving his permission."

"One has always known that he values your services highly." Mr. Tan was making the pace again now. The use of the phrase "values your services" would, he was sure, bring the matter to a head.

"And yet," said Girija, "I was glad he did not ask me questions." He paused.

Mr. Tan was silent. He was certain that the moment had arrived.

Girija flashed a smile. "For if he had, I would have been forced to hurt his feelings or to lie. I would not wish to do either of those things."

"Both are offenses against good taste," agreed Mr. Tan sententiously.

"Mr. Wright has been my father," said Girija. "How could I tell him that, being in need of the wisest advice on a matter of great importance, I was turning not to him but to Mr. Tan Siow Mong?"

Mr. Tan said nothing. He had nothing relevant to say. He was hurriedly revising his estimate of the situation. If the clerk were choosing this way of leading up to a request for money, he must have some absurdly large sum in mind.

Girija leaned forward earnestly. "Nowhere in Kuala Pangkalan is there a wiser head in important matters of business," he said. "It is well known."

Mr. Tan noted the qualifying phrase, "in important matters of business." He said: "You pay me an undeserved compliment."

"My friend," continued Girija, "could think of no one else whose advice on this matter would be so valuable."

"Your friend?" Mr. Tan was becoming confused again and in consequence also a little annoyed; but his tone remained polite.

"You do not know him, sir," said Girija, "and he knows you only from your high reputation. When I said that I would ask your advice on this important matter that is troubling him, he begged me not to mention him by name. The matter is highly confidential."

"Most business matters are." Mr. Tan spoke dryly. He guessed that "confidential" in this context probably meant "criminal."

Girija's smile became tentative. For the first time Mr. Tan saw him ill at ease, and decided to offer a word of reassurance. It would be irritating if the man took fright and left without revealing the object of his visit.

"If your friend respects my wisdom," he remarked, "he must also acknowledge my discretion."

Girija's smile went back into place and his eyes met Mr. Tan's. "Of course. But he is a nervous man. You will see why when I explain." He paused to choose his words before going on. "It appears that some years ago, during the emergency, when the terrorists were bringing in arms from the north, my friend found some of these arms—rifles, machine guns, ammunition." He looked up to see how Mr. Tan was taking this.

Mr. Tan smiled, but very faintly. "And so he turned them over to the police?"

"That, of course, is what he should have done." Girija shrugged. "But, as I said, my friend is a nervous man. He did not wish to call attention to himself. At the time, it seemed best to do nothing. Now he is in a difficulty."

"Yes?"

"My friend is in need of money. He thought of these arms. If he told the police about them now, there would be questions and trouble. But if a buyer for the arms could be found, perhaps his debts could be paid, and no one would be the worse. The emergency is over. No harm could come of it, only good for my friend."

Mr. Tan sat very still. "You wish me to advise your friend?"

Girija nodded. "That is what he hopes you may do, sir. Yes."

"He should still take the matter to the police. It would be very wrong to try to sell them. He need not say that he found them long ago, but he should certainly go to the police."

Girija spread out his hands. "But, sir, my friend has debts."

"It is better to go to a money lender than to risk going to prison."

Girija smiled triumphantly. "That was exactly my own advice to him, sir. To risk going to prison for a few hundred dollars is the act of a fool. I told him so."

Mr. Tan hesitated. The agreement baffled him. He knew instinctively that somewhere, somehow, he had mismanaged the conversation. He knew that he was left with only one question to ask, and that when he had asked it he would have lost a battle of wits. But he also knew that his curiosity would have to be satisfied. Mentally he shrugged off the humiliation.

"And what was his reply?" he asked.

Girija's hand went to the row of ball-point pens in his shirt pocket and drew from behind it a folded sheet of paper. He opened it out and handed it across the desk.

"This paper, sir," he said. "My friend gave me this paper."

Mr. Tan took the paper, spread it out on the desk in front of him, and looked down. It was a typed list with the word INVENTORY at the head of it. He read on:

Description	Type	Quantity	Today's Free Market Value ($ Straits)
Rifles	.303 Military S.A. Belge	54	16,000
.303 Ammo	For above	5,000 rds	6,000
Machine pistols	Schmeisser	25	18,000
.300 Ammo	With magazines for above	8,000 rds	7,000
Bazookas	U.S. Govt. pattern	4	6,000
Ammo for same	" " "	35 rds	1,000
Grenades	Mills unfused ⎱		
Fuses	For same ⎰	100	2,000
Land mines	Teller	40	4,000
		Total	60,000
		Equals £ (Sterling)	7,500
		Equals $ (U.S.)	21,000

Note   All items in brand new mint condition in original mnfrs. packings, containers, etc.

Prices   All prices f.o.b. vicinity Kuala Pangkalan

Terms and Conditions   Items sold separate subject 20% increase.

Mr. Tan looked up.

"You see, sir," said Girija softly, "I was wrong. It is not just a matter of a few hundred dollars, but of many thousands."

Mr. Tan pretended to read the list through a second time in order to give himself time to think. He had little doubt that the "friend" for whom the clerk claimed to be acting was nonexistent. The Indian must have been desperate for money to take the risk of approaching a comparative stranger in this way, or very sure of himself as a judge of character. Mr. Tan had an uneasy feeling that the latter explanation might be the more likely. The fellow looked confident enough, and not at all desperate. Of course, he could be lying, and the whole story could be a mere trick to get money; but Mr. Tan did not really think so. In any case, it would be simple to find out. He looked up again and met the clerk's eyes.

"My friend," said Girija, "would be willing to pay a commission of fifty per cent to anyone who found a buyer, and who would take delivery of the goods."

Mr. Tan shook his head. "But this would be a serious criminal matter. Does your friend not understand that?"

"That was my first thought, too," said Girija approvingly, "but he did not agree. This is not stolen property, he says. It has no owner. If it should leave the country, the police would have no interest in it. The emergency is over."

"But the laws remain."

"That is true." Girija nodded thoughtfully. "You think, then, sir, that I should tell my friend that you advise him to go to the police?"

"I think you should tell him to put the whole matter out of his mind." Mr. Tan paused and then added: "Perhaps later the law will not be so strict."

"Yes, that is so."

"Such merchandise as this is always saleable." Mr. Tan looked down again at the list. "Have you seen any of these items?"

"My friend is naturally careful."

"But do you believe him? You say he wishes to find a buyer. A list is not proof that there is something to sell. Could he produce samples?"

"He would be more than ready to do that, sir."

Mr. Tan refolded the inventory. "I know little about these matters," he said, "but I have heard that buyers in this market are not easy to reach. Contacts must be found. Time must be spent. There can be no urgency."

"My friend is very patient."

"Then, do as I suggest. Tell him to forget for a while." He looked up at Girija. "You agree?"

"Of course, sir."

Mr. Tan held up the list. "And I may keep this paper?"

It was a test question.

Girija smiled. "My friend will be happy for it to remain in such wise hands, sir."

He rose. The interview was over. When the usual courtesies had been exchanged, he left.

Mr. Tan watched him walk away across the yard, then sent for the Chiang Thye Phu Syndicate estate's files.

The first thing was to find out whether the clerk's discretion and sense of self-preservation were as lively as they had appeared to be. If he had been foolhardy enough to type out his list on Mr. Wright's estate-office typewriter, and then leave it with someone who could, if it seemed advantageous, go to the authorities and gain credit by reporting the incident, Mr. Tan wanted no more to do with him and would burn the paper at once. If, as he suspected, the young man had been careful to leave himself in a position to deny effectively all knowledge of the conversation they had just had, and of the list, then something might be made of the situation.

He looked through Mr. Wright's office consignment notes and compared the typing on them with that of the list. It was obvious that the list had not been typed on the same machine. So far so good. He read through the list once more and then locked it in his private office safe.

Later that day, when he had had further time to think, he wrote to his brother in Singapore.

ii

TAN YAM HENG was the disreputable member of the family. Such, at least, was the view of his brothers in Kuala Pangkalan and Manila.

He was one of the founders of the Singapore Democratic Action Party and organizer of a waterfront trade union which, though small in membership, had sufficient nuisance value to levy tribute on two of the bigger stevedoring companies. As the fruits of these negotiations were always handed over to him personally, privately, and in cash, he did not consider it necessary to report their receipt either to the union auditors or to the income-tax authorities. He had no time to waste on the pettifogging rituals of accountancy and other hindrances to social progress. He saw himself as a man of power, a manipulator of puppets, choosing to work behind the scenes until the strategic moment came for him to step forward and lead his party on to victory.

If that had been all there was to say of him, his brothers would have been content. His political pretensions they could ignore, and, devious men themselves, they did not seriously object to his methods of augmenting his income. What they did object to, strongly, was what he did with it.

Most Chinese like to gamble, and with some this liking becomes an addiction as compulsive as those of drugs or alcohol. Yam Heng was a gambler of this kind. Moreover, he was a stupid gambler. Games of chance are at least subject to the law of averages, race horses do sometimes run true to form, and skill can often qualify bad luck at poker; but Yam Heng's conceit and fantasies of omnipotence had in the end demanded more esoteric gratifications. He had taken to gambling on the "pickle" market.

This unofficial market in raw rubber is conducted by freebooters operating outside the respectable Singapore brokerage houses, and they are speculating on small price fluctuations over short periods. On the pickle market a consignment of rubber in transit may theoretically change hands several times in the course of a day. Large sums of money are made and lost on feverish, bull-and-bear transactions. The successful speculators are Chinese with great experience, cool heads, and reliable intelligence organizations. Much use is made of the time difference between the London and Singapore markets, and a few minutes' lead on a piece of cabled information can make thousands of dollars for its possessor. It is the efficient who generally win; the gamblers who generally lose.

The pickle market was no place for Yam Heng. The acquaintance who had introduced him to it was one of a syndicate of small men, and they had been perfectly willing to let an outsider buy in; the stronger the syndicate, the better; but his arrogant impatience with their wariness and caution had soon antagonized them. Eventually he had taken his money out of the syndicate and started to operate on his own.

If he had immediately and heavily lost, the blow to his self-esteem might have caused him to think twice about continuing. Unfortunately, he had won. After that, it had been too late for second thoughts.

His early appeals for loans had been received by his brothers with fraternal tolerance, and responded to in the belief that the money lent would be repaid. They had known, of course, that he was overfond of gambling, but had believed his profligacy in that respect to be confined to horse racing or fan-tan. The discovery of the true nature of the "investments" they were so innocently subsidizing had been a disagreeable shock; so had the realization that Yam Heng had been deceitfully making his applications simultaneously, and in identical terms, to both of them.

There had been worse to come. In the face of their joint refusals to lend him another cent, Yam Heng had blandly informed them that the various union funds in his charge were some thousands of dollars short, and that unless the shortages were made good before the annual audit, the consequences for the Tan name might be serious. There had been hasty consultation between Kuala Pangkalan and Manila. The brothers had paid up in the end, but only after both of them had been to Singapore and personally checked the union books. The days when Yam Heng could be trusted had gone. Thereafter, he had the status somewhat of a poor relation—a responsibility to be discharged as inexpensively as possible.

It was with this responsibility in mind that Mr. Tan had written his letter. Some weeks earlier he had received one of Yam Heng's periodic requests for money and noted a veiled belligerence in the wording. It had reminded him that the annual audit of the union books was due shortly, and that Yam Heng would soon be making his annual attempt to extort money by hinting at another raid on the union funds. Mr. Tan's nerves were strong, and for the previous three years he had successfully refused to be intimidated; but he knew gamblers, and there was always the chance that one day Yam Heng might become desperate.

At that moment, in fact, Yam Heng was merely depressed. He had had two small wins in the past two weeks and a bigger loss which had canceled out the winnings. His brother's letter annoyed him.

It contained a polite inquiry after his health, a detailed account of their mother's most recent illness, and a proposal that he visit Kuala Pangkalan at a convenient moment in the near future. It mentioned that the junk *Happy Dawn* would be unloading in Singapore the following week, and that the master would be instructed to offer him a free passage. It gave no hint of a possible reason for the visit.

Yam Heng knew his brother too well to suppose that the visit had been proposed for any social or family reason. Their mother was senile. Her current state of health could only have been mentioned to make the invitation seem logical to some stranger reading the letter. Yam Heng disliked having his curiosity aroused unless he had the means on hand to satisfy it. The offer of the junk passage irritated him also. It was his brother's way of saying that if he wanted to travel in comfort by train or plane, he could pay his own fare. He considered sending a dignified reply regretting that pressure of work compelled him to decline the invitation; but, finally, curiosity and the faint hope of another loan decided him to accept. He had just enough money for the train fare.

His brother met him at the station, greeted him warmly, and drove him to the ornate brick-and-stucco house in Willoughby Road. The first evening was spent in celebrating the family reunion. Old Mrs. Tan emerged from her room, an elaborate dinner was consumed, the young children made their Uncle Yam tell them about Singapore, and the eldest son showed his Voigtlander camera and some of the color-slide photographs of birds which he had made with it. Yam Heng found it all very agreeable. His brother remained friendly and courteous. There were no references, oblique or otherwise, to their long estrangement, or to the reasons for it. He permitted himself a few restrained smiles, some delicate compliments to his sister-in-law, and a joke or two with the younger children.

It was not until the following day that his brother revealed the reason for the invitation. In the morning they toured the godowns, visited the truck-maintenance shed, and watched one of the junks unloading fifty-gallon drums of fuel oil. Then they went to the office and tea was served.

"And how," Siow Mong inquired at last, "is the pickle market?"

Yam Heng gave him an impassive stare.

"I ask," Siow Mong continued after a pause, "not in a spirit of criticism, but because I want information."

For one wild moment Yam Heng wondered if his brother were contemplating a foray of his own. Then he shrugged. "Some make money, some lose."

His brother nodded sagely as if he had had a suspicion confirmed. "I did hear," he went on, "that there is another thriving market now in Singapore."

"There are markets there in most things."

"Yes. But I heard—I cannot remember from what source—that the market in arms is particularly active at present."

"Oh, yes." Yam Heng spoke indifferently. "The Indonesian rebels are trying to buy. They have several purchasing agents there."

"Several?"

"There is one from Sumatra, one from Java, another from Celebes. They are united only in their opposition to the central government."

"They compete?"

Yam Heng shrugged. "They must. There is not so much to buy. It is not easy."

"How do they pay? Rupiahs?"

"Nobody would take rupiahs. Pounds or dollars, I suppose."

"Dollars U.S.?"

"Straits or Hong Kong dollars, I would think. Why?"

"Cash?"

"I suppose so."

His brother nodded approvingly. "I would think this a very satisfactory business."

"No doubt it is."

"These agents you speak of—you know them?"

"I know who they are, yes."

"Have you not thought of taking an interest in the business yourself?"

Yam Heng smiled sourly. "The peddler cannot do business with an empty tray."

"And if the tray were to be filled?"

Yam Heng hesitated. His brother was not in the habit of making idle remarks. "That would require capital," he said cautiously.

"Not necessarily."

Siow Mong went over to his private safe, got out the piece of paper Girija had left with him, and handed it to Yam Heng.

"That was brought to me by a man who wants a buyer for those goods," he said.

Yam Heng read the list through carefully. His expression did not change. When he had finished, he glanced up at his brother. "It says that delivery must be taken in the *vicinity* of Kuala Pangkalan. What does that mean?"

Siow Mong told him about Girija's visit and summarized the conversation they had had.

Yam Heng listened without interrupting, and then read through the list again. He spoke as he read.

"Is this Indian to be trusted?"

"I think so. If he gets what he wants."

"I know very little about this market. Are these prices realistic?"

"I was able to make only one inquiry. There is a dealer in machinery here who used to import sporting rifles. Naturally, I had to be careful how I asked, but from what I was able to learn I would think these prices are three times what they should be. But in a sellers' market, who knows?"

"I could find out in Singapore." Yam Heng paused. "What is your proposal?"

Siow Mong sat down behind his desk and leaned forward across it. "You are a gambler, brother," he said pleasantly, "and you know what I think of that. Especially as, in the game you play, you cannot win. I am inviting you to try a different one."

"Selling arms is no game."

"It can be very profitable." Siow Mong's smile faded. "Let us have no misunderstandings. I have a good business here. I do not like risks. I do not have to take them. If you can find a way to handle this transaction without personal risk to me, I will help you, for a small handling charge of ten per cent. But I must know exactly what you intend to do, first. If I agree with your plan, I will put you in touch with the Indian. Is that understood?"

Yam Heng had been listening absently and did not reply to his brother's question. "There are two problems here," he said slowly. "The first is to get the goods out of the country. That is a matter of careful organization. The second problem is more difficult. They must be made respectable."

Siow Mong waited. Yam Heng might be a fool in many respects, but he could sometimes be shrewd.

"You see," Yam Heng continued after a moment or two, "if I were to sell these goods in Singapore, I might never receive payment. They would deal, yes; but these are not normal business dealings. There is no trust. 'Payment on delivery,' they would say. But when I had delivered, they could give me a five-thousand-dollar tip and tell me to go to the police for the rest. What could I answer in such a case? You say that these are not stolen goods, and no doubt you are right. But I would be as helpless as if they were, if I had to deal illegally."

"What is the alternative? How do you make such property respectable?"

"There must be an intermediary, someone who will sign papers, admit ownership if necessary, and take perhaps five per cent for his trouble."

"What sort of person? An Englishman?"

"It would be better if he were not a subject of the Federation or of Singapore. I am thinking of the emergency regulations."

"A Frenchman or an American, perhaps?"

"There are Americans doing such business."

"Could you approach one of them?"

Yam Heng pursed his lips. "This would be too small for those men, I think. Besides, they would want too much for themselves. We do not need an experienced man."

Siow Mong thought for a moment. Then he asked: "Have you met Khoo Ah Au?"

"Who is he?"

"I was forgetting that you have been out of touch with family affairs. He married our niece in Manila last year. They live in Hong Kong now. Perhaps he would know of a suitable American. I shall be going there next month. I might discuss the requirements with him. Possibly . . ." He broke off. "But this is all talk. You say that to ship the goods is only a matter of organization. How would you do it?"

Yam Heng told him.

His brother listened and was impressed. "It might be done," he admitted grudgingly at last.

They discussed some details, and later that day Siow Mong telephoned Girija. He referred to their recent conversation and then said that although he, Mr. Tan, could do nothing in the matter, he had heard of a Mr. Lee who might be able to give useful advice. A meeting was arranged.

iii

GIRIJA never guessed that "Mr. Lee" was Mr. Tan's brother. Mr. Tan was refined. Mr. Lee had coarse, heavy features, a sullen expression, and a hectoring, impatient way of speaking that bordered on rudeness. Girija did not like him.

They met at a rest house not far from the estate. Mr. Lee had taken a room there for the night, and they identified one another without difficulty.

The first meeting was brief. Mr. Lee produced Girija's list and asked him if he were prepared to prove the existence of the items listed by producing a sample of any one of them that Mr. Lee himself selected.

Girija nodded. "I have already said that my friend could give a sample if required. I ask only that the item chosen should be small and light."

"How small? How light?"

"Small and light enough to be carried in the pocket. You would not ask me to cycle along the road with a rifle on my back."

"Is a machine-pistol loading clip small enough?"

"Yes. And I will bring a few rounds of ammunition with it."

"When?"

"Monday."

"Today is Thursday. Why not tomorrow?"

"It cannot be arranged before Monday."

"Very well. But I have no time to waste."

On Sunday Girija went out to Awang and made his way up to the dump. It was several months since he had last repaired the shelter, and the screens were in a bad state. The termites were back again, too. He hoped that Mr. Lee was in as much of a hurry as he professed to be.

On Monday he met Mr. Lee again and showed him some ammunition and a clip.

Mr. Lee wiped the grease off the clip and examined the German markings carefully. Finally he put the clip in his pocket.

"That would seem to be in order," he said. "Naturally, I will have to check these marks. In the meantime I must have some information. Where would delivery take place?"

"In this area."

"What do you consider would be needed to transport the goods?"

"One thirty-hundredweight truck."

"Are the goods near a road?"

"Not at present. They can be brought to a loading point fifty yards from a road, but that operation will require three days' advance notice."

"That may be difficult."

"It must be allowed for." Girija spoke with assurance. He had had three years to solve this problem in logistics, and knew that there was only one answer to it.

"You say fifty yards from a road. Would you and your friend be there to help with the loading? It would have to be done at night."

"I or my friend would be there. Two men could do the loading in less than an hour. The heaviest boxes are those with the rifles. There are nine of them, and they weigh about forty pounds each. But they have rope handles."

Mr. Lee looked at him with interest. "You speak as if you have had experience before."

"I am a businessman, Mr. Lee." Girija paused. "Perhaps, now that you have examined the samples, we should discuss financial arrangements and terms."

Mr. Lee took the list from his pocket. "These prices you mention are foolish. You knew that, of course."

Girija smiled. "I knew that you would say they were foolish, Mr. Lee. And, of course, I understand. These are always difficult goods to sell. The right buyer may not be found immediately. The demand fluctuates. Handling and storage charges are high. You must work on a very small margin of profit. That is why I am prepared to pay fifty per cent of these estimated prices to the selling agent."

"*You* are prepared, Mr. Krishnan? What about your friend?"

Girija was not disconcerted. "I am authorized to speak for him at present," he said. "I say 'at present' because my friend is considering the possibility of going to Singapore and investigating the market personally."

"Could your friend move the goods?"

"He is a patient man. He could wait."

Mr. Lee did not reply immediately. He was tired of Girija's toothy smile and the knowing lilt in his voice. "Your prices are foolish," he repeated coldly.

Girija smiled again. "Then I will reduce them, Mr. Lee. I will accept thirty thousand dollars Malay net."

"That is an insignificant reduction."

"It is the only one I can make."

"I will pay twenty thousand."

They compromised in the end on twenty-five thousand, to be paid one month after the goods were handed over. A protocol for the transaction was also agreed. Under this, each of the high contracting parties was protected against murder or trickery on the part of the other. The meeting ended in an atmosphere of goodwill and mutual respect.

The following day Tan Yam Heng took the train back to Singapore.

The following week Tan Siow Mong flew up to Hong Kong. He was there for only two days; but he was able to spend an entertaining and constructive evening with his niece and her husband, Khoo Ah Au.

CHAPTER III

TWELVE HOURS OUT OF KOBE, the *Silver Isle* ran into bad weather and more than half her ninety passengers took to their cabins.

She was owned by the Isle Line, which operated a freight run between San Francisco and Calcutta, calling at Yokohama, Kobe, Hong Kong, Manila, Saigon, Singapore, and, occasionally, Rangoon. With the growing popularity of round-the-world trips, the company's passenger traffic had increased rapidly, and they had refitted two of their newer ships so as to enlarge and improve the cabin accommodation. The *Silver Isle* was one of these. Unfortunately, the improvements, which included an extra deck, had also added considerably to her top hamper, and in any but the calmest sea she rolled heavily.

For Greg Nilsen, however, the bad weather came as a blessing. Both he and Dorothy, his wife, were good sailors and could go down to the dining room with their appetites unimpaired. True, Dorothy did complain that the incessant rolling made her tired; but he could only view that as a minor inconvenience. As far as he was concerned, any weather conditions that kept Arlene Drecker confined to her cabin were fine.

Greg was an engineer and the owner of a precision die-casting business in Wilmington, Delaware. He and Dorothy had been planning their round-the-world trip for over two years—ever since their younger boy had gone to college.

They could have done it earlier if they had been prepared to fly most of the way, but Dorothy had said no. She had wanted to do it properly— by sea, and in small, slow boats.

"After all," she had said, "we're only going to be able to do it once in our lives. All the tourists go to Tokyo and Hong Kong and Paris and Rome, places like that. I think we ought to see some of the little out-of-the-way places as well; the ones most people just read about, or see pictures of in photographic books; wonderful places like Tahiti, where the cruise ships don't go."

Greg had agreed with her. However, a few evenings spent with maps, sailing lists, and an eighteen-inch globe had modified their views. They had found, for example, that if they wanted to go to Japan and Hong Kong, a one-day visit to Tahiti would add two weeks to their travel schedule. In the end it was plain that, even if they compromised on the size and speed of the boats, confined themselves to the regular ports of call, and cut out South America completely, the trip would still take at least two months. If they did not want to spend all the time traveling, it would take three.

Greg had some very capable men working for him, but, at the management level, Nilsen Die-Casting and Tools was very much a one-man business. A three-month vacation could not be embarked upon just when he felt like it; and although he had for some time been planning a reorganization that would enable him to delegate more responsibility, it involved changes that could only be made gradually. He had allowed two years—one in which to make the changes, and one in which to see that they worked—but, even so, it had still not been easy to get away. There had been some moments in the month before they had sailed when difficulties over a new government contract had made it look as if the trip would have to be called off. However, the difficulties had been ironed out in time and they had left Wilmington early in October. Because of the amount of baggage they were taking, they had gone by train to San Francisco. They had sailed on the seventh.

Neither of them had traveled much by ship before. During the war Greg had gone to Europe on a troopship. Together they had been to England and France and back on the *United States* and the *America*. That was all. They had received much advice from more experienced friends. One of them, Greg remembered later, had had a solemn warning to deliver.

"It's the first two or three days you want to be careful of," this man had said, "and especially the first day just after you sail. You're going to be with those people for weeks. But you'll be feeling strange and want to be friendly. You'll go into the bar and have a drink to celebrate the start of the trip. Watch it. Don't start getting friendly with anyone. Wait. You start talking to someone, and before you know it, bingo, you're stuck with the ship's bore. It can ruin a trip."

Arlene Drecker was not the ship's bore, but, as far as Greg was concerned, she became an even more maddening affliction.

After the ship had sailed, he and Dorothy had stayed on deck until they had cleared the Golden Gate. They had promised the boys to make a complete photographic record of the trip, and Greg had been up on the boat deck with the 16 mm. Bell and Howell for the best part of an hour. It had been a sunny day, but with a cool breeze. They had been glad, when there was no more to see aloft, to get down into the warmth of the bar for a pre-lunch drink.

Arlene had been sitting by herself at a small table about six feet away from them. She had been writing radio telegrams and sipping a Martini. Then the pen she had borrowed from the writing room had run out of ink, and she had looked round in exasperation. Greg had politely offered her his. She had accepted. Later, when she returned his pen, she had asked them to have a drink.

"No, no. You join us," Dorothy had said.

Arlene had smiled. "You know, a gal traveling alone has one big problem—how to persuade people to sometimes let her buy a drink."

Nevertheless, she had joined them and had another Martini. They had gone down to lunch together. Later that day the chief steward had approached Greg with the permanent seating plan for the dining room and asked if he and Mrs. Nilsen minded having Miss Drecker sit at their table. There were no single tables, he had explained, and Miss Drecker did not want to be with a crowd. Greg had had little choice but to agree.

That night, when they went down to dinner, there had been a bottle of champagne on the table—to thank them, Arlene had explained, for letting her sit with them, and to drink a toast to the voyage.

Later, in their cabin, Greg had grumbled about this. He did not care for champagne, which always gave him indigestion; but Dorothy had not been sympathetic. It showed, she had said, that Arlene did not intend to impose on them. The champagne had been a very nice way of telling them that. The fact that it gave him indigestion was beside the point. Dorothy had taken a liking to Arlene.

She was a tall, angular blonde with large white teeth, a beige complexion, and very thin legs. Dorothy deduced from things said that she was probably in her late forties, but she certainly looked younger. She dressed smartly and in a vaguely masculine style that suited her, although she was inclined sometimes to overload herself with chunky gold bracelets and wear earrings which accentuated the narrowness of her head. She talked freely, and not unamusingly, about herself in a carefully mellifluous voice which creaked slightly on each change of register. Her father had been a Los Angeles real-estate man. During the war she had been in the American Red Cross and had stayed on with that organization in France and Germany until '47. Then her father had died and she had gone back to California. She had a house in Palm Springs now, which she rented when she went away on her trips. She had never had any great desire to get married, although she liked married people and was crazy about kids. But things had to work out right, or it was no good. She had a sister who had been married four times, and what a mess and misery all that had been. Her attitude toward men was one of sardonic camaraderie tinged with disdain.

By the fourth day out, Greg's dislike of her had become intense. The bottle of champagne had been a minor irritant; but when at dinner on the second night a bottle of claret had appeared, he had objected.

"It was very thoughtful of you Miss Drecker," he had said, "but Dorothy and I don't drink wine as a regular thing. So if you don't mind . . ."

"But the steward's already opened it. Oh, come on, Mr. Nilsen. Live dangerously."

Dorothy had giggled. The steward had smiled and poured the wine.

"Now, look, Dorothy," Greg had said when they were alone, "Arlene Drecker can drink all the wine she wants and so can you, for that matter. But I'm not having her tell me what I'm going to drink."

"She didn't mean it that way."

"I don't care what way she meant it. The way it worked out was that I had to drink something I didn't want or seem boorish. Dammit, she's not our hostess on this ship. I wish she'd stop behaving as if she were."

"She's only trying to be friendly."

"Listen. If you want wine or we want wine, I'll order it."

The following night Arlene had ordered burgundy; but Greg had taken the precaution of ordering in advance a bottle of rosé and the two wines arrived together.

"Too bad," Greg had said blandly. "What about joining us and having rosé, Arlene?"

"Rosé with roast beef?" Arlene had raised her eyebrows. "Thanks, I prefer burgundy."

But the next night, when the steward had produced the partly consumed bottle of burgundy, Arlene had not pressed them to share it with her. Greg had succeeded in making his point. It had not been until later in the evening that he had discovered that she had paid his bar bill for the day. Dorothy had not been able to help laughing.

Two days before they had reached Yokohama, a notice had gone up announcing that, during the ship's stay in port, conducted sightseeing tours ashore had been arranged. Those passengers wishing to take advantage of the special rates offered should inform the purser's office within the next twenty-four hours.

Greg had put his and Dorothy's names down. At lunch Dorothy had mentioned the fact.

Arlene had stared at her incredulously. "Sightseeing tours! Honey, you must be out of your mind."

"What's wrong with sightseeing tours?" Greg had asked. "After all, that's what we're making the trip for—to see sights."

"Oh, Greg!" Arlene had laughed tolerantly. "Have you ever been on a Japanese sightseeing tour?"

"Have you?"

"Yes, and I can tell you it's the end. They just cram you into a bus, give you a box lunch, and then drive you from one clip joint to another. They don't want to show you what you want to see. They just want you to buy things—cameras, fans, bits of fake jewelry."

"That's not what it says on the notice board."

"Naturally. Look, if you want to go rubber-necking, let me take you. I've been before. All you do is hire a car and have the man drive you around. You're on your own. You can stop when you want and go on when you want."

Dorothy had turned to him uncertainly. "What do you think, Greg?"

"Well, we've put our names down now."

Arlene had sighed. "Well, take them off again. Why not? If you want to be tourists, you may as well do it properly. This is not the best time of the year to come to Japan, but, since you are here, at least make yourselves comfortable."

Unhappily, she had been right. Those who had gone on the sightseeing tour had returned exhausted, ill-tempered, and late for dinner. Dorothy had had a fascinating day and bought a pair of carved soapstone hairpins which the barman said were worth at least three times what she had paid for them.

The following day, and then later at Kobe, the performance had been repeated. It could have been his fancy, but Greg suspected that both Dorothy and Arlene had a tacit agreement to ignore his leadership and run things their own way. When the table steward had reported that Miss Drecker was staying in her cabin, seasick, it had required an effort of will to utter the appropriate words of regret.

The bad weather lasted for two days and Greg thoroughly enjoyed them both. When on the third day Arlene made a wan appearance at lunch, he was almost as solicitous as Dorothy.

Then came the misunderstanding over the ship's shuffleboard tournament. The doctor had wanted Greg and Dorothy on his team, and Greg, without consulting Dorothy, had accepted. When the first round was announced over the ship's loudspeakers, Dorothy was missing. Greg found her eventually in Arlene's cabin playing Scrabble. By the time he had explained what had happened and they had reached the deck, the teams had been rearranged and they were out of the tournament.

Greg was annoyed. He did not mind about the shuffleboard, which he thought an old man's game, but he did mind having to apologize to the doctor.

Dorothy was very reasonable about it. "I'm sorry, dear, but you didn't tell me, did you?"

"I thought you were around on deck."

"Well, you were reading and Arlene suggested Scrabble. I know how you hate that, so I didn't bother you."

"Did you have to play down in the cabin?"

"She's got a very comfortable cabin. You haven't seen it. It's twice the size of ours. Look, dear, I'm sure the doctor didn't mind a bit. He understood."

"Yes, I know. But all the same . . ."

All the same, he was annoyed. That evening, when Arlene and Dorothy began to talk about the shopping they were going to do in Hong Kong, his annoyance returned.

"The big stores are in Victoria," Arlene was saying. "That's on Hong Kong island itself. But for us gals the best places are over in Kowloon. That's on the mainland. There's one called Star of Siam in the Peninsular Hotel that's a must."

"Shops in a hotel?" asked Dorothy.

"That's right. There are two whole floors of them."

"Sounds like a tourist trap to me," said Greg.

Arlene smiled at him. "What would you say to a suit in the best English tropical worsted, made to order, for twenty-five dollars?"

"Oh, sure, I know all about that. They just copy a suit you have and it falls to pieces the first time you wear it."

Arlene smiled again, very gently. "Is that what happens? I've never heard that, not from anyone who's really been there and bought one."

"Why don't you try, dear?" said Dorothy. "I mean, twenty-five dollars for a suit is cheap. And you do need some more summer outfits."

"Brooks Brothers is good enough for me." He knew it was a dull, foolish remark even as he said it.

"Well, it's not important." Dorothy spoke a trifle grimly.

Arlene's silence was monumentally tactful.

It was a Sunday night and there was no dancing after dinner. When Arlene had gone to her cabin, Dorothy suggested a walk around the deck before they went to bed.

After a while she said: "Darling, I'm worried. I'm having a good time, a wonderful time. You don't seem to be."

"Because I don't happen to want to buy a suit in Hong Kong?"

"Now you're being tiresome."

"All right. That woman gets on my nerves."

"Arlene? But she's really a very nice person."

"Well, I don't like her and I wish she'd get out of our hair."

"She's not in *my* hair. I think she's being very sweet and helpful. Can you imagine what it would have been like in Tokyo if we hadn't been lucky enough to have her to show us around? It couldn't have been very exciting for her. She'd seen it all before. She went to a lot of trouble for us."

"Well, I wish she'd go to a lot of trouble for somebody else. Anyway, if she's seen it all before, why does she come on the trip?"

"Greg, dear, you're usually more understanding and tolerant. She's a very lonely woman."

"And for some very good reasons."

"That's an unkind thing to say. It doesn't sound like you."

"Well, it is me. I told you, I don't like the woman. The chief steward told me she didn't want to sit with a crowd. Why not, if she's so lonely? Why did she have to pick on us?"

Dorothy did not reply immediately, and they walked once around the deck in silence.

"Look, darling," she said finally, "we didn't come on this trip just for a vacation, but because we wanted to travel and because we wanted to see something of the world outside America. If we were multimillionaires, maybe we could have done it in our own private yacht. As it is, we have to go with other people. We're not in a position to choose our traveling companions, any more than they're in a position to choose us. So, we've all got to make the best of one another. Isn't that common sense?"

Greg chuckled. "It's a poem, and beautifully delivered."

"Greg, I'm serious."

"I know you are, dear." He drew her arm through his. "That's why you're so cute."

He had recovered his good humor. Dorothy's homilies usually had that effect on him. Before they were married, she had taught at a kindergarten school, and in moments of stress traces of the old Montessori manner were still discernible.

"You're maddening," she said.

"I know it." He stopped and kissed her cheek. "All right, darling, we'll be nice, well-behaved American tourists spreading sweetness and light and hard currency wherever we go."

"If you'll just spread a little of that sweetness in Arlene's direction, that's all I ask."

"You said make the best of one another. Okay, I'll make the best of her, whatever that is."

"Thank you, dear."

He sighed. "Anyway, I'll try."

And, for some days, try he did.

ii

THE *Silver Isle* was to be in Hong Kong for forty-eight hours, discharging and taking on cargo, and she docked on the Kowloon side of the harbor by the wharfs on the Canton Road.

This was convenient for the passengers. They could go ashore any time they wanted, and were within easy walking distance of both the ferry to Victoria and the Peninsular Hotel.

Left to themselves, Greg and Dorothy would probably have taken the ferry straightaway and gone across to see Hong Kong itself; but Arlene led them first to the hotel.

"There'll be plenty of time for sightseeing later," she told them. "Let's get organized first. I suppose you've heard that these Chinese can make anything from a pair of earrings to a man's tuxedo overnight. Well, it just is not true. If you want anything properly made, you have to give them at least thirty-six hours. So let's do our shopping first, and then we don't have to worry."

They window-shopped for a while in the hotel, and then the girls left Greg with a tailor named Mr. Yu and went back to the Star of Siam to order Thai silk skirts. They had arranged to meet in the hotel lobby. When Greg had chosen his suit materials and had his measurements taken, he made his way down there.

He knew that he had at least half an hour to wait. It was too early for a drink. There was a row of travel agents' booths in the lobby, most of them offering sightseeing tours. It might be a good idea, he thought, to see about renting a car and driver.

The moment that thought came into his head another one followed it: "Maybe I'd better check with Arlene first." It was enough. He said "God dammit" between his teeth, and went over to the nearest booth.

A Chinese in a black business suit came forward.

"Good morning, sir. What can I do for you?"

"I want to rent a limousine with a driver to take us around. Do you have cars?"

"We do not have our own cars, but we can arrange that for you, sir. An American car, if you wish. When and for how long would you want it?"

"Well, we only have two days. We'd like to see as much as we can. We could start right after lunch from here."

"Then I would suggest, sir, that this afternoon you go across on the car ferry to Hong Kong and drive up to the Peak. There is a magnificent view from there. After that I would suggest a drive to Deep Water Bay and Repulse Bay, with tea at the hotel there. Tomorrow you could tour Kowloon and the New Territories."

"Would that take us as far as the Red Chinese border?"

"Certainly, sir. And you could lunch at Shatin. But I will get you a good driver who will know all these things and make helpful suggestions."

"How much would it cost?"

By the time Arlene and Dorothy arrived it was all settled.

Arlene clearly resented having the arrangements taken out of her hands in this fashion, but had difficulty in finding anything in them to criticize. She did the best she could, however.

"We didn't have to have a car this afternoon," she said. "We could have gone across to the island by the Star ferry and taken a cab on the other side."

"In all this humidity?" said Dorothy. "It's worse than August in New York."

"Humidity?" Arlene smiled knowingly. "You wait until we get to Singapore."

Greg congratulated himself on this small rift in the female alliance; but his satisfaction was short-lived. They went to a Chinese restaurant for lunch and Arlene insisted on their all using chopsticks. It was considered discourteous, she said, to use a fork. Dorothy thought it great fun; but Greg, who liked Chinese food and was hungry, became impatient and dropped some egg on his tie.

After lunch they went back to the Peninsular Hotel to pick up the car and driver.

The car proved to be a three-year-old Chevrolet Bel-Air, and Arlene looked at it disdainfully. The driver was a young Chinese wearing gray flannel trousers, a dark blue blazer, and a chauffeur's cap. He took off the cap and stood respectfully at attention as he held the rear door open for the ladies.

"Want me to go in front with you?" Greg asked him.

"If you do not object, sir, I think you will be more comfortable."

"Okay."

When they were in the car the driver turned to him.

"I see you have a camera, sir. There are certain places on the road up to the Peak where particularly good shots can be obtained. Would you like me to stop at those places?"

"That'd be fine. By the way, what's your name?"

"My Chinese name is Khoo Ah Au, sir." The driver smiled. "American clients find it easier to call me Jimmy."

iii

KHOO AH AU liked American tourists. He found them, on the whole, generous, easygoing, and completely predictable. They were rarely ill-tempered, as the British often were, or eccentric in their demands, as were the French. They did not harass him with questions he had not been asked before, and listened politely, if sometimes inattentively, to the information he had to impart. They used their light meters conscientiously before taking photographs and bought their souvenirs dutifully at the shops which paid him commission. Above all, he found their personal relationships very easy to read. It was probably a matter of race, he thought. His own people were always very careful not to give themselves away, to expose crude feelings about one another. Americans seemed not to care how much was understood by strangers. It was almost as if they enjoyed being transparent.

This American and these two women, for example. You had only to listen for a few minutes to what they said and how they said it, and everything was clear. The woman called Arlene was attracted to the wife, and the husband was jealous. Possibly he had no cause; possibly the two women had done no more than exchange confidences or touch each other's hands; but he was jealous. And the hungry woman was jealous of him. Only the wife, personable but middle-aged, seemed unconcerned. She did not appear flattered by the situation, or even aware of it. Perhaps she was more subtle than she sounded. When he had listened a little more, he would be able to decide.

They were on the car ferry when he heard something that interested him keenly. "If we'd gone across by the passenger ferry," the Arlene woman was saying, "you'd have been able to get a beautiful shot of the boat in dock."

"Well, maybe I'll do that tomorrow," the American said. "Anyway, there'll be plenty of chances of seeing her in dock."

It was the word "boat" that had interested him. He had assumed that the trio were staying at the Peninsular Hotel because he had been engaged from there. The possibility of their being transit passengers off a boat had not occurred to him.

"You've come by boat, sir?" he inquired diffidently.

"Yes, the *Silver Isle*. Know her?"

"Oh, yes, sir. And are you staying here?"

"No, we're going on in her. Manila, Saigon, Singapore, Rangoon, Calcutta. My wife and I are on a world trip."

"Ah, that is very nice."

They were coming in to the landing ramp now, and his passengers had plenty to engage their attention. It gave him time to think.

Almost two months had elapsed since his wife's uncle had visited them; and, so far, all his attempts to find an American who would meet Mr. Tan's specifications had failed. Moreover, his last attempt had been a frightening failure. The American, a department-store executive from Cleveland, had accused him of trying to work a confidence trick and threatened to go to the police. After that, he had made up his mind to do nothing further in the matter. Unfortunately, Mr. Tan was a highly respected member of his wife's family, and she had begun nagging him about it—not in an angry way, but reproachfully, intimating that his failure to do what her uncle wanted would cause her to lose face. There was also the money to be considered. With the five hundred dollars (Hong Kong) that Mr. Tan had offered for the service, he could go to Cheong Ming and Co. and buy a hi-fi set. But was it worth the risk?

He began to study the American beside him.

He was tall and thin with loose-fitting clothes and short, graying hair. He spoke quietly and with a slight smile in one corner of his mouth. His eyes were watchful and shrewd; but there might be innocence there, too. Not an easy man to deceive; but one who might sometimes deceive himself.

Ah Au drove up toward the Peak. Near the lower cable-car station he stopped so that they could admire the view of the port from the road. The American took his camera and got out of the car.

The Arlene woman said: "There's a much better view from the top." She and the wife stayed in the car.

Ah Au went over to the American and began pointing out various landmarks in the panorama below them.

"Yes, it's a great place," the American said. "By the way, Jimmy, *is* the view better from up top?"

"There is a fine view there, too, sir, which I will show you in a minute, but this is better for photography. From the Peak there is more haze."

"I see." He was winding the camera.

"Are you using Kodachrome, sir?"

"Yes. Why?"

"From here, sir, at f 8 with a haze filter you will get a very good picture."

"Thanks. You take many pictures?"

"No, sir, but I have such information for my clients."

The camera whirred. As they were walking back to the car, the American said: "Is this your car or do you just drive for someone else?"

"It is my car, sir. I like to give personal service to clients."

"I expect you make more money working for yourself, too."

Ah Au smiled. "There is also that, sir."

The American smiled back.

Ah Au drove on up to the Peak. Some progress had been made, he thought. They had established a personal relationship.

The tour continued. His passengers had tea at the Repulse Bay Hotel. Then he drove them on to the fishing village of Aberdeen and showed them the floating Chinese restaurants. At the Arlene woman's suggestion, it was decided that he should drive them out there to dine the following night. It was on the way back to the ferry that Jimmy had the glimpse of his client's mind for which he had been hoping.

He was driving along Connaught Road, by the long quay where the junks tied up for unloading, when the American turned to him.

"Jimmy, what are all those barges lined up along there? I mean the green painted ones with the yellow stars on them."

"They are junks from Canton, sir."

"But that's in Red China."

"Yes, sir. Canton is only ninety miles away."

"Stop the car. I've got to have some shots of this."

Ah Au parked the car and, leaving the women sitting in it, walked back along the quay with the American. The man seemed curiously excited and was almost tripping over himself in his eagerness to get a closer look at the junks.

"What are they doing here?" he asked.

"They come and go all the time, sir."

"Doing what?"

"Carrying cargo." Ah Au was puzzled. He could not understand why the man was so interested.

"What sort of cargo?"

"Any sort of cargo, sir. That is rattan cane they are unloading. It is made into chairs and baskets here."

"But I don't see any police about. Do you mean they're allowed just to come and go as they please?"

"They are ordinary people. They make no trouble, sir."

"Well, I'll be . . ."

He began to take pictures. When they got back to the car, Ah Au listened thoughtfully as the American told his wife and her friend what he had found out.

The women were interested, and the Arlene one said that it showed what the British had come to when they didn't worry about Communists going in and out of one of their Colonies; but they were not interested the way the man was. As they drove on toward the ferry, Ah Au saw him looking about him intently, as if he were discovering a new meaning in everything he saw.

By the time they reached the mainland Ah Au had decided to take matters a stage further. As he drove them back along the Canton Road to the ship, he asked a question.

"Tomorrow morning, sir, for your tour of the New Territories, do you wish me to go to the Peninsular Hotel, or shall I take the car to the ship?"

"Can you do that?"

"Oh, yes, sir. If I have your name to give at the dock gate."

"My name's Nilsen. Would ten o'clock be okay?"

"Perfectly, sir." He frowned as if making an effort of memory. "Mr. Nilsen, there was another Mr. Nilsen here last year. He was in the textile business. He had a big plant at a place called Dayton, I think. Perhaps you know him."

Mr. Nilsen smiled tolerantly. "No, Jimmy, I don't. I'm an engineer and I have a small die-casting plant at a place called Wilmington. Nilsen's a pretty common name in the United States."

"I beg your pardon. I did not know that. Someday, perhaps, I will be able to go to America."

He congratulated himself. The chances of his being caught out in the lie about a textile man named Nilsen from Dayton had been small. The information gained had been reassuring. Mr. Nilsen was neither a government official, who might consider it his duty to notify the authorities, nor a newspaperman, who might become indiscreet in other ways. He was a respectable businessman of just the type that Mr. Tan had described, and traveling by just the specified route. The problem now was to find a way of putting Mr. Tan's proposition in an attractive light without being either compromised or misunderstood.

When he returned home, Ah Au said nothing to his wife about Mr. Nilsen. He had already decided to make this further attempt to oblige Mr. Tan; but only if a favorable opportunity presented itself. The pressure of her expectations could distort his judgment.

During the night he lay awake for an hour, going over every moment of the afternoon and re-examining his image of Mr. Nilsen. When he was sure that nothing had escaped his attention, he went back to sleep.

The Arlene woman was late, and they did not leave the dock until nearly ten-thirty. Mr. Nilsen controlled his impatience too obviously. It was an inauspicious beginning. Ah Au wanted Mr. Nilsen in as relaxed a mood as possible, and took an early opportunity of suggesting that, as they had plenty of time in hand, they might like to stop at the Castle Peak Hotel for coffee. It was about four miles out on the Tai Po Road, and they would be passing it anyway.

Mrs. Nilsen thought this a good idea, and the tension seemed to slacken. By the time they left Castle Peak and were heading for the frontier, the atmosphere had improved still further. Soon, as they began to pass farms and paddy fields, Ah Au was hearing the familiar exclamations—*Look at that wooden plow! This is really old China! What about those hats with curtains! My God, the smell!*—which told him that his passengers were enjoying themselves.

He drove absently, answering the questions put to him promptly and fully, but not elaborating on his answers. He was waiting for a British army truck to come along. Presently they overtook one, and he slowed to stay behind it. It was, happily, full of troops.

He glanced at Mr. Nilsen and smiled. "We are getting near Red China," he said. "This is the beginning of the military zone."

Mr. Nilsen was leaning forward, staring at the truck. "Are those British troops?"

"Yes, sir, a Scottish regiment. There is a camp farther along this road."

"How many do they have to guard this frontier?"

"One or two battalions, I think."

"One or two battalions!" He turned around. "Did you hear that, Dorothy? Only one or two battalions to guard this frontier. My God, the Reds could walk in here any time they wanted. Isn't that right, Jimmy?"

Ah Au smiled. "Oh, yes, sir. But I think they could do that even if there were two divisions to guard the frontier."

Mr. Nilsen nodded grimly. "You could be right at that. How near to the frontier can we get?"

"About a mile, sir. It is dangerous, you see."

"How dangerous?"

"Sometimes they shoot from the other side at persons moving too close to the frontier line."

"Nice people."

The army truck turned off the road into the camp entrance, and Ah Au put on speed again. He could feel the mounting excitement of the man beside him and wanted to satisfy it.

About a mile and a half from the frontier the road turned sharply to the right and ran parallel to it. However, there was a narrow cart track heading straight on, and Ah Au drove down it until they reached a small farmhouse. The track continued, but a few yards past the house there was a large signboard prohibiting movement beyond that point. Ah Au stopped the car, took a pair of binoculars from the glove compartment, and they all got out.

For about a mile ahead the landscape was flat. Then there was a line of low hills, the sides of which were dotted with groups of burial urns, and a ridge. Along the ridge and near the top of it ran a thin black line.

"That is the frontier, sir." Ah Au handed Mr. Nilsen the binoculars.

"That black line?"

"Yes, it is a barbed-wire fence. There are machine-gun towers, too, but you cannot see them well from here."

Mr. Nilsen scanned the line of the fence from side to side, then handed the binoculars to his wife and got out his camera.

"F 11 with the haze filter," Ah Au murmured.

Mr. Nilsen nodded and went to work. He did a panning shot first, beginning close on his wife as she looked through the binoculars, then going on to the signboard, then moving into an extreme long shot of the frontier. Then he switched the turret onto the telephoto lens. He used two magazines of film before he was finished.

The Arlene woman became bored and went back to the car. Small children from the farmhouse came out to peer at her through the car windows and hold out their hands for money. Ah Au had to chase them away.

Mr. Nilsen returned to the car reluctantly, and insisted on taking some shots of the farmhouse and the giggling children before he could be persuaded to leave. Even as they bumped along the track back to the road, he kept looking over his shoulder toward the frontier. Ah Au was pleased with the impression it had made.

When they passed the Kowloon-Canton Railway where it curved toward the frontier station, there were more questions.

"Is there a lot of railroad traffic between Kowloon and Canton?"

"Oh, yes, sir. People go to see friends and family in Canton."

"I don't get it. You mean they just go?"

"They must get a permit from the Chinese government office in Hong Kong, but it is quite easy."

"Hear that, Dorothy? So that's the bamboo curtain!"

"You wish to go to Canton, sir?"

"Me? No, thanks!" He laughed. "I have United States government contracts to think about."

They stopped at Tai Po market so that the two women could look at the small shops there and buy coolie hats. Ah Au bargained for the hats and, when they had been paid for, took them back to the car.

He was about to return and render further assistance when Mr. Nilsen joined him.

"They've gone into a silk shop," he said. "They're not going to buy, but they'll be there an age. You smoke?"

"Not when driving, sir. But now, thank you."

They sat in the car and smoked. A ring of children collected to stare at them, but Mr. Nilsen took no notice.

"Have you ever been to Canton?" he asked.

"No, sir. I have been to Macao, where my wife has some relatives, but my family is in Manila."

"Is that so? Don't you like the Philippines?"

"My family went there from here, sir. But I was born here and I am British. There are more opportunities here, I think."

"I don't get it. I should have thought this was the last place where you could look forward to any sort of security for your family. This section, for instance. You call it the New Territories. But it's leased, isn't it, from the government of China?"

"Yes, sir, in eighteen ninety-eight. It was leased for ninety-nine years."

"So in nineteen ninety-seven you'll have to give it back to the Reds, if they're still in business."

"That is so."

"Or if they don't walk in and take it back before?"

"There is always that possibility, sir, but I do not think the risk is great. Hong Kong is no danger to them and it is a useful outlet to the West. That is why, too, the Portuguese are allowed to stay in Macao."

Ah Au spoke almost without thinking. He had planned to wait until after lunch at Shatin before attempting to broach the subject of Mr.

Tan's proposition. Now, he was being offered an opening of a kind he could not possibly have contrived. His heart began to beat faster. Then, he made up his mind.

"All that could change overnight," Mr. Nilsen was saying. "Some shift in the Cold War or another Korea over the Formosa situation, and I wouldn't give you a nickel for the Peninsular Hotel."

Ah Au smiled. "You are probably right, sir. But, meanwhile, there are advantages to both sides, and not only for the big bankers and trading companies here."

"That so?"

"In fact, I can tell you a story that may amuse you, sir."

"What's that?"

"Well, sir, it is a little confidential, but you are not a policeman or a newspaperman, so I can tell you." He paused.

"Sure, go ahead."

"You see, sir, we Chinese are all pirates at heart." He shrugged. "Chinese piracy is as old as history. When the Reds began sending arms and ammunition down by sea in junks to the terrorists in Malaya, there were naturally some men, both here and in Macao, who thought it a pity that such valuable cargoes should arrive at their destinations. It was a great temptation. So as often as they could, they . . ." He spread his hands deprecatingly.

"They hijacked them?" Mr. Nilsen smiled.

"Yes, though that was not the best part of the joke, sir. You know that arms and ammunition are very valuable in this part of the world."

"They are in most places."

"Particularly in the Far East, sir. But the trouble is that there are government regulations and embargoes that make it difficult to sell military equipment. It was not easy to seize these cargoes, and although the Reds could not make international complaints without admitting openly that they were supplying the terrorists, these pirates, these hijackers you would call them, they ran great risks. There had to be profit." He paused again. He could see that he had Mr. Nilsen's whole attention.

"Well, how did they get rid of the stuff?"

"It was very simple, sir. They took the Communist arms down to Indonesia and sold them to the anti-Communist rebels."

Mr. Nilsen stared and then began to laugh.

Ah Au sighed inwardly with relief. He saw the holes in his own story so clearly that he had been afraid Mr. Nilsen would see them, too.

He did see one an instant later. When he had stopped laughing, he said: "What I don't see is why the Reds sent the stuff down by sea at all. What about the British navy? Couldn't they intercept the shipments to Malaya?"

"They intercepted many, sir, but, you know, there are a lot of junks in the China Seas. Last year there were over twenty-five thousand of them using Hong Kong alone. You cannot intercept and search every junk at sea between here and Singapore."

"I suppose not."

"Though you are right, sir. The illegal arms traffic was stopped in the end. A friend of mine in Manila was very sad about that."

"Yes?"

"Some time ago he took a shipment of arms and ammunition out of a Red junk off Hainan. It was modern equipment—rifles, machine guns, bazookas—worth sixty thousand dollars. And it is still in Manila."

"Why? Aren't there any more anti-Communists in Indonesia?"

"Plenty, sir, but it is not as simple as it was before. This is no longer a small business. The buying agents for the rebels are in Singapore, and they must be careful. They will not buy illegal arms any more. My friend has tried to sell. Now he says he must try to make the arms legal."

"How does he propose to do that?"

But Ah Au had seen the two women approaching and was already getting out of the car to open the door for them. Mr. Nilsen's forecast that they would buy nothing had proved incorrect. His wife had a Shantung dress length and the Arlene woman had some jade earrings. They got into the car, showing their purchases and chattering about the other things that the shop had for sale.

Ah Au drove on toward Shatin.

The interruption of his conversation with Mr. Nilsen had not dismayed him. On the contrary, he was glad of it. He was quite sure that Mr. Nilsen was sufficiently intrigued to want an answer to his last question, and it was much better that he should be the one to return to the subject.

Ah Au did not have to wait long. When the three Americans had had lunch at the Shatin Hotel, the women went for a walk in the gardens overlooking the valley. Mr. Nilsen had gone to the toilet, but when he came out, he did not join the women in the garden. Instead, he came out to Ah Au, who was sitting in the car.

Ah Au got out to open the door, but Mr. Nilsen waved him back.

"I've seen enough sights for the moment," he said with a smile. "I want to hear more about your friend in Manila."

"Yes, sir?"

"What did you mean about making that shipment of arms legal?"

"You understand, sir, this is very confidential."

"Sure, I understand."

"For arms to be legal, sir, they have to have a legal owner and a legal place of origin. What my friend needs is a nominee."

"How do you mean?"

"What my friend would like to do is ship the arms to be held in bond at Singapore, and then sell them."

"Why can't he do that?"

"Sir, the authorities at Singapore would not accept the consignment in bond without a proper certified bill of lading from a reputable shipper at the port of origin. Unfortunately, residents of Manila cannot trade in arms without a government permit. That is difficult and expensive to obtain. So, he must have a foreign nominee."

"Why? I don't get it."

"After the war in Manila, sir, a lot of surplus American war material was sold to dealers who exported it. The regulations about permits do not apply to non-resident foreigners exporting arms."

"I see."

"Also, sir, the nominee would have to go to Singapore to sign clearance papers. My friend has tried to find the right person, but although he is willing to pay as much as five per cent for the service, he has been unsuccessful. He will not deal with crooks."

"Hijackers aren't usually so particular."

"A crook would cheat him, sir. Once the papers are signed, what is to prevent the nominee from claiming the goods are his and keeping all the money? Sixty thousand Straits dollars is a lot. Twenty-one thousand dollars American."

"And five per cent of that is a thousand and fifty." Mr. Nilsen grinned amiably. "Jimmy, you couldn't be telling me all this for a reason, could you?"

Ah Au's heart missed a beat. Was Mr. Nilsen going to be like the man from Cleveland after all?

"A reason, sir? But you asked me."

"I know it. But you sort of raised the question in the first place, didn't you? Come on, now, Jimmy. Didn't you have some idea that I might be suckered into acting as your friend's nominee?"

Ah Au looked amazed. "You, sir? I had not thought of it."

"All right. Never mind." He started to turn away.

Ah Au spoke quickly. "But would you consider such a proposition, sir?"

Mr. Nilsen looked at him coldly. "What's the angle, Jimmy?"

"Angle, sir?"

"What's your friend in Manila trying to smuggle? Opium?"

"Sir, that is not a good thing to say. You asked me questions. I answered the truth."

"All right. Let me ask you some more questions. What's your friend's name?"

"Sir, if you believe that he is smuggling opium, you will go to the police. How can I tell you?"

"All right, I promise not to go to the police. What's his name?"

Ah Au hesitated, then bowed slightly. "As you promise, I must accept your promise. Please note that, sir. His name is Mr. Tan Tack Chee."

"Right, then why does Mr. Tan Tack Chee have you touting for him? Why doesn't he find a nominee himself?"

"Because he has no contacts, sir, with passengers off boats. He cannot go up to strangers and make his request. And it has to be someone who is going to Singapore. How would he know?"

"Why doesn't he get hold of an officer on one of the ships and ask him to do it?"

"A ship's officer dealing in arms would be an object of suspicion to the authorities in Singapore, sir."

"So would I."

"No, sir. Many of the dealers in war material are American businessmen. You are an engineer with a business in America. You would be perfectly acceptable."

"Don't you mean innocent-looking? Don't you mean I'd be a good cover? You say no opium. Okay, but there are other kinds of contraband. How do I know what'd be in that shipment."

Ah Au smiled. "Mr. Nilsen, sir, no person who wished to make an illegal shipment of any kind would describe it on a bill of lading and a ship's manifest as arms and ammunition. That is asking for it to be examined by port authorities."

"Is that how it would be described?"

"Of course, sir." Ah Au spread out his hands. "That is my friend's need, to be able to have the shipment legally bonded in Singapore. I explained this."

Mr. Nilsen thought for a moment, then nodded. "Yes, you did. This Mr. Tan, now. You say he's a friend of yours. How did you get to know him?"

Ah Au drew himself up a trifle stiffly. "He is my wife's father, sir," he said.

Mr. Nilsen began to laugh, then checked himself. "Sorry, Jimmy, I was just amused at the idea of a man calling his father-in-law his friend."

"You are not friendly with Mrs. Nilsen's father, sir?"

"Oh, sure, but . . . no, skip it. I'd better go and see where those women have got to."

He had started to go. Ah Au followed him.

"Then you will consider the proposition, sir?"

Mr. Nilsen grinned affably. "Oh, sure, I'll consider it."

"When will you decide, sir?"

"I'll let you know tonight. Now back the car up, Jimmy, will you? I have to stop off at the Peninsular Hotel for a fitting at the tailor's."

iv

GREG was feeling good that evening. The idea of his having been asked, in all seriousness, to act as front man for a Chinese pirate had appealed to his sense of humor.

At least, that is how he chose to explain the sudden lightness of heart that had come to him as he was changing for dinner. He regarded himself, not without reason, as a mature and level-headed man. If anyone had suggested that somewhere in the back streets of his mind another Greg Nilsen—a roistering, romantic, ten-year-old swashbuckler—had escaped from custody and was out enjoying a game of cops and robbers, he would have been angrily incredulous. It had not yet occurred to him to ask himself why, if the whole thing were simply a good joke, he had not told Dorothy about it.

Jimmy Khoo brought the car to the boat at seven o'clock and drove them across to Aberdeen.

The trouble with Arlene started in the sampan which took them out from the quayside to the floating restaurant. Halfway out across the harbor, she suddenly jumped up out of her seat.

"I've been bitten," she said to Dorothy.

"Oh, no!"

"I've been bitten."

"Where?"

The light sampan rocked dangerously.

"Better sit down," Greg cautioned them. "You're rocking the boat."

Dorothy sat down, but Arlene ignored him. "I've been bitten," she repeated maddeningly and, pulling up one side of her skirt, began examining the back of her leg.

The sampan lurched over in the other direction. The Chinese girl, standing on the stern counter with the oar, was thrown off balance. The old woman who owned the sampan screamed. Greg felt the wicker chair he was sitting on start to slide. He grabbed at the side of the boat.

"For God's sake, sit down!" he shouted.

Arlene sat down, the Chinese girl giggled, and a minute later they were at the restaurant steps. Greg paid off the sampan and joined Dorothy and Arlene on the veranda. They appeared to be having some sort of argument.

He heard Dorothy saying: "I'm sure Greg didn't mean to . . ." And then Arlene turned to face him. Her nose and mouth were pinched and white with anger.

"I'm not used to being yelled at like that," she said.

"Arlene, I only asked you to sit down. That sort of boat upsets pretty easily."

"There was no need to yell at me like that."

"I yelled because I didn't want to have to swim the rest of the way."

"Oh, really, Greg!" This was Dorothy. "I do think you ought to apologize to Arlene. I know you meant well, but it wasn't very polite."

"All right, I'm sorry. Now, for goodness' sake, let's go eat."

It was not a gracious apology and nobody attempted to pretend it was. The situation was not improved when they found that the desirable tables on the upper deck were all reserved, and that they would have to sit down below surrounded by very noisy mah-jong players. Arlene had said that it was unnecessary to make table reservations. Greg pointedly refrained from reminding her of the fact. The critical moment came, however, when they went with the waiter to the big traps moored alongside the vessel to choose the fish they would eat.

There was a man with a long-handled landing net standing by the traps. As the customers pointed to the fish they wanted, he would scoop them dextrously out of the water and fling them on to a long tiled slab which led to the kitchen.

One of the fish he pulled out was some kind of grouper. It was a heavy fish and it landed on the slab with a force that stunned it. For a moment or two it lay there almost still, its eyes staring vacuously, its big slack mouth gaping in an expression of the deepest gloom.

Arlene glanced at Dorothy. "Isn't that someone we know?" she asked slyly.

She did not look at Greg; but Dorothy did, and then burst out laughing.

"Oh, really, Arlene," she said, "he's not looking as miserable as all that."

Then she squeezed Greg's arm in affectionate apology; and, of course, he had to laugh, too.

But there was murder in his heart, and at that moment a resolution was born. Somewhere, somehow, their plans, his and Dorothy's, would have to be changed. He was not going to go all the way to Calcutta in the *Silver Isle* with Arlene Drecker.

When they arrived back at the ship, the two women went on board while Greg stayed to settle the account with Jimmy. He added a generous tip.

"Thank you very much indeed, sir." Jimmy took off his cap and bowed, but made no move to leave. He was looking at Greg expectantly.

Greg smiled. "Oh, yes. You want to know about that proposition."

"I hope you can accept, sir."

"Well, I don't know, Jimmy."

"Sir, all that is necessary is that you sign some papers in Manila and Singapore."

"People have been hanged before now just for signing papers, Jimmy."

"In this case, sir . . ."

"No. I tell you what I will do. When we get to Manila I'll see your Mr. Tan, if you'll have him contact me on the ship. And *then* I'll decide. Okay?"

Jimmy beamed. "Certainly, sir. That will be entirely satisfactory. Thank you very much indeed, sir."

"There's nothing to thank me for. And mind you explain the exact position to him. I don't want any misunderstandings."

"There will be none. And may I say what a pleasure it has been to serve you, sir?"

"The pleasure's mutual. Be seeing you again someday, maybe."

"I sincerely hope so, sir."

When Greg got back on board, he found that some mail had been sent up to the cabin from the purser's office. Among it was a progress report from his vice-president in charge of production. Everything at the plant was running smoothly. He didn't have to worry about a thing; just enjoy the trip.

v

THE following morning Khoo Ah Au dispatched two cables: one to his wife's father in Manila, the other to his wife's uncle in Kuala Pangkalan.

The cable to Mr. Tan Tack Chee read:

CONTACT POSSIBLE PROSPECT MR. G. NILSEN PASSENGER S. S. SILVER ISLE ARRIVING MANILA 14TH RESPECTFUL AFFECTION WIFE AND SELF. KHOO.

The cable to Mr. Tan Siow Mong read:

HAVE ADVISED MANILA SUITABLE PROSPECT ARRIVING S. S. SILVER ISLE 14TH RESPECTFUL AFFECTION WIFE AND SELF. KHOO.

That night Mrs. Khoo had the unusual and elevating experience of receiving an overseas telephone call from her father in Manila. The only disappointing thing about it was that more time was devoted to the business talk with her husband than to the discussion of her possible pregnancy.

CHAPTER IV

Two DAYS LATER the *Silver Isle* docked in Manila, and hordes of scarlet-shirted Filipino stevedores swarmed on board. They seemed to penetrate into every corner of the ship. Some even found their way into the writing room, where they lounged with their feet up on the tables until indignant stewards shooed them away.

The passengers had been warned that Manila was one of the worst ports in the Far East for pilfering. Greg was depositing a package containing Dorothy's jewelry in the purser's safe, when a steward came up with the message that Mr. Tan Tack Chee would like to see him. The gentleman was in the bar.

Dorothy was waiting for him by the notice board. They—or, rather, they and Arlene—had decided not to go ashore immediately, but wait until after lunch. When the purser's clerk had made out the receipt, Greg went over to her.

"Darling, I meant to tell you before. There's a man here who wants to see me on business. It'll only take a few minutes. I'll see you up on the sports deck."

Dorothy pulled a face. "Business? I though we'd left that behind."

"It's nothing important."

"I didn't know you did any business here."

"It's just a man I promised to see." There was nothing untrue about the statement; nevertheless, he did not feel quite easy about it. "I'll tell you the story later," he added. "Look, darling, do you mind holding on to the camera for me?"

He went up to the bar. It was crowded with dock police, customs officials, and the usual collection of "business" visitors thirsty for free drinks. The steward who had brought him the message pointed to a table in the corner of the bar. Greg made his way over.

Seated at the table with an open briefcase in front of him was a middle-aged Chinese. He wore a well-pressed light gray suit and thick tortoise-shell glasses. He was writing busily in a loose-leaf notebook. As Greg approached, he glanced up.

"Mr. Tan?"

"Mr. Nilsen?" As he spoke he rose and they shook hands.

Mr. Tan's voice and manner were subdued, and his hand was like a soft bag of chicken bones. It would have been difficult to conceive of anyone less piratical. Greg, whose imagination had had three days to prepare for the encounter, was disconcerted.

"My son-in-law in Hong Kong cabled me that you would be passing through Manila," Mr. Tan said easily. "He hoped that I might perhaps be of some service to you and Mrs. Nilsen."

"Well, that's very kind of you, Mr. Tan. But I rather understood that there was a matter of business you wanted . . ."

"Do you or Mrs. Nilsen know Manila?" Mr. Tan's interruption was so gentle in tone that Greg scarcely noticed the firmness of it.

"No, we don't."

"Then, may I make a suggestion? I have my car on the wharf. It would be a favor if you would allow me to place it at your disposal."

"Mr. Tan, I don't think . . ."

Mr. Tan held up a slender hand. "And an additional favor if you would allow me to be your host at lunch. You understand, I do not have the professional skills of my son-in-law, but my driver knows Manila well and can show you what there is to see."

"As a matter of fact, Mr. Tan, we've sort of committed ourselves to taking another passenger along with us. A lady."

"She is included in the invitation," Mr. Tan said promptly.

"I think . . ."

"I understand perfectly, Mr. Nilsen. Please feel free to consult with your wife before you accept."

Greg hesitated. "Mr. Tan, I think I had better explain that I have not mentioned to my wife the business we might have to discuss."

"Naturally, Mr. Nilsen, one does not trouble ladies with business." He smiled. "I am in the so-called import-export market. That is a very loose term covering everything from powdered milk to earth-moving equipment."

Greg nodded uncertainly. "I guess so. If you'll excuse me, I'll go and find my wife."

Half an hour later the four of them left the ship and walked along the quay to the car park. As they approached, a pink Cadillac swung out of the parking line and pulled up alongside them. A Filipino driver sprang out to open the doors and they all got in.

Mr. Tan took them to his house for lunch. It was in the Spanish style and built on a hillside overlooking the bay. Mrs. Tan, obviously a second wife, proved to be young, very attractive, and a graduate of the University of Southern California. She wore toreador pants, and barbecued steaks for them on the patio. Arlene was enchanted. Mr. Tan talked about Philippine politics, skin diving, and the amusing misfortunes of an American motion-picture company who were trying to shoot on location up in the hills. He did not once mention business.

After lunch the car dropped him back at his office, which was in a modern, American-style building, and then the Filipino driver took them on a tour of the city. When they returned to the office Mr. Tan's secretary informed them that he had had to go out, but that he hoped Mr. and Mrs. Nilsen and Miss Drecker would dine with him that evening. The car would call for them at seven. Mr. Tan would wear a white tuxedo.

Dorothy glanced at Arlene with a smile of triumph. "We're certainly getting the full treatment," she said. "He must want those die-castings pretty badly, eh, darling?"

Even Arlene was looking at him with approval.

Greg mumbled something noncommittal. He was feeling thoroughly confused. His neglecting to tell Dorothy about the conversation with Jimmy Khoo in Hong Kong had been natural enough, he assured himself. The commercial technicalities about nominees, manifests, and shipping in bond would only have bored her; and, besides, they had agreed from the start that business talk was to be taboo on the trip. The last thing he had been prepared for was having to account for Mr. Tan in the role of a generous host. When he had first reported the invitation to lunch, Arlene had been there, and it had been impossible to go into long explanations. "He's in the import-export business," had been all that he had said; but Dorothy had jumped to the conclusion that the man wanted to buy die-castings.

He had not realized it until later, or he could have said something to her in time. As it was, the first he had heard about it had been during the afternoon's sightseeing. He had been listening to the driver talking about the village he came from, when a fragment of conversation from the back seat had caught his attention.

"You see," Dorothy had been saying, "Greg's plant only does this special precision work. Most of his contracts are with the government, or people like airplane manufacturers, or those other people who develop the missiles. He's never had much time for export business before."

"Well, you ought to encourage it."

"Why?"

"Won't it make part of your trip tax-deductible?"

Dorothy had laughed. "I'd never thought of that."

"I'll bet Greg has."

Greg had pretended not to hear. An explanation at that moment would merely have made his wife look foolish and gratified Arlene's appetite for discord.

Now he was almost sorry that he had not taken the risk. He had maneuvered himself into one false position where Dorothy was concerned; and it looked very much as if Mr. Tan had maneuvered him into another. It was going to be embarrassing now to say "no" to Mr. Tan, or even to question him closely, when the questions could only imply doubt of his good faith. The fact that Mr. Tan's hospitality had a clear purpose was beside the point. Wisely or unwisely, the hospitality had been accepted; and so, an obligation, of courtesy at least, had been incurred.

Dinner was at a country club just outside the city, and had been specially ordered by Mr. Tan. The rum drinks were innocent-tasting but very potent. Toward the end of the evening Arlene became emotional and, in trying to express her gratitude for the wonderful day she had had, was moved to tears of joy. Her mascara ran and she was forced to retire to the powder room. Mrs. Tan and Dorothy decided to join her there. Greg and Mr. Tan were alone.

There was a pause.

"This has been a very enjoyable day," Greg said.

Mr. Tan smiled. "For me, too, Mr. Nilsen. Although—" he smiled again—"it would have been more enjoyable if you had not been so troubled by your suspicions."

"Suspicions?"

"My son-in-law in Hong Kong is a very praiseworthy young man. He is not a man of great substance as yet, but he is honest and hard-working. Otherwise, I would not have allowed my daughter to marry him. But he has a weakness."

"Oh, yes?"

"A taste for melodrama. Did he mention piracy, Mr. Nilsen?"

"He did, yes."

"I was afraid so. He lives in the richly flavored past of lions and dragons. It is an engaging weakness, but embarrassing in business."

"I guess it would be."

"You know, Mr. Nilsen, this small parcel of arms was acquired by accident, but, as far as I am concerned, perfectly legally. I will confess to you that its existence is inconvenient, and I would like to disembarrass myself. A technicality makes this difficult. You, as you know, are in a position to overcome the technicality. That is the length and breadth of the problem."

Greg pushed his drink away. "Mr. Tan, are you on the level?"

"Sir?"

"I want to get this straight. These are arms from Red China originally intended for Red terrorists in Malaya. Is that correct?"

"Perfectly correct. As I said, they fell into my hands by accident."

"What sort of accident?"

"The man who seized them off Hainan left them with me as a pledge for a loan. Later, I am afraid, he went bankrupt."

"And now you want to sell them to the *anti*-Red people in Indonesia. Is that correct?"

"Entirely correct, Mr. Nilsen."

Greg considered for a moment and then nodded. "Okay, it's a deal."

Mr. Tan stroked his chin thoughtfully before he said: "Very well. I will bring the papers to you to sign in the morning." He hesitated and then went on. "I will be frank with you, Mr. Nilsen. I am not entirely happy with this arrangement."

Greg stared at him. "You mean you've changed your mind?"

"Indeed no. On the contrary, I am quite satisfied with the arrangement as far as it goes. My regret is that it does not go further."

"How do you mean?"

"My brother in Singapore is capable of handling the shipping and delivery arrangements, but when it comes to dealing with the buyers, I am not sure that he is the best man. An American can always drive a harder bargain in that business. How long will you be in Singapore, Mr. Nilsen?"

"Two days."

"Not very long. I had hoped you might consider conducting the negotiations personally. For an additional consideration, of course."

Greg shook his head. "I don't think I'm qualified to do that, Mr. Tan. And, as you say, I won't be there long enough."

"I quite understand. Ah, here are the ladies."

The ship was sailing at midday. At ten-thirty Mr. Tan arrived with the papers for signature.

The first was a consigner's note requesting the Anglo-Malay Transport Company of Kuala Pangkalan to ship the goods listed from the Tak Wah Godown and Storage Corporation, Manila, to the Chen Warehouse Company, Singapore, to be held in bond there pending further instructions. The second was an export license giving Greg's name and address in the

United States and a list of the goods to be exported. This required his countersignature and passport number to become effective.

When Greg had signed, Mr. Tan gave him copies of the documents. "As soon as you arrive in Singapore, Mr. Nilsen," he said, "my brother Tan Yam Heng will contact you. I have written his name down here. He will have copies of the bill of lading, and go with you to make the proper customs declaration. He will then ask you to sign a paper transferring the ownership of the goods in bond to a company or person to be designated later. When you have signed that paper, he will hand you a check for one thousand and fifty dollars U.S."

"Not going to have any trouble with the customs people, am I?"

"No. The goods are being held in bond. It is merely a formality." Mr. Tan stood up. "It has been a pleasure to meet and do business with you, Mr. Nilsen."

Dorothy was ashore with Arlene, doing some last-minute shopping and arranging for flowers to be sent with their note of thanks to Mrs. Tan. She did not get back until half an hour before the ship sailed. By that time Mr. Tan had left.

"What a pity," she said when Greg told her. "I think he's nice. I hope you decided to let him have his castings after all."

Greg hesitated and then side-stepped the question. "As a matter of fact, he wanted to see me about something else, something he wants me to do for him in Singapore."

"Are you going to do it?"

"I think so."

Dorothy nodded approvingly. "After all, they did put themselves out for us, didn't they?"

ii

That afternoon a cable went from Manila to Kuala Pangkalan:

DOCUMENTS SIGNED AIRMAILED YOU TODAY. TACK CHEE

That evening Girija was in the estate office when the telephone rang. As he lifted it off the cradle he heard the operator telling Kuala Pangkalan to go ahead.

"Mr. Krishnan?" said a voice a moment later.

"Yes."

"I am speaking for Mr. Lee."

"Yes?" He did not recognize the voice, which was that of Mr. Tan Siow Mong's eldest son.

"Mr. Lee wishes for delivery three days from now of the goods previously discussed."

"Very well."

"Mr. Lee will be at the rest house on Thursday evening at eight o'clock, if you will meet him there."

"Very well."

The caller hung up.

Girija sat down again at his desk. His heart was pounding, but whether from excitement at the prospect of having a long-cherished dream realized, or from fear of the things he would now have to do, he did not know. He sat there for a while until he felt himself calmer. Then he looked at his watch.

It was half past six. He had three nights in which to move the arms and ammunition to the pick-up point near the road. If everything went according to plan, that was only just sufficient time. His instinct was to lock the office and set out at once for Awang; but he restrained himself. The first thing to remember was that his behavior must not appear in any way unusual.

At seven o'clock he left the office and went to his house. There were the remains of some food which he had prepared at midday, and he forced himself to eat it. At eight o'clock he took his bicycle and left the compound.

His first care was to see that he was not followed. The possibility of Mr. Lee's attempting to discover where the arms were hidden, so that he could remove them without payment, had to be considered. All appeared to be well, however, and he reached the tin workings without encountering anyone he knew on the way.

He had been up to the camp site at night only once before. That had been months ago, when he had been planning the operation; but he still remembered the panic that had seized him when he left the open ground by the tin workings and entered the terrifying blackness of the jungle. The track to the lower end of the dried stream bed was the worst part. It was too near the village for him to risk using a flashlight, except intermittently, and, well as he knew it in daylight, at night there was always the danger of his getting lost. Above all, there was his fear of leopards. It was at night that they raided villages on the edge of the jungle, carried off chickens and goats, and killed men. He knew the fear to be largely irrational—there had been no reports of leopards in the area for some time—but still it haunted every step he took. He plunged on desperately along the track, living for the moment when he would reach the stream bed and be able to keep the flashlight on all the time.

His plan for moving the boxes of arms and ammunition fell into three parts.

On the first night he would move them from the shelter to the cane thicket at the edge of the stream bed. On the second night he would move them to the foot of the stream bed where it met the track. On the third night he would move them to the pick-up dump that he had contrived in one of the derelict mining-company buildings.

It had taken a long time to prepare the dump. The building he had selected for it was a windowless Nissen hut that had formerly been used as a store for drums of diesel oil. The corrugated-iron sections were so badly rusted that it was possible to put a fist through them in most places; and there were several big holes near the ground where the rusting process was more advanced and the metal had simply disintegrated. From Girija's point of view, it had three things to recommend it. There was still enough metal there to prevent a casual passer-by seeing inside; it contained some empty oil drums which had been punctured for some reason, and so had not been stolen for use as waterbutts by the villagers; and it had a door with a hasp on it to take a padlock.

Once the arms and ammunition were out of the shelter, the risk of their being discovered increased as they were moved nearer the road. While they were in the cane thicket, the risk was small. The second stage at the foot of the stream bed was a greater risk, but, for twenty-four hours, an acceptable one. For the third stage, however, there had to be an effective hiding place. Girija had never read *The Purloined Letter*, but the technique he employed was similar in principle to that used in Poe's story: concealment by familiarity.

The first thing he had done was to buy a padlock, grease the interior mechanism carefully, and leave it in the underbrush for the exterior to rust. Then, one day he had gone to the oil store and padlocked the door. A gleaming new padlock would have excited too much interest in a passer-by. The rusty one, if noticed at all, would only arouse mild curiosity. When he had returned a week later, the padlock had still been there; but there had been signs that someone had crawled through one of the holes near the ground to find out what was behind the locked door. As there had still been nothing inside but the useless oil drums, nothing had been touched. Girija's next move had been to move the oil drums about inside, so as to cover the bigger holes in the corrugated iron, and draw a series of squares and circles on the dirt floor with a stick, to make it seem as if children had been playing there. The following week he had found that one of the drums had been pushed aside. He had replaced it. He had considered defecating on the floor as an additional discouragement to the curious, but had finally decided that it would require too many visits to make that form of deterrent completely effective. In the event, additional measures had not been needed. That had been the last time the drums had been touched. The former oil store with the padlocked door had become accepted as a place where children sometimes played, containing nothing worth stealing and nothing of interest. It would look no different during the twenty-four hours it held the arms and ammunition.

By the time he reached the camp site, it was after nine thirty; but he rested a few minutes before starting work. He had calculated that it would take him less than two hours to move all the boxes to the cane thicket, and was determined to reserve his strength as much as possible.

The hardest part of the job would come on the third night, and he must be prepared for that.

The problem of handling the boxes, he had solved almost by accident. At intervals Mr. Wright received catalogues from a mail-order house in Singapore, and in one of them Girija had seen a device that had interested him. It was a gadget for those with heavy suitcases who could not afford porters, and consisted of a strap attached to a bracket with two small trolley wheels mounted on it. The strap was fastened lengthwise around the suitcase, with the wheels at one corner. There was a handle on the strap. The owner of the suitcase simply grasped this handle and walked along, trailing the case behind him, with half the weight of it carried on the trolley wheels. The price was six dollars.

Girija had sent for one and experimented. The thing worked on firm ground; but up at the camp site, and with a heavy box of rifles, the small wheels sank into the spongy surface of the hillside and were useless. Larger wheels with broader tires were needed. He had found them eventually on the estate. Before the Wright children had been sent away to school in England, one of them had had a scooter. It had been left in Mr. Wright's garage, and Girija had had no difficulty in removing the wheels. Mounted on an axle made out of a spare jack handle, they worked quite well.

The transfer to the cane thicket was completed by midnight, and Girija began the journey back. In spite of his resolve to conserve his energies, he was very tired, and realized that he could no longer rely upon his wits to see him through. Now it would be a question of stamina.

There was a compensation. As his weariness increased, his fears seemed to diminish. By the time he had completed the next night's work, he had forgotten about leopards, and feared the dark track from the stream bed to the tin workings only because it threatened his powers of endurance.

The nine boxes containing the rifles were the most awkward to handle, and only one could be moved at a time. It required twenty stumbling journeys each way to shift all the boxes and ammunition containers, and the final move from the stream bed to the oil store took five and a half hours. When he had secured the padlock he sank down onto the ground in a state of collapse. It was another hour before he could summon the strength to get on his bicycle and ride back to the estate; and only his fear of being seen returning to the estate compound at daybreak, and before he had had time to wash and put on clean clothes, drove him to make that final effort.

He was in the office that morning on time, as usual, but he knew that unless he could get some rest during the day, he would be unable or unfit to keep his appointment with Mr. Lee in the evening. If he pleaded sickness, Mrs. Wright, a keen amateur physician, would dose him with pills and order him to bed; and she would see that he stayed there, too. In the end, on the pretext of looking into some minor pay dispute among the tappers, he left the compound, walked to a part of the estate which he knew was not being worked, and went to sleep under the trees. He awoke at sundown and hurried back to the office. His body ached almost intolerably, but he was no longer stupid with fatigue. When Mr. Wright looked in at the office on his way to the bungalow, Girija was able to report, with his usual air of efficiency, that the pay dispute had been satisfactorily settled.

Girija's business arrangements with Mr. Lee were somewhat complex.

When they met at the rest house, Mr. Lee would give him a draft on the Hong Kong and Shanghai Bank for twenty-five thousand Straits dollars, postdated thirty days and guaranteed by Mr. Tan. He would also give him a receipt for the arms and ammunition. Girija would, in return, give Mr. Lee a promissory note for twenty-five thousand dollars, acknowledging the sum as a loan repayable within thirty days. Then, Girija would return alone to the estate compound, put the check in an envelope marked "To be opened in the event of my death," and leave it in a safe place of his own choosing.

An hour later he would meet Mr. Lee at a rendezvous on the Awang Road. Mr. Lee would have a truck. Guided by Girija, they would then drive to the dump, where Mr. Lee would be allowed to inspect what he was buying.

This would be a critical moment for both of them; but both would feel reasonably secure. If there were no arms and Girija had brought Mr. Lee there merely in order to kill him and keep the check, Mr. Tan would know and be in a position to inform on Girija. If, on the other hand, Mr. Lee contemplated killing Girija and making off with the arms, there would be the telltale check to accuse Mr. Lee. The promissory note and the receipt were safeguards of a more genteel nature. The promissory note was Mr. Lee's insurance against Girija's making off with the check and failing to deliver the goods. The receipt for the arms was Girija's insurance against Mr. Lee's declining to return the promissory note when the arms had been delivered. These two documents would be formally exchanged at the conclusion of the transaction.

Girija reviewed the procedure once more as he cycled out to the rest house. He knew that Mr. Lee could trust him; he was quite certain that he could not trust Mr. Lee. His tired mind began to imagine new ways in which he could be betrayed. Supposing Mr. Lee had henchmen hiding in the truck. What was there to prevent their pouncing on him, retrieving the receipt for the arms, and then seizing the whole consignment? Mr. Lee could still use the promissory note, and Girija would be in no position to complain to the police of what had happened. Or supposing Mr. Lee had a confederate in the estate compound who would watch where he put the check, and then steal it while he was away delivering the arms.

There were countless opportunities for treachery remaining in the situation. Only one possibility did he refuse to consider: that the check guaranteed by Mr. Tan might not in the end be honored.

Mr. Lee was already at the rest house when he arrived. His attitude was wary but businesslike. He merely grunted a greeting and handed Girija the promissory note to sign. He then produced the check and the receipt. When the documents had changed hands, he nodded.

"That is satisfactory. Now, where do we meet?"

"At the twenty-one-mile post near Awang."

"Where is that?"

Girija told him how to get there, and then stood up to go. His whole body was aching, and a spasm of pain shot up his spine as he moved.

Mr. Lee was eying him thoughtfully. "Are you sick?" he asked.

"No, I am tired."

"Will your friend be there?"

"No, but I will help you load the boxes."

"Then I will meet you in one hour's time."

The whole transaction had taken no more than five minutes. Girija cycled back to the estate compound and went to his house. When he had written the inscription on the envelope, he put the check inside and locked it in his tin trunk. If he did not return, Mr. Wright would probably take charge of the trunk and ultimately hand it over to the authorities. It was not an ideal arrangement, but it was the best Girija could think of. As long as Mr. Lee did not know how he had disposed of the check, that was all that mattered.

He had ten minutes to wait before setting out for the rendezvous. He considered opening up the tin trunk again and passing the time with his bus catalogues, but made no move to do so. Through his weariness, he knew that the time for dreams was over. The next time he looked at the catalogues, if there were to be a next time, he would be seeing them through different eyes. There was half a tin of butterscotch on the table by his charpoy. He sat and ate that until it was time to go.

The truck was already at the rendezvous when he arrived. About a hundred yards short of it, he dismounted, switched off his bicycle lamp, and walked along the edge of the road. As he approached, he saw that the canvases above the tailboard of the truck were drawn and tied. He did not like this, and made up his mind to see that the truck was empty before they moved off.

Mr. Lee looked out of the driver's cab window as Girija came up.

"You are late," he said.

"I am two minutes early," Girija replied evenly. "Would you open the back of the truck, please?"

"Why?"

"I wish to put my bicycle inside."

"Why can't you leave it among the trees there? No one will steal it. We have to come back this way."

"I prefer to have it with me."

Mr. Lee got down impatiently and went to the rear of the truck. Girija joined him. In silence they unfastened the tailboard. Girija knew the truck. It belonged to a copra dealer in Kuala Pangkalan. The Anglo-Malay Transport Company hired it sometimes when their own trucks were busy. Mr. Lee must have learned of it from Mr. Tan.

The back of the truck was empty. Girija put his bicycle inside and they set off. Mr. Lee was a fast and bad driver. Luckily, they met little traffic on the way. After ten minutes they reached the road leading to the tin workings.

"You turn off here," said Girija; "and I must ask you to put your lights out."

"On this cart track? We shall run into a tree."

"If you drive slowly, you will be all right. If you keep your lights on, we may be seen from the kampong and someone will come to see what is happening."

Mr. Lee grumbled, but submitted. The truck ground along the road as far as the derelict pump shed.

"We stop here," said Girija.

They got down from the cab and Mr. Lee looked around. "What is this place?"

Girija told him. "We go this way," he added.

"One moment. Are the cases open?"

"Of course not."

Mr. Lee took a case opener and a hammer from the cab of the truck. In his hands they looked like weapons. Girija's scalp crawled as he led the way to the oil store. However, Mr. Lee's main concern at that moment seemed to be to avoid tripping on the uneven ground beneath the scrub. He muttered a complaint about the darkness.

Girija took no notice. Not until they were inside the oil store with the door firmly shut did he switch on his flashlight.

Mr. Lee looked at the stacked boxes. "Is this all of it?"

"Everything on the list is there."

Mr. Lee produced the list from his pocket. "Which are the rifles?"

"Those long boxes there."

Mr. Lee began opening them. He opened every one. When Girija suggested that this was a waste of time, Mr. Lee straightened up.

"Cases full of stones have been sold before now," he said. "I am buying only what I see. If you want to save time, you can refasten the cases after I have examined them."

When he had finished with the rifles, he went on in the same methodical way with the rest—the machine pistols, the bazookas, the grenades, the land mines. Only when he approached the ammunition did Girija protest again.

"If you open those, Mr. Lee, you will not be able to reseal them. You will reduce their market value."

Mr. Lee looked at the ammunition boxes. They were air-tight metal containers with soft inner lids which had to be cut or torn open with a tool. He nodded reluctantly.

"Okay. I will accept them unseen. Now we can start loading."

He grabbed the rope handle of one of the rifle boxes and looked up at Girija.

Girija smiled, but made no move to take the other handle. Once the boxes were in the truck, there was nothing to prevent Mr. Lee's hitting him on the head with the case opener and taking the receipt from him while he was unconscious. He had a feeling that Mr. Lee was aware of the fact.

"Do you not think, Mr. Lee," he said, "that we should complete our business first?"

"There is plenty of time for that."

Girija held up the flashlight. "By the time we have finished the loading, this battery will be very weak. Let us complete our business now, Mr. Lee, while there is light."

Mr. Lee stared at him resentfully, then shrugged. "As long as you help with the loading, I do not care."

"I will certainly help you." Girija produced Mr. Lee's receipt from his pocket and held it up.

Mr. Lee shrugged again and got out the promissory note. The two pieces of paper changed hands. The moment he had his note, Girija lit a match and burned it. Mr. Lee did the same with his receipt. The transaction was complete.

It took an hour to load the truck, and Mr. Lee became abusive over Girija's refusal to use the flashlight to guide them across the scrub. When the job was finished, Girija went back alone to the oil store to replace the padlock on the door. As he did so, he heard the truck start up and drive off. Mr. Lee had not had the elementary courtesy to wait and say good-by.

Girija went back to the track, picked up his bicycle, and started for home. When he had gone about a mile, he remembered that he had left the trolley with the scooter wheels in the oil store. For a moment or two he wondered if he should go back and get rid of it; then the absurdity of the notion struck him. What could a pair of wheels and a strap tell anybody? He had nothing to hide any more; nothing, that is, except a check for twenty-five thousand dollars.

When he reached his house he examined the tin trunk to see that the lock had not been tampered with. He did not open it. He did not even wait to undress before he lay down on the charpoy and went to sleep.

iii

IT WAS one in the morning when Tan Yam Heng drove the truck up to the gate of the Anglo-Malay Transport Company's compound. The Sikh night watchman came out of his hut and opened the gate. Yam Heng told him to remain at the gate and then drove through to the unloading bay of number-two godown.

The unloading platform was level with the tailboard of the truck. It did not take him long to drag the boxes out and stack them inside the two large machinery crates he had brought in some hours earlier. He had only been able to guess at the various dimensions of the boxes, and they had to be wedged and braced inside the crates; but he had anticipated this, and had provided himself with the wood and tools he would need to do the job. By two thirty both crates were ready to ship. He left them on the platform and drove himself in the truck back to his brother's house. Tan Siow Mong had waited up for him.

"Was everything in order?" he asked.

"Yes."

"Were the goods according to specification?"

"I opened and counted everything except the ammunition. Those boxes are sealed."

"And he has the check."

"Of course."

"You do not seem pleased. Has anything gone wrong?"

"That Indian clerk is insufferable. He treated me as if I were a crook."

His brother nodded calmly. "I warned you he was no fool," he said.

The following morning Tan Siow Mong had a brief interview with Kwong Kee, master of the Anglo-Malay Transport Company's motor junk *Glowing Dawn,* just back from her weekly run to Manila.

Kwong Kee was a square, pot-bellied man with a cheerful disposition and a venereal appetite that bordered on satyriasis. He was not greatly interested in the commercial reasons Mr. Tan gave him for switching the *Glowing Dawn* temporarily to the Singapore run. Nor was he interested in the cargo she carried. And if Mr. Tan's young brother were fool enough to want to go home by sea instead of comfortably by train, that was no business of his either. He was quite content to do as he was told. It was some time since he had sampled the Singapore brothels.

The *Glowing Dawn* sailed that afternoon with a cargo of latex and two machinery crates. When she was well out to sea, Yam Heng went down into the hold and stenciled the consignee's name and address on the crates: "G. NILSEN, c/o CHEN WAREHOUSE CO. SINGAPORE. IN BOND."

iv

THE night before the *Silver Isle* reached Saigon, there was a ship's gala dance. The notice had said: "Fancy Dress Optional."

On the advice of his cabin steward, who had lived through many of these occasions, Greg went as a Spanish hidalgo. It was easy. All he had to do was wear the black pants belonging to his tuxedo, an evening dress shirt with a black string tie, and two cummerbunds instead of one to raise the waist line. The steward provided the extra cummerbund and also a flat-topped black hat with a wide brim. He always carried them in his baggage. They had earned him many an extra tip. As he explained to Greg, the advantage of the costume was that a gentleman did not have to wear a jacket with it, and in the steamy heat of the South China Sea that was a real blessing. Dorothy painted on the long sideburns he needed with her eyebrow pencil.

She herself had been undecided what to wear. She had discussed the problem with Arlene; but Arlene had been curiously unhelpful, and had even refused to say what she was going to wear herself; she wanted it to be a surprise. Finally, with the aid of the stewardess, Dorothy had settled for a German doll costume. The stewardess happened to have the dirndl skirt and the blouse with embroidered smocking. Dorothy made herself a coif with two white napkins from the dining room, and put big dabs of rouge on her cheeks.

Both she and Greg were ready early, but lurked in their cabin with the door on the hook until, by watching their fellow passengers passing along the alleyway outside and listening to their conversation, they had assured themselves that they were not going to be the only ones who had opted for fancy dress. Then they went up to the bar.

Most of the passengers had decided on some form of fancy costume for the evening, and, although many had contented themselves with funny hats, false noses, and other easily discarded fripperies, a few had allowed their enthusiasm to run away with them. In the bar, the pirates, Al Jolsons, hoboes, and Indian maharajahs were already drenched with sweat and in difficulty with their burnt-cork make-ups. Over their Martinis, Greg and Dorothy congratulated themselves on having hit it off just right; they had taken trouble, but not too much trouble; and they were comfortable.

Arlene did not appear until just before the ship's speakers announced dinner. Then she made a slow, regal entrance through the double doors leading to the lounge. She was wearing a *cheong sam*, the silk formal dress with the high collar and split skirt that Chinese women wear, and long jade earrings. Just inside the door, she stopped and smiled as if expecting a round of applause.

The *cheong sam* can be an attractive and becoming garment; but it makes certain demands on the wearer. She must be small-boned and very slender, with invisible hips and near-to-invisible buttocks, a flat stomach, and minute breasts. Her arms and neck must appear fragile, and her face must be round with high cheekbones. She must, in other words, be Chinese. On Arlene's shapely but large and well-padded body, and surmounted by her equine head, it looked grotesque.

Greg said: "My God!"

"She bought it in Hong Kong," muttered Dorothy. "It's the most lovely material."

"It still looks ridiculous."

"I didn't see it on her at the fitting."

"She must be out of her mind."

Arlene's entrance created a minor sensation, and there were one or two uncertain whoops of gallantry as she swayed over to the Nilsens' table. If she were kidding, everyone was prepared to laugh. If she were serious, they were ready to be polite. Meanwhile, they were embarrassed.

Arlene sat down beside Dorothy and the splits in her skirt gaped to reveal, on Greg's side, a large area of thigh and one pink suspender. She smiled archly.

"Well, what do you think of Chinee laundly girl?"

"It's a lovely dress," said Dorothy eagerly.

"It certainly is," said Greg. "Martini?"

"No." Her smile was challenging now. "Tonight I am drinking champagne."

They went down to dinner twenty minutes late, and had to run a gauntlet of eyes as they crossed to their table. Arlene's half-bottle of champagne seemed to have gone to her head, and she began calling Greg "Don Gregorio" and Dorothy "Gretchen." She was thoroughly pleased with herself, looking about her with the calm assurance of a woman who knows that she is the most attractive in the room.

When the dancing began, she became skittish, breaking away from her partners to execute little hip-waggling solos in the middle of the deck. Greg and Dorothy, dancing sedately on the outskirts, glanced at one another.

Dorothy was worried. "I don't understand it," she muttered; "she usually has such good taste in clothes."

"Yes."

"Well, you must admit she *has*."

"If you ask me," said Greg, "she had a few belts in her cabin before she came up."

"Now, darling, that's a nasty thing to say."

"Well, look at her."

Arlene, with her arms stretched out wide, her head turned over her right shoulder, and her chin tilted imperiously, was now dancing a flamenco. Her partner, one of the ship's officers, was rotating around her somewhat helplessly. He had an uneasy grin on his face.

"She's just a little excited," said Dorothy defensively. "Anyway, she's having a good time."

"In my opinion, she's making a horse's ass of herself."

"Really, Greg!"

Arlene did not return to their table. When a "Leap Year" dance was announced, she made a beeline for the Captain. After that dance she returned with him to his table; whether by invitation or not it was impossible to determine.

The following morning, when they were going up the river to Saigon, she did not appear at her usual time; but Greg and Dorothy were too busy shooting with their movie camera and watching the sampans and the riverbanks go by to give her much thought. They found her, immaculate but a trifle pensive, sitting in the bar after the ship had docked.

"What happened to you last night?" she asked Dorothy as they joined her.

"We went down around eleven thirty."

"Four o'clock, me," Arlene said grimly. "The barman opened up a can of wienies. He's got an electric grill back there. That was after I'd switched to Scotch."

"Who else was there?" Dorothy asked.

"Nobody. Just the barman and me. He comes from L.A. and he's a Dodger fan," she added sourly.

But after lunch she felt fine again and they all went ashore. At Arlene's suggestion, they crushed into a small Renault taxi for a tour of the city.

It was insufferably humid, and the driver, a handsome young Vietnamese, smelled peculiarly of rotting fish. Arlene explained that the smell came from a sauce used in all Vietnamese cooking and was no reflection on the driver's personal cleanliness.

The driver grinned. "Is made from fish," he said suddenly in English. "You like me show where make it?"

Up to that moment he had spoken nothing but French, and Arlene had been the interpreter. Nobody had troubled to ask him if he understood English, Greg remembered. Arlene, proud of the French she had acquired in her Red Cross days, had just gone ahead and spoken for them. As a result, they had unwittingly hurt the man's feelings. That was precisely the sort of stupid incident, Greg thought, that made Americans unpopular abroad.

However, the driver did not seem offended. "I show you on way back ship," he went on. "Make bad smell, but many vitamins."

"That so?"

They were traveling along a broad, tree-lined street that reminded Arlene and Dorothy of Paris, when the driver turned to Greg.

"Now I show you where Quiet American made bomb explosion," he said.

"How's that?"

"That café there." The driver pointed. "That was where Quiet American made bomb explosion. Many killed."

They were crossing a square now. Greg looked from the café to the driver.

"But *The Quiet American* was a novel," he said.

"Yes, sir. That is café back there. I was near at time of explosion. Was very bad."

"But it was fiction," Dorothy said. "It didn't actually happen."

"Apparently there was a bomb explosion there," Arlene explained. "I had this when I was here before. Somebody told me Graham Greene was in the city at the time."

"Graham Greene, yes." The driver nodded emphatically. "Presently I will show you bridge where Fowler found dead body of correspondent, and place where there was restaurant where they talk. Real restaurant now gone, pulled down."

"You mean people here believe that story?"

"Is true, sir. I show you the place."

"But it was just a novel."

"Look," said Arlene impatiently, "if you go to Marseille, they take you out to the Chateau d'If and show you the hole in the wall that the Count of Monte Cristo made when he scratched his way through to the Abbé Faria. They show you the dungeon occupied by the Man in the Iron Mask. It doesn't mean anything. It's just to make the tourists feel they're getting their money's worth."

"But that was an anti-American novel. If they believe all that stuff, my God! We're giving these people millions in aid."

"That's right," said Dorothy.

Arlene smiled. "I can see you two have got a few surprises coming to you on this trip."

They returned to the ship hot, tired, and out of temper. On their way down to shower and change, Greg and Dorothy had to squeeze their way past a pile of baggage in the alleyway. Their steward told them that three new passengers had come on board. When they went up on deck, they saw Arlene sitting talking animatedly to a florid, thick-set man in a khaki bush shirt. They were drinking Pernod.

At cocktail time Greg and Dorothy were sitting in their usual corner when Arlene appeared with the same man. He had changed into a white sharkskin suit. Evidently he was one of the new passengers. They came over.

"Ces sont mes amis Greg et Dorothy Nilsen," said Arlene. "Je veux vous présenter Monsieur Seguin."

"How do you do?" said Monsieur Seguin.

They shook hands. Greg said: "Will you join us?"

"Thank you." With a courteous bow to Dorothy, Monsieur Seguin sat down.

He had small blue eyes, a merry smile, and large pudgy hands with little mats of gleaming blond hair on the backs of them.

"Monsieur Seguin est ingénieur civil," Arlene explained. "Il va nous accompagner jusqu'à Calcutta. Monsieur Nilsen est ingénieur aussi."

"Indeed?" Monsieur Seguin looked interested. "In what branch of our profession, sir?" His English was excellent.

"How do you say die-casting in French?" Arlene asked.

Greg shrugged helplessly.

"Oh, but I understand," said Monsieur Seguin affably. "Mr. Nilsen makes the small pieces of all those things that the world thinks of when it hears an American use the phrase 'standard of living.'"

Arlene laughed heartily. Greg and Dorothy smiled. More Pernods were arriving.

"Isn't it lucky?" Arlene said. "I had a word with the chief steward and he's fixed it for Monsieur Seguin to sit at our table."

The *Silver Isle* was an American ship and most of her passengers were Americans. Not unnaturally, the cooking was American, and served in the American style.

Monsieur Seguin did not like it. He did not like the shrimp cocktail and tried to remove all the sauce from it. He asked for his steak *bleu* and, when it came rare, regretted that it had been overcooked. He did not want his salad on the side, but as a separate course, and requested that the slices of avocado pear be removed. He ignored the baked Idaho potato, and refused the ice cream. He took one mouthful of the Wisconsin Brie, made a face, and ate no more. However, he remained, apparently, good-humored. His only comment seemed mild enough for a Frenchman who had not enjoyed his dinner.

"I needed to lose some weight," he said with a smile. "This ship will be very good for me. Here it will be easy to maintain a regime."

"I don't know what they think they're doing," Arlene burst out angrily. "You could get better food at a drugstore."

Dorothy chuckled. "The other day you were saying you thought the food was great."

"Great is a relative term, dear. Even an American chef must be able to cook eatable food *one* day in thirty." She was sharing a bottle of wine with Monsieur Seguin, and now she drained her glass.

Monsieur Seguin refilled it. "Mademoiselle, I think you are being very unfair to America," he said. "She has made some very important contributions to world civilization. Let us see—" he pretended to search his memory—"she has given us chewing gum, and Coca-Cola, and gangster films, and she has given us atomic bombs." He smiled slyly at Greg. "As well as a lot of advice."

Greg raised his eyebrows. "Aren't you forgetting popcorn?"

"Ah, yes. Pardon. And I was forgetting democracy also. McCarthy style, of course."

Arlene laughed. "That's telling 'em!"

Dorothy's face froze.

Greg smiled placidly at Monsieur Seguin. "I expect you have a lot of jokes about American tourists, too. And foreign aid."

Monsieur Seguin shrugged. "It is sad," he said. "You Americans give away billions of dollars to defend yourselves against Communism, but you ask everyone to believe that you give it because you are good and kind. Why?"

"Because big daddy-o wants to be loved," said Arlene promptly.

"America," said Monsieur Seguin, "is rich, and behaves like the rich always behave. When they begin to fear death, they become philanthropists."

"Well, most Americans aren't rich," said Greg, "and they certainly don't feel particularly philanthropic when they're paying their taxes."

"That's just childish," snapped Arlene. "Monsieur Seguin was talking about us as a nation."

Dorothy's face went pink. "I don't think Greg's the one who's being childish," she said.

"What I meant to say," Monsieur Seguin went on evenly, "was simply that American foreign policy has always, from the first, been made by men who saw the world through the eyes of money, of riches."

"If you don't mind my saying so, Monsieur Seguin," said Greg, "that is one of the stupidest remarks I've ever heard."

Monsieur Seguin smiled. "You know, Mr. Nilsen, there was an American who owned fifteen thousand acres of some of the best land in America. He owned land in New York and Pennsylvania and Virginia and Maryland and the city of Washington. When he died he was one of the richest men in your country."

"Who was that, Rockefeller?"

"His name was George Washington," said Monsieur Seguin quietly; "but, of course, you knew that."

Arlene laughed so much that she had the whole dining room looking at their table.

Dorothy sat with a face like stone.

After dinner she and Greg went straight to their cabin.

"I think Arlene behaved disgustingly," Dorothy said; "and as for that ghastly little Frenchman . . . Was it right what he said—about Washington, I mean?"

Greg shrugged. "Probably. He's the sort of man who collects facts of that kind. Of course, they weren't relevant to the point he was trying to make, but that wouldn't interest him. He's a debater."

"It's Arlene I don't understand. Encouraging him to go on talking all that anti-American nonsense. And on an American ship, too. I mean, it's such bad taste. And how dared she ask the steward to put him at our table, without even consulting us?"

"I tell you one thing, dear," said Greg, "and you'd better be ready for it. The next time that guy starts any anti-American stuff, I'm going to take a poke at him."

"You mean we have to go on eating with him?" Dorothy demanded.

Greg stared at her, a wild hope surging through him. "Darling, the ship's full. You know that. They can't rearrange the seating now."

"You mean we're stuck with them all the way to Calcutta?"

"Unless we complain to the purser and make a personal issue of it, I'm afraid we are."

"Oh, Greg!" She sat down miserably on her bed. "Our lovely trip!"

He sat down beside her and put his arm around her waist. "You said it yourself, darling. We're not in a position to choose our traveling companions."

Dorothy stuck out her chin. "Maybe not. But we *are* in a position to choose the way we travel."

"Darling, we're booked through on this ship to Calcutta."

"Maybe we are, but we can change our minds. We could stop over at Singapore, take a side trip or two, and then go on by air to Calcutta. You said you were going to do something for Mr. Tan in Singapore. All right! It's business. If you explained that, I know we could get a refund on the passage."

Greg had never loved her more. "That's right. Pan-Am and B.O.A.C. go via Bangkok. Maybe we could stop over there instead of Rangoon before we go on to Calcutta."

"Bangkok! That would be wonderful!"

"As a matter of fact, it wouldn't cost us any extra, even allowing for side trips. I didn't tell you, but this business that Mr. Tan asked me to do will net me a thousand dollars."

"Hong Kong?"

"No, real American dollars. And I could make a thousand more if we spent a day or two extra in Singapore."

"How?"

"Signing papers. Anyway, I'll tell you about that later. The main thing is that we enjoy ourselves. We don't have to worry about the extra expense. If we decide we want to get off at Singapore, then that's all there is to it."

Dorothy was silent for a moment. Then she said: "I know you never liked Arlene. I suppose she's not really a very likable person. I think that's why I felt sorry for her."

Later that evening Greg had a talk with the purser and then sent a radiogram to Mr. Tan Tack Chee in Manila.

CHAPTER V

At the upper social levels of the British community in Singapore, Colonel Soames was known as "The Policeman."

There was nothing derogatory about the name. It had been applied originally to distinguish him from another Colonel Soames, who had been a retired Ghurka officer and a prominent member of the Turf Club. The fact that its use had continued after "Ghurka" Soames' death, however, had been only partly the result of habit. Although Colonel Soames' status as a senior police official was well known, the nature of his duties was not. He never discussed them, and any attempt to draw him out on the subject was met by him with a frosty silence. It was generally assumed that he was not, strictly speaking, a policeman at all, but something to do with Intelligence. To go on calling him "The Policeman" was a mildly sardonic way of underlining that assumption.

It was, in a sense, correct. Singapore was a naval, military, and air base of crucial importance to the British Commonwealth; but it was also a free port and a trading post, largely dependent for its economic existence on international commerce. In the latter capacity it was obliged to receive many strange guests. Colonel Soames' job was to detect the undesirables among them, and to see that their interests and those of Singapore as a whole did not seriously conflict. He worked in collaboration with the immigration department, the service intelligence organizations, the port and airport authorities, and the customs. He never ordered arrests. If any major criminal activity came to his attention, he either turned the facts over to an appropriate colleague for action, or, if, in his judgment, inaction would be more productive, he merely watched and waited. Occasionally he might suggest a deportation or the refusal of an entry permit; but most of his results were obtained simply by contriving to let the objects of his attentions know that they were observed and understood. Officially, he was in charge of a branch of the internal security forces. His own definition of his function was "discouraging the bad boys."

His second-in-command was a plain-clothes inspector named Chow Soo Kee. Every morning at ten they met to discuss the reports of the previous day. It was at one of these meetings that the name "Nilsen" first came to Colonel Soames' attention.

They had reviewed the current activities of a Belgian who was attempting to set up a central distribution agency for "blue" films from Bangkok, an Austrian who was buying girls for a new brothel in Brunei, and an Australian couple who seemed to be doing too well at the badger game. They had discussed the steps to be taken in the case of the consul of a Central American republic who, comfortably shielded by his diplomatic immunity, was making money in the opium market. It had been decided to advise a man posing as a theatrical booking agent that his record had been forwarded by Scotland Yard. Inspector Chow was getting up to leave, when he remembered something.

"By the way, Colonel," he said, "we have another arms dealer."

"Not that Italian again?"

"No, sir, a new one. Customs told me about him. There was a parcel of arms consigned in bond to a G. Nilsen from Manila."

"How big?"

Inspector Chow told him. "Probably Korean war surplus," he added. "They could be samples."

"Rather a lot for samples, don't you think? Sounds more like a small man trying to get his toe in."

"Well, that's the funny thing, sir. He isn't the usual type. Full name is Gregory Hull Nilsen. American citizen. Engineer. Comes from Wilmington, Delaware, where he has his own light engineering business. Traveling with his wife. They arrived on the *Silver Isle* two days ago. Staying at the Raffles Hotel. They have an air-conditioned suite. Highly respectable sort of people, apparently."

"Well, that's a comfort."

"Yes, sir." Inspector Chow paused. "Except for two things. He made a false statement to the immigration people. Said he and his wife were here just as tourists. Made no mention of the arms business."

"How long did he ask for?"

"Two weeks. Immigration visa'd them for thirty days. The other thing was that he was brought to the hotel by Tan Yam Heng."

"You mean that union thug who's always losing his shirt on the pickle market?"

"Yes, sir. Apparently on friendly terms with him. That's what I didn't like. Tan's a member of the Democratic Action Party."

"Who else has this man seen?"

"Nobody, as far as I can gather. Yesterday he and his wife hired a car and drove round the island—to see the sights, they said. The driver says that's all they did do."

"Could be establishing their cover. I wonder why he lied, though. Stupid thing to do, if he's just a dealer. Who'd be in the market now for what he's got to sell?"

Inspector Chow thought for a moment. He knew that what he had to say would not please Colonel Soames, and he wanted to phrase it as delicately as possible.

Indonesia, the young republic which claimed sovereignty over the three thousand islands of the former Dutch East Indies, was an uneasy neighbor. The Central Government in Java was weak, unstable, and hag-ridden by Communism. In the big outer islands, especially Sumatra and Celebes, there were powerful revolutionary movements demanding secession and independence. The political thinking of these movements was religious in tone and strongly anti-Communist; and they had made fighting alliances. For three years or more, parts of Sumatra and Celebes had been virtually in a state of civil war, with insurgent forces in control of large areas and Central Government troops having in some places to defend even the big towns. With the long coastline of Sumatra only thirty miles away across the Straits of Malacca, Singapore was, whether it liked it or not, the natural supply base for the Sumatran insurgents. Their "liaison officers" and purchasing agents were the bane of Colonel Soames' existence.

"As you pointed out, sir," Inspector Chow said finally, "it is a small consignment. I don't think the Darul Islam people would be interested at present. You know they had a shipment of eighty machine guns and fifty three-inch mortars three weeks ago."

"Not through here, I hope."

"No, sir. Direct from Macao."

"That Dutchman handle it?"

"Yes. But he shipped the ammunition separately—over three tons, apparently—and an Indonesian Government destroyer intercepted it. They'll be wanting to replace that ammunition first. I don't think they'll bother about a few more rifles. I would say that at the moment the most interested buyer would be Captain Lukey."

He was careful to say the last two words very casually. Captain Lukey was the liaison officer and representative in Singapore of a small insurgent force that had recently begun to operate in Northern Sumatra. Colonel Soames' dislike of him was personal and intense.

Herbert Henry Lukey had been a regular soldier in a British county regiment, and commissioned as a lieutenant quartermaster during World War II. He had served, without distinction, until 1950, when the final period for which he had signed on had expired. His regiment had been stationed in Egypt at the time, and much of his last six months of service had been spent answering questions at Courts of Inquiry appointed to investigate the virtual disappearance of a number of emergency gasoline storage dumps of which he had been in charge. His answers had revealed qualities of imagination and ingenuity not hitherto apparent in his military career; and a secret, though unauthorized, investigation of his bank balance had shown him to be in the possession of funds far exceeding his total army pay for the previous five years. However, the smoke screen of confusion which he had succeeded in creating had, in the end, led to the inquiries being abandoned for lack of evidence. The gasoline losses had been written off, in the way he had originally advocated, as "due to evaporation." He could, and frequently did, claim that his army record was as clean as a whistle.

His subsequent record, as a civilian in North Borneo, Malaya, and Singapore, was not. He had worked in minor executive posts for several big trading concerns, most of which had, like the army, suffered some evaporation of assets before dispensing with his services. Eventually one of them had thought forthrightly and unconfusedly enough about its losses to go to the police. There had been talk, too, of forged references. He had left Singapore hurriedly, and after a while the charges against him had been dropped. Occasional inquiries over the next three years from police authorities in Colombo, Cape Town, Mombassa, and Bombay had made it possible to chart his subsequent progress. The report of his return to Singapore had been referred immediately to Colonel Soames.

"The Policeman" was not an intolerant man. He disapproved of the crooked and the *louche*, but he did not generally dislike them. Admittedly, his attitude was not as objective as he thought it was, and had a paternalistic, schoolmasterish quality about it; but that was largely a result of his training. He had come late to police work, and was inclined to treat most of the adult transgressors who came his way as if they were delinquent members of a regiment of which he was in command, and to which both he and they owed a common loyalty.

However, with Captain Lukey it was different; and the difference resided in the word "captain."

The day after Lukey had returned, Colonel Soames had summoned him to his office for an interview.

"According to your statement to the immigration authorities," Colonel Soames had begun, "you are here as a liaison officer and purchasing agent for the armed forces of the Independent Party of the Faithful of North Sumatra. Is that correct?"

"Perfectly correct."

"You say you are a liaison officer. What is the liaison between, may I ask?"

"The army of the Party of the Faithful and other forces in Sumatra hostile to those Commies in Djakarta, sir."

"I see. And in your role as purchasing agent, what are you intending to purchase?"

"Supplies, Colonel."

"Arms?"

"Supplies of various kinds, Colonel."

"Do you have funds for these purchases?"

"Naturally, Colonel."

"And where do these funds come from?"

"They are subscribed by loyal Sumatrans and certain friendly parties."

"Have you a banking account?"

"Yes, Colonel. Hong Kong and Shanghai, Orchard Road. All perfectly respectable."

"Are you empowered to sign checks?"

"With a counter-signature, yes."

"Whose counter-signature?"

"A member of the Executive Committee of the Party of the Faithful."

"Is the Committee aware of your previous record?"

"My British army record, Colonel? Certainly."

"I was thinking more of your record here, and in Borneo."

"I wasn't aware that I had one, sir."

"Weren't you?"

"I don't think I understand you, Colonel. Are you suggesting I have a criminal record in Singapore?"

That had been just what Colonel Soames had been suggesting, but he knew better than to say so. There had been no convictions recorded against the man in that area.

"All I am suggesting is that while you are in Singapore you are careful to respect the law. Do you understand, Mr. Lukey?"

"*Captain* Lukey if you don't mind, Colonel."

Colonel Soames had smiled unpleasantly. "And that brings me to another point. I don't think that there is much sense in my pointing out that the use of a military title to which one is not entitled is bad form and caddish. Perhaps I should simply remind you that it is an offense in law."

Captain Lukey had smiled back, equally unpleasantly. "And perhaps I should simply tell you, Colonel, that the British army isn't the only army in the world. Here, take a look at this."

He had handed over a paper. It had been a commission from the Commander in Chief of the army of the Independent Party of the Faithful of North Sumatra, appointing his loyal servant Herbert Henry Lukey a staff captain.

It had touched Colonel Soames in a very sensitive place. He had lost his temper.

"This is meaningless. You cannot accept such a commission."

"Why not, Colonel?"

"In the first place, you are a British subject. In the second place, you are, unhappily, an officer in the armed forces of Her Majesty the Queen."

"Not any more, Colonel."

"You may not be a serving officer, but you are on the reserve. You could be recalled to active duty if necessary."

Captain Lukey had grinned. "Do you take me for a fool, Colonel? I came off the reserve two years ago. I'm overage."

"Well, that's something to be thankful for, but don't expect me to recognize this rubbish." Colonel Soames had tossed the paper contemptuously back across the desk.

Captain Lukey had picked it up, folded it carefully, and put it back in his pocket before speaking. Then he had said: "Is that your considered opinion, Colonel?"

"It is."

"Then you won't have any objection, I take it, if I report it back to my commanding officer in Sumatra as the official British view."

Colonel Soames had hesitated. The Independent Party of the Faithful was probably little more than a gang of dissident Sumatran officers greedy for the spoils of local political power. But in Sumatra anything might happen. Within a few months those same officers could be members of a lawfully constituted government. A senior Singapore police official who had gratuitously insulted its leaders would find himself most unpopular with the British Foreign Office, to say nothing of Government House. The fact that H. H. Lukey was, in his opinion, a cad would not excuse the indiscretion.

He had swallowed his annoyance. "No, it's not an official British view. It merely represents my personal opinion of you."

Captain Lukey had not been deceived by the evasion. He had grinned infuriatingly. "Good show, Colonel. I'll tell my masters I'm getting full co-operation and all proper respect."

"You can also tell them that if there's any hanky-panky here you'll be out on your ear, and pretty damn quick."

It had been a feeble threat and Captain Lukey had known it. He had still been grinning when he left.

Colonel Soames had not forgotten the humiliation. He looked up sharply at Inspector Chow. "Why Lukey?"

"He doesn't seem to have much money to spend, sir. I should think he could just about manage this deal, though. Another thing: he's been trying to buy three-oh-three ammunition. They must have rifles of that caliber already. It would make sense to buy more. Most of the stuff going about at present is three-oh-oh."

"I see." The Colonel was thoughtful for a moment, then he nodded. "Put a man on to Tan Yam Heng. See if he tries to contact Lukey. Keep me posted."

"Very good, sir."

"What did you say that American's name was? Nilsen?"

"Yes, sir. Do you want me to . . . ?"

"No. I think I may look into that myself."

ii

GREG and Dorothy were enjoying Singapore. They had made two tours of the island and also crossed the causeway into Johore; and although they had had to admit to themselves that there was not really all that much to see, they were so glad to be on their own again that it did not seem to matter. In any case, they were having fun arranging side trips. There was a Garuda Indonesian Airways flight that could take them down to Bali, and they had made provisional reservations for early the following week. The only snag was that they would have to have an Indonesian tourist visa, and that took several days to get. Until it came through they would not know for certain what their plans were. So they had applied for the visa and decided that, if it did not come through in time, they would console themselves with a trip up to Penang. The man in Thos. Cook's had shown them some pictures of the island that made it look almost as enchanting as Bali.

The only area of dissension between them was that surrounding the Tan arms deal.

When Greg had, finally, explained it to her in detail, Dorothy had stared at him almost incredulously.

"But, darling, it sounds to me completely crooked."

"What's crooked about it? It's just a question of helping Mr. Tan to avoid a technicality in the Philippine law. Nothing more."

"Well, that's something, isn't it? It's their law."

"It wasn't made to cover this sort of eventuality."

"What sort is that?"

"Well, I think the idea of selling Communist arms to the anti-Communists is a pretty good idea."

"Maybe. But how do you know they *are* Communist arms? Who told you they were? How do you know he's telling the truth?"

It had been a long, inconclusive, and uncomfortable discussion. One passage of it had stayed in his mind to trouble him later.

"Supposing someone back home had come to you with a proposition like this," she had said.

"How could they?"

"But supposing they did. You know what? I think you'd call the police or the FBI."

"Well, this isn't America, and the circumstances and the people are all entirely different."

She had nodded calmly. "That's just my point."

"I don't get it."

"Maybe we don't know *how* different they are."

Their first encounter with Mr. Tan Yam Heng in Singapore had not improved the situation. They had found his appearance unprepossessing and his manner furtive. Indeed, when he had contacted them on the boat, Greg had at first mistaken him for some sort of tout. Then he had tried to hustle them through the immigration and customs before they had had a chance to say good-by to anyone on the ship. Greg had had to be very firm.

Later, at the hotel, Tan had produced an airmail letter from Manila confirming that Greg would act as sole selling agent for Mr. Tan Tack

Chee, and revising their financial arrangements accordingly. That had been all right; but, although the letter had been addressed to Greg personally, Tan Yam Heng had already opened it and read the contents.

When he had gone, Dorothy had raised her eyebrows. "Not much like his brother, is he?"

"No."

"Do you think opening other people's letters is an old Chinese custom?"

"Well, I don't suppose it matters. By the way, Mr. Tan sends you and Arlene his best wishes."

The meeting at the Customs House the following morning had been no more propitious. After Greg had signed the appropriate papers, they had gone outside.

"The next thing, Mr. Nilsen," Tan Yam Heng had said briskly, "is for me to arrange meetings with buyers."

Greg had smiled and shaken his head. "No, Mr. Tan. The next thing is for you to give me a check for one thousand and fifty dollars."

"But that is not until you sign the papers transferring ownership of the goods. That is the arrangement."

"That *was* the arrangement. You read your brother's letter. The arrangement is changed. The first five per cent is to be paid over on signature of the customs documents. The *second* five per cent will be paid when ownership is transferred to the actual buyer."

It had been at that moment that Greg had understood why Mr. Tan in Manila had been so anxious for him to act as his agent. Under the earlier arrangement, there would have been nothing to stop Mr. Tan in Singapore from completing the blank transfer of ownership in his own favor. Under the new arrangement, ownership would only be transferred to the buyer. The explanation was simple: Mr. Tan in Manila did not trust Mr. Tan in Singapore, and probably for very good reasons.

Tan Yam Heng had scowled almost threateningly. "Between associates in business enterprise," he had said, "there must be trust and personal dignity in all negotiations."

"I couldn't agree more. And I think the best way of keeping that trust and personal dignity, Mr. Tan, is for everyone to do just what they've agreed to do right along the line. No more, no less."

Mr. Tan Yam Heng had had the check, drawn on the Manila office of an American bank, ready in his pocket, and had handed it over in the end, but with a bad grace. He had left, saying that he would telephone when he had arranged the meetings.

Since then, two days had elapsed and Greg had heard nothing. He had not told Dorothy about the argument over the check; nor had he thought it necessary to discuss with her his other misgivings. He was on the point of cabling to Mr. Tan in Manila to remind him of the time limit they had agreed on, when Tan Yam Heng called.

"Mr. Nilsen," he said, "I have an interested buyer."

"Oh."

"He would like to meet with you and discuss the proposition."

"Who is he?"

"A British army captain, now acting for a group in Indonesia."

"What sort of group?"

"I think it is religious."

"What do you mean, religious?"

"Does it matter? We wish to sell, he wishes to buy."

"It matters a great deal. Anyway, what's the man's name? How do I meet him?"

"His name is Captain Lukey, and, if convenient, I will bring him to your hotel this afternoon at five."

"Okay."

"And the price is agreed?"

"We ask seventy-five thousand, accept anything over sixty."

"Yes. This is very confidential."

"I'll see you at five."

He told Dorothy.

"What's a religious group want with rifles and machine guns?" she asked.

"How should I know? I don't think Tan knew what he was talking about. Anyway, there's a British officer acting for them, so they must be fairly respectable."

"I suppose you'll have to see him alone."

"You can stay in the bedroom and listen through the door, if you want."

Tan Yam Heng arrived ten minutes early, looking more furtive than ever.

"I wished," he explained, "to find the best route from the courtyard entrance to your suite. As soon as he arrives I will bring him straight here without telephoning from the reception desk first, if you agree."

"It's all right with me."

"The fewer people who see us together, the better."

"Why all the cloak-and-dagger stuff?"

"In such negotiations it is important to be secret. If some spy of the Indonesian Government got to know of this, it would be dangerous."

Greg avoided looking at Dorothy. "I see."

"Captain Lukey may wish to search the suite before discussions begin."

"Well, he can't. My wife's going to be in the bedroom."

"These are serious matters. I am sure Mrs. Nilsen understands."

"Look, there's not going to be any searching, and if the gallant captain doesn't like it, he can lump it. How well do you know him?"

"I have talked to him."

"Did he say he wanted to search the place?"

"No, but . . ."

"Then suppose we let him speak for himself. He'll be here in a minute. Now, why don't you just go down and wait for him, Mr. Tan?"

Tan Yam Heng went, sullenly. Twenty minutes later he returned with Captain Lukey.

The Captain was a tall man in the late forties with a slight paunch, a florid complexion, graying brown hair, and a large handlebar mustache stained on one side by nicotine. He wore the Singapore business uniform—white duck slacks, white long-sleeved shirt with breast pockets, and a regimental tie. He had a reverberating voice and a hearty manner. He came into the room with hand outstretched.

"How do you do, Mr. Nilsen? Sorry I'm late. Got held up in a spot of traffic."

"Glad to know you, Captain," said Greg. "Won't you sit down?"

Captain Lukey seemed not to have heard the invitation. He smiled broadly, put his hands on his hips, and looked around the room. "Well, now," he said, "the last time I was in this suite, General Blacklock had it. That was before he became C. in C. of course. I was his A.D.C. for a time. Rum bird, old Blackie."

"Can I get you a drink?" Greg asked.

"Very handsome of you. I'll have a stengah, if you don't mind."

"That's Scotch and soda, isn't it?"

"Little Scotch, lot of soda. Got to keep the old waterworks going in this climate."

"Oh, yes, I see." Greg was having trouble placing Captain Lukey's accent. Behind the stage British there was another intonation that he could not identify. Colonel Soames could have told him that it came from Liverpool.

"You know," said Captain Lukey, "lots of people say business before pleasure." He sat down heavily. "Never been able to understand it myself. But then people say all sorts of things they've never thought about. They've got rule-of-thumb minds. The shortest distance between two points is a straight line. Agreed?"

"Agreed."

"Is the hypotenuse of a right-angled triangle a straight line?"

"It is."

"And the sum of the lengths of the other two sides is greater?"

"Yes."

Captain Lukey gave him a cunning leer. "Yet the *square* of the hypotenuse is *equal* to the sum of the squares of the other two sides. How do you account for that?"

"Euclid accounted for it quite satisfactorily." Greg put some more soda in the Captain's drink. He was wondering if the man were as sober as he had at first appeared to be.

"Euclid!" The Captain laughed shortly, as if Greg had mentioned some long-discredited mutual acquaintance, and glanced over his shoulder at Tan Yam Heng. "You never bothered your head about that sort of thing, eh, Tan?"

"I do not understand." Tan Yam Heng had stationed himself in front of the door like a character in a trench-coat melodrama.

The Captain eyed him sourly. "I'll bet you don't. Shortest distances, maybe. Straight lines? Don't make me laugh."

"Are you meaning to insult me, Captain?"

"Me? Perish the thought."

Greg finished mixing the drinks and crossed over to them.

"Shall we talk business?" he said. There was a touch of impatience in his voice that he could not quite conceal.

Captain Lukey chuckled. "That's what I like," he said. "American hustle. Okay, brother, where do we go from here? You name it."

He was speaking now with what he evidently imagined to be an American accent.

Greg smiled. "All right. I understand you're in the market for small arms and ammunition. Did Mr. Tan show you a list of the stuff I have in bond here?"

"Yup," said Captain Lukey sportively.

"He's told you the price?"

"Yup."

"And I gather you're interested."

"Nope."

Greg stared at him coldly. "Then, why are you here?"

"Because I just *might* become interested." He had abandoned his American accent.

"In what circumstances?"

"Well, if the stuff were really new and not re-conditioned, for instance."

"You can inspect it."

"And if you cut your asking price by fifty per cent, so that I could make a reasonable offer at something like the current market price."

"There is no current market price."

"Mr. Nilsen, I'm just a simple soldier, but even I know better than that. I can buy rifles at twenty dollars apiece."

"Then you should."

"I'm not all that interested in rifles. Now, if you were to put a fair price on the machine pistols, we might talk. As it is . . ." He broke off, swallowed the rest of his drink, and got to his feet. "Tell you what. You think it over and we'll be in touch tomorrow. What do you say?"

"I might come down a little, but the price'll still be in the same range."

Captain Lukey nodded, almost appreciatively. "Well," he said, "there's no taste in nothing."

Greg found the statement obscure, but he, too, nodded. The Captain wrung his hand and went, exuding good will.

The moment the door had shut, Tan Yam Heng went to it, listened, and then flung it open suddenly.

The corridor outside was empty.

Tan shut the door again and turned to Greg. "Of course, he is bluffing," he said.

"How far? You did check the going prices thoroughly, I suppose?"

"Oh, yes. If he does not come back to us, it will only be because he does not have the money to pay."

"What happens in that case?"

Tan looked shifty. "There is another buyer, but he is away in Macao at present."

"When's he coming back?"

"Next week, perhaps."

"Well, he won't find me here. All right, Mr. Tan, we'll check in the morning."

When he had gone Dorothy came out of the bedroom.

"What a curious man," she said. "Do you think he really is a British officer?"

"Why not? I've met some pretty curious American officers in my time. Why shouldn't the British army have some dogs, too?"

The telephone rang. Greg answered it.

"Mr. Nilsen?" It was Captain Lukey.

"Yes."

"I'm speaking from downstairs. I wonder if I could slip up and see you again for a tick."

"Very well."

"Be up in a brace of shakes."

Greg looked at Dorothy. "Lukey again."

"I'll go back into the bedroom."

"No, you stay here."

Captain Lukey returned looking bland and businesslike. When he saw Dorothy, however, he became stickily gallant.

"Well, this is a delightful surprise. I'd no idea."

Dorothy said: "How do you do, Captain?"

The Captain did not miss the lack of warmth in her tone. "Terribly sorry to butt in like this, Mrs. Nilsen. Frightfully bad form, but I did want another word with your good husband. Ghastly shop talk, I'm afraid."

Dorothy sat down. "That's quite all right, Captain."

"I'm afraid Tan's not here," said Greg.

"I know. Saw him go." The Captain smiled boyishly. "As a matter of fact, I waited downstairs until he did."

"Oh?"

"Mind if I sit down?"

"Do."

"You see, it was a bit awkward."

"What was?"

The Captain smoothed his mustache. "Well, it's a funny sort of game, this. I didn't know quite what to expect here. No offense meant, of course. As soon as I met you, I knew that you were a good type." He hesitated.

"But . . . ?" said Greg encouragingly.

"Well, as I say, it's awkward." Captain Lukey gave the impression of a simple man wrestling with an unfamiliar problem in ethics. "I'm no saint myself, and if you tell me to run along and mind my own confounded business, I'll understand, but I do think white men ought to stick together a bit. Nothing against Asians, mind you, but, well, sometimes . . ." He broke off, his pale, anxious eyes searching Greg's face for understanding.

"Captain, if you'll just tell me what you're talking about."

The Captain turned apologetically to Dorothy. "So sorry about all this, Mrs. Nilsen."

Dorothy smiled sweetly. "Oh, I'm just as interested as my husband."

The Captain did not seem reassured. He went on with knitted brow. "Well, it's awkward, you see," he said again, and then appeared to make up his mind. "Look, Nilsen, man to man, how long have you known this fellow Tan?"

"Three days. Why?"

"I see. Thought it might be like that."

"Like what?"

"Nilsen, I'm not asking you how you came to meet him or who put him in touch with you or who recommended him as a contact man." He paused and then added somewhat unexpectedly: "Ask no questions and you'll be told no lies, I always say."

Greg shrugged. "I may not answer your questions, Captain, but I'm certainly not going to lie to you."

"Very decent of you to put it that way." Captain Lukey seemed genuinely pleased.

"Is it?"

"Frankness begets frankness, Nilsen. So I'll be frank with you. How much do you know about Tan?"

"Very little."

"Do you know what he does for a living?"

"Import, export—at least, that's what I gathered."

"Did he tell you that?"

"Not in so many words, no."

"What would you say if I told you that he ran a labor protection racket down at the docks?"

"How do you know?"

"Made inquiries about him. You see, I know most of the people in this business. Part of my job. I didn't know you and I didn't know him. Could have been a trap."

"A what?"

The Captain looked surprised. "Well, of course. Naturally the Indonesian Government knows what's going on. You know as well as I do that they've only got a few old destroyers and gunboats to patrol a huge area. They can't stop more than a fraction of the stuff getting through. So, naturally, they go for our weak spot."

"What's that?"

"Money. If they can get me tied up in a phony deal, they will."

"I'm afraid I don't get it. Are you suggesting I'm operating a phony deal?"

"Good God, no! Please don't misunderstand. This is nothing personal."

"Then, what's the problem? You inspect the stuff first. You don't pay until you take delivery, do you?"

"No. But I take delivery in bond. As soon as I start to move it, things happen. First some cheap lawyer comes along and claims that the goods have been obtained by trickery and gets a court order holding them. By the time that's straightened out, there's some other stooge claiming that all the ammunition is phony, and that instead of having cordite inside them the cartridges are loaded with morphine. So then the narcotics people have a go. And so on."

"But the stuff gets there in the end."

"If you're lucky."

"But you said yourself that the Indonesian Government can't maintain an effective patrol."

"If they know exactly when the stuff is going, the size of the consignment, and the approximate delivery area, they've got at least a fifty-fifty chance of intercepting it. It stands to reason."

"You said money was the weak spot."

"You don't know these people, Nilsen."

"What people?"

"The people I work for. Oh, they're good types in lots of ways, but when they pay out money, that's something special."

"Who are they? Tan said something about their being a religious group."

"They're devout Moslems, if that's what you mean. Most of the anti-Communists are. That doesn't mean they're not tough, though. Life and death don't mean much to them. They'd kill a man or be killed themselves without turning a hair. But they're funny when it comes to money. If things go badly, they give up."

"And you think Tan's working for the Indonesian Government?"

"I don't know. In my opinion, he's the type who'd work for anyone who paid enough. Anyway, I don't want to risk it."

"Then you don't want to deal?"

"I didn't say that. I said I don't want to deal with Tan."

"But Tan already knows about all this. If what you say is true, he can cause just as much trouble, whoever deals."

"Not if you're the principal. Are these goods bonded in your name?"

"They are."

"Then we don't need Tan at all."

Greg was silent. He was inclined to believe what the Captain had said, or some of it, anyway; and his own instincts were against having business dealings of any kind with Mr. Tan. Unfortunately, they were almost equally against having dealings with Captain Lukey. And there was the overriding complication of the fact that he was not in reality a principal at all, but an agent. To some extent he was deceiving Captain Lukey. He temporized.

"I'll have to think about that, Captain."

"Sure. Don't get me wrong—" the Captain was Americanizing again— "I'm not trying to pressure you, old boy."

The sudden lapse into British made Greg smile. "Oh, I didn't think you were, Captain," he said hastily.

His smile and his tone of voice combined to create an effect he had not intended.

"No need to apologize," said Captain Lukey cheerfully. He suddenly snapped his fingers. "I tell you what. Have you and Madame made any plans for the evening?"

Greg looked quickly at Dorothy. "Well, we . . ."

But it was too late. The Captain swept on enthusiastically. "I tell you what. Why don't we stop talking shop now and all go out to dinner, the four of us?"

"Four?" For one wild moment Greg thought that the Captain was proposing to include Tan in the invitation.

"I know my good lady will be dying to meet you. She's mad about America. Do you like Indian food? I mean the real stuff, not those ghastly Madras curries the planters ruin their livers on. There's a little restaurant we found where it's absolutely the real thing. You know India, of course?"

"Well, no. But I'm sure you don't want to . . ."

"Then that's settled, then." The Captain smiled broadly at them both. "Sorry to butt in again like this. Supposing I pick you up at seven. No jackets. Just a tie. We might have a spot of the cup that cheers first."

He gave them a mock salute and left.

Greg looked at Dorothy. "Sorry, darling," he said, "I didn't think fast enough."

But Dorothy did not seem unduly put out. "Well, at least we'll go somewhere we wouldn't have been to on our own," she said. "I wonder what Mrs. Lukey's like."

Promptly at seven Captain Lukey called up from the lobby and they went downstairs. He was alone.

"Left my good lady outside in the taxi," he explained.

It was dark, and Mrs. Lukey was sitting in the shadows at the back of the taxi; but even in the brief glimpse Greg had of her as they were introduced, he saw that she was strikingly beautiful. Her husband got in beside the driver and told him to go to the Cathay Hotel. On the way there he talked almost continuously, identifying buildings which they could not see, and having rapid conversations in Malay with the driver which they did not understand. Dorothy, sitting next to Mrs. Lukey, exchanged one or two brief courtesies with her. From her English, which was fluent but overprecise, Greg deduced that Mrs. Lukey was not British. It was not until they were in the elevator which took them up to the Cathay Hotel bar that he saw her clearly.

She had dark hair, cut short, and a long face with a delicate, high-cheeked bone structure that reminded him of a bust of Queen Nefertiti which he had seen illustrated in *Life*. Her skin was pale without being pallid. She wore no powder and very little lipstick. Her figure was slender, with a small waist that the flared silk skirt she was wearing made seem even smaller. Only her legs were disappointing. Greg thought them too straight and shapeless. Nevertheless, she was an exquisite creature, and it was difficult to understand how she had been captivated by Captain Lukey. Beside her, he looked oafish and gross. She smiled readily, revealing excellent teeth. However, the smile did not reach her eyes, and at those moments she became less beautiful. It was possible, Greg thought, that she had a dull mind.

Her husband was an overpowering host. He drank deeply and talked incessantly, mostly about people whom he had known in South Africa and Egypt. Many of the stories he told seemed pointless to Greg until he realized that, in deference to Dorothy, and possibly also to his own wife, the Captain was censoring his tongue. He was the kind of man who has a stock of anecdotes packed away in his mind like the contents of a kit bag. He cannot rummage about and select what he wants; everything must be pulled out as it comes to hand, dirty clothes as well as clean. It was noticeable, too, as the evening progressed, that the social pretensions of those who peopled his memories became more and more modest. Brother army officers, generals, senior civil servants, important businessmen, and embassy attachés gradually gave way to sergeant majors, canteen managers, stewards, bartenders, and seedy men encountered in pubs. Captain Lukey's accent also deteriorated, or at least changed, earthier tones and racier speech rhythms replacing the plummy affectations of the afternoon. Greg and Dorothy found him easier to understand and, as some of his stories were quite funny, even began to warm to him.

Captain Lukey the officer and gentleman might verge on the odious, but Lukey the soldier of fortune was not unengaging.

The Indian restaurant was in a street off Orchard Road. It was small and squalid. The waiters were Indians wearing dhotis and striped shirts with the tails hanging out. They spread sheets of white wrapping paper on the table instead of a cloth. A single fan stirred the warm, curry-laden air. There were a great many flies. Greg made up his mind that the first thing he and Dorothy would do when they got back to the hotel would be to take full doses of the Entero-Vioforme which they had bought in Saigon.

Mrs. Lukey ordered dinner in a language which she told Dorothy was Urdu. The food took a long time to prepare, and Captain Lukey had drunk four more stengahs and paid two visits to the toilet before it arrived. There were four dishes, two of them curries, and a bowl of boiled Patna rice. To Greg's surprise, it was all delicious. He often ate curried dishes—the University Club in Wilmington always had curried shrimps or curried turkey on the lunch menu—but he had never tasted curries like these. They were hot but not harsh, and there were undertones of flavor that he could not begin to identify.

"In the West you use curry powder already made," Mrs. Lukey explained. "Here the spices are ground fresh and mixed according to the needs of the dish. In this case, for instance, there is less turmeric and more cumin. That is what you taste."

A plate of Indian condiments was put on the table. Among the seeds and sauces and shredded coconut there were sliced bananas.

"If a curry is too hot," said Mrs. Lukey, "you add sliced banana and it becomes milder."

"You mean it seems milder?"

"No. It *is* milder. I do not understand why. Some say it is the juice of the banana. Try."

Dorothy tried and was impressed.

Mrs. Lukey smiled. "Some curries are so hot," she said, "that even I could not eat them without banana, even though I have lived many years in India."

The Captain, returning from yet another visit to the toilet, overheard her.

"If you think this is a good curry," he said, "you wait until you taste Betty's. She's a wonderful cook."

This was the first time they had heard Mrs. Lukey's first name. The Captain's endearments, which had ranged from "darling" through "the memsahib" to "old girl," had not hitherto included it.

Suddenly the Captain slapped the table. "I tell you what. One night you must come over to our place and have a binge. The old girl will cook, and if we can still move afterwards we'll have a rubber of bridge. You play bridge?"

Greg admitted that they did.

"Then, it's a date. As a matter of fact, why don't we go back now and have a drink? It's only a furnished place we've taken while we look around, but it's not all that bad, and at least we'll be able to drink some decent whisky."

Greg had opened his mouth to hedge, but Dorothy spoke first. "I think that would be a lovely idea," she said.

The Lukeys' apartment was a few minutes' walk from the restaurant. It was over an electrical-appliance showroom and was approached by a long steep stairway at the side. The living room had pale green walls and contained a polished teak table and some bamboo-framed lounge chairs. In one corner there was a card table with some papers and a desk pad on it. Light came from a frosted-glass ceiling fitting. The effect was bleak.

"Make yourselves at home," said the Captain. Going to a wardrobe in the small hallway, he got out bottles and glasses.

Dorothy and Mrs. Lukey retired to the bedroom. Greg sat down in one of the lounge chairs.

"You know," Captain Lukey continued as he made the drinks, "the trouble with my job is that you never know where you're going to be next. Can't put down any roots."

"I suppose not." Greg had not thought of the Captain's occupation as one about which it was possible to generalize in such terms. Acting as purchasing agent for Sumatran insurgent forces scarcely seemed the basis of a career. Whether the insurgents won or lost, their need for a foreign representative with Captain Lukey's special qualifications seemed bound eventually to disappear; and, while there might be other insurgent forces in other parts of the world who could use his services when available, the business of contacting them would be hazardous as well as difficult. The Captain did not strike him as being a particularly robust type of adventurer. "How did you come to get into the job?" he asked.

"Oh, I don't know. Friends, influence." The Captain grinned. "Never could stand the ordinary desk job. 'Sing ho for the open road,' that's me." He reached for the soda siphon. "Say when."

"That's enough, thanks." Greg went over and took the drink.

"Yes, always on the go." The Captain shook his head ruefully. "Take next week, now. I'll probably have to go off to Macao for a few days."

"On business?"

"You can bet your sweet life I wouldn't go for pleasure."

Greg was beginning to understand the Captain. When dissembling he had the too artless look of a boy telling a lie.

"I shouldn't have thought there'd be much for you there at the moment," he said casually. "My information is that the buyers are all moving in here."

The Captain looked at him quickly. "The Dutchman's still there."

"I'm only telling you what I heard."

The Captain stared at him gloomily for a moment and then, with a visible effort, relaxed. "No shop in the mess," he said. "Cost you drinks all round in the old days. All the same, I'd like to know where we stand pretty soon. About Tan, for instance, you said you'd think it over. How long do you want?"

"Twenty-four hours."

"Cards on the table, Nilsen. Got another buyer on ice?"

"Could be." Greg was enjoying this.

"Is he dealing with Tan?"

"Look, I said I want twenty-four hours to think it over. Until tomorrow evening. I'd like to deal with you, Captain, and as long as there's no misunderstanding about price range, I'm sure we can work something out. If you want to save time, you can arrange with Tan to inspect the stuff at the warehouse in the morning."

"I told you, I don't want to deal with Tan."

"He's merely holding the customs documents at present. You wouldn't be committing yourself to anything."

"All right. As long as we understand one another."

The women came out of the bedroom and the Captain returned to his reminiscences. Soon Greg and Dorothy left.

As they were walking to the taxi rank by the Cathay Hotel, Greg told her about his brief business discussion.

"You know," he added, "I'm a bit sorry for that man."

Dorothy laughed.

"Oh, I know he's a phony," Greg said. "All that gobbledygook he talks, all those stories, all that false bonhomie."

"And all those trips to the men's room."

"It's not his fault if he has a weak bladder."

"He shouldn't drink so much."

"I think he's a pretty depressed character. I think he has to have a few drinks to stay in one piece. You know, he wants those arms badly and tried to pretend that he didn't. It was pathetic, bush-league stuff. It made me feel like a con man."

"Famous last words."

"All right. We'll see."

They walked on in silence for a moment or two. "I liked her," said Dorothy.

"Yes, what about that! How in the world did he do it? She looks like something out of Vogue. Do you think she really likes him?"

"Oh, yes."

"Attraction of opposites, I suppose. What nationality is she? 'Betty' sounds British enough, but she's got a funny sort of accent."

Dorothy glanced at him wonderingly. "You mean you didn't get it?"

"Get what?"

"She's Eurasian."

"She's what?"

"Well, Anglo-Indian, she called it. Her mother came from Bombay. She didn't say much, but I think it must have been very important to her to marry an Englishman."

"Even that one?"

"I told you, she's very fond of him."

He drew her arm through his. "I'm glad we came on this trip together," he said.

Dorothy smiled.

When they got back to the hotel, there was a message for Greg. Mr. Lane Harvey of the American Syndicated Wire Service had telephoned, and would call again in the morning.

Before he went to sleep that night, Greg booked a person-to-person call to Mr. Tan Tack Chee in Manila.

iii

WHILE they were at breakfast the following morning, the Singapore overseas operator called to say that Mr. Tan was not then in Manila but was expected back that afternoon. Greg placed a call for 4 p.m. Manila time.

Just as he put the telephone down, it rang again.

"Mr. Nilsen? This is Lane Harvey, American Syndicated Wire Service."

"Yes?"

"You're from Wilmington, Delaware, I believe."

"That's right."

"And you have a die-casting business there?"

"Yes. What's all this about? The plant hasn't burned down, has it?"

Mr. Harvey chuckled. "No, nothing like that. It's just that I'd like to send back a story on you, if you could spare me half an hour sometime today."

"Well, yes, of course. But, Mr. Harvey, it's not a very big plant, you know, and I'm not an important man. Mrs. Nilsen and I are just tourists stopping over for a few days. I don't want to waste your time."

"Mr. Nilsen, you wouldn't be wasting my time. That's the very reason I want to talk to you. More Americans are traveling now than ever before. New York's doing a survey on the problems they run into, what they don't like, what they do like, and so on. We don't get many stopping over here in Singapore, so if you could spare the time I'd be grateful."

"Okay, if you think it's worth it. When do you suggest?"

"Well, let's see. Are you doing anything for lunch?"

"I don't think so."

"Then why don't you and Mrs. Nilsen come along to the American Club?"

"Well, that's very kind of you, but . . ."

"Mr. Nilsen, I've got to try and justify my expense account sometimes."

Greg laughed. "All right, Mr. Harvey."

"Twelve thirty, then? I'll send the office car for you."

"We can take a cab."

"No trouble. The car'll pick you up at twelve thirty."

Greg gave Dorothy the gist of the conversation.

"Isn't it a bit unusual?" she said. "Why doesn't he just come over here?"

"I don't know. Perhaps that's the way they like to do things in Singapore."

Lane Harvey was a balding man of about forty with an unhealthy complexion and sleepy eyes. He spoke slowly and carefully, as if he were under some emotional pressure that he was striving to ignore, or as if he were listening all the time to the voice of a doctor telling him to relax or suffer the consequences.

"For a wire-service man," he said, "this place is Siberia. Politically, Southeast Asia is one of the most important areas in the world. In Vietnam, Laos, Cambodia, Thailand, Sumatra, Java, the Islands, everywhere around, there's history being made. But all around. Not in Singapore. We're in the eye of the storm here."

"So all you have to do is interview American tourists," said Dorothy. "It's a shame."

Lane Harvey smiled. "I'll tell you a secret, Mrs. Nilsen. It's more comfortable here than those other places, and I like being comfortable. But an American correspondent who doesn't wail for the dangers and discomforts of the battlefront is guilty of unprofessional conduct." He signaled to the waiter for another round of drinks. "Now tell me about your trip."

Greg began to do so. Lane Harvey listened attentively, nodding understandingly now and then, but asking no questions. After a few minutes Greg, beginning to hear the sound of his own voice droning on, broke off.

"Look, Mr. Harvey, this must be very boring for you."

"No, no."

"Isn't there something else we can talk about?"

"You've given me just what I wanted." He looked across the ranch-style patio. "By the way, I hope you don't mind. I asked someone else to join us for lunch. He's very British, pukka sahib and all that, but he knows a lot about Singapore. You might find him interesting."

A lean, gray-haired man with a long, narrow head and a receding chin was advancing across the patio toward them. He was one of the few men there wearing a jacket. He came up to the table.

"Hallo, Harvey. Hope I'm not late."

"Not a bit. Sit down and have a drink. Mr. and Mrs. Nilsen, this is Colonel Soames."

Over lunch, Lane Harvey insisted on telling the Colonel all about their trip, the details of which he recalled with remarkable accuracy. Greg became embarrassed.

"Now, wait a minute," he said. "Thousands of Americans must do this trip every year. There's nothing special about it."

"Yes, but we ought to do more about them in Singapore," said the Colonel. "All we get as a rule are the transient passengers off the boats. They buy a few batik sarongs and that's the end of it. Now, you, for instance—what made you decide to stay in Singapore? It would be interesting to know."

Greg glanced at Dorothy and grinned. "We were escaping," he said.

The Colonel looked startled. "Indeed?"

"From the ship's bore."

"Oh, now, that isn't fair," Dorothy protested. "Arlene may have been difficult, but she wasn't a bore." She turned to the Colonel. "You see, we were going on to Calcutta, but—well, we thought it might be better to get off here and take a side trip. Anyway, there was some business Greg wanted to attend to here, so it fitted in quite well."

The waiter came over and said something to Lane Harvey. He got up apologetically. "Call from New York," he said. "I'll only be a few minutes, but don't you wait for me, please." He left them.

The Colonel nodded genially. "Nothing like combining business with pleasure," he remarked.

"Harvey was saying that you knew a lot about Singapore," Greg said. "Are you in the tourist business here?"

The Colonel began eating his steak. "I suppose you might call it that," he replied.

"Then I expect you know quite a lot of the local people."

The Colonel shrugged. "Big place, Singapore," he said. "Over a million now. Mostly Chinese, of course."

"I suppose you don't happen to know of a Chinese named Tan Yam Heng?"

Dorothy said: "Oh, darling, I don't think you ought to bother the Colonel with all that."

"No bother, Mrs. Nilsen," the Colonel said cheerfully. "As a matter of fact, I do happen to know the chap. Trade-union organizer. That the one you mean?"

"Well, I heard it put a little more crudely," Greg said.

"Labor thug?"

"Something like that."

"Who told you?"

"A Captain Lukey. Perhaps you know him, too?"

"Met him, yes. Having trouble with Tan?"

"It's a long story. I won't bother you with it. Captain Lukey doesn't want to deal with Tan. I wondered why. You confirm what Lukey said. That answers the question. I'm much obliged to you."

The Colonel gave him a toothy grin. "Could be another answer though, couldn't there?"

"How do you mean?"

"You're selling something?"

"Yes."

"Lukey wants to buy?"

"Yes."

"And Tan Yam Heng's the contact man?"

"Yes."

"Could be that Tan's trying to get a commission out of Lukey as well as you, couldn't it?" The Colonel smeared English mustard on a large piece of steak and popped it into his mouth.

Greg stared. "But . . ." he began, then stopped. The possibility had simply not occurred to him.

The Colonel chewed for a moment or two and then swallowed. "Squeeze," he said. "Old Chinese custom."

"But why didn't Lukey tell me that?"

"Might think you already knew. Might think you didn't want to know. Might think a lot of things. What's your impression of Lukey?"

"I only met him yesterday. We had dinner. Do you happen to know anything about these people he represents?"

The Colonel shrugged. "They're called the Army of the Independent Party of the Faithful," he said. "All I know about them is that their Committee seems to have some sense of self-preservation."

"Oh?"

"They don't allow Lukey to sign checks on his own. One of them has to countersign. Met that chichi wife of his?"

"Chichi, Colonel?" Dorothy said. "What does that mean?"

"Indian slang for Eurasian, Mrs. Nilsen." He grinned. " 'Anglo-Indians,' as they like to call themselves nowadays."

The diversion had given Greg time to think. "Colonel," he said, "you told us that your business was with tourists. You didn't mean that quite literally, did you?"

"I said you could call it that."

"What are you really? Police of some kind?"

"I work for the government, yes."

"And this little party was prearranged, I take it." Greg's smile was wide but hostile.

The Colonel nodded. "We try to do these things in a friendly fashion."

"What things? Is there something wrong, Colonel?"

"Wrong?" He appeared to consider the adjective. "That rather depends upon your point of view, doesn't it? Of course, there are some cranks who think that gun running and the arms traffic are evil things in themselves, ethically indefensible. I think that's a lot of nonsense myself. In your country and mine the people can change their governments, if they want to, by voting. But there are a lot of places where it takes a revolution to do that. Look at Cuba. If somebody hadn't supplied that fellow Castro with arms, Batista would still be a dictator. Some people might say that those gun runners deserved a vote of thanks. Take Sumatra. The people there are afraid that Java's going to go Communist. They want to secede from Indonesia before that happens. Maybe they're right. Sumatra could be a self-supporting country. There are quite a few people here who think that she might one day join the Federation of Malaya. But, whatever they do, they'll have to win their independence first. They won't do that with words. Mind you, these are only my personal views."

"Do they conflict with your official views, Colonel?"

The Colonel shook his head. "No, Mr. Nilsen, they don't. And for a very simple reason. I have no official views. I am not entitled to any. My job is to obey orders. The British government recognizes the Indonesian government, and is in normal, friendly, diplomatic relations with it. That means that we don't like to add to its difficulties by helping its enemies. At the moment, that means you."

"Well, that's certainly laying it on the line, Colonel."

"I'll go farther." The Colonel took a cigar case from his pocket and offered it to Greg.

Greg shook his head. "No, thanks."

The Colonel took a cigar for himself and glanced inquiringly at Dorothy. "Do you mind, Mrs. Nilsen?"

"Not in the least." Dorothy's tone was icy.

"You were going farther, Colonel," said Greg.

"Yes. I should tell you that I was considering having you deported."

"I beg your pardon."

"Making false statements to the immigration authorities is a serious offense."

"False statements? What the hell are you talking about?"

"Steady, darling," Dorothy said quietly.

Greg took no notice. He was glaring across the table at the Colonel.

The Colonel stared back coldly. "Nature of visit—tourism. Isn't that what you told the immigration inspector?"

"Of course. It happened to be the truth."

"No. Only part of the truth. You are also here dealing in arms."

"Oh, for God's sake! Look, I also had a letter from the man I left in charge of my plant back in America. I even replied to it. So I'm in the die-casting business here, too."

"There's no point in losing your temper, Mr. Nilsen, and it's bad for the digestion. I said I had considered deporting you. Of course, now that I have met you and Mrs. Nilsen, I have no doubt of your good faith."

"Is that intended as a compliment, Colonel?"

"No, reassurance."

"The American consul will be glad to hear that."

The Colonel smiled. "You can't threaten me with your consul. I know him very well, and he doesn't have much patience with empty indignation."

"How does he feel about petty officiousness?"

"If I'd wanted to be officious, Mr. Nilsen, we would not be sitting at this table, but in my office. I don't expect you to like what I'm saying, but I think you might try to understand the political reasons for it. Singapore is a free port and a center of international trade. I admit that, legally, there is nothing to stop you or anyone else using its warehouse facilities as you are using them. But we don't like it, and you can't expect us to welcome your presence here." He smiled at Dorothy. "I'm speaking officially, of course, Mrs. Nilsen."

"But you don't disapprove of selling arms to anti-Communists?" demanded Greg.

"Personally, not in the least."

Greg laughed shortly. "You change hats rather easily, don't you, Colonel?" he said, and had the satisfaction of seeing the Colonel redden.

"I'm sorry you think that," he said stiffly. He looked at his watch. "I think it's time I was getting back to my office."

The look at the watch was evidently some sort of signal, for almost immediately Lane Harvey returned to the table.

"Sorry to have to leave you like that," he said when the Colonel had gone. "You know how it is."

"Yes," said Greg acidly. "The Colonel explained."

Lane Harvey was unembarrassed. He even grinned. "Funny old guy, isn't he?" he said. "I thought you'd like him."

iv

LATE that afternoon Inspector Chow interviewed the driver of the American Syndicated Wire Service car. Then he reported to Colonel Soames.

"They went straight back from the American Club to the Raffles Hotel. The man was expecting a telephone call from Manila. The driver had no difficulty in hearing their conversation."

"Well?"

"The man was very angry, sir."

"I imagine he was."

"With Mr. Harvey, mainly. He used strong language and talked of reporting the incident to Mr. Harvey's superiors in New York, with a view to having him dismissed."

"He'll think better of that."

"Yes, sir. He spoke of humiliation and feeling ridiculous. He also apologized to the woman and talked of forgetting the whole deal. That was a reference to the arms, I take it."

"Pulling out, eh? Good show. I was pretty sure he was an amateur."

"Later, sir, he changed his mind."

"Oh?"

"The woman said that he had a business obligation to Captain Lukey." Colonel Soames stared. "Mrs. Nilsen said that? Are you sure?"

"That is what the driver reports, sir."

"But she was on my side right from the start. I could see it."

"According to the driver, sir, Mrs. Nilsen made some highly unfavorable remarks about you. She appeared to think that you had insulted Mrs. Lukey."

"I?" Colonel Soames was genuinely bewildered. "I only asked her if she'd met the woman."

"Yes, sir." Inspector Chow's face was quite expressionless. "It appeared that you used the word 'chichi.'"

"What about it? She asked what it meant. I told her."

"She appeared to think that it was equivalent to using the word 'jigaboo' in America."

"What the hell does that mean?"

"I don't know, sir, but I assume that it must be something to do with the race question." Inspector Chow hesitated. "The woman used one very unladylike phrase."

"Well?"

Colonel Soames could not be quite certain, but he thought he detected a hint of relish in Inspector Chow's tone as he answered.

"She said you were a bigoted old bastard, sir."

CHAPTER VI

THE CALL TO MANILA came through on time.

Greg was still out of temper, and cut through Mr. Tan's preliminary courtesies almost brusquely.

"Mr. Tan, I'll come to the point. The prospective buyer doesn't want to deal through your brother."

"Oh. Does he give a reason?"

"He says he doesn't trust him, but I have an idea that that's not the real reason."

"I see. And what do you think the real reason is, Mr. Nilsen?"

"Are you paying your brother a commission?"

"Of course."

"Well, I think he's trying to make the buyer pay him a commission for the introduction as well."

There was a pause. "What do you propose, Mr. Nilsen?"

"That I negotiate on my own with the buyer, and that you tell your brother to behave himself."

"Leaving everything in your hands, Mr. Nilsen?"

"You're covered. Your brother has the customs documents. He can hold on to those as security."

There was another pause before Mr. Tan said: "Very well. I will cable to my brother."

"Today?"

"At once. It is a pleasure to do business with you, Mr. Nilsen."

At five o'clock there was a call from Captain Lukey.

"Did you inspect the stuff?" Greg asked him.

"Yes. It seemed pretty fair. What about Tan?"

"He's taken care of."

"Good show."

"Do you want to talk business?"

"Be over in a jiffy."

Despite his admitted eagerness to buy, the Captain proved to be a stubborn bargainer. It took an hour and three stengahs to force his price up to fifty thousand dollars. His method of haggling was to isolate two items, the machine pistols and the bazookas, admit their worth, and then insist on putting a nominal valuation on the remaining items. He wore a tortured expression throughout, gnawed steadily at his mustache as if it were hurting him, and covered sheets of hotel stationery with pointless calculations. In the end Greg became impatient.

"Captain, we're not getting anywhere. Sixty-five thousand is rock bottom. If you don't want the stuff, just say so."

"But if we disregard the rifles . . ."

"Well, let's not disregard them. They're there, and that's the price."

Eventually, at sixty-two thousand five hundred, there was a meeting of the minds. When they had shaken hands on the deal, the Captain grinned.

"I'd have paid sixty-five if you'd stuck out."

"Well, I'd have gone down to sixty if you'd stuck out," Greg replied, "so we're both happy. Now, about terms. Cash on delivery, of course. Okay?"

"Okay."

"Good. If you'll get a certified check made out and meet me at the Customs House tomorrow morning, we'll square it all away."

The Captain stared at him indignantly. "I'm afraid I can't do that, old boy."

"Why not?"

"Well, I'm only the liaison officer, the agent. I have to follow the drill."

"What drill?"

"Well, I told you. Those people are funny about money. They like to do the paying out themselves."

"As long as it's clearly understood that the stuff stays where it is until I have sixty-two thousand five hundred dollars in my hand, I don't care who does the paying."

"You needn't worry about that, old boy. They want that stuff and the sooner the better. This is how we handle it. I give you a draft on the Hong Kong and Shanghai Bank, made out but unsigned. It requires two signatures, mine and a member of the Central Committee's. When you present that check to him, he knows that I've inspected the stuff and agreed to the price. He signs. Then you and I go down to the Customs House, you sign the transfer, I countersign the check, and Bob's your uncle."

"Will the check be certified?"

"We can go to the Bank and cash it first, if you like."

"Well, it sounds unnecessarily complicated to me, but if that's the way they want it, okay. Where do I see this Committee man?"

"In Labuanga."

"Where's that?"

"Oh, it's only half an hour or so by air. Anyway, my good lady will arrange all that side of it." He spoke rather too airily.

Greg was suddenly suspicious. "Where is it?"

"Just across the other side of the straits, opposite Penang."

"In Sumatra?"

"Well, naturally."

Greg took a deep breath. "Now, wait a minute. Why didn't you say something about this before? I'm not going gallivanting off into the wilds of Sumatra in order to get a check signed."

"Labuanga isn't in the wilds, old boy," the Captain said patiently. "It's a coast town with its own airport and a hotel. Pretty little place, as a matter of fact."

"I don't care how pretty it is."

"But that's the drill. There's nothing to it, really. It's always worked out fine. Don't misunderstand, old boy. I'm not asking you to pay your own expenses."

"I tell you, it's out of the question. Quite apart from anything else, I don't have an Indonesian visa."

"Well, that's easily fixed."

"Is it? I understood it took a week."

The Captain threw up his hands in exasperation. "Old boy, this isn't my idea. You want cash on delivery, Singapore. All right. Cash it is. I'm not arguing about that. But you've got to look at things from their point of view. They've been let down before now, and they like to know who they're dealing with. You only have to go the first time. After that it's plain sailing."

"Don't they trust you?"

"Of course they trust me. I tell them what to buy and what they ought to pay. They just finalize the first deal."

"Well, I don't like it. If you can't produce the money here without this drill, as you call it, the deal's off."

The Captain drew himself up. "I'm sorry, old boy, but I can't accept that. I thought we shook hands on it."

"We didn't shake hands on a trip to Sumatra."

"Old boy," the Captain said wearily, "there's a plane every day. You can be there and back in twenty-four hours. It's perfectly simple. Betty goes along with you, calls up when you get there, arranges the meeting, and takes you to it. You don't have to bother about a thing. Take Dorothy along with you for the ride, if you like."

"I don't get this. Why does your wife have to go? Why don't you go yourself?"

"I would, but the Indonesians won't give me a visa any more."

"Why not?"

"Naturally, they know what I'm up to."

"But they let your wife in?"

"She's got her passport in her maiden name. As a matter of fact, she looks forward to these little trips. Makes a change for her. Look, old boy," he went on persuasively, "you admit the deal's a good one for you. All I'm asking you to do is finalize it."

"You could have said something about this before."

"It never occurred to me that you'd object, old boy. Most of you chaps are popping in and out all the time."

"Well, I'm not."

"A half-hour plane trip, that's all. Surely, old boy . . ."

"All right, all right," Greg snapped irritably, "I'll think about it."

"I'll have to know tomorrow. They're waiting to hear about this stuff." He was looking tortured again.

"I understand."

The Captain smiled bitterly, shook his head, sighed, finished his stengah, and went.

Dorothy came out of the bedroom.

"You heard?" Greg asked.

"Yes. Do you think he meant that if I went with you he'd pay my expenses too?"

Greg chuckled. "I wonder. That colonel was certainly right about his needing a counter-signature on checks. What a way to do business!"

"What will you do?"

"I'm darned if I know. The trouble is that, as Mr. Tan's appointed

agent, I'm virtually the legal owner, as far as Singapore customs are concerned. If I don't sell it to Lukey, what happens? After all, I do have an
obligation to Tan. I can't just do nothing at this stage. As for that
crooked brother of his, I'd be crazy if I expected him to find another
buyer while I'm around to stop him picking up two commissions. It's got
to be Lukey."

Dorothy shrugged. "Well, we'll never get another chance to see Sumatra."

"Are you serious?"

"Why not? Why shouldn't we both go? You know, while you two were
arguing about money, the Cook's man called up. He said our Indonesian
visa has come through. All we have to do is take our passport around in
the morning."

ii

MRS. LUKEY, or, as her British passport somewhat incongruously pro-
claimed her, Miss Elizabeth O'Toole, met them at Singapore Airport
with the tickets. The plane, a Garuda Indonesian Airways Convair with
an Australian pilot, was reassuring. The discovery that the flying time to
Labuanga was not thirty minutes, as the Captain had claimed, but a full
two hours seemed a matter for amusement rather than annoyance. They
were getting off the beaten track—and not merely as tourists, but in order
to sell arms to a band of freedom-loving anti-Communists. Moreover,
they were traveling at someone else's expense. The spirit of high ad-
venture tingled in their veins.

Mrs. Lukey had explained the whole thing to them while they had
been waiting in the departure lounge. The Captain's contact man in
Labuanga was a Sumatran oil-company employee who had legitimate
reasons for cabling regularly to Singapore. This man also had access to a
clandestine radio, through which he kept in touch with insurgent headquarters in the hills. On these check-signing occasions he notified headquarters and arranged the rendezvous three days in advance. This gave
the Committee member time to make the journey to the coast without
running the risk of traveling by day.

"What sort of people are they?" Greg had asked her. "The Committee
members, I mean."

"I've only seen two of them. One is a lawyer from Medan, the other is
an army officer. I think those two are sent because they both speak English. A European comes with them, but only as a guard, I think. All the
Committee members are Moslems."

"What sort of European?"

"He is Polish. Hamid, who is our contact, said that he had been in the
French Foreign Legion in Indochina and was training them to use the
arms."

The plane reached its cruising altitude and headed north along the coast of Sumatra. The Malacca Strait moved slowly beneath them, green among the shoals of the offshore islands, brown where the river mouths discharged the silt carried down from the hills, slate blue where the colder currents flowed down from the Bay of Bengal. Then, as the Strait widened, they altered course and began to fly over land. Soon, from their seats on the port side, all they could see below was something that looked like a vast sand dune covered with green moss.

"Jungle," said Mrs. Lukey.

The Indonesian stewardess began to serve bottled lemonade and stale cheese sandwiches. Twenty minutes before they were due at Labuanga they ran into a local storm and had to fasten their seat belts. The plane bucketed about wildly for a time, and they came in to land under a huge black cloud and in a deluge of rain. A sheet of spray went up as the plane touched down; but by the time it had taxied in to the arrival apron, the rain had stopped and the sun was out again. Their first impression of Labuanga airport was the smell of steaming mud.

It was the most favorable impression they received.

Mrs. Lukey had warned them about the immigration and customs officials. "They are appointed from Djakarta," she had said, "and they are not friendly to anyone here. Europeans especially they do not like. The last time I was here, they made two Europeans undress to be searched; but the papers in Singapore were very angry about it, and I do not think we shall be troubled in that way if we are careful. It is better not to smile or look impatient."

Greg and Dorothy did their best to remain impassive, but it was difficult. One immigration official took their passports away for examination and did not return. A second official then demanded the production of the passports. When Mrs. Lukey had explained to him what had happened, they were told to wait. It took an hour to recover the passports. Next the currency-control official ordered Greg to turn out his pockets and, for some unexplained reason, decided to confiscate his Diners' Club Credit Card. Finally, the customs inspector insisted on taking the lens numbers of his camera and impounding the exposed film in it.

Mrs. Lukey seemed to be as shaken as Greg and Dorothy by the experience. "I am sorry," she said. "They have never been so bad before."

"What the hell were they trying to prove?" demanded Greg. "Why take a credit card? I don't particularly mind. I can replace that. But what's the idea?"

"Darling, at least they didn't make us undress."

Greg, whose cotton and Dacron shirt was clinging wetly to his body, muttered that he wished they had. The loss of the film had particularly annoyed him.

The airport was three miles from the town, and the airline bus had already gone. There were no taxis. They found that they had to wait for another bus. There was a painful silence.

Mrs. Lukey made an unfortunate attempt to dispel the gloom. "Well, anyway," she said, "I don't suppose the same men will be on duty tomorrow when we leave."

"You mean we have to go through all that again?" asked Dorothy.

"If we are careful about our exit visas, it will be all right."

Greg swung around. "What exit visas?"

"We have to get those tomorrow morning at the police office. As long as we give the man who makes them out a good tip, there will be no trouble." She gave them an anxious smile.

There was another silence.

As the mud dried, other, more human smells were beginning to emerge from the vicinity of the airport. The heat was stupefying. Dorothy could feel the sweat trickling down her legs. She made a determined effort to be objective.

"Well," she said lightly, "it's their country."

Mrs. Lukey turned to her eagerly. "Yes, they are really gay, laughing, happy people, but they are not always understood. It is the same in India. Because a European coming to Bombay cannot buy alcoholic drinks without a permit, he thinks that the Indians are not friendly people. That is not true. One must live in a country to know it. One should not judge a country from the airport. Nor from its customs officials."

She had spoken quickly and vehemently, and, in doing so, had suddenly become more Asian than European. It was a disconcerting transformation.

Dorothy started to make some sort of reply. Fortunately, a bus drew into the yard at that moment and she did not have to complete it.

Almost as soon as the bus left the airport they passed through a village. The houses were of the small teak-framed atap kind with which they were becoming familiar, but on most of them the atap was faded and torn or patched. Only one house looked new and cared for. There was a signboard across the veranda. On it, painted in Malay and English, were the words: LABUANGA DISTRICT COMMUNIST PARTY.

Dorothy and Mrs. Lukey were on the other side of the bus. Greg did not draw their attention to it.

iii

LABUANGA was a port, and the terminal point of a system of pipelines connecting the oil fields in the area. The town sprawled over a broad alluvial tongue of land jutting out into the sea beside a river delta. It had been built by the Dutch, and the tree-lined streets and public gardens of the civic center had been laid out like those of a provincial town in Holland. The effect was bizarre. The trees were not lindens or sycamores, but casuarinas. Flower beds which should have contained orderly rows of tulips, narcissi, and hyacinths were lush with crotons, wild orchids, and scarlet lilies. Hibiscus rioted over the iron railings surrounding a plinth which had supported a statue of Queen Wilhelmina. The portico of the Stadhuis looked raffish under the burden of a monstrous bougainvillaea. The center of Labuanga was like a respectable Dutch matron seduced by the jungle and gone native.

Radiating out from it were the wide roads and bungalow compounds of the former European quarter. There were still a number of Europeans living there, mostly oil-company employees; but many of the buildings had been taken over by the security forces and other agencies of the Central Government. It was now called the "Inner Zone."

The change had a military as well as a social significance. The District of Labuanga covered an area of several hundred square miles and included oil fields, pipelines, copra plantations, over fifty villages, and substantial tracts of virgin jungle in addition to the city and port. An effective system of defenses against the insurgents operating from the hills would have absorbed at least three divisions of reliable and well-equipped troops. Major General Iskaq, the military governor of Labuanga, had at his disposal a garrison consisting of two demoralized infantry battalions, with three small field guns, ten decrepit armored cars, and sixty policemen. So far, the insurgents had confined themselves to night raids on outlying oil-storage installations, the dynamiting of bridges, and harassing reconnaissances in force. But the General knew that the day must come when the Party of the Faithful would feel itself strong enough to mount an all-out assault on the city, capture it, defend it against counterattack, and proclaim an autonomous regional government. When that day (or night) did come, the Inner Zone would become a fortress within which the garrison could hold out until help came from Medan. The problem had been to guard against surprise. At every road junction on the perimeter of the zone, concrete defense positions had been built. Now, at the first sign of any insurgent activity at all in the vicinity of the city, an alarm button was pressed, the defense positions were manned, and the rest of the garrison withdrew behind them. Only a small mobile column was left outside the zone to deal with the raiding party which had been the cause of the trouble.

The Inner Zone plan was one of those dreamlike pieces of military thinking which even their authors know to be unsound, but which are solemnly acted upon, nevertheless, because any plan is preferable to none. The General was well aware of the illusory nature of this one. The zone contained the police headquarters, the Stadhuis, and a number of office buildings and houses. From a tactical point of view, it was a mere geographical location, no easier to defend than any other part of the city. The power station, the water-pumping station, the port installations, and the telephone exchange were all outside it, together with the bulk of the population. But there were similar disadvantages to every other area that had been considered. The truth was that, with only two infantry battalions, ten armored cars, and three field guns, there was no right way of defending a place the size of Labuanga against superior forces.

General Iskaq was a cunning and ambitious man with a deep contempt for Djakarta politicians and a sensitive regard for his own interests. He knew that many of his officers were in sympathy with the insurgents and that he had only to hint at such a sympathy himself to initiate secret negotiations with the Committee. He had a reputation as a patriot, and the price they would pay for his defection would be high. He had never heard the axiom "if you can't lick 'em, join 'em" expressed in just those terms, but it exactly described his own ideas about power. Only one thing secured his allegiance to the Central Government.

His father had been a Javanese coolie. All through his childhood the General had seen his father kicked, shouted at, and bullied by white men, or *mandurs* working for white men. There had been nothing strange about this. His friends' fathers had been treated in the same way. That white men should drive Javanese coolies to work, coolies who would otherwise have idled in the shade, had been in the natural order of things, just as it had been natural to stop work when a white man drove by in his car or carriage, and turn toward him, and bow. Then, one day, a white man who had drunk too much gin had accused the General's father of smiling at him. When the General's father had denied it, the white man had started to beat him about the head and shoulders with a thick cane. The General's father had been strong, but the cane had been stronger, and, as his face had become covered with blood, he had fallen to his knees crying like a child.

From that moment, and for many years after, the General had found nothing natural in a relationship with white men but hatred. It was not until the Japanese army had surrendered and the white men had tried to reclaim Java as a colony that he had been able to assuage much of his hatred by killing. What was left of it had in time been transformed into the irrational but unshakable belief that white men and Asians could have no interests in common, and that what was good for one must be bad for the other. The Party of the Faithful was financed by white men, its forces were trained by white men, and, if it came to power, it would be friendly with white men. For the General, the idea of coming to terms with such an organization was totally unacceptable.

His repeated requests to the area commander for reinforcements had been refused—and for a good reason. The area commander had no reinforcements to send. The General had been in a mood of bitter desperation when his new intelligence officer, Captain Gani, had come to him with an interesting proposal.

According to the Captain's estimates, the insurgents had roughly three thousand men in the hills and many unarmed sympathizers in the city ready to help them when the time came. The General had only two thousand men at present. Yet, did he but know it, he could have a powerful ally with over fifteen hundred men to throw in on his side. That ally was the local Communist party. If the General were prepared to arm the Party men, he would have a disciplined auxiliary force at his side and superior fire power.

The General had stared at him angrily. "Are you mad?"

"Far from it, sir. What I am proposing is the creation of a loyal militia to meet an emergency."

The General had laughed harshly. "You know the area commander. He is one of Dr. Hatta's men. Are you fool enough to imagine that he would give me permission to arm the Labuanga Communists? He would have me arrested for suggesting it."

"You are responsible for the defenses here, sir, not the area commander. You are entitled to take emergency measures without consulting him. Besides, until it is equipped, the militia should remain a secret force."

"Only the area commander can authorize the issue of arms and ammunition. What is your militia to be equipped with? Stones?"

Captain Gani had had an answer for that, too.

Two months later the General had promoted him to major and made him his personal aide.

iv

THE Harmonie Hotel was in the Inner Zone and consisted of a number of porticoed colonial bungalows built inside a rectangular, wire-fenced compound. The reception clerk, a handsome young Indonesian in European dress, was courteous but firm. The only accommodation he could offer them was a bungalow with three beds in it. All other bungalows in the hotel were occupied by permanent residents. This was by Government order.

Greg and Dorothy stared at one another in dismay, but Mrs. Lukey nodded as if she had anticipated the difficulty. "There is a sitting room," she said. "I can sleep in there."

The clerk took them along to the bungalow. The sitting room was an unscreened veranda with a tiled floor. The bedroom beyond contained three cubicles completely enclosed by perforated zinc screens and looking rather like old-fashioned meat safes. As the clerk turned on the ceiling fan, a thing like a soft-shelled crab with black fur on it flopped onto the floor at their feet and began scuttling toward the wardrobe.

Dorothy let out a yelp of fear. Giggling, the boy who had brought their bags in picked the creature up by one of its hairy legs and tossed it out through the sitting room.

"My God!" said Greg. "What was that?"

"They are quite harmless," Mrs. Lukey said. "It is better to leave them. They eat the insects."

But the thing had unnerved Dorothy. While Mrs. Lukey was away telephoning the contact man, she insisted on Greg searching every inch of the bungalow. He found some lizards and a mildewed slipper, but no more of the black creatures. He did make the discovery that the bungalow contained no bathroom.

When Mrs. Lukey returned, she showed them the row of bathhouses, separated, for hygienic reasons, from the living quarters. One of those gloomy cement caverns had the number of their bungalow on it. Inside, there was a toilet, a large urn full of water, and a metal scoop.

"It is a Siamese bath," Mrs. Lukey explained. "You throw the cold water over you. It is very refreshing."

The rendezvous was for seven o'clock at a house outside the Inner Zone.

It was then a little after four. They had had no lunch. They bathed awkwardly and, when they had changed, walked over to the hotel restaurant. There was a noisy group of Dutchmen drinking in the veranda bar, and they did not stay there long. With some difficulty they found a waiter and persuaded him to produce some food. It was a warmed-over rice dish and not very appetizing, but they were hungry enough to persevere with it. While they were eating, darkness fell, and the square on the far side of the gardens, which had been deserted before, suddenly came to life. Market stalls were set up among the trees, people congregated, and food sellers appeared. A boy, squatting on his haunches by the roadside, began to play a bamboo xylophone.

It was a gentle, plaintive sound and curiously moving. Dorothy looked at Greg and he smiled at her understandingly. They were in a strange, far-off land, with no tourists within hundreds of miles of them. For a moment the discomforts of the day were forgotten. It was a brief moment.

Mrs. Lukey had said that it would take half an hour to walk to the rendezvous, and that they would probably be back at the hotel by eight o'clock. When they had had their coffee, they returned to the bungalow.

As soon as they switched the lights on, a large insect flew in and blundered about the sitting room, hitting the walls and light fittings with the force of a ricocheting pebble. Greg killed it eventually by knocking it down with a towel and treading on it. It was like a huge grasshopper made of brown plastic. Its hard shell crunched sickeningly beneath his foot. Two more came in immediately after.

Mrs. Lukey said that they were harmless and that it was best to ignore them; but Dorothy had seen the one Greg had killed and was afraid of the things getting into her hair. The prospect of remaining there by herself while Greg and Mrs. Lukey went off to their business appointment was becoming more unattractive every minute. She announced her intention of shutting herself inside one of the screened bed cubicles while they were gone.

Greg looked at Mrs. Lukey. "Is there any reason why all of us can't go? If we took a cab, Dorothy could sit and wait outside while we did our business."

"Of course, if she will not be bored."

"I'd sooner be bored than fighting these things," Dorothy said.

They had some difficulty in getting a taxi, but the reception clerk sent boys out and eventually one was captured. Shortly after seven they set off.

The taxi was a diminutive Fiat, and Greg and Dorothy, crouching in the back, found it difficult to see where they were going. After they left the Inner Zone there were fewer lights in the streets, and soon they lost all sense of direction. They had glimpses of the port, of the flashing beacon at the end of a mole mirrored in the water, and of a cluster of oil-storage tanks. Then they turned onto a road with a bad surface and broken fences on either side, bumped along it for two or three hundred yards, and stopped.

The house was about twenty yards from the road, and surrounded by an untidy litter of banana trees. It was built on teak piles and there were steps leading up to the veranda. Light showed through the plaited window blinds.

Greg pressed Dorothy's hand. "You'll be all right here?"

"Of course."

As Greg clambered out to join Mrs. Lukey, she said something to the taxi driver. He switched off his lights. As they walked toward the house, Greg asked her if she had used this rendezvous before.

"Once," she said.

The car's arrival had been heard, and, as they approached, a door opened and a man came out on the veranda. He had a flashlight in his hand. He shone it in their faces for a moment before motioning them up the steps.

He was very small and thin, with slightly bowed shoulders. He wore a black *petji*, a sarong, and bifocal glasses. He inclined his head courteously to Mrs. Lukey, and then looked at Greg.

"Mr. Nilsen?"

"Yes."

He held out his hand and said in good English: "I am Mr. Hamid. That is not my real name and this is not my house, of course, but you will understand that I have to be careful."

"Sure."

"Please come in."

The walls were of corrugated iron. Nightfall had not brought any noticeable drop in temperature, and the single room interior was like an oven. In one corner there was a bed with a mosquito net looped back over it, but most of the space appeared to be used as an office. There was a desk, a steel filing cabinet, and a table piled high with small cartons apparently in the process of being labeled. Against one wall were stacked some larger cartons with the words FRAGILE—MADE IN JAPAN stenciled on their sides.

There were two men in the room: one Indonesian, one European. The Indonesian was a slender, graceful man and tall for his race. The skin of his face was stretched tightly over a prominent bone structure, and the veins on his forehead stood out too plainly. There was a look of hunger and tension about his face that seemed to contradict the ease and grace of his body. His hair was long and unkempt. The European was thick-set and muscular, with cropped gray hair, lined gray cheeks, and a thin half-smile which exposed a set of stainless-steel false teeth. Both men were dressed in sweat-stained khaki shirts and slacks, and wore pistol belts. The Indonesian was sitting by the desk. The European lounged on the bed.

As Greg and Mrs. Lukey came in, the Indonesian got to his feet.

"This is Major Sutan," said Hamid.

The Major did not offer to shake hands. "The woman can wait outside," he said.

Mrs. Lukey looked at Hamid, who nodded and ushered her out again. The Major moved across and shut the door after them before turning to face Greg again.

"Your passport, please," he said.

Greg took the passport from his hip pocket and handed it over.

The Major examined the photograph in it and handed it back. "This is Captain Voychinski," he said.

Greg nodded. "How do you do, Captain?"

The man on the bed stared at him without speaking.

"Captain Voychinski is Polish," said the Major. "He is one of our technical staff advisers. Sit down, please, Mr. Nilsen."

He himself sat down behind the desk. Greg got the Singapore check out and laid it on the desk. Major Sutan glanced at it.

"We have not done business together before," he said. "You will not object if I ask you some questions?"

Greg smiled amiably. "As long as you don't object if I ask you a few, no."

Major Sutan considered him for a moment before he said: "Perhaps you had better ask your questions first."

"All right. To begin with, why do I have to come all this way to get a check signed? Captain Lukey says you like to know whom you're dealing with. I don't get it. Don't you trust him?"

Major Sutan shrugged. "We trust ourselves."

Captain Voychinski got up off the bed and came over. "That's right, mister," he said. His English was only just intelligible. "That fool in Singapore know nothing."

"He knows how to drive a bargain."

"Does he know agent provocateur when he see?" Captain Voychinski demanded. He spat the French words out as if they were fish bones.

"Are you suggesting that's what I am?"

"How we know? You sell arms. How do we know you not take our money and tell the Central Government?"

"I went through all this with Captain Lukey," Greg said patiently. "It's not my business to deliver the arms here. I sell them in Singapore. When and how they reach you is your business."

Major Sutan leaned forward. "We have lost too many shipments lately, Mr. Nilsen."

"Sorry about that, but I don't know what it's got to do with me."

"I am explaining our caution, Mr. Nilsen."

"Well, I'm not proposing to tell the Indonesian Government about the deal, and I don't know anyone who is. That's if there is to be any deal to tell about."

"If, Mr. Nilsen?"

"That's right—if. You like to know whom you're dealing with. So do I."

Captain Voychinski laughed unpleasantly.

Greg turned and stared at him. "You're a long way from home, Captain," he said.

"Home?"

"Isn't Poland your home?"

"What is meant by that?" Captain Voychinski's hand had gone to his pistol.

Major Sutan intervened. "Captain Voychinski is an ardent fighter against Communism," he said. "He fought in Russia and Italy and Vietnam."

"Italy?" Greg raised his eyebrows.

"Captain Voychinski was an officer in a Polish division of the Wehrmacht."

"I see."

"Any more questions, Mr. Nilsen?"

Greg shook his head. Captain Voychinski smiled grimly and took his hand from his pistol.

"Very well." Major Sutan picked up the check and looked down at it. "Where did these arms come from, please?"

"Manila. Why?"

"You are not a regular dealer, Mr. Nilsen, and the composition of the shipment is unusual. Naturally, we are curious."

"I got the stuff from a man who'd taken it as collateral for a loan.

He was left with it on his hands and wanted to get rid of it. I understand that it came originally from Red China."

"How?"

"I was told that it was intercepted at sea on its way to Malaya."

"At sea?"

"That's right. Does it matter? Captain Lukey has inspected the stuff."

"Arms from China to Malaya do not go by sea."

"Well, these did."

"What is the name of the person who told you?"

"Tan Tack Chee."

Major Sutan looked down at the check again and then took a pen from his shirt pocket. "I do not know this Tan, Mr. Nilsen, but I would suggest you do not deal with him again."

"Why not?"

"If you are not lying to me, then he lied to you. I do not think you can be lying."

"Thanks."

"On that point you would have no reason to lie." He signed the check and pushed it across the desk. "That is all, Mr. Nilsen. Will you be returning to Singapore tomorrow?"

"Yes." Greg picked up the check and slipped it inside his passport.

"Then the transaction could be completed the following day?"

"It could."

Major Sutan got to his feet and held out his hand. "Next time," he said, "I think that our dealings will be more friendly. It will not be necessary for you to come here again, I think."

"Thanks." Greg shook hands with Major Sutan, nodded to Captain Voychinski, and went to the door.

Mrs. Lukey and Hamid were waiting on the veranda.

"Is everything in order?" Hamid asked.

"Yes, the check's signed." Greg glanced at Mrs. Lukey. "Shall we go? Good night, Mr. Hamid."

They had reached the bottom of the veranda steps when he heard Dorothy cry out.

He started to run toward the road.

There were lights there now, and he saw the soldiers almost immediately. Two of them were dragging the driver out of the taxi. Three more were coming toward him across the clearing. From behind, near the house, there was a sudden confused shouting and then the ear-shattering din of a submachine-gun burst.

At that moment one of the soldiers saw him, yelled to the others, and started to bring his carbine up to his shoulder.

Mrs. Lukey was screaming at him to stop.

Greg stopped; and then, as the other two soldiers ran toward him, he took a step backward and put up his hands.

CHAPTER VII

GENERAL ISKAQ ATE a second honey cake and poured himself a third cup of coffee. It was cool enough to drink, but he left it to get still cooler. He was in no hurry. He knew that he was going to enjoy the day which lay before him. A little delay in approaching it could only serve to increase the ultimate satisfaction. Meanwhile, there were more modest pleasures at hand. He picked up his binoculars.

From the window of his apartment on the top floor of the Stadhuis he could see the port, the river delta, and the sea beyond. The sky was cloudless, and at that early hour there was little heat haze. The previous day's rains were pouring down from the hills, and the silt-laden water was swirling out in fantastic patterns across the choppy waters of the bay. When the river was in flood like that, the currents interacted with the tides to produce a mill-race effect at the harbor mouth. Plans had been made to eliminate this navigational hazard by extending the mole; but the Government had refused to pay for the work. Now a tanker in ballast, trying to get alongside the oil company's wharf, was having to be warped in cautiously a foot at a time. The morning sun was glittering on her wheelhouse windows, and the General could see the white-topped caps of her European officers out on the wings of the bridge. Other white blobs on the wharf marked the presence of the oil company's Dutch undermanager and the English representative of the tanker's owners. They, too, would be impatient at the delay.

The General watched through his binoculars and was content. Admittedly, the situation had richer possibilities. For some minutes he had toyed with the vision of one or, better still, both of the warps parting under the strain, and of the tanker drifting helplessly across the basin to crunch into the side of a dredger moored there; but that, he knew, had been idle daydreaming. One should not expect too much of life. It was enough that the Europeans were inconvenienced and irritated. Enough for the present, anyway. One of them, the Englishman, was British vice-consul in Labuanga, and there were further tribulations in store for him.

The tanker was nearing the wharf now, and the brown water eddying around her sides was losing its power over her. The General continued to watch, but his thoughts began to stray. There was an important question to be decided. Whom should he tell first—the American vice-consul or his British colleague?

It was not easy. The Englishman, Mr. Wilson, was the local agent of the North Borneo and Federation Shipping Company, and his post as British vice-consul was merely honorary. In fact, it was said that the only reason for appointing a British vice-consul in Labuanga had been to enable Mr. Wilson to import his supplies of whisky and tobacco duty free. When told that a female British citizen had been arrested the night before and was in jail on charges of conspiracy against the Government, illegal trading in arms, illegal entry, consorting with criminals, and espionage, the inexperienced Mr. Wilson might well become confused and behave incorrectly. That would be most enjoyable. On the other hand, he might consult with the British consul in Medan or, worse, ask Mr. Hallett, the American vice-consul, for advice. They were very friendly. In that case, Mr. Hallett would have less of a shock when he discovered that there were two American citizens also in jail on similar charges.

The General wanted Mr. Hallett to have a big shock. Mr. Hallett's post was not honorary. He was a career member of the Foreign Service of the United States, and acted not only as his country's vice-consul, but as a local information officer as well, organizing subversive things like American book centers and documentary film shows, and corrupting promising young Indonesians by arranging for them to take courses in American technical institutions. He was also closely associated with the World Health Organization office in Labuanga, and had been known to accompany malaria-control and B.C.G. field units into the interior. On several occasions he had even penetrated into insurgent-held areas with such units, returning not only unscathed but impertinently unwilling to talk about what he had seen. There were a number of American technicians working in the oil fields; and when they came into Labuanga, they could be as riotous as Dutchmen. Mr. Hallett had a disagreeable way of making the arrest of one of these drunken gangsters appear as either a calculated affront to the President of the United States or the result of some ridiculous mistake on the part of the security forces under the General's command. The prospect of confronting Mr. Hallett with two American arms smugglers, disguised as tourists and caught red-handed in the company of notorious traitors, was infinitely alluring.

From the other end of the apartment he could hear his wife upbraiding one of the servants for not answering the doorbell promptly. A moment or two later he heard the voice of Major Gani. He decided to hear his aide's report before making up his mind how he would handle the situation.

The General did not really like Major Gani, who had spent a year as a student at a Japanese university and did not always trouble to conceal his belief that he was cleverer and more cultivated than his commanding officer. He had, too, an annoying habit of quietly snapping his fingers while the General was speaking. The General, a religious man himself, had also realized by now that Gani was a Communist. However, it was impossible to get rid of him at this juncture. The man had made himself indispensable; and so had the Communist Party.

The idea of seizing the insurgent arms shipments in the Labuanga area had been a good one; he was at once arming his secret militia and denying arms to the enemy; but without the Communist intelligence network to discover the times and places of the shipments it would have been impossible. The insurgents had lost four substantial shipments before they had changed their delivery arrangements; and now, thanks to Gani and the Party, the new arrangements would soon be as unprofitable to the Committee as the old.

It had been Gani, who had noted, in the immigration service's reports, the frequency and brevity of the visits to Labuanga of the British woman Elizabeth O'Toole. A more detailed study had then shown that O'Toole had always arrived from Singapore, and in the company of a male European of one sort or another. She had always left with him the following day. Out of five visits, one had been made with a Belgian, one with an Italian, one with a German, and one each with two different Australians. Since nobody in his senses, Asian or European, would regularly choose Labuanga as a place of assignation for any amorous purpose, Gani had made a further investigation and noted a relationship between the dates of three of O'Toole's visits and the dates of three interceptions of arms shipments. The Party had alerted the comrades in Singapore and inquiries had been made about her there. Two days ago a report of her true identity had been received, together with the information that she was about to make another visit to Labuanga. Arrangements had been made with the immigration service to delay the woman and her companion at the airport when they arrived, so that the necessary steps could be taken to place them under surveillance.

Major Gani came in briskly. As usual, his salute was more like an acknowledgment of applause than a mark of respect; but the General did not care today. He was hungry for information.

"Well, Major?"

Major Gani took off his cap and sat down before he answered. "The traitor Hamid Osman," he said, "died of his wounds an hour ago, sir. It is a pity because I had hoped for much information from the man. The house they were meeting in belongs to a small importer. He is believed to be in Medan at the moment. We shall find out. Hamid Osman's house was most interesting."

"Ah."

"He is unmarried and lived with his brother, who is a radio technician. We found a radio transmitter there. It was still warm from use."

"You arrested the brother?"

"He had escaped. The two houses are only three hundred yards apart. He must have heard the firing."

The General frowned. "The radio was still warm, you say. Would he have had time to report to the traitors in the hills?"

"Perhaps."

"It would have been better if we could have had complete secrecy."

Major Gani shrugged. "There cannot be complete secrecy, sir. The American and British consuls here will have to be informed. And I believe there is a Polish consul in Medan." There was a hint of malice in the way he said the last sentence. The General would have to be careful. If it became generally known that there were four non-Dutch whites under lock and key in Labuanga jail on charges other than disorderly conduct, the area commander in Medan would remove them from the General's jurisdiction within hours. The area commander had a weakness for personal publicity and would certainly not permit a subordinate to take charge of a situation of such lively interest to the press.

"I will deal with the American and British consuls myself," the General replied casually. "They will want to be discreet. The Polish consul does not matter." He brushed the subject aside with a wave of his coffee spoon. "Now, about the prisoners. What information do we have from them?"

"It is a little soon, sir, to expect real information. I interrogated the taxi driver who took them from the hotel. He heard only that the house had been used as a meeting place once before. Nothing of value. I released him." He saw the General stiffen and added curtly: "He is a good Party member."

"But the O'Toole woman—what does she say?"

"Nothing, sir." Major Gani began snapping his fingers.

"And the Americans?"

"Also nothing. The man Voychinski advised them to say nothing until instructed by their consuls. It is not important. They are not important."

The General threw his coffee spoon down with a clatter. "Not important?" he demanded. "Four European gangsters engaged in smuggling arms to the traitors, not important?"

Major Gani sighed patiently. "Very important, sir, for propaganda purposes. But for our purposes we have someone much more useful—Major Sutan."

The General controlled himself. In his daydreaming about the white prisoners he had almost forgotten that a member of the insurgent Committee had been taken, too.

"What does Sutan say?" he asked.

"He refuses to speak."

"Where are the prisoners?"

"In the police jail, sir."

"Sutan as well?"

"Yes, sir." And then Major Gani made a mistake. "He is a strong man," he went on blandly, "and will not talk easily. I have put two good men onto the preliminary interrogating work, but we do not want to injure him too much, in view of the public court-martial that must follow, and it may be twenty-four hours or more before he can be persuaded. I thought it safer not to interrogate him at your own headquarters. He has many friends in the army."

"Yes." The General pushed his cold coffee away and got to his feet. "I was one of them."

"Ah, then you understand, sir."

Major Gani was an able and astute officer with a glib command of the Marxist dialectic and a keen eye for the weaknesses of other men; but he was also a deeply conceited man and in some respects grossly insensitive. To him, General Iskaq was merely a brutish and reactionary strongarm guerrilla leader whom circumstances had thrust into a temporary position of authority—a thick-skulled clod to be deferred to and pandered to now so that he could be exploited later. The possibility of the General's disliking the idea of torturing a former comrade had not occurred to him.

The General looked him in the eyes. "Yes, I do understand. I shall take charge of these interrogations personally."

"In the case of the foreigners, sir?"

"In the cases of all these prisoners. Then we will see who will talk, and who will not."

ii

AT THE time of the arrest Greg had been too bewildered to be really frightened; it had been as if they were in some nightmare traffic accident involving a truckload of uniformed maniacs instead of another car. Later, when Dorothy and Mrs. Lukey were being yelled at, prodded with guns, and searched in front of a roomful of policemen, he had been too angry. The butt of a carbine slammed into the pit of his stomach had ended that phase. Out of the consequent pain and nausea had come at last a cold realization of their predicament—and, with it, fear. On the way to the jail Mrs. Lukey had wept hysterically. It had been Dorothy, calm and collected, who had found the words of reassurance. Handcuffed to Voychinski and Major Sutan, he had sat there in numbed silence.

At the jail, a single-story brick building in a walled compound on the outskirts of the town, Dorothy and Mrs. Lukey had been hustled off to the women's quarters. Major Sutan had been held in the control section. Greg and Captain Voychinski had been put into a cell containing one iron-framed bed, an urn of water, and a bucket. The whole place had a strong ammoniac smell thinly mingled with that of disinfectant.

Voychinski had taken their arrest philosophically, and, now that Greg's good faith had been so strikingly proved, his attitude became almost friendly. Unfortunately, he was one of those men who, in the face of danger, affect a sardonic facetiousness as nerve-racking after a while as any display of fear.

"How did they get onto us?" Greg asked him as soon as they were alone.

"When I know, I send you letter."

"What do you think they'll do?"

"To me? Pop-pop-pop." He grinned, showing his steel teeth. "Or perhaps . . ." He made the motion of castrating himself. "With you? Big trial after six months. After two years, perhaps, they let you go. With the women? If they let you go, they keep the women. If they let the women go, they keep you. Don't worry."

"Well, they'll have to inform our consuls, anyway."

"Oh, yes. Next week, perhaps."

"What about Major Sutan?"

"He no have consul here. Like me."

As there was nothing to sit on except the bed, neither of them had any sleep. Voychinski seemed unconcerned. He began to talk about his experiences with the German army in Russia and Italy. His facetiousness never flagged, but there was an unpleasant undercurrent of reality to all he said. Greg, who had served with the Fifth Army in Italy and understood what he was hearing about, listened with a mounting disgust that he found difficult to conceal. He had seen an Italian village after a unit of the sort Voychinski seemed to have enjoyed serving with had left it. He tried not to listen, and to pin his thoughts onto the moment when Dorothy and he would be regaling their friends with the hilarious account of how they were arrested in Labuanga and had to spend a night in the local hoosegow; but it was not a very convincing fantasy and was too easily overlaid by another in which Dorothy and he did not figure personally. In this, their friends were discussing with gloomy perplexity what the newspapers were referring to as "the Nilsen arms-racket inquiry" and wondering how come Greg Nilsen had made such a horse's ass of himself.

Soon after dawn a guard brought them a pot of rice and fish, which they had to eat with their fingers. Greg ate very little. His bowels were beginning to cause him uneasiness and he had been obliged more than once to make use of the bucket. Voychinski had some jokes to make about that, too. Greg's dislike of him was now complete.

The barred window of the cell gave onto an inner court, and as the sun rose, they were able to see through the zinc mosquito screen that it was an exercise yard. About twenty male prisoners, barefooted and wearing sarongs tucked between their legs like loincloths, wandered about aimlessly or squatted in groups under the supervision of guards with carbines. Inside the cell, the heat and smell were becoming unbearable. When, shortly before noon, a guard unlocked the door and beckoned to him, Greg's fondest hope was that he was to be allowed out into the yard with the other prisoners.

Instead, he was taken by two guards to a room off a corridor leading to the main entrance. Except for a long table and six chairs, it was bare. The windows were barred. One guard entered with him, motioned him to a chair, and stood by the door with his carbine at the ready. After a brief interval the door opened and an army officer entered. Greg recognized him as the officer who had attempted to interrogate him the previous night, a handsome man with angry eyes and an air of carefully controlled impatience. Behind him was a man of Greg's own race, in a very clean white shirt and gabardine slacks. He was about thirty-five, stocky, and balding, with a round, chubby face and square shoulders. He stood in the doorway with a lopsided smile on his face and looked curiously at the guard.

As Greg got to his feet, the officer inclined his head. "I am Major Gani," he said.

Greg nodded. "Major."

"And this, as you requested, is the American vice-consul in Labuanga."

Greg gave an audible sigh of relief and smiled. "Am I glad to see you, Consul!"

The man in the doorway nodded, but without looking at him. "I wish I could say the same, Mr. Nilsen. My name's Ross Hallett."

Greg started to move toward him, but the guard raised his carbine threateningly. Hallett took no notice. He looked from the guard to Major Gani.

"Good-by, Major," he said.

Major Gani's lips tightened and he began to snap his fingers. "The formalities have now been complied with," he said. "You have seen the prisoner. He is unharmed. It is now your duty to inform him that it is in order for him to be interrogated and to answer all questions."

Hallett shook his head. "Oh, no, Major. That isn't my duty."

"This is Labuanga, not Washington, Mr. Hallett. The prisoner is under our law, and so are you."

"Sure we are," Hallett replied easily, "and you have every right to ask Mr. Nilsen any questions you like. But that doesn't mean he has to answer them. You see, I've had no opportunity yet of talking privately to him. I don't think that I can advise him to co-operate with you at this stage."

He turned away as if to go, then paused as the Major said something sharply in his own language. Hallett answered him in the same language.

"What did he say?" Greg asked.

Hallett ignored him. Greg stood there, uncomprehending and irritated, while they argued. Finally the Major gave a reluctant nod and motioned the guard out of the room.

"You may have ten minutes," he said in English. "There will be a guard on the door."

He followed the guard outside.

Hallett's smile faded as the door closed.

"Sit down, please," he said.

"Now look, Mr. Hallett," Greg began, "all I'm worried about at the moment is my wife. You see . . ."

"I know, Mr. Nilsen. But we don't have that much time, so supposing you let me run things. I've seen your wife, and she seems to be okay. The British vice-consul is seeing Mrs. Lukey, and she's okay, too."

"You mean Miss O'Toole, don't you?"

Hallett sighed. "Mr. Nilsen, I don't have time for games. Whatever her passport says, these people know she's Mrs. Lukey."

"How did they find out?"

"I don't know. Anyway, that's unimportant. If you'll just answer my questions, we may get somewhere." He took a notebook from his pocket. "Now, then. Mrs. Nilsen gave me some basic facts, and, according to her, you have a joint American passport. Where is it now?"

"They took it away."

"The police or the military?"

"That officer who was just in here was in charge."

"What else did they take from you?"

"Everything—money, wallet, watch, the lot."

"They claim they have documentary evidence linking you with Major Sutan. What would that be?"

"I had a check for sixty-two thousand five hundred Malay dollars in my passport. It was drawn on the Hong Kong and Shanghai Bank and signed by Sutan."

Hallett's lopsided smile returned for a moment, but it was anything but friendly. "Do you know what sort of a spot you're in, Mr. Nilsen?"

"I have a pretty good idea."

"I wonder if you have. All right, give me the background. I want the whole history of this transaction."

Greg gave it to him.

When he had finished, Hallett was staring at him in sour wonderment. Greg shrugged.

Hallett drew a deep breath. "Mr. Nilsen," he said, "I wish you could tell me something. Why is it that when an apparently normal, intelligent, law-abiding citizen like you gets hold of a passport and a steamship ticket, he suddenly turns into a juvenile—"

"Okay, Mr. Hallett," Greg broke in irritably. "You can't say anything I haven't already said myself."

"I wouldn't be too sure of that. Our country spends millions of dollars trying to help these people become a nation of free men, trying to give them confidence in democratic processes, trying to persuade them that some version of our way of doing things offers them a better chance of happiness than the Communist Party, and then people like you . . ." He broke off. "I'll give you the rest of the lecture another time. Right now we've got to try to get you and Mrs. Nilsen out of this mess."

"Well, Mrs. Nilsen, anyway."

"As they see it, she's guilty by association." Hallett leaned forward. "Now, tell me again. Your arrangement with Lukey was just as you've stated it? You had nothing to do with the delivery of this war material and know nothing about the arrangements that were to be made for that delivery? Is that right? Don't fool with me, Mr. Nilsen. I have to know. Is that the true picture?"

"It is."

Hallett sighed. "That's too bad."

"What do you mean?"

"The military governor's terms for your release are that you inform them when and how the stuff is being delivered, so that they can intercept and confiscate it."

"But that's crazy. How can I tell them? Lukey doesn't even own the stuff until that check is cashed in Singapore."

"They won't believe that."

"But they'll have to."

"There's no 'have to' about it."

"Major Sutan'll tell them I don't know anything. Voychinski, too."

"A traitor and a hoodlum? Why should they believe what they say?"

Greg was silent for a moment. Then he nodded. "I see. It looks as if my wife and I are going to be here quite a while."

Hallett made no comment. "How much money did you have with you?" he asked.

Greg told him.

"All right, I'll try to get that released. While you're held without trial you can pay for a more comfortable cell and have food sent in from outside, if you want."

"Will I be able to see my wife?"

"I'll ask, but I doubt it."

"I don't know how Mrs. Lukey's fixed for money. If we can get these privileges for her, too, I'd be glad to pay."

"I'll speak to the British consul about that. Now, then. You're going to be interrogated by the governor personally. His name is General Iskaq, and what he'd really like to do is beat the daylights out of you. He won't, because he knows I'd raise hell in Medan and Djakarta if he did, but bear it in mind and don't push him. Do you know what xenophobia is?"

"Yes."

"Well, the General has it badly. So watch yourself. Tell him the truth. He won't believe you, but go on telling it anyway. That check is your best talking point."

"How do you mean?"

PASSAGE OF ARMS [125

"It substantiates your story that the transaction was incomplete, and that there were, therefore, no delivery arrangements. Tell him about the second signature needed. Say that, if he doesn't believe you, he should send the check to the Indonesian consulate in Singapore and ask them to try and cash it as it is. Ask him if he thinks you fool enough to trust Lukey with the goods before you had been paid."

"He knows Lukey?"

"Of course. Lukey's a crook. The oil company filed embezzlement charges against him two years ago, but couldn't make them stick. The Government deported him."

"I see."

"Another thing: don't get into any sort of political discussion. You had the stuff to sell. You were approached in Singapore. You thought you were dealing with an agent of the Central Government."

"You said I was to tell the truth."

"The Communist Party here will make all the propaganda use they can out of this. They'll try to say you're an American agent and that we're secretly backing the insurgents while pretending friendship with the Central Government. The less help they have from you, the better."

"How do I account for the meeting with Major Sutan?"

They could hear footsteps approaching along the corridor outside. Hallett began to speak quickly.

"You thought he was a Government official trying to get a secret commission on the deal. Play the innocent. You shouldn't find that too difficult." He waved Greg into silence with a gesture. "Do you smoke, Mr. Nilsen?" he went on loudly.

"A cigar occasionally. Why?"

"I'll send you in some cigarettes anyway. They are currency here. There's a pack to go on with. Liquor is not allowed, I'm afraid."

"Do you have something for an upset stomach?"

"I'll get you some pills from my doctor."

The door opened as he was speaking and Hallett got to his feet. Greg rose with him.

The man who came into the room had a stunted, barrel-chested body the ugliness of which was only partially concealed by an immaculately laundered uniform. He had a heavy, pock-marked face with thick, rubbery lips and ears. His eyes were watchful and his movements deliberate, like those of some powerful yet cumbersome animal. He wore a scrubbed webbing pistol belt, and carried a short leather-covered cane of the type Greg had seen carried by British officers during the war.

Just inside the door he stopped and looked distastefully from Hallett to Greg.

"This is Mr. Nilsen," Hallett said, and added to Greg: "The military governor of Labuanga, General Iskaq."

The General went over to the table and sat at the head of it. He was followed by Major Gani, who motioned to Greg to stand facing the General.

Hallett said: "General, I have advised Mr. Nilsen to make a frank and full statement."

The General seemed to take no notice.

"You will find that he acted in good faith and that no possible charge against him can be substantiated," Hallett continued.

Major Gani smiled ironically and began to translate what had been said into Malay. Only then did Greg realize that the General could not understand English.

When the translation was finished, the General looked at Hallett and said something in a harsh, guttural voice.

Hallett inclined his head politely and turned to Greg. "I am requested to leave now, Mr. Nilsen," he said. "You will, of course, answer the General's questions as best you can. I have no doubt that you and Mrs. Nilsen will be released very soon. In any case, I shall be watching your interests and will see you as often as I can. If it becomes necessary, I will get counsel for you."

"Thanks."

With a slight bow to the General, Hallett went. As the guard shut the door behind him, Major Gani sat down by the General.

Greg turned to face him.

Major Gani nodded. "We will begin," he said briskly. "First, let us hear what you and Mr. Hallett have arranged that you shall say. After that we will hear the truth."

iii

THE General listened absently to the white man's voice speaking the language that always sounded to him like the chattering of apes, and watched the sweat pouring off him as he talked. In his mind's eye, however, all he could see was the room he had left ten minutes earlier, and his old friend Mohamad Sutan lying on the stone floor in a pool of bloody water, moaning and choking, with blood running from his mouth and nostrils and his stomach heaving. He had told the proudly smiling men who had done it to stop for the present and let the prisoner rest; but he could not leave matters there. Soon he would have to tell them to go on again. Unless, of course, one of the whites should talk first.

As Major Gani started to tell him what the white man was saying, the General picked up the cane he had placed beside him on the table and began to tap the palm of his other hand.

iv

"IT's really my fault," Dorothy was telling Mrs. Lukey. "We'd been planning this trip and looking forward to it for so long that the reality was bound to be an anticlimax. I was prepared for that, but Greg wasn't, and I let him get angry and bored. I should have had more sense. When a man's worked so hard and successfully for so many years, and been such a wonderful husband and father, you tend to forget some things about him. Or maybe tell yourself that they're no longer there."

"What sort of things?"

Dorothy sighed inwardly with relief. After the American and British consuls had been there, Mrs. Lukey had been calmer for a while; but gradually the effect of their visits had worn off and she had begun to weep again. She was going to be tortured, she was going to be raped, she was going to be shot. She had done nothing. She did not want to die.

As almost everything she had said expressed Dorothy's own presentiments and fears, it had not been easy to reassure her with any sort of conviction. Despair can be infectious, and Dorothy had begun to cast about feverishly for some means of diverting her companion's thoughts from their immediate situation. She had found it, unexpectedly, in the subject of her relationship with Greg. Mrs. Lukey was almost avidly curious about it. Dorothy guessed that she was trying indirectly to find the key to a more secure relationship with her own husband. It was the difficulties of marriage that interested her most. Her eyes were dry now, and, although she still held the damp white ball which had been Dorothy's last piece of Kleenex, her nose had at last stopped running.

"What sort of things?" she repeated.

"Oh, I don't know," Dorothy said. "Nothing very bad, really. You know those dolls with round weights at their feet? The ones that always stand up straight again, however much you push them over? As long as he has work that's important to him, a man like Greg hardly ever does anything really silly. It's only when the weight is suddenly taken away that things go wrong. It was like that when he came home from the army. He'd been away four years working with mine-detection equipment and explosives. It was dangerous work, but it had fascinated him. All that time he'd hardly thought of anything else. When he came home safely to me and the boys, I was so happy. I thought that all our troubles were over." She paused. "The first thing that happened was that he fell in love with another woman—or, rather, a nineteen-year-old girl."

Mrs. Lukey looked at her quickly; but Dorothy's expression remained placid.

"I suppose that if it hadn't been for the children," she said, "we'd have broken up. But we didn't. Greg got his business going, and gradually everything was all right again."

"What about the other woman?"

Dorothy shrugged. "The last time we talked about it was five years ago. Greg became very upset."

"Because he was still in love with her?"

"No. Because he couldn't remember her second name."

Mrs. Lukey stared at her uncertainly for a moment. Dorothy was look-ing preternaturally solemn. Then Mrs. Lukey began to laugh. After a moment Dorothy began to laugh with her. They did not hear the foot-steps of the guard approaching, and were still laughing when the cell door opened. Mrs. Lukey's laughter became a strangled cry as they turned.

Standing in the doorway were the old woman who acted as wardress and one of the armed guards from the control section.

The wardress said something in Malay, and Mrs. Lukey began to back away.

As Dorothy started to go to her, the guard came into the cell and, reaching out, grabbed Mrs. Lukey by the arm. She screamed and tried to pull away. With a shout he flung her across the cell to the wardress and then, using his carbine with both hands, thrust them out into the corridor. The cell door slammed behind him.

As the sound of Mrs. Lukey's screams receded, Dorothy sat down on the bed and searched her bag frantically to see if by any chance there was one more piece of Kleenex that she had overlooked. There was none. She sobbed once and tried holding her breath. Then she ceased trying. Kleenex or no Kleenex, it was better perhaps to cry.

v

WHEN Greg was taken back to his cell, Voychinski was stretched out asleep on the bed.

He awoke at the sound of the cell door closing, but made no attempt to move. Greg took no notice of him. Heat, lack of sleep, stomach cramps, and the insistent questioning had exhausted him to the point of indiffer-ence to discomfort. When he had used the bucket, he sat down on the floor and rested his back against the wall.

Voychinski sat up lazily and yawned. Greg took Hallett's cigarettes and matches from his shirt pocket and tossed them onto the bed.

"Compliments of the American consul," he said.

Voychinski picked up the cigarettes and smirked. "You leave soon, hah?"

"Just as soon as I tell them when and how that stuff you were going to buy is being delivered."

"They think you know?"

"That's right. They think I know."

Voychinski swung his feet off the bed and looked down at him. "Who question you?"

"General Iskaq and that major."

"So!" The pale eyes searched for hidden clues. "What you say?"

"What could I say? I told them all I know. I told them fifty times."

"About the delivery?"

"I don't know anything about the delivery. You know that as well as I do."

"But you tell them something, a good story perhaps?"

"I told them what I know and that's all."

"Nothing about delivery?"

"That's right."

"You lie."

Greg shut his eyes wearily. "Anything you say."

Voychinski got up off the bed and stared down belligerently. "Gani would not permit you to say nothing."

"Gani wasn't conducting the interrogation."

"You are lucky."

"It's not Gani I'm worried about."

"That peasant Iskaq?" Voychinski spat derisively. "Listen, my friend. Iskaq is a soldier, a good soldier, but stupid politically. Oh, yes, he would wish to break your face, but he is not serious. Gani is the dangerous one. He want those guns to arm more of his Party men."

"What Party men?"

"You do not know he is a Red?"

"How would I?"

"Mrs. Lukey know it."

"What difference does it make?"

"My friend, if Iskaq had political sense, he would have come over to the Committee. Now he secretly help to arm the Reds and think he is fighting us when he only make firing squad for himself. It is stupid." He sat down again and stared at Greg suspiciously. "You did not tell Gani anything?"

"About the delivery? Don't be silly. I don't know anything. Is there anyone who does? Does Major Sutan? Do you?"

Voychinski's eyes narrowed unpleasantly. "Did Gani tell you to ask that?"

"Oh, for God's sake!"

Voychinski shrugged. "When a man is afraid and has nothing to lose, he will do many things. And Gani mean to find out from one of us."

Greg glowered at him. "What do you mean, 'nothing to lose'?"

"Your arms are still in Singapore."

"Exactly! So there's nothing for Major Gani to find out. That's what I keep trying to tell you."

Voychinski sighed impatiently. "My friend, do you think that you are the only man in the world who sell us arms?"

It took Greg several seconds to get the point. Then he remembered something Captain Lukey had said. "You only have to go the first time. After that it's plain sailing." With only one deal to consummate himself, he had not taken much notice of it then. He looked up at Voychinski.

"You mean there's another shipment from someone else already on the way?"

Voychinski showed his teeth, but did not reply. From along the corridor there was the sound of a door opening and a rattle of keys. A moment later the cell door was opened and a guard outside motioned to Voychinski.

He got up slowly, stretched himself, and walked out. He did not even glance at Greg. The door shut behind him.

vi

Ross and Fran Hallett were playing bridge with Dr. Subramaniam, the Indian director of the tuberculosis clinic, and his wife that evening when the lights went out. It was a little before eight o'clock.

They were not unduly concerned. Power failures were common enough. Dr. Subramaniam lit some oil lamps, and they went on with the rubber. Twenty minutes later the lights were still out, and Dr. Subramaniam, wondering if the failure could after all be due to a fuse in his own house, went out to the road to see if there were lights elsewhere. He saw immediately that the failure was general; but as he walked back he heard the sound of distant machine-gun fire. It seemed to come from the other side of the town, by the port.

He called Ross Hallett. The sounds of firing were becoming more insistent, and intermingled with them now there were faint thudding noises.

"What is it, do you think?" asked the doctor. "Another raid on the storage tanks?"

"Possibly. Difficult to tell from here."

"What else could it be?"

"I wouldn't like to say. Anyway, I think I have to get back."

"Why? There's nothing you can do. We've got a spare bed you and Fran can have for the night."

Hallett shook his head. "I'll be grateful if you'd let Fran stay, but I have to get back."

"They'll have shut the Inner Zone."

"I'll get through on my pass."

Fran Hallett recognized what she called the "State Department" look on her husband's face when he returned to the house, and made no attempt either to dissuade him from going or to insist on going along herself. She did not even tell him to take care. She merely reminded him that there were fresh eggs in the water cooler and kissed him good night.

He drove very slowly. Once, when a column of army troop carriers began to pass him, he pulled off the road and stopped. During these emergencies the Labuanga garrison became trigger-happy, and moving vehicles, including their own, were frequently shot at. As he approached the Inner Zone check point, he became even more cautious. A hundred yards short of it, he stopped the car and, leaving the headlights on, got out and walked toward the guardhouse. With the lights behind him, the sentries could see clearly that he was unarmed and alone.

The N.C.O. in charge of the check point had never seen a diplomatic pass before, and could not read. An officer had to be summoned to approve the pass before Hallett was allowed through. The sounds of firing were louder there, and it was possible to determine the direction from which they were coming. The officer was excited and on edge, but Hallett decided to take a small risk.

"What do they want?" he asked. "To burn one more oil tank?"

There was a local joke implicit in the form of the question. From time to time Government spokesmen had accused the oil company of secretly subsidizing the Party of the Faithful. Insurgent propaganda leaflets had indignantly denied the charge and listed the attacks made on oil-company property. The list had been unconvincing, and a Government newspaper had run a sarcastic article about it. Why was it, the writer had asked, that the insurgents were never able to blow up more than one oil-storage tank at a time? Why didn't they use a little more explosive while they were about it and blow up two or three? And why did they bother with oil-storage tanks at all when they could, at much less risk to themselves, cut the pipelines? The writer had gone on to offer helpful suggestions of how this might be done, and to suggest that the insurgents apply to America for technical assistance. Even the strongly pro-Faithful had smiled a little at this.

The officer looked at Hallett uncertainly.

Hallett said: "Maybe they brought two sticks of dynamite this time."

The officer grinned. "Tuan, it will take more than two sticks to blow up the power station."

Hallett chuckled, but said nothing more. He had confirmed an earlier suspicion.

He went back to his car and drove through into the Inner Zone.

CHAPTER VIII

KEITH WILSON, Her Britannic Majesty's honorary vice-consul in Labuanga, had been born in Shanghai. When he was eight, his parents had sent him "home" to school in England. When he was eighteen, he had returned to the Far East. Most of his working life had been spent in Borneo and Malaya. He looked and, in a sense, was a typical middle-class, pipe-smoking Englishman. His wife had died in a Singapore internment camp during the war, and he had never remarried. The ruling passion of his life was cricket, and his only complaint against Labuanga was that there were not enough cricketers there to form two teams. He had a powerful radio receiver and spent much of his spare time listening to broadcast cricket commentaries on the Australian and B.B.C. short-wave services. He held that the political stability of India and Pakistan owed as much to the legacy of cricket as to the existence of the British-trained Indian Civil Service. When not on the subject of cricket, he had an agreeable sense of humor. He also had the insight necessary to translate obscure Malay and Chinese jokes into meaningful English. The Halletts, who had read their Somerset Maugham, referred to him, not unaffectionately, as "The Taipan."

He answered Hallett's telephone call promptly. "I tried to get you at the Subramaniams," he said. "They told me you were on your way back. Are you at home now?"

"Yes." Hallett could hear the breathing of the switchboard operator listening to their conversation, and knew that Wilson could hear it, too. "What about a drink?" he asked.

"Fine. Why don't you come over here and enjoy the view?"

"Be with you in a couple of minutes."

Wilson's apartment was on the top floor of the oil company's building and overlooked the western half of the city. That was the area in which the power station was situated. Earlier, when the firing had started, he had been able to see through his binoculars a sparkle of tracer bullets in that direction. By the time Hallett telephoned, however, the firing had almost ceased. He had switched the radio over to battery operation, and was listening to the voices on the garrison communication frequency when Hallett arrived.

"What do you make of it, Keith?" Hallett asked.

"As far as I can gather, the Faithful sent a strong force in to take over the power station, and the army got in first. The Faithful took up encircling positions. Now they're all just sitting there. I don't understand it. If they wanted to dynamite the place, why didn't they use a small party and their usual hit-and-run tactics?"

"Why indeed?"

Wilson was lighting another candle. Something in Hallett's voice made him look up. "Any ideas?"

"A hunch. You know the night defense plan. The moment there's an attack alarm, the main body concentrates in the Inner Zone. No dispersal of forces. All that's left outside is the mobile column. Where's that now?"

"Holding the power station."

"Which is on the opposite side of town from the jail."

"What about it?"

"That power-station attack could be a diversion. The Faithful could be going for the jail to spring Major Sutan."

Wilson thought for a moment. "It's a possibility," he said finally. "Do you think Sutan's worth it to them?"

"He's an important member of the Committee. Besides, if they do nothing, don't they lose face?"

Wilson thought again. "If they did get inside that jail," he said, "what they'd do there wouldn't be very nice."

"That's what I was thinking. Once they started killing . . ."

"Yes. You know, I tried to call our consul in Medan earlier. I wanted him to go to the area commander and get Mrs. Lukey moved out of here. They wouldn't put me through. Said the line was down."

"I know. They gave me the same treatment. I'd made up my mind to fly over there in the morning if necessary. As it is . . ."

"What do we do? Call General Iskaq and request him to move troops out to the jail just in case?"

Hallett frowned. "I don't know. Let's think. Supposing he did take the idea seriously enough to send part of the garrison out there. Is that necessarily better for our people? Supposing the troops were given orders to shoot all prisoners in the case of an attack. It's happened before. Supposing someone like Major Gani decided to use them as hostages. Look at it another way. The more fighting there was, the more killing there would be after the fighting was over. After all, the jail doesn't matter to us, only those three persons inside it."

"I gather you're against requesting reinforcements," said Wilson dryly.

"I'm against hypothetical reinforcements in that hypothetical situation."

Wilson switched the radio off. "Well, it may be hypothetical, but I must confess you have me worried. Mrs. Lukey's a highly strung woman. Anglo-Indian, you know. Even with your Mrs. Nilsen to help, she's in a pretty bad state. I didn't like leaving her there today."

"Do you think she knows anything they want to know?"

Wilson hesitated before he said: "I'm afraid she might."

Ross Hallett nodded. Mrs. Lukey was a British subject and, common humanity aside, no concern of his. He thought about the Nilsens, who *were* his concern. To Fran he had referred to them as "rogue tourists." They had been irresponsible and stupid—more irresponsible and more stupid than the booziest oil driller spoiling for a fight. So far, he had been able to view their predicament with a certain amount of detachment. Now it was beginning to frighten him. Men like General Iskaq and Major Gani were not easily deterred from violence by the fear of diplomatic consequences. The Nilsens could be murdered that very night, and he would be powerless except to protest and listen to polite expressions of regret.

"I'm going out to the jail," he said. "Do you want to come with me?"

"What are we going to do?"

"Ask to see the prisoners."

"At this time of night? They won't let us."

"No, but we'll be there. It can't do any harm, and if there is going to be trouble, it just might do some good."

"Then we ought to put on a show. Flags on our cars, neck-ties, lots of protocol."

"Whatever you say, Sir Anthony."

They had to make a wide detour to avoid going through the Inner Zone, and approached the section in which the jail was situated from the Chinese quarter to the south of it. It was probably that which saved them. If they had been coming from the Inner Zone, they would almost certainly have been fired upon before they had had time to identify themselves.

As Hallett's car was the more imposing, it had been agreed that he should lead the way. Skirting the Chinese quarter there was a deep drainage canal that was bridged in only two places. He was driving very slowly over the ruts and potholes of the approach road to one of the bridges when something he saw in the headlights made him pull up quickly. He heard Wilson stopping behind him.

They were about fifty yards from the narrow earth ramp which led up to the bridge. At the foot of the ramp was an overturned cart completely blocking the way. Hallett got out of his car. Wilson joined him.

"What do you think, Keith?"

"We could probably move it out of the way between us."

"Think we ought to try?"

"I don't know. Does it look like an accident to you?"

"Pretty funny sort of accident."

On one side of the road there were a few small houses, but they were in complete darkness. The only sounds were those of crickets and of the car engines idling.

"What about leaving the cars here with the lights on and going a bit closer to have a look?"

"Okay."

They walked forward into the beam of the headlights, heard the quick rustle of sandaled feet, and saw the long shadows of the men behind them flickering across the road ahead. As they swung around and stopped with their hands in the air, the men closed in.

ii

IT HAD been mid-afternoon when Voychinski had been taken away, and Greg had immediately used the opportunity to get some sleep.

It had been dark when he had wakened. Voychinski had not returned. After a while, a guard had come in with food and water. With it had been a package from Hallett containing a carton of cigarettes, two paperbacked novels, a tube of Entero-Vioforme, and a note saying that he hoped to secure further amenities the following day. The package had been opened and most of the cigarettes stolen. Greg had given one of the remaining packs to the guard and received in return a cup of weak tea. His watch had been taken from him with the rest of his personal belongings, and he had had no means of telling the time. It had been about two hours later, it seemed, when the lights had gone out. He had thought that this must be part of the jail routine. Then, through the grille in the cell door, he had seen oil lamps being brought to light the corridor.

The cells had been left in darkness. As he could no longer read, he had gone to sleep again.

To Dorothy the power failure had brought a curious kind of relief.

Some time after nightfall Mrs. Lukey had been brought back to the cell sobbing incoherently. It appeared that after being questioned for over two hours by Major Gani she had been taken to another room and confronted by Captain Voychinski. Already he had been so badly beaten by his guards that he was scarcely able to stand; then, in front of her, they had knocked him down and kicked him until he became unconscious. After that, she had been taken out and warned, meaningly, that her own interrogation would shortly be resumed. Meanwhile, she should try to remember useful facts.

Dorothy had done her best to calm her, but without success. It had been all she could do to remain calm herself. If they could beat Captain Voychinski, they could beat Greg. The American consul had said that Greg would not be physically harmed; but how could he be sure? These horrible little madmen might do anything.

"But what do they want to know?" she had asked. "Mr. Hallett said he was going to tell Greg to make a full statement."

"There is another shipment already on the way." Mrs. Lukey had hesitated. "They want to know about that."

"Did you know about it?"

"Yes, I knew."

"Did you tell them what they wanted?"

"I told them what was in the shipment. That is all I know. But they want the route so that they can intercept it. They said that if I did not know the route myself, I must tell them who did know."

"What did you say?"

Mrs. Lukey raised her panic-stricken eyes to Dorothy's. "I told them Captain Voychinski knew."

"And *does* he?" Dorothy was beginning to feel sick.

"He might." The eyes pleaded for understanding and forgiveness. "I could not help it. I had to say something or they would have beaten me."

And then the lights had gone out, and Dorothy had no longer had to watch Mrs. Lukey's eyes and wonder if, the next time she were questioned, she would become desperate enough to implicate Greg as well as Captain Voychinski.

There were two beds in that cell. After a while Dorothy said: "It looks as if we're not going to have any more light. I think we ought to try to get some sleep."

"They will be coming for me again."

"If you don't listen for them, maybe they won't."

"I could not sleep."

"Try."

A few minutes later Mrs. Lukey began, in a quiet, ladylike way, to snore.

Dorothy dozed fitfully. Hours seemed to go by. She was half awake, half asleep, when she heard a sound like a huge air-filled paper bag bursting somewhere near at hand. A moment later the sound came again. This time the bed shook a little. Mrs. Lukey woke up and started to whimper.

iii

ONLY convicted prisoners serving sentences of less than ninety days, and suspects on remand or awaiting trial, were held in Labuanga jail. It was built around two small quadrangles which were used as exercise yards— one for the male prisoners, one for the female. Separating the two quadrangles was the so-called "control section." This contained the guards' quarters, some interrogation rooms, a kitchen, and the head jailer's office. A high outer wall enclosed the whole compound. The main gates, two imposing slabs of iron-braced teak, were opposite the control-section entrance.

What Dorothy had heard were the explosions of two P.I.A.T. mortar bombs, stolen some months earlier from a British army ordnance depot in Kuala Lumpur and purchased from the thieves by Captain Lukey. They were fired, with some accuracy, from a projector which looked like a truncated Lewis gun, and the first one hit the junction of the gates just by the drop bar. Two of the brackets which supported it snapped, and a piece of the flying metal wounded one of the duty guards. The second bomb completed the work. The drop bar fell to the ground, and one of the gates swung open. The unwounded guard was too dazed by the blast of the explosions to do more than stare as the attackers poured in. Then, as he turned and started to run, he tripped and fell to his knees. An instant later a parang sliced down into the muscles of his neck, and he slid forward to die.

The grilles at the entrance to the control section were less imposing than the outer gates, but more efficient. A Very pistol was fired to give the P.I.A.T. crew light to aim by, but the bomb only bent and jammed the long sliding bolts. A second bomb aimed at the hinges was equally unsuccessful. By this time, too, the defenders had come to their senses. A flare was lobbed from the roof of the building onto the road, and a burst of rifle fire from behind the grille forced the P.I.A.T. crew to take cover behind the outer wall, where they could do no more damage. The flare from the roof was now followed by grenades. Caught in the narrow space between the outer wall and the jail itself, the assault party began to suffer casualties.

However, they were well trained and ably led. The surprise attack having failed, they set about blasting their way in. With the aid of smoke grenades and covering fire from across the road outside, more men were rushed through the broken outer gates. They had orders to work around the sides of the building, deal with the defenders on the roof, and then dynamite their way through from the rear.

Inside the control section, Major Gani, whose interrogation of Voychinski had been interrupted at an interesting point, was on the telephone to General Iskaq at his headquarters in the Inner Zone.

"No, sir," he was saying, "I cannot tell you how strong the attacking force is. It is impossible to estimate. But they are well armed, with machine guns and an anti-tank weapon of some kind. Our guards are armed with only rifles and grenades. It is imperative that you send armored cars and troops."

"Anti-tank weapons?"

"They burst open the main gate with two shots."

The General hesitated. Only four of his ten obsolete armored cars were at that moment capable of taking the road. The rest had mechanical trouble of one sort or another. Three, which were awaiting spare parts from Italy, had been out of commission for months. The thought of exposing even one of the effective cars to the fire of anti-tank weapons made his heart sink.

He put a touch of impatience into his voice. "Unless they destroy the outer wall first, they cannot use such long-range weapons against the building. The jail is of brick. Every window is barred. You have the main gate covered. Why do you need more troops?"

"These guards are not troops," Major Gani replied. He knew that he had made a mistake in mentioning the anti-tank weapons, and tried to regain the initiative. "I must remind you, sir," he went on quickly, "that we are holding important prisoners here. This is an attempt to free them."

"Of course. But they will not be freed."

"Then send troops, sir."

"They will not be freed," the General repeated sharply. "Better if they should all be killed."

"You authorize me to kill those five prisoners, sir, including the American and British subjects?"

"It would be the insurgents who would be held responsible. But that will not be necessary. We will keep them. Has the white man talked yet?"

"No, sir. He . . ."

Somewhere overhead a grenade burst, and slabs of plaster fell down from the ceiling of the head jailer's office from which Major Gani was speaking. As the plaster dust billowed up, he heard the General asking if they had been cut off.

He managed to croak into the mouthpiece: "Send troops," before the dust forced him to start coughing; then he hung up. If the General were left wondering what had happened, so much the better. The troops would be dispatched with more urgency.

He had misread the General's thought processes. The General was a hard man to stampede. So far, only half of the available Party men had been armed with weapons from the intercepted shipments, and they had very little ammunition. Subsequent interceptions would no doubt improve that position, but, until they did, the "militia" was not effective. As far as the General was concerned, the Inner Zone plan was still in force. That meant that the garrison did not dissipate its small strength by chasing off in all directions to fight wherever the rebels chose to attack. The thrust at the power station was obviously a diversion for the attempt on the jail; but that knowledge changed nothing. The power station was difficult to defend. The jail was virtually a stronghold. Gani was an Intelligence officer, unused to battle and therefore overanxious. His reckless demand for armored cars showed that. He must learn that there was more to soldiering than he had realized. The experience might make him more respectful.

The General's only misgiving at that moment concerned his authorization to kill the white prisoners. It would be annoying if Gani lost his head and killed them prematurely. For a moment or two he considered telephoning the jail and countermanding the authorization; but he concluded finally that any hint of indecision on his part could be misinterpreted just then. If there were a serious change in the situation at the jail, Gani would obviously report it. Meanwhile, it was best to leave things as they were.

At that moment, in fact, the situation at the jail was changing more rapidly than even Major Gani knew. There had been fighting on the roof, and the jail guards up there had been cornered by the water tank. It was only a matter of time before the enemy winkled them out and gained access to the stairs leading below. With a steadiness and decision which would have surprised the General, Major Gani prepared to evacuate the control section and fall back behind the grilles and steel doors of the men's cell block. What he did not know was that, under cover of the roof fighting, a party had made its way to the rear of the building and was at that moment setting demolition charges in one of the drains.

Orders had been given to remove Sutan and Voychinski from the interrogation rooms and transfer them immediately to cells in the men's block, when the man who had taped the charges lighted the fuse.

iv

GREG's cell was less than a hundred feet from the explosion. The blast wave slammed him against the wall, smashed the light fitting, and snatched the zinc screen out of the window embrasure as if it had been paper.

Since the attack had begun, he had been sitting there as wretched and perplexed as a child listening to a quarrel between adults. Outside in the corridor, there had been some confused shouting at first, and then the guards, apparently in response to an order, had all left. The other prisoners in that section had begun to carry on excited conversations in Malay through the door grilles. The exercise yard had been quiet. The sounds had been coming from the other side of the jail. He had started then to worry about Dorothy. If, as it seemed, there were some sort of jail riot going on, she could be in danger.

Now, as he got to his feet and went to the unscreened window, he could see a cloud of dust and smoke drifting across the moonlit yard. At the same moment there was the crash of a grille opening along the corridor behind him and the sound of running, struggling, shouting men. Then the air was shattered by a long burst of submachine-gun fire and the shouts changed to screams.

v

THE Committee member in charge of the raiding force was a former army officer, Colonel Oda, whom Hallett had met on one of his trips into insurgent territory.

The Colonel had a protruding lower lip which curled inauspiciously at the smallest hint of opposition to his wishes; but he was not wholly unreasonable, and had been persuaded in the end that the proposal of his second-in-command to kill the American and British vice-consuls and commandeer their cars was both politically unsound and tactically unnecessary. On the subject of those in the jail, however, he had been adamant. He and he alone would decide what was to be done with them, prisoners and guards, white or brown. After further discussion he had agreed, reluctantly, to allow the foreign diplomatic representatives to accompany the attacking force. They would go as neutral observers of the justice meted out by the Committee of the Faithful.

The reason for even that concession had soon become apparent. Neutral or no, the observers had been ordered, before the assault began, to park their beflagged cars bumper to bumper fifty yards from the jail entrance, in order to provide cover for the Colonel's battle headquarters among the trees beside the road. During the early stages of the fighting, Hallett and Wilson had been obliged to crouch behind the cars while carbine bullets from the roof of the jail had ripped through the door panels into the upholstery.

Half an hour after the first P.I.A.T. mortar bomb had been fired, the demolition charge blew out the rear wall of the control section. Two minutes after that, the sound of firing ceased. There was some shouting. Then the second-in-command appeared at the main gate and called out that the place was taken. The Colonel walked across the road. He took no notice of Hallett and Wilson. They exchanged questioning glances, then left the cars and followed him.

As they went through the main gate, the damaged grilles beyond were being levered open by the men inside. Lanterns had been brought. By their yellow light it was possible to see a group of guards huddled by an office door with their hands clasped behind their heads. The bodies of the guards who had been killed in the forecourt were lying face downward at the foot of the steps. Their blood had drained into a broad puddle. The Colonel did not trouble to walk around it.

The blast of the demolition charge had brought down a great deal of plaster. The dust of it hanging in the air made Hallett and Wilson cough. It did not seem to affect the Colonel. He was talking to his second-in-command. When he saw the captured guards, however, he stopped and glanced over his shoulder at Hallett.

"Do you know where your American and British prisoners are in this place?" he asked.

"I know where they were, Colonel." Hallett began coughing again.

The Colonel looked at one of the soldiers covering the guards. "Keys," he said.

The soldier looked at the six terrified guards. Three of them had long key chains at their belts. The soldier grinned and took out a knife. Then he stepped forward and swung the knife upward. The guard screamed as the double blade of the knife slashed through the belt and across his stomach simultaneously. As he doubled up in agony, the soldier snatched the belt away and handed the keys to the Colonel. The other two guards with keys hastily unfastened their belts and let them drop to the floor. The soldier with the knife laughed.

The Colonel pulled his lip in and nodded to Hallett. "You may release your prisoners," he said, "but do not try to take them away from here."

"Very well, Colonel."

But the Colonel was already walking on. "Voychinski can wait," he was saying to the second-in-command. "The one who matters is our Sutan."

The guard with the stomach wound had sunk to the floor and was looking down stupidly at the blood pouring over his hands. Wilson picked up one of the belts and took the key chain off it. His face was white as he looked at Hallett.

"If you want to see that Nilsen's all right," he said quietly, "I'll look after the two women."

Hallett nodded. "Okay."

He took the remaining set of keys and went on down the corridor. The demolition charge had wrecked the building here, and he had to pick his way over piles of rubble to get to the passage leading to the men's cell block. The soldiers there had seen him with their officers and made no move to stop him. In any case, they were too busy stripping the bodies of the dead guards to care much about a white man. He stumbled on, using the flashlight from his car to light the way and shutting his ears to the cries of two men who were not yet dead. From beyond the open grille ahead of him came the sound of prisoners calling to one another and pounding on the doors of their cells. One man was screaming hysterically that the place was on fire and that they would all be burned alive. As Hallett went along, trying to make out the cell numbers, he shouted in Malay that everything was all right and that all prisoners would soon be released. Under cover of the excited cries that followed this announcement he called out quietly: "Mr. Nilsen."

"Here."

He had already passed the cell. He went back, fumbling with the flashlight and the keys, and called again. "Where are you? Keep talking."

"Right here. Is that Hallett? What's going on? Is my wife all right? What's happened?" He was trying, not quite successfully, to keep a tremor out of his voice.

Hallett began trying the keys. "Take it easy, Mr. Nilsen. I've got to find the right key. The jail's been taken over temporarily by the insurgents. The British consul's gone along to get your wife and Mrs. Lukey."

"Is she all right?"

"There was no fighting on that side. They may be scared, but I'm pretty sure they're not hurt. Wait a minute. This looks as if it might be the right one."

A moment later he had the cell door open and saw the prisoner's face livid and desperate in the beam of the flashlight.

Hallett made himself smile. "Dr. Livingstone, I presume," he said and then: "Steady, Mr. Nilsen. Sit down a moment."

"I just want to get out of here." But he did as he was told. "It sounded as if they'd blown the whole place up," he added weakly.

"Only a bit of it. Now, listen. We're in a curious sort of spot. Sutan's friends came to get him. Okay, they've got him. They won't hold this place for long, though. As soon as it starts to get light, they'll be hightailing it back to the hills. Where that leaves you and Mrs. Nilsen, I don't know, unless you ask them to take you along. Even if they'd agree, I wouldn't advise that."

"You mean we've got to stay here in jail?"

"I hope not. I don't know. I'm just warning you. At the moment it's

all up to the commander of the raiding party, and he's a tough proposition. I'm taking you to him now. He doesn't speak much English, so he
won't question you direct, but don't say anything unless I tell you to.
Above all, don't get mad or try to protest. Just keep quiet. Is that clear?"

"I don't have a protest left in me."

"Good. How's your stomach?"

"Queasy."

"Well, keep close to me and don't look around too much, or it may
give you trouble."

He led the way out of the cell and back toward the control section.
He went quickly, holding the flashlight ahead of him and ignoring the
prisoner's complaints that he could not see where he was going. Hallett
judged that the man had reached a point of mental exhaustion at which
he could very easily become unnerved. Anger was sometimes a useful
restorative.

"Come on," he said impatiently, "we don't have much time."

"Time for what?"

Hallett did not have to reply. They had reached the main corridor of
the control section and Colonel Oda's second-in-command was approaching. He was a square, muscular man with a wispy mustache and bright,
stupid eyes. He had not forgotten that the Colonel had earlier accepted
Hallett's arguments in preference to his own. He looked at the prisoner
contemptuously.

"Is this your American?"

"This is Mr. Nilsen, yes."

"You will both come to see the Colonel immediately."

"Very well."

The second-in-command turned on his heel, and they followed him
along the corridor. Hallett felt the prisoner's hand on his arm.

"What did he say?"

Hallett frowned warningly and told him loudly in Malay to hold his
tongue. The second-in-command spoke no English and Hallett did not
want to irritate him unnecessarily.

The room into which they were taken was the one in which Hallett
had last seen Major Gani; and Major Gani was the first person he saw
there now. He was standing against one of the barred windows, with a
soldier on either side of him and blood running from his head and left
shoulder. Sitting at the table beside Colonel Oda was a man whom Hallett guessed to be Major Sutan. His head was drooping and his face a
deathly yellow in the lamplight. It was obviously all he could do to remain upright. The Colonel was talking to him quietly.

Across the table from them was Wilson with the two women. Mrs.
Lukey was crying. As soon as he saw his wife, Nilsen went over and put
his arms around her. She began to cry, too. The Colonel looked up in
exasperation.

"Ah!" He rapped on the table as if for silence. "I have told Mr. Wilson. Now I tell you, Mr. Hallett. Major Sutan has confirmed the friendly status of these European prisoners. You may take them with you and go. That is all."

Hallett's eyes met Wilson's. The latter shrugged resignedly.

The Colonel frowned. "That is all," he repeated sharply.

"Thank you." Hallett bowed slightly. "May I ask where you suggest they should go to?"

"That is their affair. They are free to go."

"Just a moment, Colonel." Hallett went forward to the table. "You asked Mr. Wilson and me to come here as neutral observers to witness the administration of justice by the Committee of the Faithful. You say now that Major Sutan has confirmed the friendly status of these persons. Yet you are prepared to send them away from here, without protection, to be rearrested by the Central Government, put back into prison like common criminals, perhaps shot as your collaborators. Is that the justice of the Committee of the Faithful?"

"They are free to go. I do not understand what you want."

"He understands, all right," Wilson said in English. "I've just finished explaining it to him."

Hallett kept his eyes on the Colonel. "It has been instructive to see how the Committee of the Faithful keeps faith with its friends," he said. He put a sarcastic inflection on the word "Faithful."

The second-in-command stepped forward. "You do not have to hear these insults, Colonel. Give the order and I will see that they cause no further trouble."

The Colonel ignored him. "What can we do?" he demanded angrily. "What do you expect?"

"A safe-conduct for these persons to the airport, and permission to embark on the first Malayan Airways plane to Penang or Singapore."

"You are a fool or mad."

"I don't believe so."

"This is a raiding force, not an army of occupation. Only General Iskaq could give such a safe-conduct."

"I know that."

The Colonel laughed shortly. "Then you must know also that you are wasting my time. We have released these persons. They are in your care. We can do no more."

"You can obtain a safe-conduct for them from General Iskaq."

"Impossible."

"Is it? Why not ask Major Gani?" Without waiting for a reply, Hallett looked across the room at the man by the window. "Major, do you think that General Iskaq values your services highly enough to grant a safe-conduct for Mr. and Mrs. Nilsen and Mrs. Lukey in exchange for your release unharmed?"

He saw Gani's eyes flicker. Then there was a crash as Colonel Oda stood up quickly and his chair shot back against the wall.

Wilson started to move toward Hallett. The second-in-command snapped back the cocking handle of his machine pistol.

Hallett looked from the machine pistol to the Colonel's lower lip and shrugged. "Violence is the fool's answer for every difficulty," he remarked. "I did not think it was yours, Colonel."

"Get out, before we think too much."

Hallett inclined his head. "Very well. It is a pity. I had hoped that Mr. Wilson and I could have been of help to you."

The Colonel's lip curled proudly. "We did not need your help to take this prison. We will not need your help to take all Labuanga when we wish."

"Maybe not. But you will find that taking Labuanga is easier than keeping it. One day—soon, perhaps—you will proclaim an autonomous government here and declare your independence of Djakarta and Medan. It is then you will need the help of friends."

"These are our friends." The Colonel tapped his pistol holster.

"They will not win your government recognition. Think, Colonel. The Central Government will denounce you as brigands and bandits and destroy you as they destroyed your comrades in Celebes. To whom will you appeal for justice? To the United Nations? The Central Government is there before you. To the Soviet Union? You are anti-Communist. The only ears that will hear you are in the United States and Britain. Our countries, Mr. Wilson's and mine, admire good fighting men, but they also value moderation. No doubt Major Sutan has been vilely ill-treated by this man Gani. But how will you explain that, merely in order to have your revenge by torturing and killing Gani, you endangered the lives of two Americans and a British subject? Supposing General Iskaq puts them back here tomorrow, has them killed, and then tells the world that they were savagely murdered by you when the jail was attacked. How could you deny it?"

"You would know that was not true," the Colonel said indignantly.

"Would I? It seems to me that there is a very small difference between that and what you are planning. And how foolish that plan is. Simply by using Gani as a hostage, you could not only cause General Iskaq to lose face, but also show yourselves as humane and honorable men, infinitely more worthy of governing Labuanga than these lackeys from Djakarta. These things are not forgotten. When the day comes on which you need the friendship of the United States and the nations of the British Commonwealth, which memory will you prefer—that of killing Major Gani or that of having saved American and British lives?"

The Colonel stared at him for a moment and then sat down again. He looked at Sutan inquiringly.

Sutan's haggard eyes looked up at Hallett. "Captain Voychinski has died from the beatings this man gave him," he said slowly in English. "Perhaps the gentleman does not know that. Voychinski was a white man. Perhaps if the gentleman saw Voychinski's body, he would not feel so merciful."

"It's not mercy he's asking for," Wilson put in, "but some protection for these people who came here to do business with you."

"They came at their own risk."

"Oh, no. They came because you wanted them to. They were told there was no risk. Personally, I feel they were unwise, but I also feel that you people have a responsibility. Besides, have you thought about what would happen to your future arms deliveries if you turn these three persons over to the authorities? You wouldn't be able to buy a bow and arrow after that."

The Colonel hammered on the table with his fist. "We are *not* turning them over to the authorities," he shouted.

"In effect you are." Hallett had taken over again. "That is, unless they have a safe-conduct out of the country."

The Colonel turned to Sutan again.

Sutan shrugged wearily. "Gani learned nothing that matters. Do what is best."

The Colonel looked with disgust from the white men to Major Gani. His eyes hardened.

"We had good plans for you, Gani," he said. "Perhaps, if your General does not love you enough, we shall still carry them out. Or perhaps, if you stay in Labuanga, there will be another day."

"Perhaps," said Major Gani.

The Colonel motioned to the telephone. "Then, see if your fine General will speak to you."

vi

GENERAL ISKAQ had not been unduly worried by the absence of news from the jail. An explosion had been heard in that direction; but the sounds of firing had later ceased. He had assumed that the situation at the jail was now similar to that at the power station. When he heard Gani's voice on the telephone, he was prepared to be calm and matter-of-fact. By making no reference at all to Gani's hysterical behavior earlier, he would emphasize its absurdity far more effectively than by drawing attention to it.

When he heard what Gani had to say, a spasm like an electric shock seemed to jolt him from his heels to the top of his head. His ears began to sing.

Through the singing he became aware of Gani's repeating urgently: "General! General! Can you hear me?"

He controlled himself carefully before he answered: "You say you are a hostage?"

"Yes, General. You see, sir, the position is this. . . ."

"Answer my questions!" He had heard the brisk self-assurance flowing back into Major Gani's voice, and, in a sudden rage, shouted the order.

"Certainly, General. But you see . . ."

"What steps were taken about the white prisoners?"

"Unfortunately, Captain Voychinski died. The others are alive. It is about those persons . . ."

"And Sutan?"

"Major Sutan is beside me, sir, and Colonel Oda."

"Why have they not killed you?"

"If you will permit me to explain, sir."

He explained.

The General listened with mounting bitterness. Fantasies began to crowd into his mind. He would countermand his standing orders about night operations and the Inner Zone, take his armored cars and field guns out, and blast the jail into a heap of rubble. He would kill everyone in it, including Major Gani. The anti-tank weapons of the raiding force would be crushed beneath the wheels of the armored cars. There would be a holocaust. Or, simpler, he would refuse the safe-conduct, tell them to kill Gani, and then hang the three whites publicly in front of the Stadhuis. Or, wiser, more cunning, he would put a cordon around the jail area, cover it with the field guns, and starve them all into submission. He knew that none of those things was really going to happen, that he could never be sure that the power station and jail attacks were not tricks to lure him out of the Inner Zone so that the garrison could be chopped to pieces by the main body of the insurgents. He also knew that, however much he might want to discard Major Gani, the time had not yet come when he could safely do so. Without Gani, the arming of the militia could not be completed, and he, the military governor, would be left again to plead impotently for reinforcements which would never arrive. He knew, too, that he could never justify, even to himself, the proposition that the life of one Indonesian officer was worth sacrificing for the pleasure of punishing three whites.

He heard himself saying: "Very well. I understand. But what guarantees do we have that they will keep the agreement?"

"One moment, sir."

"I had better speak to Oda myself."

"One moment, please, sir."

There was a pause and silence. Gani had had the impertinence to put his hand over the mouthpiece. Then another detested voice addressed him.

"General, this is Ross Hallett. I am at the jail in order to protect the lives of two American citizens. Colonel Oda, who commands the troops now in control of the jail compound, has requested my assistance and that of the British vice-consul in the matter of this proposed exchange of prisoners."

"What kind of assistance?"

"As referees, General. It will be five hours before a Malayan Airways freight plane leaves that could take Mr. and Mrs. Nilsen and Mrs. Lukey out of Indonesian territory. During that period Colonel Oda's troops will leave the jail compound. They will take Major Gani with them. So that there will be no misunderstandings or unfortunate incidents, Mr. Wilson will accompany Major Gani and remain with him. I shall remain at the airport with Mr. and Mrs. Nilsen, Mrs. Lukey, and three of Colonel Oda's officers until the plane leaves. I shall then telephone Mr. Wilson, and the exchange will be completed. Major Gani will report to you. Colonel Oda's officers will report back to him."

"You expect me to trust you?"

"Colonel Oda is prepared to trust us, General. However, should either side attempt to take advantage of the situation, Mr. Wilson and I will personally offer ourselves as hostages until the agreement is carried out."

The General thought for a moment. The possibilities of trickery inherent in such a situation were many. Mr. Hallett had obviously envisaged some of them. For instance, he had stipulated a Malayan Airways plane. That precluded the use of an Indonesian plane to take the prisoners into the air and set them down at Labuanga again after Gani's release. But, what was to prevent Oda, on learning that his white accomplices were free, from killing Gani and laughing at Mr. Wilson's protests? The lives of three expendable junior officers? The General sighed. He knew the answer to that. No insurgent leader who hoped to survive would dare to abandon so treacherously even the most useless of his men.

"How can I believe that you will not favor the traitors in arranging this exchange?" he said at last.

"Do you really believe, General, that Mr. Wilson and I are dishonest?"

The General examined his inner thoughts and found, somewhat to his surprise, that his truthful answer to that question would be "no." He decided to ignore it.

"Very well," he said coldly.

"Then perhaps I may discuss the detailed arrangements for the exchange with a member of your staff?"

"I will discuss the arrangements personally."

When the conversation was finished, the General made a few notes and sent for his senior colonel.

Only one thing puzzled him. Gani had tortured Sutan. Sutan and Oda were friends. How was it that such men, whom he himself knew and had once respected, could forgo the satisfaction of tearing Gani to pieces with their own hands in order to permit three whites to escape without a scratch on their ugly skins? It seemed incredible. And yet, from another point of view, it showed how easily Asians became weak and corrupt through association with white men. It showed how right he had been himself to resist the temptation to come to terms with the Party of the Faithful. The thought was comforting.

vii

It was four o'clock in the morning when Hallett set out in his bullet-scarred car to drive Greg, Dorothy, and Mrs. Lukey from the jail to the airport. Following him, in Major Gani's personal jeep, were the three insurgent officers who would replace them as hostages when the plane took off three and a half hours later.

Hallett had managed to retrieve the two passports and an envelope with the prisoners' valuables in it from the wreckage of the head jailer's office; but, at his lukewarm suggestion that some way might later be found of picking up their other belongings from the Harmonie Hotel, Greg had shaken his head.

"We've caused enough trouble," he had said. "As far as Dorothy and I are concerned, they can keep everything, camera included. We just want out."

Mrs. Lukey had not been so accommodating. Hallett had explained briefly to Greg and Dorothy the substance of the negotiations for their release; but Mrs. Lukey had understood them at the time and, as a result, had acquired an exaggerated idea of the strength of their position.

"I do not see why someone should not be sent from the hotel to the airport," she had said. "I have a very nice overnight case. It was very expensive. I do not want to lose it. These people are all thieves."

Hallett had started to remind her that the Inner Zone was still closed, when Dorothy had firmly taken Mrs. Lukey aside. Neither man had heard what she had said, but thereafter Mrs. Lukey had been subdued, and there had been no more talk of her overnight case.

The General had evidently decided that the opportunity of impressing three insurgent officers with the strength of the Labuanga garrison had been too good to miss, and the airport building was bristling with troops when they arrived. As Hallett presented himself to the officer in charge, an armored car moved in menacingly, if pointlessly, to cover the approaches to the bus yard.

They were taken to a large storeroom in the customs section to await the arrival of the plane. Hallett asked for food and tea, and, rather to his surprise, some was presently brought. Access, under escort, to a nearby washroom was also granted, providing that not more than two persons went at a time. Dorothy and Mrs. Lukey were away taking advantage of this concession when Greg raised a question that was beginning to trouble him.

"Does everybody know about all this?" he asked. "I mean, will it get in the newspapers back home?"

Hallett's smile was not entirely free from malice. "If it gets in the newspapers here," he said, "you can bet your life it'll be picked up back home. So far, it's all been kept secret. I don't imagine the General'll want to give it any publicity now. The press do what they're told here, anyway. Where you'll have to be careful is in Singapore."

"How do you mean?"

"Well, you'll be put on this plane under armed guard. You can't stop the crew talking when they get back. You might be questioned when you arrive. If I were you, I'd have a nice dull story ready in advance for the pilot."

"Like what?"

"Technically, your visa's not in order. You were only cleared for Bali. You've been held here under guard. You could be pretty mad about it. Why didn't Garuda Indonesian Airlines check your visa carefully before flying you out from Singapore? Goddam Asian inefficiency. That sort of stuff. I'm not telling you to say that, mind. That's just advice."

"Thanks. I wish there were something I could do for you."

"Don't worry about that, Mr. Nilsen. There's no real harm been done."

"Major Gani's going back to work, isn't he? That's harm. You can't have enjoyed making that deal."

"No?" Hallett laughed. "I was never so relieved in my life. When the General agreed to swap you three for that sadistic bastard, I thought he must be kidding."

Greg stared. "Why?"

"You don't know General Iskaq. I'd have said he'd have ditched his own wife for the chance of keeping his hands on you three. He hates the whites. Always has."

"So you said. But you knew he couldn't ditch Gani."

"Couldn't? I was almost sure he would. You don't know how lucky you are."

"But in view of what he and Gani are doing, surely he *had* to have him back."

Hallett frowned. "What are you talking about?"

"Well, aren't they hijacking all these insurgent arms shipments to arm the Communists? Isn't Gani the Party go-between?"

Hallett said nothing for a moment, then looked across at the three officers. They were curled up on top of some packing cases, asleep. He looked again at Greg.

"Who told you that?"

"Voychinski. Didn't you know? He spoke as if it were common knowledge."

"Well, it isn't. Can you remember exactly what he said?"

Greg could. He would remember every moment he had spent in that jail for the rest of his life.

"Is it important?" he ended.

"If it's true—and that could easily be checked—it's important enough to relieve Iskaq of his job and start a clean-up. Assuming the area commander in Medan were to find out, of course."

"Will he?"

"That's not for me to say. All I'll have to do is send an information report through. You'll be quoted as the source, naturally."

"Do I have to be?"

"I'll have to send through a report about your arrest and the reasons for it." His smile was no longer unfriendly. "This could just about square the account," he added.

"That's something, I suppose."

"It is. By the way, was that check of Sutan's with your other things? I didn't look to see."

"I don't know." Greg got his passport out and opened it. The check was still there. He looked up at Hallett. "Did Major Sutan mention it to you at all?"

"No."

"That's funny. He must have known they'd found it, but he said nothing to me before we left. I know he was in pretty bad shape, but you'd think he'd have been anxious about that."

"Perhaps he took it for granted that an experienced arms peddler like you would have asked for another check if he needed it." There was a gleam of amusement in his eyes.

Greg was silent for a moment; then he folded the check carefully and put it in another pocket. "Did you see Voychinski's body?" he asked.

Hallett seemed to find nothing inconsequential in the question. He nodded. "Major Sutan evidently felt that a mutilated corpse ought to prove something about the Central Government. All it proves really, of course, is that in civil wars there are always men around like Major Gani."

"I think that Voychinski was that kind of man himself." Greg remembered something. "By the way, did you or Wilson tell Dorothy *how* he died?"

"I didn't, and I don't imagine Wilson would. Maybe Mrs. Lukey told her. Why?"

"Well, she didn't appear to worry too much about those guards who were killed. But Voychinski dying—that really seemed to upset her."

viii

THE freight plane from Koetaradja and Medan landed at seven-thirty and took off again for Singapore at eight. The captain was a New Zealander. Greg had no difficulty in boring him with complaints about Indonesian red tape and a garbled tale of mislaid overnight bags. He listened absently, lent Greg an electric shaver, and returned to his seat in the nose. They did not see him again.

Most of the interior space was taken up by pieces of machinery going to Singapore and beyond for repair, and mail bags. The plane was unpressurized, cold, and noisy. They sat on the mail bags, dozing fitfully, until the Malay radio operator came aft to warn them that in five minutes they would be landing in Singapore. The plane taxied in to the freight sheds and the operator led them across to the passenger arrival section so that they could go through immigration and customs. He left them there, politely declining the tip Greg offered him.

It was the first time the three of them had been alone together and able to talk freely since the evening of their arrest. Mrs. Lukey, hollow-eyed and plaintive when she had been awakened on the plane, now became flustered and embarrassed. As soon as they were through the customs, she hurried off to telephone her husband.

Greg sighed. "Oh, my God! Do we have to wait for her? All I want in the world at the moment is the Raffles Hotel, a bath, and a drink."

"Me, too, darling," said Dorothy, "but I think we have to wait a moment."

"I suppose so. Don't you think one of us ought to tell her that we're not holding her responsible for anything?"

"I don't think so." Dorothy's tone was surprisingly firm.

"Just as you say. Only she looked perfectly miserable to me."

"I don't think we're feeling exactly gay, are we, darling?"

He kissed her, but she drew away.

"Don't. We both smell of that place still."

"I know."

They stood there unhappily until Mrs. Lukey returned.

"I had to telephone," she explained breathlessly. "I knew he would be terribly worried when we did not get back yesterday. He sent a cable off, but there was no reply. He is coming over immediately with the car."

Dorothy nodded. "That's good, but I don't think we'll wait, Betty."

"Oh, but you must."

"No. We'll get a cab to the Raffles."

"That's right," said Greg. "Maybe we'll talk later, or tomorrow morning when we're rested up a bit."

"But he said he wanted to see you."

"Sure, but not right now, eh? We'll be in touch."

She seemed both relieved and distressed to see them go.

In the taxi they were silent until, as they were nearing the hotel, Dorothy said: "Did you get that check back?"

"Yes, it was still in the passport." He paused. "We don't even have a toothbrush," he went on. "I suppose we'd better stop at a drugstore and buy a few things."

By the time they had bathed, it was twelve-thirty. Greg rang down to the bar for double dry Martinis, but neither he nor Dorothy wanted any lunch. While they were drinking the Martinis, he telephoned Cook's.

"This is Mr. Nilsen. . . . Yes, we're back from Indonesia. . . . Yes . . . Well, we decided to cut it short. Now, look. I'd like you to check up for me on boats sailing during the next couple of days for Calcutta. . . . No, that doesn't matter. British, Norwegian, German, anything you like, as long as it's comfortable. We'd want a large stateroom with bath, air-conditioned if possible. . . . I see. Okay, but not too slow, and it's got to be comfortable, with good food. At the same time, I'd like to know about flights to Calcutta. . . . Via Bangkok. We might want to stop over there for a couple of days. . . . Yes, that's right. . . . No, not today. We'll come around and see you in the morning. . . . Thanks."

He hung up and his eyes met Dorothy's.

"Could we afford the Bangkok trip?" she asked.

"I don't know. Let's see what it would cost, anyway."

He smiled at her, but she was looking down at her drink now.

"Greg, what are you going to do about Captain Lukey?"

He got up with a sigh. "I don't know. While we were in the plane I tried to think about it. We went to get a check signed and—" he hesitated—"get off the beaten track. Well, we did both. Logically, all I have to do now is go to the customs office with Tan and Lukey, sign some papers, and collect sixty-two thousand five hundred dollars. But . . ." He broke off.

"But you don't know if you want to be logical."

"That's right. What do you think?"

She went over and kissed his cheek. "Maybe we should get some sleep," she said.

CHAPTER IX

GREG WOKE AT SIX-THIRTY in the evening. His body ached all over and he had a metallic taste in his mouth. Dorothy was still asleep. He went into the sitting room, shut the bedroom door softly behind him, and rang for some ice. When it came, he got out the remains of the bottle of whisky purchased for his first meeting with Captain Lukey, and made himself a drink. As he drank it, he realized that he would be feeling very hungry, but for one thing: he could still smell the jail.

He thought carefully about that. Before they had gone to bed, both he and Dorothy had thoroughly washed every inch of themselves, their hair included; and they had given every stitch of clothing they had been wearing to the room boy with orders to burn or otherwise dispose of it. There could be only one reason for the phenomenon. "Thank *you*, Dr. Freud," he muttered sourly.

He reached for the telephone and asked the operator to see if Mr. Lane Harvey of the American Syndicated Wire Service could be found at his office or at the American Club.

Harvey was at the club, and sounded as if he had been there for some time.

"And how was fabulous Bali?" he asked.

"Great."

"And those nubile young ladies with the fecund breasts and the side-long looks? How were they? Or maybe I'd better ask Mrs. N. about them."

"Maybe you had. Look, I want to have a word with Colonel Soames. Do you mind telling me how I can get in touch with him?"

There was a momentary pause before Harvey answered. "The Policeman? Sure. Just call up police admin. They'll put you through to his office."

"I meant this evening."

"Oh. Well, I don't have my book with me right now, but I'll be going back to my office sometime. Supposing I call you later."

"Thanks. I'm at the Raffles."

"I'll call you."

His tone was careless and he hung up almost before the last word was out. Greg suspected that the promise had already been forgotten. He put some more ice in his drink and then looked up the word "Police" in the telephone directory. There was a long list of entries, none of which was "Police admin." He was edging his way through the listings under "Government" when the telephone rang.

"This is Soames," said a well-remembered voice.

"Colonel Soames, I was just trying to contact you."

"So I gathered. That's why I'm phoning. What can I do for you?"

"I need advice. I'd like to see you as soon as I can."

"Won't the morning do?"

"I was hoping . . ." Greg broke off. "Look, I've been in Labuanga. I got back today. It's sort of urgent."

There was a pause. "Very well, Mr. Nilsen. I'll meet you in the Raffles lounge in fifteen minutes. Will that be all right?"

"Fine. Thanks."

He went back into the bedroom. Dorothy was fast asleep. Very quietly he collected the clothes he needed and returned to the sitting room. When he was dressed, he left a note for Dorothy telling her where he was, and went down to the lounge.

ii

COLONEL SOAMES arrived with the sandwiches Greg had ordered. He was wearing a white dinner jacket.

"Hope this won't take long," he said briskly. "I'm due at a dinner party at eight-thirty."

"It's a longish story," said Greg, "but I'll cut it as short as I can. What are you drinking?"

"Is that coffee you've got there?"

"Yes."

"I'll have some of that. Now, what's the trouble?"

The Colonel was a good listener. He did not stir as Greg told him the history of his dealings with the Tan brothers, Captain Lukey, and the Party of the Faithful. Twice only, he interjected brief questions to obtain a clarification of detail. Once he signaled to the waiter to bring some more coffee. When Greg had finished, he sat back.

"That all?"

"Yes."

"What did you say that fellow's name was? Gani?"

"Yes, Major Gani."

"Very interesting. Might come in handy to our people sometime. Much obliged to you." He paused. "You said you wanted advice, though."

"Help would be a better word."

"For a rank amateur, you don't seem to have done so badly without help. You've been lucky, of course, but didn't someone say luck was a form of genius?"

Greg leaned forward. "Colonel, you said at lunch the other day that you'd considered having me deported."

The Colonel chuckled amiably. "If I'd known what I know now, I probably would have. Can't have amateurs fooling about in the arms racket. Disgraceful state of affairs!"

"Supposing you had deported me," Greg went on, "and supposing I'd just been on the point of concluding a piece of business that netted me sixty-two thousand five hundred Straits dollars. Would I have been allowed to complete it?"

The Colonel's smile faded and he eyed Greg curiously. "That would have depended. I was only gingering you up a bit. You wouldn't have been deported unless the Indonesians had made a formal and specific complaint against you. In that case, naturally, we'd have tried to stop you completing."

"Once I was out, could I have come back?"

"Of course not."

Greg nodded. "That's what I wanted to know. Right, Colonel. As a favor to me, I'd like you to have a deportation order made out against me."

"I beg your pardon."

"Naturally, I'd like it done without any fuss or publicity. I figure there wouldn't be any, unless I tried to contest the order, and, obviously, I wouldn't do that. I'm sure that if I were to have a word with the American consul first there'd be no trouble there."

The Colonel was staring at him angrily. "If this is your idea of humor, Nilsen, I think it's in very poor taste."

"I'm quite serious."

"Then you must be up to some game I don't know about. I think you'd better tell me what that is."

"Certainly. I want to call this whole deal off."

The Colonel scowled. "I see. Had a better offer for the stuff. My dear chap, if you think you're going to use me to get you off the hook, you're very much mistaken."

"I haven't another offer. I don't want another offer. I just want out from the whole filthy business."

"But not neglecting to take your commission, I imagine."

"No deal, no commission, nothing."

The Colonel shook his head wearily. "All right, what are you up to? Come on, let's hear it."

"I've told you. I want out." Greg paused, then shrugged. "You may as well know the whole idiotic truth. When I went into this thing, it was a sort of a joke. I was told those arms had been hijacked from the Communists. I thought it would be highly amusing to help put them into the hands of anti-Communists. Don't ask me how I managed to sucker myself into thinking that I was doing something pretty smart. That's another cute little story. The thing is, I fell for all that double talk of Tan's in Manila like a kid. No, that's unfair. My own sons would have had more sense." He paused again. "Well, then I got what I deserved. I had a chance of seeing a bit of both sides of this fascinating little war. Oh, yes, I found a Communist bastard, all right, and he was right where you might have expected him to be. But I found a Fascist bastard there as well."

The Colonel laughed shortly. "And wasn't *he* where you might have expected *him* to be?"

"I guess he was." Greg's lips thinned. "But you have to remember this, Colonel. I'd been dealing in make-believe. Now, for a real hundred-percent Rover Boy like me, just a lick of reality can be terribly uncomfortable and disturbing. To say nothing of the fact that Rover Boy managed to put his wife as well as himself into a very dangerous situation, where they not only became a source of acute embarrassment to their country's representative, but had to be rescued by him as well. So you see, Colonel, the joke's now over. My wife's a very tolerant woman. She hasn't said 'I told you so,' and she won't. But I have a bad conscience, and she knows it. I think she'd like me to do something about that. So, that's what I'm trying to do."

The Colonel sneered. "I see. You'd like to wash your hands of the whole thing and make believe none of it ever happened."

"Yes, that's about the size of it, I guess. More make-believe, as you say. Well, maybe that won't work, but there are some things I can do."

"Like having yourself deported? What would that accomplish?"

"One thing. It would put Tan back right where he started. Originally, he couldn't move those arms from Manila because of some legal snag, or so he said. I'm his sole authorized agent. If I'm expelled from here, I can't sign them out of bond or transfer ownership. That means he can't move the arms from Singapore because of a legal snag. So he's back where he was before I came along, and those arms are back behind the eight ball. He can't take legal action against me because the circumstances are beyond my control. He can have his check for a thousand dollars back. Finish."

The Colonel looked perplexed. "I see your point, but, my dear fellow, you're not seriously asking me to have you deported, are you?"

"I am."

"I'm not Himmler, you know. I'd have to justify such a request, and I don't see how I could."

"Why not? You said yourself that a complaint from the Indonesian Government could do the trick. I bet there's one on the way right now."

"If what you say about General Iskaq is true, I should think that extremely unlikely. He'd have to send his complaint through Medan, and that'd mean he'd have to answer a lot of awkward questions first." He shook his head. "No, I'm afraid it won't do. If that's your idea of washing your hands, you can forget about it."

"Well, thanks for listening, anyway."

The Colonel glanced at his watch. "I'll have to be off." He hesitated. "Of course, it's none of my business really, but I can't help thinking that you're being a bit hard on yourself, Nilsen."

"Yes?"

"And on one or two other people as well."

"Including Tan?" Greg asked sarcastically.

"I wasn't thinking of him. You see," the Colonel went on thoughtfully, "I'm something of a prig myself, too, on occasions, so I can understand how you feel. But one thing I have noticed. When all the hand-washing, clean-slate stuff begins, it usually has the effect of landing someone else in the soup. Funny thing, moral indignation."

Greg said nothing.

"This idea of yours, for instance." The Colonel broke off to murmur something in Malay to a passing waiter. "It wasn't such a bad idea really, selling Communist supplies to anti-Communist forces, hoisting them with their own petards or whatever the phrase is. Not bad at all."

"Maybe. If they really had been Communist supplies."

"They were that, all right."

"You don't mean to say you believe that story of Tan's about collateral for a debt?"

"No, but I had one of my chaps take a closer look at the stuff. The types of weapons, the manufacturers, the ammunition batch numbers, the quantities—it all corresponds to a very familiar pattern."

"What pattern?"

"Terrorist arms cache. That's exactly the kind of parcel the Chinese were shoving across the Thai border into Malaya four or five years ago. Couldn't mistake it."

"Where did Tan get it, then?"

"How should I know? Probably stole it. Does it matter?"

"No, except that, if he did, that makes me a receiver of stolen goods as well."

The Colonel sighed. "As well as what, my dear fellow? Of what other crimes against God or man are you accusing yourself?"

"Arrogance, ignorance, stupidity, and trying to make a fast buck out of men trying to kill one another. Will that do for the moment?"

The waiter put down two stengahs in front of them.

"As I doubt if I shall reach my hostess in time to be offered a drink before dinner, this is just a precaution," the Colonel explained. "After all the breast-beating you've been doing, you could probably use one, too."

Greg was silent.

The Colonel drank half the contents of his glass, and then dabbed his lips with a black silk handkerchief. "Nowadays," he said, "we don't hear the phrase 'merchants of death' very much. It's all very sad. The idea that the act of selling arms somehow tricked people into making wars they didn't want never really stood up to very close inspection, did it? But it was good to have a fine, top-hatted bogeyman to put all the blame on. The trouble is we've learned a thing or two since nineteen thirty-nine. Now we can't even blame the politicians—not with much conviction, anyway. The real bogeyman crawled out of the mud with our ancestors millions of years ago. Well, we all have a piece of him, and when we start to put the pieces together, it's like one of those nuclear-fission things —when the mass reaches a critical point, a chain reaction starts, and poof!"

Greg raised his eyebrows. "I always thought there was a standard justification for any sort of illicit peddling, whether it was in drugs, smut, or arms. 'If I don't, somebody else will.' Isn't yours a bit new?"

"I wasn't talking about illicit peddling," the Colonel replied huffily, "and I wasn't attempting to justify anything. I was merely trying to correct your rather muddled view of your obligations at this moment. Selling arms or selling the wherewithal to make them—what's the difference?

What does your government do with the die-castings you make for them —feed the hungry or put them into ballistic missiles?"

"The United States Government isn't selling arms for profit."

"I must remember that when the nuclear war starts. It'll be a great comfort."

Greg's temper was beginning to fray at the edges. "As I said before, Colonel, you change hats rather easily. Which one are you wearing at the moment?"

"Major Sutan's, probably."

Greg looked at him, startled.

The Colonel picked up his drink and examined it dubiously. "Of course," he said slowly, "you've had a trying time, a surprise or two, and not very much sleep. Apt to warp a man's judgment, those things. Same as a hangover. Alcoholic remorse and all that." He looked up with a small smile.

"What are you getting at, Colonel?"

"Well, now. Let's suppose I'm Sutan. Rightly or wrongly, I'm buying arms with which to fight for something—freedom, power, social justice, or one of the other delusions. You offer to sell me arms and I accept your offer. We're both men of good faith, eh? I give you a check. Then something unforeseen happens. As a result, I and my friends have a choice. We can wash our hands of you and your wife and leave you both to rot, or we can, at some cost to ourselves, see that you go free. It's not an easy choice, but we decide in your favor and you go free. To show your appreciation, you promptly call off the deal we've made, and try and arrange things so that nobody else can call it on again. How does that sound to you?"

Greg sighed. "As it was intended to sound, of course. However, the facts are a bit different."

"I'm sure they are. But you began by asking for advice. Then you asked me to help you. I couldn't do that, so perhaps you'll accept some advice after all. It's not your conscience that's troubling you, Mr. Nilsen, but a slight injury to your self-esteem. Officially, I'm not particularly interested now either in you or in what happens to those arms. Unofficially, though, I would suggest that you do something about recovering your sense of humor."

"So that I can laughingly go ahead with the deal as planned?"

"Oh, I've no doubt you'll find a way of penalizing yourself in the process, like sending that thousand-dollar check back to Tan." He got to his feet. "I really must be going now. I think I'll let you pay for my drink."

"Good-by, Colonel."

The Colonel hesitated, then sat down again. "I don't like to leave you in this despondent mood," he said. "If it's laughter you need, it's just possible that I may be able to help you."

"I'll stop you if I've heard it."

The Colonel ignored the remark. "What was your arrangement with Tan in Manila about payment?" he asked. "What were you to do with the money from Lukey?"

"Pay it into the Merchants' Security Bank here for the credit of his account."

"Was anything particular said about what you were to do if you received the money in cash?"

"No. Why? I seem to be missing the point of this story, Colonel. You know, I doubt very much if we laugh at the same things."

"How about poetic justice? That can sometimes be quite entertaining, can't it?"

"Oh, sure."

"Well, your Mr. Tan in Manila wasn't what you might call frank with you, was he? Don't you think you're entitled to a little joke at his expense?"

"What sort of joke?"

"You could give Tan Yam Heng here the money to bank for his brother."

"And give him a chance to take his double commission after all? Is that the idea?"

The Colonel pursed his lips. "Something like that. Of course, you'd make the fellow give you a receipt in duplicate for the full amount. Keep one copy for yourself, send the other to Manila."

Greg smiled doubtfully. "Well, it's not exactly the biggest belly laugh of the year." He shrugged. "In fact, it's sort of petty, isn't it?"

"I can assure you that Mr. Tan won't think so."

"You mean he'll lose face, or whatever they call it?"

"Undoubtedly."

"Well, I'll think about it. There's no chance of Tan Yam Heng being restrained by any feelings of family loyalty, I suppose?"

The Colonel grinned. "Don't worry. I know a little about that chap. · No chance at all."

When he had gone, Greg remained there for a few minutes, finishing his drink and thinking about what the Colonel had said.

He had, he reflected, been called, directly or by implication, a prig, a simpleton, a hypocrite, a pompous ass, a self-satisfied ingrate, and a man who could mistake his self-esteem for his conscience. Together with the adjectives he himself had applied, it all made quite a picture. Dorothy would have been highly indignant. The odd thing was that he did not feel at all indignant himself. For the first time in several days, in fact, he felt like laughing—not at anything in particular, certainly not at the Colonel's feeble vision of poetic justice, but because he had suddenly seen his own face.

He signed a chit for the sandwiches and drinks, and went back up to the suite. Dorothy had not stirred. He undressed, brushed his teeth, and got back into bed beside her.

iii

THE following morning he met Captain Lukey and Tan Yam Heng at the Orchard Road branch of the Hong Kong and Shanghai Bank.

The Captain was boisterously cheerful, and countersigned the check with a flourish. The "spot of bother in Labuanga," as he had called it over the telephone, had now, it seemed, been forgotten.

Greg watched Tan as the money was being paid out. His face did not move, but his eyes followed every bundle of notes as it was pushed across the counter, and the fingers of his right hand twitched in sympathy with the Captain's as he checked the bundles. It was more than likely, Greg decided, that the Colonel had been right. Once Tan Yam Heng had his hands on the money, brotherly love would not deter him from taking a triple or even quadruple commission if he had a mind to.

From the bank they went to the Customs House. There Greg signed the necessary papers transferring the ownership of the arms and ammunition to Captain Lukey, and received the bulky canvas bag containing the money.

Captain Lukey beamed. "Signed, sealed, and delivered," he said fatuously. "What about a drink to celebrate?"

They went to the lounge bar of a nearby hotel. When the drinks had been ordered, Captain Lukey left them to go to the toilet. Greg looked at Tan.

"I think this is where you give me another check for a thousand and fifty dollars," he said.

"Ah, no." Tan pointed to the bag on the table in front of Greg. "That must be paid into the Merchants' Security Bank first."

"Where is the bank?"

"In Coleman Road. We will take a taxi there."

Greg frowned. "I've got a lot to do today. Look, you're acting for your brother. Why don't I give you the money, and you pay it in? Then we can square everything away right now."

He had been prepared for some visible indication that the suggestion met with Tan's approval, but had not expected the reaction to be so manifest. It was remarkable. Not a muscle of the man's face moved; but suddenly it was glistening with sweat.

His lips moved slowly. "If that is what you wish, Mr. Nilsen, yes, I will go to the bank."

"Fine. Just a moment." Greg got up and, going over to one of the writing tables, wrote out on hotel stationery two copies of a receipt for sixty-two thousand five hundred Straits dollars cash received from Gregory H.

Nilsen as payment in full for the goods listed on bill of lading number so-and-so, and the date. Then he addressed an envelope to Tan Tack Chee in Manila, marked it "airmail," and went back to the table.

Captain Lukey had stopped to talk to someone on his way back from the toilet, and they were able to complete the transaction before he returned. Tan filled in the bill-of-lading number on the receipts, signed both copies, and handed Greg a check for a thousand and fifty dollars. Greg put the check and one copy of the receipt into his pocket. Across the other copy he wrote "Compliments of Gregory H. Nilsen," then put it in the envelope and sealed it.

Tan was sitting tensely, watching. Greg pushed the canvas bag over to him and smiled. "I guess you don't want to count that again."

"No." Tan took the bag and rested it on his knees.

Greg held up the envelope. "You don't happen to have an airmail stamp for Manila, do you?"

"I will get one from the barman."

"Don't trouble. I'll get one later."

"No trouble, Mr. Nilsen."

Tan put the bag under his arm and went to the bar. Captain Lukey came back to the table and began talking about the "dear old chum" he had just run into. "White man through and through, which is more than you can say for some of the murkey types who work for Afro-Asian nowadays."

Tan came back with a stamp and put it on the table at Greg's elbow. He did not sit down.

"If you will be good enough to excuse me now," he said with strained civility, "I think I will go to the bank."

"Won't you have a drink first?"

"No, I will go to the bank." He was still sweating, and obviously yearning to be gone.

"Okay. I'll be seeing you."

"Good-by, Mr. Nilsen, Captain."

He hurried away.

Captain Lukey chuckled. "You must have a trusting nature, old boy. If it was mine, I wouldn't let him hold that money even while I tied a shoelace."

Greg smiled. He was putting the stamp on the envelope. "I don't think I need worry," he said.

As they were leaving, Greg went over to the hotel mailbox. He was about to drop the envelope in it when Captain Lukey stopped him.

"By the way, old boy. Couldn't help noticing, but if you want that to go airmail to Manila you'll have to put some more stamps on. That's the surface rate. It may take a week or more to get there."

Greg shrugged and put the envelope into the box. "It's not particularly urgent," he said.

iv

ON HIS way back to the hotel, Greg called in at the Chase National, who were his own bankers' agents, paid in Mr. Tan's two American-dollar checks, and asked for special clearance on them.

At the hotel he wrote out a check for two thousand one hundred dollars payable to the Wilmington Chapter of the American Red Cross. Dorothy, who knew a woman on the Volunteer Service Co-ordination Committee, wrote a covering letter. They mailed it on their way to see the man at Thomas Cook's.

CHAPTER X

TAN TACK CHEE AND TAN SIOW MONG were bland men with level heads and strong nerves; but the arrival of Yam Heng's receipt in Manila threw them into a state of flustered consternation that Greg would have found gratifying, if puzzling.

Tack Chee took one long, appalled look at the receipt and then put through an overseas call to the Raffles Hotel in Singapore. He was told that Mr. and Mrs. Nilsen had sailed two days previously on the S.S. *Camboge* for Colombo and Bombay. Next he tried to call Yam Heng at the union office where he worked. A clerk there told him that Yam Heng had not been to his office for several days. He was presumed to be indisposed. Yam Heng had no telephone at his home, and Tack Chee knew that it would be useless to cable. Despairingly, he put through a call to the Merchants' Security Bank. The manager was helpful and efficient. No payment of any kind had been made into his account for the past month. Tack Chee hung up, turned his air-conditioner on to FULL, and told his secretary to place a person-to-person call to his brother in Kuala Pangkalan.

Siow Mong had not been unduly concerned at the delay in collecting the twenty-five thousand dollars due to him in respect of Girija's check. He had received a satisfactory progress report from Singapore, saying that the sale was about to be completed. As there was still a clear week to go before the Indian could present the check for payment, he did not expect to have to draw upon his own resources in order to honor it. Only one thing was troubling him a little. So far, the clerk had shown himself to be shrewd, careful, and discreet. But would he go on being shrewd, careful, and discreet with twenty-five thousand dollars in the bank? Money could affect people strangely, and for a young man in his position this would be a fortune. What did he propose to do with it? Something foolish, like buying an expensive sports car and driving about ostentatiously advertising his sudden wealth? And, if so, how was he proposing to explain where he had got it? Tan Siow Mong had decided to have a talk with him before the thirty days were up, to caution him if that seemed necessary, and to make sure that any explanations the young man contemplated using did not compromise either the Anglo-Malay Transport Company or its proprietor.

The telephone call from Manila came through late on Thursday afternoon.

As soon as he heard his brother's voice, Siow Mong knew that something was wrong; but Tack Chee was an ingenious breaker of bad news, and it was two minutes before Siow Mong fully realized what had happened. Then he lost his temper, and for a further minute there was a loud and demeaning exchange of generalities in which words relating to the excretory organs and functions of the body were freely used. Finally, however, Siow Mong began to recover his self-possession and to think again.

"It is the American who is responsible," he declared. "If the money is gone, he must pay."

"Impossible," Tack Chee replied. "Yam Heng signed the receipt as my authorized agent. We can only hope that he has not yet lost it all. You must go to Singapore immediately."

"Both of us must go."

"My expenses in this business have already been heavy enough. Twenty-one hundred dollars American plus entertainment, and now overseas telephone calls."

"Those are trifles, brother." Siow Mong was becoming angry again. "When I stand to lose twenty-five thousand dollars Malay, plus five hundred dollars Hong Kong, plus shipping and other handling charges, I am surprised that you commit the indelicacy of speaking about them."

"There is nothing indelicate about two thousand dollars American. The whole transaction was your idea."

"You had no criticisms of it. If you had properly instructed this Nilsen . . ." He broke off. "There is no sense in our bickering. It is a waste of time. Obviously, we shall get nothing unless Yam Heng can be persuaded to co-operate. You know what that means. This time it may be necessary to bring in the police and threaten charges of embezzlement. You are the legal principal in this, and the receipt will be required as evidence. You must be there."

"The police? He would know we were bluffing."

"I am not bluffing," Siow Mong said. "This time he has gone too far. Charges of misappropriation of funds brought against him by that union would have been damaging to our names. We should have lost face. Charges brought against him by us would give rise to no such indignity, except for Yam Heng."

"They might cause pain to our mother."

"She has endured worse," Siow Mong said unfeelingly. "If I leave immediately for Kota Bharu, I can get a plane to Singapore tonight. I will meet you at the Cathay Hotel tomorrow morning."

Yam Heng had had a bitterly frustrating week on the pickle market, and was querulous when the brothers eventually confronted him. He had, he explained indignantly, merely borrowed the money for a few days. Was not part of it due to him anyway, for all his work on their behalf? Why was he hounded in this way? Yes, he had incurred certain losses; but these would at any moment be more than offset by substantial gains. In three days' time he would be able to give them a hundred thousand dollars if they needed money so badly.

Mention of the police, however, changed the character of the debate. There was abuse, and much harsh, contemptuous laughter and snapping of fingers. It was only when he realized that his brothers were not simply ready to press charges against him, but beginning to feel vindictive enough to relish the prospect of doing so, that Yam Heng agreed sulkily to an accounting.

Of the sixty-two thousand five hundred dollars there remained seventeen thousand, three hundred; and threats of violence as well as police prosecution were necessary to persuade Yam Heng to part with that. His brothers left him, glutinous with self-pity, and returned to the Cathay Hotel.

Minor expenses disregarded, they were fourteen thousand dollars (Straits) out of pocket on the deal. They were also tired. They had little difficulty in agreeing how they should divide the salvaged remains. Tack Chee took the equivalent of eight hundred American dollars to set off against his outlay of twenty-one hundred. Siow Mong, as the heavier loser, took the balance of fifteen thousand dollars (Straits).

He arrived back in Kuala Pangkalan late on Friday night. When he went to his office the following morning, he found a message. Mr. Krishnan had telephoned and would like to see Mr. Tan. In the hope that Mr. Tan would find it convenient, he would call in on Saturday afternoon at four.

ii

MR. TAN, sitting gloomily at his desk, watched the Indian cross the yard from number-one godown and thought that he detected a certain impudent jauntiness in the fellow's walk.

In spite of its obvious absurdity, he could not quite rid himself of the fear that the Indian had somehow learned of the Singapore disaster and had come there merely to gloat over and humiliate him. If that should indeed be the case, he told himself darkly, the fellow would regret his temerity.

As matters now stood, he, Siow Mong, was prepared to be generous. The Indian would be solemnly warned of the dangers of so much sudden wealth, and of the impossibility of his being able to account satisfactorily to the police for its acquisition. It would then be relatively simple to persuade him to return the check. In exchange, he would be given a deed of annuity guaranteeing him a yearly income of two thousand five hundred dollars for ten years. Mr. Tan was reasonably sure that he could buy such an annuity for around fifteen thousand dollars.

Should the fellow be in any way disagreeable, however, Mr. Tan had an alternative scheme ready. He would stop payment of the check and invite the young blackguard to sue him in open court. There, if his challenge were accepted, he would tell the judge that the Indian had undertaken to buy for him, through a relative, a certain valuable tract of tin-bearing land, and that the postdated check had been written, at the Indian's request, to impress the relative and to use as a deposit if the purchase went through. When he had discovered that the Indian's landowning relative was nonexistent, he had stopped the check. Perfectly simple. If the Indian chose to tell the truth, he would either be disbelieved and lose his case, or believed and prosecuted for selling arms. Mr. Tan did not think that he would be fool enough to risk either of those alternatives.

When he was announced, Mr. Tan assumed the mask of courtesy and ordered tea.

Girija flashed a smile as they shook hands. "I am sure that if Mr. Wright had been aware that I was to have the pleasure of seeing you, Mr. Tan, he would have wished me to convey his personal regards." He had a box file under his arm. He placed it on the floor beside him as he sat down.

"Mr. and Mrs. Wright are well and happy, I hope."

"Oh, yes, thank you. I trust that your own fine family are equally blessed."

The tea came and was consumed to further light conversation. Then Girija picked up the box file and rested it on his knees. Mr. Tan accepted this as an intimation that business might begin.

"I was hoping to have the pleasure of seeing you again in the near future, Mr. Krishnan," he said. "In fact, when I returned from Singapore yesterday, it was already in my mind to telephone you."

"Perhaps there was the same thought in both our minds, Mr. Tan."

Mr. Tan stiffened involuntarily.

"I refer," Girija continued, "to the thought, sad for me, that, under present arrangements, our very satisfactory association will shortly end."

Mr. Tan relaxed. He had noted the words "under present arrangements" and decided to wait for the Indian to explain them.

"I am assuming," Girija added politely, "that the association also proved satisfactory from your point of view."

"Oh, yes. Very satisfactory," Mr. Tan replied manfully.

"And Mr. Lee's?"

"Sufficiently so, I believe."

"I am glad of that," said Girija, "because it gives me the courage to submit a further problem to you, in the hope of receiving further good advice."

Mr. Tan was silent.

Girija flashed another smile. "I am so sorry to have to tell you that the friend I spoke of to you before has since died."

Mr. Tan permitted himself a faint twitch of the lips. "You have my sympathy."

"Thank you. However, as you know, my friend had money. That now passes to me. Unfortunately, he left no will. My difficulty at the moment is to find a substitute for that will."

Mr. Tan hid his satisfaction perfectly. "I can appreciate the difficulty," he said. "In fact, if you will allow me to say so, I had anticipated it. I even had a possible solution to suggest to you if you were interested."

"I am indeed most interested."

Mr. Tan proceeded, somewhat elliptically, to explain his annuity proposal. As he began to enlarge upon its virtues, however, he was disconcerted to see, for the first time, a smile of pure amusement spread over the Indian's face. He felt himself getting angry, and stopped in the middle of a sentence.

The smile vanished instantly and Girija leaned forward. "Mr. Tan, I beg your pardon. Perhaps I should have explained first. For the project that I have in mind, twenty-five thousand dollars will be the minimum capital required if we are to operate at a profit."

Mr. Tan never discovered whether the Indian had used the words "we" and "profit" at that moment intentionally; just as he was never quite clear how it had come about that, twenty minutes later, the contents of the box file had been scattered over his desk and he had been listening bemused to a dissertation on the economics of public transport operation in rural areas. It had been quite difficult to break in and regain the initiative; and even then he did not keep it long.

"Why don't you begin with one bus? Why must you have two?"

"People must learn quickly that the buses are reliable or they will keep to their bicycles. The service must become indispensable, Mr. Tan. With only one bus it cannot be guaranteed."

"But if you were to buy one new one, you would have the reliability you want."

"We cannot afford an experienced mechanic full time, to begin with. Therefore we cannot carry out maintenance at night, as the big operators do. What I propose is that we buy two of these reconditioned buses. I know this firm at Acton in London. They have long experience of the work. The chassis are old, but very good. The engines are new. The bodies have been adapted for Far East work. Look, here is a picture."

Mr. Tan waved the picture aside. "Yes, yes. It is all very interesting. But why have you brought this project to me?"

Girija returned to his seat on the other side of the desk before he replied, slowly and methodically: "Firstly, Mr. Tan, because a bus service such as I have described would be a logical extension of the Anglo-Malay Transport Company's business. Secondly, because of the trade journals I subscribe to, Mr. Wright knows of my interest in such matters. He knows of my respect for you. He would not think it too strange that a new bus company which you owned should employ me as manager. Thirdly, because if a new company called Kuala Pangkalan Transport Limited were formed, with a nominal capital of fifty thousand dollars, and if, in consideration of my signing a service agreement as managing director of that company, I were allotted fifty per cent of the ordinary shares free, I could return your check to you without presenting it for payment. Fourthly, because a company with your reputation behind it would have no difficulty in securing a franchise to operate the service. Fifthly, because I think you know that I can be trusted and would serve our interests well."

Mr. Tan thought carefully. What the Indian had said about the need for a bus service was undoubtedly true. As a business venture, it was probably sound. The capital of a new company would not have to be fully paid up. Fifteen thousand would buy the two reconditioned buses. On the other hand, if the project were a success, a fifty-per-cent interest in it was eventually going to be worth a lot more than twenty-five thousand dollars. He would certainly be wise to keep the ordinary shares in his own hands. A counter-offer of non-voting preference shares might be the answer. Ingeniously worked out, it could, he was sure, be made to seem advantageous. Meanwhile, he would employ delaying tactics, wear the Indian down by keeping him waiting, and then, if necessary, dictate the terms. He fingered the papers from the box file as if they were of small importance, and then pushed them aside.

"Very well," he said. "I will look through these estimates and proposals, and perhaps make some other inquiries. Later, possibly, we could meet again and continue the discussion."

Girija nodded. "Of course, Mr. Tan. On the terms I have mentioned, the whole matter can be very easily settled—" he paused and flashed his most annoying smile—"any day before your check falls due for payment next week."

iii

THE day after Greg and Dorothy arrived back in Wilmington, Kuala Pangkalan Transport Limited took delivery of its first vehicle at Singapore.

W. W. Belden, the maker's Far Eastern representative, was on hand to promote an atmosphere of goodwill. The new owners' managing director, G. Krishnan, was there to sign the necessary documents on behalf of his company.

A ten-ton crane picked the bus off the deck of the ship and placed it on the dockside.

Privately, Mr. Belden thought that the thing looked like a cattle truck; but, as most of its passengers would presumably be coolies, that probably did not matter. The important thing was that the Indian seemed to be pleased. With all this German competition in the low-price field, you had to be on your toes. When the second reconditioned unit had been delivered, he would start plugging their own new economy job. Meanwhile, he had a luncheon date at the Yacht Club. As soon as he could gracefully do so, he left.

The two drivers Girija had brought with him had both spent some years on army vehicles, and knew the type of chassis well. When everything had been checked, the new battery installed, the temporary registration plates fitted, and the tank filled, the engine was started. It had a leisurely, powerful sound that was very satisfying.

One driver got up into the cab, the other sat behind him on one of the passenger benches.

The driver at the wheel grinned down at Girija. "Can we drive the tuan to his hotel?"

Girija smiled and shook his head. "I'll be waiting for you in Kuala Pangkalan," he said.

He did not ride in buses; he operated them.

But he stood there, listening and watching, as the big gears grated, the big tires began to turn, and the bus rumbled away toward the dock gates and the journey north. He wished that his father, the subahdar, could have been there.

STATE OF SIEGE

STATE OF SIEGE

CHAPTER I

THE WEEKLY DAKOTA from Selampang had never been known to arrive at the valley airstrip before noon, or to leave on the return journey before one. After the farewell party they had given for me the previous night, I should have slept until eleven at least. But no; I was wide awake, packed and ready to go at dawn.

Not that I had had much packing to do. Most of my clothes—the *dobi*-battered slacks and bush shirts, the mosquito boots and the sweat-stained hats—I had given, with my camp bed, to Kusumo, who had been my servant for the past three years. The few things that were left—shoes, some white shirts, underwear and other personal oddments—had gone easily into one small metal suitcase. The only suit that I possessed, I wore. Like a fool, I had ordered it by mail from an outfitters in Singapore, and it hung on me like a shower curtain; but that morning I did not care how I looked; nor, indeed, how long I had to wait for the plane. What mattered most to me just then was the fact that I was leaving, and that in my breast pocket, along with my passport and a ticket for a B.O.A.C. Qantas flight from Djakarta to London, was a letter. It was from the Singapore branch of the Hongkong and Shanghai Bank, and advised me that, on the completion of my contract as resident consulting engineer to the North Sunda Power and Irrigation Project, there stood to my credit the sum of fifty-eight thousand eight hundred and ninety-six Straits dollars.

Soon after eleven, I borrowed one of the maintenance department jeeps and drove across to the Chief Engineer's office to say goodbye.

Now that I was leaving the place I could look at it with friendlier eyes. As the jeep bounced along the corduroy road past the new *attap* houses and the row of quonset huts in which the European employees lived, I was even aware of a feeling of pride in what had been done.

It was a Colombo Plan project, and there had been no shortage of American and British Commonwealth capital to finance it; but it takes more than money and good intentions to build dams in places like the Tangga Valley. When I had first arrived at the site with the advance party, there had been nothing but swamps, jungle, leeches and a colony of twenty-foot pythons. It had taken the contractors nearly a month to get their first two bulldozers up from the coast; and there had been a period during the first year, just after the monsoon broke, when we had had to abandon all the equipment and move up to the high ground in order to stay alive. Yet now there was a camp as big as a small town on the site, and an airstrip, and, there, wedged in the throat of the valley, the huge mass of stone and steel and concrete that was the keystone of the whole project. Because of that dam, it had been possible to turn something like two hundred square miles of scrub country down by the Tangga delta into rich padi fields. That year, for the first time, Sunda would have surplus rice to sell to the neighbouring islands of Indonesia; and when the power station below the dam was completed and the trans-mission lines began to reach into the tin- and tungsten-bearing areas to the north, there was no telling how prosperous the young state might not become. The Tangga Valley scheme was something to be proud of. My own motives for going to Sunda had been in no sense noble or disinter-ested. I had been paid as much for working for three years in the Tangga Valley as I would have been paid for working for ten years, and tax free, in England. But there had been satisfaction in the job for its own sake, too. I might be sick to death of Sunda and delighted to be leaving it, but I had come to like the Sundanese and was glad that I had been of service to them.

There were two other men already in the Chief Engineer's office when I put my head round the door, but Gedge beckoned me in.

"Sit down, Steve. Won't keep you a moment." He turned and went on with what he had been saying. "Now, Major Suparto, let's get this straight . . ."

I sat down and listened.

Gedge, the man in charge of the job for the contractors, was a South African civil engineer of great ability and experience who had spent most of his working life in the East. Moreover, he had done so from choice. He had worked for many years in China and, since the Japanese war, in India and Pakistan. There, he had made no secret of the fact that he preferred Asians to men of his own race, not merely as working as-sociates but also as friends. Among the Europeans, he had, not unnatu-rally, a reputation for eccentricity, and from time to time inaccurate rumours that he had Communist sympathies, or six Eurasian concu-bines, or that he had secretly become a Buddhist, would find their way across the bridge tables.

At the moment, however, his feelings towards his Asian collaborators were anything but friendly. He was having trouble with them. Indeed, since Major Suparto and his five brother officers had arrived from Selampang six months earlier, there had been practically nothing but trouble.

Sunda used to be part of the Netherlands East Indies. In 1942 it was occupied by the Japanese. When the Dutch returned three years later, they were confronted by a Sundanese "Army of Liberation" and a demand for independence which they were unable in the end to resist. In 1949 Sunda became a Republic.

The moment of greatest difficulty for all revolutionary leaders seems to be the moment of success; the moment when, from being rebels in conflict with authority, they themselves have suddenly become the authority, and the fighting men who procured the victory wait jealously, and inconveniently, for their reward. Armies of liberation are more easy to recruit than they are to disarm and disband.

At first, it looked as if the Provisional Government of the new Republic of Sunda were dealing shrewdly with this embarrassment. A policy of dispersal was applied to break down *esprit de corps*. No unit was disbanded as a unit. Men who came from the same district were collected together and then transported back to that district, before being disarmed and demobilised. Meanwhile, the Government rapidly built up the small regular army on which their authority was to rest in the future, and used it against any of their former supporters who showed fight. And, of course, some did; particularly the younger soldiers, who frequently banded themselves together and terrorised the people in the villages. But this sort of brigandage had little political importance. For some months after the proclamation of independence by President Nasjah all seemed to be going fairly well.

Unfortunately there was an aspect of the problem that the Government had neglected. In their anxiety to dispose of the rank and file, they had not troubled to do anything about disposing of the officers; and by the time they had realised the gravity of that mistake, it was too late to retrieve it.

There were several hundreds of these surplus officers; many more than could conceivably be absorbed by the regular army or by the new police force. Moreover, many were not officers in the ordinary sense of the term, men sensitive in matters of loyalty, but guerrilla leaders and ex-bandits who had both fought and collaborated with the Japanese occupation forces before doing those same things with the Dutch colonial troops, and who might reasonably be expected to start fighting the new Government in Selampang if the promised Utopia did not immediately materialise; or if they became dissatisfied with their share of the spoils. With such men, making revolutions may easily become a habit. Machiavelli thought that the wise usurper should, as soon as he comes to power, trump up charges against his more ambitious supporters and have them killed off before they can get into mischief. But not all politicians are so wary or so practical.

Even when the danger had become manifest, the Nasjah Government underestimated it. Struggling with vital day-to-day problems of administration and caught up in the political battle being waged over the new Constitution, they felt that they had no time to spare just then to deal with petty discontents. No doubt something would have to be done soon, but not now. With the peculiar innocence of politicians in office, they even assumed that as long as the surplus officers continued to draw their pay and allowances they would remain loyal to the leaders of the Republic. Had these men not fought to make it all possible? Were they not, after all, patriots?

The politicians soon had their answer. By the time they were ready to submit the Draft Constitution to the General Assembly, there was an insurgent force of nearly three thousand men operating in the central highlands. It was led by an ex-colonel named Sanusi, who promoted himself to general and rapidly gained administrative control of an area which straddled the only two roads connecting the capital with the northern provinces. Moreover, Sanusi was a devout Moslem and issued a series of manifestos calling upon all True Believers to join his Sundanese National Freedom Party and declare a Holy War on the infidels in Selampang who had betrayed the new state at the very moment of its birth.

The riots which ensued caused some casualties among the Eurasian population of the capital, but order was eventually restored without much bloodshed. Although most Sundanese are Moslems and a majority of the men wear the black cap of Islam, religion is not an important factor in their lives. It was General Sanusi's hold on the interior of the country which constituted the real problem. A punitive expedition sent against him had to withdraw ignominiously when one of its regimental commanders deserted, together with all his men and most of the expedition's ammunition supply. A subsequent series of air attacks on what was believed to be Sanusi's headquarters resulted, because of the hazardous flying conditions in the mountains, in the loss of two out of the ten obsolete planes that constituted the Government air force.

Having swallowed these humiliations, the Government were forced to examine the problem more realistically. They believed that Sanusi possessed neither tanks nor artillery, and that without them he would be obliged to remain in the hills. They knew, too, that any further loss of face on their own part would shake the public's confidence badly. Foreign sensibilities had also to be considered. Arrangements were almost completed for large United States dollar credits to be placed at their disposal. An appearance of calmness and stability must be preserved at all costs.

So they decided to bluff.

A communiqué issued by the Minister of Public Enlightenment announced that the "Sanusi gang" had been rounded up and liquidated, and a directive to newspaper editors ordered them to refrain from all further allusions to the "incident." Political murders committed by Sanusi's undercover agents in Selampang were to be blamed on "colonialist reactionaries." For inquisitive foreigners who wanted to know why it was still impossible to travel by road from the capital to the north, there was a bland statement that, in view of the extensive damage to bridges and mining of roads carried out by the retreating Dutch forces during the war, land communications would take at least a year to restore. Meanwhile, both sea and air transport were readily available.

At the same time, the Minister of Defence was instructed to take special and secret precautions against any further treachery in the armed forces. The reliability of every army officer was to be carefully tested by the use of *agents provocateurs*. A list of the dissident was to be compiled and steps taken to render them harmless. Sanusi was to be left to cool his heels in the mountains until a full-scale offensive could be mounted against him.

The feeling of security which the Government derived from the making of these decisions did not last long. The inquiries made by the Minister of Defence soon provided the frightening information that there was open talk of a *coup d'état* among the officers, that a group was already in secret communication with Sanusi, and that it was doubtful if more than a third of the officers of the Selampang garrison could be relied upon in an emergency.

The Council of Ministers' first reaction was to panic, and for an hour or so, apparently, there was wild talk of asking for a British warship from Singapore to stand by. Then, they pulled themselves together and gave General Ishak, the Minister of Defence, special powers to deal with the conspirators. Within twenty-four hours, sixteen senior officers had been shot and a further sixty were in prison awaiting court-martial.

The immediate crisis was over; but the Government had been badly frightened and they did not forget the experience. The news from Indonesia of the "Turko" Westerling incident intensified their anxiety. If a small force of Javanese counter-revolutionaries led by a few mad Dutchmen could capture a city like Bandung under the very noses of the lawful Indonesian Government, a large force of Sundanese insurgents under Sanusi could probably capture Selampang. Only the Selampang garrison, with its Japanese tanks and armoured cars and its six German eighty-eights, prevented their trying. If Sanusi could ever neutralise the garrison by allying himself with a Fifth Column conspiracy of the kind that had so nearly succeeded before, the game would be up. From now on there must be extreme vigilance. Reliable police spies must be found to report on the activities of all officers and former officers. The malcontents must be dealt with shrewdly. With a determined trouble-maker, a knife in the back would be the only safe solution. With a more self-interested man, however, a well-paid civil appointment might be the best answer. If, besides purchasing his loyalty, you could also expect to gain his services as an informer, an even more lucrative post could be awarded.

As self-interest seemed to be the dominating characteristic of most of the officers on the list of suspects, the new policy worked. From time to time there were plot scares and midnight executions, and for one period of a month martial law was declared; but although the roads to the north were now permanently in insurgent hands (Sanusi impudently collected taxes from the villages in his area), the Government did not lose any more ground. The losses they suffered from now on were in terms of morale rather than territory.

The black market, for example. There were simple economic reasons for its growth. The American credits had been spent not on capital goods, but dissipated on such things as cars, refrigerators, radios and air-conditioning equipment, the importation of which had produced huge personal commissions for members of the Government and their subordinates. Efforts to control the resulting inflation had been half-hearted. "Inducement taxes" had been imposed only to be evaded. In Selampang there was a black market in practically everything. In the tuberculosis clinics set up by the World Health Organisation, a *mantri* would even inject water into his patients so that he could steal the B.C.G. vaccine and sell it on the black market. All kinds of racketeering flourished. In Asia, admittedly, the giving and taking of bribes is a normal, accepted part of the daily business of getting things done; but in Sunda it assumed stultifying proportions.

Yet, the Government, although recognising the need for measures to deal with the problem, were quite unable to agree what those measures should be. It was not mere indecision, and it was not simply because there were some ministers with personal interests to consider. Their inability to deal effectively with this or any of the other social and economic problems which confronted them had a deeper cause. The Sanusi affair had in some subtle way served to demoralise them completely. Certainly, after the discovery of the conspiracy of 1950, the whole business of government in Sunda was conducted in a deadly atmosphere of guilt, greed and mutual suspicion that made any major decision seem horribly dangerous. The Nasjah Government, in fact, was suffering from a recurrent nightmare, and their fear of it incapacitated them. A watertight plan for eliminating Sanusi was the only thing that could have produced unanimity.

Up in the Tangga Valley we were to some extent isolated from all this madness; at least during the first year. We used to be told about what was going on by visitors, especially World Health Organisation and UNICEF people who came to work in our area, and be surprised that such intelligent men should expect us to believe the fantastic stories they told. Later on, when our own contact with the capital became closer, we knew better. But as long as Gedge had the labour force he needed and supplies continued to come up to us from our small port on the coast, we were able to feel that what went on in Selampang was no concern of ours.

And then the "government nominees" began to arrive.

It is one of the basic principles of Colombo Plan policy that, when aid is given for a project like the Tangga River dam, as many of the managerial posts as possible should be held by Asians. If qualified Asians are not immediately available and Europeans (i.e., whites) have to be employed under contract, then every effort has to be made to replace them with Asians when those contracts expire. Obviously, this is good sense, and, naturally, a man like Gedge was in eager sympathy with the principle. But the operative word is "qualified." Asia is desperately short of technicians of all grades, and at the managerial level the shortage is acute. In Sunda, the position was as bad as could be.

However, that fact did not deter the authorities in Selampang. When a government depends for its physical safety on a policy of "jobs for the boys," highly paid jobs become scarce. Furthermore, the salaries were paid by the Colombo Plan contractors, not by the Government. When the Europeans' service contracts began to expire, the Tangga Valley project must have looked like a gold mine in Selampang. Innocently, Gedge assumed that his formal, routine requests for Asians to replace the departing Europeans (requests that he was legally obliged to make) would be acknowledged and then forgotten in the usual way. He knew perfectly well that they had nobody suitable to send him. And he was right.

The first surplus officer to report for duty was a brutish-looking man in the uniform of a captain of infantry, who announced that he was taking up the post of surveyor to the project and then demanded a year's salary in advance. On being questioned as to his qualifications, he stated that he was a graduate of the new School of Economic Administration at Selampang, and produced a certificate to that effect. He also produced a pistol which he fingered suggestively during the remainder of the interview. I was there and it was a nerve-racking hour. In the end Gedge gave him a warm letter of recommendation for a post on the central purchasing commission (whose salaries were paid by the Government) and held the plane so that the captain could return at once to the capital and present the letter.

The captain soon proved to be a fairly typical example of what we had to expect. After three other would-be surveyors had been returned, together with a dozen or more candidates for other jobs, the Ministry of Public Works had changed its tactics. Instead of sending the applicant in person, it would send his name, together with an imposing account of his alleged qualifications, certified as correct by the Minister of Public

Works. This left Gedge with the choice of accepting the applicant unseen at the Ministry's valuation, or of questioning the valuation, and
thus, by inference, the Minister's honesty.

In the end, both sides had to compromise. The Ministry promised to
stop sending half-witted gangsters who had been found unemployable
even by Sundanese standards. Gedge agreed to take on six Sundanese
officers with experience of administrative duties as "liaison managers."
The real jobs were filled, as Gedge had always intended they should be,
partly by re-engagement, partly by promotion and partly by bringing in
new men, Asian and European, from outside.

I think that we all thought that he had made a good bargain. Friendly
relations with the Government had been preserved. His own authority
had been unimpaired. His employers' interests had been safeguarded.
The work could now go forward smoothly to its completion (as per specification and on schedule) and to the moment when he would stand bare-
headed in the breeze above the eastern spillway accepting the President's
congratulations. Permission had arrived from the contractors' head office
to debit the salaries of six useless Sundanese officers to the contingency
account. All that remained now was to see if the Government kept faith
with him.

In their own tortuous way they did keep faith. They did not send half-
witted gangsters. They sent intelligent ones.

They arrived all together, four majors and two captains, by special
plane from the capital, and began by complaining that the Chief Engineer was not there to welcome them officially. They then announced
that they would wait until he arrived. I was with Gedge when he got the
message.

He sighed. "I see. Prima donnas. They mustn't get away with that.
Would you mind going over, Steve?"

"Me?" Strictly speaking, it was no concern of mine. Labour relations
were the contractors' business. I was there to represent the firm of consulting engineers who had planned the project, and to see that the contractors did the work according to our specifications. But I had always got
on well with Gedge and could see that he was genuinely concerned.

"If someone senior doesn't go they'll lose face," he explained; "and you
know I can't afford to start off badly with these people."

"All right. But it'll cost you a couple of large Scotches."

"Done. And if you go right away I'll make it three."

I was not to know that he was, in a way, saving my life.

I found the new arrivals standing in the shade by the radio shack, glow-
ering into space. The jeep drivers who had been sent to collect them
looked terrified. I got out of my jeep and walked over.

They were all very smartly turned out, their uniform shirts spotless
and their pistol holsters gleaming. I was a bit impressed.

As I approached, they turned and stiffened up. One of the majors took a pace forward and nodded curtly. He was a slim, handsome little man with the flat features and high cheekbones of the southern Sundanese, and a tight, arrogant mouth. His English was almost perfect.

"Mr. Gedge?"

"No. My name's Fraser. I'm the resident consulting engineer. You are . . . ?"

"Major Suparto. I am glad to meet you, Mr. Fraser." We shook hands and he turned to the group behind him. "I introduce Majors Idrus, Djaja and Tukang, Captains Kerani and Emas." There were more curt nods as he turned to me again.

"We had expected Mr. Gedge to give us the honour of welcoming us on our arrival, Mr. Fraser."

"You are certainly welcome, Major. Unfortunately, Mr. Gedge is rather busy just now, but he would like to see you gentlemen in his office."

Major Suparto appeared to consider this. Then, suddenly, he smiled. It was such a charming, good-humoured smile that it deceived me for a moment; as it was meant to. I nearly smiled back.

"Very well, Mr. Fraser. We will accept you as Mr. Gedge's deputy." The smile went as suddenly as it had arrived. "You do not think that if we went to his office immediately he would be busy merely in order to keep us waiting?"

"We haven't much time here for protocol, Major," I said; "but you will have no reason to complain of discourtesy."

"I hope not." He smiled again. "Very well. Then we can go. Perhaps I may drive with you, Mr. Fraser."

"Certainly."

The rest followed in the other jeeps. As we went, I explained the geography of the camp, and stopped at a point on the track from which they could all get a view of the dam. There were exclamations of wonder from the jeeps behind us, but Major Suparto did not seem greatly interested. As I drove on, however, I saw him examining me out of the corners of his eyes. Then he spoke.

"What is a liaison manager, Mr. Fraser?"

"I think it's a new appointment."

"And unnecessary, no doubt. No, do not answer. I will not embarrass you."

"You're not embarrassing me, Major. I just don't happen to know the answer to your question."

"I admire your discretion, Mr. Fraser."

I took no notice of that one.

"I am a reasonable man, Mr. Fraser," he went on after a bit. "I shall be able to accept this situation philosophically. But my companions are a little different. They may look for other satisfactions. Things may grow difficult. I think that it would be as well for Mr. Gedge to remember that."

"I'll tell him what you say, but I think you'll find that he'll be very understanding."

He did not speak again until we pulled up outside Gedge's office; but as I went to get out, he put a hand on my arm.

"Understanding is a fine thing," he said; "but sometimes it is better to carry a revolver."

I looked at him carefully. "If I were you, Major, I wouldn't make any jokes like that in front of Mr. Gedge. He might think that you were trying to intimidate him, and he wouldn't care for that."

He stared at me, and, although his hands did not move, I was for a moment acutely aware of the pistol at his belt. Then, he smiled. "I like you, Mr. Fraser," he said; "I am sure that we shall be friends."

The meeting with Gedge passed off fairly well. All the liaison managers claimed to have had administrative experience. A more surprising thing was that they all spoke some English. Although English is now a second official language in Sunda (Malay being the first), not many Sundanese can speak it yet. There was some tension when the discrepancies between what they had been told about their jobs in Selampang and what they were told by Gedge became apparent, but, in the end, they seemed to accept the situation good-humouredly enough. Major Suparto nodded and smiled like a father pleased with the behaviour of his children in adult company. Later that evening, there was a further meeting with heads of departments. They had all been warned in advance and were ready. Each one had to take a liaison manager. In effect he would be a kind of trainee. Let him potter around. If he could make himself useful, so much the better. If not, it would not matter.

None of them claimed any technical knowledge. Major Suparto asked to go to transport. The supply, plant, electrical, construction and power-lines departments took the rest.

The first hint of trouble came three days later from the construction department. Captain Emas had attacked and badly beaten up one of the men working in number-three bay of the power house. Questioned about the incident, Captain Emas stated that the man had been insufficiently respectful. The following week two more men were beaten up by Captain Emas for the same reason. The truth emerged gradually. It appeared that Captain Emas was organising a construction workers' union, and that the men who had been beaten up had shown a disrespectful reluctance to pay dues. The secretary and treasurer of the union was Captain Emas.

Gedge was in a difficult position. All the project labour had been recruited locally and such minor disputes as had arisen had hitherto been settled by consultation with the village headmen. No formal union organisation had been found necessary. Unfortunately, under the Sundanese labour charter, membership of a union was obligatory for manual workers. Captain Emas obviously knew that. If he were fired and sent back to

Selampang, he would simply complain to the Ministry of Public Works that he had found an illegal situation and been victimised for trying to remedy it. The Ministry would be delighted. In no time at all, Captain Emas would be back armed with special powers to organise all Tangga Valley labour.

Gedge chose the lesser evil. He called a meeting of headmen, reminded them of the law, and secured their agreement to his applying to the labourers' union in the capital for an official organiser. He also instructed them that a record of all dues paid to Captain Emas must be kept in future so that Captain Emas could be held accountable for them later. He then called Captain Emas in and repeated the instruction in his presence.

That took care of Captain Emas for a few weeks, but it soon transpired that Majors Djaja and Tukang had been operating the same racket in the plant and electrical departments. Further meetings of headmen proved necessary.

All this was tiresome enough. The headmen felt that their authority was being undermined and were being obstructive; the workmen resented having to pay union dues just because somebody in Selampang said they had to, and were slacking on the job; small difficulties were beginning to cause big delays. But there was worse to come.

About fifteen miles east of the valley camp, on the road up from Port Kail which was used by the supply trucks, there were several big rubber estates. Two of these were still run by Dutchmen.

The position of the Dutch who remained in Sunda was both difficult and dangerous. The majority were employees of the few Dutch business houses which, under Government supervision, were still permitted to operate; banks, for example. The rest were mostly rubber planters in outlying areas where anti-Dutch feeling had been less violent; men who, rather than face the bitter prospect of having to abandon everything they possessed and start afresh in another country, were prepared to accept the new dangers of life in Sunda.

For the Dutch, those dangers were very real. When there was trouble in the streets, the greatest risk that any European ran was in being taken for a Dutchman. After a ghastly series of incidents in Selampang, the Chief of Police had even made a regulation authorising any European in charge of a car involved in an accident to drive right on for a kilometre before stopping to report to the police. If he stopped at the scene of the accident, both he and his passengers were invariably beaten up, and often murdered by the crowd. Men or women, it made no difference. The explanation that the victims had seemed to be Dutch would always serve to excuse the crime. Dutch owners of rubber estates were in an almost hopeless position. They were not allowed to sell or mortgage their estates, except to the Government, who would pay them in blocked currency which could not be exported. If they continued to operate their estates they had to sell their entire output to the Government at a price fixed by the Government. On the other hand, they had to pay their estate workers at minimum wage rates which made it virtually impossible for the estate to remain solvent. If they wanted to survive, their only chance was to conceal a proportion of their output from the Government inspectors and sell it for Straits dollars to the Chinese junk masters who made a rich business out of buying "black" rubber in Sunda and running it to Singapore.

Mulder and Smit were both men of about fifty, who had spent most of their lives in Sunda. Mulder had been born there. Neither had any capital in Holland. Every guilder they had was in their estates. Moreover, both had Sundanese wives and large families of whom they were very fond. Inevitably, they had decided to stay.

In the early days at the camp we had seen a good deal of both men. During the first few months, indeed, before the road was properly completed, we had used their guest rooms almost as if we rented them. Smit was a huge, red-faced man with a fat chuckle and an incredible capacity for bottled beer. Mulder had a passion for German *lieder*, which he would sing, accompanied by a phonograph, on the smallest pretext. With each other they played chess; with us, poker. Later, we had been able to repay some of their hospitality, but they never really liked coming to the camp. No women were allowed in the European club, so we could not ask them to bring their wives; and there were many Sundanese in the camp for whom the mere presence of a Dutchman was an irritant. When the liaison managers arrived I had seen neither of them for weeks.

Early one morning about three months before I was due to leave, Mulder drove into the camp with the news that Smit and his wife had been murdered.

The first part of the story was easily told. At one o'clock that morning, Mulder and his wife had been wakened by the Smits' eldest son, a boy of sixteen. He said that two men had driven up to the bungalow half an hour earlier and battered on the door until they were admitted. The noise had wakened him. He had heard his father speaking to them and there had been an argument. His father had become angry. Suddenly, there had been four shots. His mother had screamed and more shots had been fired. The men had then driven away. His mother and father were wounded. He had left the ayah to look after them and run for help.

By the time Mulder had arrived at the bungalow, Smit was dead. The wife had died shortly afterwards. Later, he had taken the children and their ayah back with him to his bungalow. Fearing for the safety of his own family, he had stayed with them until daylight before driving up to the camp to ask us to report the matter by radio to the police at Port Kail.

From the way he told it, it was fairly obvious that he knew more than he was saying. When I got him alone and had promised to keep my mouth shut, he told me the rest.

A week earlier two Sundanese had come to see him with a proposal. They said that they knew that he was smuggling rubber out of the country and being paid for it in Straits dollars. They wanted a half share in the proceeds of all future consignments. If they did not get it, unpleasant things would happen both to his family and to him. They would give him two days to think it over. Meanwhile, he was to tell nobody.

He went to Smit and found that the men had been to see him also. The two planters discussed the situation carefully. They knew that they were helpless. There was, of course, no question of their appealing for police protection. Apart from the fact that they would have to admit to the smuggling, which for Dutchmen would be suicidal, there was also the possibility that the men themselves might be connected with the police. They decided, in the end, to pay up, but to bargain first. They thought that an offer of ten per cent might satisfy the men.

It did not. The men became angry. They gave Mulder a further twenty-four hours to agree, and also demanded two thousand Straits dollars in cash as an earnest of his intentions.

That had been the previous night. The men must have gone straight to Smit, realised from what he said that the victims had been consulting together, and decided to show Mulder that they meant business. They had succeeded. Mulder was ready now to give them his whole estate if they asked for it.

But I was still a bit puzzled. Smit had not been the sort of man who is easily intimidated. It was difficult to think of his opening the door to a couple of thugs in the middle of the night without a loaded gun in his hand. As for Mulder; if he had asked me to help him to ambush the two men and leave their bodies for the kites, I should not have been greatly surprised.

It was not until I had persuaded him to talk about the two men that I understood. It would have been death to touch either of them. They were Sundanese army officers, a major and a captain. The descriptions that he gave left me in no doubt as to their identity. I persuaded Mulder to go with me to Gedge and repeat the story.

That night when Major Idrus and Captain Kerani arrived at Mulder's bungalow, Gedge and I were waiting behind the screen doors into the bedroom. We heard them describe what they had done to Smit and his wife, and threaten Mulder with the same treatment if he did not pay. Then we came out armed with shotguns and a shorthand record of what we had heard. For a while the air was thick with protestations. In the end, however, a deal was made. If Major Idrus and Captain Kerani left Mulder alone, we would take no further action. Mulder would lodge our signed statements at his bank, so that if anything happened to him the statements would go to the police. It was a miserable arrangement, but, short of involving Mulder in police inquiries, it was the best that we could do. Idrus and Kerani were smiling when they left to drive back to the camp in a supply-department truck. They had reason to smile; they had got away with murder.

We stayed behind with Mulder for a while and drank too much gin. For Gedge it did not improve the occasion.

"How would you like to stay on here, Steve?" he asked suddenly as I drove the jeep back to the camp.

"What do you mean?"

"You can have my job if you like."

"No, thanks."

"Wise man. It's not going to be pleasant having murderers about the place."

"Understanding is a fine thing," I said; "but sometimes it is better to carry a revolver."

"What's that?"

"Something that Major Suparto said."

And now I was sitting in Gedge's office for the last time, listening to what was being said, yet knowing that in less than three hours what I was hearing would seem as remote as a dream.

Unlike his five brother officers, Suparto had been an unqualified success. The ability to plan and organise is rare among the Sundanese; but, in this respect, Suparto was exceptional by any standards. Secure in a two-year contract, the Transport Manager had no qualms at all about delegating authority to so able and energetic an assistant, and had resisted the efforts of other departmental managers to lure him away.

Suparto had outlined the situation crisply.

There had been a strike of stevedores down at Port Kail the previous week and some important machinery had been unloaded on to the quay-side by the ship's crew. Now, the Customs people were making difficulties about identifying the individual items on the ship's cargo manifest, and were refusing to clear it. In his opinion they were turning a small confusion into a big one in the hope of getting a substantial bribe. He believed that if he were to go down to Kail and see the head of the Customs himself, the problem would very soon disappear. The Transport Manager shared that belief.

"We've never had trouble with the Customs before," Gedge was saying; "even in the early days when they could have made things good and tough for us."

"Major Suparto thinks that the local men may be getting squeezed from above," the Transport Manager said.

"I think it is possible," said Suparto; "but that is not something which can be discovered by radio telephone. I must talk with these men privately."

Gedge nodded. "Very well, Major. We'll leave it to you. The main thing is to get that machinery on its way up here. How long will you be away?"

"Two days, perhaps three. I propose to leave at once." He turned to me. "Mr. Fraser, I shall not have another opportunity. May I wish you a safe journey and a happy future?"

"Thanks, Major. It's been a pleasure knowing you."

We shook hands and he went out with the Transport Manager. Then began the rather more elaborate business of saying goodbye to Gedge.

The Dakota arrived at twelve thirty. When they had off-loaded the two mailbags, some cartons of dried milk and a couple of small air-compressor sets, they put my suitcase aboard and slung the outgoing mail in after it. My successor and one or two particular friends had come out to the airstrip to see me off, so there was more nonsense to be talked and hand-shaking to be done before I could get aboard myself.

Roy Jebb was the pilot. The first officer was a Sundanese named Abdul. They never carried a full crew on those trips, so, as I was the only pas-senger, I sat in the radio operator's seat just behind them. The plane had been standing in the sun for an hour and was suffocatingly hot inside; but I was so glad to be going that I did not even think to take my jacket off. I could see the men who had been seeing me off walking back to where the jeeps were standing, and wondered vaguely if I would ever see any of them again. Then the sweat began to trickle into my eyes and Jebb called to me to fasten my seat belt.

Two minutes later we were airborne.

CHAPTER II

THE DARK GREEN MASS of the jungle moved away beneath us and we began to follow the coast line with its ragged fringe of islands and turquoise-coloured shoal water.

Jebb glanced over his shoulder at me. He was lean, rangy and very Australian.

"Done anything about getting yourself a room, Steve?" he asked.

"I thought of trying the Orient."

"You might get a bed there. You won't get a room to yourself. Isn't that right, Abdul?"

"Oh yes. You can't sleep alone in Selampang. That is what they say." The first officer giggled deprecatingly. "It is a joke."

"And not a very funny one. They've got six beds now in some of those fly-blown rooms at the Orient. It's a fair cow."

"I'll buy my way in," I said; "I have before. Anyway, it's only for three days. I'm hoping to get a plane to Djakarta on Friday."

"You can try if you like, but you'll still have to share with a stranger. Why don't you come over to the Air House with me?"

"I didn't know they let rooms."

"They don't. I've got a little apartment up top there over the radio station. You can doss in the sitting room if you like."

"It's kind of you, but . . ."

"No 'buts' about it. You'd be doing me a favour. I've got to go to Makassar tomorrow and won't be back till Friday. It's asking for trouble these days to leave an apartment unoccupied."

"Thieves?"

"Either that or you come back and find some bloody policeman's wangled a requisition order and moved in with his family. I lost my bungalow that way when I went on leave last year. Now, I always try and get a pal to stay, even if it's only a couple of days."

"Then, I'll be glad to."

"It's a deal. What do you want to do on your first night of freedom?"

"Where's the best food now?"

"The restaurants are all pretty bloody. Did you know we've got a new club? The New Harmony it's called."

"It's a year since I've been down here."

"Then that's settled. Your evening's made. Now then, Abdul, what about some tea? Where's that thermos?"

Selampang lies at the head of a deep bay looking westward across the Java Sea. It used to be called Nieu Willemstad, and along the canals near the port there are still a few of the old houses, with brown-tiled roofs and diamond-paned windows, built by the early Dutch colonists. It stands on what was once swamp land, and the network of canals which covers the whole city area is really a system of drainage ditches; ditches in which the majority of the inhabitants, serenely ignoring the new sanitary regulations, continue to deposit their excreta, wash their bodies, and launder their clothes. When the Dutch left it, Selampang had a population of about half a million. Now it has over a million and a half. Yet, when you drive along the wide, tree-lined streets of the modern sections, past the big solid bungalows standing in their spacious compounds, there are no signs of overcrowding. It is only the pervasive smell of the canals and the occasional glimpses you get of the teeming *attap* villages which encrust their banks that remind you. The new slum city has grown like a fungus behind the colonial façade of the old.

The Air House was on the south side of the big Van Riebeeck Square, next to an eighteenth-century Residency which housed a department of the Ministry of Public Health. The highest and the newest building in

Selampang, it had been put up by a consortium of oil companies and airline operators as an office block, and was nearing completion when the Japanese occupied the city in 1942. For a time the Japanese had used it as a military headquarters; then their psychological warfare people had moved in, erected lattice masts on the roof and made a short-wave radio station of it. After the war it had remained a radio station. Only the ground floor had been handed back to the airline operators, and this was now a booking office and the terminal for the airport bus.

Jebb's apartment was on the top floor. The lift only went to the fifth; after that you walked along a rubber-floored corridor, through some swing doors and up a flight of stairs. Beyond the doors the building was still unfinished. The concrete of the auxiliary staircase was as the builders had left it in 1942. Footsteps echoed dismally down the staircase well. The window openings were roughly boarded up and it was not easy to see where you were going.

"Mind yourself here. You'll catch your coat," Jebb said.

We rounded a concrete upright bristling with the ends of reinforcement rods and walked a short way along a dusty passage. Then Jebb stopped at a door and took a key out.

"They'd just started to put the drains in these apartments when the Japs came," he said. "This is the only one they finished. The other five are still empty. After all this time and with a housing shortage, too! What a country! I had to bribe the whole of the city hall before I could even get the water turned on."

He opened the door and we went in.

My spirits had been drooping a little as we mounted the stairs, and I was remembering the camp bed I had so confidently given away; but inside things were different. There was a small tiled hall with a kitchen leading off it and another door into the sitting room. This was long and narrow, but almost the whole of the outer wall was taken up by french windows leading on to a deep terrace with a concrete balustrade. Over the terrace there was a plaited bamboo sun roof and, at the sides, *attap* screens. There was not much furniture; apart from the usual bamboo long chairs and a divan that was clearly used as a spare bed, there was a radio, a portable phonograph, a bookcase full of paper-backed novels and a bamboo serving trolley with drinks on it. On the walls were some Balinese pictures. It was cool and comfortable. I said so.

"The girl-friend helped me fix it up." He started the ceiling fan going very slowly. "Got to watch this bastard. Don't switch it on too quickly or it'll blow the main fuses down on the floor below. Now, what's it to be, Steve? Drink first or shower first? I'll tell you what. We'll have a long drink first while I show you where everything is. Then we'll shower and go on from there. What'll it be? Brandy dry? Gin fizz? Scotch if you like, but if you want to stay on the same thing all the evening, brandy or gin are easier. I'll go and get the ice."

When he had made the drinks, he showed me his bedroom and then took me out on to the terrace. It faced north, and from one end you could see out over the funnels and masts of the shipping in the port and across the bay. Beyond one of the *attap* screens at the other end was a Dutch bathhouse with a big stone ewer of water and a galvanised iron scoop.

"What do you know about it?" he demanded. "My word! Fancy putting a thing like that in a new building."

"Some people say it's the best sort of shower there is."

"Not me. Sloshing the water all over yourself with a thing like a saucepan, when you could pipe it up another four feet to a sprinkler—it's crazy! Besides, you have to be a bloody contortionist to rinse the soap off all over. The can's okay though—ordinary civilised type. Last place I had, it was practically the old pole-over-the-pit."

"How long have you been here, Roy?"

"In this country? Four years. Don't get me wrong. There's a lot I like about it besides the fat salary they pay me. But they're a funny lot. For instance, all these things they're getting now, like cars and fridges and radios, they don't look on them just as things to use. They *wear* them like lucky charms. Doesn't matter if the thing's any use to them or not, or even if it works. They've got to have it to feel all right. Abdul saw an American wearing a gold wrist-watch in a movie, so *he* had to have a gold wrist-watch. He starved himself for three months to pay for it. Why? He never looks at the time, he doesn't wind the bloody thing, he's not even particularly proud of it. It's just *his*. They're mostly like that, and that's what fools you. You think they're simply a lot of show-off kids trying to ape western civilisation."

"Until one day you find out that they're not simple at all, and that you haven't even begun to understand them."

"Too right. You know, when I was new here, I once asked a bunch of them at the airport what they thought was the most serious crime a man could commit. Know what they said?"

"Not murder anyway. They think we're too fussy about that."

"No, not murder. To steal another man's wife, that was the worst, they thought."

"I've never heard that one before."

"Neither had I. I didn't know then that it's no use asking questions in this country. You only get the answer they think you want to hear. During the war my wife went off with another man. I'd just divorced her. Those jokers happened to have found out, that's all." He grinned. "You married, Steve?"

"Not any more. Same story."

He nodded. "Mina'll fix you up all right."

"Who's she?"

"The girl-friend. Tell you what. You have the shower first. I'll go and call her up now and tell her to bring a friend along."

It was dark when we went down into the square again and the whole place had come to life. There were people everywhere. The casuarina trees and travellers' palms which ringed the gardens in the centre were festooned with lights, and market stalls had been set up beneath them. Chinese food-sellers surrounded by little groups of eaters squatted in the dust. A boy of about ten sat on his haunches playing a bamboo xylophone, while another beside him beat a drum. The road which ran round the square was jammed with crawling cars, and the *betjak* drivers rang their bells incessantly as they manoeuvred their brightly painted tricycles through the gaps. It was a tribute to the wealth and influence of the Selampang black-market operators that, in a city where the cheapest American car cost three times as much as it cost in Detroit, there should be a modern traffic problem.

There was a line of empty *betjak* by the Air House entrance and, as soon as he saw Jebb, one of the drivers swung out of the line and pedalled up to us, smiling eagerly.

"We need two this evening, Mahmud."

"I can take both, *tuan*."

"Maybe you can, sport, but we want to be comfortable. Where's your friend?"

Another driver was summoned and we set off.

Once you have learned to disregard the laboured breathing of the driver pedalling behind you and have overcome the feeling that you are the sitting target for every approaching car, the *betjak* is an agreeable form of transport, especially on a hot night. You are carried along just fast enough for the air to seem cool, but not so fast that the sweat chills on your body. You can lean back comfortably and look up at the trees and the stars without being bitten by insects; and, providing the driver does not insist on muttering obscene invitations to the nearest brothel in your ear, you can think.

I was glad of the respite. After the Tangga hills Selampang was suffocatingly humid, and even a light cotton shirt seemed like a blanket. Also, I had had three large brandies at the apartment; one more than I really wanted. I would be busy the following day and had no intention of burdening myself with a hangover. I had no intention either, I told myself, of spending the night with some local drab selected by Jebb's girl-friend. I had heard his telephoned instructions, and decided that there was a point at which hospitality became officiousness. Besides, the breaking of a habit of continence, especially if it has been enforced, should not be too casually enjoyed. I had my own ideas about the occasion, and they did not, at that moment, include Selampang.

The New Harmony Club was outside the city. Beyond the race track there was a stretch of about a mile of straight, unlighted road, with large bungalow compounds on either side of it. It was very quiet on this road, and you could hear an approaching car almost as soon as you saw its lights. Even the cicadas seemed muted, and we had left behind the smell of the canals.

"Nice part this," Jebb said; "as long as you're not too near the race track." The two *betjak* were travelling abreast now.

"Who lives here?"

"Foreign legations mostly. One or two rich Chinese. They have to pay through the nose for the privilege though. Look, there's the club. That light ahead. Shove it along, Mahmud! We need a drink."

It was a bungalow much like the rest, but with an electric sign by the entrance to the compound, and a gatekeeper in a peaked cap who peered at us intently as we turned in. As we stopped, the warm, humid air seemed to close in again, but now it was heavily scented by the frangipani growing in the forecourt; and from inside came the lush, sentimental, international sound of a night-club pianist playing American music.

In the vestibule a Chinese doorman in a sharkskin dinner jacket made out a temporary membership card for me, and sold me a pack of American cigarettes at double the black-market price. Then, we went through into the room beyond.

Once it had been two rooms, but arched openings had been cut in the old dividing wall to make it one. There was a teak-panelled bar at one end and a platform with the piano on it in an alcove. The rest of the space inside was filled with tables, about a dozen of them. Out on the covered terrace there were a few more tables and a small raised dance floor. The walls were painted to imitate stonework, and the light came from electric candles in wrought-iron wall brackets.

It was early, and only two or three of the tables were so far occupied. The bar, however, was crowded. Most of the men were Europeans, though there were a couple of slick young Sundanese in air-force uniforms sitting on bar stools and a neat Chinese with rimless glasses. The pianist was a supercilious-looking Indian wearing a gold bracelet and a ruby ring. A Dutch couple were leaning on the piano with glasses in their hands, listening to him raptly. The wife's hair was untidy and she seemed to be a little drunk. The Indian was ignoring them.

"'A bunch of the boys were whooping it up in the Malamute saloon,'" Jebb quoted facetiously, and began to elbow his way towards the bar, exchanging greetings with people as he went. "Hullo, Ted. How're you doing, sport? Hi, Marie."

Marie was a stout, dark girl with big, protruding teeth and a tight silk dress. She smiled mechanically and blew cigarette smoke at the ceiling. Jebb winked at me. I had no idea what the wink meant, but I grinned back understandingly. The effort was wasted. He was greeting the Chinese with the rimless glasses.

"Evening, Mor Sai. Want you to meet a pal of mine, Steve Fraser. Steve, this is Lim Mor Sai. He owns the joint."

As we shook hands, a middle-aged blonde with haggard eyes and a foolish mouth came through the door beside the bar and slipped an arm through Jebb's. "Hullo, Roy love," she said. "I thought you were going to Makassar."

"No, that's tomorrow. Molly, this is Steve Fraser. Steve, this is Molly Lim."

She gave me a glassy stare. "Another bloody Britisher, eh? Why don't you people stay at home?"

I smiled.

"One day, my darling," said her husband primly, "you will make such a joke too often. Then, a lot of our furniture will be broken and there will be trouble with the police."

"Oh, go on with you!" She fondled his cheek. "He knows I'm pulling his leg. I'll give you three guesses where I come from, Mr. Fraser, and the first two don't count."

"Lancashire?"

"Of course. Mor Sai says I even speak Cantonese with a Liverpool accent. Isn't that right, love?"

Lim looked bored with her. "As this is your first visit to the club," he said to me, "you must have a drink on the house."

"That's what we've been waiting to hear," said Jebb. "We're drinking brandy."

"You'll find it on the bill," said Mrs. Lim sardonically and moved away.

Lim snapped his fingers for the barman and gave the order. Jebb nudged me. I glanced across the room and saw Mrs. Lim snatch a glass out of a man's hand and swallow the drink at a gulp. The man laughed.

Lim saw it, too. The moment our drinks came, he excused himself and went over to where she was standing.

"I ought to have warned you about our Molly," Jebb said. "Don't buy her a drink, whatever you do."

"It doesn't look as if she waits to be bought one."

"Yes, you have to hold on to your glass when she's around. That bastard should know better. He'll be unpopular with Lim if he's not careful."

"Is that a bad thing?"

"It's as well to keep on the right side of him. Lim's got friends in the police department. You know the time they take over exit papers? A week sometimes if they feel bloody-minded. Last time I went on leave, Lim got everything for me in a couple of hours, and I bet you . . ." At that moment he broke off, grinned over my shoulder and said: "Hi, Mina baby!"

I looked round.

Eurasian women are difficult to describe accurately. One's first impression is always dominated by one set of racial characteristics to the virtual exclusion of the other; but closer acquaintance always seems to reverse that first impression. It is not just a matter of clothes; a European dress can make the same woman look both more Asian and less; the change is as unpredictable as it is with those optical illusions with which you may make a pyramid of solid cubes become a pyramid of empty boxes, merely by blinking.

At first sight Mina looked completely European. She was a slim, attractive brunette with the sort of aquiline bone structure that you find mostly in the Eastern Mediterranean; Greek, you might have guessed. Her friend, Rosalie, on the other hand, looked like a Filipino girl of good family who had learned to wear her clothes at an American university. Yet, after ten minutes, Mina's features had become for me unmistakably Sundanese, while Rosalie looked like a European girl who was modelling her appearance on that of her favourite ballerina. Their voices had something to do with it. Both spoke good English with Dutch accents; but in Mina's voice you could hear the Sundanese gutturals as well. She was tense and emphatic. Rosalie was quieter and more self-assured.

Jebb had explained that they both taught Western dancing at a school run by a Chinese, and that we would be expected to pay them for spending the evening with us at the club. After midnight, further negotiations would become necessary; but I would have to conduct those myself. With Mina, he had a more or less permanent arrangement. Rosalie was known to be very choosey; if she did not like you, there was nothing doing, even if you were a millionaire. It was up to me.

I was resigned, then, to a dull and probably squalid evening. It turned out to be neither. I think that the thing which broke the ice for me was the realisation that, unsentimental though it might be, the relationship beween Mina and Jebb had at the same time a basis of genuine affection. I don't think I was being ingenuous. You can be deceived about loving, but not so easily about liking.

Mina talked a great deal at first. Most of the time she was playing a favourite Sundanese game. If you owe a man money, or if he has caused you to lose face in any way, or if he is someone in authority whom you dislike, you invent a scandal about him, preferably with a wealth of scatological detail, suggesting that he is impotent, cuckolded or perverse. Nobody believes the story, but the more circumstantial you make it, and the more carefully your audience listens, the more superior to your enemy do you become. Mina's scandals were pungent and outrageous and she told them like a good comedienne, with a sort of bland amazement at their strangeness. Jebb's part was to refuse to believe a word she said. If, for example, the story was about the Chief of Police, Jebb would de-

clare that he knew the man personally and that her story was impossible.
This in turn would lead to a further extravaganza in order to prove the
first.

It could have been boring, but for some reason it wasn't. Once or twice,
when I laughed outright, she would laugh too, and then hasten to persuade me that what she had said was no laughing matter. Rosalie only
smiled. Her attitude towards Mina was that of an adult towards a pre-
cocious child who may become overexcited; amused but guarded. Now
and again I saw her out of the corner of my eye watching me shrewdly
and weighing me up. I was surprised to discover that I did not mind.
Once, she realised that I was examining her. She was saying something
to Jebb at the time, and the realisation made her hesitate for a word; but
otherwise she seemed completely self-possessed.

The dinner was Vietnamese and very good. After it we moved out on
to the terrace and drank tea. Then, Lim switched on a record-player and
we danced for a while; but the small floor soon became too crowded for
comfort and we wandered out into the compound.

Once there had been a garden neatly laid out with stone walks and
flower beds and ornamental fish pools; now, it was all overgrown, the
crotons and banana trees had run wild, and the pools were choked with
Java weed. But the air was pleasantly scented and I was glad to get away
from the noise of the record-player. I lit a cigarette and for a minute or
so we walked along a path that had been roughly cleared to one side of
the compound. Then a bat fluttered close to my head and I swore. The
moon was very bright and I saw the girl look up at me.

"You do not have to be polite to me," she said.

"What do you mean?"

"It is eleven o'clock. Mina and Roy will not leave for two hours yet.
You have had a long journey today. I think you must be very tired."

"I've enjoyed this evening, but now, yes, I am tired."

"Then you should go and sleep." She smiled as I hesitated. "We can
meet again tomorrow if you wish."

"Yes, I'd like to do that. Roy's going to Makassar tomorrow morning and
I know no one else in this place. No one, that is, that I want to see."
I hesitated again. We had stopped and she was looking up at me.

"What is it you wish to say?"

"There is my side of the bargain too."

"I do not think we need to talk about that. You will be here for two,
three days. When you leave you will give me a present of money. If we
have not liked each other, you will give it in contempt. If we have liked
each other, it will make the parting easier. In any case you will be generous."

"Are you sure about that?"

"Yes, I am sure."

That was all that was said. She took my arm and, in silence, we continued the circuit of the compound. It was a fine night and I suddenly felt peaceful.

We were walking along the path that ran parallel to the lane beyond the boundary fence, when I saw a light flickering through the bamboo thicket ahead of us.

"What's that light?" I asked.

"There are some old kampong houses there. When the Dutch people were in the bungalow, that is where the servants lived. But I did not think that they were used now."

The stone surface of the path had ended and we were walking on soft earth that deadened the sound of our footsteps. Then we heard voices ahead, and our pace became slower. One of the voices was Mrs. Lim's and neither of us, I think, wanted to encounter her just at that moment. I was about to suggest that we turn back, when she began to shout at the top of her voice.

"And I say they can't! Do you want us all murdered? You're out of your bloody mind!"

A man said something quickly. Mrs. Lim uttered a sort of gasp, as if she had been hit, and then began to weep.

Rosalie's hand tightened on my arm. Suddenly, there was a faint clatter of feet on wooden steps and then the sound of someone, Mrs. Lim presumably, hurrying back towards the bungalow.

For a moment we stood there uncertainly. We had half turned to go back; but the shortest way back to the bungalow was straight ahead, and there seemed no point now in retracing our footsteps. We walked on.

The servants' houses were among some palm trees on the far side of a rough track that led from a gateway on to the lane. It was wide enough for a bullock cart and had probably been used as a sort of tradesmen's entrance. The houses were built on teak piles, and the frames were substantial enough, but the *attap* walls had suffered in the monsoons and both places looked derelict. The light, which looked as if it came from a kerosene vapour lamp, was in the house farthest away from the track, and it shone through the tattered walls. A low murmur of men's voices came from within. There seemed to be four of them. By the steps up to the verandah of the nearer house stood a jeep.

Jeeps are common enough in that part of the world. It was a bracket welded on to the side that made me stop and look at it. Quite a number of the ex-army jeeps had that bracket; it had been fitted originally to support a vertical exhaust pipe when the jeep was water-proofed for driving out of a landing-craft; but this one was bent in a vaguely familiar way. I glanced down at the number.

In a place where you depend on mechanical transport for practically every move you make, even a highly standardised vehicle like a jeep acquires character, has its own subtle peculiarities, its special feel. You prefer some to others, and because they all look the same you learn to differentiate between them by their numbers.

I knew the number of this one only too well. I had already seen it once that day. It had been standing outside Gedge's office.

I must have made a startled movement, for Rosalie looked up at me quickly.

"What is it? What's the matter?"

"Wait here a moment."

The house with the light was about twenty yards away. I walked towards it. At that moment my intention was to go in and ask what the hell a jeep from the Tangga Valley project was doing down in Selampang. Luckily, by the time I had covered half the distance, I had come to my senses and stopped. It had been about 11 a.m. when I had last seen the jeep in Tangga, and yet here it was just over twelve hours later in Selampang. It could not have come by sea in that time. It could not have come by air. That meant that it had been driven down two hundred miles by road. Which meant, in turn, that it had been passed quickly and safely through every road block manned by the insurgents in Sanusi's area, as well as the outposts manned by the Selampang garrison. That meant that the person who had been in it was someone to stay well away from at that moment; and that applied to his friends, too.

I stood there for a second or two with my heart thumping very unpleasantly. I could distinguish the voices inside now. They were speaking Malay. One man was repeating something emphatically. His voice was light and ugly and sounded as if he were trying to speak and swallow at the same time.

"All of them. We must have all," he was saying.

The voice that replied was certainly Major Suparto's. It was very calm and controlled. "Then it must be delayed until the second day," he said. "There must be patience, General."

I turned quietly and went back to Rosalie. She said nothing and took my arm again as we walked back towards the club.

When we had gone a little way she said: "Is there something wrong?"

I hesitated. I thought she might think that I was being stupid. "That jeep back there," I said at last. "It was in Tangga this morning. A Sundanese army officer drove it here today—by road. A major. He's in there now."

I need not have worried. The implication, when she saw it, made her draw in her breath.

"With Lim Mor Sai?" she said quickly.

"I suppose so. There were others there, one of them a general. I think we'd better forget about it."

"Yes, we must forget."

We went on back to the terrace. Mina and Jebb were in the bar and the floor was fairly clear, so we decided to have one more dance before I went.

CHAPTER III

JEBB WAKENED ME at seven o'clock the next morning to say goodbye and to introduce me to the cleaning woman, Mrs. Choong.

"There's a fair amount of stuff in the Frigidaire," he said; "but if there's anything else you want, just write out a list and she'll do the marketing. Isn't that right, Mrs. Choong?"

Mrs. Choong nodded. "I buy for good prices. I cook, too, if you like. You want eggs for breakfast, mister?"

"Yes, please."

She was a ball of fat and the seams of her black trousers stretched almost to bursting-point as she bent down to pick up Jebb's breakfast tray. As she waddled away into the kitchen, Jebb said: "I told her you'd be sleeping in the bedroom. There are two beds there. Tell her to make both of them up if you want to. Liberty Hall, this is."

"And I'm very grateful. I can't tell you."

"Forget it, sport. Like I said, you're doing me a favour. Let's see. It's Tuesday today. I should be back Thursday night or Friday morning. When exactly do you reckon on getting away, Steve?"

"I'm hoping to get the Friday plane to Djakarta."

"Well, if they try and twist your arm too much over your exit papers, you see Lim Mor Sai and ask him to talk to his pals in the police department."

"I'll do that." It was on the tip of my tongue to tell him that the police department was not the only place where Lim Mor Sai had pals. Then, I decided not to. No doubt there were hundreds of people in Selampang who were secretly in touch with the insurgents in the north. If Lim were one of them, Jebb, as a Government employee, would probably rather not know about it. I said instead: "If you're not back before I leave, what would you like me to do about the key you lent me?"

"Leave it with Mrs. Choong. You can trust her. She's got her own anyway. But I hope I'll see you."

"So do I."

He hesitated. "She's a classy kid, Rosalie, you know," he said awkwardly.

"Don't worry. I'll do right by her. Mina's not going to be waiting for you with a hatchet."

He laughed. "Okay, sport. Sorry I spoke. By the way, if you see Lim Mor Sai, tell him I'll be bringing him some cheroots back with me. He usually asks me when I go Makassar way. He must have forgotten this time."

"I'll tell him. And thanks again."

"If you're still here Friday, you can buy me a drink."

When he had gone, Mrs. Choong brought me a breakfast of fried eggs, coffee and papaya. Later, when I had bathed and shaved, I considered my clothes. Up in Tangga, I had seen myself making do with what I had until I reached Singapore. Now, the situation was different. My ridiculous suit did not matter; I would not be needing a jacket while I was in Selampang; but I would certainly need some more slacks and shirts. I consulted Mrs. Choong. She told me that she could get shirts *dobi*-ed for me in a few hours, but that if I wanted them properly laundered I would have to wait twenty-four. She also gave me the address of a good Chinese tailor.

I went to the tailor first and ordered two pairs of slacks and four shirts for delivery late that afternoon. Then, I paid my first call on the police department.

Sundanese officials are peculiarly difficult to deal with, especially if you are an English-speaking European. The first thing you have to realise is that, although they look very spruce and alert and although their shirt pockets glitter with rows of fancy ball-point pens, they have only the haziest notions of their duties. The language problem is also important. All the forms you have to fill up are printed in English as well as Malay, because English is an official language and the officials are supposed to be bi-lingual. The trouble is that they will never admit that they are not. If you speak in Malay they feel bound to reply in English. Unfortunately, the few words they have soon run out, and although they may continue to *look* as if they understand what you have said, they are in fact hopelessly at sea. Their technique for dealing with the resulting impasse is to pretend that they have to consult a colleague, and then go away and forget about you. The form you have completed gets lost. Your only chance is to say and write everything very distinctly both in English and Malay, and to keep fingering your wallet as if you are getting ready to pay. You are, indeed, going to have to pay eventually; and not merely the legal fee for the service in question. When the formalities are almost completed, it will suddenly be discovered that you ought to have produced another "clearance," and that without it you cannot have whatever it is you want. A Kafka-like scene ensues. Nobody can tell you precisely what this mysterious clearance is or how you set about obtaining it. The shifty brown eyes peer at you. It is your move now. You ask what the fee for the clearance would be if one knew where to obtain it. A figure is named. You ask if, as a special favour, you may deposit this sum so that when more is known about it, the clearance may be obtained for you. There is a shrug, then a grudging assent. The eyes watch sullenly as you count the money out. You agreed too quickly. He is wishing he had asked for more and wondering if it is too late. No, it is not. He made a mistake. He forgot the price of the Government stamp. You smile politely and pay that, too. There is no answering smile. Other brown eyes have observed the transaction and there will be a share-out when you have gone. To get out again into the open air is like emerging from a depression.

The granting of an exit visa to a resident European is a big operation. My first visit to the visa section of the police-department headquarters lasted an hour. In that time I managed to secure the five different forms that had to be completed, and countersigned by various other authorities, before the formal application could be submitted. This was good going. I went next to the agents for the Hongkong and Shanghai Bank, cashed a cheque and had one of the forms countersigned. After I had deposited it, together with another form, at the Internal Revenue Department, I called in at the Indonesian Consulate and applied for a transit visa. By then, it was time for lunch.

I went to the Orient Hotel, where they had an air-conditioned bar. I also hoped to find De Vries, the Sunda-Pacific Airways traffic manager, and thus save myself the trouble of calling in at his office. He was there all right, nursing a de Kuyper's gin as if it were all that he had left to live for. Sunda-Pacific Airways ran the scheduled passenger services out of Selampang under a Government franchise that was due to expire later that year. The Government had recently announced that it would not be renewed, and that a new national airline authority would take over. He knew only too well that, while international air safety requirements would necessitate their retaining the Dutch pilots, no such necessity would protect the rest of the Dutch staff. He had been one of the original members of the company. His bitterness was understandable.

After he had promised to see that a seat was held for me on the Friday plane to Djakarta, he asked me how things were up in Tangga. I told him, and asked how things were in Selampang. It was a foolish question; but I had nothing to do until the offices opened again, and I thought, somewhat virtuously, that the least I could do was to listen to him.

I received the answer I deserved.

"You know damn well how things are in this city. I would be pleased if you would stop encouraging me to become a bore. Have another drink."

Over luncheon, however, he did unburden himself a little.

"I wouldn't like a Government spy to hear me saying this," he said; "but people like me have only one chance of survival here."

"What's that?"

"A revolution."

"You mean Sanusi?"

"Why not? Did you know that he'd appointed a representative in New York to lobby the United States, and that for the past six months he's had agents in Malaya and Pakistan, meeting religious leaders and canvassing support for the movement?"

"No, I didn't."

"The censorship has been quite efficient, but in my business news gets around. I can tell you, they're badly worried down here. Sanusi controls more than half the total area of the country as it is. The Nasjah Government has failed completely. The country's bankrupt, the elections were a farce and the Communists are getting stronger every day. If Sanusi were to take over tomorrow, the Americans and British would probably sigh with relief."

"I don't see how you'd be better off, though."

"We couldn't be worse off. At least, we could come to terms with Sanusi."

"Are you sure of that?"

"Sanusi may be a fanatic in some ways, but in others he is open to reason."

"You speak as if you knew him."

"Oh yes, I know him. You forget, he commanded the garrison here." He paused, then added: "There are lots of people in this place who know Sanusi."

"I'm sure there are. Has he any weaknesses?"

"Wishful thinking. Same as me."

A waiter was hovering near us. De Vries began to talk of other things. It was not until we were sitting on the terrace having our coffee that he reverted to the subject. A column of army trucks with troops aboard them went by. The troops were in full marching order, with steel helmets and machine pistols. They were clinging on for dear life as the trucks bounced over the pot holes outside the hotel. I remembered something I had read in the Government newspaper that morning about an important army exercise.

"Sanusi has another weakness," De Vries remarked sombrely.

"Oh?"

"He does not like to take chances."

When the Government offices reopened I made another tour, beginning with the Ministry of Public Works, who were required to certify that I was leaving the country with their knowledge and without any of their property in my possession, and ending with the police department, where I deposited the completed forms, together with my passport and a substantial sum to cover "fees." A sour police lieutenant then agreed reluctantly that, if I returned the following day at about the same time, the exit permit might be stamped in my passport. When I arrived back at the tailor's it was no surprise to find that the slacks and shirts I had or-

dered were ready for me; nevertheless, I was pleased. After a day with
official Sunda, it was refreshing to deal with the businesslike Chinese.

Back in the apartment, I slept for an hour or so. When I awoke, I
found that it had rained heavily and that the air smelt of, and felt like,
hot mud. However, the water in the bathhouse was cool, and, after I had
showered, I was able to dress without too much discomfort.

I had arranged to meet Rosalie at the New Harmony Club at eight
thirty. Soon after eight, I locked up the apartment and set out. The lift
was not working, and I had to walk down the stairs past the floors occupied by the radio station. The corridors had sponge-rubber carpets laid
along them and there was a lot of external wiring on the walls; but otherwise they looked much like floors in an ordinary office building. On one
landing workmen were manhandling a heavy piece of electrical equipment
that looked like a meat safe out of the lift. When I reached the ground
floor I could hear a big diesel generator set thudding away in the basement. The radio station, Jebb had told me, was independent of the city
power supply. The two policemen on the door glanced at me casually,
but did not trouble to look at the temporary pass their predecessors had
given me earlier in the day.

Mahmud pedalled over grinning when he saw me come out, and soon
we were splashing through the rain-filled pot holes along the Telegraf
Road towards the racecourse.

I would like to be able to say that I sensed something strange about
the city that evening—an inexplicable tension in the air, a brooding calm
that foretold the storm—but I cannot. Most of the drains had overflowed
with the rain and added their own special stench to the normal canal
smell, but there seemed to be just as many people about as there had
been the previous night, and they all seemed to be behaving in the normal way. On one patch of wasteland beside the road, there was even a
small fair in progress. A carousel had been set up, and a small stage on
which two Indian conjurors were performing. Mahmud slowed down as
we went past. One of the conjurors was holding a tin chamber pot, while
the other pretended to defecate coins into it. As the coins clattered into
the pot, the crowd applauded happily.

When I got to the club, I went through into the bar. It was fairly
crowded, but I was relieved to find that neither Lim Mor Sai nor his wife
was there. The Dutch couple were at their place by the piano. I had a
drink and watched them for a time. Once, the pianist nodded vaguely to
them and began to play what was evidently their favourite tune. The man
touched his wife's hand, and she looked at him fondly. The man smiled
and said something to the pianist; but he was bored with them again.
For him, no doubt, they were merely two pathetic Europeans who drank
too much and breathed across the piano at him every evening, distracting
him with their tiresome adulation from his private world of soft lights,
rich boy-friends and American recordings. It was all rather depressing.

Then, Rosalie arrived and things were suddenly different.

She was wearing a light cotton dress that should have made her look more European, but for some reason had the reverse effect. As soon as she saw me, she smiled and came over, nodding to someone she knew on the way. There was nothing self-conscious about her greeting, no arch pretence that she had not really expected to find me there. She was glad to see me and I was glad to see her, and, as I was drinking gin, she would drink that, too.

It was a good evening. I don't remember all the things we talked about; Mina and Jebb for a while, I know, and the police department, food, clothes, Singapore, air travel, and the black markets; but after we had dined, and then danced a bit, we talked about ourselves. I learned that she had a sister who worked for a shipping company, that her father, who had been in the Dutch army, had died in a Jap P.O.W. camp, and that her mother preferred to live now with relatives who owned land near Kota Baru. She learned that, after a spell in the Western Desert, I had spent most of the war building airfields, that my wife had gone off with a Polish army officer while I had been away, and that my firm in London had written asking me if I would like to do a job in Brazil.

Lim Mor Sai showed up later in the evening and went round the tables making himself agreeable to the customers. When he stopped at our table I gave him Jebb's message about the cigars. Just for a moment it seemed to disconcert him.

"Cigars? Ah yes. That is most kind." He paused. "May I ask where you are staying, Mr. Fraser?"

"Jebb's lent me his apartment. Why?"

He hesitated, then shrugged apologetically. "Here one always asks. The hotels are so full. You are fortunate." He bowed slightly and moved on; but I had a feeling that he had left something unsaid. So had Rosalie. I saw her look after him in a puzzled sort of way; then our eyes met, she smiled as if I had caught her out in an indiscretion, and we got up to dance again.

We left the place soon after eleven. Mahmud was waiting outside. There is just room for two reasonably slim persons in a *betjak*, and he waved away a colleague who tried to muscle in. Rosalie gave him an address, and he set off enthusiastically, the chain making cracking sounds as he threw his weight on to the pedals.

The street to which he took us was on the outskirts of the Chinese quarter. The pavements were arcaded, and between the shops there were broad, steep staircases leading to the upper floors. About halfway down the street, Rosalie told him to stop. Then she got out and hurried up one of the staircases. I lit a cigarette and waited. A little way along the street, an old man was sitting on the edge of the open drain with his legs dangling into it, solemnly combing a long grey beard. On the opposite pavement there was a Sikh watchman asleep on a charpoy placed across the doorway of a furniture shop. Only two or three windows in the street showed any light. It was so quiet that I could hear Mahmud breathing.

Rosalie was gone about ten minutes. When she returned, she had a small dressing case with her. I told Mahmud to drive us to the Air House.

There, the policemen on duty at the door glanced casually at my pass and nodded. They paid no attention to Rosalie. The generator in the basement was silent; presumably, the radio station had shut down for the night. The lift was working again and lights had been left on in the fifth-floor corridor. Beyond the swing doors at the end of it, however, there was pitch darkness and I had to strike matches to light the way to the apartment. I remembered how unprepossessing it had seemed to me the previous day.

"It's not all as bad as this," I said.

"I know, Mina told me. Besides, I helped her choose the furniture."

When I had left the apartment, I had locked all the windows on to the terrace. She sat down while I opened up the living room, but when I came back from doing the bedroom, I found that she had gone into the kitchen and was looking at the refrigerator.

"Thirsty?" I asked.

"A little." She patted the refrigerator. "Does it work?"

"Oh yes."

I got a tray of ice out and showed her. She smiled and wandered off into the living room. When I went in there with the ice and glasses, however, she was out on the terrace.

I watched her. For a moment or two she stood quite still, looking round at everything as if she were making an inventory, then she walked away slowly past the *attap* screen to inspect the bathhouse. She was out of sight now, but I could hear her shoes clicking on the concrete. The sound receded and then got louder again. I heard her go into the bedroom. The sound of her footsteps ceased, and I knew that she was standing there taking in everything and getting used to it. The drinks were made, but I left them where they were and stretched out on one of the long chairs. I did not want to interrupt her.

A minute went by, and then I heard her move.

"Steven?" It was the first time she had used my name.

"In here."

She came through from the bedroom and smiled when she saw me on the chair.

"I have been looking at everything," she said.

"Yes, I know."

I handed her a drink. She drank about half of it, but thoughtfully, as if she were up against a serious problem. I asked her what it was.

"It is very warm," she explained carefully. "I was thinking that I would take a bath."

"Is that all? Well, I'm going to take one, too. You go first."

She came back from the bathhouse wearing a sarong. The towel was draped modestly over her breasts and her black hair hung loose on her shoulders. I left her standing by the terrace balustrade, looking down into the square below.

The water was deliciously cool. I dried myself slowly so as not to get warm again, tied a towel round my waist and walked back along the terrace.

She was no longer there, and there was only a single light on in the living room. It shone indirectly through the open door into the bedroom. It was there that I found her.

It was still dark when I awoke and the terrace outside was almost white in the moonlight. I knew that it was a sound that had wakened me, but I did not know what sound. I looked across at Rosalie asleep on the other bed; but she was quite still. There was a small table between the two beds and I could see the dial of my watch glowing there. It was three forty-five.

Just then I heard the sound again. It came from away along the terrace. A man said something sharply and there was a noise like a packing case being moved on concrete.

I swung my legs to the floor and stood up. My bath towel was lying between the beds and I wrapped it around my waist. If I were going to have to tackle an intruder, I preferred not to do so stark naked.

I bent over Rosalie and kissed her. She stirred in her sleep. I kissed her again and she opened her eyes. I kept my head close to hers.

"Wake up, but speak softly."

"What is it?" She was still half asleep.

"Listen. There's somebody trying to get along the terrace from one of the empty apartments. Thieves, I suppose. I'm going to scare them away."

She sat up. "Have you a revolver?"

"Yes, but I hope I won't have to use it. They're making a lot of noise. They probably think there's no one here."

My suitcase was under the bed. I got the revolver out, rotated the cylinder until one of the three rounds in it would fire when I pressed the trigger, and went over to the window.

There was a wall separating this section of the terrace from that belonging to the unfinished apartment next door, and it had iron spikes on it. I heard one of the men cursing as he tried to negotiate them. Now was the moment to act, I thought. As I had told Rosalie, all I wanted to do was to scare them away. If either of them got down from the wall, he would be cornered with nowhere to run to.

I stepped out on to the terrace.

I could see very clearly. The moon was behind me, shining directly along the terrace. A man was standing on the top of the wall astride the spikes. He was wearing an army steel helmet and a belt of ammunition pouches. As I watched, he bent down and took something handed up to him from below. When he straightened up I saw that it was a Japanese-pattern machine pistol. He held it up for a moment, regaining his balance, then he brought his other leg over the spikes and jumped.

As he landed on the terrace, I moved back into the bedroom. I was confused and scared now, but I had some sense left. I went straight back to the suitcase and dropped the revolver inside it.

"What's the matter?" Rosalie whispered.

I took her hand and held it tightly, motioning her not to speak. The soldier was walking along the terrace now, not cautiously, but as if he were uncertain of the way. Then, he came into view, the machine pistol held across his body as if he were on patrol. Rosalie started violently and I gripped her tighter. For a moment the man outside stood silhouetted in the moonlight. He looked round and stared at the bedroom window. Rosalie began to tremble. He took a step towards it.

Suddenly, a loud hammering noise came from the living room, and I realised that someone was beating on the outer door of the apartment.

The man on the terrace peered round and then went through the open window into the living room. The door into the bedroom was open and we saw him cross towards the hall. A moment later there was the sound of the bolts of the door being shot back and a murmur of voices. The lights in there went on.

I stood up. My dressing gown was lying on a chair and I tossed it to Rosalie. Then, putting my finger to my lips, to warn her to keep quiet, I walked through into the living room.

There were several voices murmuring in the corridor now. Suddenly, there was a sound of sharp footsteps approaching and the voices were hushed.

A Sundanese voice said: "At your service, Major *tuan*."

A moment later, Major Suparto walked into the room.

CHAPTER IV

HE DID NOT RECOGNISE ME at once. His pistol holster was unfastened and his hand went to it quickly. At the same moment he called sharply to the soldiers in the corridor. As he levelled the pistol, two of them ran in through the doorway. They had the long chopping-knives called *parangs* in their hands, and as soon as they saw me they started forward with a shout.

I had opened my mouth to tell him who I was, but it all happened so quickly that I was still gagging over the words when he yelled to the two men to halt. They were within a yard of me with their *parangs* raised to strike, and their teeth clenched in the mad killing grimace. Another second and he could not have stopped them hacking me to pieces. As it was, they stood there dazed, their faces gradually regaining a stupid sort of sanity as they lowered their arms.

Suparto came towards me, thrusting them aside.

"What is this?" he demanded. "Why are you here?"

I was so unnerved that it did not occur to me that those should have been my questions. Idiotically, I started to explain about hearing someone climbing on to the terrace. He cut me short.

"The owner of this apartment is in Makassar."

"I know. He lent it to me."

He swore, stared at me bitterly for a moment and then motioned to the two soldiers to stand back.

They retreated, awkwardly, as if they had been reprimanded. I was coming to my senses again now and realised that there was something unfamiliar about their uniforms. The trousers were of khaki drill, but it was not the same khaki that I had seen on other troops in the city. And both men were wearing a sort of yellow brassard on the left arm. So was Suparto.

"Are you alone?"

"No."

"Who is here with you?"

"A woman."

He moved past me swiftly to the bedroom door and went in.

Rosalie stood in the centre of the room. She was turning back the sleeves of my dressing gown. As she swung round to face him, her hands dropped to her sides, but she made no other movement.

"Your name?" he said.

"Rosalie Linden, *tuan*."

He turned the light in the bedroom on, then looked from one to the other of us.

"You can see we're both quite harmless, Major," I said.

"Possibly. But your presence is inconvenient. Are you armed?"

"There's a revolver in that case under the bed."

He looked at Rosalie. "Pull the case out. Do not open it."

As she obeyed, he called in the N.C.O. and told him to take the revolver. Then he looked at me, his lips tightening.

"Armed men enter your apartment in the middle of the night and steal your property. Yet, you say nothing, you make no protest. Why, Mr. Fraser?"

"The men are wearing uniforms and this is Selampang, not London."

"You do not even ask questions?"

"That would be a bit pointless, wouldn't it?"

"Because you think that you already know the answers?"

I knew that it was dangerous to go on pretending to be stupid. I shrugged. "Less than forty-eight hours ago you were in Tangga, Major. You didn't come here by sea or air and those men outside are not Government troops. I presume then that they are General Sanusi's, that you are in sympathy with his aims, and that the long-awaited day has arrived. No doubt you've taken over the radio station below and will shortly begin broadcasting the good news to the rest of the country. Meanwhile, other troops are occupying the central telegraph office, the telephone exchange, the power station and the railroad station. The main body of your forces is taking up positions surrounding the police barracks, the ammunition dump, the forts defending the outer harbour and the garrison . . ." I hesitated. I had remembered something.

"Yes, Mr. Fraser?" His face was very still.

"Most of the garrison moved out today on manoeuvres."

"The moment, of course, has been carefully chosen."

"Of course. However, I'm a foreigner, and it's no concern of mine. Now that you've satisfied yourself that there is nobody up here who could possibly do anything to interfere, I take it that you will allow us to go back to sleep again."

He considered me coldly. "I like you, Mr. Fraser," he said at length; "and I am sorry to see you here. At the moment, however, I am wondering if I have a sufficient excuse for allowing you to remain alive."

"You need an excuse? We're no danger to you, for God's sake!"

"As I have said, your presence is inconvenient."

"Then let us go somewhere else."

"I regret that that is impossible."

I said nothing and looked across at Rosalie. She was still standing by the open suitcase. I went over to her, put my arm round her shoulders and made her sit down on the edge of the bed.

Suparto seemed to hesitate; then he beckoned impatiently to the N.C.O. and nodded in our direction.

"These two persons," he said, "will remain in this room. Post a sentry on the terrace. They may go one at a time to the bathhouse, but they will go by the window. This door will remain locked. If either attempts to leave without permission, they are both to be killed."

The N.C.O. saluted and eyed us sullenly.

Suparto looked at me. "You understood what I said?"

"Yes, I understood. May I ask a question?"

"Well?"

"Was I right? Is this part of a *coup d'état*?"

"The National Freedom Party of Sunda has taken over all the functions of government and assumed control of the country."

"That is what I meant."

"The so-called Democratic Government of the colonialist traitor, Nasjah, has proved unworthy of the people's confidence." He was speaking Malay now, and as if he were addressing a public meeting. Behind him, the N.C.O. nodded approvingly. "The guilty will be punished. The Unbelievers will be destroyed. Colonial influences will be eliminated. The Faithful will rally to the standard of Islam. As soon as the emergency is over, elections will be held. But order must be maintained. Hostile elements will be wiped out ruthlessly."

"Do we count as hostile elements?"

"It might be thought so." He lapsed into English again. "At present the decision is my responsibility. Later, it may be different. My superior officers, who will arrive here shortly, are sensitive men and the presence of Unbelievers at such a time may not be tolerated. In your own interests, I would advise you to be as silent and unobtrusive as possible."

"I see. Thank you, Major."

"I can promise you nothing."

With a nod he turned and went out of the room. The N.C.O. shut the door and the key turned in the lock. A moment later a soldier appeared on the terrace outside the window, peered in and then sat down with his back against the *attap* screen and his machine pistol cradled in his lap.

I looked down at Rosalie and she smiled uncertainly.

"Why does he like you?"

"I don't know that he really does. He has no special reason that I know of. That is the officer who was up at Tangga, the one with the jeep."

"Oh. Perhaps if you explained how discreet you had been, he would let us go."

"I don't think so. We know too much."

"What do we know?"

"That this is their headquarters. He spoke of other officers who will arrive. That'll be General Sanusi and his staff, I suppose. They knew Jebb was away. Having ear-marked this place for their headquarters, they may even have arranged that he should be. It's logical enough. There aren't many buildings in the city as strong as this one, and Sanusi would naturally want to be near the radio station. He'll be using it quite a bit, I imagine."

"Do you think that they will kill us?"

"I don't know."

"I think they will." Her tone was quite even and matter-of-fact.

"Why should you think that?"

"They kill very easily. During the war of liberation I saw them. Men like that major. They smile and then they kill. For them it is easier to kill than to have doubts, to be uncertain."

She stood up and then went over and switched off the light. Outside on the terrace, the sentry turned his head quickly. Rosalie crossed to the window and drew one of the curtains so that the man could see only half the room. He stirred, and I moved across to watch him. He was waiting to see if the other curtain would also be drawn. When it was not, he relaxed.

Rosalie had taken off my dressing gown and dropped it on the chair. The strong moonlight was visible even through the curtains, and I could see her standing there running her hands over her body as if she had never touched it before. Then she realised that I was watching her and laughed softly.

"I saw the men with the *parangs*," she said; "and I knew that if they killed you, they would also kill me, because they would not have been able to stop. So, I was ready to die. Now, I am alive again."

I went over to her. I think I meant to make some futile apology for having brought her there, but instead I kissed her.

From far away across the city there came a sudden rattle of machine-gun fire. The sentry got up and went to look out over the parapet. We stood behind the curtain, listening. There were several more bursts of fire and one or two small explosions that might have been from mortars. After about ten minutes, the firing ceased and there was an uncanny silence. It was broken by a murmur of voices from the square below, and a series of crashes as the windows of the Air Terminal offices were knocked out. I guessed that the ground floor was being fortified against a counter-attack. Once, a truck whined and clattered along on the other side of the square, but otherwise the streets seemed to be deserted. A little before five, there was a glow in the sky from a fire which Rosalie thought might be in the neighbourhood of the police barracks, and, soon after, a single explosion just heavy enough to make the windows vibrate. It could have been a small demolition charge of some kind.

When the first bout of firing had ceased, we had feverishly hurried into our clothes, as if we had overslept and were late for an appointment. There was, I suppose, a logical need for haste; Suparto had warned us to expect further visitors; but I think that the true reason was less rational. Until that moment, what we had been facing had been like a nightmare; terrifying, yet also unreal. The sound of firing had sharply disposed of the unreality, and we were left with our fears. Our scramble for our clothes was a scramble for cover of a different sort. We wanted to feel safer. In fact, we only felt hotter. After a time, we sat on one of the beds, and smoked and listened and sweated and suffered the twin ills that afflict everyone who finds himself on a battlefield: the knot of fear in the stomach, and the desperate desire to know what is really going on.

Thanks, no doubt, to the treachery of Suparto and others like him, Sanusi's army had been able to make its approach march in secrecy, and to mount an attack at a moment when the capital was almost unguarded. Surprise having been achieved, it seemed unlikely that General Sanusi would have much difficulty in the early stages. Nothing we had heard so far suggested that he had encountered anything more than token resistance, and very little of that. Probably, he was already in complete control. The testing time for him would come when the Government forces counter-attacked; *if* they counter-attacked, that is; if there were not too many Supartos in their ranks.

I remembered the snatch of conversation I had overheard in the garden of the New Harmony Club. "We must have all," the General had said. "Then it must be delayed until the second day," had been Suparto's reply. All what? Reinforcements? Arms? Hostages? And what was it that had to be delayed? A movement of troops? The assassination of the President? The offer of an amnesty? I worried at the questions as if the answer really mattered. It was more agreeable to do that, than to reflect that what was going to happen on the second day was possibly of only theoretical interest to Rosalie and me.

It was nearly six o'clock when the sky lightened and then flushed with the sudden glow of the equatorial dawn. For the past half-hour there had been sounds of activity from the square below. Several cars had driven up and there had been sharp words of command. There had been a murmur of voices from the next room also. It had been difficult to distinguish what was said. We heard some isolated phrases: ". . . medical service . . . damage to installations . . . rice distribution . . . police situation . . . guns fire out to sea . . . transport arrangements . . . hour of curfew . . ." And then someone switched Jebb's radio on.

For several minutes there was only the crackling of static. The set was near the open living-room window and we could hear it plainly. Then, as the station carrier wave started up, the static faded and presently the usual *Soeara Sunda* recognition signal, five notes played on the bamboo xylophone, came on. Rosalie seemed to find the sound reassuring. I did not.

Whether the insurgents had forcibly rounded up the engineers and were now standing over them below with guns, or whether they were relying on sympathisers among the technical personnel was immaterial. The fact that they already had the station on the air was an impressive demonstration of efficient staff-work. If their other arrangements were working as smoothly, the possibility of an early change in the situation was remote. I wondered what had happened to Nasjah and his followers. Had they managed to get away, or had they been taken by surprise and hacked to pieces in their homes?

At six thirty the xylophone sound ceased and a man's voice gave the station identification. This was followed by the announcement, repeated three times, of an important government statement and a request to stand by. At six forty-five the same voice read out the statement.

It began with a recital of the "crimes" committed by the Nasjah Government, and then went on to say that, in order to save the nation from the colonialist vultures gathering over its helpless body, the People's National Freedom Party had taken over the functions of government. The Nasjah gang had run away. Insignificant bands of their adherents, incited by foreign agents, might make isolated attempts to resist the authority of the new government; but these would quickly be eliminated. In the capital, order had been restored and all was calm. However, as a precaution against reactionary elements and to protect life and property, certain temporary security measures had been ordered by General Sanusi, head of the People's National Freedom Party.

There followed a list of ordinances, amounting in effect to a declaration of martial law, and an intimidating series of instructions to provincial mayors. It was stated finally that, within the next few hours, General Sanusi would himself broadcast a message of hope and encouragement to the loyal people of Sunda from his secret headquarters. Meanwhile, they should stay quietly in their houses. Groups of more than three persons assembling in the streets would be treated as hostile and dealt with accordingly. Admittedly, this was harsh, but if the people were to be protected against the Godless forces of reaction, harshness was necessary. All loyal, right-thinking men would understand the necessity. Through discipline the way lay open to freedom.

The voice stopped. A few seconds later the recognition signal began again.

The sunlight was pouring on to the terrace now. At that time yesterday I had lain half-awake on the spare bed in the living room, trying to ignore the sounds of traffic coming up from the square below. Today, there was scarcely a sound. Now and again a vehicle drove up to the Air Terminal entrance, but apart from that the square was silent. Like a wary animal, the whole city seemed to have gone to ground. Six floors down, in the roadway, a soldier hawked and spat, and the noise interested the soldier on the terrace sufficiently to make him look down over the balustrade.

"Freedom!" said Rosalie sharply. She used the Sundanese word "*merkeda*" and made it sound like a curse.

She was sitting in the chair behind the drawn curtain, the sunlight casting the pattern of the material across her face. I could not see her eyes, but her hands were gripping the arms of the chair tightly and her whole body was tense.

I shrugged. "All political parties use that word." I paused, then added: "Why don't you lie down and try to get some rest?"

She did not answer, and after a moment or two I went over and put my hand on her shoulder. As I touched her, she sobbed and began to cry helplessly. I put my arm round her and waited. When I felt that the worst of it was over, I led her to the bed and made her lie down. Then, I went back to the chair, took my shirt off and wondered what it was she did not like about freedom. In the next room the recognition signal stopped again and the voice began to repeat the earlier announcement.

I was quite sure that she had gone to sleep, but, as the announcement ended, I heard her sigh and looked over at her.

She was watching me.

"There is something I wish to say," she said.

"Go to sleep. You will feel better."

She shook her head. "It is about my father. I did not tell you the truth. I said that he died in a Japanese prison camp. That is not true."

"Is he alive then?"

"No. He died, but not in that way."

I waited.

For a moment or so she stared at the ceiling, then she went on. "My father was in a camp in Siam. When he came back, we went outside the city to a small place where my father owned a plot of land. We thought that for us it would be safer where there were other Eurasian families, because of the way the *pemoedas* hated us."

"*Pemoedas?*"

"That is what we called the young soldiers of the liberation army. Anyone who was not Sundanese they wanted to kill. When the Amboina troops left, there was nothing to stop them. Even the police were afraid of them, or perhaps they did not care."

She paused, and then went on slowly. "One day, a lot of them came in trucks. They had guns, and they made everyone in the village leave their houses and stand in the square while they searched the houses. They said that they were looking for hidden arms, but they were really looting. They took everything of value that there was and put it in the trucks. Then, one of them saw my father. Some of the other men in the village had made him stand among them so that he would not be noticed, but this *pemoeda* saw him and shouted to the others that he had found a Dutchman. The others came running up. Some of them were boys of fifteen or sixteen." She drew a deep breath. "They took my father, and tied him by the wrists to a hook at the back of one of the trucks. They said that he should stay there until there was nothing left of him but his hands. Then they drove the truck fast up and down the road and round the square in front of us. And while my father was battered to death, the *pemoedas* clapped and laughed and ran along behind the truck shouting 'Merkeda! Merkeda!' "

She stopped, still staring up at the ceiling.

"Why did you say that he'd died in a prison camp?" I asked.

"That is something that everybody understands. Sometimes I almost believe it myself. It is easier to think of."

Her eyes closed. When I went over to her a few minutes later I saw that this time she was really asleep. The voice on the radio in the next room finished the second reading of the announcement and the bamboo xylophone began again.

I needed to go to the bathhouse. I picked up a towel, went to the window and snapped my fingers. The sentry turned quickly and raised his gun.

I explained what I wanted. He said something that I did not catch; but he nodded, too, so I went along the terrace. I had left my shaving things in the bathhouse, and by the time I had finished there, I felt less depressed. I have always sympathised with those legendary Empire-builders who changed for dinner in the jungle. When I came out, I did something which I would not have done when I had gone in. Although the sentry was watching me, I walked over to the balustrade of the terrace and looked down into the square.

There were even more troops there than I had imagined; over a hundred, I thought, split up into squads of about a dozen. Rough barricades had been erected at the four entrances to the square, and the squads manning them either sat on the ground smoking or lounged in nearby doorways. Between the trees on the edge of the gardens, four machine guns had been set up covering the approaches, and parked in the centre under tarpaulins were two anti-tank guns. They looked like old British two-pounders. I had always been given to understand that Sanusi's army had no artillery of any description. Possibly two-pounders had not been reckoned as artillery; possibly the situation had changed.

The sentry was fidgeting, so I went back to the bedroom, bowing to him politely on the way.

Rosalie was still asleep. I got out some new slacks and a clean shirt and changed into them. Then, I considered another matter.

I had taken a bottle of water into the room the previous night, but most of it was now gone; and the water from the bathhouse main could not safely be drunk without boiling it first. There were bottles of drinking-water in the refrigerator; but that was in the kitchen and therefore inaccessible. And there was the matter of food. With some people fear creates a craving for food; but with most, I think, it has the opposite effect. It has with me. But I knew that, if we survived the next few hours, a moment would come when food would become really necessary. I also knew that when the men murmuring in the next room grew hungry, they would soon eat what was in the refrigerator. It would be as well to see if I could appropriate a little of it, some fruit and eggs, perhaps, before that happened.

I went to the window, beckoned the sentry over and explained what I wanted. He stared back at me resentfully. I had begun to repeat my request when, without a change of expression, he suddenly drove the muzzle of the gun he was holding straight into my stomach.

I staggered back, doubled up with pain; then one of my feet slipped on the polished wood floor of the room, and I fell forward on my knees, retching helplessly. The sentry began to shout at me. The noise woke Rosalie. She saw the sentry standing over me with his gun raised, and cried out. That brought the men in the next room out on to the terrace.

There were two of them, both officers. While I struggled to get my breath, I was dimly aware of the sentry's voice telling them what Suparto's orders had been. As Rosalie helped me up, one of them came into the room.

He was a squat, bow-legged, dark-complexioned man with a jagged wound scar on his neck. He looked down at me angrily.

"It is ordered you stay here," he said.

I managed to find the breath to answer. "I only asked if I might get some food and drinking-water from the kitchen."

"If you attempt to escape you will be shot."

"I wasn't attempting . . ." I did not trouble to finish the sentence. I could see by his eyes now that he had not understood what I had said. If I translated it into Malay, he would know that I knew, and therefore lose face. It was better to keep quiet.

He still glowered at us though, waiting for the next move.

"The soldier did not understand," I said carefully.

He hesitated. He had got that all right and was now fumbling among his English sentences for a suitable reply. I felt Rosalie stir and gripped her arm to stop her from speaking. At last, he shrugged.

"It is ordered you stay here," he repeated, and went out on to the terrace.

"What really happened?" Rosalie asked.

I told her. She made no comment, but I could see that she thought I had been stupid. I knew it myself, now. Because I had been able to bathe and shave, because the sentry had not prevented my going to the balustrade to look down into the square, because I had been able to change into clean clothes and feel for a few minutes like a rational European, I had made the mistake of behaving like one. As a result, I had a bad pain in the stomach; worse, I had reminded the men in the other room of our existence, which was what Suparto had expressly warned me not to do.

"We can't go without water," I said defensively.

"We have water. There is still some in the bottle."

"That won't last long."

"I am not thirsty now."

"But you will be later. And hungry, too."

"Perhaps."

"Well, there you are."

"We shall not die of thirst or hunger," she said.

I had no answer for that. She was not being ironical. She was merely expressing a Sundanese point of view. In lush Sunda nobody dies of thirst or hunger; only of disease or violence. There is no winter for which to prepare, no drought to fear. The harvests are not seasonal as we understand the term. Tread a seed into the warm, rich earth and shortly you will have a tree heavy with fruit. Survival is achieved not by taking thought for the future, but by manipulating as best one can the immediate present. By thinking like a European, by anticipating bodily needs instead of waiting passively for them to present themselves, I had modified unfavourably the present situation of the bodies in question.

I sat on the edge of the bed and looked down at the smear of black grease that the gun had left on my shirt. Rosalie had moved away. Now she returned and sat down beside me. She had a box of Kleenex and a can of lighter fluid that Jebb had left on the dressing table. She began to wipe off the grease.

"It seemed a reasonable thing to do," I said.

"These are not reasonable people."

"I know that now."

"Why do you think that I told you about the *pemoedas* who killed my father? I know these people. Mostly they are quiet and gentle. In the kampongs you will see a boy of twelve run to his mother and suck her breast when he is frightened or hurt. They smile a lot and laugh and seem happy, though they are also sad and afraid. But some are like those madmen nobody knows about, who have devils inside them waiting. And when there are guns to fire and people to kill, the devils come out. I have seen it."

"Do you think that Major Suparto has a devil?"

"Perhaps. But he does not wish to kill you. I do not know why. But his advice was good. If they do not see you or hear you, they do not think of you, and you are safe."

I said nothing. In the silence, the sound of the radio xylophone in the next room became distinct again. The five notes were in the form of a scale. *Doh-ray-me-soh-lah.* What was the name of it? The pentatonic? Ah yes. If only they would play it descending for a change; or play the Japanese National Anthem; that used the same scale. After all, it was the Japanese who had originated the signal.

It ceased abruptly. I waited for the announcement to begin again. There was a long silence. The men in the next room were no longer talking. The sentry was staring at the living-room door. Then, there was the hiss of a disc recording surface and a rendering of the Sunda battle song. This was different from the Republican National Anthem, which was a westernised song, composed, it was said, by the Dutch saxophone-player who led the Orient Hotel orchestra. The battle song was chanted by male voices to the accompaniment of drums, many small cymbals and one cumbersome string instrument that was twanged like a zither. Gedge, who was interested in such matters, said that the battle song was not really native to Sunda, but had been imported from the Spice Islands. However, in Sunda it was supposed to evoke memories of the old warrior sultans and the early struggles against the colonial powers. The reason it had not been used as a national anthem was that, even to the most sympathetic western ears, it had no identifiable melody, and a national anthem that could only be played in Sunda would, it had been felt, cause the Republic's representatives abroad to lose face.

The noise went on for three or four minutes. During it, I glanced at the sentry on the terrace. The battle song did not seem to have evoked any patriotic emotions in him; he was busy lighting a twig-like cheroot. When the music stopped, however, he looked up expectantly.

The announcer came on and gave the station identification twice. There was another pause, then another man began to speak. He announced himself as Colonel Roda, Secretary of the National Freedom Party and new Minister of Internal Security. Shortly, he said, we would hear the voice of the new Head of the State. General Sanusi, he went on, was a great patriot, a true son of Islam, who had fought against the colonial usurpers in the name of the Republic, believing that by doing so his country would be made free to follow its destiny as a political unit, and at the same time conform to the forty-two precepts of An-Nawawi. So, he had attempted to serve the Republic. But evil men had made it impossible to serve as Allah had commanded that a man should serve, with his whole heart. Questions had arisen in his mind. He had taken to his heart the first precept, which stated that actions are to be judged only in accordance with intentions. The intentions had been plainly bad. Therefore the actions were bad. He had gone further. He had examined the men at the heart of the Republic with eyes unclouded by alcohol. He had turned to An-Nawawi again for guidance and there, in the sixth precept, had been the knowledge he had sought. "Is it not a fact," the holy man had written, "that there is in the body a clot of blood, and that if it be in good condition, the whole body is also?" Certainly! And was it not also written that if the clot of blood be in a rotten condition, so also was the whole body? Was not that clot of blood the very heart? Indeed, yes. Therefore, the heart must be purified. With other True Believers he had taken to the hills to prepare for the act of purification that had now been accomplished. As a result, a new era of peace, discipline and happiness had come to Sunda. Let all offer prayers for the author of this good fortune, *Boeng* General Kamarudin ben Sanusi.

There was a brief pause, a moment of rapid whispering, and then Sanusi began to speak.

He had a soft, pleasant voice which he used slowly and deliberately, as if he were none too sure of the intelligence of his audience.

He began by recalling the high hopes with which the Republic had been founded, and went on to describe the way in which the Nasjah Government had falsified those hopes. Power without Godliness had led to corruption. Corruption had led to the breakdown of the democratic machinery set up by the Constitution. Unconstitutional action had become necessary if the country were not to fall into anarchy, and become dominated, either by more powerful neighbours, or by the forces of colonialism which still threatened all the young nations of South-East Asia. And when the safety of the Republic was threatened, there was no time for legal quibbling. If your brother's house caught fire while he was working in the fields, you did not wait until he returned so that you could ask his permission before you poured water on the flames. If a hungry leopard came looking for food in your village, you did not call a council meeting to discuss what should be done.

And so on. It was, in effect, the speech of every military dictator who seizes political power by force of arms, and seeks to justify himself.

He went on to proclaim the suspension of the authority of parliament (until such time as it was considered advisable to order new elections) and the establishment of a new People's Army of Security (*Tentara Keamanan Ra'jat*), recruiting for which would begin immediately. All young men should offer their services. A delegation of the National Freedom Government was already in New York awaiting orders. Today it would be ordered to request recognition of the new Government from the United Nations. Prompt recognition would be sought also from friendly Indonesia, and from the other powers represented at the Afro-Asian Conference at Bandung.

Finally, there were the carefully worded threats. The transfer of power which had taken place had been swift and complete. Inevitably, however, a few small areas remained in which, through lack of efficient communications, control was not yet fully established. Inhabitants of such areas were cautioned against giving aid to disaffected political elements, or to troops still bearing arms against the newly constituted Government of National Freedom. Reprisals would be taken against villages committing such offences against the new military ordinances, and collective fines would be imposed. All troops and police were required to signify their adherence to the new Government forthwith. Failure to do so would be interpreted as a hostile act. Terms of a political amnesty would shortly be announced, but no mercy would be shown to those whose loyalty was suspect. He concluded: "The killing of a True Believer is not lawful but for one of three reasons: that he is an adulterer, an avenger of blood, or because he offends against religion by splitting the community. Remember that. But if a man shows himself faithful, then, so far as I am concerned, his life and property will be protected. His only account will be with Allah Ta'ala. Long live our glorious country!"

The battle song was played again. The men in the next room began talking excitedly. I looked at the time. It was eight o'clock. Less than twenty-four hours earlier I had been told that Sanusi was a man who did not like to take chances. Now he was the head of the state. I wondered what sort of man he really was.

There was one thing I did know. The voice of Sanusi was not the voice of the General I had heard talking to Suparto in the garden of the New Harmony Club two nights ago.

CHAPTER V

TEN MINUTES AFTER THE END of the speech there was a stir in the next room and talk ceased. In the quiet that followed, I heard Suparto's voice out in the corridor. Then, there were footsteps and the door of the apartment closed. A moment or two later, Suparto and two other men walked out of the living room on to the terrace.

I had never seen a picture of Sanusi, but he had been described to me once and it was not hard to recognise him. In a country where maturity is reached early and the average expectation of life is low, a man of forty-eight is almost elderly and generally looks it. Sanusi did not. The close-cropped hair showing beneath his black cap was grey and his cheeks were cadaverous, but his body was lean and muscular and he moved with an alert grace that was anything but elderly. His companion, whom I took to be the sanctimonious Colonel Roda, was plump by comparison and had long black hair bulging from under his cap. I could not see his face. His uniform shirt was soaked with sweat and he was carrying a leather document case.

Suparto followed them over to the balustrade, and waited while they looked out over the city. Sanusi was smoking a cheroot, and after a moment or two he pointed with it down into the square and said something which I did not hear. There was no hint of triumph in his attitude, no suggestion that he found it pleasant to contemplate the city he had conquered; he was simply a military commander casting an eye over his defences.

Rosalie was getting worried by my standing so near to the window. The sentry could not see me because I was hidden from him by the one drawn curtain, but she was afraid that if the men further along were to turn round suddenly, I should be seen watching them. I knew that she was right and moved away.

It was as well that I did so, for almost immediately they began to move along the terrace in our direction. I saw the shadow of the sentry move as he straightened up.

"An ultimatum," Roda was saying; "surrender of the forts within an hour on reasonable terms or total destruction. Surely, *Boeng . . .*"

"No." It was Sanusi's voice and, as he spoke, the footsteps ceased. "They will surrender anyway when they are hungry enough. But if you offer them terms now and they refuse, you will have to attack. We shall certainly lose men and I cannot spare them. In any case, it does not trouble me. A few stupid gunners shut up in forts with guns they cannot point at us. Let them stay there until they starve. What is important is to find out what we have to expect from the enemy at Meja. Which way are they moving? Which of their units can we be sure of? These are the uncertainties I do not like."

They began to move towards us again.

"We know the units loyal to you, *Boeng*." This was Suparto.

"We know those who promised loyalty, but how many will commit themselves to us before the result is certain?"

"All," said Roda.

"If we had only one plane for reconnaissance . . ." Sanusi began and then broke off. He was level with the bedroom window now and had seen the sentry. "Why is this man here? We do not need him."

I took Rosalie's hand.

"He is guarding two prisoners, *Boeng*," said Suparto evenly. "They were in the apartment when it was requisitioned for your use."

"Prisoners? Are they hostile?"

"No, *Boeng*. But it would be unwise to release them yet. Your whereabouts must remain secret at present."

"That is true," said Roda. "There must be no failure of security. That is Suparto's responsibility. The enemy would be glad to talk to such people."

"Who are they?"

"One is an Englishman. He has been the consulting engineer up at the Tangga River dam. He is a good technician and an employee of the Colombo Authority. I thought that you would wish him to be treated with consideration."

"You said two prisoners," put in Roda.

"The other is a woman, an Indo"—he used the slang term for Eurasian —"from the New Harmony Club."

There was a silence. Rosalie's hand lay absolutely still in mine.

"The apartment," Suparto continued, "is owned by an Australian pilot. He had lent it to the Englishman. Admittedly, it is a disagreeable situation."

"They should have been handed over to the troops for disposal," Roda said irritably. "If . . ." He paused.

In the next room the telephone had begun to ring. One of the men there answered it. The call was for the General.

Sanusi turned away to go into the living room. "The matter is unimportant," he said; "it can be considered later."

A moment or two after, we heard him curtly answering the telephone. I looked at Rosalie. Her whole body was rigid.

"You see, now," she whispered; "I am the danger to you."

"Nonsense."

"It is always the same when there is trouble. There must be someone to blame, someone to hate. The Chinese are too powerful and would combine together. But nobody cares about the Indos because we are weak. Besides, I am here with you. That will make them want to kill. They will say that I have made this place unclean, and there will be a pleasure for them in the killing."

I managed to smile. "Oh now, wait a minute. I don't think it's as bad as that. What you say might be true of some of them, but Sanusi's not a savage."

"A good Moslem does not speak as he does."

"I wouldn't know. He sounds reasonable."

"And Colonel Roda?"

"I expect he does what he's told. And you heard Suparto. He doesn't want us harmed. In any case, they're all going to have far too much to do to trouble about us. They may not even stay here. This is only a tactical headquarters. If things go on as they're going now, Sanusi'll soon be moving into the Presidential Palace. We'll be able to laugh at all this."

"You are very kind to me."

"Kind?"

"You know very well that if I were not here there would be no great danger for you."

It was she who was smiling now, faintly, as she watched my face. I got up impatiently and lit one of my dwindling supply of cigarettes, but I knew that she was not deceived. Neither was I. I had heard the change in their voices when Suparto had told them about her. For these men, with their desperate pride of race and hatred of Europeans, she already stood for treachery; and the fact that she was there with me made the iniquity of her existence doubly obscene. To kill us both might seem like an act of purification. Everything depended, really, on how necessary such an act might become to them. And that in turn depended on events. I had been right, I felt, about one thing. If things went well, Sanusi would be quick to install himself in more becoming surroundings. We would be forgotten. What we had to fear was a set-back to their plans.

I went as near as I dared to the open window. Sanusi was still on the telephone. Occasionally he would ask a question. "How many?" "Who is in command?" Evidently, he was receiving a report. Probably, it concerned the dispositions of the "enemy's" forces about which he had expressed so much uneasiness. I thought again of De Vries and his assertion that Sanusi was reluctant to take chances. There might have been something in that after all. Was it Colonel Roda who had tipped the scales in favour of the move? Or Suparto?

The telephone in the next room tinkled as Sanusi hung up. At the same moment, I became aware of a faint throbbing sound. For a moment, I thought that it was something to do with the radio station below. Suddenly, the sentry outside shouted: "*Kapal terbang!*"

The men in the next room hurried out on to the terrace. I could hear the planes clearly now, and it sounded as if there were several of them. There were shouts from the square below. Colonel Roda began pointing up into the sky.

I looked round. Rosalie was sitting passively on the edge of her bed. I blundered over to her, grabbed one of her arms and dragged her down with me on to the floor.

From where I was lying, I could see through the open window on to the terrace. There was nobody standing there now. Then, I saw the planes. They were coming in over the north-west corner of the square; three old twin-engined American fighter-bombers, flying in a ragged line-abreast formation at about twenty-five hundred feet. As they roared overhead I could see extra bombs in the racks below the wings. The whole Republican Air Force, or, at least, all of it that could get off the ground, was out.

The bow-legged officer ran on to the terrace and gazed up after the planes. Rosalie started to get to her feet. I pressed her back on to the floor. It was possible that the Air Force was throwing in its lot with Sanusi, in which case the planes would be going in to land at the civil airport out by the racecourse; but it was also possible that they were not. The behaviour of the men on the terrace had not suggested that they were expecting such a welcome reinforcement. The low altitude and steady course of the planes might simply mean that their pilots knew that there were no ground defences for them to worry about, and that they had time to make their bombing runs carefully. If there were going to be any bombing, of course; if this were not just a threatening gesture.

A moment or two later, I knew that it was not. The sound of the engines which had almost died away was beginning to get louder again, and the bow-legged officer hastily retreated into the living room.

After Sanusi's broadcast, I suppose it was inevitable that the Government would make some attempt to put the radio station out of action; but when it came, the attempt was still a very unpleasant shock. In war it is relatively easy to be philosophical about being bombed or shelled indiscriminately; but when you become, or the building you are in becomes, a selected target for enemy fire, things are different. It is not just that the degree of danger has changed; quite often it hasn't; but that the affair is no longer impersonal. From being a man like yourself, dutifully scattering high explosive where it seems likely to inflict the most casualties, the enemy has suddenly become a vindictive maniac intent on your personal destruction. You become resentful, and begin, most sensibly, to think of ways of killing him first. There is nothing more enraging than to have to stay where you are, a passive, stationary, impotent target, and let him take pot shots at you. That is what it was like at the top of the radio building.

They came in one after the other in line-ahead, and just high enough to avoid bomb blast from the ground. As I heard the first one beginning his run, I realised that there were big glass window panes two feet from our faces, and dragged a rug from the floor over our heads. At the same moment, someone down in the square opened up with a machine gun.

The sound of the plane became suddenly louder and there was a series of slithering noises as the bombs started to fall. Then, the explosions came. He must have let go everything he had, for the floor bucked and trembled for close on ten seconds. There was a pandemonium of falling plaster and breaking glass and then, as a sort of finale, a torrent of earth and stones poured down on to the terrace.

One of the bombs had fallen into the garden of the Ministry of Public Health next door, and the earth and stones were merely the falling débris of that explosion; but, of course, it sounded as if the building were collapsing. Rosalie cried out and there was a yell from the terrace. I flung back the rug and saw that the sentry was still at his post outside the window, crouching against the balustrade under the bamboo sun roof, which had collapsed. He had been hit by the roof when it fell, and was gingerly rubbing his shoulder. The curtains had been sucked out by the blast and were now caught up on the open window frame, but the glass was still intact and so was the ceiling. The blast damage was probably on the lower floors. Then I heard the second plane on its way, and dived under the rug again.

The first stick of bombs had straddled the Air House, and it was just as well that the pilot in question had no more bombs. He was too accurate. Next time, he might have scored a direct hit. The second stick was wide and ploughed along a street running parallel to our side of the square. It made a lot of noise and a few more windows went in the rear of the building; but, as far as we were concerned, that was all. It was the third plane that did the most damage to the sixth floor. Most of its bombs fell in the square, but one of them hit the portico of the Ministry of Public Health. We did not know that until later, however; at the time, it seemed like a direct hit on our own building. It was not a big bomb, but it exploded on a level with the second floor and most of the blast came our way. The floor heaved. Something hit me hard in the back. Then, there was a long, low rumbling and silence. I became aware of a thin, high singing in my ears.

My right arm was across Rosalie's shoulders and I could feel her trying to get up. I went to fling back the rug and found that there was a weight pressing on the top of it. That made me panic. I struggled to my knees and fought my way out of the rug. Suddenly, I choked, and then began coughing as I breathed in a cloud of plaster dust. I still could not hear properly, but I knew now what had hit me in the back. It was a large piece of the ceiling.

I dragged the rug off Rosalie and helped her to her feet. She was white with dust and coughing helplessly. I led her over to the bed, dragged a sheet of plaster off it and made her sit down. My ears were still painful, but the drums in them were beginning to function again. I could hear coughs and hoarse shouts coming from the next room. Through the cloud of dust, I saw that the windows had shattered and that the curtains were hanging in ribbons. I started to cough again, and, at the same moment, I heard the planes returning. Then, one of them opened up with his cannons and roared overhead.

I don't think Rosalie even heard it; in any case, she was too dazed to respond to the sound. I did nothing. I guessed that, finding their target still standing, they were trying to shoot up the radio masts. However, they had no ammunition that would penetrate the reinforced concrete roof over our heads; and, with most of the ceiling down and the windows gone, there was nothing more they could do to us.

They made six runs in all and, from what I heard, only managed to hit the roof twice. They were not very good at their jobs. Then, at last, having circled a couple of times to inspect the results of their work, they flew off.

The plaster had begun to settle now. I gave Rosalie a towel to wipe her face with, and then I went to the window.

The first thing I saw, lying on the terrace amid the broken glass, was the sentry's machine pistol. I peered through the tattered curtains looking for its owner.

He was sitting on the concrete with his head lolling between his knees, and blood pouring from a deep gash in his neck. I called to him sharply. He raised his head slightly and then sagged over on to his side.

I dragged a sheet off my bed, rummaged in my suitcase until I found a razor blade, and went out to him.

Something had hit him on the head, almost knocking him out; there was blood coming from just above his right ear. Probably, he had been flung against the balustrade by the blast. The cut in his neck, however, had been done when the windows flew to pieces. A piece of the glass was still sticking in the wound. Something had to be done about that. I cut through the hem of the sheet with the razor blade and then tore the material into strips. With one strip I made a pad. Then, as gently as I could, I eased the glass out of the wound. It bled a little more profusely, but not much more so. I clapped the pad over it, and then began to bandage it into place. He did not utter a sound. He scarcely moved. Once, when I pulled the glass out, he opened his eyes and looked at me, but he was no longer really interested in what was happening to him.

Feet crunched on the broken glass behind me, and I looked round.

The bow-legged officer was picking his way across the terrace towards me. He was covered from head to foot in plaster dust and there was blood trickling down his forehead.

"It is ordered you stay in," he said.

I went on with the bandaging. He went to the living room and called for two men. They came running out, and he told them to look after the sentry. They stood over me while I finished tying the bandage, but made no attempt to stop me.

When I stood up, they hauled him to his feet and helped him away. The officer picked up the gun.

"He has a head wound," I said. "He should have medical attention."

"You go in." He levelled the gun at me, but without very much conviction. He was a stupid man, and the fact that I had helped the sentry had evidently confused him. I decided to take advantage of the fact.

"It is still permitted to go to the bathhouse?" I asked.

He hesitated, then nodded.

I went into the bedroom and told Rosalie that she could go and wash the dust off. She was still shaken, but the prospect of a bath made her feel better. As she went along the terrace, I saw that the bow-legged officer was posting a new sentry. The dust had made me intolerably thirsty. While the officer was still there, I asked again for a bottle of drinking-water and some fruit. He seemed to take no notice; but a few minutes later, while I was trying to clear up the mess in the room, the sentry appeared at the window and put a bottle of water on the floor and a bowl of fruit beside it.

I thanked him. He grinned, shrugged, made a gesture of cutting someone's throat, and, with another grin, pointed to me. I grinned back and he went through the pantomime again. Then, he explained it in words. "Man's throat cut, man cannot eat, food fall out." A comedian, this one. I smiled until my jaw ached.

Rosalie, when she returned, was impressed. The fact that they had remembered my request meant, she said, that they were ashamed of their earlier behaviour, which meant in turn that they did not hate us too much. I did not tell her that I had asked again in order to get the fruit and water; nor did I tell her about the new sentry's little joke.

We ate half the fruit and drank a third of the water. I was still filthy from the plaster dust. When the rest of the fruit and water had been put away to keep cool, I got permission from the sentry to go along to the bathhouse and clean up. There, I found that the water supply was no longer working. It did not matter at that moment. The Dutch ewer was full and there was a further supply in the storage cistern on the roof, but I could hear that there was no more water coming in.

As I walked back along the terrace, I was surprised to see Rosalie at the window talking to the sentry. When he heard me coming, he smiled and moved away.

Rosalie's eyes were gleaming with excitement.

"Why did you not tell me that you helped the man who was wounded?" she began, as I went back into the room.

"It didn't seem important."

"It has made a very good impression. That man is his friend. He told me he would bring us more fruit later."

"You mean they've decided not to kill us after all?"

"Oh no, but now they do not hate us so much."

"That's something, I suppose."

"He told me that there are machine guns being mounted on both sides of the roof in case there is another air attack, also that the Nasjah army is advancing from the direction of Meja."

"How does he know that—I mean about the army?"

"He heard one of the officers on the telephone. It is curious," she went on thoughtfully; "before, that man would not have looked at us except to think how it would feel to kill us. Now, because you bandage his friend, it is different. He speaks to us and brings us fruit."

"That's because of the bombing, and because we were all covered in dust just as he was. He's not used to air attack. He was frightened, and now because he isn't dead he feels generous and friendly and wants to talk. It's nothing to do with my bandaging his friend. It always happens. Besides," I added, "you're a woman. That would make a difference, too."

She thought for a moment or two and then nodded. "Yes, I understand. It was the way I felt when the men with the *parangs* did not kill us last night. I wanted you to take me to bed at once. If it had not been for the guns beginning to fire and making me frightened in another way . . ."

I kissed her, and she smiled. "Was it like that in the war?" she said. "When you had been very frightened of being killed or wounded and were not, did you always want a woman afterwards?"

"Well, there wasn't much to be frightened of building airfields, and when we were in the desert there weren't any women to have."

"But you would want one?" she persisted.

"Oh yes. There was nothing to stop you wanting."

"Now you are making a joke of it. I think it is very good that people should feel that way."

"There's a simple biological explanation."

"Is it biology that I am here with you?"

"Well, not exactly."

"No. It is because it is good for a man and a woman to have pleasure together. If they are sympathetic, that is . . ."

"And if they aren't being threatened by men with *parangs*, and bombed, and peered at by sentries."

She looked startled, but did not turn her head. "He is watching us now?"

"With great interest."

Without once letting her eyes stray in his direction, she walked over to the window and looked up at the torn curtains. "If you will take these down," she said, "I will pin the pieces together. Then we can put them back again as we wish. If we do it now, he will think it is because of the sun. If we wait until the sun has moved, he will know that we do not wish to be seen and will be offended."

"All right."

It was a good idea in any case. The sentry had managed to hoist the bamboo roof back into position, but the blast and débris had split it in several places, and the sun was pouring through the gaps into the room. Every slight movement raised the dust again, and even the sight of it swirling about in the shafts of sunlight made me thirsty.

I made a great show of shielding my eyes from the glare as I unhooked the curtains. The sentry, squatting in one of the patches of shade, watched idly while Rosalie, with the few pins and a needle and thread that she had in her case, tacked the pieces of curtain together. When I put them up again, I was able to cover almost the whole of the window space.

Since the air attack, the telephone in the next room had been in constant use, but the voices had been those of the junior officers. I had concluded that Sanusi, Roda and Suparto had temporarily abandoned the sixth floor for some less exposed command post. When, as I finished rehanging the curtains, I heard footsteps crunching towards us over the broken glass on the terrace, I assumed that it was the bow-legged officer on his way to the bathhouse. Then, the footsteps ceased, the curtains were brushed aside and Major Suparto stepped into the room.

I saw Rosalie freeze into the passive immobility with which she had faced him before, but he did not even glance at her. He looked at the ceiling, at the débris piled in one corner of the room, finally at the curtains.

"Aren't these repairs a waste of time, Mr. Fraser?"

"I don't think so."

There was no trace of plaster dust on his uniform. I guessed that he had been in the corridor when the ceilings of the apartment had come down.

"The planes may be returning soon," he said.

"They will have to score a direct hit to do any more damage here. And I understand that you are putting machine guns on the roof. If they couldn't manage to hit the place before, they're not likely to do better when they're under fire."

"I hope you're right, Mr. Fraser. Now, I am sorry to disturb you, but you must come with me."

The knot in my stomach tightened. "Where to?"

"I will show you."

"Both of us?"

"Only you."

"Shall I be coming back here?"

"I am not taking you to be executed, if that is what you mean. If you behave intelligently it is possible that you will be sent back here. Now, please."

Rosalie had not moved. There was nothing I could do to reassure her. I pressed her arm and followed Suparto out on to the terrace. He turned into the living room.

The sentry stared blankly as I crunched past him.

The living room was in a wretched state. No attempt had been made to clear the rubble. Two pictures were lying on the floor. Some of the chairs had gone.

There were three officers there, one of them on the telephone. Suparto stopped and addressed himself to the bow-legged one.

"Nobody is to go into the next room unless this Englishman is there," he said. "Is that understood?"

"*Ya, tuan.*" He eyed me curiously.

Suparto nodded to me.

I followed him out into the passage, past a sentry and down the stairs to the next floor. There were two more sentries on guard at the swing doors. As Suparto approached they stood aside for him to pass.

The ceiling had come down in the corridor beyond, and some of the doors belonging to the offices leading off it were propped against the walls. Just beyond the main stairway landing, a group of officers stood outside an office door listening to a captain reading out orders for the requisitioning of rice. They made way for Suparto and I followed him through an office, where a man sat loading machine-gun magazines, to a door marked "TECHNICAL CONTROLLER." Suparto knocked on the door and went in.

There were three men in the room: Sanusi, Roda and a man in civilian clothes whom I recognised as the editor of a Selampang newspaper subsidised by the Nasjah Government. I had met him when he had visited Tangga with a party of other journalists; but if he now remembered me, the memory was inconvenient, for he gave me no more than a blank stare. Sanusi and Roda were reading a copy of a printed proclamation which was spread out on the desk. Suparto and I stood just inside the door, waiting. When the reading was finished, there was a muttered conference among the three men, and then the editor took the proclamation away. Sanusi looked at me.

"Mr. Fraser, *Boeng*." Suparto prodded me forward.

I went up to the desk. Sanusi examined me thoughtfully as I approached, but it was Colonel Roda, sitting at the corner of the desk, who spoke.

"You are an engineer?"

"Yes."

"At Tangga Valley?"

"I have been resident consulting engineer there for the past three years."

"Then you are a fully qualified and experienced person, no?"

I did not hear this properly for the first time. He spoke English with a Dutch accent, but it was his determination to be peremptory that made it difficult to understand. He had broad, fleshy lips, and the words rattled about in his mouth like pebbles.

"I beg your pardon, Colonel."

He repeated the question loudly and even less articulately, but this time I got the meaning.

"Yes, I am qualified."

"Then you will consider yourself under the orders of the National Freedom Government. Any delay or negligence in the carrying out of such orders will be punished immediately by death. Major Suparto . . ."

"A moment, Colonel." It was Sanusi who had spoken.

Colonel Roda stopped speaking instantly, his eyes alert and respectful within their nests of fat.

Sanusi considered me in silence for several seconds, then he smiled amiably. "Mr. Fraser is a European," he said; "and Europeans expect high payment for their services to natives. We must fix a good price."

Roda laughed shortly.

"Were you paid a good price in Tangga, Mr. Fraser?"

"Yes, General."

"And yet you hope to leave us?"

"A man must return to his own country sometimes."

"But what is a man's own country, Mr. Fraser? How does he recognise it?" He still smiled. "When I was a child here in Sunda and worked with my family in the fields, I did not know my country. If we were near a road and a Dutchman came by, or any European, my father and mother had to turn and bow respectfully to him. Us children, too. It was the Dutchman's law and, therefore, the Dutchman's country. Are you married, Mr. Fraser?"

"No, General."

"The woman with you. Is she a Christian?"

"I don't know, General."

"There are three fine Christian churches in Selampang. Did you know that?"

"Yes, I knew."

"And the Buddhist and Brahmin places of worship, they are also very fine. Have you seen them?"

"Yes."

"Tell me, where are the mosques?"

I hesitated. Roda laughed again.

"I will tell you," Sanusi continued; "one is by the cattle market, the other is by the Chinese fairground. They are small, decayed and filthy. They are insults to God."

He was probably right; but I could not see what it had to do with me.

"And yet President Nasjah wears the cap." He touched his own significantly. "And so do the members of his Government. Which mosque do they go to for prayer? The cattle market or the fairground? Or do they worship in the toilets of the Presidential Palace?"

I stood there, woodenly.

"They say they won our independence as a nation from the Dutch," he went on. "They lie. It was the Japanese forces who defeated the Dutch, and the forces of circumstance that gave us our independence. But the hands of Nasjah and his gang were there to receive it, and so they seemed to the people like great men. The people are loyal but misguided. We have no great men. Under the Dutch, no Sundanese was permitted to rise in the public service above the rank of third-grade clerk. So now we have an administration controlled by third-grade clerks, and a government of petty thieves and actors. We are corrupt, and only discipline can save us from the consequences. To you, to any European, that much is certainly obvious. But it will not come from outside. Not from China, not from America. It will come from what is already in us, our faith in Islam. Of that you may be sure. Meanwhile, we need help. That we must ask help from Europeans and Unbelievers is humbling to us, but we are not vain men."

There was a pause. Some comment seemed to be expected of me.

"What is it you wish me to do, General?"

"A trifling service. Major Suparto will explain."

"One of the bombs that fell in the square just outside damaged the main water conduit," said Suparto, evenly. "The lower basement of this building was flooded and the generator equipment which supplies the power for the radio transmitter has been put out of action. It is necessary that it should be repaired immediately."

"But I don't know anything about generators."

"You are an engineer," snapped Colonel Roda.

"But not an electrical engineer, Colonel."

"You are a technician? You have a university degree? And are there not generators at Tangga?"

"Yes, but . . ."

Sanusi raised his hand. "Mr. Fraser is a technician and also a man of resource. That is sufficient. For a suitable inducement he will lend us his skill. Yes, Mr. Fraser?"

"It's not a question of inducement, General."

"Ah, but it is." His smile faded. "This woman, Van der Linden, whose religion you do not know, does she please you?"

"I like her, yes."

"To us her presence is offensive," he said. "Perhaps, if you do what is required, you will persuade us to tolerate it."

"I've tried to explain, General. It's not a question of whether I want to help you, or don't want to. It's just that I don't happen to have the right kind of knowledge. There must be someone in this city better qualified to help you than I am."

"Coming from Tangga, you should know better than that, Mr. Fraser. Obviously, if there were a technician here better qualified to repair the damage, we should use him. But we have no one available, and work must begin at once. You must be ingenious. You must acquire the knowledge."

"With all due respect, General, you don't know what you're talking about."

Roda sprang to his feet with an angry exclamation, but I took no notice of him. "I'll see what I can do to help," I went on; "but, for goodness' sake, leave Miss Linden out of it."

Sanusi stared at me for a moment, then shrugged. "Certainly, if you wish. What is it you want instead?"

I did not immediately understand what he was getting at, but from behind me Suparto spoke quickly. "Mr. Fraser did not mean that, Boeng. If he is successful, he will hope that the woman's presence may be tolerated, as you suggest."

"Ah, good." Sanusi glanced at Roda. "For a moment, Colonel, I was afraid that what happened to his woman was of no interest to our engineer."

Roda chuckled. He had seen the joke coming.

Sanusi looked up at me. "We understand one another?"

"Yes, General."

"Then there is no more to be said." He nodded dismissal. "God go with you."

I went.

CHAPTER VI

SUPARTO LED THE WAY back to the stairway and we began to walk down.

"Was this your idea?" I demanded.

"No. It was the General's."

"Do you agree with it?"

"I am not in a position to agree or disagree. But I think he has had worse ideas."

I glanced at him, but he did not seem to be aware of having said anything odd.

"What's the extent of the damage?"

"That you will have to discover for yourself. There are two of the station engineers below. Perhaps they will be able to help you."

"Station engineers? Why can't they do the job themselves?"

"That is a polite way of describing them. They know how to operate the transmitter, which switches to press, which dials to turn, but they are not technicians. They know nothing about the generator except how to start it."

"But somebody on the staff must know."

"Possibly, but we have only certain members of the staff with us. The sympathisers."

"You're in control of the city. Can't you round up the others?"

"The three senior technicians are all Chinese. We have sent patrols into the Chinese quarter with instructions to find the men, and they may eventually succeed. But not today, and perhaps not tomorrow either. The General cannot wait."

"Why not? What's so important about the radio? I shouldn't have thought that there were very many people in the country with short-wave receivers."

"It is not the people inside the country who matter to the General. It is the impression outside that he is concerned about. Later today, he proposes to broadcast again in English. His speech will be addressed to the cities whose good opinion matters most to him at the moment: Djakarta, Singapore, Canberra and Washington. The speech, part of which you have already heard, will be issued to the world press correspondents here at a special conference afterwards."

"What do you mean, 'part of which I have already heard'?"

"Surely you did not believe that so much eloquence could be unrehearsed? 'To you, to any European, that much is certainly obvious.' Come now, Mr. Fraser, admit it. You must at least have wondered."

He was smiling slyly at me. It was an invitation to share a joke and I distrusted it deeply.

I said non-committally: "I had other things to wonder about."

"Ah yes. But you see why it is so important that the station should be working properly. If the General does not speak to the world, the world may think that he cannot speak, that he is not yet really in control and that they had better withhold their gestures of friendship until they see more clearly who has won. The General attaches great importance to the power of radio propaganda. He believes that it can be of decisive political importance." There was a distinctly critical note in his voice.

I said: "And you do not?"

"I think that the realities of power are important, too."

"You make the General sound a bit naïve."

"Not naïve, Mr. Fraser. Simple, like all great men."

We had been picking our way down the rubble-strewn stairs. Now we were at the ground floor. In the hall there were troops stacking rice sacks half-filled with earth to make a blast screen. The elevator gates were open and a man's body in a police uniform lay across the threshold in a mess of congealed blood. I caught a glimpse of his face as we came down the stairs. It had been one of the guards who had passed Rosalie and me into the building the previous night.

Suparto stopped and shouted for the N.C.O. in charge of the sand-bagging. The man came running and Suparto told him to have the body taken outside. As the man went off to carry out the order, Suparto looked after him unpleasantly.

"They are animals," he said.

We started down the stairs to the basement. From below there came a sound of voices and a smell of fuel oil and drains. On the landing half-way down, I stopped.

"May I ask you a question, Major?" I said.

His face became impassive. "About what, Mr. Fraser?"

"Last night you were good enough to say that you liked me. I have been wondering why."

His face cleared. "Ah, I see. You wish to assess the value of my friend-ship, the extent to which it might be relied upon and used. Well, I will explain. You remember the day I arrived in Tangga with my colleagues?"

"Very well."

"We were stiff-necked, presumptuous, and arrogant. I most of all, be-cause I did the talking. There were reasons, but"—he shrugged—"we will not discuss them now. You had reason to be annoyed, and you *were* annoyed with me, were you not?"

"A bit."

"You made it plain. But it was the way in which you made it plain that impressed me. You did not say to yourself: 'Here is another of these tiresome little brown men, these pathetic little upstarts in uniform, whom I must pretend to treat respectfully in order to show that I do not think of him as an inferior human being.' You did not patronise, as Mr. Gedge does, and you were not more tactful than was necessary. You dealt with me frankly as you would have dealt with a European in the same circumstances, and there was no calculation in your attitude. You treated me neither as a dog, nor as a pet monkey who may bite. And so I liked you."

"Oh. Well, that's very civil of you. But it wasn't to assess the value of your friendship, as you put it, that I brought the matter up. What I wanted to know was if you would trust me."

"With what, Mr. Fraser?"

"A confidence. Which side are you really on, Major? The National Freedom Party's or the Government's?"

"Naturally, Mr. Fraser, I am on the side of the General. How could you doubt it?" He smiled easily.

"I don't, Major. But which General do you mean?"

For once, I saw him disconcerted; but it was a short-lived pleasure. His lips narrowed and his hand went to his gun.

"You will explain that remark," he said softly.

"Certainly. I was in the garden of the Harmony Club two nights ago. I saw your jeep. I knew it came from Tangga. I knew it could only have come by road, so . . ."

"How much did you hear?" he demanded abruptly.

"Not much, but enough to know that there are two Generals in this. Who is the other one?"

He ignored the question. "Whom have you told?"

"Nobody. It wasn't my affair."

"You said nothing of this last night."

"Why should I? Until I heard Sanusi's voice I thought that he was the other man whom you called 'General.'"

"Was Miss Linden with you?"

"She only saw the jeep. She heard nothing."

"I can believe you?"

"Yes."

He sighed. "But why do you risk your life by telling me?"

"Because I want to save my life if I can, and Miss Linden's. If what I suspect about this business is true, I don't think either of us has very much of a chance. Do you?"

He looked me in the eyes. "Nobody here has very much chance."

"By showing you that I can be trusted not to betray you, I increase what chance we have."

"How?"

"If you can help us, you will."

"Why should I help you? A moment ago, I was on the point of shooting you like a dog."

"You will help me because, if the occasion arises, you can trust me to help you. Also, because you are a humane man."

He stared at me grimly. "I would not depend too much on my humanity, Mr. Fraser. It may still become necessary for me to shoot you."

"If it becomes necessary, of course, you will. I said that you were humane, Major. I didn't accuse you of sentimentality. Now, you'd better show me this generator."

We went on down the stairs.

"One thing I should like to know, Mr. Fraser," he said. "Is your ignorance on the subject of generators as complete as you claim?"

"I have a certain amount of theoretical knowledge, naturally, but I don't think that's going to be much use. If the windings are damaged, and they probably are, there's nothing I can do."

"I ask, because if the generator is not running again by sundown, I am afraid that harsh disciplinary measures may be taken against you. I would regret that, but I could do nothing to stop it. And now, here we are."

We had come to a short flight of steel stairs leading down to the sub-basement. There were lights on below and at the foot of the stairs there was a gleam of black, oily water. There were sounds of splashing. The bottom two stairs were under the water. Suparto went down as far as he could without getting his feet wet and called sharply.

There was more splashing and then two bedraggled young men waded to the foot of the stairs.

"What progress?" Suparto asked curtly.

One of them shrugged. "The water is no longer coming in, but we cannot make the drain work."

"The *tuan* here is an engineer from Tangga. He understands these matters. You will take orders from him now. Mr. Fraser, these men are Engineer Osman and Engineer Alwi."

I nodded to them and made my way down to the water level. From there I could see the whole area of the room. It was about thirty feet by twenty. The generating set and two five-hundred-gallon fuel tanks occupied most of the space. The diesel part of the set stood clear of the water but the generator itself was half-submerged. To one side was a slate switchboard.

I looked at Osman. "You say that there is a drain that won't work."

"Yes, *tuan*. We have put rods down it, but it will not work."

I looked at Suparto. "How close did the bomb fall?"

"In the roadway at the side. You wish to see the crater?"

"No. But what happened?"

"The crater filled up with water from the broken pipe before a man who knew how to turn the water off could be found. Then it was found that the water was coming in here."

"Where did it come in? A crack in the floor? Down the walls? Where?"

"Up through the drain, *tuan*." This was Engineer Alwi, wide-eyed with wonder. "It bubbled up through the drain. I saw it."

"Then what the hell's the good of poking about trying to get it to run back *down* the drain?" I demanded. "Don't you see what happened? The bomb collapsed the drain conduit as well and the water from the crater took that way out. We must be below the crater here. Naturally the water won't run back uphill. We'll have to pump it out."

"What do you need, Mr. Fraser?" This was Suparto.

"A powerful rotary pump. A fire-truck would do the job, or maybe there's a sewage-disposal unit. Any pump that will lift water twenty feet at a reasonable speed. There's nothing to be done until we get it."

But Suparto was already hurrying up the stairs. Osman and Alwi stood there in the water looking at me sheepishly.

"Where does the exhaust from the diesel go?" I asked.

"There is a pipe, *tuan*," said Osman. "It comes out at the back of the building."

"There must be a venilator shaft. Where is it?"

"There in the corner, *tuan*."

"Where does that come out?"

"I don't know, *tuan*." He wrung his hands. "How should I know?"

"All right, Osman. Don't worry. Just go upstairs and see if you can follow it. It looks as if it may come out where we can reach it from the outside. You understand? Then, when the fire-truck comes, we can run the hose down through the ventilating shaft and reach the water that way. It will be quicker."

"Yes, *tuan*." He was smiling eagerly as he clambered out of the water and squelched away up the stairs.

I was left with Alwi. He was waiting attentively for his orders. It occurred to me suddenly that all I had to do was to invent some task for him that would take him out of sight for a few minutes, to be free to walk out of the building. It was unlikely that anyone would try to stop me. If anyone did, I could say that I had gone to inspect the ventilator. If all went well, I could be at the British Consulate in ten minutes. True, my passport was at the police department awaiting an exit permit; but providing that I was not stopped by a patrol, that would not matter. I would be safe.

When the day-dream was over, I sat down on the stairs and wondered idly if Suparto were counting on my reluctance to abandon Rosalie to keep me from escaping, or whether he had preferred to rely upon more direct methods.

"Alwi," I said, "a guard should have been posted at the top of the stairs to prevent unauthorised persons interfering with our work. Go and see if he is there."

He looked a bit mystified, but he went readily enough. I lit my last cigarette. He was back before I had taken two puffs.

"The guard is there in position, *tuan*."

Suparto was, after all, a realist.

"Very well," I said. "Now tell me. Was the generator set running when the water came in?"

"Yes, *tuan*. There was a loss of power. My colleague, Osman, came down and found the water. The motor stopped running as he came in."

"Did any fuses blow?"

"We have not looked, *tuan*."

I lowered myself into the water and waded over to the switchboard. The generator set itself had been made by the Krupp engine works at Kiel, but the board was Japanese. There was a "no-volts" circuit-breaker on it and that had tripped. After a bit, I discovered that the motor control box was linked to the circuit-breaker. It seemed likely that the motor was undamaged and that it had cut out automatically as a result of the electrical failure. No fuses had blown. It was possible, I decided, that the generator windings had not burnt out and that the loss of power had been due simply to the damp insulation; but it would be a long time before I knew for certain one way or the other. There was one other hope, a faint one.

"Can't you adapt the equipment to use the main's power?"

Alwi looked at me reproachfully. "But that is direct current, *tuan*. One hundred and thirty volts."

So that was that.

It was eleven thirty then. Soon, Osman came to report that he had found the ventilator shaft opening and that it was near enough to the ground to serve as a duct for the hose pipe. There was an extractor fan fitted to the basement end of the shaft. So that there should be no delay when the pump arrived, I told them to get some tools and remove the fan. When that was done, we sat on the stairs and waited.

Just before noon there was another air raid. This time the target seemed to be on the outskirts of the city. Presumably, the fact that the radio station was no longer on the air had satisfied them. Down in the sub-basement we could feel the concussion of the bombs. The lights flickered once, and Alwi said that it must be the power station that was being attacked; but, to my relief, the lights stayed on. About ten minutes later, Suparto arrived, accompanied by a terrified fireman wearing a steel helmet, and reported that a motor pump was outside.

I sent Osman up to show them the ventilator shaft. At twelve thirty they started to pump. There was a delay when Suparto noticed that the water was being allowed to run back into the bomb crater; but after another hose had been fitted to carry the water from the pump to a drain farther along the road, the work was uninterrupted. By one fifteen, the water in the basement had sunk to the level of the intake hose nozzle, and further pumping was impossible. There was still an inch or so of water on the floor, but it was well clear of the generator housing and could be dealt with later.

Suparto was looking pleased. "You must admit, Mr. Fraser," he said sportively, "that the General's methods sometimes produce results."

"What results?"

"You have made progress."

"We haven't even started yet."

I called for a hand lamp and made a careful inspection of the generator. This told me nothing that I did not know already. The thing was designed to deliver alternating current at five hundred volts, and the windings were soaking wet. I also knew there was only one course open to me; that was to dismantle the thing, dry the windings out as best I could, reassemble it and hope to God it worked.

Suparto was standing over me, watching expectantly. To get rid of him I explained that I should want heating appliances of some sort, preferably blow lamps, a couple of electric fans, some thin sheet iron and a block and tackle. When he had gone to give the necessary orders, I began, with Osman and Alwi, the dismantling process.

In one of the ceiling joists there was a ring bolt that had obviously been put there to lower the generator into place when it had been originally installed. I managed, eventually, to get a rope sling round the armature; then, by using the block and tackle rigged to the ring bolt above, I was able to sway the armature clear of the housing. But the job took well over an hour. The coupling to the generator had proved all but inaccessible, and we had had much more dismantling to do than I had anticipated. We had, moreover, removed the fan from the ventilator shaft to get the hose through, and the heat down there became overpowering. By the time we were ready to start drying out, we were too exhausted to go on without a rest.

Suparto had food brought to us—*nassi goreng* and fruit—and we squatted on the stairs while we ate. I got some cigarettes, too. Suparto watched us keenly, like a trainer; with us but not of us.

"What about Miss Linden?" I asked him. "Has she had any food?"

"I will see that she gets some."

"And drinking-water, and cigarettes?"

"Very well." He looked at his watch. "It is three hours to sundown, Mr. Fraser. It will be necessary soon for me to report to the General."

"I can't tell you a thing. I shan't know whether it's going to work until we're able to try it."

"He has called a press conference at the Presidential Palace for six.

There, he will distribute copies of the proclamation; also the radio address he expects to deliver tonight. If the radio is not working he will be exposed to serious humiliation."

There were a number of replies I should have liked to have made to that; but Osman and Alwi were listening. They were looking worried, too.

"Well, we'd better get on with it," I said.

My plan for drying the windings was simple; it had to be. What I did was to bend the sheet metal into two big tubes, wrapping wire round each one to hold it together. Then I kept the sides of the tubes heated by the blow lamps and blew air through them with the fans. They were, in effect, like two large hair-driers. One I set up to blow into the field windings inside the housing. The other I directed at the armature suspended in its sling from the ceiling. Neither of them was very efficient, as a lot of the heat was wasted; but I could think of no better way of doing the job.

There were two blow lamps to each tube, and, once their most effective positions had been determined, all we had to do was to keep them going. The atmosphere rapidly became stifling, but we had time to replace the ventilator fan now, and when that was set going, things improved. After a while, I momentarily switched off the fan blowing on to the armature to feel if the ropes round it were getting too hot, and was rewarded by the sight of a whiff of steam rising from the windings.

At about four o'clock there was another air raid, and Suparto went up to find out what was happening. To us, it sounded as if the planes had returned to the same target as before, and I was terrified lest they should succeed in cutting off the power supply to the fans; but this time the lights did not even flicker. Osman and Alwi said, gleefully, that it was because the enemy were such timid pilots, but I was not so sure. Isolated, easy to identify and, doubtless, undefended, the power station was a much simpler target than the Air House. If they had really been after the power station, I thought, even those pilots would have been able to hit it. When Suparto returned he was blandly uncommunicative; however, I was beginning to know him, and I thought I detected a hint of satisfaction in his manner. For him, at any rate, things might be going according to plan.

At five o'clock we turned off the fans and the blow lamps and began the task of reassembling. The windings felt dry outside, but that meant little. Even if there were nothing else wrong with them, there might still be enough damp inside to break down the insulation. I should have liked to cook them longer, but Suparto would not allow it. I tried to persuade him that it was better to have a generator that did work at seven rather than one that did not work at six; but he merely shrugged.

I could see why, too. From his point of view, it did not matter whether the generator worked or not; all that mattered was that the verbose, ridiculous but dangerous Sanusi should continue to trust him until it was too late to withdraw from the trap that had been so carefully set. Sanusi had ordered me to repair the generator by sundown. For my sake, Suparto hoped that I would succeed in doing so; but if I failed, he had no intention of sharing the blame with me. As a loyal servant of the Nasjah Government, a patriotic *agent provocateur*, his responsibility was to the other General, the one he had been with in the garden of the New Harmony Club, the General who was now on his way to close the jaws of the trap, and liquidate Sanusi and his National Freedom Party once and for all.

The reassembly went far too well for my liking. I wanted difficulties and delays; I wanted to postpone the moment when the whole thing would be started up and I should know for certain that I had failed. But Osman and Alwi worked with feverish efficiency. Every part fitted neatly into place first time; every nut went on to every bolt as if it had been machined by an instrument-maker; Osman even began to sing as he worked. When I told him to stop it, he giggled happily.

At a little after five thirty, we were ready to test. I held the no-volts circuit-breaker trip plate into position, closed the circuit and told Osman to start up.

The diesel fired within about ten seconds. When it was up to speed, I let the trip plate go. It dropped instantly, the breaker flew out with a bang and the diesel chuffed to a standstill.

There was a horrified silence. I thought that Osman was going to burst into tears. Suparto raised his eyebrows.

"Well, Mr. Fraser?"

I took no notice of him. I was not so worried now; I knew that there was power there, because I had seen the meters kick. There just had not been enough to hold the circuit-breaker in.

I nodded to Osman. "Start up again."

When it started this time I kept my finger on the trip plate and watched the meters. The voltage was all over the place and I guessed that there was still a lot of damp in the windings; but the probability now was that the heat of the diesel and the heat generated in the windings themselves would gradually complete the drying-out process; either that, or the insulation would break down disastrously. I kept the trip plate up. After about twenty minutes' running the voltage had steadied appreciably. I gave it another five minutes and then tried releasing the plate. It held.

Osman grinned.

"Is it all right?" Suparto asked.

"I think it may be. It's not delivering anything like full power yet, but it'll improve, I think."

"The General will be pleased. I congratulate you, Mr. Fraser."

"The rest of this water ought to be mopped up. The drier the air in here, the better."

"That shall be attended to." He glanced at Osman and Alwi. "One of you had better stay here to supervise the work. I will send men down."

"I will stay," said Osman. "Alwi should test the transmitter."

I was covered in grease and filth from head to foot, my shoes were full of water, my muscles ached and my legs were trembling. Suddenly, I felt so tired that I had to go over to the stairs and sit down.

Suparto followed me. "Are you sick, Mr. Fraser?"

"No, just tired. I didn't have much sleep last night, you may remember."

"But not too tired to report to the General, I hope?"

"Can't you report to him?"

"It will be better for you and for the woman if you speak to him yourself."

"All right."

Alwi had already gone ahead. Suparto and I mounted the stairs slowly. When we reached the guard on the stairs, Suparto told him to report back to his N.C.O. The man followed us up to the ground floor, where Suparto made arrangements for the sub-basement to be cleaned up. The lift was working again now. It was the kind you operated yourself. When we were inside and the gates were closed, I asked Suparto about the air raids we had heard below.

"Were they trying for the power station?"

"No. The road and rail bridges over the river east of the city."

"Did they destroy them?"

"They damaged them badly enough."

"Badly enough for what?"

"Enough to prevent a retreat to the hills before the city is completely surrounded."

"Doesn't he realise that?"

Suparto pressed the button for the fifth floor and the lift started up.

"The General and Colonel Roda place a more optimistic interpretation on the attacks. They see them as a move to delay the Government troops who have mutinied, and who are on their way to join us here in the city."

"That interpretation having been suggested by you, I take it?" When he said nothing, I asked: "Have any Government troops, in fact, mutinied?"

"The loyalty of one infantry unit was considered doubtful. It was disarmed yesterday."

The lift stopped and we got out.

The General was preparing to leave for the foreign press conference at the Presidential Palace, and I had to wait in the outer office. While I was there, a station monitor speaker in the corner began to emit a frying sound and then the xylophone signal came on. Alwi had got the transmitter working again.

When the General appeared at the door of his office, I saw why I had been kept waiting. He had changed into a clean uniform and was wearing a tie. Roda and Suparto followed him out.

I stood up and the General came over to me. He nodded graciously; his thoughts were already in the Presidential Palace.

"Major Suparto has told me of your hard work," he said. He glanced at the monitor speaker. "We can hear for ourselves that it has been successful, eh, Colonel?"

"As we expected, the *tuan* was too modest about his qualifications." Roda grinned.

I ignored him. "I am glad to have been of service, General."

"Sunda has need of good engineers," he replied; "especially those of proved loyalty. It is my intention to set up intensive technical training schemes for the youth of our country. For a man like you, Mr. Fraser, there might be exceptional opportunities for advancement here."

"You are very kind."

"Those who serve us well will be well rewarded. Do not forget that, Mr. Fraser."

"I have every reason to remember it, General."

"Ah yes. We made a bargain. It shall be kept."

Roda grinned again. " 'Deal gently therefore with the infidel,' " he quoted facetiously; " 'and grant them a gentle rest.' "

Sanusi frowned at the blasphemy but continued to look at me. "By this time tomorrow, Mr. Fraser, I shall have moved my headquarters and the security considerations which have compelled us to detain you here will no longer apply. You and the woman will then be free to leave. You agree, Major?"

"Of course, *Boeng*." Suparto's face was completely impassive.

"Meanwhile, the Major will see that your detention is not made too disagreeable."

"Thank you, General."

"We keep our promises, you see."

With a proud lift of his chin, he strode on out of the office. Roda, with a nod to me, followed.

Suparto looked at me. "You see? It was as well that you reported yourself."

"Was it? I can see why you find them easy to despise."

He shrugged. "At least you will get a comfortable night's sleep."

He led the way out of the office. We went back along the corridor, through the swing doors and up to the apartment.

The man by the telephone was asleep. The bow-legged officer kicked him to his feet as Suparto entered.

Suparto looked round, then went over to the radio and switched it on. The announcer had begun to read a communiqué issued by National

Freedom Party headquarters claiming that calm and order had been restored in all provinces. Suparto switched it off again.

"This morning," he said, "an enemy bomb damaged the radio power supply. At the request of *Boeng* Sanusi, the *tuan* here repaired the damage and restored the power. Our *Boeng* has congratulated the *tuan* on his loyalty and skill, and given strict orders that both he and the woman with him should be treated with the greatest politeness and respect. They will remain in this apartment, but a guard on the terrace will no longer be necessary. Is it understood?"

There was a murmur of agreement. Suparto walked over to the drink table, picked up a bottle of whisky, and went out on to the terrace.

I followed.

Outside the living-room window he stopped and called the guard over. When the man came he dismissed him.

"You will not be so foolish as to try to leave the apartment, I hope, Mr. Fraser?"

"All I want to do is to rest."

He put the bottle of whisky into my hand. "We have no use for this," he said; "perhaps it will help you to sleep."

He turned on his heel and went inside again.

I walked along the terrace.

Rosalie had heard our voices and was standing by the window waiting for me. As I approached, she switched on the light.

My appearance must have been a shock to her; it was a shock even to me when I saw myself in the mirror; but she did not say anything. She was waiting for me to make the first move.

I put the bottle down and kissed her. She held on to me for a moment, then she smiled.

"I heard what the Major said. Was it true?"

"More or less. Anyway, we have a reward. We are to be treated with consideration. You see, the sentry has already gone."

"Does it mean they will let us go?"

"Well . . ." I hesitated. "Not yet. I'll tell you about it in a minute. I must clean myself up first."

She was watching me closely, and I knew that I was not going to be able to pretend to her for very long. I turned away as if to take my shirt off and saw that there were bowls of food and fruit on the table.

"You haven't eaten," I said. "I asked them to send it up for you."

"Do you think I would eat when I did not know what had happened to you?"

"The rice will be cold," I said stupidly.

She did not answer. She was still wondering what it was that I had not told her. I looked round the room. In some way she had managed to get rid of the plaster dust and rubble and make the place tidy. I wanted to comment on the fact, but I could not get the words out.

I sat down on the edge of the chair and started to unbutton my shirt. As I did so, she knelt down in front of me and took off my waterlogged shoes. I fumbled with the shirt. My fingers were scratched and sore, and one of the buttons caught in a loose thread. In a weak rage I tore it free. She looked up, and then, with a murmured apology, began to help me. Every stitch of clothing I had on smelt of oil and sweat and dirty water. When I had undressed, I gathered it all up and threw it out on to the terrace.

She smiled. "While you are bathing I will get out some clean things."

Luckily there was still plenty of water left in the bathhouse; I had to soap myself several times from head to foot before I could get rid of the smell of oil.

When I got back to the room, she had switched off the top light so that there was not so much glare, and had put the bedside lamp on. There was a set of clean clothes ready for me on my bed, and also a neatly folded batik sarong.

"I can wash some of our clothes," she explained, "but I cannot iron them. You have only those white trousers clean and two more shirts. There are some of Roy's things there, but they will not fit you. Perhaps it is foolish to think of such things now but . . ."

"No. You're quite right. Anyway, a sarong will be more comfortable. Up in Tangga I often wore one."

"You do not object that it is one of mine?"

"Object? It's a beauty."

She watched me critically while I put it on.

"There are, perhaps, more suitable materials for a man," she said at length; "but it does not look effeminate."

"Good. Have you another one for yourself?"

"Oh yes. But while you were not here and the guard was outside, it was better that I looked as European as possible. In batik I look more Sundanese."

"Then look Sundanese."

She smiled, and, going to the other end of the room, began to take off her dress. In the next room they switched on the radio.

I opened the bottle of Jebb's whisky that Suparto had given me, and poured out two drinks. I drank one straight down. Then I refilled the empty glass and took it over with me to my bed. The bruise on my stomach was beginning to be painful and I lay down gingerly. When I was stretched out flat, however, the muscles began to relax, the pain went and a delicious drowsiness began to steal over me. In the next room a voice on the radio was announcing that General Sanusi would shortly address a message to the world. I closed my eyes.

There was something moving against the fingers of my right hand and I half opened my eyes. Rosalie was gently removing the glass that I had been holding. Her hair was down over her shoulders, the sarong was fastened at her waist and she had a narrow scarf draped loosely over her breasts like a country woman. She looked beautiful. I remained still and watched while she placed the glass gently on the bedside table. Then, she glanced at me and saw that I was not asleep. She smiled and sat down on the edge of the bed. I took her hand.

"There's something I'd better tell you," I said.

"I know, but you are very tired. Sleep first."

"Sanusi said that by this time tomorrow he would have moved his headquarters, and that we would be free."

"And does he not mean it?"

"Oh yes, he means it, but there are things he doesn't know."

"Tell me."

"He's in a trap. It was all a trap; the garrison leaving the city unprotected; promises from men he thought he could trust that they would bring over their troops to his side; assurances that the country was waiting for his leadership, appeals to his vanity, warnings that if he hesitated he would be lost; anything to trick him into coming down from the hills with all his men so that the Government tanks and guns could move in and cut him to pieces. Well, it's worked. Tomorrow he thinks that he'll be moving over into the Presidential Palace. He won't. He'll be fighting for his life, here, and I don't imagine that he has any chance at all of winning."

She had been looking down at my hand. Now, her eyes looked into mine. "How do you know this? Who told you?"

"You may be better off if you don't know."

"Major Suparto." It was a statement, not a question. I said nothing.

"They might still get away to the hills."

"Not very many of them. And none from this building, I think. They know where Sanusi is, all right."

"It will be bad again for us here."

"I'm afraid it will."

She took my hand and, leaning forward over me, held it against her breast so that my fingers touched one of the nipples. I felt it harden, and she smiled.

"You see," she said, "I am not afraid."

She pressed my hand, and then moved away. "You must sleep now, and I think I will sleep, too."

She lay down on her bed and stared up at the ceiling. I watched her face for a while, and then my eyes closed. After a moment or two, I heard her say my name.

"Yes, Rosalie?"

"Perhaps we should wear our clean clothes tomorrow."

CHAPTER VII

THE ATTACK on the city began just before dawn. I thought at first that it was the voices of the men in the living room that had awakened me. Some sort of argument was going on, and another man was speaking on the telephone. He kept repeating the word "impossible." The argument seemed to be about someone named Dahman who had moved his troops without authority.

Then, I became aware of an irregular thudding that sounded as if, somewhere in the building below us, the wind was slamming a heavy padded door. Only there was no wind.

I opened my eyes and saw Rosalie standing by the window. There were lights flaring in the sky behind her. I sat up and gasped as I realised how sore my body was. She looked round. I got off the bed carefully and went over to the window.

Rosalie was looking over towards the bay. As I joined her, two cones of orange flame stabbed the darkness there. The sound took about three seconds to reach me, and, as it thudded against the windows, there were two more flashes. This time I caught a momentary glimpse of the shape behind them, and knew why the forts commanding the sea approaches to Selampang had not surrendered to Sanusi. The Sundanese navy consisted of only five ships: one lighthouse tender, three small patrol vessels and the flagship, an elderly destroyer which the Government had bought from the British and re-named *Semangat*. I had seen her in Port Kail. She had four 4.7-inch guns.

She was firing into an area to the left of the racecourse, and you could see the flashes of the bursts reflected on the smoke drifting away from earlier ones. Rosalie said that the barracks were in that direction.

"What should we do?" she added.

"There's nothing we can do."

She came back with me and we lay together on my bed, listening. Two men from the next room had gone out on the terrace now and were discussing the situation in low tones.

"What will happen?" Rosalie asked.

"I don't know enough about it. I suppose these people have established some sort of defence line on the outskirts. If so, the other side, with their tanks and guns, will find the weakest spot and blast their way through. This naval bombardment is just the preliminary softening up. I suppose it's meant to impress the civil population, too. But it's the tanks and guns that will decide the thing. Unless Sanusi has tanks and guns to fight back with, there's nothing he can do to stop them. I'm certain he has no tanks."

"Has he guns?"

"There are a couple of anti-tank guns down in the square. I suppose he has a few more dotted about the city. I don't know how old the Government tanks are, but unless they are very old indeed, the shot that those guns fire won't even knock a dent in them. They might stop a light armoured car, but nothing heavier."

"What will happen, then?"

"That depends on how hard these people fight."

"But you said they cannot win."

"I don't think they can. It's only a question of how long it takes to defeat them."

She was silent for a moment, then she said: "To kill them all, you mean?"

"Most of them, anyway."

"They might surrender."

"They might, yes. Let's hope they will."

"Yes, let us hope." She must have guessed from my tone that I did not think that there was much likelihood of it. The Government were certainly not going to let Sanusi get out of the trap once he was in it, and Sanusi would not be such a fool as to believe in any promises they might make. Besides, when street-fighting began and men began to kill at close range, it became difficult to surrender.

I was remembering a Fusilier sergeant I had met in Burma. It was some weeks before we went into Mandalay. My company had been clearing a forward airstrip and were waiting to be flown out to another job. This sergeant had come out from the Eighth Army in Italy, and because we had both been in the desert with Auchinleck, we had started talking. He had had experience of street-fighting against the Germans, and had later become an instructor on the subject. He had developed a passion for it that even he, I think, suspected to be a trifle unhealthy. All the same, he could not wait to get into Meiktila and try his skill on the Japanese.

"It's an art, sir, rushing a building," he had told me eagerly; "a bleeding art. They can't stop you if you know how. You just have to get near enough first. That's the dodgy bit. There's usually plenty of cover, though, shell holes, ruins and that, but you've got to have patience. Crawl, dig your way there if you have to, but don't start until you're within thirty yards of a window. Then go mad. Put a four-second grenade in first and follow it. By the time you're there they'll be wetting themselves, if they've got anything left to wet with. Then, you go through the whole house. Quick as lightning. Every room. First a grenade, and then yourself. Doesn't matter what's there. Doesn't matter who's there. Then, comb it out with your machine pistol. If it's a soft house, put a burst up through the ceiling and catch them bending. But don't stop for a second. Be as quick as lightning. First a grenade, and then yourself with the old machine pistol, trigger happy. Don't be afraid of anything. They're more frightened of you than you are of them because you're attacking. Blind 'em and then hit 'em with everything. And when you run out of ammo, still keep going while they're dazed. Knife, shovel, the lot! Keep going and there's nothing that can stop you, sir. I've seen it. I've done it. I know."

I felt sure that he did know.

The sky lightened, and then the sun rose.

We went to the window again.

A pall of smoke hung over the area where the barracks were. The destroyer had ceased firing and was lying there innocently on the smooth, sparkling surface of the bay. There were some bursts of light automatic fire and one or two faint thuds that might have been two-pounders in action. The radio in the next room had been switched on. The station was transmitting a recording of Sanusi's "foreign policy" speech of the previous night, translated into Hindustani. I realised that the station had probably been transmitting in various languages all through the night, and wondered vaguely what sort of output Osman was getting from the generator. Down in the square there was a sound of trucks being started and driven off.

"I am hungry," Rosalie said.

"So am I."

We divided the cold rice between us and then ate some fruit. While we were eating, the destroyer's guns opened up again, but this time we took no notice. I thought that I could imagine what was going on. In the darkness their shooting had not been too good. As a result, when the tanks and infantry had moved in, they had met with more opposition than they had expected. The guns had been called upon to put down some properly observed fire before the attack was resumed. I told Rosalie this fiction as if it were fact.

She said: "How do you know?"

"That is how these things happen. Soon, the General will issue a communiqué. He will say that an enemy attack on the outer defence ring was beaten off with heavy losses to the enemy and at practically no cost to the defence. But he will also announce a tactical withdrawal to previously prepared positions of greater strength, in order to straighten the line."

"What does that mean?"

"It is the language of retreat. We shall be having plenty of it soon, I think . . ."

We both heard the planes at the same moment. As we dived for the floor, one of the men on the terrace began shouting orders to the machine-gunners on the roof. I started to drag the rug over our heads and then, remembering that there was no glass left to worry about now, dropped the rug and pulled the curtains aside.

"There," said Rosalie.

I saw them then. They were the three planes which had bombed us the previous day, but now they were flying at over six thousand feet. There was a noise like a pneumatic drill over our heads as the machine guns on the roof opened fire, and a few more bits of plaster fell from the ceiling. They had one of the things mounted almost directly above us. As the gunner traversed, a shower of ejected cartridge cases came tinkling down on to the terrace. The gunners must have known that, at that range, they could not have hit a house, but they went on firing just the same.

Something began dropping from the planes. It looked for a moment like a load of incendiaries. Then, the black dots in the sky seemed to split up and stop falling, and I realised that it was leaflets that were being dropped. The men in the next room realised it at the same moment and ran out on to the terrace, staring up and exclaiming excitedly.

The Sundanese Air Force may not have been very good at hitting its targets with bombs, but with leaflets it was superbly accurate. A minute after the drop, the sky above the Van Riebeeck Square was filled with them, evenly distributed and fluttering down in perfect formation. Suddenly, the men on the terrace began running about wildly, capering up and down, snatching at the air as the first of the leaflets came within reach. It was a fantastic spectacle. Two of them, intent on the same leaflet, cannoned into one another as the paper swooped capriciously over the edge of the balustrade. There were shrill cries of protest, and Rosalie began to giggle uncontrollably.

We were still on the floor and she hastily crawled away to the bed to smother her laughter. I stayed by the window, and, some seconds later, about a dozen leaflets fell on the terrace. One was within a yard of me and, when I saw that the men were not picking all of them up, I reached out and got it.

The same message was printed on both sides in Malay and English. Rosalie had recovered now and I took it over to show her.

It was not long. It was addressed: *"To All Loyal Citizens of The Republic of Sunda."* It said:

"During the past thirty-six hours, a terrorist criminal organisation calling itself the People's National Freedom Party, and led by a former officer named Kamarudin b. Sanusi, has taken advantage of the absence of the Republican Army on manoeuvres to occupy certain public buildings in Selampang and other towns in the Southern Provinces, including newspaper offices and premises used by Radio Sunda. Statements put out by the terrorists, both by radio and in certain newspapers, indicate that it is their intention to attempt, in contravention of the provisions of the Constitution of the Republic, to overthrow the elected Government of the Republic by force. By my lawful authority as President of the Re-

*public, a State of Emergency has, therefore, been stated to exist, and
the said Kamarudin b. Sanusi and his associates are declared to be enemies of the Republic.*

*"Under the Public Security Law of 1948, any person giving aid to a
declared enemy of the Republic or permitting such aid to be given by
others, may be punished by death. The Army of the Republic will now
proceed to administer justice. The innocent, who have nothing to fear,
will welcome their defenders. It is likely, too, that there are some persons
who now regret their part in the disorders that have taken place. Providing that they surrender immediately to the advancing troops and give
them all assistance, such persons will be treated leniently. This applies
also to members of the so-called T.K.R., or People's Army of Security.
Failure to obey promptly all orders issued by, or in the name of, the
Officer Commanding the Army of the Republic, General Ishak, will be
an offence punishable by death. We fight for Freedom and the Constitution."*

There followed the printed signature of President Nasjah and the date.
The ink smudged off on my fingers. Presumably, they had been printed
in Meja during the past twelve hours; but someone had had the fore-
thought to have stereos of the signature ready in advance. In dealing
with its enemies, at least, the Government could be efficient.

I remarked on the fact to Rosalie. She shrugged.

"No doubt there are others like Major Suparto. It is said this swine
Ishak is intelligent. What do you think that they will do to us before they
kill us?" It was said quite evenly, but there was something in the tone
of her voice that should have warned me to be careful. It did not, however; I was re-reading the leaflet.

"To us?" I said vaguely.

"Of course. It says that we are criminals now."

"What do you mean?"

She pointed to the leaflet. "You have helped them with the radio. I
am with you. We have taken part. We shall not be able to surrender.
Perhaps it will be better if we are killed here."

"Let's hope we won't be killed at all."

"Hope? That is amusing, I think."

"There's not much else we can do."

"We can kill ourselves."

Two minutes earlier she had been laughing because some men were
jumping about, making fools of themselves. The change was so fantastic
that I smiled. The smile was a mistake.

"Are you afraid?" Suddenly, she was breathing quickly and her eyes
were gleaming with hatred. "It would be quite simple. We could jump
from the terrace. It would be quick and not painful. But if you are afraid,
I will do it myself."

She started up and I gripped her arm. "Rosalie, listen to me."

"What does it matter if a filthy Indo dies?" Then, she broke into Dutch and I could not understand much of what she said.

"Rosalie, listen!"

She hit me in the face and tried again to get away. I grabbed her arms, swung her round and forced her down on to the bed.

"For God's sake, stop it!" I said angrily.

She spat at me; then, for about a minute, she fought like a maniac; a maniac with closed eyes who cursed me savagely all the time in Dutch. When, at last, she went limp, I thought that she had fainted or that it was a trick to make me release my hold; but it was neither. After a moment, she caught her breath in a sob and began to cry helplessly. I took my hands away and sat down on the other bed to wait.

The leaflet lay crumpled on the bed beside me. After a bit, I picked it up and looked at it again. To me it had been no more than a smudgy proclamation of martial law; but to her it must have brought the smell of death. I tore it into small pieces, and wished that I could deal with my memory of the street-fighting sergeant in the same way.

She was quiet now. I fetched her a glass of water. She had pulled her hair down over her face so that I could not see her. When she had taken the glass from me, I turned away and began to pick up the fresh bits of plaster that had fallen from the ceiling.

The sounds of the battle had changed perceptibly. The attack was still coming from the west, but it had become possible to distinguish the firing of individual guns. At intervals there was the short, sharp crack of an eighty-eight. The destroyer was silent again. There was nothing new to be seen. Smoke from burning buildings had drifted across the whole area. I thought of the people in the crowded kampongs along the canal banks near the firing, and wondered what was happening to them. Were they swarming out, trying to get away towards the centre of the city, or were they huddled trembling inside their houses, waiting for the terror to pass them by? The latter, I hoped. The tanks and guns would stay on the metalled roads as much as they could, and the defenders would choose solid buildings from which to fight back rather than canal banks. Later, perhaps, when the defenders broke and the mopping-up process began, it might be wise to join in the killing and so demonstrate one's loyalty to the victors; but, for the present, it would be safer to remain passive.

I heard Rosalie put the empty glass down and move over to the mirror. I finished picking up the plaster and glanced at her. She was brushing her hair. She saw me in the mirror, looking at her, and stopped brushing. I went over to her and put my hands on her shoulders. She turned to face me.

"You do not dislike me now?"

"No."

"You are not pretending because you feel sorry for me?"

"No."

"If you were angry and beat me for what I said, I should feel more certain."

"Most of what you said I didn't understand."

"It was not polite."

"I know. There was something about my skin."

She flushed. "You understood that? I am sorry. I said it to humiliate myself."

"Does a European skin disgust you?"

"Sometimes." She looked up at me defiantly. "You see, I do not pretend with you. And sometimes, my own skin disgusts me because it is so dark. My father's was light, much lighter than yours. You are nearly as brown as I am. I like to touch and smell your body and to feel the strength of it. I do not think: 'He is a European, I am an Indo.' I think: 'It is good to be a woman with this man.'" She paused. "But sometimes it is different. You know how these men here can feel about me. That is how I can feel about myself. Part of me is European. Sometimes I hate it and want to kill it."

"What made you feel like that just now? Was it the leaflets? They don't really alter anything, you know."

"Perhaps not. I do not know. But I laughed at those officers dancing about like little boys when someone is throwing them coins, and forgot to be frightened. Then, when you showed me what was on the paper, it was worse than it had been before. It was like waiting for the *pemoedas* to come, and I wanted us both to die." She looked at me anxiously. "Do you understand?"

"Not altogether. Perhaps you have to be an Indo to understand completely."

She nodded. "Yes, perhaps you do." She hesitated. "It is curious to hear you use that word."

"You used it."

"And you do not dislike me for what I said?"

"No."

"Put your arms round me."

A few minutes later she said: "I do not really mind if I have to die, but I am afraid of being hurt."

"I know. So am I. The men in the next room are. The men firing those guns are. Everyone is—Indos, Sundanese, Europeans—everyone. There's nothing special about you."

"That is not polite."

"I don't have to be polite to you. It was part of the arrangement."

She smiled then. "You remember? That is very businesslike."

"Certainly. And dying was no part of the arrangement. If one of us is to be killed or wounded because we happen to be here, that is another matter, but we are not going to kill ourselves."

"It is not much to kill oneself." She was still smiling.

"It is to me. Whatever happens, don't get that idea again, will you?"

Her smile faded and she looked up at me curiously. "Does it truly matter to you?"

"Yes, it matters."

After a moment she nodded. "Then as long as you are here, I will not think of it." She gathered up her hair and began to twist it into a bun on top of her head. "There is still water left in the bathhouse," she remarked; "perhaps we should use it while we can."

It was such a determined change of subject that it made me laugh.

She raised her eyebrows. "It will not be amusing if we cannot wash."

"You're right. It won't."

"Do you wish to go first?" She was still uneasy because I had laughed at her.

"No, you go ahead. If you use too much water, I shall beat you."

She smiled. I had made a feeble joke and she had regained face. All was well.

"May I wear your bathrobe?"

"Of course."

When she had gone, I ate a slice of papaya, lit a cigarette and went out on to the terrace. The bow-legged officer was standing at the far end, looking out gloomily at the smoke haze. He nodded curtly when he caught sight of me, and I nodded back. We did not speak.

The firing had slackened off considerably and there were only occasional flurries of activity. It was as if both sides were weary of the argument, but could not quite make up their minds to abandon it. I found that a comforting notion. Unfortunately, I could not altogether conceal from myself the fact that what sounds there were seemed to come from very much nearer than they had an hour earlier.

Down in the leaflet-strewn square there was feverish activity. Fox-holes were being dug and the two-pounders were being manoeuvred into sand-bagged pits so that they could cover the two western approaches to the square. One of the bomb craters was being used as a headquarters, another as an ammunition dump. Sounds from the Ministry of Public Health next door suggested that it, too, was being placed in a state of defence. Immediately below, beside the crater that had flooded the generator room, some men were unloading three-inch mortars from a truck. There were other men sitting on the ground fusing grenades. As far as I could see, there was only one small group of men in the entire square to whom a tank commander would have given a second thought. They were squatting under the trees, placidly scooping rice out of their bowls with their fingers. Laid out neatly on a groundsheet beside them were two American bazookas.

Someone came into the living room. Out of the corner of my eye, I saw the bow-legged officer turn and then go in quickly. A moment later

I recognised Suparto's voice. There was a lot of firing going on just then and a truck down in the street below was spitting and back-firing as the driver revved it up, so I went back into the bedroom to see if I could hear what he was saying through the door.

It was not much better there. I could tell by the tone of his voice that he was giving orders, but that was all. Then, there was a pause, and I heard steps on the terrace. I had just time to move away from the door before Suparto came in by the window.

He nodded to me and glanced quickly round the room.

"She's bathing," I said.

He nodded. "That is as well. I have not much time and what I have to say is private."

"You might be heard in the next room."

"For the present, there is no one in the next room. Sanusi is shortly transferring his headquarters there." He sat down wearily and stretched his legs. His cheekbones stood out sharply and his skin was the colour of parchment. I realised that it was probably three days since he had slept. His uniform, however, was as neat as ever.

"May I know what's happening out there?"

"There will be an official statement issued at the first opportunity. Colonel Roda is writing it at this very moment."

"No jokes, Major, please."

He smiled. "My apologies. I was indulging myself. The thought of Colonel Roda, whom I greatly dislike, trying bravely to misrepresent a situation which is already hopeless is very enjoyable."

"Are you sure there's nobody in there who can hear you?"

"I can see that you are nervous this morning, Mr. Fraser."

"Yes."

"Well, I admit that this waiting is disagreeable. As far as I know, the present situation is this. General Ishak's troops broke through the outer defence positions without difficulty. Some rebel troops, however, were commanded with more skill than he expected. Instead of waiting to be swallowed up, they moved. As a result, General Ishak's teeth met on nothing, and he will have to take another bite."

"You said that the situation was already hopeless."

"It is. The rebels have postponed defeat by a few hours, that is all. They cannot get out now."

"Does General Sanusi know that?"

"Not yet." He paused. "That is what I wanted to tell you about, Mr. Fraser. During the next few hours Sanusi is going to discover some very disagreeable facts, and there is going to be a moment when he realises what has happened. He is a misguided man, but not a fool. He will look at the faces of those about him and wonder whom he has to thank for his defeat. He will think back over the past two years and try to remember

all that has been said and done, and relate it to the present situation.
You understand?"

"Yes, I do."

"He is not, as I have said, a fool, and it may be that he will come to a
correct conclusion. If he does and I am there, he will be looking into my
face. In that case, I have no doubt that I could kill him before he killed
me, but I would certainly be killed myself a moment later. Do you still
understand?"

"I think so. You've done your job. You're getting out."

He eyed me carefully. For the first time, I felt sorry for him. He was a
brave man who had taken nerve-racking risks to serve his country's government; and although I knew nothing of his motives, I found it hard
to believe that personal ambition figured very prominently among them.
It was even possible that he was a patriot. But patriot or no, he was not
sufficiently insensitive to enjoy that moment of success. It was understandable that he should suspect me of irony.

"You do not seem surprised, Mr. Fraser."

"Why should I be? You've been risking your life because you felt it
necessary. Why go on doing so when the need no longer exists?"

"These things cannot always be decided so logically. I ask you to believe me when I say that treachery does not come naturally to me."

"I'm sure it doesn't. I said that you were a humane man. But, forgive
my asking, why did you take this risk? Supposing Sanusi had succeeded.
Would it have been such a disaster? The present Government may have
your loyalty, but I cannot believe that it has your approval."

"Approval? Mr. Fraser, I dislike the Nasjah gang quite as much as I
dislike Colonel Roda. Sanusi is right about some things. We did not win
our independence from the Dutch. Force of circumstances delivered it
into hands which were unfit to receive it. But we do not have hands that
are fit. Revolution is therefore pointless. What this nation must have is
time to learn about government. Meanwhile, we must choose between
evils. The Nasjah Government is corrupt and incompetent, and foreigners
laugh at us for it. But you have heard Sanusi. He is not himself an evil
man. As a commander in the field he is excellent. As a Minister of Propaganda he might perform useful service. But what has he to offer as the
leader of the nation? More mosques in Selampang? Excellent. But what
else? Only the discipline of men like Roda, men hungry for power. I prefer
the Nasjah gang. They are weak, but with them, at least, the machinery
of representative government is preserved and gradual change is possible.
In the end, if the Americans and you British do not interfere, there will
be fresh, healthy growth. But we must have time and patience."

"It may not be the Americans and British who do the interfering."

"Communism? That is your bad dream, not ours. Ah yes, I know. You
see the propaganda in the kampongs. But that is all you see, and all there
is. If I could believe that among all the ordinary people of Sunda there

were enough able and determined men to create one effective district political organisation of any kind, I should be happy."

"Then I wish you luck, Major. How are you going?"

He stood up. "I shall decide to make a reconnaissance of the situation in the city. Sanusi's troops are falling back to the centre here and there is a certain amount of confusion. It will not be difficult to walk through their lines. And I am expected."

"I see. It's good of you to come and tell me."

"That was not the only reason I came. Of course, I shall inform the commander of the assaulting forces of your detention here, so that the troops may be warned that you are friendly."

"Thank you."

He looked embarrassed. "I cannot promise that it will help you."

"No, I understand."

"Also, I had some advice to offer you. This building will probably be shelled. Our naval gunners are not highly skilled, but it is possible that they will score some hits. Unless you are forced to do so, however, do not move down from this floor. You will be safer here in the end. I need not tell you to keep out of Roda's way if you can. Desperate men are always dangerous."

"Yes."

"Have you enough food and water in here?"

"Enough for how long?"

"Until tonight."

"We could do with some more drinking-water, I think."

"Come with me."

I followed him out on to the terrace and through the empty living room to the kitchen.

There were three bottles of water left in the refrigerator.

"Will one bottle be sufficient?"

"I think so."

"Good. One other thing. It will be better if you dress as a European."

"I've kept some clean clothes specially for the occasion, Major. But it's a hot day. Do you think I need to wear a tie?"

He gave me a wintry smile. "A sense of humour is an excellent thing at times like these. It helps a man to be philosophical." There were voices along the corridor outside. "Go back now, Mr. Fraser," he added, and then turned and walked out quickly. As I went back through the living room, I could hear his voice in the corridor. "Everything is prepared, *Boeng*. Shall I give orders for coffee to be sent to you?"

Rosalie had just returned. She had heard us talking in the kitchen and was eager to know what was going on.

I told her briefly most of what I had learned.

"And it will be ended by tonight?" she asked.

"Apparently."

We looked at one another in silence for a moment; then she drew a deep breath and nodded.

"So."

"Yes." I picked up my towel. "I think that it's about time I went and shaved."

CHAPTER VIII

THE SHELLING of the area around the Van Riebeeck Square began at one o'clock.

For three hours before that, insurgent troops had been straggling back from the forward positions and occupying the block of buildings which included the Air House and the Ministry of Public Health. On my way back from the bathhouse, I had looked over the balustrade and seen two more two-pounders being manhandled through the big doorway of the Air Terminal offices below, and a truck full of wounded being driven in the direction of the Telegraf Road. The only civilians to be seen were children. Some of them stood in awe-struck silence, watching the troops; others, bolder, were playing a war game round a bomb crater and jumping in and out of the fox-holes.

A little after eleven, there were several violent outbursts of firing. They seemed to come from about a mile away to the north. Immediately after the first one, the telephone in the next room began to ring. During the half-hour that followed, there was scarcely a moment when Sanusi or Roda was not on the telephone; but for most of the time there was such a lot of noise going on outside that, although I could distinguish odd words and sentences, I could not make sense of what was being said. Eventually, Sanusi and Roda went out on to the terrace, and there was a muttered conference over a map. If the bad news was beginning to filter through to them, they clearly did not want their staff inside the room to know too much about it. In the middle of the conference, Roda was called in to the telephone again; but Sanusi remained on the terrace, fidgeting uneasily with the map and staring down into the square. After a minute or two, Roda came back and there was another furtive discussion. Some decision seemed to come out of it, for in the end Sanusi nodded, and the two men turned and walked back inside. A few minutes later the radio was switched on, and I guessed that the staff had been left to their own devices.

The official communiqué was being broadcast at intervals of fifteen minutes, and part of it was similar enough to the one I had invented earlier that morning to make us both laugh. The rest was not so amusing, however. Six persons attempting to obstruct the movements of the National Freedom Army had been shot; twenty others had been arrested on suspicion of sabotage, and were being questioned. There was a warning that persons failing to obey orders promptly, or displaying reluctance to assist the National Freedom Army in its fight against the colonialist reactionaries who were attempting to defeat the will of the people, would be liable to summary trial and imprisonment with forfeiture of all property.

Rosalie began to worry about her sister and Mina. The fighting seemed to be moving towards the quarter in which they lived, and she was afraid that, in trying to get away from it, they would run into worse trouble when the Government forces began to close in from the east. We talked about it for some time, but I made no effort to reassure her; not merely because I knew that my reassurances would be worthless, but because I hoped that the more she worried about Mina and her sister, the less she would worry about herself.

A little after mid-day there were two extra-violent explosions that brought down some more fragments of plaster, and a few moments later we saw two columns of smoke mushrooming up over the warehouses in the direction of the old town. Rosalie said that one of the oil companies had their gasoline storage tanks in that area, but the smoke looked to me more like the result of demolition charges. I thought it probable that the defenders were now trying to delay the Government's encircling movements by blowing up canal bridges, and wondered if they yet knew that there were enemies, not friends, waiting across the line of their retreat.

I did not have to wait long for the answer. During the morning I had found a pack of cards in a drawer of Jebb's belongings, and at intervals since then I had been teaching Rosalie to play gin rummy. We had just sat down to resume our interrupted game when there was a sound of movement from the next room and the radio was switched off. Sanusi and Roda had returned.

For a few minutes, there was a steady murmur of voices punctuated by sharp monosyllables from Roda. Suddenly, chairs grated on the tiled floor and a door closed. Then, footsteps sounded on the terrace, the curtain was pushed aside, and the staff captain whom I had seen the previous day on the floor below peered in at us.

I looked up, and he beckoned.

"You, come."

"Where to?"

"See *Boeng*."

My heart was beating too insistently for comfort; but, for Rosalie's benefit, I put my cards down with a sigh of irritation and a word of apology before I stood up.

"You, come." He was belligerent now.

"I am coming."

I walked out on to the terrace and, with his hand on his pistol, he stood aside to let me pass. I took no notice of him and walked along to the living-room windows. There was no glass in them and I could clearly see the four men inside. Apart from Sanusi and Roda, there were a major and a lieutenant-colonel, both of them grey with dust and wearing steel helmets.

As before, it was Roda who took the initiative. He beckoned me in. The captain followed and stood behind me. Sanusi was sitting on the side of one of the long chairs, staring at the floor. He took no notice of me.

Roda glanced at the other two. "It was this *tuan* who repaired the radio power generator when a bomb damaged it yesterday. He is an engineer from Tangga."

The lieutenant-colonel nodded absently. The major stared. Sweat had caked the dust on their faces and their eyes were swollen with fatigue.

Roda stood up. "Mr. Fraser, you will answer some questions. Some of the answers we already have, so that we shall know whether you tell the truth or not. So, be careful."

I said nothing and waited.

"Have you see Major Suparto today?"

"Certainly I've seen him."

"When?"

"I think it was shortly before the General and you came up here, nearly an hour after the planes came over that dropped leaflets."

"Where did you see him?"

"Here, naturally."

"What was said?"

"He told me that the General was returning to this apartment, and that I should respect his desire for privacy by keeping off the terrace outside."

"What else?"

"He allowed me to fetch some drinking-water from the kitchen."

"What else?"

"Nothing more, I think. Oh yes, he mentioned that he was going to make a reconnaissance in the city."

Roda laughed shortly. Inside the room there was a silence. Not very far off, an eighty-eight was slamming away like a pair of double doors in a gale.

Sanusi raised his head. "Was nothing else said, Mr. Fraser?"

"No, General."

"Why should he tell you where he was going?"

"I've no idea, General."

"You knew Major Suparto when he was at Tangga. Were you friendly with him there?"

"Not particularly. He was employed by the contractors as a liaison manager. His duties were very different from mine."

"What was the opinion of Major Suparto at Tangga?"

"Very high. In fact . . ." I broke off.

"Go on, Mr. Fraser. Say what there is to be said."

"I was only going to say that Major Suparto was exceptional. The Government sent quite a lot of unemployed officers to work with us there. Major Suparto was the only one of them who had any real ability."

There was another brief silence. Sanusi looked at Roda. Roda stared back at him bitterly for a moment and then swung round to face the other two.

"You hear?" he said in Malay. "You remember the meeting at Kail? I asked then. Why should they send him to Tangga where it was so easy for him to contact us? Luck, you all said. Luck, and more. It showed that they did not have the smallest suspicion that he was one of us." He glared round the room. "Well, now you know better. Now you know . . ."

"That is enough," Sanusi broke in impatiently. "Many mistakes have been made. I did not believe that we were ready. I was for waiting another year, for letting them destroy themselves before we moved. I yielded to the Committee's judgment."

"A judgment based on information supplied by a traitor, *Boeng*."

"I am not reproaching you. We are men, not gods, Ahmad. We cannot read souls." Sanusi stood up and walked over to the table.

Perhaps because they were now speaking Malay they thought I did not understand. Perhaps they had forgotten me. I just stood there. They watched him as if they were waiting for an oracle, while he smoothed out a map and bent over it.

"Here are the possibilities," he said at last. "We can try to break out of the city and regain our base."

Roda shrugged. "That is their greatest hope, that we will try," he said.

Sanusi eyed him coldly. "We will consider all the possibilities, Ahmad. Your advice will be asked later. The second possibility is that we attempt to hold the centre of the city." He paused and this time Roda was silent. "The third possibility is that we negotiate with them." He looked at the lieutenant-colonel. "Well, Aroff? Your opinions?"

Aroff wiped his forehead with the back of his hand. "As to the first possibility, *Boeng*, I agree with Ahmad." He spoke huskily and kept clearing his throat. "As to the second, I have no objection to dying. As to the third, I do not understand how we can negotiate anything except surrender, and for us that only means dying in a different way. I say that it is better to die like men than to die shamefully in a prison yard."

"Major Dahman?"

"I say the same, *Boeng*."

"Ahmad?"

Roda stared round at them belligerently. "Are we whipped dogs? What is all this talk of dying?"

Aroff stiffened. "Can you give us guns, Ahmad?" he snapped. "Can you give us tanks? Can you, at this late hour, persuade the men who were to have fought with us to desert General Ishak? If so, we will talk of living."

"We are not whipped dogs," Sanusi interposed; "and neither are we children. What is your opinion, Ahmad?"

"We should negotiate, *Boeng*. Consider. We are in a strong position here. They have tanks, yes, and they have guns, but they cannot stand at a distance and kill us all with high explosive. At Cassino, a few Germans held an army corps. At Stalingrad, it was the Germans who broke, not the Russkis. Ah yes, I know it is different with us. We are cut off from our supplies. Our ammunition will not last for ever. But if they want to kill us they will have to assault us, and that will be an expensive operation for them. They will prefer to negotiate."

"For our surrender, certainly they will negotiate," retorted Aroff; "but what terms can we expect?"

"An amnesty within two years. The terms to be witnessed by a neutral observer, the Indonesian Ambassador perhaps."

"They would be fools to agree."

"Why? We have a following in the country. They will not make themselves secure by killing us. Besides, think of the good impression it would create abroad."

Aroff turned protestingly to Sanusi. "*Boeng*, this is madness."

Sanusi started to say something and so did Roda. At the same instant, there was a quick rushing sound. Then, the floor jumped, a blast wave that felt like a sandbag clouted me in the chest and my head jarred to the whiplash violence of exploding T.N.T.

For a second I stood there, stupidly staring at the other men in the room who were staring stupidly at me. Then, I turned and blundered out on to the terrace. The shell had burst against a window embrasure on the floor below, and fumes and smoke were pouring up over the balustrade. As I began to cough, the staff captain pushed past me with an angry exclamation that I was too deafened to hear, and went to look down over the balustrade. Then, the fumes got him, too, and he turned away. I looked back into the room. Roda was holding the back of his hand against his forehead as if he were dazed. Sanusi was shouting something at him. I stumbled along the terrace to the bedroom.

Rosalie was sitting on my bed with her hands over her face, trembling violently. I was not feeling too good myself. If that was a sample of the shooting we could expect from the naval gunners, we were not going to last very long.

I put my arms round her and she looked up at me. The whistle of the second shell rose to a climax and we both ducked involuntarily. The burst that followed made a glass on the table tinkle against the water bottle standing beside it, but that was all. It was about three hundred yards over.

I produced the old platitude: "If you can hear it coming it's going to miss you."

It has never yet comforted anyone who was badly frightened, and it did not comfort her. The destroyer was firing its four guns singly, so that the bombardment was reasonably steady, but I soon realised that the first hit had been a fluke. When, after twenty minutes, the first burst of firing ceased, they had not succeeded in dropping another shell within fifty yards of the Air House. Perhaps they were not trying for it. For Rosalie, however, every round was aimed, not merely at the building we were in, but at our room in it. I moved one of the beds around so as to give us some protection from a burst on the terrace, and we lay down on the floor behind it, but I don't think she felt any more protected.

When the lull came, however, I made her go out on to the terrace with me to see what damage had been done. There were some craters in the square, and a small building on the far side was on fire; but that was about all that was visible. In fact, the closely built-up area behind us had taken the brunt of the shelling; but there was no point in telling her that. The damage to our own building was also out of sight. As she had clearly expected to find the entire square in ruins, all this produced a very satisfactory sense of anti-climax. We kept to the bathhouse end of the terrace, and saw nothing of the men in the living room. I guessed that the council of war had been resumed on the other side of the building. Rosalie had heard something of what had been said while I was there, and now I told her the rest. The possibility of negotiation cheered her up considerably. I did not say what I thought of it. When we went back into the bedroom, I was able to persuade her to eat some fruit and begin another game of gin.

It was just after three when the staff captain came for me again.

Since two, the sounds of street-fighting had steadily been getting nearer, and we had had another twenty-minute bombardment from the destroyer. This had been both worse and better than the first; worse, because the gunners had dropped the range slightly and managed to put every shell into or around the square itself; better, because Rosalie, having decided that her earlier fears had been quite groundless, proposed that we should continue our game of gin on the floor. Admittedly, it was my hands that shook now, not hers, and she who was concerned on my account when a near miss made me fumble and scatter my cards; but on the whole it was an improvement on the earlier situation.

The staff captain was more polite this time. It was Colonel Roda who wished to see me, he explained; but why, he did not know. The radio in the next room was silent, and, with a sinking heart, I wondered if the generator had broken down again. The staff captain shrugged when I suggested this; he knew nothing. I told Rosalie that if I were going to be away for any length of time, I would try to get a message to her, and then went off with him.

He led me to an office on the third floor at the back of the building. The shell that had burst on the fifth floor had gutted three offices and brought down part of the wall along the corridor, but there had been no casualties, and no structural damage of any consequence. It had short-circuited the lights, however, and Alwi was along there trying to rectify the trouble. I asked him about the generator, but he said that it was running perfectly. By the time I reached Colonel Roda's office, I was both puzzled and worried.

The office into which the staff captain ushered me had the look of a board room after a directors' meeting. The air was full of tobacco smoke, and there was a litter of dirty coffee cups and crumpled scribbling paper. There had been seven men in there, but now there were only two: Roda and Aroff. The latter had cleaned himself up and wore a black cap in place of the steel helmet; but he looked even wearier than before. Roda's face was the colour of putty. It did not seem to have been a very successful meeting.

They were sitting at one end of the table reading through a document and comparing it with what was evidently the draft from which it had been typed. To my surprise, Roda waved me to a chair. I sat down as far away from them as possible and waited. When they had finished, Roda looked at Aroff inquiringly. Aroff nodded, but with the air of a man agreeing to something against his better judgment. Roda pursed his lips and turned to me.

"Mr. Fraser, we have sent for you because we believe that you may be willing to assist us."

"Oh yes?"

"The General and I were much impressed by your co-operation in the matter of the generator. Under circumstances of the greatest difficulty, without proper assistance or equipment, you employed your skill and knowledge to such good effect that the enemy's attempts to silence Radio Sunda were totally defeated." He smiled.

This was fantastic. For one wild moment I thought that he was about to pin a decoration on me: the Order of *Boeng* Sanusi (2nd Class) perhaps. I smiled back guardedly. Aroff, I noticed, was absently studying his fingernails, as if none of what was being said were any business of his.

"That being so," Roda continued amiably, "we do not think it unreasonable to assume that, as a British friend of Sunda, you are sympathetic to the policy and aspirations of the National Freedom Party and its leader."

I could have thought of several brief replies to that, but by now I was curious to know what he wanted.

I shook my head doubtfully. "As a foreigner, of course, it would be a gross impertinence for me to express an opinion about a political matter."

"Nevertheless, Mr. Fraser, we feel that you are not unsympathetic to the principles for which we stand. It is for that reason that we propose to take you into our confidence."

"I see." I did not see, but he evidently expected me to say something.

"Good. As you know, the Nasjah forces have counter-attacked. At this moment a battle is being fought in the streets of our city. Now, I must tell you, Mr. Fraser, that but for the activities of certain enemy agents and the unconstitutional action of the Nasjah gang in arresting many of our supporters on false charges, this battle would not be going on. We should be in complete control. As it is, Sunda is faced not merely by civil war, but also by the devastation of large areas of our capital. Mr. Fraser, we are patriots, not savages. Sunda cannot tolerate civil war. Selampang cannot be permitted to suffer needlessly. General Sanusi has, therefore, taken the initiative in proposing to General Ishak, as between equals, an armistice, during which negotiations can take place for the evacuation of all armed forces from the city and the setting up of a joint commission of conciliation under neutral supervision."

It was not a bad bluff. If I had not talked to Suparto I might have swallowed it for a while. I glanced at Aroff. He had a knife out and was cleaning his fingernails now. I looked back at Roda.

"I wish you every success, Colonel. But I don't see how I can help you."

"I will explain, Mr. Fraser. We have been in telephone communication with General Ishak's headquarters and certain conditions have been agreed for a preliminary meeting to discuss the terms of the cease-fire. That meeting will take place, under flags of truce, in front of the police barracks at four o'clock. That is in half an hour." He paused and stirred uncomfortably.

"Yes, Colonel?"

"We asked that independent foreign observers should be present, so that any promises made or undertakings given should be properly witnessed. Consular or diplomatic representatives would have been suitable, but this was not agreed. The enemy refuse to permit accredited representatives of foreign powers to participate in what they say is a domestic political matter. They pretend that it would be contrary to protocol and an encroachment on our national sovereignty. In fact, of course, they are afraid to lose face. It has been agreed, however, that two foreign observers not of diplomatic status may attend, one for each side, providing that neither is a newspaper representative and neither of Dutch nationality. We would like you to attend for us, Mr. Fraser."

"Me? Why me? Surely there is someone more suitable in the area you control, some business man who fulfils the agreed conditions."

"There may be, Mr. Fraser, but we do not know where to find him at this moment. There is not much time."

"Frankly, I don't see why you need anyone at all." This was pure malice. I did see. Having nothing whatsoever to offer in exchange for the terms he was asking, and merely hoping to pull off a bluff, he was doing his best to make the negotiations seem formal and portentous. If the other side were the slightest bit unsure of themselves, it was just possible, too, that the presence of neutral observers might influence their judgment.

"The procedure has been agreed," he said coldly. He was tired of persuasion, and the fact that he would sooner be cutting my throat than asking for my co-operation was beginning to show in his eyes.

"Very well. What do I do?"

"Colonel Aroff will be our delegate. You will accompany him."

"What are my duties?"

"Firstly, to take note of what is said." He hesitated. "Should you feel, of course, that the other side are not viewing the situation correctly, you would be entitled to consult with their observer, and perhaps to protest." His eyes held mine. "I am sure you realise, Mr. Fraser, that it is in everyone's interest that an acceptable agreement is reached."

There was sufficient emphasis on the word "everyone." I understood now.

"May I know what terms you would accept?"

"Colonel Aroff has his instructions. He will explain them to you on the way. You should be leaving now."

Colonel Aroff put his knife away, stuffed the document they had been studying into his pocket and stood up. Then, with a nod to me he walked out of the room. He did not even look at Roda.

The staff captain was waiting in the corridor and, as I followed Aroff out, he joined the procession. I noticed that he was carrying something that looked like a long cardboard tube in his hand. We followed Aroff down the stairs to the sandbagged entrance. There was a guard there who demanded passes before we were allowed to leave the building; Suparto having got away, the stable door was now bolted. The staff captain had the passes and we went through.

Outside in the road there was a jeep waiting which I recognised as the one from Tangga that Suparto had used. There was a soldier sitting in the driving seat. Aroff stopped and looked at the tube the staff captain was holding.

"Is that the flag of truce?"

"Yes, Colonel *tuan.*"

"It must not be shown here. Can you drive?"

"No, Colonel *tuan.*"

Aroff looked non-plussed. "Neither can I."

"I'll drive if you like, Colonel."

For the first time he looked at me directly. After a moment's thought, he nodded. "Good." He told the staff captain to go and dismiss the driver.

"When men see a flag of truce," he added to me, "they begin to think of safety. After that it is hard to make them fight. The driver would have come back here and told them."

As we walked towards the jeep, a shell from the destroyer burst among the trees across the square and sent a lot of torn-off branches spurting up into the air. Another bombardment had begun. I remembered that I had not tried to send a message to Rosalie; but it was too late to do anything about that now. Another shell landed near one of the gun positions. As my ears returned to normal, I could hear a wounded man screaming.

"A waste of ammunition," Aroff remarked dourly. "Nearly two hundred rounds and what have they done with them? Six men killed and twenty wounded. It is absurd."

Absurd or not, they had also made a mess of some of the buildings in and around the square. One of the streets I tried to drive along was completely blocked by fallen rubble, and we had to make a detour. It was not easy. The area now being defended by Sanusi's troops was not much more than a quarter of a mile across in some places, and twice we had to reverse out of streets which had come under enemy fire. At several points, buses and trucks had been turned on to their sides and teams of civilians, women as well as men, were being forced by squads of troops to drag the vehicles broadside on to form tank obstacles. I saw no other civilians on the streets and the shops were all shuttered. Once, I caught a glimpse of a child's face at a window, but I was too busy driving to look about me much.

The police barracks were opposite the telephone exchange in a long, straight road that began somewhere in the Chinese section and ended at the airport. About two hundred yards short of the barracks, we came to a canal crossing with a cinema on one corner and a barricade of overturned cars across the roadway. There was a two-pounder behind one of the cars, and in the deep storm drains on either side of the road a couple of machine-gunners. As I pulled up at the barricade, an officer who looked like a recently promoted N.C.O. moved out of a doorway and hurried over.

Aroff returned the man's salute casually.

"Have you been notified of the arrangements, Lieutenant?"

"Yes, Colonel *tuan*."

Aroff looked up at the bullet-scarred walls of the godown that stretched along one side of the road.

"You were under fire here until when?"

"Until ten minutes ago, Colonel *tuan*." He pointed with pride to the empty cases lying on the ground behind the two-pounder. "And they did not have it all their own way. The armoured car they sent did not like our gun."

"Did you destroy the armoured car?"

"Ah no, *tuan.*" He smiled tolerantly, as if at a foolish question. "But they did not return for more. They have brought up a tank now."

"Where are the rest of your men?"

"On the roof of the godown, *tuan.*"

Aroff looked at his watch. "We have five minutes, Mr. Fraser. We must discuss the situation."

He climbed out of the jeep, and I followed him as he walked over to the barricade. The staff captain seemed about to follow, then he thought better of it and began to talk to the lieutenant.

Aroff peered through the gap between two of the overturned cars which the gunners were using as an embrasure, and motioned to me to do the same. The crew squatting in the shade of one of the trucks looked up at us drowsily.

Except for a dead dog lying just beyond the canal, the road between the barricade and the police barracks was empty. The only visible sign of life in the ramshackle apartment houses which flanked it was a line of washing strung between two of the windows; but the sound of gunfire was comparatively distant now, and I could hear a man coughing in one of the houses. Outside the police barracks, in the centre of the road, and with its gun pointing directly at us, stood a medium tank.

Aroff was watching me as I straightened up.

"Are you a soldier, Mr. Fraser?"

"I was in the British army."

"An officer?"

"Yes, in the Engineers. Why?"

He drew me away and we walked back along the road for a few yards. When we were out of earshot of the gunners, he stopped.

"Should that tank you see there decide to move along this road, Mr. Fraser, what do you think will happen?"

"How do you mean?"

"Do you see anything here to stop it?"

"Not a thing. The two-pounder's shot will bounce off it. It'll just push this road block out of the way and drive on. Unless, that is, you've got an anti-tank mine under that crossing."

"We have no mines."

"And no other anti-tank weapons?"

"Here, none."

"Then there's nothing to stop it."

"Exactly." He produced the document from his pocket, and held it out to me. "Do you wish to read this?"

"I think Colonel Roda made its contents clear."

"Then we understand one another. All I have to offer them, in fact, is a small saving of effort. The rest is pretence, and, of course, they will know that."

"What do you want me to do, Colonel?"

He shrugged. "Is it of interest to you what happens to us?"

"If there is any prospect of a cease-fire, naturally I'll do everything I can to help."

"Then I will make only one request to you, Mr. Fraser."

"Yes?"

"General Ishak is a military man. If you should have to refer to Roda, please do not call him Colonel Roda. In General Ishak's army he was a captain."

"And General Sanusi?"

"Colonel Sanusi would be more discreet."

"What about you, Colonel?"

He smiled slightly. "I received no promotion. But I do not think that General Ishak will regard that as a point in my favour. We shall, of course, speak Malay."

He looked at his watch again, then turned and walked towards the jeep.

The staff captain came forward and, when Aroff nodded, he took the white flag of truce out of its cardboard wrapping and fixed it on to the windscreen of the jeep.

I saw the gunners staring at it incredulously. Then, the lieutenant shouted an order and they scrambled to their feet. Another order, and they rolled the gun back clear of the barricade. The machine-gunners helped them to swing one of the cars aside a foot or two, so that there was space for the jeep to go through.

Aroff took no notice of these preparations. He had got into the jeep and was sitting there woodenly under the flag. I went and sat beside him in the driving seat while the staff captain clambered into the back. We sat there for a moment or two, then Aroff looked at his watch again and nodded to me.

I drove through the gap in the barricade on to the road ahead.

"Slowly, Mr. Fraser," Aroff said; "and keep to the centre."

I needed no telling. The moment we were clear of the barricade I felt horribly exposed; I was almost sure that the tank was going to open fire on us. The white flag drooping on its stick above us seemed a totally inadequate protection. It only wanted one trigger-happy idiot to start, I thought, and every gun in Selampang would be firing at us. I had no hat and was already far too warm. As I drove, sweat began to trickle into my eyes.

The first hundred yards was the worst. After that, although I could see the muzzle of the tank's gun dropping gradually as the gunner kept us in his sights, I knew that unless we suddenly drove straight at him brandishing anti-tank grenades, he was not going to fire. Also I could see a group of officers standing in the shade by the gate of the police barracks, waiting.

When we were within ten yards of the tank, a lieutenant in the Government uniform stepped out from behind it and held up his hand. I stopped with a jerk that made the staff captain lurch against the back of my seat.

Aroff got out stiffly and stood beside the jeep. When the staff captain and I had joined him, the lieutenant advanced and stopped in front of us.

"Follow me, please," he said curtly.

He turned then, and we followed him past the tank and over to the gateway. The group of officers was no longer there, only two sentries who stared at us curiously. The lieutenant led the way through into the courtyard of the barracks and the two sentries closed in behind us.

There was a big sago palm in the centre, and a table and chair had been placed in the shade of it. General Ishak sat at the table. Standing behind him were four officers and a civilian. I had never seen Ishak before. He was a thin, bitter-looking man with angry eyes and one of those wispy Sundanese moustaches that look as if they have just been stuck on with spirit gum. More interesting to me at that moment, however, was the fact that just behind him, still haggard but crisp and clean in his proper uniform, stood Major Suparto. As we came up to the table, I saw his eyes flicker towards me, but he gave no sign of recognition.

Aroff stopped and saluted the General.

Ishak did not return the salute. For a moment the two men stared at one another in silence. I was standing a little behind Aroff and I could see the muscles of his jaw twitching. Ishak looked at me.

"Who is this?" I recognised the voice. It was light and ugly, and sounded as if he were trying to speak and swallow at the same time. I had heard it once before that week.

"Mr. Fraser, an engineer from the Tangga Valley project, General. He is here by agreement as an observer."

"Very well." He glanced at the civilian who stood next to Suparto. "This is Mr. Petersen of the Malayan Rubber Agency."

"Dutch?" Aroff demanded sharply.

"Danish," said Mr. Petersen. He was a stout, fleshy-faced man in the late fifties, wearing a suit as well as a tie and looking as if he might at any moment collapse from the heat. I nodded to him and he smiled nervously.

Ishak yawned. "Although why foreign observers should be necessary to witness a simple police operation is not easy to understand," he said, and looked up at Aroff. "Well, this meeting is at Sanusi's request. He can only wish to surrender. It remains for me to inform you about the time and place. You agree?"

"No, General. All I am instructed to discuss are the terms of an armistice."

"What armistice? What terms?"

Aroff fumbled in his pocket and drew out the document. "I have the proposals here."

Ishak took the document, glanced through it impassively and then passed it to a colonel, presumably his chief of staff, who was standing behind him. Suparto read it over the colonel's shoulder. When they had finished, the colonel handed it back to Ishak. The latter glanced through it again and then looked at Aroff.

"Before you became a traitor, Aroff," he said, "you used to be an intelligent man." He tore the document in half and dropped the pieces on the table. "What has happened to you?"

"I am here to discuss terms, General." Aroff's voice was very carefully controlled.

Ishak flicked the torn paper away from him. "That discussion is ended. If you do not wish to make any personal explanation, then we will waste no more time. You may go."

Aroff did not move. "The document, General, was intended as a basis for negotiations. It can be modified."

Ishak shook his head. "It cannot be modified. You are not here to negotiate or to discuss terms. If you are not here to offer surrender, then we are wasting time." He stood up. "You have five minutes to get back to your lines."

Aroff hesitated, then he gave in. "On what terms would you accept a surrender, General?"

"I will tell you. Your masters say that they wish to avoid useless suffering and damage to property. So do I. On that point we agree. Very well. I will accept the surrender of all members of your rebel force who disarm themselves, form themselves into separate parties of not more than twenty-five, and march under flags of surrender to the square in front of the railroad station. Each party should appoint a leader who will carry the white flag, and every man must bring any food he has with him. All arms and ammunition must be left behind under guard in the Van Riebeeck Square until our troops arrive there."

"What treatment would those who surrender receive?"

"For the present they will be treated as if they were foreign prisoners of war under the terms of the Geneva Convention. Later, no doubt, after a year, perhaps, an amnesty will be granted. That is all, I think. Do those terms seem harsh to you, Aroff?"

Aroff shook his head.

Ishak smiled unpleasantly. "After what has happened, they seem to me absurdly lenient. Politicians' terms, Aroff! You should be laughing."

Aroff sighed. "You were good enough to say that I was an intelligent man, General. You would have more dignity if you treated me as one."

"What more do you want, Aroff? A free pardon?"

"The list of exceptions, General. The list of those whose surrender will not be accepted."

"Ah yes, the outlaws." He held out his hand and Suparto gave him a paper. "Let us see. Sanusi, Roda, Aroff, Dahman . . . I am sorry to tell you that you are on the list. Shall I read any more?"

"If Major Suparto drew it up, I am sure it is complete." Aroff looked straight at Suparto, and I was glad I could not see his eyes.

Suparto stared back impassively.

Ishak handed Aroff the paper. "Your masters will want to see that. They have half an hour in which to let us know that they accept our terms."

"Terms, General?" Aroff said bitterly. "You mean a death sentence, surely!"

"No, Aroff." Ishak's eyes narrowed. "That sentence has been passed already. It is no longer a question of whether you all die or not, but only of how you die and of how many of your men die with you. We shall see now what value your leader puts on his men's lives." He turned to Suparto. "Send them back."

Ishak began to walk towards the barrack entrance. Suparto moved after him quickly and said something. Ishak paused. I saw him glance back at me and then nod to Suparto before walking on.

Suparto came over to Aroff.

"Mr. Fraser is a foreigner and a non-combatant. Is it necessary for him to return with you?"

Aroff shrugged. "I don't know. I suppose not."

"It is very necessary," I said.

They both stared at me.

Suparto frowned. "Why?"

"Roda left me in no doubt that he regards Miss Linden as a hostage."

"That is absurd."

"It wasn't absurd yesterday, Major. You should know that."

"The situation is now different."

"Not for Miss Linden. She's still up there in that apartment. I'm very grateful to you for the suggestion, but I think I must go back."

He sighed irritably. "This is foolishness, Mr. Fraser. The woman is not your wife."

"Perhaps Mr. Fraser has scruples about betraying those who trust him," said Aroff.

Suparto stood absolutely still, his face a mask. For a moment he stared at Aroff, then he nodded to the lieutenant who was waiting to escort us back to the jeep.

Aroff was smiling as he turned away.

The jeep had been standing out in the sun and the metal on it was painful to touch. I made a clumsy job of turning it between the deep drains. My movements were hampered, too, by the staff captain, who was leaning forward across the back of my seat, pleading with Aroff.

"The list, Colonel. May I see the list?"

"Not now."

"A man has a right to know if he is to die."

"All men have to die, Captain."

"If I could see the list."

"Not while they are watching us. Have you no dignity?"

"For the love of Allah, tell me."

"Are you a renegade? Did you formerly hold a commission from the Republic?"

"You know that I did, Colonel."

"Then you will be on the list."

I managed to get the jeep round at last and drove back towards the barricade. Behind me, the staff captain began to weep.

From this side of the canal crossing I could see the front of the cinema. Above the portico there was a big advertising cut-out. Next week, it said, they would be showing *Samson and Delilah*.

When we arrived back at the square, the shelling had stopped. The Ministry of Public Health had had a direct hit on the roof, and smoke was drifting up from the smouldering débris below. Outside the Air House there was a pile of rubble that seemed to have fallen from one of the upper floors. All over the square there were men still digging in. There was an insistent racket of machine-gun fire. It seemed to be coming from somewhere only two or three streets away.

Rosalie had been alone for nearly an hour and I was worried about her. The only time Aroff had spoken since we had re-crossed the canal had been to tell me to stop so that the wretched staff captain could remove the flag of truce. When we left the jeep, I drew him aside.

"I don't think I can be much help to you with Roda, do you, Colonel?"

He thought for a moment and then he said: "No. This captain will escort you back. I will tell Roda that I ordered it."

"Is there any reason why Miss Linden and I should remain here?"

"None, except that you would need Roda's permission to leave. At this moment, it would not be wise to ask for it."

"I see what you mean."

"Besides, where would you go? The streets would be more dangerous for you than this place, and who would take you into his house at such a time?"

"Perhaps there will be a surrender?"

He shook his head. "They will never agree. They will dream of miraculous escapes. Ishak knows that. He is only humiliating us. He means to destroy us all."

"If it rested with you, Colonel, would you accept?"

He shrugged wearily. "If it had rested with me, I would never have attempted to negotiate. I am not so afraid of death. Now, we have lost face and will die ashamed." He hesitated and then gave me a little bow of dismissal. "Your company has been a pleasure, Mr. Fraser."

The staff captain left me at the door of the apartment and hurried back downstairs, presumably to make his own panic-stricken contribution to the discussion of Ishak's surrender terms.

The door from the hall into the living room was shut. If there were any officers inside I did not want to walk in on them unexpectedly. I knocked. There was no reply; but as I opened the door I had a shock.

When I had left, the sun roof over the terrace had been propped up fairly securely, and the screens were in place. Now there was no sun roof and the screens were flattened. One of the long chairs was lying across the balustrade. I ran through on to the terrace.

The shell had landed on the terrace of one of the unfinished apartments about thirty feet beyond the barrier wall with the spikes on it, and had dislodged a whole section of the balustrade there. The barrier wall was sagging like an unhinged door, and the blast had lifted the roof off the bathhouse.

As I saw this and started towards the bedroom shouting for Rosalie, I stumbled over one of the screens. Then, I saw her running towards me along the terrace and went to meet her.

For a minute or so she clung to me, sobbing. It was only relief, she explained after a while; relief that I was back. She had really not been very frightened when the shell burst; it had been so sudden. It was right what I had told her about shells and the noise they made. She had not heard this one coming.

All this time she had been holding the water scoop from the bathhouse in her hand. Now, she explained that the cistern had collapsed into the bathhouse when the roof had lifted, and that she had been trying to transfer what was left of the water into the ewer before it all leaked away.

I went along there with her and had a look at the damage. If the cistern had been full it would have crashed through to the floor. As it was, the pipes had held it up, though one of them had fractured and was gradually draining it. I got a jug from the kitchen and between us we managed to get most of the water into the ewer. While we were doing this, I told her about the surrender offer and what Colonel Aroff had said.

She took the news calmly.

"General Ishak is a swine," was her comment.

"You know him?"

"Everyone knows about him. Mina has a very funny scandal. He sleeps with young men, you know. They say that even so he can do nothing. When you spoke to Major Suparto, did he say anything about us?"

"I only had a word or two with him."

"Do you think he will try to help us?"

"If he can, he will."

She fell silent. The cistern just above our heads was vibrating to the concussion of an eighty-eight which was slamming away somewhere along the Telegraf Road. I knew that she was listening to the noise carefully and beginning to wonder about the violence it represented. She had a standard of comparison now.

"I think it's time we had a drink," I said.

CHAPTER IX

THE FIRST TANK reached the Van Riebeeck Square just before sundown.

No great flights of military imagination had been needed to devise General Ishak's plan of attack. The modern dock area south of the river had been quietly occupied by Government troops after the bombing of the road and rail bridges the previous afternoon. It was only the semi-circle of city north of the river, and centred on the Van Riebeeck Square, that he had to take by force. The rebel outer defence ring had been held together by three strong points: the canal network of the old port, the garrison barracks and a rubber factory in the suburbs. He had decided to make his break-through a little to the south of the barracks under a covering bombardment from the destroyer, then fan out right and left, rolling up the outer defences as he went. Finally, he would turn east again and send three armoured columns to converge on rebel headquarters. In view of the superior forces at his disposal, there was no likelihood of the plan failing. All that remained to be learned was how soon it would succeed.

The reduction of the outer defences had been all but completed by mid-day, though it had not been quite as easy as Ishak had expected. At several points, the defenders had been agile enough to slip through his cumbersome enveloping movements and re-establish themselves in new positions; but in the end, they were squeezed back, and all they succeeded in gaining for themselves by their efforts was a little time that they could not use. By three o'clock the turn to the east had been made, and the armoured columns were carving their way through towards the centre, the speed of their advance controlled only by that of the infantry mopping up behind them.

Not long after five, there was a tremendous burst of firing along the Telegraf Road; machine guns, mortars, a two-pounder; the noise was deafening. The sun was low now, and I could see smoke drifting up over the roofs less than a quarter of a mile away. Where the Telegraf Road entered the square there was a sudden flurry of activity. There were men running back out of the road and other men running forward into it. Then, one of the two-pounders out in the square began to fire. I heard Rosalie give a startled gasp and turned round. She was crouching behind the balustrade with her fingers in her ears. When I looked back across the square, there were no running men. One of them was lying face downwards in the centre of the road. The rest had taken cover against the walls of the building that jutted out on the corner. The two-pounder was firing rapidly, bouncing about in its shallow pit, sending up a cloud of yellow dust and adding to the racket of the machine guns; then, for an instant, there was a gap in the sound, and through it I heard the shrill squeaking of a tank's tracks.

It nosed out of the end of the road, and seemed to hesitate there for a moment like a dull-witted bull blinking in the sunlight of the arena. There was a black stain down the side of it that looked as if it had been made by an oil bomb. The two-pounder fired twice and I saw a streak of silver appear on the turret. Every automatic weapon in the square seemed to be firing at that moment, and the sound of the tank's own machine gun was lost in the din. But it was the tank's gun that was effective. Dust spurted up all around the two-pounder, and suddenly it was no longer firing. I saw one of the gunners start to crawl out of the pit, and then a second burst finished him. Two more bursts wiped out the crews of two of the machine guns.

The tank lurched forward and then made a left turn. It controlled the square now, and was ready to demonstrate the fact to anyone foolish enough to dispute it. Apparently, nobody was. The crew of the other two-pounder out in the square were scrambling for cover among the trees, and the remaining machine-gunners who, a moment ago, had been blazing away so fiercely at the tank's armour plating, were now crouching discreetly in their fox-holes. The tank began to move along the north side of the square searching for targets. From away across the square some optimist began dropping mortar bombs near it. And then, suddenly the situation changed. There was a noise like an enormous paper bag being exploded. Immediately on top of it there was a spine-jarring crack. At the same moment the tank swung round broadside on and stopped in a cloud of dust.

The commander of it knew his job. Within a few seconds, he was putting down smoke; though not before another bazooka bomb had sent fragments of the broken track screaming up through the trees overhead. As the smoke drifted back across the tank, I could see the turret traversing rapidly and knew that the commander had spotted the bazookas' position. If the men handling them did not move quickly, they would become sitting targets as soon as the smoke thinned; but, like innocents, they were settling down expectantly to wait for another chance to knock the tank out.

Rosalie touched my arm. I looked round and saw that Roda had come into the living room. We went back quickly into the bedroom.

After a moment, Sanusi walked out on to the terrace and looked down on to the square. Roda was talking to someone in the next room, but it was impossible to hear the conversation. When the other person went, Roda joined Sanusi at the balustrade.

There was some sort of disagreement between the two men. Roda was trying to persuade Sanusi of something and Sanusi would appear to be listening; then he would turn away abruptly and Roda would have to go after him and begin all over again. Once Sanusi turned sharply and asked a question. Roda had his document case with him, and in reply he held it up and patted it.

Down in the square, the tank's turret gun began firing suddenly and the building shook as something crashed into it. Rosalie looked at me inquiringly. I said I thought that the tank was firing at the place where the bazooka crews were dug in, and that the shot had probably ricocheted into the building down below. She nodded understandingly, as if I had been apologising for the noise made by an inconsiderate neighbour.

Another tank had entered the square now. I could hear it squeaking along the road in the opposite direction to the first one and firing bursts from its machine gun.

Then, the sun went down, and for nearly a minute there was no sound from the square except the squeaking of the tank tracks. Along the Telegraf Road, however, the firing intensified and I could hear the thumping of grenades. The infantry were moving up now, clearing the defended houses that the tanks had left behind them. Now and again, the drifting smoke would be illuminated momentarily by the flash of an explosion below.

A shoe grated outside on the terrace.

"Mr. Fraser." It was Roda's voice.

I went to the window. There were no lights on in the apartment, nor was there a moon yet. He was about ten feet away and for a moment I did not see him.

"Yes, Colonel?"

"Come here, please."

I went over. Beyond him, along the terrace, Sanusi stirred and rested his elbows on the balustrade.

Roda lowered his voice. "I must speak in confidence to you, Mr. Fraser."

"Yes?"

"It has become necessary for the General and myself to leave this headquarters."

"Yes?"

"We have done all we can here. It is better to live for a cause than to die for it uselessly. That is our choice now. I have persuaded our *Boeng* that it is his duty to live."

"I see."

"It has been a difficult decision, you will understand." He paused.

"I can see that."

"More difficult than you might think."

"No doubt." I was trying unavailingly to understand the reason for these confidences.

"For two men, withdrawal from this headquarters is still possible. If more should attempt it, all will fail. There must be secrecy."

"Of course." That, at least, I could understand.

"As there was when Napoleon withdrew from Egypt."

For a moment, I thought that he was making a tasteless joke. But no; his lips were pursed solemnly. He saw himself as the Marmont of this occasion.

I mumbled agreement.

"I tell you this, Mr. Fraser, because there is a matter in which you can help us."

"Yes?"

"If we are to withdraw successfully we cannot go in our uniforms."

"I see that."

"It is the shirts. Our pants will attract no attention. We merely need civilian shirts. I think you have some."

"Shirts?" I stared at him stupidly.

"Two will be enough. You have clean ones?"

"Yes, I have." I also had a terrible desire to laugh.

"Then perhaps you will get them."

"Now?"

"At once, please."

I turned and went back into the bedroom. In there, I tried switching on the light, but the power was off. Rosalie watched me incredulously, while I struck a match and began fumbling in the drawers. I knew that I had only one clean shirt left. This round would have to be on Jebb. I found the right drawer eventually, picked out two of the oldest shirts there, and took them out on to the terrace. Roda nodded approval.

"I'm afraid they will be a bit large for you, Colonel."

"That is unimportant." He folded them carefully and put them in his document case. "They are light-coloured but not . . ."

"Colonel!" It was Sanusi's voice.

Roda turned inquiringly.

Sanusi had moved away from the balustrade and was standing in the centre of the terrace. I thought I saw a pistol in his hand, but it was too dark to see properly. At the same moment, there were footsteps in the living room, and Aroff and Major Dahman came out on to the terrace.

"*Boeng*," Aroff began, "you sent for us?"

"Yes," said Sanusi; and then he fired.

The first bullet hit Roda in the stomach. For a second, he stood quite still; then he dropped the document case and took a step forward. The second bullet hit him in the right shoulder and he twisted forward on to his knees. He began to say something, but Sanusi paid no attention to him.

To Aroff and Dahman, he said: "I sent for you to witness an execution." Then, he went up to Roda and shot him again in the back of the head.

Roda slid forward on to his face.

Aroff and Dahman did not move as Sanusi turned towards them. Across the square, one of the tanks began firing its turret gun.

"What was the offence, *Boeng*?" Aroff said.

"He was attempting to desert. You will find the evidence in there." He shone a flashlight on to the document case. "Open it."

Aroff walked over to the document case and opened it up. The shirts fell out. He looked up at me.

"Yes, they were from the Englishman," said Sanusi. "I leave that matter to you. All officers of the defence force must be informed of the execution and the reason. The body should be put where they can see it. For the public I shall issue a simple statement informing them that, in view of the pressure of Colonel Roda's military duties, I have taken over the Secretaryship of the Party for the time being. There must be no suggestion at this moment of a division in our ranks. I also have to consider world opinion. Firmness in such matters is not always understood."

He made these announcements with the cool authority of a leader secure in the possession of great power and the habit of using it with wisdom and restraint. He seemed totally unaware of their absurd incongruity. I saw Aroff look at him sharply.

"We have yet to hear from Djakarta," Sanusi added; "I think the time has come for me to speak to President Soekarno personally." With a nod to Aroff, he turned and walked away through the living room.

Aroff looked at Dahman, who shrugged slightly, and then at me. "What happened, Mr. Fraser?"

I told him. He made no comment. When I had finished he looked at Dahman.

"Well, Major, what do you think?" He nodded towards Roda's body. "Perhaps he was right. Of two men, one might be lucky."

Dahman smiled grimly. "And the other? I have seen Ishak's way of putting a renegade to death. I would prefer to shoot myself now rather than risk that."

"Are you a coward, Dahman?"

"About some things, Colonel."

"So am I." Aroff handed the shirts to me. "You see, Mr. Fraser? We have no use for them either." A gun flash lit up his face for an instant as he looked out across the square. "They will have their artillery up soon," he remarked; "then, there will be no more doubts to trouble us."

He turned to leave but at the living-room window he paused and looked back. "Mr. Fraser, if Roda had anything else belonging to you, something that you may need, you should take it at once."

I stood there staring after him uncertainly as he went through into the corridor. Then, Rosalie was at my elbow.

"Steven! He means the pistol."

"Are you sure?" I was still trying not to be sick.

"Yes. He means you to take the pistol."

"All right."

The holster was near enough to the side for me to get the pistol out of it without getting blood on my hands, but the spare magazines were on the other side of the belt, and I knew that I would have to turn the body over to get at them. There was a sound of footsteps in the corridor. We hurried back to the bedroom and I slipped the pistol into a drawer with the shirts on top of it.

The guards had a simple way of moving the body. They rolled it on to a mat that they had taken out of the living room and dragged it away. As they went, they made jokes about Roda's plumpness. They seemed in excellent spirits. In one respect, at least, Sanusi's officers had been successful; they had managed to conceal the truth about their predicament from the unfortunate rank and file.

When they had gone, I got a flashlight out of my suitcase and examined the pistol. It had a full magazine in it and there was a round in the breech. Rosalie watched intently, and when I had unloaded it to make sure that I knew how it worked, she asked if she might handle it.

The possession of the pistol obviously pleased her a great deal more than it pleased me. I remembered how, when I had wakened her the first night, thinking that there were thieves getting into the apartment, her first thought had been to ask if I had a revolver.

When I had shown her how to load and fire it and had explained the safety catch, I thought that I had better try to modify her enthusiasm for the thing.

"Pistols are not really very much use except for frightening people," I said.

"Colonel Roda would not agree with you."

"The General was six feet away and Roda wasn't expecting it. I've seen people miss a target in broad daylight with a pistol at that range."

"But if anyone attacks us, we can kill him."

"The fact that you have a pistol can be more dangerous than being unarmed. A soldier might not kill an unarmed civilian, but if he sees someone facing him with a gun in his hand, he may shoot rather than take a chance."

"I think it is better to have it."

"As long as we don't have to use it, it's fine."

"You had a revolver."

"There was a time up in Tangga when there were a lot of snakes about, and sometimes they got into our rooms. So I had a revolver. But the only time I tried to use it I missed, and after that I kept a shot-gun. I left that behind."

"Then the pistol is no good?" She sounded bitterly disappointed.

"It's an excellent pistol, and, as you say, it's better to have it than not. But what we need at this moment is somewhere to go when the fighting starts."

"When it *starts*? What is all that going on over there?"

There was, indeed, a fierce machine-gun and mortar battle going on around the College of Agriculture on the far side of the square. Some of Sanusi's troops had dug themselves in in the College grounds, and now the Government infantry were having to ferret them out.

"When it starts here, I mean. It's not going to be easy for them to take this building. They'll have to do it floor by floor. I don't want to be here when they start throwing grenades about."

"But where is there to go?"

"The roof would be safer. It's not so enclosed. I want to try and find the way up there. Will you come with me or would you sooner stay here?"

"I will come with you."

I hung the pistol by its trigger guard on a nail at the back of the cupboard, and we went out on to the terrace.

A car outside the big building at the end of the Telegraf Road was on fire, and the immobilised tank was using armour-piercing shot to break up a sandbagged defence position in one of the corner shops. The smoke and the glare and the noise made it all seem like a sequence from a somewhat improbable war film. The glare, however, was useful.

We went along the terrace past the bathhouse to the barrier wall which had been dislocated by the shell burst. There was a gap between the wall and the balustrade, and it was not too difficult to squeeze through. Beyond it we had to walk carefully. This terrace did not broaden out as Jebb's did, and the rubble was piled up against the balustrade. Farther along, where the balustrade had broken away and fallen down into the roadway, it was impassable; but by going through what should have been the bed and living rooms, it was possible to get round on to the terrace again beyond the obstruction. No more barrier walls had yet been erected, and from there on it was easy. I knew that somewhere on that floor there must be a stairway up to the roof. What I had wanted to find was a way of getting to it without being seen or having to pass the sentry stationed outside the apartment. By going along the terraces of the unfinished apartments for most of the way, it was possible to reach the stairway without using any of the passage visible to the sentry.

The roof was quite flat with an eighteen-inch parapet running round it. At intervals along the parapet concrete blocks had been let in to hold the guy wires for the radio masts. There were the usual water tanks and ventilating shafts.

The sounds of the battle for the College of Agriculture had died down, and we had just started to walk over to the parapet, when there was a bright flash from somewhere way across the square, a stab of pain in my ears and the whole building jumped as if it had been dynamited. For one absurd instant, I even thought that it had. Then there was another flash, and the same thing happened again. General Ishak had brought his guns into action.

We hurried down the stairs and back to the apartment. There was no point in hurrying: I suppose that it was just a panic desire to be in familiar surroundings. As we went along one of the terraces, I could see that there were two more tanks in the square now, and that they were moving round the perimeter into positions from which they could give covering fire to the assault troops. The eighty-eights were firing at twenty-second intervals and with shattering effect. At that range they could not miss. When the first rounds had landed there had been shouts and screams from below. Now, those had stopped. After about five minutes the guns changed their targets. One of them began to take pot shots at the first-floor windows. The others started to pound the Ministry of Public Health.

There was nobody in the apartment when we returned, but I guessed that it would not be long before a general movement away from the lower floors began. I told Rosalie to put anything of special value that she had there into her handbag. My money and air ticket, and the few personal papers that I had, I stuffed into my pockets. Then, I took the pistol and a bottle of water and hid them along the terrace where they could be picked up easily when we moved out.

The din was appalling now and the whole place shook continually. Rosalie seemed more bewildered by the noise than frightened. When she had collected what she wanted to take with her and I gave her a glass of whisky, it was my hand that was shaking. I had made up my mind that the moment to move would be when the assault began. From then on, there would be little chance of anyone caring where we were; it would be everyone for himself. The trouble with me was that I could no longer see what was going on. Once or twice, a machine gun in the square had sprayed the windows of the floor below with bullets, and I knew that if I tried looking over the balustrade now I should almost certainly be seen and draw fire. So I had to sit there drinking whisky, listening and trying to imagine what was happening.

At about seven thirty there was a sudden lull, and from down in the square there came a series of small plopping bangs that sounded as if someone were letting off fireworks. A moment or two later, there was a lot of confused shouting from the floor below. I put my glass down and went out on to the terrace. As I did so, there were some more bangs. The

Ministry next door was burning and the smoke from it was drifting over to mingle with the stink of shell fumes rising from below. My eyes were smarting anyway. Then, I became aware of another smell and a sudden pain between the eyes. I turned quickly and went back into the room.

"We're going now," I said.

"What is it?"

"Tear gas. If we get too much of it we shan't be able to see to get up to the roof."

As we scrambled through the gap on to the next terrace, our eyes began to stream, but I managed to find the bottle of water and the pistol, and once we were past the rubble we did not have to be so careful about looking where we were going.

I did not have to see now to know what was happening below. The bigger guns were silent, but there was incessant automatic fire and the frame of the building was transmitting an intermittent thudding that was certainly from bursting grenades. There were other sounds, too; the hoarse, inhuman screams and yells that come from men's throats when they are killing at close quarters.

The moment the tear gas had gone in and the defenders were blinded by it, a party of assault troops in respirators had rushed the Air Terminal. Now, with grenades, machine pistols and *parangs*, they were clearing the ground floor and basements. Other parties would be storming the rear of the building. The business of clearing the upper floors would soon follow. First, more tear gas; then, up the stairs. *"Quick as lightning. Every room. First a grenade, and then yourself. Doesn't matter what's there. Doesn't matter who's there. Then, comb it out with your machine pistol."*

I had already decided where we would go on the roof. There was no cover worth speaking of, and if the defence did last long enough to make a stand there, all we could do would be to lie flat on our faces and hope for the best. The important thing for us was to stay close to the apartment. If Suparto had remembered his promise to warn the assault troops of our presence, we wanted to be there when they arrived. The place I had chosen, therefore, was the section of parapet immediately above the apartment terrace.

We soon found it. The anti-aircraft machine gun which had showered the terrace with cartridge cases had been mounted there, and that part of the roof was strewn with empties. There was a good deal of tear gas about, but most of it seemed to be coming up from below through the ventilators, and when we got to windward of them the air was better. By leaning forward, I could see the terrace below. There was nobody there, and, as far as I could tell, the apartment was still empty. We sat down beside the parapet to dab our eyes and blow our noses and try not to listen to the massacre going on beneath us.

We had been there about twenty minutes when there was a sound of men blundering through the living room immediately below. A moment later Sanusi and Major Dahman came out on to the terrace, coughing and gasping for breath. I could hear others moaning and retching and stumbling about behind them.

It was Dahman who managed to find his voice first.

"Not here, *Boeng*," he said hoarsely.

"Where is Aroff?"

"Aroff is dead, *Boeng*. You saw him."

"Yes. I shall stay here."

"They will take you alive."

"No, they will not do that."

There was a commotion from the passage beyond. A man was shouting something about surrender.

"You are in command, Dahman."

"I will return for you if I can, *Boeng*. But we cannot die like women begging for mercy. We must counterattack."

He started to cough again as he went back through the living room, but a moment later I heard him gasping out an order about assembling on the stairs. I leaned forward cautiously and looked down on to the terrace.

Sanusi was walking slowly towards the balustrade. He had a machine pistol in his hand. At the end of the terrace he stopped and looked round, drawing deep breaths and wiping his face with the back of his hand. Then, he knelt down and, putting the gun beside him on the ground, began to say his prayers.

He went through the *Rakats*; then, he began to intone a passage from the Koran.

"But what shall teach thee what the night-comer is? It is the star of piercing radiance. Truly every soul has a guardian over it. Let man then reflect out of what he was created. He was created of the poured-forth germs which issue from between the loins and breastbones. Well able truly is Allah, the all-seeing, the all-knowing, the all-merciful, to restore him to life, on the day when all secrets shall be searched out, and he shall have no other might or helper."

I looked down at Rosalie. She took my hand and pressed it against her face.

He was still kneeling there when there was a series of violent explosions that felt as if they were coming from right underneath us, and somewhere not far away a man began screaming. Then, the screaming was drowned by a blast of automatic fire as the assaulting troops reached the head of the staircase.

I saw Sanusi grab the machine pistol, get to his feet and start towards the window. At the same moment a grenade burst in the living room.

The blast flung him across the terrace like an empty sack, but he was on his feet in an instant, and as he rose he pressed the trigger of the machine pistol. Someone inside was firing back, and for a few seconds the air was torn to pieces. I saw the grenade land on the terrace outside the bedroom windows just in time to drop behind the parapet. Then, there was an ear-splitting concussion, another burst of automatic fire and silence. When I dared to look down again, three men in steel helmets were walking out slowly on to the terrace.

Two of them looked round warily and then began to move along towards the bathhouse, their arms at the ready. The third man went over to Sanusi's body and shone a flashlight on it. Then, he turned and looked at the bedroom window.

"Mr. Fraser," he called.

"We're up here, Major," I said.

The moon had risen. Down in the square, the dead were still being piled into trucks and driven away, so that, in the morning, when the Minister of Public Enlightenment issued a statement minimising the importance of the whole affair, no sceptical foreign newspapermen would be able to refute his casualty figures. The few surviving wounded were already in sick quarters at the garrison barracks, and therefore inaccessible. The disabled tank had been hauled on to a transporter and removed. The other tanks had retired together with the self-propelled eighty-eights. The square was being patrolled by two small armoured cars. Now and again there would be a faint rattle of fire from the outskirts of the city as stragglers or would-be escapers were rounded up and killed. The building next door had nearly burned itself out.

There were some eggs left in the kitchen and a Primus stove. While I held the flashlight, Rosalie made an omelette. I salvaged a couple of broken chairs from the chaos in the living room and we ate out on the terrace. It was not comfortable and the smoke still drifted over, but we were very hungry and did not care. We were eating the last of the fruit when Major Suparto returned.

I offered him fruit, but he declined stiffly.

"No, thank you, Mr. Fraser. I have to report to General Ishak and must leave immediately."

"I see. Well, what's the news?"

"I do not think that Miss Linden need feel alarmed for her sister's safety. I am told that there is little damage in that quarter. Apart from that, I regret that the news I have for you is not good. The streets about here are forbidden to civilians at present. If you insist on leaving, I will provide you with an escort, but I do not advise it. The hotels are being searched for rebel sympathisers and many arrests are being made. Emotions have been aroused and matters are a little out of hand. You would be wiser to remain here."

"Oh."

"I can understand your reluctance to stay in this apartment a moment longer than is necessary, but in your own interests it is better that you do."

"Yes. All right."

"There are troops in this building. There is much to be done here. But you will not be disturbed. I have given strict orders. By the morning, perhaps . . ."

"Yes, of course. It's good of you to come and tell us yourself."

He hesitated. It was clear that he was desperately tired, but he also seemed ill at ease, even embarrassed. I wondered why.

"Mr. Fraser," he said, "I may not have the opportunity of seeing you again."

"I'm sorry to hear that."

"You, I think, will soon be leaving Selampang."

"If the police haven't lost my passport in the confusion."

"Should you have difficulties, Lim Mor Sai will arrange matters for you. If you will mention that I suggested that he should."

"Thank you. I was forgetting he was a friend of yours. Will you be going back to Tangga?"

"No. I believe that I am to be given other duties now."

His face had become impassive, and I knew now what was troubling him. He was going to be promoted for his services to the Government, and he had a bad conscience. Aroff's sneer about his treachery had hurt, and I had been there to hear it. He believed that in my heart I despised him. I wished that there were some way of telling him that I did not; and knew that there was no way that would not humiliate us both.

"Gedge will be sorry to hear that," I said; "and so will the Transport Manager."

He smiled sourly. "As Mr. Gedge will shortly be losing his other liaison managers also, perhaps he will feel compensated." The smile went. "And now I regret that I must go."

"Major, I wish that I could begin to thank you . . ."

He broke in hastily. "Please, Mr. Fraser, no thanks. We are both civilised and—what was your word?—humane men. Are we not? Yes. I will wish you, as I wished you the other day in Tangga, a safe journey and a happy future."

"Thank you."

He gave Rosalie a curt little bow, and then went back through the living room to the passage door. I followed. As he opened the door, I held out my hand.

"Goodbye, Major."

His handshake was limp; a perfunctory concession to European manners.

"Goodbye, Mr. Fraser."

He went. There was another officer waiting for him in the passage.

I shut the door and bolted it. Then, I walked back through the living room and stood for a moment looking round at the litter and wreckage and filth on the terrace. Where Roda and Sanusi had died there were two large stains, congealed, glistening, and black in the moonlight.

I went over and sat down by Rosalie.

"Do you mind very much that we have to stay here?"

"Now that I am not so worried for my sister, it does not matter."

"Are you still hungry?"

"Not any more."

"Would you like a drink?"

She shook her head. "Do you think that we could have baths?"

"There should be enough water for you."

"For both of us if we use the water carefully. I will show you."

"All right."

So we bathed, pouring the water carefully over one another so that none was wasted, soaping ourselves, and then each rinsing the other. And gradually, as we stood there in the warm darkness, our bodies began to come alive. Nothing was said. We had not touched. We could not see. Yet both of us knew suddenly that it was happening to the other as well. For a moment or two we stood there motionless, each listening to the other's breathing. It became intolerable. I put out my hands and touched her. She drew in her breath sharply; and then her body pressed with desperate urgency against mine.

I picked her up and carried her along the terrace. Somewhere in the wreckage of the bedroom there was a bed. Later, when our bodies had celebrated their return to life and the smell of death had gone, we slept.

CHAPTER X

Soon after eight thirty the next morning I was awakened by someone knocking on the outer door of the apartment. By the time I had found my dressing gown, the knocking had ceased, but there were voices in the passage, one of them a woman's. She sounded annoyed. When I opened the door, Mrs. Choong was waving her door key angrily in the face of a soldier who had come to ask what she was doing there.

She gave a cry of triumph as she saw me. Not only, she said, had she been prevented from coming to work the last two mornings by soldiers in the street, but now, when the soldiers in the street did let her pass, there were other soldiers waiting to accuse her of looting. Her trousers quivered with indignation. When I sent the soldier away she shouted insults after him.

Then, she came in and saw the apartment.

For several seconds she stood there staring; then, she waddled through slowly into the living room.

It looked awful in the daylight. The bombing had made a mess, but it had been a tolerable mess; in two days a decorator could have put everything right again. The grenades and machine-pistol fire had savaged the place. The furniture was torn and splintered, the floor and walls and doors were scarred and pitted. Nothing was unspoiled; a pleasant room had become a hideous disfigurement.

To my dismay, I saw tears beginning to roll down Mrs. Choong's plump cheeks.

"Soldiers!" she said bitterly, and then looked at me. "Bedroom also?"

"That's pretty bad, too, I'm afraid, Mrs. Choong."

"Poor Mr. Jebb! But you, mister? You here?"

"Most of the time. Last night, when the attack came, Miss Linden and I went up on the roof."

"Miss Linden? That is Miss Mina's friend?"

"Yes."

"Ah." She brushed the tears away. "You want breakfast?"

"I'm afraid there isn't any food left."

"I bring." She held up the bag she was carrying. "I promise, I bring. Miss Linden, too? She want breakfast?"

"Yes, please, Mrs. Choong. There's no electricity, though. We used the Primus stove."

But she was already in the kitchen. I heard her swearing to herself over the confusion she found there.

After breakfast, Rosalie and I cleaned ourselves up as best we could with the dregs of the water in the bathhouse, and made ready to leave. We had arranged to meet later at the Harmony Club. Meanwhile, she would go home and I would see the police about my passport. I would also have to buy some clean clothes. Mrs. Choong took away the dirty ones to get them *dobi*-ed.

Nobody was allowed inside the radio station without a new sort of pass that I did not have, and we had to use the auxiliary staircase to get down into the square. The road was still closed to four-wheeled traffic, but the *betjak* drivers were back, and Mahmud was there, grinning knowingly as if we had all been on a wild two-day party together and were suffering a common hangover. There were a lot of people about, staring awe-struck at the damaged buildings or excitedly discussing their experiences. The children were having a fine time playing in the shell holes. As he pedalled along, Mahmud talked continuously about what had happened where he lived; but I don't think either of us listened to a word he said. We were enjoying our freedom.

When we arrived at Rosalie's apartment house, I waited outside until she had satisfied herself that all was well there, and then went on to the tailor's shop. He had a pair of khaki slacks from another order that he said he could alter for me in an hour, and showed me where I could get a shirt ready-made. After I had bought the shirt, I set out for police head-quarters.

As we approached, I could see that there was a big crowd collected at the end of the street in which the headquarters were situated. It soon became apparent that we were not going to be able to get through, and I waited while Mahmud went ahead on foot to see what the trouble was. He was gone five minutes and came back looking troubled. Barbed-wire barricades had been set up at both ends of the street, he said, and troops were preventing anyone entering or leaving who did not have a special pass. The crowd consisted mainly of people with relations who had been arrested during the night. Many of those arrested, he added with gloomy satisfaction, were themselves policemen, but there were others whose only crime was that they had not refused to give food and water to the rebel troops; or so their relatives said.

I went to De Vries' offices, but they were closed. Then, I tried the Orient bar. That was closed, too. As I was coming away, I saw a man I knew slightly who said that there was rumour going around that both the Dutch manager of the Orient and De Vries had been arrested. I went back to the tailor's shop and waited while he finished altering the slacks; then I told Mahmud to take me out to the Harmony Club.

It was a little after eleven and the club did not open until noon, but the doorman was there and he fetched Mrs. Lim.

She was only just sober, and obviously could not remember a thing about me; but she did her best.

"Hullo, love. Fancy seeing you here!"

"Hullo, Mrs. Lim. I'm looking for your husband."

"Oh, he's gone into town. I don't know where. Hasn't it been awful? Where were you all the time? The Orient?"

"Roy Jebb lent me his apartment."

"Dear old Roy. Is he back yet?"

"He should be back today." I could see her memory fumbling dimly with the fact that I knew Jebb.

"And you want to see Mor Sai?"

"That's right. Major Suparto suggested that your husband might be able to advise me about a business matter."

Suparto's name jolted her. She was suddenly wary.

"Major who?"

"Suparto."

"Never heard of him. But Mor Sai'll be here soon. You'd better come in and wait."

"Thanks. While I'm waiting, is there anywhere in the club where I can have a bath and change my clothes?"

"Oh, sure. Charlie there'll show you. I expect you'd like a drink after. I'll see you later in the bar, love."

It was Lim who was waiting for me in the bar when I got there. He nodded politely and we shook hands.

"A drink, Mr. Fraser? Brandy dry?"

"Thanks."

There was no barman there. He went round and poured two, one for himself.

"I hear that you have had a bad time during these troubles, Mr. Fraser."

"Mrs. Lim told you that?" I smiled. "I must have looked rougher than I thought."

"It was not my wife who told me." He pushed a glass across to me and raised his own. "Your health, Mr. Fraser."

"And yours, Mr. Lim."

I took a drink from my glass. He sipped at his, and then put it down and felt in his pocket.

"I think that this is what you wished to see me about," he said, and put my passport on the bar in front of me.

I stared at it uncertainly, then picked it up and looked through the visa pages.

"The exit permit is in order," he said; "and the Customs and exchange clearance papers are clipped to the back."

"This is remarkable, Mr. Lim."

"Oh no. Our friend told me that you had left your passport with the police. I knew that you would not be able to get it, and would come to me. So, to save a journey, I brought it with me."

"You make it sound very simple. I'm deeply grateful."

"What have you been able to arrange about your air passage?"

"Nothing. The airline offices are shut. Someone told me that De Vries has been arrested. Is that true?"

"He will be released later, perhaps. But planes can fly without his assistance. Naturally, the scheduled services have been suspended, but foreign airports have been notified now that all is well again. There will be a plane in from Djakarta early this afternoon. It will leave again at five thirty. A passage will, I am certain, be arranged for you."

I smiled. "It sounds as if the Major is in a hurry to get rid of me."

The eyes behind the rimless glasses considered me attentively for a moment. Then, he shrugged. "Why not, Mr. Fraser? You know a little more than is convenient. The longer you are here, the more likely you are to talk to a newspaperman or to a friend who might himself talk."

"I can talk just as well in Djakarta."

"The Major thinks not. He has great confidence in you. Also, he believes that you will not wish to cause difficulties for Miss Linden. No, no,

Mr. Fraser. Do not misunderstand. You are not being threatened. Neither is she. It will be no hardship for her to be discreet. We merely ask that you permit her to remain so for the moment. Later, in a week or two, nobody will be interested."

"Well, she'll be here soon. I'll let you know." I paused. "You could have warned me the other night. Why didn't you?"

"I am an agent, not a principal, Mr. Fraser. In such a delicate situation, I was not free to consult my own personal wishes. I was very pleased to hear that you had come to no harm. Another drink?"

"No, thanks."

"Then, if you will excuse me now."

"Of course. And thanks again for the passport."

"If you decide to leave this afternoon . . ."

"Sure, I'll let you know."

Rosalie arrived wearing a dress I had not seen before and looking delightful. She had spoken both to Mina and to her sister. Everything was all right. Mina had not dared to go to the apartment this morning; she had been afraid to find the whole thing blown to pieces and our bodies lying among the ruins. She was going to find a place for Roy to stay while the repairs were being done.

"Poor Roy," I said.

"He will not blame us. We could not help what happened."

"No."

She looked at me quickly. "What is wrong?"

There was nobody else in the bar. I told her about my passport and the plane that afternoon and what Lim had said. When I had finished, she thought for a moment, then nodded.

"Yes, I see. What is it you wish to do?"

"I want to know what you think. I'm not going to leave here if they're going to make things difficult for you."

"But it is you they are worried about. They know I will say nothing. Isn't that what Lim said?"

"Do you believe him?"

"Oh yes. They know I would not dare."

I knew enough about her now to know when she believed what she was saying; but I persisted.

"Are you sure?"

"Do you not want to go?"

I hesitated. "No, I don't."

"Because of us?"

"Yes."

"I am glad. I, too, had hoped that we could be together again as we were last night. I keep thinking about it. But if they mean you to go, it is better that you go today."

"Yes, I suppose it is."

The barman came in and I ordered some drinks. We drank them and then went in to eat. The food was delicious, but I could not eat very much of it. She scarcely looked at hers. After a bit I gave up trying.

"Rosalie."

Her eyes met mine. She said softly: "Yes, it is the same with me. I cannot stop thinking. What time must you be at the airport?"

"Five, I should think."

"If you went back to the Air House and packed your things, we could be together until it is time for you to go."

"Where?"

"At my home. My sister will not be there. It is very small and not like Roy's apartment, but you will not mind that."

"No, I won't mind."

As soon as we were ready to leave, I went into the bar and found Lim.

"About that air passage. What do I do about the ticket?"

"It is at the airport reception office, waiting for you, Mr. Fraser."

"You were pretty sure of me, weren't you?"

"Not of you, Mr. Fraser. But I was sure of Miss Linden. She is an honest and clear-thinking person. Do you not agree?"

Back at the apartment, I found that Jebb had returned and was surveying the damage with Mrs. Choong.

"Well, Roy," I said.

"Well, chum," he answered grimly; "I bet that's the last time you mind anybody's place for them."

"I'm sorry, Roy. But first the bombing and then the grenades and stuff. There was nothing we could do. You see . . ."

"I'm not blaming you, you silly bastard, I'm apologising! How do you think I felt in Makassar, sitting there listening to the bloody radio and wondering how you were getting on up here? I'd sooner have been here myself. I was afraid I'd killed you, dammit! Where were you when all this happened?"

I told him a bit about it. He listened and swore at intervals, and then asked after Rosalie.

"She's fine. I'm going to see her in a minute. I'm leaving today."

"My word! On that five-thirty plane?"

"That's right."

"Who fixed that? People are fighting to get on it."

"Lim Mor Sai."

"What did I tell you? He can fix anything. Well, I'll see you out at the airport. I've got to go out there to clear some stuff through Customs. I came straight in as soon as I touched down. Seen anything of Mina?"

"No, but she's trying to find somewhere for you to live while this is being repaired."

"That means a camp bed in her place. See you later, Steve."

When he had gone, I packed. It did not take long. Mrs. Choong fetched my things from the *dobi* laundry. They were still damp. But I stuffed them into my suitcase anyway. Then I gave Mrs. Choong a present and went downstairs again for the last time.

I had told Mahmud to wait for me and he was there at the door. On the way, I stopped at a shop in the Chinese quarter and bought a silver box with an amethyst set in the lid. When I had paid for it, I took out all the money I had left on me, set aside what I would need to pay Mahmud, buy my ticket to Djakarta and bribe the Customs at the airport, and put the rest in the box. Then I went on to see Rosalie.

There were two rooms, one hers, one her sister's. They were clean and simple, like rooms in a kampong house, with bamboo blinds on the windows and mosquito nets over the beds. There was a small verandah with orchids growing in pieces of tree bark.

When it was time for me to go, I went over to the bed and looked down at her. She was lying there with her eyes closed and her body shiny with sweat. There was a smile on her lips. I thought that she might be asleep.

I put the box down on the small table as quietly as I could, but she heard and opened her eyes. For a moment she looked up at me; then her eyes went to the table and she sat up quickly.

"No."

"You said that if we had liked one another it would make the parting easier."

"That was before."

"For me it needs to be made easier."

"And for me."

"Then this is the best way. Open it later when I've gone."

I bent over and kissed her once more.

"We love each other," she said.

"Yes."

"But we are also wise."

"I believe so."

"Yes." She smiled. "This way we shall always remember each other with love."

A few moments later I carried my suitcase down the long, steep staircase and walked out into the blinding sun.

Mahmud had put the hood up, and I sat in the shade of it trying to think of the journey ahead as he pedalled me out to the airport.

THE SCHIRMER
INHERITANCE

to Sylvia Payne

THE SCHIRMER INHERITANCE

PROLOGUE

IN 1806 NAPOLEON set out to chastise the King of Prussia. Both at Auerstadt and at Jena the Prussian armies suffered crushing defeats. Then, what remained of them marched east to join a Russian army under Bennigsen. In the following February, Napoleon met this combined force at the town of Preussisch-Eylau, near Königsberg.

Eylau was one of the bloodiest and most terrible of Napoleon's battles. It began in a blizzard and in a temperature well below freezing-point. Both armies were half starved and fought with desperate ferocity for the bleak shelter of the buildings of Eylau itself. Casualties on both sides were heavy, nearly a quarter of those engaged being killed. When, at nightfall on the second day, the fighting ended, it was from exhaustion rather than because a decision had been reached. Then, during the night, the Russian army began to retreat northward. The survivors of the Prussian corps, whose flank-guard action against Ney's troops had nearly served to win the day, now had no reason to remain. They made their withdrawal through the village of Kuttschitten to the east. The cavalry screen of their rear guard was provided by the Dragoons of Ansbach.

The relationship between this unit and the rest of the Prussian army was absurd, but, in the middle Europe of the period, not unusually so. Not many years before, and well within the memories of the older soldiers in it, the regiment had been the only mounted force in the independent principality of Ansbach, and had taken its oaths of allegiance to the ruling Margrave. Then, Ansbach had fallen upon evil times and the last Margrave had sold his land and his people to the King of Prussia. Fresh oaths of allegiance had had to be sworn. Yet their new lord had eventually proved as fickle as the old. In the year before Eylau the Dragoons had experienced a further change of status. The province of Ansbach had been ceded by the Prussians to Bavaria. As Bavaria was an ally of Napoleon, this meant that, strictly speaking, the Ansbachers should now have been fighting against the Prussians, not beside them. However, the Dragoons themselves were as indifferent to the anomaly they constituted as they were to the cause for which they fought. The conception of nationality meant little to them. They were professional soldiers in the eighteenth-century meaning of the term. If they had marched and fought and suffered and died for two days and a night, it was neither for love of the Prussians nor from hatred of Napoleon; it was because they had been trained to do so, because they hoped for the spoils of victory, and because they feared the consequences of disobedience.

Thus, as his horse picked its way through the woods on the outskirts of Kuttschitten that night, Sergeant Franz Schirmer was able to consider his situation and make plans for extricating himself from it, without much inconvenience to his conscience. Not many of the Dragoons of Ansbach were left, and of those who were, few would survive the hardships to come. The wounded and the badly frostbitten would die first, and then, when the horses had been lost or eaten, starvation and sickness would kill off all but the youngest and strongest of the remainder. Twenty-four hours earlier the Sergeant could reasonably have expected to be one of the enduring few. Now he could not. Late that afternoon he had himself been wounded.

The wound had affected him strangely. A French cuirassier had slashed with a sabre, and the Sergeant had taken the blow on his right arm. The blade had sliced obliquely through the heavy deltoid muscles and down to the bone just above the elbow. It was an ugly wound, but the bone had not broken and it had therefore been unnecessary for him to seek torture at the hands of the army surgeons. A comrade had bound up the wound for him and strapped the arm against his chest with a crossbelt. It throbbed painfully now, but the bleeding seemed to have stopped. He was very weak, but that, he thought, might be due to hunger and the cold rather than to any serious loss of blood. The thing he found so strange was that with all his physical distress there went an extraordinary feeling of well-being.

It had come upon him as the wound was being bandaged. The feelings of surprise and terror with which he had first regarded the blood pouring down his useless arm had suddenly gone, and in their place had been an absurd, splendid sense of freedom and light-heartedness.

He was a bovine young man of a practical turn of mind, not given to fancies. He knew something about wounds. His had been bound up in its own blood and could therefore be reckoned healthy; but there was still no more than an even chance of his escaping death from gangrene. He knew something about war, too, and could see not only that the battle was probably lost but also that retreat would take them into a countryside already picked clean by armies on the move. Yet this knowledge brought no despair with it. It was as if he had received with his wound some special forgiveness for his sins, an absolution more potent and complete than that which any mortal priest could give. He felt that he had been touched by God Himself, and that any drastic steps he might be obliged to take in order to stay alive would have Divine approval.

His horse stumbled as it fought its way clear of a snowdrift, and the Sergeant reined in. Half the officers had been killed and he had been put in command of one of the outlying detachments. He had orders to keep well out on the flank away from the road, and for a while it had been easy to do so; but now they had emerged from the forest, and in the deep snow the going was bad. One or two of the Dragoons behind him had already dismounted and were leading their horses. He could hear them floundering about in the snow at the rear of the column. If it proved necessary for him to lead his own horse he might not have the strength to get back into the saddle.

He thought about this for a moment. After a two-day battle fought so desperately, the chances of there being any French cavalry still capable of harrying the retreat from a flank were remote. The flank guard was therefore no more than a drill-book precaution. Certainly it was not worth taking risks for. He gave a brief word of command and the column began to turn into the forest again towards the road. He had no great fear of his disobedience being discovered. If it were, he would simply say that he had lost his way; he would not be severely punished for failing to do an officer's duty. In any case, he had more important matters to consider.

Food was the first thing.

Luckily, the haversack beneath his long cloak still contained most of the frozen potatoes he had looted from a farm building the previous day. They must be eaten sparingly; and secretly. At times like these, a man known to have private stores of food went in some danger, whatever his rank. However, the potatoes would not last long and there would be no soup pots bubbling at the end of this march. Even the horses would be better off. None of the supply wagons had been lost and there was a day's fodder still in them. The men would starve first.

He fought down a rising sense of panic. He would have to do something soon and panic would not help him. Already he could feel the cold eating into him. Not many hours could elapse before fever and exhaustion took irrevocable charge of the situation. His knees tightened involuntarily on the saddle flaps, and at that moment the idea came to him.

The horse had started and passaged a little at the pressure. Sergeant Schirmer relaxed his thigh muscles and, leaning forward, patted the animal's neck affectionately with his left hand. He was smiling to himself as the horse walked on again. By the time the detachment reached the road his plan was made.

For the rest of that night and most of the next day the Prussian corps moved slowly eastward towards the Masurian Lakes; then it turned north to Insterburg. Soon after nightfall, and on the pretext of rounding up a straggler, Sergeant Schirmer left the detachment and rode south across the frozen lakes in the general direction of Lötzen. By morning he was south of that town.

He was also nearly at the limit of his strength. The march from Eylau to the point at which he had deserted had been bad enough; the cross-country journey from there would have taxed even an unwounded man. Now, the pain of his arm was at moments intolerable and he was shaking so much from fever and the bitter cold that he could scarcely stay in the saddle. He was beginning to wonder, indeed, if he might not have been mistaken in his estimate of God's intentions, and if what he had supposed to be a sign of Divine favour might not prove to have been an intimation of approaching death. He knew, at all events, that if he did not very soon find shelter of the kind his plan called for, he would die.

He reined in and with an effort raised his head again to look about him. Far away to the left across the white desolation of a frozen lake he could see the low black shape of a farmhouse. His eyes moved on. It was just possible that there was a nearer building to investigate. But there was nothing. Hopelessly he turned his horse's head in the direction of the farmhouse and resumed his march.

The area into which the Sergeant had ridden was, although at that date part of the Kingdom of Prussia, inhabited mainly by Poles. It had never been very prosperous; and after the Russian army had passed through it, commandeering the winter stores of grain and fodder and herding away the livestock, it was little more than a wasteland. In some villages the Cossack horses had eaten the very thatch from the roofs, and in others the houses had been gutted by fire. The campaigns of the armies of Holy Russia could be more devastating for her allies than for her enemies.

The Sergeant, himself an experienced campaigner, had not been unprepared for devastation. Indeed, his plan had depended upon it. Country that had just supplied a Russian army would not attract another army for some time to come. A deserter might consider himself reasonably safe there. What he had not been prepared for, however, was the absence of a starving population. Since dawn he had passed several farmhouses, and every one had been abandoned. He had realized by now that the Russians had been more exacting even than usual (perhaps because they had been dealing with Poles), and that the inhabitants, unable to conceal enough food to keep them alive until the spring, had trekked to places farther south that might have been spared. For him, therefore, the situation was desperate. He could perhaps stay in the saddle for another hour. If all the peasants in the immediate vicinity had gone with the rest, he was finished. He raised his head again, blinking to free his eyelashes from the ice that clung to them, and peered ahead.

At that moment he saw the smoke.

It came in a thin wisp from the roof of the building he was heading for, and he saw it for only a moment before it disappeared. He was still some way off, but he was in no doubt as to what he had seen. This was a peat-burning area and that was smoke from a peat fire. His spirits rose as he urged his horse forward.

It took him another half-hour to reach the farmhouse. As he approached he saw that it was a wretched and dilapidated place. There was a low wooden building which was both barn and living-quarters, an empty sheep-pen, and a broken-down wagon almost hidden under a drift of snow. That was all.

The horse's hoofs made only a faint crunching sound in the frozen snow. As he drew nearer, he let go the reins and carefully eased his carbine from its long saddle-holster. When he had primed it he wedged the weapon across the saddlebags and against the rolled blankets at the pommel. Then he took up the reins again and went on.

At one end of the building there was a small shuttered window, and beside it a door. The snow outside had been trodden since the last fall, but except for the slight trickle of peat smoke from the roof, there was no other sign of life. He stopped and looked about him. The gate of the sheep-pen was open. Near the cart was a slight mound of snow that probably covered the remains of a hayrick. There were no cattle droppings on the fresh snow, no sounds of poultry. But for the faint sighing of the wind, the silence was absolute. The Russians had taken everything.

He let the reins slip through his fingers, and the horse shook its head. The jangling of the bit seemed very loud. He looked quickly at the door of the building. If the sound had been heard, the first response to it would be that of fear; and, providing that it led to the immediate opening of the door and prompt compliance with his wishes, fear would be useful. If it led to the door's being barricaded against him, however, he was in a difficulty. He would have to break the door down, and he could not risk dismounting until he was sure that this was to be the end of his journey.

He waited. There was no sound from within. The door remained shut. His Dragoon's instinct was to slam the butt of his carbine against it and yell at those inside to come out or be killed; but he put the temptation aside. The carbine butt might have to come into play later, but for the present he would try the friendly approach he had planned.

He tried to call "Ho!" but the sound that came from his throat was no more than a sob. Disconcerted, he tried again.

"Ho!"

He managed to croak the word this time, but a deadly feeling of help-lessness swept over him. He, who a moment ago had been thinking of battering on a door with his carbine and even of breaking it down, had not enough strength left to shout. There was a roaring in his ears and he thought he was going to fall. He shut his eyes, fighting down the horrible sensation. As he opened his eyes again, he saw the door slowly open.

The face of the woman who stood in the doorway looking up at him was so ravaged by hunger that it was hard to tell what her age might be. But for the braids of hair wound round her head, even her sex would have been in doubt. The voluminous peasant rags she wore were quite shapeless and her feet and legs were bound with sacking like a man's. She stared at him dully, then said something in Polish and turned to go inside. He leaned forward and spoke in German.

"I am a Prussian soldier. There has been a great battle. The Russians are defeated."

He said it as if he were announcing a victory. She stopped and looked up again. Her sunken eyes were quite expressionless. He had the curious idea that they would remain so even if he were to draw his sabre and cut her down.

"Who else is here?" he said.

Her lips moved again and this time she spoke in German. "My father. He was too weak to go with our neighbours. What do you want here?"

"What's the matter with him?"

"He has the wasting fever."

"Ah!" If it had been the plague, he would have chosen to die in the snow rather than stay.

"What do you want?" she repeated.

To answer her, he undid the fastenings of his cloak and threw it back to reveal his wounded arm.

"I need shelter and rest," he said; "and someone to cook my food until my wound is healed."

Her eyes flickered from his bloodstained tunic to the carbine and the bulging saddlebags beneath it. He guessed that she was thinking that if she had the strength she might seize the gun and kill him. He put his hand on it firmly and her eyes met his again.

"There is no food to cook," she said.

"I have plenty of food," he answered; "enough to share with those who help me."

She still stared at him. He nodded reassuringly; then, holding his carbine firmly in his left hand, he brought his right leg across the saddle and slid to the ground. As his feet touched it, his legs gave way under him and he sprawled in the snow. A burning shaft of agony shot from his arm through every nerve in his body. He screamed, and then, for a moment or two after, lay there sobbing. At last, still clutching the carbine, he clambered dizzily to his feet.

The woman had made no attempt to help him. She had not even moved. He pushed past her through the doorway into the hovel beyond.

Inside, he looked round warily. By the light from the doorway that filtered through the peat smoke he could dimly see a rough wooden bed with what looked like a pile of sacking on it. A whimpering sound came from it now. The peat fire glowed dully in a crude clay stove in the centre.

The dirt floor was soft with ash and peat dust. The reeking air made him choke. He blundered round the stove and between the roof supports into the space where the animals had been kept. The straw under his feet here was filthy but he kicked a pile of it together against the back of the stove. He knew that the woman had followed him in and gone over to the sick man. Now he heard a whispered conversation. He arranged the pile of straw into the semblance of a bed and when he had finished spread his cloak on it. The whispers had ceased. He heard a movement behind him and turned.

The woman stood there facing him. She had a small axe in her hands. "The food," she said.

He nodded and went out into the yard again. She followed and stood watching as, with his carbine held between his knees, he awkwardly unstrapped the blankets. He succeeded at last and flung the roll in the snow.

"The food," she said again.

He raised the carbine and, pressing the butt against his left hip, slid his hand down to the lock. With an effort he managed to cock it and move his forefinger on to the trigger. Then he put the muzzle to the horse's head just below the ear.

"Here is our food," he said, and pulled the trigger.

His ears sang with the noise of the shot as the horse sank kicking to the ground. The carbine had leaped from his hand and lay in the snow, smoking. He picked up the blankets and tucked them under his arm before retrieving it. The woman still stood watching him. He nodded to her and, motioning to the horse, went towards the house.

Almost before he reached the door, she was on her knees by the dying animal, at work on it with the axe. He looked back. There was the saddle and its contents; his sabre too. She might easily kill him with it while he lay helpless. There was a fortune, by her standards, in the flat leather pouch beneath his tunic. For a moment he watched the quick, desperate movements of her arms and the dark mess of blood spreading in the snow beneath her. His sabre? She would not need a sabre if she had a mind to kill him.

Then he felt the periodic agony of his arm returning and heard himself beginning to moan. He knew suddenly that there was nothing more he could do now to order the world outside his own body. He stumbled through the doorway and to his bed. The carbine he put on the ground under the cloak. Then he took off his helmet, unrolled his blankets, and lay down in the warm darkness to fight for his life.

The woman's name was Maria Dutka, and she was eighteen when Sergeant Schirmer first set eyes on her. Her mother had died when she was young and, as there were no other children and her father had failed to find a second wife, Maria had been brought up to do the work of a son and heir on the holding. Moreover, the chronic disease from which Dutka suffered was now of long standing and the periods of relief from it had become rarer. She was already accustomed to thinking and acting for herself.

She was not headstrong, however. Although the idea of killing the Sergeant, in order to avoid having to share the dead horse with him, did occur to her, she discussed the matter with her father first. She was by nature deeply superstitious, and when he suggested that some supernatural agency might have had a hand in the Sergeant's providential appearance, she saw the danger of her plan. She saw, too, that even if the Sergeant were to die of his wound—and he was very near to death in those first days—the supernatural powers might consider that her murderous thoughts about him had turned the scale.

She nursed him, accordingly, with a kind of anxious devotion which it was easy for the grateful Sergeant to misunderstand. Later, however, she did something that appealed to him still more. When, during his convalescence, he made an attempt to thank her for so faithfully keeping her part of their bargain, she explained her motives to him with great simplicity and candour. At the time he was both amused and impressed. Afterwards, when he thought about what she had said and the fact that she had said it, he experienced rather more surprising sensations. As the food they shared restored her youthful appearance and vitality, he began to watch the movements of her body and to modify pleasurably his earlier plans for the future.

He stayed in the Dutka house for eight months. Preserved under the snow, the carcass of the horse supplied them all with fresh meat until the thaw came, and then with the smoked and dried remains. By that time, too, the Sergeant was able to take his carbine into the woods and bring back deer. Vegetables began to grow. Then, for a few remarkable weeks, old Dutka rallied and, with the Sergeant and Maria doing a horse's work in the traces, was even able in the end to plough his land.

The Sergeant's continued presence was taken as a matter of course now. Neither Maria nor her father ever referred to his military past. He was a victim of war, as they were. The returning neighbours found nothing strange in his presence. They themselves had spent the winter working for strangers. If old Dutka had found a strong, hard-working Prussian to help him set things to rights, so much the better. And should the curious wonder how old Dutka paid him or why a Prussian should trouble to work so poor a patch of land, there was always someone to remind them of Maria's broad hips and strong legs and of the harvest to be reaped between them by such a lusty young fellow.

The summer came. The battle of Friedland was fought. The Emperors of France and Russia met on a raft moored in the river Niemen. The Treaty of Tilsit was signed. Prussia was stripped of all her territories west of the Elbe and all her Polish provinces. Bialla, only a few miles south of the Dutkas' holding, was suddenly on the Russian frontier, and Lyck had become a garrison town. Prussian infantry patrols came seeking recruits, and the Sergeant took to the woods with the other young men. He was away on one of these excursions when Maria's father died.

After the burial ceremonies he got out his leather money-pouch and sat down with Maria to count his savings. The proceeds of many looting forays and the peculations of four years as a non-commissioned officer, they were more than sufficient to match the small amount that Maria would get from the sale of her father's holding to a neighbour. For there was no question now of their remaining to work the land. They had seen what could happen when the Russian armies came, and with this new frontier the Russians were no more than a day's march away. To them this seemed a weightier argument for leaving the holding than the Sergeant's precarious position as a deserter. The place for them to go was clearly somewhere where there were neither Russians nor Prussians, and where Maria, already pregnant, could bring up their children in the certainty of being able to feed them.

Early in the November of 1807 they set out, with a handcart contrived from Dutka's old wagon, to walk towards the west. It was a hard, dangerous journey, for their road lay through Prussia and they dared travel only at night. But they did not go hungry. They had brought their food with them in the cart and it lasted until they reached Wittenberg. That was the first town they entered in broad daylight, too. They were free of Prussian soil at last.

They did not remain in Wittenberg, however. To the Sergeant it seemed uncomfortably near the Prussian border. Towards the middle of December they arrived in Mühlhausen, newly incorporated into the Kingdom of Westphalia. There, Maria's first son, Karl, was born; and there, Maria and the Sergeant were married. For a time, the Sergeant worked as an ostler; but later, when he had added to their savings, he set up in business as a horse-coper.

He prospered. The tides of the Napoleonic wars washed gently in the harbour that he and Maria had found. For several years it seemed as though the evil days were over. Then, the disease from which her father had suffered attacked Maria herself. Two years after the birth of her second son, Hans, she died.

Eventually Sergeant Schirmer married again and had ten more children by his second wife. He died in 1850, a respected and successful man.

Only once during all those happy years in Mühlhausen was Franz Schirmer disturbed by memories of the military crime he had committed. In 1815, by the Treaty of Paris, Mühlhausen became a Prussian city.

It was the year of the Sergeant's second marriage, and while he did not think it likely that church records would be combed for the names of deserters, there was always a chance that they might be used in checking mobilization lists. He could not bring himself to be fatalistic about the risk. After so many years' immunity from arrest he had lost the habit of living for the moment. The prospect of death before a firing-squad, however remote it might be, could never be endured with the old fortitude.

Then what was to be done? He gave the matter careful thought. In the past, he reminded himself, he had trusted in God; and in times of great danger God had been good to him. But could he *still* simply trust in God? And was this, he asked himself critically, a time of *great* danger? After all, there were plenty of other Schirmers in the Prussian army records; and some of them, no doubt, were men named Franz. Was it really necessary to call upon God to insure against the possibility of the list of those citizens who had purchased army exemptions in Mühlhausen being compared with the list of army deserters in Potsdam? Or really wise to do so? Might not God, who had done so much for His servant, be displeased at having this minor responsibility thrust upon Him and so neglect it? Was there not, therefore, something that His servant could do for himself in the matter, without invoking the aid of the Almighty?

Yes indeed, there was!

He decided to change his name to Schneider.

He encountered only one slight difficulty. It was simple to change his own surname and that of the baby, Hans. He had good friends in the mayor's office, and his excuse that there was another horse-dealer of the same name in a near-by town was readily accepted. But the first son, Karl, presented a problem. The boy, now seven years old, had just been classified for future conscription by the Prussian military authorities, and the Sergeant neither had nor wanted friends in Prussian military circles. Moreover, any official move to change the boy's name might easily invite the very inquiries into origins which he most dreaded. In the end he did nothing about Karl's name. So it was that, although the sons of Franz and Maria were baptized in the name of Schirmer, they grew up with different surnames. Karl remained Karl Schirmer; Hans became Hans Schneider.

The Sergeant's change of name never caused him a moment's anxiety or inconvenience in his lifetime. The anxiety and inconvenience resulting from it descended, over a hundred years later, on the head of Mr. George L. Carey.

CHAPTER I

GEORGE CAREY came from a Delaware family that looked like an illustration for an advertisement of an expensive make of car. His father was a prosperous doctor with snow-white hair. His mother came from an old Philadelphia family and was an important member of the garden club. His brothers were tall, solid, and handsome. His sisters were slim, strong, and vivacious. All had fine regular teeth, which showed when they smiled. The whole family, indeed, looked so happy, so secure, and so successful that it was difficult not to suspect that the truth about them might be different. But no, they actually were happy, secure, and successful. They were also exceedingly smug.

George was the youngest son and, although his shoulders were not so broad as those of his brothers nor his smile as self-satisfied, he was the most talented and intelligent member of the family. When the glories of their football-playing days had departed, his brothers had made their ways aimlessly into business. George's plans for the future had been clearcut from the moment he left high school. Despite his father's hope for a successor in his practice, George had declined to pretend to an interest in medicine which he did not feel. What he wanted to go in for was law; and not the criminal, courtroom kind, but the kind that led in early middle age to the presidencies of railroads and steel corporations or to high political office. But while the war, which came just after he had been graduated from Princeton, had removed much of his solemnity and smugness and had had beneficial effects upon his sense of humour, it had done nothing to change his mind about his chosen profession. After four and a half years as a bomber pilot, he went to Harvard Law School. He graduated, *cum laude*, early in 1949. Then, having spent a useful year as secretary to a learned and famous judge, he joined Lavater, Powell and Sistrom.

The firm of Lavater, Powell and Sistrom of Philadelphia is one of the really important law offices of the eastern United States, and the long list of partners reads like a selection of promising candidates for a vacancy on the Supreme Court. No doubt its massive reputation still derives to some extent from memories of the vast utilities manipulations with which it was concerned in the twenties; but there have been few corporation cases of any magnitude during the last thirty years in which the firm has not held an important brief. It remains a virile, forward-looking concern, and to be invited to join it is a mark of approbation most flattering to a young lawyer.

Thus, as he arranged his belongings in one of Lavater's comfortably furnished offices, George had reason to feel satisfied with the progress of his career. Admittedly, he was a little old for the somewhat junior position he occupied, but he was shrewd enough to realize that his four years in the Air Corps had not been wholly wasted from a professional point of view, and that the distinction of his war record had had quite as much to do with his presence at the Lavater firm as his work at law school or the warm recommendations of the learned judge. Now, if all went well (and why shouldn't it?), he could look forward to rapid advancement, valuable contacts, and an expanding personal reputation. He felt that he had arrived.

The news that he was to do some work on the Schneider Johnson case came, then, as a disagreeable blow. It was also a surprise of another kind. The sort of business that Lavater, Powell and Sistrom normally handled was the sort that made reputations as surely as it made money. From what George remembered of the Schneider Johnson case, it was just the sort of slapstick affair that a corporation lawyer with a thought for his reputation would pay to stay clear of.

It had been one of the notorious missing-heir-to-a-fortune absurdities of the pre-war years.

In 1938, Amelia Schneider Johnson, a senile old woman of eighty-one, had died in Lamport, Pennsylvania. She had lived alone in the decrepit frame house which had been the late Mr. Johnson's wedding present to her, and her declining years had been passed in an atmosphere of genteel poverty. When she had died, however, it had been found that her estate included three million dollars in bonds which she had inherited in the twenties from her brother, Martin Schneider, a soft-drink tycoon. She had had an eccentric distrust of banks and safe-deposit boxes and had kept the bonds in a tin trunk under her bed. She had also distrusted lawyers and had made no will. In Pennsylvania, at the time, the law governing intestacy had been determined by an act of 1917 which said, in effect, that anyone with even a remote blood-relationship to the deceased might be entitled to a share in the estate. Amelia Schneider Johnson's only known relative had been an elderly spinster, Miss Clothilde Johnson; but she had been a sister-in-law and therefore had not qualified under the act. With the enthusiastic and disastrous co-operation of the newspapers, a search for Amelia's blood-relations had begun.

It was, George thought, all too easy to understand the newspapers' eagerness. They had scented another Garrett case. Old Mrs. Garrett had died in 1930, leaving seventeen million dollars and no will, and here was the case eight years later, still going strong, with three thousand lawyers still chiselling away, twenty-six thousand claimants to the money, and a fine smell of corruption over all. The Schneider Johnson thing could last as long. True, it was smaller, but size wasn't everything. It had plenty of human angles—a fortune at stake, the romantic isolation of the old lady's declining years (she had lost her only son in the Argonne), the lonely death without a relative at the bedside, the fruitless search for the will—there was no reason why it should not have staying-power, too. The name Schneider and its American modifications were widely distributed. The old girl must have had blood-relatives somewhere even if she hadn't known them. Or him! Or her! Yes, there might even turn out to be a one hundred per cent non-sharing heir! All right, then, where was he? Or she? On a farm in Wisconsin? In a real-estate office in California? Behind the counter of a drugstore in Texas? Which of the thousands of Schneiders, Snyders, and Sniders in America was going to be the lucky one? Who was the unsuspecting millionaire? Corn? Well, maybe, but always good for a follow-up, and of nation-wide interest.

And of nation-wide interest it had proved. By the beginning of 1939, the administrator of the estate had been notified of over eight thousand claims to be the missing heir, an army of disreputable lawyers had moved in to exploit the claimants, and the whole case had begun to soar rapidly into the cloud-cuckoo land of high fantasy, skullduggery, and courtroom farce in which it was to remain until, on the outbreak of war, it had fallen suddenly into oblivion.

What business Lavater, Powell and Sistrom could have with the resurrection of so unsavoury a corpse, George could not imagine.

It was Mr. Budd, one of the senior partners, who enlightened him.

The main burden of the Schneider Johnson estate had been borne by Messrs. Moreton, Greener and Cleek, an old-fashioned Philadelphia law firm of great respectability. They had been Miss Clothilde Johnson's attorneys and had conducted the formal search for a will on her instructions. The intestacy duly established, the matter had come before the Orphans' Court in Philadelphia, and the Register of Wills had appointed Robert L. Moreton as administrator of the estate. He had remained the administrator until the end of 1944.

"And very nice too," said Mr. Budd. "If only he'd had the sense to leave it at that, I wouldn't have blamed him. But no, the cockle-brained old coot retained his *own* firm as attorneys for the administrator. Jeepers, in a case like that it was suicidal!"

Mr. Budd was a pigeon-chested man with a long head, a neat, clipped moustache, and bifocal glasses. He had a ready smile, a habit of using out-of-date colloquialisms, and an air of careless good-humour of which George was deeply suspicious.

"The combined fees," George said carefully, "must have been pretty big on an estate of that size."

"No fees," declared Mr. Budd, "are big enough to make it worth while for a decent law office to get mixed up with a lot of ambulance-chasers and crooks. There are dozens of these inheritance cases hanging fire all over the world. Look at the Abdul Hamid estate! The British got tied up in that one and it's been going on for thirty years or more. That'll probably never be settled. Look at the Garrett case! Think how many reputations that's damaged. Shucks! It's always the same. Is A an impostor? Is B out of his mind? Who died before whom? Is the old photograph Aunt Sarah or Aunt Flossie? Has a forger been at work with faded ink?" He waved his arms disparagingly. "I tell you, George, in my opinion the Schneider Johnson case pretty well finished Moreton, Greener and Cleek as a regular law firm. And when Bob Moreton got sick in '44 and had to retire, that was the end. They dissolved."

"Couldn't Greener or Cleek have taken over as administrator?"

Mr. Budd pretended to look shocked. "My dear George, you don't take over an appointment like that. It's a reward for good and faithful service.

In this case, our learned, highly respected, and revered John J. Sistrom was the lucky man."

"Oh. I see."

"The investments do the work, George, our John J. takes the fees as administrator. However," Mr. Budd continued with a trace of satisfaction in his voice, "it doesn't look as if he's going to do so much longer. You'll see why in a moment. From what old Bob Moreton told me at the time, the position was originally this. Amelia's father was named Hans Schneider. He was a German who'd immigrated in 1849. Bob Moreton and his partners were pretty well convinced in the end that, if there were anybody at all entitled to take the estate, it was one of the old man's relatives back in Germany. But the whole thing was complicated by the representation question. Do you know anything about that, George?"

"Bregy, discussing the 1947 act, gives a very clear summary of the former rules."

"That's dandy." Mr. Budd grinned. "Because, frankly, I don't know a thing about it. Now, leaving out all the newspaper nonsense, here's what happened to the case. In '39 old Bob Moreton went off to Germany to check up on the other side of the Schneider family. Self-preservation, of course. He needed facts to go on if he was going to deal with all those phony claims. Then, when he got back, the damnedest thing happened. The damnedest things were always happening on that screwy case. It seemed that the Nazis had got wind of Bob's inquiries. What they did was to take a quick look into the thing themselves and produce an old man named Rudolph Schneider. Then they claimed the whole estate on his behalf."

"I remember that," George said. "They hired McClure to act for them."

"That's right. This Rudolph was from Dresden or some such place and they said that he was a first cousin of Amelia Johnson. Moreton, Greener and Cleek fought the claim. Said the documents the Krauts produced were forged. Anyway, the case was still before the courts when we got into the war in '41, and that finished it as far as they were concerned. The Alien Property Custodian in Washington moved in and filed a claim. Because of the German claim of course. The case froze. When he retired, Bob Moreton handed over all the documents to John J. There were over two tons of them and they're down in our vaults right now, just where they were left when Moreton, Greener and Cleek delivered them in '44. Nobody's ever troubled to look them over. No reason to. Well, now there *is* a reason."

George's heart sank. "Oh, yes?"

By choosing this moment to fill his pipe Mr. Budd avoided George's eyes as he went on. "This is the situation, George. It seems that with the appreciation of values and interest the estate is worth over four million now and the Commonwealth of Pennsylvania has decided to exercise its rights under the act and claim the lot. However, they've asked

John J., as administrator, if he proposes to fight them on it, and, just for form's sake, he feels we ought to check through the documents to make sure that there's no reasonable claim outstanding. So that's what I want you to do, George. Just check through for him. Make sure he's not over-looking anything. O.K.?"

"Yes, sir. O.K."

But he did not quite succeed in keeping a note of resignation out of his voice. Mr. Budd looked up with a sympathetic chuckle. "And if it'll make you feel any better about the job, George," he said, "I can tell you that we've been getting short of vault space for some time now. If you can get that load of junk out of the way you'll be earning the heartfelt thanks of the entire office."

George managed to smile.

CHAPTER II

HE HAD NO DIFFICULTY in finding the Schneider Johnson records. They were parcelled up in damp-proof wrappings and had a stor-age vault to themselves, which they filled from floor to ceiling. It was clear that Mr. Budd's estimate of their total weight had not been exag-gerated. Fortunately, all the parcels had been carefully labelled and ar-ranged systematically. Having made sure that he understood the system which had been employed, George made a selection of the parcels and had them carried up to his office.

It was late in the afternoon when he started work and, with some idea of getting a general picture of the case before settling down to work seri-ously on the claims, he had brought up a bulky parcel labelled: "Schneider Johnson Press Clippings." The label proved to be slightly misleading. What in fact the parcel contained was the record of Messrs. Moreton, Greener and Cleek's hopeless battle with the press and their efforts to stem the flood of nonsensical claims that was overwhelming them. It made pathetic reading.

The record began two days after Mr. Moreton had been appointed administrator of the estate. A New York tabloid had discovered that Amelia's father, Hans Schneider ("the Old Forty-niner," as the paper called him), had married a New York girl named Mary Smith. This meant, the paper had contended excitedly, that the name of the missing heir could be Smith as well as Schneider.

Messrs. Moreton, Greener and Cleek, as attorneys for the administrator, had properly hastened to deny the contention; but instead of pointing out, more or less simply, that, as Amelia's first cousins on her mother's side had all been dead for years, the Smith family of New York did not qualify in law as heirs, they had stuffily contented themselves with quoting the act as saying that "there could be no representation admitted among collaterals after the grandchildren of brothers and sisters and children of aunts and uncles." This unfortunate sentence, quoted derisively under the subheading "Double-Talk," was the only part of the statement that had been printed.

Most of the partners' subsequent statements had suffered the same kind of fate. From time to time some of the more responsible papers had made serious efforts to interpret the intestacy laws to their readers, but never, as far as George could see, had the partners attempted to assist them. The fact that, as Amelia had had no close relatives living, the only possible heirs were any nephews and nieces of the late Hans Schneider who had still been alive when Amelia died, was never explicitly stated by the partners. The nearest they had come to clarity had been in a statement suggesting that it was unlikely that there were any "first cousins of the intestate decedent who had survived the decedent" in America, and that if any did exist they would most probably be found in Germany.

They might have saved themselves the trouble. The suggestion that the legal heir to the estate might be in Europe instead of somewhere like Wisconsin had not been interesting to the newspapers of 1939; the possibility of his not existing at all they had preferred to ignore altogether. Besides, the enterprise of a Milwaukee paper had just then given the story yet another twist. With the help of the immigration authorities, this paper's special investigator had been able to discover the number of families named Schneider who had emigrated from Germany in the latter half of the nineteenth century. The number was large. Was it too much to suppose, the paper had asked, that at least one of the Old Fortyniner's younger brothers had followed his example in emigrating? No indeed! The hunt had been on again, and squads of special investigators had gone forth to pad hopefully through city records, land registers, and state archives in the footsteps of the immigrant Schneiders.

George repacked the parcel with a sigh. He knew already that he was not going to enjoy the next few weeks.

The total number of claims made was just over eight thousand and he found that there was a separate file for each. Most had only two or three letters in them, but many were quite thick, while some had parcels to themselves and bulged with affidavits, photostats of documents, tattered photographs, and genealogical tables. A few had old Bibles and other family souvenirs in them, and one, for some inexplicable reason, even contained a greasy fur cap.

George set to work. By the end of his first week he had been through seven hundred of the claims and was feeling sorry for Messrs. Moreton, Greener and Cleek. Many, of course, had come from lunatics and cranks. There was the angry man in North Dakota who said that *his* name was Martin Schneider, that he was *not* dead, and that Amelia Johnson had stolen the money from him while he lay sleeping. There was the woman who claimed the estate on behalf of a Californian society for the propagation of the Cataphrygian heresy, on the grounds that the spirit of the late Amelia had entered into Mrs. Schultz, the society's honorary treasurer. And there was the man, writing in multi-coloured inks from a state hospital, who said that he was the legitimate son of Amelia by a secret first marriage to a coloured man. But the majority of the claimants seemed to be persons who, while not actually insane, had rudimentary notions of what constituted evidence. There was, for instance, a Chicago man named Higgins who had evolved an elaborate claim from the memory of having heard his father say that Cousin Amelia was a wicked old miser; and another man had pressed for a share of the estate on the strength of an old letter from a Danish relative named Schneider. Then there were those who warily declined to send evidence to support their claims lest it should be stolen and used to prove the case of another claimant, and others who demanded travelling expenses in order that they might present their cases in person to the administrator. Above all, there were the lawyers.

Only thirty-four out of the first seven hundred claims which George examined had been handled by attorneys, but it took him over two days to get through those particular files. The claims in question were mostly of doubtful validity, and one or two were patently dishonest. In George's view, no reputable lawyer would have touched any of them. But these had been disreputable lawyers; they had both touched and held on. They had quoted non-existent precedents and photographed useless documents. They had hired dishonest inquiry agents to conduct pointless investigations, and quack genealogists to draw up faked family trees. They had written portentous letters and uttered obscure threats. The only thing, apparently, that none of them had ever done was to advise his client to withdraw a claim. In one of these files there was a letter to the administrator from an old woman named Snyder, regretting that she had no more money left to pay her attorney to act for her, and asking that her claim should not on this account be overlooked.

In his second week on the records, George managed, in spite of a severe cold in the head, to push his score of examined claims up to nineteen hundred. In the third week he topped three thousand. By the end of the fourth week he was at the halfway mark. He was also feeling very depressed. The boring nature of the work and the cumulative effect of so much evidence of human stupidity were lowering in themselves. The amused commiseration of his new colleagues and the knowledge that he was beginning his career in Lavater, Powell and Sistrom at the wrong end of an office joke had done nothing to improve matters. Mr. Budd, when last encountered in the elevator on his way back from lunch, had talked cheerfully about baseball and had not even troubled to ask for a progress report. On the Monday morning of the fifth week George surveyed with loathing the stacks of records that still remained to be examined.

"Finish the O's, Mr. Carey?" The speaker was the janitor who looked after the vaults, cleaned up the parcels, and carried them to and from George's office.

"No, I'd better start on the P's now."

"I can ease the rest of the O's out if you like, Mr. Carey."

"All right, Charlie. If you can do it without bringing the lot down." The inroads he had already made on the towering stacks of parcels had gradually reduced the stability of the remainder.

"Sure, Mr. Carey," said Charlie. He took hold of a section near the floor and pulled. There was a slithering noise and a crash as an avalanche of parcels engulfed him. In the cloud of dust that followed the subsidence, he stumbled to his feet coughing and swearing, his hand held to his head. Blood began to pour from a long cut over his eye.

"For God's sake, Charlie, how did that happen?"

The janitor kicked something solid under the heap of parcels about him. "This damned thing caught me on the head, Mr. Carey," he explained. "Must have been stacked up in the middle somewhere."

"Do you feel all right?"

"Oh, sure. It's only a scratch. Sorry, Mr. Carey."

"You'd better get it fixed anyway."

When he had handed the janitor over to the care of one of the elevator men and the dust in the vault had settled again, George went in and examined the confusion. Both the O's and the P's had vanished under a rubble of S's and W's. He pushed several of the parcels aside and saw the reason for the janitor's cut eye. It was a large, black, japanned deed box of the kind that used to line the walls of old family lawyers. Stencilled on it in white paint were the words: "SCHNEIDER—CONFIDENTIAL."

George dragged the box clear of the parcels and tried to open it. It was locked and there was no key attached to either of the handles. He hesitated. His business in this case was with the claims files, and it was foolish to waste time satisfying his curiosity about the contents of an old deed box. On the other hand, it would take an hour to straighten out the mess at his feet. There was little point in his covering himself with dust and cobwebs in order to hasten the process, and Charlie would be back in a few minutes. He went into the janitor's room, took a cold chisel and a hammer from the tool rack, and returned to the box. A few blows cut through the thin metal around the tongue of the lock, and he was able to wrench the lid open.

At first sight, the contents seemed to be simply some personal belongings from Mr. Moreton's office. There was a calf-bound appointment book with his initials stamped on it in gold, an onyx desk set, a carved teak cigar box, a tooled leather blotting pad, and a pair of leather-covered letter trays to match it. In one of the trays there was a hand towel, some aspirin tablets, and a bottle of vitamin capsules. George lifted the tray. Beneath it was a thick loose-leaf binder labelled: "GERMAN INQUIRY RE SCHNEIDER BY ROBERT L. MORETON, 1939." He glanced through a page or two, saw that it was in diary form, and put it aside for later reading. Underneath was a Manila folder containing a mass of photographs, mostly, it appeared, of German legal documents of some sort. The only other things in the box were a sealed package and a sealed envelope. On the package was written: "Correspondence between Hans Schneider and his wife, with other documents found by Hilton G. Greener and Robert L. Moreton among effects of late Amelia Schneider Johnson, Sept. 1938." On the envelope was written: "Photograph handed to R. L. M. by Father Weichs at Bad Schwennheim."

George put Mr. Moreton's personal things back in the deed box and took the rest of the contents up to his office. There the first thing he did was to open the sealed parcel.

The letters in it had been carefully numbered and initialled by Mr. Greener and Mr. Moreton. There were seventy-eight of them, all tied up in small packets with silk ribbon and with a pressed flower in each. George undid one of the packets. The letters in it belonged to the courtship period of Amelia's parents, Hans Schneider and Mary Smith. They showed that Hans had been working in a warehouse at the time and learning English, and that Mary had been learning German. George thought them formal, graceless, and dull. However, their value to Mr. Moreton must have been considerable, for they had probably made possible the speedy tracing of the Smith family concerned, and led to its elimination from the list of claimants.

George tied the packet up again and turned to an album of old photographs. In it there were photographs of Amelia and Martin as children, of their brother Frederick, who had died at the age of twelve, and, of course, of Hans and Mary. More interesting, because it was even older, was a daguerreotype portrait of an old man with a vast beard.

He sat erect and very stern, his big hands grasping the arms of the photographer's chair, his head pressed hard against the back of it. The lips were full and determined. There was a heavy, strong face beneath the beard. The silvered copper plate on which the portrait had been made was glued to a red velvet mount. Beneath it Hans had written: "*Mein geliebt Vater, Franz Schneider. 1782–1850.*"

The only other document was a thin, leather-bound notebook filled with Hans's spidery writing. It was written in English. On the first page, elaborately decorated with ornamental pen-strokes, was a description of the book's contents: "An Account of My Beloved Father's Heroic Part in the Battle of Preussisch-Eylau, fought in the year 1807, of His Wounding, and of His Meeting with My Beloved Mother, who Saved His Life. Set down by Hans Schneider for His Children in June 1867, that They may be Proud of the Name They Bear."

The Account began with the events leading up to Eylau and went on with descriptions of the various actions in which the Ansbach Dragoons had engaged the enemy, and of spectacular incidents in the battle: a Russian cavalry charge, the capture of a battery of guns, the decapitation of a French officer. Obviously, what Hans had written down was a legend learned at his father's knee. Parts of it still had the artless quality of a fairy tale; but as the account progressed, the middle-aged Hans could be seen perplexedly trying to reconcile his boyhood memories with his adult sense of reality. The writing of the Account, George thought, must have been a strange experience for him.

After his description of the battle, however, Hans's touch had become surer. The emotions of the wounded hero, his certainty that God was with him, his determination to do his duty until the end—these things were described with practised unction. And when the terrible moment of treachery came, when the cowardly Prussians had abandoned the wounded hero while he was helping a stricken comrade, Hans had let loose a torrent of Biblical denunciation. If God had not guided the hoofs of the hero's horse to the farmhouse of the gentle Maria Dutka, all would certainly have been over. As it was, Maria had been understandably suspicious of the Prussian uniform, and (as she had later confessed to the hero) her humane instincts had been all but overcome by her fears for her virtue and for her ailing father. In the end, of course, all had been well. When his wound was healed, the hero had brought his rescuer home in triumph. In the following year Hans's elder brother, Karl, had been born.

The Account concluded with a sanctimonious homily on the subjects of prayer-saying and the obtaining of forgiveness for sins. George skipped it and turned to Mr. Moreton's diary.

Mr. Moreton and an interpreter whom he had engaged in Paris had arrived in Germany towards the end of March 1939.

His plan had been simple; simple in intention, at all events. First he would retrace Hans Schneider's steps. Then, when he had found out where the Schneider family had lived, he would set about discovering what had happened to all Hans's brothers and sisters.

The first part of the plan had proved simple of execution. Hans had come from somewhere in Westphalia; and in 1849 a man of military age had had to have a permit to leave it. In Münster, the old state capital, Mr. Moreton had been able to find the record of Hans's departure. Hans had come from Mühlhausen and gone to Bremen.

In Bremen, a search in the port authority files of old ships' manifests had revealed that Hans Schneider of Mühlhausen had sailed in the *Abigail*, an English ship of six hundred tons, on May 10, 1849. This had checked with a reference, in one of Hans's letters to Mary Smith, to his voyage from Germany. Mr. Moreton had now concluded that he was tracing the right Hans Schneider. He had gone next to Mühlhausen.

Here, however, a baffling situation had awaited him. He had found that, although the church registers recorded marriages, baptisms, and burials as far back as the Thirty Years' War, none of them covering the years 1807 and 1808 contained any reference to the name of Schneider.

Mr. Moreton had brooded on this disappointment for twenty-four hours; then he had had an idea. He had gone back to the registers.

This time he had turned to those for 1850, the year of Franz Schneider's death. The facts of his death and burial had been recorded, and the location of the grave. Mr. Moreton had gone to inspect it. Now he had had a most disturbing surprise. A decaying memorial stone had supplied the confusing information that this was the resting place of Franz Schneider and his much beloved wife, Ruth. According to Hans's Account, his mother's name had been Maria.

Mr. Moreton had returned to the registers again. It had taken him a long time to work back from 1850 to 1815, but by the time he had done so, he had had the names of no less than ten of Franz Schneider's children and the date of his marriage to Ruth Vogel. He had also learned to his dismay that none of the children's names had been either Hans or Karl.

The idea that there must have been a previous marriage in some other city had soon occurred to him. But where could this earlier marriage have taken place? With what other towns had Franz Schneider been associated? From what town, for instance, had he been recruited into the Prussian army?

There had been only one place where that sort of question might be answered. Mr. Moreton and his interpreter had gone to Berlin.

It had taken Mr. Moreton until the end of March to cut through the swathes of Nazi red tape and dig far enough into the archives at Potsdam to get at the Napoleonic war diaries of the Ansbach Dragoons. It had taken him less than two hours to find out that between 1800 and 1850 the name of Schneider had figured only once in the nominal rolls of the regiment. A Wilhelm Schneider had been killed by a fall from his horse in 1803.

It had been a bitter blow. Mr. Moreton's entry in his diary for that day ended with the despondent words: "So I guess it's a wild-goose chase after all. Nevertheless I will make a check search tomorrow. If no result, will abandon inquiry as I consider inability to link Hans Schneider positively with Mühlhausen family in records makes further efforts pointless."

George turned the page and then stared blankly. The next entry in the diary consisted entirely of figures. They filled the page, line after line of them. The next page was the same, and the page after that. He flicked the pages over rapidly. With the exception of the date headings, every entry in the diary from then on—and it continued for over three months—was in figures. Moreover, the figures were in groups of five. Not only had Mr. Moreton decided after all *against* abandoning his inquiries in Germany, but he had thought it necessary to record the results of them in cipher.

George abandoned the diary and glanced through the file of photographed documents. He did not read German with great confidence even when it was printed in roman type. German handwriting of the traditional kind defeated him completely. These were all handwritten. Careful scrutiny of two or three of them revealed the fact that they referred to the births and death of people named Schneider, but this was scarcely surprising. He put them aside and opened the sealed envelope.

The photograph "handed to R. L. M. by Father Weichs at Bad Schwennheim" proved to be a dog-eared, postcard-size portrait of a young man and a young woman sitting side by side on a professional photographer's rustic bench. The woman had a certain fluffy prettiness and was possibly pregnant. The man was nondescript. Their clothes were of the early 1920's. They looked like a prosperous working-class couple on their day off. There was a painted background of snow-covered pines behind them. Across the corner of it was written, in German script: *"Johann und Ilse."* The photographer's imprint on the mount showed that it had been taken in Zurich. There was nothing else in the envelope.

Charlie, the janitor, came in with a piece of adhesive plaster on his forehead and another load of parcels, and George got back to work on the claims. But that night he took the contents of the deed box back to his apartment and went through them carefully again.

He was in a difficulty. He had been asked to check on the claims to the estate received by the former administrator; nothing else. If the deed box had not fallen and cut the janitor's head, he would probably not have noticed it. It would have been moved out of the way of the parcels of claims files and then left in the vault. He would have worked his way through the claims and then, no doubt, simply reported to Mr. Budd what Mr. Budd wanted to hear: that there were no outstanding claims worth discussing and that the Commonwealth of Pennsylvania could go ahead. Then he, George, would have been free of the whole wretched business and ready to be rewarded with an assignment more suited to his abilities. Now it looked as if he had a choice of two ways of making a fool of himself. One was by forgetting about the contents of the deed box and so running the risk of allowing Mr. Sistrom to make a serious blunder; the other was by plaguing Mr. Budd with idle fancies.

High political office and the presidencies of railroads seemed very far away that night. It was not until the early hours of the morning that he thought of a tactful way of putting the thing to Mr. Budd.

Mr. Budd received George's report with impatience.

"I don't even know if Bob Moreton's still alive," he said irritably. "In any case, all that this cipher stuff suggests to me is that the man was in an advanced stage of paranoia."

"Did he seem O.K. when you saw him in '44, sir?"

"He may have *seemed* O.K., but from what you show me it looks very much as if he wasn't."

"But he *did* go on with the inquiry, sir."

"What if he did?" Mr. Budd sighed. "Look, George, we don't want any complications in this business. We just want to get rid of the thing, and the sooner the better. I appreciate that you want to be thorough, but I should have thought it was very simple, really. You just get a German translator on these photographed documents, find out what they're all about, then check through the claims from people named Schneider and see if the documents refer in any way. That's straightforward enough, isn't it?"

George decided that the time for tactful handling had arrived. "Yes, sir. But what I had in mind was a way of speeding up the whole thing. You see, I haven't got through to the Schneider claims yet, but, judging by the volume of paper in the vault, there must be at least three thousand of them. Now, it's taken me nearly four weeks to check through that number of ordinary claims. The Schneider files are certain to take longer. But I've been looking into things and I have a hunch that if I can check with Mr. Moreton it may save a lot of time."

"Why? How do you mean?"

"Well, sir, I checked through some of the reports on that case he fought against the Rudolph Schneider claim and the German government. It seemed to me quite clear that Moreton, Greener and Cleek had a whole lot of facts at their disposal that the other side didn't have. I think they had very definite information that there was no Schneider heir alive."

Mr. Budd looked at him shrewdly. "Are you suggesting, George, that Moreton as administrator went on and established beyond doubt that there was no heir, and that he and his partners then kept quiet about the fact so that they could go on drawing fees from the estate?"

"It could be, sir, couldn't it?"

"Terrible minds some of you young men have!" Mr. Budd suddenly became jovial again. "All right, what's your point?"

"If we could have the results of Moreton's confidential inquiries, we might have enough information to make any further examination of all these claims unnecessary."

Mr. Budd stroked his chin. "I see. Yes, not bad, George." He nodded briskly. "O.K. If the old chap's alive and in his right mind, see what you can do. The quicker we can get out from under the whole thing, the better."

"Yes, sir," said George.

That afternoon he had a call from Mr. Budd's secretary to say that a check with Mr. Moreton's former club had disclosed that he was now living in retirement at Montclair, New Jersey. Mr. Budd had written to the old man asking him if he would see George.

Two days later a reply came from Mrs. Moreton. She said that her husband had been bedridden for some months, but that in view of former associations, and providing that Mr. Carey's visit was brief, Mr. Moreton would be glad to put his memory at Mr. Carey's disposal. Mr. Moreton slept afternoons. Perhaps Friday morning at eleven o'clock would be convenient to Mr. Carey.

"That must be his second wife," said Mr. Budd.

On the Friday morning, George put the deed box and all its original contents into the back of his car and drove out to Montclair.

CHAPTER III

THE HOUSE was a comfortable-looking place surrounded by several acres of well-kept garden, and it occurred to George that the financial fate of Messrs. Moreton, Greener and Cleek had not been quite as disastrous as Mr. Budd had implied. The second Mrs. Moreton proved to be a lean, neat woman in her late forties. She had a straight back, a brisk manner, and a patronizing smile. It seemed probable that she had been Mr. Moreton's nurse.

"Mr. Carey is it? You won't tire him, will you? He's allowed to sit up in the mornings at present, but we have to be careful. Coronary thrombosis." She led the way through to a glass-enclosed porch at the rear of the house.

Mr. Moreton was big and pink and flabby, like an athlete gone to seed. He had short white hair and very blue eyes, and there was still a trace of boyish good looks visible in the slack, puffy face. He was lying, propped up by cushions and swathed in a blanket, on a day-bed fitted with a book-rest. He greeted George eagerly, thrusting the book-rest aside and struggling into a sitting posture in order to shake hands. He had a soft, pleasant voice and smelled faintly of lavender water.

For a minute or two he asked after the people at George's office whom he had known, and then about a number of men in Philadelphia of whom George had never even heard. At last he sat back with a smile.

"Don't ever let anyone persuade you to retire, Mr. Carey," he said.

"You live in the past and become a bore. A dishonest bore, too. I ask you how Harry Budd is. You tell me he's fine. What I really want to know is whether he's gone bald."

"He has," George said.

"And whether, in spite of all that studied bonhomie, he's got ulcers yet, or high blood-pressure."

George laughed.

"Because if he has," continued Mr. Moreton amiably, "that's fine. He's one son of a bitch I don't have to envy."

"Now, Bob!" his wife said reproachfully.

He spoke without looking at her. "Mr. Carey and I are going to talk a little business now, Kathy," he said.

"Very well. Don't overtire yourself."

Mr. Moreton did not reply. When she had gone, he smiled. "Drink, my boy?"

"No, thank you, sir. I think Mr. Budd explained why I wanted to see you."

"Sure. The Schneider Johnson matter. I could have guessed anyway." He looked sideways at George. "So you found it, did you?"

"Found what, sir?"

"The diary and the photographs and all Hans Schneider's stuff. You found it, eh?"

"It's outside in the car, sir, with some of your personal belongings that got put in the box with it."

Mr. Moreton nodded. "I know. I put them there myself—on top. I figured that, with any luck, a person opening the box would think that it was all just my personal junk."

"I'm afraid I don't quite follow you, sir."

"Of course you don't. I'll explain. As administrator I was ethically bound to hand over everything, lock, stock, and barrel. Well, that confidential stuff was something I didn't want to hand over. I wanted to destroy it, but Greener and Cleek wouldn't let me. They said that if anything came up afterwards and John J. found out, I'd be in trouble."

George said: "Oh." He had not really believed in his suggestion that Moreton, Greener and Cleek had concealed important information. It had merely occurred to him as a means of beguiling Mr. Budd. Now he was a trifle shocked.

Mr. Moreton shrugged. "So all I could do was to try and camouflage it. Well, I didn't succeed." He stared out gloomily at the garden for a moment, then turned to George briskly as if to dismiss an ugly memory. "I suppose the Commonwealth of Pennsylvania's after the loot again, eh?"

"Yes. They want to know if Mr. Sistrom's going to fight them on it."

"And Harry Budd, who doesn't like soiling his dainty fingers with such things, can't wait to get the thing out of the office, eh? No, you don't have to answer that, my boy. Let's get down to business."

"Would you like me to get the papers out of the car, sir?"

"We won't need them," said Mr. Moreton. "I know what's in that box as well as I know my own name. Did you read that little book Hans Schneider wrote for his children?"

"Yes."

"What did you think of it?"

George smiled. "After reading it I made a resolution. If I have children, I'm never going to tell them a thing about my war experiences."

The old man chuckled. "They'll get it out of you. The thing you want to watch out for is having a drip of a son like Hans who writes down what you say. That's dangerous."

"How do you mean?"

"I'll tell you. I was administrator all right, but I went to Germany because my partners sent me. Tail wagging the dog. The case had been in our hair too long and they wanted to have done with it. My instructions were to confirm what we already believed—that there was no legitimate heir to the estate. Well, when I found that Hans was probably a son of Franz Schneider's first marriage, I had to know about that marriage in order to complete the picture. As you know, I went to Potsdam to see if I could trace him through the regimental archives. To begin with, I failed."

"But next day you went back for another check through."

"Yes, but I'd had a night to think. And I'd thought again about what Hans had written. If there was any truth in the thing at all, Sergeant Schneider had become a casualty at the Battle of Eylau and been lost in the retreat. Surely the war diary would record that fact in a casualty list. So that next day, instead of going all over the nominal rolls again, I got the interpreter to translate the regimental account of the battle for me." He sighed reminiscently. "There are some moments in life, my boy, that always feel good no matter how many times you go over them again in your mind. That was one of them. It was late in the morning and getting very warm. The interpreter was having trouble with that old writing and was stumbling over the translation of it. Then he began on the account of the long march from Eylau to Insterburg. I was only half listening. As a matter of fact, I was thinking about a bad march I'd done in Cuba during the Spanish-American War. And then something the interpreter had said made me jump right out of my skin."

He paused.

"What was that?" George asked.

Mr. Moreton smiled. "I remember the words exactly. 'During this night'—I quote from the war diary—'Franz Schirmer, a Sergeant, left the detachment under his command, saying that he was going to succour a Dragoon who had lagged behind because of a lame horse. When morning came, Sergeant Schirmer had not rejoined his detachment. There was found to be no other man missing from it, nor any who had lagged behind. Accordingly, the name of Franz Schirmer was posted in the list of deserters.' "

For a moment or two there was silence. "Well?" added Mr. Moreton. "What do you think of that?"

"Schirmer, did you say?"

"That's right. Sergeant Franz Schirmer, S-c-h-i-r-m-e-r."

George laughed. "The old bastard," he said.

"Exactly."

"So all that stuff he told his son Hans about the cowardly Prussians leaving him for dead was—"

"Bull," said Mr. Moreton dryly. "But you see the implications."

"Yes. What did you do?" George asked.

"The first thing I did was to take security precautions. We'd already had trouble enough with the newspapers' finding out stuff about the case and printing it, and before I went to Germany I'd agreed on a policy with my partners. I was to keep what I was doing as secret as possible; and to make sure that I didn't get an interpreter with German newspaper contacts, I was to engage him in Paris. The other thing we'd agreed on was a cipher for confidential matters. It may sound funny to you, but if you've ever had experience of—"

"I know," George said. "I saw the newspaper clippings."

"Ah. Well, I'd been sending my partners progress reports in diary form. When I found out about Schirmer, I began to use the cipher. It was a simple key-word affair, but good enough for our purpose. You see, I had visions of the newspapers' getting hold of the Schirmer name and starting another flood of claims from Schirmers, Shermans, and the rest. The final thing I did was to fire the interpreter. I said I was abandoning the inquiry and paid him off."

"Why was that?"

"Because I was going on with it and I didn't want anyone outside the firm to have a complete picture. It was just as well I did fire him, too, because later on, when the Nazis were after the estate and France was occupied, the Gestapo pulled in the second man I used, for questioning. If he'd known what the first one knew, we'd have been in a spot. I got the second one through our Paris Embassy. By the time he arrived, I'd had the war-diary entry photographed—you'll find it in the file—and was ready to move on."

"To Ansbach?"

"Yes. There I found the record of Franz Schirmer's baptism. Back in Mühlhausen again, I found the register entries for the marriage of Franz and Maria Dutka, the births of Karl and Hans, and the death of Maria. But the really important thing I found was when I went back to Münster. The boy Karl was down in the recruits' muster-roll for 1824 as Karl *Schirmer*. Franz had changed his own name but not his eldest boy's."

George thought quickly. "I suppose Franz changed his name when Mühlhausen was ceded to Prussia."

"That's what I thought. As far as the Prussians were concerned, he'd be a deserter. But I guess he just didn't trouble about Karl."

"He changed Hans's name."

"But Hans was a baby then. He'd naturally grow up a Schneider. Anyway, whatever the reason, there it was. Hans had had six brothers and five sisters. All were surnamed Schneider except one, Karl. His surname was Schirmer. All I had to do was to find out which of those persons had had children—cousins of Amelia—and whether any one of those children was alive."

"That must have been quite a job."

Mr. Moreton shrugged. "Well, it wasn't quite as bad as it sounds. Death rates were higher in the last century. Out of the eleven brothers and sisters, two boys and two girls died in a typhoid epidemic before they were twelve, and another of the girls was killed by a runaway horse when she was fifteen. That meant I had only six to worry about. Four of them I handed over to a private inquiry agent specializing in that kind of thing. The other two I looked after."

"Karl Schirmer was one of your two?"

"He was. And by the middle of July I had finished with the Schneiders. There had been children all right, but none of them had survived Amelia. So there was still no heir. The only one left to check on was Karl Schirmer."

"Did he have any children?"

"Six. He'd been apprenticed to a printer in Coblenz and married the boss's daughter. I spent from mid-July on, chasing around the towns and villages of the Rhineland. By mid-August I'd traced all but one of the six, and there was still no heir. The missing child was a son, Friedrich, born in 1863. All I knew about him was that he'd married in Dortmund in 1887, and that he was a bookkeeper. And then I had trouble with the Nazis."

"What sort of trouble?"

"Well, in the summer of 1939 any foreigner who travelled about the Rhineland asking questions, checking official records, and sending cables in cipher was bound to become suspect, but, like a dope, I hadn't thought of that. In Essen I was interviewed by the police and asked to give an account of myself. I explained as best I could and they went away, but the next day they came again. This time they had a couple of Gestapo boys with them." Mr. Moreton smiled ruefully. "I don't mind telling you, my boy, I was glad I had an American passport. Still, I made them believe me in the end. The fact that I was trying to prevent the papers' knowing what I was doing helped, I think. They didn't like newspapers either. The main thing was that I managed to keep the name of Schirmer out of it. But they made trouble all the same. Within two weeks I had a cable from my partners to say that the German Embassy in Washington had notified the State Department that in future the German government would represent any German national claiming the Schneider Johnson estate, and had requested complete information about the present state of the administrator's inquiries in the matter."

"You mean the Gestapo had reported what you were doing to their Foreign Office?"

"They certainly had. That's how that phony Rudolph Schneider claim of theirs started. You have no idea how difficult it is, politically and in every other way, to challenge the validity of documents produced and attested by the government of a friendly power—I mean a power enjoying normal diplomatic relations with your own government. It's like accusing them of forging their own bank-notes."

"And what about the Schirmer side of the family, sir? Did the Nazis ever get on to that?"

"No, they didn't. You see, they didn't have Amelia's documents to help them as we did. They didn't even have the right Schneider family, but it was difficult to prove."

"And Friedrich Schirmer, Karl's son? Did you trace him?"

"Yes, my boy, I traced him all right, but I had hell's own job doing it. I got on his trail at last through a clerical employment agency in Karlsruhe. They found out for me that there had been an elderly bookkeeper named Friedrich Schirmer on their files five years previously. They'd found a job for him in a button factory at Freiburg-im-Breisgau. So I went to the button factory. There they told me that he had retired three years earlier at the age of seventy and gone into a clinic at Bad Schwennheim. Bladder trouble, they said. They thought he'd probably be dead."

"And was he?"

"Yes, he was dead." Mr. Moreton looked out at the garden as if he hated it. "I don't mind telling you, my boy," he said, "that I was feeling pretty old and tired myself by then. It was the last week in August and there wasn't very much doubt, from what the radio was saying, that Europe was going to be at war within the week. I wanted to go home. I've never been the sort of man who likes being in the thick of things. Besides, I was having trouble with the interpreter. He was a Lorrainer, France was mobilizing, and he was afraid he wouldn't have time to see his wife before he was called to his regiment. It was getting difficult to buy gasoline for the car, too. I was tempted to forget about Friedrich Schirmer and get out. And yet I couldn't quite bring myself to go without just making a final check-up. Twenty-four hours more, that was all I needed."

"And so you did check up." Now that he had the facts he wanted, George was getting impatient with Mr. Moreton's reminiscences.

"Yes, I checked up. But without the interpreter. He was so darned scared that I told him to take the car, drive it to Strasbourg, and wait for me there. That was a lucky thing, too. When the Gestapo got hold of him later, he knew no more than that I'd gone to Bad Schwennheim. Real luck. I went there by train. Do you know it? It's near Triburg in Baden."

"I never got down that way."

"It's one of those scattered little resort towns—pensions, family hotels, and small villas on the edge of the fir forest. I'd found that the best person to make for on those inquiries was the priest, so I set out to find him. I could see the church—like a cuckoo clock it was, on the side of the hill— and I had just about enough German to find out from a passer-by that the priest's house was beyond it. Well, I sweated up there and saw the priest. Luckily, he spoke good English. I told him the usual lies, of course—"

"Lies?"

"About its being a trifling matter, a small legacy, all that stuff. You have to play it down. If you go telling the truth on a job like that you're a dead duck. Greed! You'd be surprised what happens to perfectly sane people when they start thinking in millions. So I told the usual lies and asked the usual questions."

"And the priest said Friedrich Schirmer was dead?"

"Yes." Mr. Moreton smiled slyly. "But he also said what a pity it was that I'd come too late."

"Too late for what?"

"For the funeral."

"You mean he'd survived Amelia?"

"By over ten months."

"Had he a wife?"

"She'd been dead for sixteen years."

"Children?"

"A son named Johann. That's his photograph in the box you have. Ilse was the son's wife. Johann would be in his fifties now."

"You mean he's alive?"

"I haven't any idea, my boy," said Mr. Moreton cheerfully. "But if he is, he's certainly the Schneider Johnson heir."

George smiled. "*Was* the heir you mean, don't you, sir? As a German, he could never receive the estate. The Alien Property Custodian would vest himself with the claim."

Mr. Moreton chuckled and shook his head. "Don't be so certain, my boy. According to the priest, Friedrich spent over twenty years of his life working for a German electrical manufacturer with a plant near Schaffhausen in Switzerland. Johann was born there. Technically, he'd be Swiss."

George sat back in his chair. For a moment or two he was too confused to think clearly. Mr. Moreton's pink, puffy jowls quivered with amusement. He was pleased with the effect of his statement. George felt himself getting indignant.

"But where did he live?" he asked. "Where *does* he live?"

"I don't know that either. Neither did the priest. As far as I could make out, the family returned to Germany in the early twenties. But Friedrich Schirmer hadn't seen or heard from his son and daughter-in-law in years. What's more, there was nothing in the papers he left to show that they'd ever existed, barring the photograph and some things he'd said to the priest."

"Did Friedrich make a will?"

"No. He had nothing to leave worth troubling about. He had lived on a small annuity. There was scarcely enough money to bury him properly."

"But surely you made an effort to find this Johann?"

"There wasn't much I could do right then. I asked Father Weichs— that was the priest—to let me know immediately if anything was heard of or from Johann, but the war broke out three days later. I never heard any more about it."

"But when the German government claimed the estate, didn't you tell them the situation and ask them to produce Johann Schirmer?"

The old man shrugged impatiently. "Of course, if it had got to the point where they had a real chance of substantiating their Schneider claim, we'd have had to. But, as it was, it was better not to show our hand. They'd already produced a phony Schneider. What was to stop them producing a phony Johann Schirmer? Supposing they'd discovered that Johann and Ilse were dead and without heirs! Do you think they'd have admitted it? Besides, we didn't expect the war to last more than a month or two; we were thinking all the time that at any moment one of us would be able to go back to Germany and clear the whole matter up in a proper way and to our own satisfaction. Then, of course, Pearl Harbor came and that was the end of the thing as far as we were concerned."

Mr. Moreton sank back on his cushions and closed his eyes. He had had his fun. Now he was tired.

George was silent. Out of the corner of his eye he could see the second Mrs. Moreton hovering in the background. He got to his feet. "There's only one thing I'm not clear about, sir," he said hesitantly.

"Yes, my boy?"

"You said that when you handed over to Mr. Sistrom in '44 you didn't want these facts to come to his attention. Why was that?"

Slowly Mr. Moreton opened his eyes. "Early in '44," he said, "my son was murdered by the S.S. after escaping from a prisoner-of-war camp in Germany. My wife wasn't too well at the time and the shock killed her. When the time came to hand the administration over, I guess I just couldn't accept the idea of a German getting anything out of this country as a result of my efforts."

"I see."

"Not professional," the old man added disapprovingly. "Not ethical. But that's the way I felt. Now—" he shrugged and his eyes were suddenly amused again—"now all I'm wondering is what Harry Budd's going to say when you tell him the news."

"I've been wondering the same thing myself," said George.

Mr. Budd said: "Oh my God!" with great force and asked his secretary to see if Mr. Sistrom was available for consultation.

John J. Sistrom was the most senior partner in the firm (Lavater and Powell had been dead for years) and had been well thought of by the elder J. P. Morgan. A remote, portentous figure who entered and left his office by a private door, he was rarely seen except by other senior partners. George had been presented to him on joining the firm and received a perfunctory handshake. He was very old, much older than Mr. Moreton, but skinny and spry—an energetic bag of bones. He fidgeted with a gold pencil while he listened to Mr. Budd's disgusted explanation of the position.

"I see," he said at last. "Well, Harry, what do you want me to do? Retain someone else, I suppose."

"Yes, John J. I thought that someone like Lieberman might be interested."

"Maybe he would. What's the exact value of the estate now?"

Mr. Budd looked at George.

"Four million three hundred thousand, sir," George said.

Mr. Sistrom pursed his lips. "Let's see. Federal tax will account for quite a bit. Then, the thing has been held up for over seven years, so the 1943 legislation applies. That means eighty per cent of what's left to the Commonwealth."

"If a claimant were to get half a million out of it, he'd be lucky," said Mr. Budd.

"Half a million free of tax is a lot of money these days, Harry."

Mr. Budd laughed. Mr. Sistrom turned to George. "What's your opinion of this Johann Schirmer's claim, young man?" he asked.

"On the face of it, sir, the claim looks sound to me. A big point in its favour would seem to be the fact that although the intestacy itself comes under the 1917 act, this Schirmer claim would satisfy the tougher provisions of the '47 act. There's no question of representation. Friedrich Schirmer was a *first* cousin *and* he survived the old lady."

Mr. Sistrom nodded. "You agree with that, Harry?"

"Oh, sure. I think Lieberman will be glad to act."

"Funny things, some of these old inheritances cases," mused Mr. Sistrom absently. "They make perspectives. A German Dragoon of Napoleon's time deserts after a battle and has to change his name. Now here we sit, over a hundred years later and four thousand miles away, wondering how to deal with a situation arising out of that old fact." He smiled vaguely. "It's an interesting case. You see, we could argue that Friedrich inherited the estate prior to the appointment of the Alien Property

Custodian and that it should therefore have descended to Johann Schirmer under the German law. There have been one or two cases of German-Swiss claims against the Custodian which have succeeded. There are all sorts of possibilities."

"And won't the papers have fun when they get hold of them!" said Mr. Budd.

"Well, they don't have to get hold of them, do they? Not for the present anyway." Mr. Sistrom seemed to have come to a decision. "I don't think you ought to be too hasty about this business, Harry," he said. "Naturally, we're not going to get involved in any newspaper nonsense, but we're in the possession of certain information that nobody else has access to. We're in a strong position. I think that before we come to any decision about who's going to act we ought at least to send someone quietly to Germany to see if this Johann Schirmer can be traced. I don't like the idea of just letting the Commonwealth take all this money because we can't be bothered to fight them. If he's dead and without issue or heir, or we can't find him, then we can think again. Maybe I'll just tell the Commonwealth the facts and leave it to them in that case. But if there is some chance that the man may be alive, no matter how slight, we should bend our effort to find him. There is no need to hand over a substantial fee to another firm for doing so. Our charge for services is made irrespective of whether we are successful or not. I see no reason for turning down the opportunity."

"But, my God, John J.—"

"It's perfectly ethical for the administrator's attorneys to endeavour to find the heir and be paid for their efforts."

"I know it's ethical, John J., but jeepers—"

"In this kind of office one can get too narrow," said Mr. Sistrom firmly. "I don't think, either, that just because we're afraid of being annoyed by a little newspaper publicity we should let the business go out of the family."

There was a silence. Mr. Budd heaved a sigh. "Well, if you put it that way, John J. But suppose this man's in the Russian zone of Germany or in jail as a war criminal?"

"Then we can think again. Now, whom will you send?"

Mr. Budd shrugged. "I'd say a good, reliable, private inquiry agent was what we needed."

"Inquiry agent!" Mr. Sistrom dropped his gold pencil. "Look, Harry, we're not going to make a million dollars out of it. Competent private inquiry-agents are far too expensive for a gamble like this. No. I think I have a better idea." He turned in his chair and looked at George.

George waited with a sinking heart.

The blow came.

Mr. Sistrom smiled benevolently. "How would you like a trip to Europe, Mr. Carey?" he said.

CHAPTER IV

Two weeks later George went to Paris.

As the plane from New York banked slowly and began to lose height in preparation for the landing at Orly, he could see the city turning lazily into view beneath the port wing. He craned his head to see more of it. It was not the first time he had flown over Paris; but it was the first time he had done so as a civilian, and he was curious to see if he could still identify the once familiar landmarks. He was, besides, at the beginning of a new relationship with the place. For him it had been, successively, an area on a map, the location of an Army Air Corps headquarters establishment, a fun fair in which to spend leave periods, and a grey wilderness of streets to wander in while you sweated it out waiting for transportation home. Now it had become a foreign capital in which he had business to attend to; the point of departure for what, in a facetious moment, he had thought of as an Odyssey. Not even the knowledge that he was acting merely as an inexpensive substitute for a competent private inquiry agent could quite dispel a pleasurable feeling of anticipation.

His attitude towards the Schneider Johnson case had changed somewhat during those two weeks. Though he still regarded his connection with it as a misfortune, he no longer saw it as a major disaster. Several things had conspired to fortify his own good sense in the matter. There had been Mr. Budd's protest against sending so able a man on so pedestrian a mission. There had been his colleagues' blasphemously expressed conviction that, having become bored with examining claims, he had cunningly misrepresented the facts in order to get himself a free vacation. Above all, there had been Mr. Sistrom's decision to take a personal interest in the matter. Mr. Budd had crossly attributed this to vulgar greed; but George suspected that Mr. Sistrom's apparently simple desire to milk the estate while he had the chance contained elements of other and less businesslike wishes. It was fantastic, no doubt, to suggest that, in a financial matter of any kind, a partner in Lavater, Powell and Sistrom could be influenced by romantic or sentimental considerations; but, as George had already perceived, fantasy and the Schneider Johnson case had never been very far apart. Besides, the belief that a schoolboy lurked in Mr. Sistrom was somehow reassuring; and reassurance was a thing of which he now stood in need.

After a further visit to Montclair, he had set to work deciphering Mr. Moreton's diary. By the time he had completed the task and identified all the photographed documents in the deed box he was aware of an unfamiliar feeling of inadequacy and self-doubt. Münster, Mühlhausen, Karlsruhe, and Berlin—he had dropped bombs on many of the places in which Mr. Moreton had worked to piece together the history of the Schirmer family. And killed quite a few of their inhabitants, no doubt. Would he have had the patience and ingenuity to do what Mr. Moreton had done? He was inclined to doubt it. It was humiliating to be comforted by the knowledge that his own task was likely to prove simpler.

The morning after his arrival in Paris, he went to the American Embassy, established relations with the legal department there, and asked them to recommend a German-English interpreter whom they had themselves used and whose sworn depositions would later be accepted by the Orphans' Court in Philadelphia and by the Alien Property Custodian.

When he returned to his hotel a letter awaited him. It was from Mr. Moreton.

MY DEAR MR. CAREY:

Thank you very much for your letter. I am, of course, very interested to hear that my old friend John Sistrom has decided to take the Schirmer inquiry further, and very pleased to know that you are to have the responsibility. I congratulate you. You must stand well with John J. to be entrusted with this job. You may be sure that no newspaper will get a word out of me on the subject. I note with pleasure your flattering intention of taking the same precautionary measures as I did to ensure secrecy. If you will permit me to give you a word of advice on the interpreter question—don't take anyone you feel you do not like personally. You will be so much together that if you do not quite like him to begin with, you will end by hating the sight of him.

As to the points in my diary on which you were not clear, I have set out my answers to your questions on a separate sheet of paper. Please remember, however, that I am relying upon my memory, which in some instances may have failed me. The answers are given "to the best of my knowledge and belief."

I have given some thought to your problems in Germany and it seems to me likely that Father Weichs, the Bad Schwennheim priest, will be among those with whom you will be getting in touch at an early stage. But when I tried to recall what I had said to you about my interview with him, it seemed to me that I had left out several important things. My diary, I know, gives only the barest facts. It was my last interview in Germany and I was in a hurry to get home. But, as you may imagine, I remember the occasion vividly. A more detailed account of it may prove of some service to you.

As I told you, he informed me of Friedrich Schirmer's death and I gave him a cautious account of my reasons for inquiring about the man.

We then had some conversation which, as it concerned Johann Schirmer to some extent, I will give you as I remember it.

Father Weichs is, or was, a tall, fair man with a bony face and sharp blue eyes. No fool, I warn you. And nothing passive about him. My halting German set the muscles of his jaws twitching impatiently. Fortunately, he speaks English well, and after the courtesies were over, that was the language we used.

"I hoped you might be a relative," he said. "He spoke once of an uncle in America whom he had never seen."

"Had he no relatives here? No wife?" I asked.

"His wife died about sixteen years ago, in Schaffhausen. She was a Swiss. They had lived there for over twenty years. Their son was born there. But when she died he returned to Germany. During his last illness he used to speak of his son, Johann, but he had not seen him for many years. Johann was married and he had lived with the couple for a time, but there had been a quarrel and he had left their house."

"Where did they live?"

"In Germany, but he did not tell me where. The whole subject was very painful to him. He spoke of it only once."

"What did they quarrel about?"

Father Weichs hesitated at this question. Evidently he knew the answer to it. What he said was: "I cannot say."

"You don't know?" I persisted.

He hesitated again, then answered very carefully: "Friedrich Schirmer was not, perhaps, as simple a man as he appeared. That is all I can say."

"I see."

"De mortuis . . . the old man was very sick."

"You have absolutely no idea then, Father, of the whereabouts of Johann?"

"I regret, none. I looked among the old man's things for the address of someone to tell of his death, but I did not find anything. He lived at the sanatorium for old people. The woman director there said that he received no letters, only his annuity every month. Will the son receive the legacy now?"

I had been prepared for the question. At one moment I had thought of trusting this priest, but the habit of caution was very strong. I answered evasively. "The money is in trust," I said, and changed the subject by asking what had happened to his belongings.

"There was little more than the clothes he was buried in," he said.

"No will?"

"No. There were a few books and some old papers—records of his army service, such things. Nothing of value. I have charge of them until the authorities tell me they may be destroyed."

Naturally, I was determined to go through these things myself, but tact was necessary. "I wonder if I might see them, Father," I said. "It would be fitting, perhaps, if I could tell his relatives in America that I had done so."

"Certainly, if you wish."

He had made a package of the papers and put the dead man's rosary in with them. I looked through them.

It was, I must tell you, a pathetic collection. There were old Swiss concert programs and catalogues of Swiss electrical trade exhibitions, an accountancy diploma from a commercial college in Dortmund, and the autographed menu of a banquet held in 1910 for the German employees of the Schaffhausen plant he had worked in. There were letters from business houses all over Germany replying to applications for book-keeping posts. Dates from 1927 and on. The applicant had written from Dortmund, Mainz, Hanover, Karlsruhe and Freiburg, in that date order. There were the army papers and the documents connected with the annuity he had purchased with his savings. In expansive moments I have been known to contend that the apparently unimportant things a man keeps, the private souvenirs, the clutter he accumulates during his lifetime, are an index to the secrets of his soul. If this is so, then Friedrich Schirmer must have led a singularly uneventful inner life.

There were two photographs—the one you have seen of Johann and Ilse and another of the late Frau (Friedrich) Schirmer. I knew that I must have the one of Johann at all costs. I put them down casually.

"Nothing of interest, you see," said Father Weichs.

I nodded. "But," I said, "I wonder if it would not be a kindly action for me to take some remembrance of him back to his relatives in America. If these things are to be destroyed, it seems a pity not to save something of him."

He thought for a moment but could see no objection. He suggested the rosary. I immediately agreed and only brought up the matter of the photograph as an afterthought. "If, by any chance, it should be wanted, I could always copy it and return the original to you," I said.

So I took it with me. I also had his promise that in the event of his learning anything of the whereabouts of Johann Schirmer, I should be informed. As you know, I have never heard from him. In the early hours of the following day, the German army crossed the frontier and began to advance into Poland.

Well, there it is, my boy. My wife has been good enough to type it all out for me and I hope it will be of some use to you. If there is anything else I can do, let me know. And if you feel that you can, without betraying your firm's confidence, let me know how you get on, I shall be more than pleased to hear. You know, the only one of all the Schneiders and Schirmers I got to know about that I really liked was that old Sergeant Franz. I imagine that he was quite a tough proposition. What happens to blood like that? Oh yes, I know that only certain physical characteristics get transmitted, and that it's all a matter of genes and chromosomes; but if you do happen to run across a Schirmer with a beard like Franz's, let me know. Good luck anyway.

> *Sincerely,*
> ROBERT L. MORETON

George refolded the letter and looked at the accompanying sheet of paper with the answer to his questions. As he did so, the telephone by his bed buzzed harshly and he turned to answer it.

"Mademoiselle Kolin to see you, sir."

"All right. I'll come down."

This was the interpreter who had been recommended to him by the Embassy.

"Miss Kolin?" George had said. "A woman?"

"Sure, she's a woman."

"I assumed you'd get a man. You know I've got to travel all over the place staying at hotels. It's going to be awkward if—"

"Why? You don't have to sleep with her."

"Isn't there a man available?"

"Not as good as Miss Kolin. You said you wanted someone we could vouch for if it came to getting the interpreter's testimony accepted in an American court. We could vouch for Kolin all right. We always use her or Miss Harle for important rogatory commissions, and so do the British. Harle's on another job in Geneva right now, so we got Kolin. You're lucky she's available."

"All right. How old is she?"

"Early thirties and quite attractive."

"For God's sake."

"You don't have to worry." The Embassy man had chuckled in an odd way.

George had ignored the chuckle and asked about Miss Kolin's history. She had been born in one of the Serbian towns of Yugoslavia and was a graduate of the University of Belgrade. She had an almost phenomenal talent for languages. A British Major working with a relief organization had found her in a displaced-persons camp in 1945 and employed her as a secretary. Later she had worked as an interpreter for an American legal team doing preparatory work for the Nuremberg trials. When the team's work had ended, one of the lawyers, impressed as much by her secretarial ability as by the fact that she was multi-lingual, had given her introductions to the International Standards Organization and the American Embassy in Paris and advised her to try to work up a connection as an interpreter and verbatim reporter. She had soon established herself. She now had a solid reputation at international trade conferences for the speed and reliability of her work. Her services were much in demand.

There were several women waiting in the foyer of the hotel and George had to ask the concierge to point his visitor out to him.

Maria Kolin was indeed attractive. She had the sort of figure and posture that makes inexpensive clothes look good. The face and features were broad, the complexion brown against sleek straw-coloured hair. Her eyes were prominent and heavy-lidded. The only make-up she wore was lipstick, but this was boldly applied. She looked as if she had just returned from a skiing holiday.

Although she had obviously seen the concierge point her out to him, she remained staring blankly into the middle distance as George approached, and gave an unreal start of surprise when he spoke.

"Miss Kolin? I'm George Carey."

"How do you do?" She touched the hand he held out to her as if it were a rolled-up newspaper.

"I'm very glad you could come along," George said.

She shrugged stiffly. "Naturally, you would wish to interview me before deciding to employ me." Her English was very clear and precise, with only the faintest trace of an accent.

"They told me at the Embassy that you were a busy person and that I was lucky you were available." He put as much friendliness as he could into his smile.

She looked past him vaguely. "Ah, yes?"

George felt himself beginning to be irritated by her. "Shall we sit down somewhere and talk, Miss Kolin?"

"Of course."

He led the way across the foyer to some comfortable chairs near the bar. She followed a little too slowly. His irritation increased. She might be an attractive woman, but there was no reason for her to behave as if she were fending off a clumsy attempt at seduction. She was here about a job. Did she want it or didn't she? If she didn't, why waste time by coming at all?

"Now, Miss Kolin," he said as they sat down, "how much did the Embassy people tell you about this job?"

"That you were going to Germany to interview various persons there in connection with a lawsuit. That you would want verbatim reports of the interviews transcribed. That it might be necessary to attend later at an American Embassy to have these transcriptions notarized. The length of time for which you would require me would be not less than one month and not more than three. I should receive my normal fees on a monthly basis, and all travelling and hotel expenses would be paid in addition." She looked past him again, her head held high—a lady of quality importuned by a lascivious workman.

"Yes, that's about right," George said. "Did they tell you which lawsuit it was?"

"They said that it was a highly confidential matter and that you would no doubt explain what it was necessary for me to know." A faint, indifferent smile—men are such children with their little secrets.

"Right. What passport do you have, Miss Kolin?"

"French."

"I understood you were a Yugoslav citizen."

"I am naturalized French. My passport *is* valid for Germany."

"Yes, that was what I wanted to know."

She nodded but did not say anything. One could be patient with the slow-witted, but one was not obliged to pander to them.

Several sentences came to the tip of George's tongue at that moment, most of them designed to bring the interview to an abrupt conclusion. He swallowed them. Just because she wouldn't pretend to be stupider or more eager for the work than she really was, he didn't have to insult the woman. She had an unfortunate manner. All right! Did that make her a bad interpreter? And what did he expect her to do? Cringe?

He offered her a cigarette.

She shook her head. "Thank you, I prefer these." She brought out a packet of Gitanes.

He struck a match for her. "Are there any questions about the job you would like to ask me?" he said.

"Yes." She blew smoke out. "Have you had any experience of using an interpreter, Mr. Carey?"

"None at all."

"I see. Do you speak any German?"

"A little, yes."

"How little? It is not a pointless question."

"I'm sure it isn't. Well, I speak the German I learned at high school. I was stationed in Germany for a few months after the war and heard a fair amount of German spoken there. I can understand the drift of most conversations between Germans, but I sometimes misunderstand so completely that I might think I was listening to an argument about politics when what I was really hearing was a discussion of the finer points of chicken farming. Does that answer your question?"

"Very clearly. I will explain the point. When you are using an interpreter, it is not always easy to avoid listening also to the conversation being interpreted. That way confusion may arise."

"In fact, it's better to trust to the interpreter and not try to do the work for her."

"Exactly."

The barman was hovering in the background. George ignored him. The interview was as good as over and he did not want to prolong it. Her cigarette was half smoked now. When it had burned down another quarter of an inch, he would get up.

"I expect you know Germany pretty well, Miss Kolin."

"Only certain parts."

"The Rhineland?"

"A little."

"You worked on the preparations for the Nuremberg trials, I hear."

"Yes."

"As a Yugoslav you must have found that very satisfactory."

"You think so, Mr. Carey?"

"You didn't approve of the trials?"

She looked down at her cigarette. "The Germans took my father as a hostage and shot him," she said crisply. "They sent my mother and me to work in a factory in Leipzig. My mother died there of blood-poisoning from an infected wound which they refused to treat. I do not know exactly what happened to my brothers, except that eventually they were tortured to death in an S.S. barracks at Zagreb. Oh yes, I approved of the trials. If they made the United Nations feel strong and righteous, certainly I approved. But do not ask me to applaud."

"Yes, I can see you must have wished for a more personal revenge."

She had leaned forward to stub her cigarette out. Now she turned her head slowly and her eyes met his.

"I'm afraid that I have not your belief in justice, Mr. Carey," she said.

There was a curious, persecuted little half-smile on her lips. He realized suddenly that he was on the verge of losing his temper.

She rose to her feet and stood in front of him smoothing down her dress. "Is there anything else you would like to know?" she asked calmly.

"I don't think so, thank you." He stood up. "It was very kind of you to come along, Miss Kolin. I'm not sure yet when I shall be leaving Paris. I'll get in touch with you as soon as I know."

"Of course." She picked up her bag. "Good-bye, Mr. Carey."

"Good afternoon, Miss Kolin."

With a nod she went.

For a moment he looked down at the cigarette she had stubbed out and the lipstick on it; then he went to the lift and was taken up to his room.

He telephoned the Embassy man immediately.

"I've just seen Miss Kolin," he said.

"Good. All fixed up?"

"No, *not* all fixed up. Look, Don, isn't there somebody else I can get?"

"What's the matter with Kolin?"

"I don't know, but whatever it is I don't like it."

"You must have caught one of her bad days. I told you she'd had some pretty rugged experiences as a refugee."

"Look, I've talked to lots of refugees who've had rugged experiences. I've never talked to one before who made me sympathize with the Gestapo."

"Too bad. Her work's O.K., though."

"She's not."

"You wanted the best interpreter available."

"I'll take the next best."

"Nobody who's actually worked with Kolin has ever had anything but praise for her."

"She may be fine for conferences and committees. This is different."

"What's different about it? You're not on a vacation trip are you?" There was a note of irritation in the voice now.

George hesitated. "No, but—"

"Supposing there's a dispute later over the testimony. You're going to look pretty silly explaining that you passed up the chance of getting a reliable interpreter because you didn't like her personality, aren't you, George?"

"Well—" George broke off and then sighed. "O.K.—if I come back a raving alcoholic I shall send the doctor's bills to you."

"You'll probably end by marrying the girl."

George laughed politely and hung up.

Two days later he and Maria Kolin left for Germany.

CHAPTER V

A BOOKKEEPER named Friedrich Schirmer had died at Bad Schwennheim in 1939. He had had a son named Johann. Find this son. If he was dead, then find his heir.

Those were George's instructions.

There were probably thousands of Johann Schirmers in Germany, but certain things were known about this one. He had been born somewhere about 1895, in Schaffhausen. He had married a woman whose given name was Ilse. There was a photograph of the two taken in the early twenties. George had a copy. It would probably be of little help in making a positive identification at this stage, but it might serve to remind former neighbours or acquaintances of the pair. Appearances were usually better remembered than names. The photograph itself supplied another faint clue; the photographer's imprint on the mount showed that it had been taken in Zurich.

However, the first move in the plan of campaign which Mr. Sistrom had mapped out for him was, as Mr. Moreton had surmised, to go to Bad Schwennheim and start where the former inquiry had stopped.

When Friedrich Schirmer had died, he had been estranged from his son for several years; but there was always a chance that the war might have changed things. Families tended to draw together in emergencies. It would have been natural, Mr. Sistrom had contended, for Johann to try to get in touch with his father at that time. If he had done so, he would have been officially notified of the death. There might be a record of that notification giving his address. True, Mr. Moreton had heard nothing on the subject from Bad Schwennheim, but that proved nothing. The priest might have forgotten his promise or neglected it; his letter could have been lost in the uncertain wartime mails; he might have gone off into the German army as a chaplain. There were endless possibilities.

In the train on the way to Basel, George explained it all to Miss Kolin. She listened attentively. When he had finished she nodded. "Yes, I see. You can, of course, neglect no possibility." She paused. "Do you hope much from Bad Schwennheim, Mr. Carey?"

"Not much, no. I don't know exactly what the German procedure is, but I would say that when an old man like this Friedrich dies, the authorities don't fall over backwards finding relations to notify. We wouldn't, anyway. What's the point? There's no estate. And supposing Johann did write. The letter would go to the sanatorium and most likely get returned through the mail marked 'Addressee deceased' or whatever it is they put. The priest could easily not have heard about it."

She pursed her lips. "It is curious about this old man."

"Not very. That sort of thing happens every day, you know."

"You say that Mr. Moreton found nothing of the son except this one photograph among the old man's papers. No letters, no other photographs, except of his dead wife, nothing. They quarrelled, we are told. It would be interesting to know why."

"The wife got tired of having him around, probably."

"What disease did he die of?"

"Bladder trouble of some sort."

"He would know he was dying, and yet he did not write to his son before the end or even ask the priest to do so?"

"Perhaps he just didn't care any more."

"Perhaps." She thought for a moment. "Do you know the name of the priest?"

"It was a Father Weichs."

"Then I think you could make inquiries before going to Bad Schwennheim. You could find out if Father Weichs is still there from the church authorities at Freiburg. If he is not still there, they will be able to tell you where he is. You might save much time that way."

"That's a good idea, Miss Kolin."

"At Freiburg you may also be able to find out if the old man's belongings were claimed by a relative."

"I think we may have to go to Baden for that information, but we can try at Freiburg."

"You do not object that I make these suggestions, Mr. Carey?"

"Not a bit. On the contrary, they're very helpful."

"Thank you."

George did not find it necessary to mention that the ideas she had put forward had, in fact, already occurred to him. He had given some thought to Miss Kolin since making his reluctant decision to employ her.

He disliked her and, if Mr. Moreton were to be believed, would end by detesting her. She was not somebody he had chosen freely to serve him. She had, to all intents and purposes, been imposed upon him. It would be senseless, therefore, to behave towards her as if she ought to represent—as a good secretary ought to represent, for instance—an extension of part of his own mind and will. She was rather more in the position of an unsympathetic associate with whom it was his duty to collaborate amicably until a specific piece of work was done. He had encountered and dealt philosophically with such situations in the army; there was no reason why he should not deal philosophically with this one.

Thus, having prepared himself for the worst, he had found the Miss Kolin who had presented herself with suitcase and portable typewriter at the Gare de l'Est that morning an agreeable modification of it. True, she had marched along the platform as if she were going out to face a firing-squad, and, true, she looked as if she had been insulted several times already that day, but she had greeted him in quite a friendly fashion and had then disconcerted him by producing an excellent map of Western Germany on which she had drawn for his convenience the boundaries of the various occupation zones. She had accepted with businesslike comprehension his patently guarded outline of the case, and shown herself alert and practical when he had gone on to explain in detail the nature of the work they had to do in Germany. Now she was making intelligent and helpful suggestions. Kolin on the job was evidently a very different person from Kolin being interviewed for one. Or perhaps the man at the Embassy had been right and, having experienced one of her bad days, he was now enjoying a good one. In that case it would be as well to discover how, if at all, the bad might be avoided. In the meantime he could hope.

After two good days in Freiburg, his attitude towards his collaborator had undergone a further change. He was no nearer liking her, but he had acquired a respect for her ability which, from a professional standpoint at any rate, was far more comforting. Within two hours of their arrival, she had discovered that Father Weichs had left Bad Schwennheim in 1943, having been called to the Hospital of the Sacred Heart, an institution for disabled men and women, just outside Stuttgart. By the end of the following day she had unearthed the facts that Friedrich Schirmer's belongings had been disposed of under a law dealing with the intestacy of paupers and that the dead man's next of kin was recorded as "Johann Schirmer, son, whereabouts unknown."

To begin with he had attempted to direct each step of the inquiry himself, but as they were passed from one official to another, the laborious time-wasting routine of question and interpretation followed by answer and interpretation became absurd. At his suggestion she began to interpret the substance of conversations. Then, in the middle of one interview, she had broken off impatiently.

"This is not the person you want," she had told him. "You will waste time here. There is, I think, a simpler way."

After that he had stood back and let her go ahead. She had done so with considerable energy and self-assurance. Her methods of dealing with people were artless but effective. With the co-operative she was brisk, with the obstructive she was imperious, for the suspicious she had a bright, metallic smile. In America, George decided, the smile would not have beguiled an oversexed schoolboy; but in Germany it seemed to work. Its final triumph was the persuasion of a dour functionary in the police department to telephone to Baden-Baden for the court records of the disposal of Friedrich Schirmer's estate.

It was all very satisfactory, and George said so as handsomely as he could.

She shrugged. "It does not seem necessary for you to waste your time with these simple, routine inquiries. If you feel you can trust me to take care of them I am glad to do so."

It was that evening that he found out something rather more disconcerting about Miss Kolin.

They had fallen into the habit of discussing the next day's work briefly over dinner. Afterwards she would go to her room and George would write letters or read. This particular evening, however, they had been drawn into conversation with a Swiss businessman in the bar before dinner and were later invited by him to sit at his table. His motive was quite evidently the seduction of Miss Kolin, if that could be accomplished without too much trouble and if George had no objection. George had none. The man was agreeable and spoke good English; George was interested to see how he would make out.

Miss Kolin had had four brandies before dinner. The Swiss had had several Pernods. With dinner she drank wine. So did the Swiss. After dinner he invited her to have brandy again, and again ordered large ones. She had four. So did the Swiss. With the second of them he became coyly amorous and tried to stroke her knee. She repelled the advance absently but efficiently. By the time he had finished his third, he was haranguing George bitterly on the subject of American fiscal policies. Shortly after his fourth he went very pale, excused himself hurriedly, and did not reappear. With a nod to the waiter Miss Kolin ordered a fifth for herself.

George had noticed on previous evenings that she liked brandy and that she rarely ordered anything else to drink. He had even noticed when they had been going through the customs in Basel that she carried a bottle of it in her suitcase. He had not, however, observed that it affected her in any way. Had he been questioned on the point he would have said that she was a model of sobriety.

Now, as she sipped the new arrival, he watched her, fascinated. He knew that had he been drinking level with her, he would by now have been unconscious. She was not even talkative. She was holding herself very upright in the chair and looking like an attractive but very prudish young schoolmistress about to deal for the first time with a case of juvenile exhibitionism. There was a suspicion of drool at one corner of her mouth. She retrieved it neatly with her tongue. Her eyes were glassy. She focused them with care on George.

"We go, then, tomorrow to the sanatorium at Bad Schwennheim?" she said precisely.

"No, I don't think so. We'll go and see Father Weichs at Stuttgart first. If he knows something it may be unnecessary to go to Bad Schwennheim."

She nodded. "I think you are right, Mr. Carey."

She looked at her drink for a moment, finished it at a gulp, and rose steadily to her feet.

"Good night, Mr. Carey," she said firmly.

"Good night, Miss Kolin."

She picked up her bag, turned round, and positioned herself facing the door. Then she began to walk straight for it. She missed a table by a hairsbreadth. She did not sway. She did not teeter. It was a miraculous piece of self-control. George saw her go out of the restaurant, change direction towards the concierge's desk, pick up her room key, and disappear up the stairs. To a casual observer she might have had nothing stronger to drink than a glass of Rhine wine.

The Hospital of the Sacred Heart proved to be a grim brick building some way out of Stuttgart off the road to Heilbronn.

George had taken the precaution of sending a long telegram to Father Weichs. In it he had recalled Mr. Moreton's visit to Bad Schwennheim in 1939 and expressed his own wish to make the priest's acquaintance. He and Miss Kolin were kept waiting for only a few minutes before a nun appeared to guide them through a wilderness of stone corridors to the priest's room.

George remembered that Father Weichs spoke good English, but it seemed more tactful to begin in German. The priest's sharp blue eyes flickered from one to the other of them as Miss Kolin translated George's polite explanation of their presence there and his hope that the telegram (which he could plainly see on the priest's table) had arrived to remind him of an occasion in 1939 when . . . .

The muscles of Father Weichs's jaws had been twitching impatiently as he listened. Now he broke in, speaking English.

"Yes, Mr. Carey. I remember the gentleman, and, as you see, I have had your telegram. Please sit down." He waved them to chairs and walked back to his table.

"Yes," he said, "I remember the gentleman very well. I had reason to."

A twisted smile creased the lean cheeks. It was a fine, dramatic head, George thought. You were sure at first that he must hold some high office in the church; and then you noticed the cracked, clumsy shoes beneath the table, and the illusion went.

"He asked me to give you his good wishes," George said.

"Thank you. Are you here on his behalf?"

"Unfortunately, Mr. Moreton is now an invalid and retired." It was difficult not to be stilted with Father Weichs.

"I am sorry to hear that, of course." The priest inclined his head courteously. "However, it was not the gentleman himself who gave me special cause to remember him. Consider! A lonely old man dies. I am his confessor. Mr. Moreton comes to me asking questions about him. That is all. It is not as unusual as you think. An old person who has been neglected by relatives for many years often becomes interesting to them when he dies. It is not often, of course, that an American lawyer comes, but even that is not remarkable in itself. There are many German families who have ties with your country." He paused. "But the incident becomes memorable," he added dryly, "when it proves to be a matter of importance for the police."

"The police?" George tried hard not to look as guilty as he suddenly felt.

"I surprise you, Mr. Carey?"

"Very much. Mr. Moreton was making inquiries on behalf of a perfectly respectable American client in the matter of a legacy—" George began.

"A legacy," interposed the priest, "which he said was for a small amount of money." He paused and gave George a wintry smile before he went on. "I understand, of course, that size is relative and that in America it is not measured with European scales, but even in America it seems an exaggeration to call three million dollars a small amount."

Out of the corner of his eye George saw Miss Kolin looking startled for once; but it was a poor satisfaction at that moment.

"Mr. Moreton was in a spot, Father," he said. "He had to be discreet. The American papers had already caused trouble by giving the case too much publicity. There had been a whole lot of false claims. Besides, the case was very complicated. Mr. Moreton didn't want to raise anybody's hopes and then have to disappoint them."

The priest frowned. "His discretion placed me in a very dangerous position with the police. And with certain other authorities," he added bleakly.

"I see. I'm sorry about that, Father. I think if Mr. Moreton had known—" He broke off. "Do you mind telling me what happened?"

"If it is of interest to you. A little before Christmas in 1940 the police came to me to ask questions about Mr. Moreton's visit of the year before. I told them what I knew. They wrote it down and went away. Two weeks later they came back with some other men, not of the police, but the Gestapo. They took me to Karlsruhe." His face hardened. "They accused me of lying about Mr. Moreton's visit. They said that it was a matter of highest importance to the Reich. They said that if I did not tell them what they wished to know, I would be treated as some of my brothers in the church had been treated." He had been looking at his hands. Now he raised his head, and his eyes met George's. "Perhaps you are able to guess what they wanted to know, Mr. Carey."

George cleared his throat. "I should say they wanted to know about someone named Schneider."

He nodded. "Yes, someone named Schneider. They said that Mr. Moreton had been searching for this person and that I was concealing my knowledge. They believed that I knew where this person was who was entitled to the American money and that Mr. Moreton had bought my silence so that the money could go to an American." He shrugged. "The sadness of evil men is that they can believe no truth that does not paint the world in their colours."

"They weren't interested in Friedrich Schirmer?"

"No. I think that they believed in the end that it was a trick of Mr. Moreton's to mislead them. I do not know. Perhaps they only became tired of me. In any case, they let me go. But you see I have reason to remember Mr. Moreton."

"Yes. But I don't see how he could have anticipated the trouble he would cause you."

"Oh, I have no bitterness, Mr. Carey." He sat back in his chair. "But I should like to know the truth."

George hesitated. "Friedrich Schirmer's family was a branch of the Schneider family in question. The actual connection would take a long time to explain, but I can tell you that the German government did not know of it."

The priest smiled. "I see that it is still necessary to be discreet."

George flushed. "I'm being as frank as I can, Father. This has always been a pretty funny sort of a case. There have been so many false claimants to the estate already that, even if a legitimate one were found, it would be enormously difficult now to establish the claim in the American courts. The fact is that, in all probability, no claim ever will be established. The money will just go to the Commonwealth of Pennsylvania."

"Then why are you here, Mr. Carey?"

"Partly because the law firm I work for succeeded Mr. Moreton in the matter. Partly because it is our duty to find the heir. Partly because the matter has to be cleared up so that our firm may be paid."

"That, at least, is frank."

"Maybe I should add, too, that if there *is* a rightful heir, then he or she ought to have the money and not the Commonwealth of Pennsylvania. The federal government and the state will get most of it in taxes in the end anyway, but there's no reason why someone else shouldn't enjoy it too."

"Mr. Moreton mentioned a trust."

"Well—"

"Ah, I see. That also was discretion."

"I'm afraid so."

"Was Friedrich Schirmer the rightful heir?"

"Mr. Moreton thought so."

"Then why did Mr. Moreton not tell the courts so?"

"Because Friedrich Schirmer was dead and because he was afraid that if Friedrich were found to have no living heir, the German government would fake one to get the money. In fact they did produce an old man they claimed to be the heir. Mr. Moreton fought the claim for over a year."

Father Weichs was silent for a moment; then he sighed. "Very well. How can I help you now, Mr. Carey?"

"Mr. Moreton said that you promised to let him know if Friedrich Schirmer's son, Johann, appeared. Did he?"

"No."

"Do you know if any letters ever came for Friedrich Schirmer to the sanatorium where he died?"

"Up to the middle of 1940 no letter came."

"You would have known?"

"Oh yes. I visited the sanatorium often."

"And after the middle of 1940?"

"The sanatorium was commandeered by the army. It became the headquarters of a training school for radio operators."

"I see. Well, that seems to be fairly conclusive." George stood up. "Thanks a lot, Father."

But Father Weichs had made a movement of protest. "One moment, Mr. Carey. You asked if Johann Schirmer came to Bad Schwennheim."

"Yes?"

"He did not come, but his son did."

"His son?" Slowly George sat down again.

"He would be of interest to you, the son?"

"If he were a grandson of Friedrich Schirmer, he would interest me very much."

Father Weichs nodded. "He came to see me. I must explain that when the army occupied the sanatorium, I visited the Commandant of the school to offer the services of my church to those who wished them.

The Commandant was not himself of the religion, but he was sympathetic and made it as easy as possible for those who wished to come to Mass."

He looked thoughtfully at George. "I do not know if you served in the army, Mr. Carey," he went on after a moment or two. George nodded. "So! Then you may have noticed that there were some men—among the young front fighters I mean—who were not religious and yet found it necessary sometimes to seek some of the consolations of religion. It was when they had to find the courage to face death or mutilation, after they had seen what those things were, that the need seemed to come. Then the elaborate materialism of the intelligent among them proved as useless and sterile as the hero myths they had brought with them from the Hitler *Jugend*. They found that they needed something else, and sometimes they went to a priest to look for it." He smiled faintly. "Of course, it never appeared as simple as that at the time. They came to me for many commonplace reasons, these young men—to talk about their families, to ask advice on some material problem, to borrow a book or a magazine, to show photographs they had taken, to enjoy the privacy of a garden. But the outward reason was unimportant. Though they might not always realize it, what they wanted was, in some way, to come to terms with me as a priest. They wanted something that in their hearts they thought I might be able to give them—an inner peace and strength."

"And Schirmer's grandson was one of them?"

Father Weichs shrugged. "I was not sure. Perhaps, yes. But I will tell you. He had been sent to the school for special training. He was a—"

He broke off, hesitating, and then, glancing at Miss Kolin, said the word *Fallschirmjäger*.

"He was a paratrooper," she said.

The priest nodded. "Thank you, yes. He came to see me one day in September or October—I do not quite remember. He was a tall, strong-looking young man, very much a soldier. He had been wounded in Belgium in the attack on the fortress of Eben-Emael, and was not yet well enough to return to combat duty. He came to ask me if I knew of his grandfather, Friedrich Schirmer."

"Did he say where his home was?" asked George quickly.

"Yes. He came from Köln."

"Did he say what his father's occupation was?"

"No. I cannot remember that he did."

"Had he any brothers or sisters?"

"No, he was the only child."

"Did he know when he came that his grandfather was dead?"

"No. It was a great disappointment to him. When he was a boy the grandfather had lived in his parents' house and been kind to him. Then one day there had been a quarrel and the old man had gone."

"Did he say how he knew that the old man had lived at Bad Schwenn-heim?"

"Yes. The quarrel had been serious, and after Friedrich left, his name was never mentioned by the boy's parents. But the boy loved his grand-father. Even before he went to school the old man had taught him how to write and to rule his exercise books properly. Later the grandfather helped him with arithmetic problems and talked to him much of com-mercial affairs. You knew Friedrich Schirmer was a bookkeeper?"

"Yes."

"The boy did not forget him. When he was about fourteen his parents received a letter from the old man saying that he was retiring to live at Bad Schwennheim. He had heard them discussing it. They destroyed the letter, but he remembered the name of the town, and when he was sent to the army school there he tried to find his grandfather. He did not know until I told him that, by a strange chance, he was living in the building where the old man had died."

"I see."

Father Weichs looked down at his hands. "You would not have thought to see him or speak with him that he was a young man whom it was necessary to protect from disillusion. I think I failed him. I did not understand him until it was too late. He came to see me several times. He asked many questions about his grandfather. I saw afterwards that he wanted to make a hero of him. At the time I did not think. I an-swered the questions as kindly as I could. Then one day he asked me if I did not think that his grandfather Friedrich had been a fine and good man." He paused and then went on slowly and carefully as if choosing words in his own defence. "I made the best answer I could. I said that Friedrich Schirmer had been a hard-working man and that he had suf-fered his long, painful illness with patience and courage. I could say no more. The boy took my words for agreement and began to speak with great bitterness of his father, who had, he said, sent the old man away in a moment of jealous hatred. I could not allow him to speak so. It was against the truth. I said that he was doing his father a great injustice, that he should go to his father and ask for the truth." He raised his eyes and looked at George sombrely. "He laughed. He said that he had never yet had anything from his father that was good and would not get the truth. He went on to talk jokingly of his father as if he despised him. Then he went away. I did not see him again."

Outside, on the iron balconies of the hospital, the shadows were get-ting longer. A clock tolled the hour.

"And what *was* the truth, Father?" asked George quietly.

The priest shook his head. "I was Friedrich Schirmer's confessor, Mr. Carey."

"Of course. I'm sorry."

"It would not help you to know."

"No, I see that. But tell me this, Father. Mr. Moreton made a rough list of the documents and photographs that were found after Friedrich Schirmer's death. Was that all he had? Was nothing else ever found?"

To his surprise, he saw a look of embarrassment come over the priest's face. His eyes avoided George's. For a moment or two there was something positively furtive about Father Weichs's expression.

"Old documents," George added quickly, "can be very important evidence in cases like these."

Father Weichs's jaw muscles tightened. "There were no other documents," he said.

"Or photographs?"

"None that could possibly have been of any value to you, Mr. Carey," the priest replied stiffly.

"But there *were* other photographs?" George insisted.

Father Weichs's jaw muscles began to twitch. "I repeat, Mr. Carey, that they would have had no bearing on your inquiry," he said.

"'*Would* have had'?" George echoed. "Do you mean they no longer exist, Father?"

"I do. They no longer exist. I burned them."

"I see," said George.

There was a heavy silence while they looked at one another. Then Father Weichs got to his feet with a sigh and looked out of the window.

"Friedrich Schirmer was not a pleasant man," he said at last. "I see no harm in telling you that. You may even have guessed from what I have already said. There were many of these photographs. They were never of importance to anyone but Friedrich Schirmer—and possibly to those from whom he bought them."

George understood. "Oh," he said blankly. "Oh, I see." He smiled. He had a strong desire to laugh.

"He had made his peace with God," said Father Weichs. "It seemed kinder to destroy them. The secret lusts of the dead should end with the flesh that created them. Besides," he added briskly, "there is always the risk of such erotica getting into the hands of children."

George got to his feet. "Thanks, Father. There are just a couple more things I'd like to ask you. Did you ever know what unit of the paratroopers young Schirmer was serving in?"

"No. I regret that I did not."

"Well, we can find that out later. What were his given names, Father, and his rank? Do you remember?"

"I only knew one name. Franz, it was, I think. Franz Schirmer. He was a Sergeant."

CHAPTER VI

THEY STAYED that night in Stuttgart. Over dinner George summed up the results of their work.

"We can go straight to Cologne and try to find the Johann Schirmers by going through the city records," he went on; "or we can go after the German army records, turn up Franz Schirmer's papers, and get hold of his parents' address that way."

"Why should the army have his parents' address?"

"Well, if it were our army he'd been in, his personal file would probably show the address of his parents, or wife if he's married, as next of kin. Someone they can notify when you've been killed is a thing most armies like to have. What do you think?"

"Cologne is a big city—nearly a million persons before the war. But I have not been there."

"I have. It was a mess when I saw it. What the R.A.F. didn't do to it our army did. I don't know whether the city archives were saved or not, but I'm inclined to go for the army records first just in case."

"Very well."

"In fact, I think the army is a better bet all round. Two birds with one stone. We'll find out what happened to Sergeant Schirmer at the same time as we trace his parents. Do you have any ideas about where his German army records would be?"

"Bonn is the West German capital. Logically they should be there now."

"But you don't really think they will be, eh? Neither do I. Anyway I think we'll go to Frankfurt tomorrow. I can check up with the American army people there. They'll know. Another brandy?"

"Thank you."

A further thing he had discovered about Miss Kolin was that, although she probably consumed, in public or in the privacy of her room, over half a bottle of brandy every day, she did not seem to suffer from hangovers.

It took them nearly two weeks to find out what the German army knew about Sergeant Schirmer.

He had been born in Winterthur in 1917, the son of Johann Schirmer (mechanic) and Ilse, his wife, both of pure German stock. From the Hitler *Jugend* he had joined the army at the age of eighteen and been promoted corporal in 1937. He had been transferred from the Engineers to a special air training unit (*Fallschirmjäger*) in 1938 and promoted sergeant in the following year. At Eben-Emael he had received a bullet wound in the shoulder, from which he had satisfactorily recovered. He had taken part in the invasion of Crete and had been awarded the Iron Cross (Third Class) for distinguished conduct. In Benghazi later in that year he had suffered from dysentery and malaria. In Italy in 1943, while acting as a parachutist instructor, he had fractured a hip. There had been a court of inquiry to determine who had been responsible for giving the order to jump over wooded country. The court had commended the Sergeant's conduct in refraining from transmitting an order he believed to be incorrect, while obeying it himself. After four months in hospital and at a rehabilitation centre, and a further period of sick leave, a medical board had declared him unfit for further duty as a paratrooper or any other combat duty which entailed excessive marching. He had been posted to the occupation forces in Greece. There, he had served as weapons instructor to the Ninety-fourth Garrison Regiment in a Lines of Communication Division stationed in the Salonika area, until the following year. After an action against Greek guerrillas during the withdrawal from Macedonia, he had been reported "missing, believed killed." The next of kin, Ilse Schirmer, Elsass Str. 39, Köln, had been duly notified.

They found Elsass Strasse, or what was left of it, in the remains of the old town off the Neumarkt.

Before the stick of bombs which had destroyed it had fallen, it had been a narrow street of small shops with offices above them, and a tobacco warehouse halfway along. The warehouse had obviously received a direct hit. Some of the other walls still stood, but, with the exception of three shops at one end of the street, every building in it had been gutted. Lush weeds grew now out of the old cellar floors; notices said that it was forbidden to trespass among the ruins or to deposit rubbish.

Number 39 had been a garage set back from the street in a space behind two other buildings and approached by an arched drive-in between them. The arch was still standing. Fastened to its brickwork was a rusty metal sign. The words on it could be read: "*Garage und Reparaturwerkstatt. J. Schirmer—Bereifung, Zübehor, Benzin.*"

They walked through the archway to the place where the garage had stood. The site had been cleared, but the plan of the building was still visible; it could not have been a very big garage. All that remained of it now was a repair pit. It was half full of rain water and there were pieces of an old packing case floating in it.

As they stood there, it began to rain again.

"We'd better see if we can find out anything from the shops at the end of the street," George said.

The proprietor of the second of the shops they tried was an electrical contractor, and he had some information. He had only been there three years himself and knew nothing of the Schirmers; but he did know something about the garage site. He had considered renting it for his own use. He had wanted to put up a workshop and storeroom there and use the rooms over his shop to live in. The ground had no street frontage and was therefore of little value. He had thought to get it cheaply; but the owner had wanted too much and so he had made other arrangements. The owner was a Frau Gresser, wife of a chemist in the laboratories of a big factory out at Leverkusen. When women started bargaining, you understand, it was best to . . . Yes, he had her address written down somewhere, though if the gentleman were considering the property, he personally would advise him to think twice before wasting his time arguing with . . .

Frau Gresser lived in an apartment on the top floor of a newly reconstructed building near the Barbarossa Platz. They had to call three times before they found her in.

She was a stout, frowzy, breathless woman in her late fifties. Her apartment was furnished in the cocktail-bar-functional style of prewar Germany, and crammed with Tyrolean knickknacks. She listened suspiciously to their explanations of their presence there before inviting them to sit down. Then she went and telephoned her husband. After a while she came back and said that she was prepared to answer questions.

Ilse Schirmer, she said, had been her cousin and childhood friend.

"Are the Schirmers alive now?" George asked.

"Ilse Schirmer and her husband were killed in the big air attacks on the city in May 1942," Miss Kolin interpreted.

"Did Frau Gresser inherit the garage land from them?"

Frau Gresser showed signs of indignation when the question was put and spoke rapidly in reply.

"By no means. The land was hers—hers and her husband's, that is. Johann Schirmer's own business went bankrupt. She and her husband had set him up in business again for the sake of Ilse. Naturally, they had hoped also to make a profit, but it was goodness of heart that motivated them in the first place. The business, however, was theirs. Schirmer was only the manager. He had a percentage of the takings and an apartment over the garage. No one could say that he had not been generously treated. Yet, after so much had been done for him by his wife's friends, he had tried to cheat them over the takings."

"Who was his heir? Did he leave a will?"

"If he had had anything to leave except debts, his heir would have been his son, Franz."

"Did the Schirmers have any other children?"

"Fortunately, no."

"Fortunately?"

"It was hard enough for poor Ilse to feed and clothe one child. She was never strong, and with a husband like Schirmer, even a strong woman would have become ill."

"What was the matter with Schirmer?"

"He was lazy, he was dishonest, he drank. When poor Ilse married him she did not know. He deceived everyone. When we met him he had a prosperous business in Essen. We thought him clever. It was not until his father went away that the truth was known."

"The truth?"

"It was his father, Friedrich, who had the business head. He was a good accountant and he kept the son properly under control. Johann was only a mechanic, a workman with his hands. The father had the brains. He understood money."

"Did Friedrich own the business?"

"It was a partnership. Friedrich had lived and worked for many years in Switzerland. Johann was brought up there. He did not fight for Germany in the first war. Ilse met him in 1915 while she was staying with friends in Zurich. They married and remained in Switzerland to live. All their savings were in Swiss francs. In 1923, when the German mark failed, they all came back to Germany—Friedrich, Johann, Ilse, and the child, Franz—and bought the garage in Essen cheap with their Swiss money. Old Friedrich understood business."

"Then Franz was born in Switzerland?"

"Winterthur is near Zurich, Mr. Carey," said Miss Kolin. "It was mentioned in the army papers, you remember. But he would still have to apply for Swiss nationality."

"Yes, I know all about that. Ask her why the partnership broke up."

Frau Gresser hesitated when she heard the question.

"As she has said, Johann had no head for—"

Frau Gresser hesitated again and was silent. Her plump face had become red and shiny with embarrassment. At last she spoke.

"She would prefer not to discuss the matter," said Miss Kolin.

"All right. Ask her about Franz Schirmer. Does she know what happened to him?"

He saw the relief in Frau Gresser's face when she understood that the subject of Friedrich Schirmer's departure was not going to be pursued. It made him curious.

"Franz was reported missing in Greece in 1944. The official letter addressed to his mother was forwarded to Frau Gresser."

"The report said: 'missing, believed killed.' Did she ever receive official confirmation of his death?"

"Not officially."

"What does she mean?"

"One of Franz's officers wrote to Frau Schirmer to tell her what had happened to her son. That letter also was forwarded to Frau Gresser. Having read it, she had no doubt that Franz was dead."

"Did she keep the letter? Is it possible for us to see it?"

Frau Gresser considered the request for a moment; finally she nodded and, going to a chest of drawers shaped as if to reduce its wind resistance, brought out a tin box full of papers. After a long search the officer's letter was found, together with the original army casualty notification. She handed both documents to Miss Kolin, making some explanation as she did so.

"Frau Gresser wishes to explain that Franz neglected to report to the army authorities that his parents had been killed and that it was the postal authorities who forwarded the letters."

"I see. What's the letter say?"

"It is from Lieutenant Hermann Leubner of the Engineer Company, Ninety-fourth Garrison Regiment. It is dated the 1st of December 1944."

"What's the date that Franz was reported missing on that army notification?"

"October 31."

"All right."

"The Lieutenant writes: 'Dear Frau Schirmer: You will, no doubt, already have been notified by the army authorities of the fact that your son, Sergeant Franz Schirmer, has been listed as missing. I write as his officer to tell you of the circumstances in which this sad occurrence took place. It was on the 24th of October—' " She broke off.

"They were pulling out. They wouldn't trouble to send casualty returns every day," George said.

Miss Kolin nodded. "It continues: 'The regiment was moving westwards from Salonika towards the Greek frontier in the general direction of Florina. Sergeant Schirmer, as an experienced soldier and a responsible man, was sent with three trucks and ten men to a gasoline dump several kilometres off the main road near the town of Vodena. His orders were to load as much of the gasoline as he could on to the trucks, destroy the remainder, and return, bringing the troops who had been guarding the dump with him. Unfortunately, his detachment was ambushed by one of the Greek terrorist bands that had been attempting to hinder our operations. Your son was in the first truck, which exploded a mine laid by the terrorists. The third truck was able to stop in time to avoid most of the machine-gun fire of the terrorists, and two men from it were able to escape and rejoin the regiment. I myself led a force immediately to the place of the ambush. Your son was not among the dead we found and buried, nor was there any other trace of him. The driver of his truck was also missing. Your son was not a man to surrender unwounded. It is possible that he was rendered unconscious by the explosion of the mine and so captured. We do not know. But I would be failing in my duty if I encouraged you to hope that if he were captured by these Greeks he would be alive. They have not the military code of honour of us Germans. It is, of course, also possible that your son evaded capture but was unable to rejoin his comrades immediately. If so, you will be informed by the authorities when there is news of him. He was a brave man and a good soldier. If he is dead, then you will have the pride and consolation of knowing that he gave his life for his Führer and the Fatherland.'"

George sighed. "That all?"

"He adds: 'Heil Hitler,' and signs it."

"Ask Frau Gresser if she heard any more about it from the army authorities."

"No, she did not."

"Did she make any attempt to find out more? Did she try the Red Cross?"

"She was advised that the Red Cross could do nothing."

"When did she ask them?"

"Early in 1945."

"And not since?"

"No. She also asked the *Volksbund Deutsche Kriegsgräberfürsorge*—that is, the war-graves organization—for information. They had none."

"Was any application ever made to have him presumed dead?"

"There was no reason for such action."

"Does she know if he married?"

"No."

"Did she ever correspond with him?"

"She wrote a letter of sympathy to him when his parents were killed, but received no more than a bare acknowledgment from him. He did not even ask where they were buried. He showed a want of feeling, she thought. She sent a parcel soon afterwards. He did not trouble to write to thank her for it. She sent no more."

"Where did his reply come from in 1942?"

"From Benghazi."

"Did she keep the letter?"

"No."

Frau Gresser spoke again. George watched her plump face quivering and her small, resentful eyes flickering between her two visitors. He was getting used now to interpretation and had learned not to try to anticipate the conversation while he waited. He was thinking at the moment that it would be unpleasant to be under any sort of obligation to Frau Gresser. The rate of emotional interest she would charge would be exorbitantly high.

"She says," said Miss Kolin, "that she did not like Franz and had never liked him even as a child. He was a sullen, sulky boy and always ungrateful for kindness. She wrote to him only as a duty to his dead mother."

"How did he feel about foreigners? Had he any particular girl-friends? What I'm getting at is this—does she think he'd be the kind of man to marry a Greek girl, say, or an Italian, if he had the chance?"

Frau Gresser's reply was prompt and sour.

"She says that, where women were concerned, he was the sort of man who would do anything that his selfish nature suggested. He would do anything if he had the chance—except marry."

"I see. All right, I think that's about the lot. Would you ask her if we can borrow these papers for twenty-four hours to have photostats made?"

Frau Gresser considered the request carefully. Her small eyes became opaque. George could feel the documents suddenly becoming precious to her.

"I'll give her a receipt for them, of course, and they'll be returned tomorrow," he said. "Tell her the American Consul will have to notarize the copies or she could have them back today."

Frau Gresser handed them over reluctantly. While he was writing the receipt, George remembered something.

"Miss Kolin, have another try at finding out why Friedrich Schirmer left the business at Essen."

"Very well."

He lingered over the writing-out of the receipt. He heard Miss Kolin put the question. There was a momentary pause; then Frau Gresser replied with a positive volley of words. Her voice rose steadily in pitch as she spoke. Then she stopped. He signed the receipt and looked up to find her staring at him in a flustered, accusing sort of way. He handed her the receipt and put the documents in his pocket.

"She says," said Miss Kolin, "that the matter is not one which can be discussed in the presence of a man and that it can have no bearing on your inquiries. She adds, however, that if you do not believe that she is telling the truth, she will make the explanation confidentially to me. She will say no more on the subject while you are here."

"O.K. I'll wait for you downstairs." He rose and bowed to Frau Gresser. "Thank you very much indeed, madam. What you have told me is of inestimable help. I will see that your papers are safely returned to you tomorrow. Good day."

He smiled affably, bowed again, and went. He was outside the apartment almost before Miss Kolin had finished interpreting his farewell speech.

She joined him in the street below ten minutes later.

"Well," he said, "what was it all about?"

"Friedrich made advances to Ilse Schirmer."

"To his son's wife, you mean?"

"Yes."

"Well, well. Did she go into details?"

"Yes. She enjoys herself, that one."

"But the old man must have been around sixty then."

"You remember the photographs that Father Weichs destroyed?"

"Yes."

"He showed them to the wife."

"Just that?"

"His meaning apparently was unmistakable. He also proposed in a veiled way that he should take similar photographs of her."

"I see." George tried to picture the scene.

He saw a shabby room in Essen and an elderly bookkeeper sitting there pushing dog-eared photographs one by one across the table to where his son's wife could see them as she sat bent over her needlework.

How the man's heart must have beat as he watched her face! His mind must have seethed with questions and doubts.

Would she smile or would she pretend to be shocked? She was sitting still, absolutely still, and she had stopped working. Soon she would smile, for certain. He could not see her eyes. After all, there was nothing wrong in a little private joke between a father and daughter-in-law, was there? She was a grown-up woman and knew a thing or two, didn't she? She liked him, he knew. All he wanted to do was show her that he wasn't too old for a bit of fun and that, even if Johann was no good, there was one man about the house for her to turn to. And now the last photograph, the sauciest of the lot. An eye-opener, eh? Good fun? She still hadn't smiled, but she hadn't frowned either. Women were funny creatures. You had to choose your moment; woo gently and then be bold. She was slowly raising her head now and looking at him. Her eyes were very round. He smiled and said what he had planned to say—that subtle remark about new pictures being better than old. But she did not smile back. She was getting to her feet and he could see that she was trembling. With what? Excitement? And then, suddenly, she had let out a sob of fear and run from the room out to the workshop where Johann was decarbonizing that Opel taxi. After that, everything had become a nightmare, with Johann shouting at and threatening him, and Ilse weeping, and the boy Franz standing there listening, white-faced, not understanding what it was all about; only knowing that in some way the world was coming to an end.

Yes, George thought, a pretty picture; though probably an inaccurate one. Still, it was the sort of scene about which nobody could ever be quite accurate; least of all, those who had taken part in it. He would never know what had really happened. Not that it mattered very much. Friedrich, Johann, and Ilse, the principal actors, were certainly dead. And Franz? He glanced at Miss Kolin marching along beside him.

"Do you think Franz is dead?" he asked.

"The evidence seemed conclusive. Did you not think so?"

"In a way, yes. If the man had been a friend of mine and had a wife and family he was fond of back home, I wouldn't try to kid his wife that he might still be alive. And if she were crazy enough to go on believing that he wasn't dead, I'd tell her as gently as I could to face the facts. But this is different. If we took the evidence we've got to court and asked for leave to presume Franz Schirmer dead, they'd laugh at us."

"I do not see why."

"Look. The man's in a truck ambushed by these guerrillas. That Lieutenant comes along some time afterwards and has a look at the scene. There are lots of dead bodies about, but not the dead body of our man. So maybe he's escaped and maybe he's a prisoner. If he's a prisoner, says the Lieutenant, then he hasn't a hope, because the Greek guerrillas had the habit of killing their prisoners. 'Just a minute,' says the judge; 'are you claiming that *all* Greek guerrillas operating in 1944 *invariably* killed *all* their prisoners? Are you prepared to prove that there were no cases at all of German soldiers surviving after capture?' What does the Lieutenant say to that? I don't know anything about the Greek campaign—I wasn't there—but I do know that if all these guerrillas were so well trained and so well organized and so trigger-happy that no German who fell into their hands was ever smart enough or lucky enough to get away, they'd have had the Germans pulling out of Greece long before the Normandy landings. All right, then, let's alter the wording of the evidence. Let's say that Greek guerrillas *often* killed their prisoners. Now, then—"

"But do you think he is *not* dead?" she asked.

"Of course I think he's dead. I'm just trying to point out there's a whole lot of difference between an ordinary everyday probability and the calculated kind that the law prefers. And the law's right. You'd be surprised how often people turn up when they've been thought dead. A man gets fired from his job and quarrels with his wife; so he goes down to the shore, takes off his coat, leaves it with a suicide note on the beach, and that's the last seen of him. Dead? Maybe. But sometimes he's found by accident years later living under a different name and with a different wife in a city on the other side of the continent."

She shrugged. "This is different."

"Not so very. Look at it this way. It's 1944. Let's suppose that Franz Schirmer is captured by the guerrillas but by luck or skill manages to get away alive. What is he to do? Rejoin his unit? The German occupation forces are trying to escape through Yugoslavia and having a tough time doing it. If he leaves his hide-out and tries to catch up with them, he's certain to be recaptured by the guerrillas. They're all over the place now. It's better to stay where he is for a while. He is a resourceful man, trained to live off the country. He can stay alive. When it is safe for him to do so, he will go. Time passes. The country is under Greek control once again. Hundreds of miles now separate him from the nearest German unit. Civil war breaks out in Greece. In the resultant confusion he is able to make his way to the Turkish frontier and cross it without being caught. He is an engineer and does not mind work. He takes a job."

"By February 1945 Turkey was at war with Germany."

"Maybe it's before February."

"Then why does he not report to the German Consul?"

"Why should he? Germany is collapsing. The war is virtually over.

Maybe he likes it where he is. Anyway, what has he to return to postwar Germany for? To see Frau Gresser? To see what's left of his parents' home? Maybe he married an Italian girl when he was in Italy and wants to get back there. He may even have children. There are dozens of possible reasons why he shouldn't go to the German Consul. Maybe he went to the Swiss one."

"If he had married, his army record would show it."

"Not if he married someone he wasn't supposed to marry. Look at the rules the Americans and British had about their troops marrying German girls."

"What do you propose?"

"I don't know yet. I'll have to think."

When he got back to the hotel, he sat down and wrote a long cable to Mr. Sistrom. First he set out briefly the latest developments in the inquiry; then he asked for instructions. Should he return home now or should he go on and make an attempt to confirm Franz Schirmer's death?

The following afternoon he had the reply.

"HAVING LOOKED UNDER SO MANY STONES," it said, "SEEMS PITY LEAVE ONE UNTURNED STOP GO AHEAD TRY CONFIRM OR OTHERWISE FRANZ DEATH STOP SUGGEST GIVING IT THREE WEEKS STOP IF IN YOUR JUDGMENT NO SERIOUS HEADWAY MADE OR LIKELY BY THEN LETS FORGET IT. SISTROM."

That night George and Miss Kolin left Cologne for Geneva.

Miss Kolin had interpreted at conferences for the International Red Cross Committee and knew the people at headquarters who could be of help. George was soon put in touch with an official who had been in Greece for the Red Cross in 1944; a lean, mournful Swiss who looked as if nothing again could ever surprise him. He spoke good English and four other languages besides. His name was Hagen.

"There is no doubt at all, Mr. Carey," he said, "that the *andartes* did often kill their prisoners. I am not saying that they did it simply because they hated the enemy or because they had a taste for killing, you understand. It is difficult to see what else they could have done much of the time. A guerrilla band of thirty men or less is in no position to guard and feed the people it takes. Besides, Macedonia is in the Balkan tradition, and there the killing of an enemy can seem of small importance."

"But why take prisoners? Why not kill them at once?"

"Usually they were taken for questioning."

"If you were in my position, how would you go about establishing the death of this man?"

"Well, as you know where the ambush took place, you might try getting in touch with some of the *andartes* who were operating in that area. They might remember the incident. But I think I should say that you may find it difficult to persuade them to refresh their memories. Was it an ELAS band, do you know, or an EDES?"

"EDES?"

"The Greek initials stand for the National Democratic Liberation Army—the anti-Communist *andartes*. ELAS were the Communist *andartes*—the National Popular Liberation Army. In the Vodena area it would most likely be ELAS."

"Does it matter which it was?"

"It matters a great deal. There have been three years of civil war in Greece, you must remember. Now that the rebellion is over, those who fought on the Communist side are not easy to find. Some are dead, some in prison, some in hiding still. Many are refugees in Albania and Bulgaria. As things are, you would probably find it difficult to get in touch with ELAS men. It is complex."

"Yes, it sounds it. What real chance would there be, do you think, of my finding out what I want to know?"

Monsieur Hagen shrugged. "Often in such matters I have seen chance operate so strangely that I no longer try to estimate it. How important is your business, Mr. Carey?"

"There's a good deal of money at stake."

The other sighed. "So many things could have happened. You know, there were hundreds of men reported 'missing, believed killed' who had simply deserted. Salonika had plenty of German deserters towards the end of 1944."

"Plenty?"

"Oh yes, of course. ELAS recruited most of them. There were many Germans fighting for the Greek Communists around Christmas 1944."

"Do you mean to say that in late 1944 a German soldier could go about in Greece *without* getting killed?"

A pale smile drifted across Monsieur Hagen's mournful face. "In Salonika you could see German soldiers sitting in the cafés and walking about the streets."

"In uniform?"

"Yes, or part uniform. It was a curious situation. During the war the Communists in Yugoslavia, Greece, and Bulgaria had agreed to create a new Macedonian state. It was all part of a larger Russian plan for a Balkan Communist Federation. Well, the moment the Germans had gone, a force called the Macedonian Group of Divisions of ELAS took over Salonika and prepared to put the plan into execution. They didn't care any more about Germans. They had a new enemy to fight—the lawful Greek government. What they wanted to fight with were trained soldiers. It was Vafiades who had the idea of recruiting German deserters. He was the ELAS commander in Salonika then."

"Can't I get in touch with this Vafiades?" George asked.

He saw Miss Kolin stare at him. An expression of anxious perplexity came over Monsieur Hagen's face.

"I'm afraid that would be a little difficult, Mr. Carey."

"Why? Is he dead?"

"Well, there seems to be some doubt as to just what has happened to him." Monsieur Hagen seemed to be choosing his words. "The last we heard of him directly was in 1948. He then told a group of foreign journalists that, as head of the Provisional Democratic Government of Free Greece, he proposed to establish a capital on Greek soil. That was just about the time his army captured Karpenissi, I believe."

George looked blankly at Miss Kolin.

"Markos Vafiades called himself General Markos," she murmured. "He commanded the Greek Communist rebel army in the civil war."

"Oh, I see." George felt himself reddening. "I told you I didn't know anything about the Greek set-up," he said. "I'm afraid this kind of name-dropping misses with me."

Monsieur Hagen smiled. "Of course, Mr. Carey. We are closer to these things here. Vafiades was a Turkish-born Greek, a tobacco worker before the war. He was a Communist of many years' standing and had been to prison on that account. No doubt he had a respect for revolutionary tradition. When the Communists gave him command of the rebel army he decided to be known simply as Markos. It has only two syllables and is more dramatic. If the rebels had won he might have become as big a man as Tito. As it was, if you will forgive the comparison, he had something in common with your General Lee. He won his battles but lost the war. And for the same kind of reasons. For Lee, the loss of Vicksburg and Atlanta, especially Atlanta, meant the destruction of his lines of communication. For Markos, also faced by superior numbers, the closing of the Yugoslav frontier had the same sort of effect. As long as the Communists of Yugoslavia, Bulgaria, and Albania helped him, he was in a strong position. By retiring across those frontiers, he was able to break off any action that looked like developing unfavourably. Then, behind the frontier, he could regroup and reorganize in safety, gather reinforcements, and appear again with deadly effect on a weakly held sector of the government front. When Tito quarrelled with Stalin and withdrew his support of the Macedonian plan, he cut Markos's lateral lines of communication in two. Greece owes much to Tito."

"But wouldn't Markos have been beaten in the end anyway?"

Monsieur Hagen made a doubtful face. "Maybe. British and American aid did much. I do not dispute that. The Greek army and air force were completely transformed. But the denial of the Yugoslav frontier to Markos made it possible to use that power quickly and decisively. In January 1949, after over two years' fighting, the Markos forces were in possession of Naoussa, a big industrial town only eighty miles from Salonika itself. Nine months later they were beaten. All that was left was a pocket of resistance on Mount Grammos, near the Albanian frontier."

"I see." George smiled. "Well, there doesn't seem to be much likelihood of my being able to talk to General Vafiades, does there?"

"I'm afraid not, Mr. Carey."

"And even if I could, there wouldn't be much sense in my asking him about a German Sergeant who got caught in an ambush in '44."

Monsieur Hagen bowed his head politely. "None."

"So let me get it straight, sir. In 1944 the guerrillas—*andartes* you call them, do you?—the *andartes* killed some Germans and recruited others. Is that right?"

"Certainly."

"So that if the German soldier I'm interested in managed to get away alive after that ambush, it would not be fantastic to give him a fifty-fifty chance of staying alive?"

"Not at all fantastic. Very reasonable."

"I see. Thanks."

Two days later George and Miss Kolin were in Greece.

CHAPTER VII

"FORTY-FIVE THOUSAND KILLED, including three thousand five hundred civilians murdered by the rebels and seven hundred blown up by their mines. Twice as many wounded. Eleven thousand houses destroyed. Seven hundred thousand persons driven from their homes in rebel areas. Twenty-eight thousand forcibly removed to Communist countries. Seven thousand villages looted. That is what Markos and his friends cost Greece."

Colonel Chrysantos paused and, leaning back in his swivel chair, smiled bitterly at George and Miss Kolin. It was an effective pose. He was a very handsome man with keen, dark eyes. "And I have heard it said by the British and the Americans," he added, "that we have been too firm with our Communists. Too firm!" He threw up his long, thin hands.

George murmured vaguely. He knew that the Colonel's ideas of what constituted firmness were very different from his own and that a discussion of them would not be profitable. Monsieur Hagen, the Red Cross man, who had given him the letter of introduction to Colonel Chrysantos, had made the position clear. The Colonel was a desirable acquaintance only in so far as he was a senior officer in the Salonika branch of Greek military intelligence, who could lay his hands on the kind of information George needed. He was not a person towards whom it was possible to have very friendly feelings.

"Do these casualty figures include the rebels, Colonel?" he asked.

"Of the killed, yes. Twenty-eight of the forty-five thousand were rebels. About their wounded we have naturally no accurate figures; but in addition to those we killed, we captured thirteen thousand, and twenty-seven thousand more surrendered."

"Do you have lists of the names?"

"Certainly."

"Would it be possible to see if the name of this German is on one of those lists?"

"Of course. But you know we did not take more than a handful of Germans."

"Still it might be worth trying, though, as I say, I don't even know yet if the man survived the ambush."

"Ah, yes. Now we come to that. The 24th of October '44 was the date of the ambush, you say, and it was near a petrol point at Vodena. The *andartes* might have come from the Florina area, I think. We shall see. So!"

He pressed a button on his desk and a young Lieutenant with horn-rimmed glasses came in. The Colonel spoke sharply in his own language for nearly half a minute. When he stopped, the Lieutenant uttered a monosyllable and went out.

As the door shut, the Colonel relaxed. "A good boy, that," he said. "You Westerners sometimes pride yourselves that we cannot be efficient, but you will see—like that!" He snapped his fingers, smiled seductively at Miss Kolin and then glanced at George to see if he minded having his girl smiled at in that way.

Miss Kolin merely raised her eyebrows. The Colonel passed round cigarettes.

George found the situation entertaining. The Colonel's curiosity about the nature of the relationship between his visitors had been evident from the first. The woman was attractive; the man looked passably virile; it was absurd to suppose that they could travel about together on business without also taking advantage of the association for their pleasure. Yet, of course, the man was an Anglo-Saxon and so one could not be sure. In the absence of any positive evidence as to whether the pair were lovers or not the Colonel was beginning to probe for some. He would try again in a moment or two. Meanwhile, back to business.

The Colonel smoothed his tunic down. "This German of yours, Mr. Carey—was he an Alsatian?"

"No, he came from Cologne."

"Many of the deserters were Alsatian. You know, some of them hated the Germans as much as we did."

"Ah, yes? Were you in Greece during the war, Colonel?"

"Sometimes. At the beginning, yes. Later I was with the British. In their raiding forces. It was a type of Commando, you understand. That was a happy time."

"Happy?"

"Were you not a soldier, Mr. Carey?"

"I was a bomber pilot. I don't remember ever feeling particularly happy about it."

"Ah, no—but the air is different from soldiering. You do not see the enemy you kill. A machine war. Impersonal."

"It was personal enough for me," George said; but the remark went unheard. There was the light of reminiscence in the Colonel's eyes.

"You missed much in the air, Mr. Carey," he said dreamily. "I remember once, for example . . ."

He was off.

He had taken part, it seemed, in numerous British raids on German garrisons on Greek territory. He went on to describe in great detail what he obviously felt to be some of his more amusing experiences. Judging by the relish with which he recalled them, he had indeed had a happy time.

". . . splashed his brains over the wall with a burst from a Bren gun . . . put my knife low in his belly and ripped it open to the ribs . . . the grenades killed all of them in the room except one, so I dropped him out of the window . . . ran away without their trousers, so we could see what to shoot at . . . tried to come out of the house to surrender, but he was slow on his feet and the phosphorous grenade set him alight like a torch . . . I let him have a burst from the Schmeisser and nearly cut him in two . . ."

He spoke rapidly, smiling all the time and gesturing gracefully. Occasionally he broke into French. George made little attempt to follow. It did not matter, for the Colonel's whole attention now was concentrated on Miss Kolin. She was wearing her faintly patronizing smile, but there was something more in her expression besides—a look of pleasure. If you had been watching the pair of them without knowing what was being said, George thought, you might have supposed that the handsome Colonel was entertaining her with a witty piece of cocktail-party gossip. It was rather disconcerting.

The Lieutenant came back into the room with a tattered folder of papers under his arm. The Colonel stopped instantly and sat up straight in his chair to receive the folder. He looked through it sternly as the Lieutenant made his report. Once he rapped out a question and received an answer which appeared to satisfy him. Finally he nodded and the Lieutenant went out. The Colonel relaxed again and smirked complacently.

"It will take time to check the lists of prisoners," he said, "but, as I hoped, we have some other information. Whether it will be of help to you or not, I cannot say." He glanced down at the bundle of torn and greasy papers before him. "This ambush you mention was most likely one of several operations undertaken in that week by an ELAS band based in the hills above Florina. There were thirty-four men, most of them from Florina and the villages about there. The leader was a Communist named Phengaros. He came from Larisa. A German army truck was destroyed in the action. Does that sound like the case you know of?"

George nodded. "That's it. There were three trucks. The first hit a mine. Does it say anything about any prisoners?"

"Prisoners would not be reported, Mr. Carey. Fortunately, however, you can ask."

"Ask whom?"

"Phengaros." The Colonel grinned. "He was captured in '48. We have him under lock and key."

"Still?"

"Oh, he was released under an amnesty, but he is back now. He is a Party member, Mr. Carey, and a dangerous one. A brave man, perhaps, and a good one for killing Germans, but such politicals do not change their ways. You are lucky he has not long ago been shot."

"I was wondering why he wasn't."

"One could not shoot all of these rebels," the Colonel said with a shrug. "We are not Germans or Russkis. Besides, your friends in Geneva would not have liked it."

"Where can I see this man?"

"Here in Salonika. I shall have to speak to the commandant of the prison. Do you know your Consul here?"

"Not yet, but I have a letter to him from our Legation in Athens."

"Ah, good. I will tell the commandant that you are a friend of the American Minister. That should be sufficient."

"What exactly is this man Phengaros in prison for?"

The Colonel referred to the folder. "Jewel robbery, Mr. Carey."

"I thought you said he was a political prisoner."

"In America, Mr. Carey, your criminals are all capitalists. Here in these times they are occasionally Communists. Men like Phengaros do not steal for themselves, but for the Party funds. Of course, if we catch them they go to the criminal prison. They cannot be sent to the islands as politicals. They have made some big coups lately. It is quite traditional. Even the great Stalin robbed a bank for the Party funds when he was a young man. Of course, there are some of these bandits from the hills who only pretend to rob for the Party, and keep what they get for themselves. They are clever and dangerous and the police do not catch them. But Phengaros is not of that kind. He is a simple, deluded fanatic of the type that always gets caught."

"When can I see him?"

"Tomorrow perhaps. We shall see." He pressed the button again for the Lieutenant. "Tell me," he said, "are you and Madame by chance without an engagement this evening? I should so much like to show you our city."

Twenty minutes later George and Miss Kolin left the building and came again into the heat and glare of a Salonika afternoon. George's excuse that he had a long report to write that evening had been accepted with ready understanding. Miss Kolin had seemed to have rather more difficulty in evading the Colonel's hospitality. The conversation, however, had been conducted in Greek and George had understood nothing of it.

They crossed to the shade on the other side of the street.

"How did you manage to get out of it?" he asked as they turned towards the hotel.

"I explained that my stomach was upset by the food and the flies and that I should probably be sick all night."

George laughed.

"I spoke the truth."

"Oh, I'm sorry. Do you think you ought to see a doctor?"

"It will pass off. You have no stomach trouble yet?"

"No."

"It will come later. This is a bad place for the stomach when one is not used to it."

"Miss Kolin," George said after a while, "what did you really think of Colonel Chrysantos?"

"What can one think of such a man?"

"You didn't like him? He was very helpful and obliging."

"Yes, no doubt. It soothes his vanity to be helpful. There is only one thing that pleases me about that Colonel."

"Oh?"

She walked on several paces in silence. Then she spoke quietly, so quietly that he only just heard what she said.

"He knows how to deal with Germans, Mr. Carey."

It was at that moment that George received the first intimations of coming discomfort in his stomach and intestines. At that moment, also, he forgot about Colonel Chrysantos and Germans.

"I begin to see what you mean about the food and the flies," he remarked as they turned the corner by the hotel. "I think, if you don't mind, that we'll call in at a drugstore."

The following day the Colonel's Lieutenant arrived at their hotel in an army car and drove them out to the prison.

It was a converted barracks built near the remains of an old Turkish fort on the western outskirts of the city. With its high surrounding wall and the Kalamara Heights across the bay as a background, it looked from the outside rather like a monastery. Inside, it smelt like a large and inadequately tended latrine.

The Lieutenant had brought papers admitting them and they were taken to the administration block. Here they were introduced to a civilian official in a tight tussore suit, who apologized for the absence of the commandant on official business and offered coffee and cigarettes. He was a thin, anxious man, with a habit of picking his nose, of which he seemed to be trying, none too successfully, to break himself. When they had had their coffee, he took a heavy bunch of keys and led them through a series of passages with steel doors at both ends, which he unlocked and relocked as they went along. They were shown eventually into a room with whitewashed walls and a steel grille running down the middle from floor to ceiling. Through the grille they could see another door.

The official looked apologetic and mumbled something in bad French.

"Phengaros," Miss Kolin translated, "is not a good prisoner and sometimes behaves violently. The commandant would not wish us to be exposed to any trouble. It is for that reason that the interview must take place in these uncomfortable surroundings. He apologizes for them."

George nodded. He was not at ease. He had spent a disagreeable and exhausting night, and the smell of the place was making it difficult for him to forget the fact. Moreover, he had never been inside a prison before, and, while he had not supposed the experience would be anything but depressing, he had been unprepared for the lively sense of personal guilt that it aroused.

There was a sound from the door beyond the grille and he looked round. A Judas window had opened in it and a face was peering through. Then a key turned in the lock and the door opened. A man slowly entered the room.

The prisoner was thin and sinewy, with dark, sunken eyes and a long beak of a nose. His skin was brown and leathery as if he worked a lot in the sun. His shaven head had a black stubble of growth on it. He wore a cotton singlet and canvas trousers tied in at the waist with a strip of rag. His feet were bare.

He hesitated when he saw the faces on the other side of the grille, and the warder behind him prodded him with a club. He came forward into the light. The warder locked the door and stood with his back to it. The official nodded to George.

"Ask him what his name is," George said to Miss Kolin.

She relayed the question. The prisoner licked his lips, his dark eyes looking beyond her at the three men, as if she were the bait in a trap of their devising. He looked from her to the official and muttered something.

"What is the game?" Miss Kolin translated. "You know my name well enough. Who is this woman?"

The official shouted something at him violently and the warder prodded him again with the club.

George spoke quickly. "Miss Kolin, explain to him in as friendly a way as you can that I am an American lawyer and that my business has nothing to do with him personally. It is a private, a legal matter. Say we only want to question him about that ambush at Vodena. There is no political angle to it. Our only object in questioning him is to confirm the death of a German soldier reported missing in 1944. Make it good."

As she spoke, George watched the prisoner's face. The dark eyes flickered suspiciously towards him as she went on. When she had finished, the prisoner thought for a moment. Then he answered.

"He will listen to the questions and decide whether he will answer when he has heard them."

Behind George the Lieutenant was beginning to mutter angrily to the official. George took no notice.

"O.K.," he said, "ask him his name. He's got to identify himself."

"Phengaros."

"Ask him if he remembers the ambush of the trucks."

"Yes, he remembers."

"He was in command of those particular *andartes?*"

"Yes."

"What happened exactly?"

"He does not know. He was not there."

"But he said—"

"He was leading an attack on the gasoline dump at the time. It was his second-in-command who caught the trucks."

"Where is his second-in-command?"

"Dead. He was shot a few months later by the fascist murder gangs in Athens."

"Oh. Well, ask him if he knows of any German prisoners taken from the trucks."

Phengaros thought for a moment, then nodded.

"Yes. One."

"Did he see this prisoner?"

"He interrogated him."

"What rank was he?"

"A private, he thinks. The man was the driver of the truck that hit the mine. He was wounded."

"Is he sure that there was no other prisoner?"

"Yes."

"Tell him we have information that there were two men in that first truck who did not return and whose bodies were not found by the German party that came on the scene later. One was the driver of the truck, whom he says he interrogated. The other was the Sergeant in charge of the detachment. We want to know what happened to the Sergeant."

Phengaros began gesturing emphatically as he talked.

"He says that he was not there, but that if there had been a German sergeant alive his men would certainly have taken him prisoner for questioning. A sergeant would have more information to give than a driver."

"What happened to the driver?"

"He died."

"How?"

There was a hesitation. "Of his wounds."

"O.K., we'll skip that. When he served in the army of General Markos, did he come across any Germans fighting with it?"

"A few."

"Any whose names he can remember?"

"No."

"Ask him if he knows of anyone who actually took part in the truck ambush who's still alive."

"He knows of nobody."

"Surely they can't *all* be dead. Ask him to try and remember."

"He knows of nobody."

Phengaros was no longer looking at Miss Kolin now, but staring straight ahead.

There was a pause. George felt a touch on his arm. The Lieutenant drew him aside.

"Mr. Carey, this man does not wish to give information that might compromise his friends," he said in English.

"Oh, I see. Of course."

"Excuse me a moment, please."

The Lieutenant went to the official and held a whispered conversation with him. Then he returned to George.

"The information might be obtained for you, Mr. Carey," he murmured, "but it would take time to do so."

"How do you mean?"

"This Phengaros is a difficult man to persuade, it seems, but, if you wish, some disciplinary pressure might be applied—"

"No, no." George spoke hastily; his knees were beginning to tremble. "Unless he gives the information quite voluntarily it can have no legal value as evidence." It was a dishonest excuse. Phengaros's evidence had no legal value anyway; it was the evidence of eyewitnesses (if any) that would be important. But George could think of nothing better.

"As you please. Is there anything else you wish to ask?" The Lieutenant's manner was bored now. He had seen through George. If the inquiry could be pursued with such lily-livered timidity, it could not be of very great importance.

"I don't think so, thanks." George turned to Miss Kolin. "Ask this prison man if it's against the rules to give the prisoner some cigarettes."

The official stopped picking his nose when he heard the question. Then he shrugged. If the American wished to waste cigarettes on such an un-co-operative type he might do so; but they must be examined first.

George took out a packet of cigarettes and handed it to him. The official glanced inside, pinched the packet, and handed it back. George held it through the grille.

Phengaros had been standing there with a faint smile on his face. His eyes met George's. With an ironic bow he took the cigarettes. As he did so he began to speak.

"I understand the feelings of embarrassment that prompt you to offer this gift, sir," translated Miss Kolin. "If I were a criminal, I would gladly accept them. But the fate of my comrades at the hands of the fascist reactionaries already rests too lightly on the conscience of the world. If your own conscience is troubling you, sir, that is to your credit. But I am not yet so corrupted here as to allow you to ease it for the price of a packet of cigarettes. No. Much as I should have enjoyed smoking them, sir, I think that their destination must be that of all other American aid."

With a flick of his wrist he tossed the cigarettes to the warder behind him.

They fell on the floor. As the warder snatched them up, the official began shouting to him angrily through the grille and he hastened to unlock the door.

Phengaros nodded curtly and went out.

The official stopped shouting and turned apologetically to George. "*Une espèce de fausse-couche,*" he said; "*je vous demande pardon, monsieur.*"

"What for?" said George. "If he thinks I'm a lousy crypto-fascist-imperialist lackey, he's quite right in refusing to smoke my cigarettes."

"*Pardon?*"

"He also had the good manners not to heave the cigarettes right back in my face. In his place, I might have done just that."

"*Qu'est ce que Monsieur a dit?*"

The official was looking desperately at Miss Kolin.

George shook his head. "Don't bother to translate, Miss Kolin. He won't get it. You understand me, though, don't you, Lieutenant? Yes, I thought so. Now, if you don't mind, I'd like to get the hell out of here before something very inconvenient happens inside my stomach."

When they got back to the hotel, there was a note from Colonel Chrysantos awaiting them. It contained the information that a search of all the relevant lists had failed to discover anybody named Schirmer who had been either killed or captured in the Markos campaign; nor had an amnesty been granted to anyone of that name.

"Miss Kolin," George said, "what can you drink when you have this stomach thing?"

"Cognac is best."

"Then we'd better have some."

Later, when the experiment had been tried, he said: "When we were in Cologne my office gave me permission to go on with the investigation for three more weeks if I thought we were making progress. One of them's gone, and all we've found out is that Franz Schirmer most likely didn't get taken prisoner by the people who shot up the trucks."

"Surely, that is something."

"It's mildly interesting at best. It doesn't get us anywhere. I'm giving it one more week. If we're no nearer the truth by then, we go home. O.K.?"

"Perfectly. What will you do with the week?"

"Do what I have an idea I should have done before. Go to Vodena and look for his grave."

CHAPTER VIII

Vodena, which used to be called Edessa and was once the seat of the kings of Macedon, is some fifty miles west of Salonika. It hangs, amid lush growth of vine and wild pomegranate, fig, and mulberry trees, in the foothills of Mount Chakirka six hundred feet above the Yiannitsa plain. Sparkling mountain streams cascade lyrically down the hillsides into Nisia Voda, the tributary of the Vadar which flows swiftly past the town on its way to the parent river. The old tiled houses glow in the sun. There are no tourist hotels.

George and Miss Kolin were driven there in a car hired in Salonika. It was not an enjoyable trip. The day was hot and the road bad. The condition of their stomachs denied them even the consolations of a good lunch and a bottle of wine at their destination. While the chauffeur went off heartily in search of food and wine, they went into a café, fought the flies for long enough to drink some brandy, and then dragged themselves off dispiritedly in search of information.

Almost immediately luck was with them. A sweetmeat pedlar in the market not only remembered the ambush well, but had actually been working in a near-by vineyard at the time. He had been warned to keep clear by the *andartes*, who had arrived an hour before the German trucks came.

When the chauffeur returned they persuaded the pedlar to leave his tray of flyblown titbits with a friend and guide them to the scene.

The fuel dump had been near a railway siding about three miles out of Vodena, on the side road to Apsalos. The trucks had been caught about two miles along this stretch of road.

It was an ideal place for an ambush. The road was climbing steadily and at that point made a hairpin turn below a hillside with plenty of cover for the attackers among its trees and thickets. Below and beyond the road there was no cover at all. The mines had been placed well past the turn so that, when the first truck hit, it would block the road for those following at a point where they could neither turn their vehicles nor find cover from which to reply to the fire from above. For the *andartes* concealed on the hillside the business must have been easy. The remarkable thing was that as many as two of the eleven Germans in the trucks had managed to get back down the road alive. They must have been exceptionally nimble or the fire from the hillside very wild.

Those who had died had been buried lower down the hill in a patch of level ground just off the road. According to the pedlar, the ground had been damp with rain at the time. The neat row of graves was still discernible in the undergrowth. Lieutenant Leubner and his men had piled stones in a small cairn on each. George had seen wayside German graves in France and Italy and guessed that originally each grave had also borne its occupant's steel helmet, and perhaps a wooden stake with his number, name, and rank. It depended on how much time there had been to spare for such refinements. He looked for the stakes, but if they had ever existed, there was now no sign of them. Under a near-by bush he found a rusty German helmet; that was all.

"Seven graves," remarked Miss Kolin as they walked up the hill again; "that is what one would expect from the Lieutenant's letter to Frau Schirmer. Ten men and the Sergeant went. Two men return. The bodies of the Sergeant and the driver of the first truck are missing. Seven are buried."

"Yes, but Phengaros said that there was only one prisoner—the driver. So where was the Sergeant? Look! The driver was wounded when the truck hit the mine, but not killed. Most likely the Sergeant was in the cab beside him. Probably he was wounded too. Lieutenant Leubner said he wasn't a man to surrender without a fight. Supposing he managed somehow to get clear of the road and was hunted down and killed some distance from it."

"But how, Mr. Carey? How could he get clear?"

They had reached the place of the ambush again. George walked along the edge of the road away from the hillside and looked down.

The bare rocky ground fell away precipitously to the valley below. It was absurd to suppose that even an unwounded man would attempt to scramble down it under fire from the hillside and the road above. The two men who had escaped had been able to do so because they were in the last truck and unwounded. The Sergeant had been a full two hundred yards farther away from cover. He had had no chance at all of getting clear.

George climbed a short way up the hillside to look at the scene from the attackers' point of view. From there, the plight of the men in the trucks seemed even more hopeless. He could imagine the scene: the trucks grinding up the hill, the ear-splitting detonation of the mine, the rattle of machine-gun and rifle fire, the thudding explosions of grenades lobbed on to the road, the hoarse shouts, the screams of the dying.

He clambered down to the car again.

"All right, Miss Kolin," he said; "what do *you* think happened?"

"I think that he was taken prisoner with the driver and that both were wounded. I think that the Sergeant died of his wounds or was killed trying to escape on the way to the *andartes*' rendezvous with Phengaros. Naturally Phengaros would think that only one prisoner had been taken."

"What about the Sergeant's papers? They would have been taken to Phengaros."

"They would also take the papers of those they had killed here."

George considered. "Yes, you may be right. At least it's a reasonable explanation. There's still only one way we can find out for certain though, and that's by getting hold of someone who was there."

Miss Kolin nodded towards the pedlar. "I have been talking to this man. He says that the *andartes* who did this were from Florina. That agrees with the Colonel's information."

"Did he know any of them by name?"

"No. They just said they were from Florina."

"Another dead end. All right, we'll go there tomorrow. We'd better start back now. How much money do you think I should give this old man?"

It was early evening when they arrived back in Salonika. Something unusual seemed to have happened while they had been away. There were extra police on duty in the streets and shopkeepers stood in the roadway conferring volubly with their neighbours. The cafés were crowded.

At the hotel they heard the news.

Just before three o'clock that afternoon a closed army truck had driven up to the entrance of the Eurasian Credit Bank in the rue Egnatie. It had waited there for a moment or so. Then, suddenly, the covers at the back had been flung open and six men had jumped out. They had been armed with machine-pistols and grenades. Three of them had immediately stationed themselves in the entrance portico. The other three had gone inside. Within little more than two minutes they had been out again with several hundred thousand dollars' worth of foreign currency in American dollars, escudos, and Swiss francs. Ten seconds later, and almost before the passers-by had noticed that anything was wrong, they had been back in the truck and away.

The affair had been perfectly organized. The raiders had known exactly which safe the money was kept in and exactly how to get to it. No one had been shot. A clerk, who had courageously tried to set off an alarm bell, had received no more than a blow in the face from a gun butt for his audacity. The alarm bell had not sounded for the simple reason, discovered later, that the wires to it had been disconnected. The raiders had saluted with the clenched fist. Quite clearly they had had a Communist confederate inside the bank. Quite clearly the robbery was yet another in a series organized to replenish the Communist Party funds. Quite naturally suspicion as to the identity of the confederate had fallen upon the courageous clerk. Would he have dared to do what he did unless he had known in advance that he was running no risk? Of course not! The police were questioning him.

That was the receptionist's excited account of the affair.

The hotel barman confirmed the facts but had a more sophisticated theory about the motives of the criminals.

How was it, he asked, that every big robbery that now took place was the work of Communists stealing for the Party funds? Did nobody else steal any more? Oh yes, no doubt there *had* been political robberies, but not as many as people supposed. And why should the brigands give the clenched fist salute as they left? To show that they were Communists? Absurd! They were merely seeking to give that impression in order to deceive the police by directing attention away from themselves. They could count on the police preferring to blame Communists. Everything bad was blamed on the Communists. He himself was not a Communist of course, but . . .

He went on at length.

George listened absently. At that moment he was more interested in the discovery that his appetite had suddenly begun to return and that he could contemplate without revulsion the prospect of dinner.

Florina lies at the entrance to a deep valley nine miles south of the Yugoslav frontier. About forty miles away across the mountains to the west is Albania. Florina is the administrative centre of the province which bears its name and is an important railhead. It has a garrison and a ruined Turkish citadel. It has more than one hotel. It is neither as picturesque as Vodena nor as ancient. It came into existence as an insignificant staging point on a Roman road from Durazzo to Constantinople, and far too late to share in the short-lived glories of the Macedonian Empire. In a land which has contained so many of the springs of Western civilization, it is a parvenu.

But if Florina has no history of much interest to the compilers of guidebooks, it has, in the Edwardian sense of the word, a Past.

In the summer of 1896, sixteen men attended a meeting in Salonika. There they founded a political organization which in later years was to become the most formidable secret terrorist society the Balkans, or for that matter Europe, has known. It was called the Internal Macedonian Revolutionary Organization; IMRO, for short. Its creed was "Macedonia for the Macedonians," its flag a red skull and crossbones on a black ground, its motto "Freedom or Death." Its arguments were the knife, the rifle, and the bomb. Its armed forces, who lived in the hills and mountains of Macedonia enforcing IMRO laws and imposing IMRO taxes on the villagers and townspeople, were called *comitadjis*. Their oath of allegiance was sworn upon a Bible and a revolver, and the penalty for disloyalty was death. Among those who took this oath and served IMRO there were rich men as well as peasants, poets as well as soldiers, philosophers as well as professional murderers. In the cause of Macedonian autonomy it killed Turks and Bulgars, Serbs and Vlachs, Greeks and Albanians. It also killed Macedonians in the same cause. By the time of the First Balkan War, IMRO was a serious political force, capable of bringing considerable influence to bear upon events. The Macedonian *comitadji* with his cartridge belts and his rifle was becoming a legendary figure, a heroic defender of women and children against the savagery of the Turks, a knight of the mountains who preferred death to dishonour and treated his captives with courtesy and forbearance. The facts, harped upon by cynical observers, that the savageries of the Turks were generally committed by way of reprisal for atrocities committed by the *comitadjis*, and that the chivalrous behaviour was only in evidence when there was a chance of its impressing foreign sympathizers, seemed to have little effect on the legend. It persisted remarkably and has to some extent continued to do so. In the main square of Gorna Djoumaia, the capital of Bulgarian Macedonia, there is even a monument to "The Unknown *Comitadji*." True, it was put up in 1933 by the IMRO gangsters who ran the city; but the Bulgarian central government of the time did not object to it, and it is almost certainly still there. If IMRO is no longer served by poets and idealists, it remains a political force and has from time to time sold itself with nice impartiality to both Fascists and Communists. IMRO is and always has been a very Balkan institution.

Florina was one of the "founder" strongholds of IMRO. Soon after the momentous Salonika meeting in 1896, an ex-Sergeant of the Bulgarian army named Marko began recruiting an IMRO band in Florina, which rapidly became the most powerful in the area. And the most distinguished. The Bulgarian poet Yavorov and the young writer Christo Silianov were among those who chose to join it, and (though Silianov, the writer, disgraced himself by showing an effeminate aversion to cutting his prisoners' throats) both saw much active service with the Florina men. Marko himself was killed by Turkish soldiers, but the band remained an effective unit and played a prominent part in the rebellion of 1903. The irredentist techniques of sabotage, ambush, kidnapping, intimidation, armed robbery, and murder are part of Florina's cultural heritage; and although it now takes invasion and a war to induce the law-abiding inhabitants of the province to turn to these old skills, there are always, even in times of peace, a few daring spirits ready to take to the mountains and remind their unfortunate neighbours that the traditions of their forefathers are still very much alive.

George and Miss Kolin arrived by train from Salonika.

The Parthenon Hotel was a three-story building near the centre of the town. There was a café beneath it, and a restaurant which could be entered directly from the street. It was about the size of a third-class commercial hotel in a town like Lyon. The rooms were small and the plumbing primitive. The bedstead in George's room was of iron, but there was a wooden frame round the springs. At Miss Kolin's suggestion, George spent his first half-hour there with an insufflator and a canister of D.D.T., spraying the crevices in the woodwork. Then he went down to the café. Presently Miss Kolin joined him.

The proprietor of the Parthenon was a small, grey-faced man with grey hair cut *en brosse* and a crumpled grey suit. When he saw Miss Kolin appear, he left a table by the bar counter, at which he had been standing talking to an army officer, and came over to them. He bowed and said something in French.

"Ask him if he'll join us for a drink," George said.

When the invitation had been interpreted, the little man bowed again, sat down with a word of apology, and snapped his fingers at the barman.

They all had *oyzo*. Politenesses were exchanged. The proprietor apologized for not speaking English and then began discreetly to pump them about their business in the town.

"We have few tourists here," he remarked; "I have often said that it is a pity."

"The scenery is certainly very fine."

"If you have time while you are here you should take a drive. I shall be happy to arrange a car for you."

"Very kind of him. Say that we heard in Salonika that there was excellent hunting to be had near the lakes to the west."

"The gentleman is intending to go hunting?"

"Not this time, unfortunately. We are on business. But we were told that there was plenty of game up there."

The little man smiled. "There is game of all sorts in the neighbourhood. There are also eagles in the hills," he added slyly.

"Eagles who do a little hunting themselves, perhaps?"

"The gentleman learned that in Salonika, too, no doubt."

"I have always understood that this is a most romantic part of the country."

"Yes, the eagle is a bird of romance to some," the proprietor said archly. Obviously, he was the kind of person who could not let the smallest joke go, once he had got his teeth into it.

"It's a bird of prey, too."

"Ah, yes indeed! When armies disintegrate, there are always a few who prefer to stay together and fight a private war against society. But here in Florina the gentleman need have no fear. The eagles are safe in the hills."

"That's a pity. We were hoping you might be able to help us to find one."

"To find an eagle? The gentleman deals in fine feathers?"

But George was getting bored. "All right," he said, "we'll cut the double-talk. Tell him I'm a lawyer and that we want, if possible, to talk to someone who was in the ELAS band led by Phengaros in 1944. Explain that it's nothing political, that we just want to check up on the grave of a German Sergeant who was killed near Vodena. Say I'm acting for the man's relatives in America."

He watched the little man's face as Miss Kolin translated. For a moment or two a quite extraordinary expression came over its loose grey folds, an expression compounded of equal parts of interest, amazement, indignation, and fear. Then a curtain came down and the face went blank. Its owner picked up his drink and drained the glass.

"I regret," he said precisely, "that that is not a matter in which I can be of any assistance to you at all."

He rose to his feet.

"Wait a minute," said George. "If he can't help me, ask him if he knows of anyone here who can."

The proprietor hesitated, then glanced across at the officer sitting at the table by the bar. "One moment," he said curtly. He went over to the officer, and bending over the table, began talking in a rapid undertone.

After a moment or two, George saw the officer look across quickly at him, then say something sharply to the proprietor. The little man shrugged. The officer stood up and came over to them.

He was a lean, dark young man with lustrous eyes, very wide riding-breeches, and a waist like a girl's. He wore the badges of a captain. He bowed to Miss Kolin and smiled pleasantly at George.

"I beg your pardon, sir," he said in English. "The patron tells me that you are here making inquiries."

"That's right."

He clicked his heels. "Streftaris, Captain," he said. "You are an American, Mr.—?"

"Carey's my name. Yes, I'm an American."

"And this lady?"

"Miss Kolin is French. She is my interpreter."

"Thank you. Perhaps I can be of assistance to you, Mr. Carey."

"That's very kind of you, Captain. Sit down, won't you?"

"Thank you." The Captain spun the chair round, swung the seat between his legs, and sat down with his elbows resting on the back. There was something curiously insolent about the gesture. He smiled less pleasantly. "You have made the patron feel very uneasy, Mr. Carey."

"I'm sorry about that. All I asked him was to put me in touch with someone who was in the Phengaros band in 1944. I told him there was nothing political about my business."

The Captain sighed elaborately. "Mr. Carey," he said, "if I were to come to you in America and ask you to put me in touch with a gangster wanted by the police, would you be prepared to help me?"

"Is that a true comparison?"

"Certainly. I do not think you quite understand our problems here. You are a foreigner, of course, and that excuses you, but it is very indiscreet to inquire into matters of this kind."

"Do you mind telling me why?"

"These men are Communists—outlaws. Do you know that Phengaros himself is in prison on a criminal charge?"

"Yes. I interviewed him two days ago."

"Pardon?"

"Colonel Chrysantos in Salonika was kind enough to arrange for me to see Phengaros in prison."

The Captain's smile faded. He took his elbows off the back of the chair.

"I beg your pardon, Mr. Carey."

"What for?"

"I did not understand that you were on official business."

"Well, to be exact—"

"I do not think we have received orders from Salonika. Had we done so, of course, the Commandant would have instructed me."

"Now, just a moment, Captain, let's get this straight. My business is legal rather than official. I'll explain."

The Captain listened carefully to the explanation. When George had finished he looked relieved.

"Then it is not on the advice of Colonel Chrysantos that you are here, sir?"

"No."

"You must know, Mr. Carey, that I am military intelligence officer for the district. It would be most unfortunate for me if Colonel Chrysantos thought—"

"Sure, I know. A very efficient man, the Colonel."

"Ah, yes."

"And a busy one. So, you see, I thought it might be better if I didn't trouble the Colonel again, but just got the names of some of these people unofficially."

The Captain looked puzzled. "Unofficially? How unofficially?"

"I could buy the names, couldn't I?"

"But from whom?"

"Well, that was what I was hoping the patron might be able to tell me."

"Ah!" The Captain at last permitted himself to smile again. "Mr. Carey, if the patron knew where the names that you want could be bought, he would not be so foolish as to admit the fact to a stranger."

"But haven't you a line on *any* of these people? What happened to them all?"

"Some were killed with the Markos forces, some are across the border with our neighbours. The rest"—he shrugged—"they have taken other names."

"But they're somewhere about here, surely."

"Yes, but I cannot recommend you to go looking for them. There are cafés in this town where, if you asked the questions you asked the patron here tonight, there would be much unpleasantness for you."

"I see. What would you do in my place, Captain?"

The Captain thought carefully for a moment, then he leaned forward. "Mr. Carey, I would not wish you to believe that I am not anxious to give you all the assistance I can."

"No, of course not."

But the Captain had not finished. "I wish to help you all I can. Please, however, explain to me one thing. You wish simply to know if this German Sergeant was killed or not killed in the ambush. Is that right?"

"That's right."

"You do not specially wish to know the name of the person who saw him die?"

George considered. "Well, let's put it this way," he said finally; "the probability is that the Sergeant *did* die. If he did and I can be reasonably certain of the fact, then that's all I want to know. My business is finished."

The Captain nodded. "Ah. Now let us suppose for a moment that such information could be obtained in some way. Would you be prepared to pay perhaps three hundred dollars for that information without knowing where it came from?"

"Three hundred! That's rather a lot isn't it?"

The Captain waved the subject away deprecatingly. "Let us say two hundred. The sum is not important."

"Then let's say one hundred."

"As you will. But would you pay, Mr. Carey?"

"Under certain conditions, yes."

"What conditions, please?"

"Well, I can tell you right now that I'm not going to pay out a hundred dollars just for the pleasure of having someone tell me that he knows somebody else who knows a man who was in that ambush and says that the German Sergeant was killed. I'd want some kind of evidence that the story was genuine."

"I understand that, but what evidence could there be?"

"Well, for one thing, what I'd want is a reasonable explanation of the fact that the Sergeant's body was not found by the German patrol that came along afterwards. There were dead men there, but the Sergeant wasn't among them. A genuine witness ought to know the answer to that one."

"Yes, that is logical."

"But is there any chance of getting the information?"

"That is what I have been thinking about. I see a chance, perhaps, yes. I can promise nothing. Do you know anything of police methods?"

"Only the usual things."

"Then you will know that when one is dealing with criminals, it is sometimes wise to give the less dangerous ones temporary immunity, and even encouragement, if by doing so one can know a little of what is going on among the rest."

"You mean paid informers?"

"Not quite. The paid informer is rarely satisfactory. One pays and pays for nothing and then, when he is about to be useful, he is found with his throat cut and the government's money is wasted. No, the types I am discussing are the lesser criminals whose activities can be tolerated because they know and are trusted by those whom we may wish to put our hands on. Such types will not inform, you understand, but by seeming to be friendly and ready to overlook their little games one can learn much of what goes on that is interesting."

"I understand. If there were money in it and nobody risked incriminating himself, such a person might find out what I wanted to know."

"Exactly."

"Have you someone in mind?"

"Yes, but I must make a discreet inquiry first to see if an approach can safely be made. I think that Colonel Chrysantos would be very annoyed with me, Mr. Carey, if I put your life in danger"—he flashed a lustrous smile at Miss Kolin—"or that of Madame."

Miss Kolin looked down her nose.

George grinned. "No, we mustn't annoy the Colonel. But all the same it's very kind of you to take all this trouble, Captain."

The Captain raised a protesting hand. "It is nothing. If you should happen to mention to the Colonel that I was of some small assistance to you, I should be well repaid."

"Naturally I shall mention it. But who is this person you think might fix it up?"

"It is a woman. Outwardly she is the proprietress of a wineshop. In fact she deals secretly in arms. If a man wishes a rifle or a revolver, he goes to her. She gets it for him. Why do we not arrest her? Because then someone else would begin to deal, someone we might not know and could not so easily keep under surveillance. One day, perhaps, when we can be sure of stopping her sources of supply, we will take her. Until then, things are better as they are. She has a love of gossip and for your purpose is most suitable."

"But doesn't she know she's under surveillance?"

"Ah yes, but she bribes my men. The fact that they take her money makes her feel safe. It is all quite friendly. But we do not wish to alarm her, so she must be consulted first." He rose to his feet, suddenly business-like. "Perhaps tonight."

"That's good of you, Captain. Won't you stay and have a drink?"

"Ah, no, thank you. Just now I have various appointments. Tomorrow I will send a note to you here to give you the address to go to if she has agreed, and any other necessary instructions."

"O.K. Fine."

There was a lot of heel-clicking and politeness and he went. George signalled to the barman.

"Well, Miss Kolin," he said when they were served again, "what do you think?"

"I think that the Captain's various appointments are almost certainly with his mistress."

"I meant do you think there's anything in this. You know this part of the world. Do you think he'll do what he said about contacting this woman?"

She shrugged. "I think that for a hundred dollars the Captain would do almost anything."

It took a moment or two for George to appreciate the implication of this statement. "But the Captain's not getting the money," he said.

"No?"

"No. That's for the wineshop woman, if she comes through with the information."

"I do not think he will give her a hundred dollars. Perhaps twenty. Perhaps nothing."

"You're kidding."

"You asked me for my impression."

"He's the Keen Young Executive type. All he wants is a pat on the back from the boss. You see."

Miss Kolin smiled sardonically.

George did not get much rest that night. The precautions he had taken against bedbugs had somehow served to convince him that the mattress frame must be alive with the creatures. In the darkness he had soon begun to imagine that he was being attacked by them. Useless now to remind himself of the D.D.T. he had applied; Balkan bugs probably ate the stuff like ice cream. After a fourth panic inspection failed to reveal even one attacker, he became desperate, stripped the bed, and made a further assault on the mattress with the insufflator. A rose-coloured dawn was glowing among the mountain peaks before he succeeded in going to sleep.

He awoke, resentfully, at nine o'clock. While he was at breakfast in the café downstairs, a letter arrived from the Captain.

DEAR SIR [George read]:

 The woman is Madame Vassiotis at the wineshop in the rue Monténégrine. She will expect you, but not until this afternoon. Say that you come from Monsieur Kliris. Do not refer to me. She has been told what you want and might have an answer for you. The price will be U. S. dollars 150, but do not give it to the woman herself or speak of it. I wish to be assured personally that you are satisfied before you pay. If, when I have seen you this evening, you tell me that all is well, I will see that the money goes to her by Monsieur Kliris.

The letter was written on plain paper and unsigned. George did not show it to Miss Kolin.

The rue Monténégrine proved to be a steep, refuse-strewn lane in the poorer quarter of the town. The houses were broken down and ugly. Lines of dingy washing were strung across the lane between some of the upper windows; others had bedding hung out over the sills. There were a great many children about.

The wineshop was near the top of the lane by a builder's yard. It had no display window. There was a bead-curtained doorway in a wall, and two or three steps led down to the interior. George and Miss Kolin entered and found themselves in a kind of cellar, with wine barrels stacked on their sides against the walls, and a massive wooden bench in the centre. Light came from an oil lamp on a shelf. The air was cool and there was a smell of stale wine and old barrels that was not unpleasant.

There were two persons in the shop. One of them, an old man in blue denim trousers, sat on the bench drinking a glass of wine. The other was Madame Vassiotis.

She was amazingly fat, with huge pendulous breasts and a vast lap. She was sitting on, and almost completely enveloping, a low stool by a doorway at the back of the shop. When they entered, she rose slowly to her feet and waddled forward into the light.

Her head was small for her body, with dark hair drawn tightly away from the brow. The face seemed as though it ought to belong to someone younger or less gross. It was still firm and delicately shaped, and the eyes under their heavy lids were dark and clear.

She murmured a word of greeting.

Miss Kolin replied. George had briefed her in readiness for the interview and she did not trouble to interpret the preliminaries. He saw Madame Vassiotis nod understandingly and glance at the old man. He promptly finished his wine and went out. Then she bowed slightly to

George and, with a gesture of invitation, led the way through a doorway at the back into a sitting-room.

There, there were Turkish carpets on the walls, a divan with plush cushions, and a few pieces of rickety Victorian furniture. It reminded him of a fortune-teller's booth in a travelling fair. Only the crystal ball was missing.

Madame Vassiotis poured three glasses of wine, sank down heavily on the divan, and motioned them to chairs. When they were seated, she folded her hands in her lap and looked placidly from one to the other of them as if waiting for someone to propose a parlour game.

"Ask her," George said, "if she has been able to get any reply to the questions put to her by Monsieur Kliris."

Madame Vassiotis listened gravely to the translation and then, with a nod, began to speak.

"She states," said Miss Kolin, "that she has been able to speak with one of the *andartes* who took part in the affair near Vodena. Her information is that the German Sergeant was killed."

"Does she know how he was killed?"

"He was in the first truck of the German convoy. It exploded a mine."

George thought for a moment. He had not mentioned either of those facts to the Captain. It was promising.

"Did the informant see the Sergeant dead?"

"Yes."

"Was he on the road?"

"He was where he fell when the truck was hit."

"What happened to the body afterwards?"

He saw Madame Vassiotis shrug.

"Does she know that the body was not there when the German patrol came along afterwards?"

"Yes, but her informant can offer no explanation of this."

George thought again. This was awkward. An experienced man would probably know that the N.C.O. in charge of a German column would ride in the leading truck; and certainly anyone who had taken any part at all in the ambush would know that the leading truck had hit a mine. The informant might well have been farther down the road, firing on the other trucks. With the prospect of earning a few dollars for his trouble, however, he would be ready to oblige with a reasonable guess.

"Ask her if her friend knows what the Sergeant's injuries were."

"She cannot say exactly. The Sergeant was lying in a pool of blood."

"Is she absolutely sure in her own mind—?" Then he broke off. "No, wait a minute. Put it another way. If the Sergeant were her own son, would she be satisfied in her own mind that he was dead from what her friend has told her?"

A smile appeared on the delicately curved lips and a chuckle shook the massive body as their owner understood his question. Then, with a grunting effort, she heaved herself up from the divan and waddled to a drawer in the table. From it she took a slip of paper, which she handed to Miss Kolin with an explanation.

"Madame anticipated your doubts and asked for proof that her friend saw the body. He told her that they stripped the dead Germans of their equipment and that he got the Sergeant's water bottle. He still has it. It has the Sergeant's number and name burned into the strap. They are written on this paper."

Madame Vassiotis sat down again and sipped her wine as George looked at the paper.

The army number he knew well; he had seen it before on several documents. Beneath it in block letters had been written: "SCHIRMER F."

George considered it carefully for a moment or two, then nodded. He had not mentioned the name Schirmer to the Captain. Trickery was quite out of the question. The evidence was conclusive. What had happened afterwards to the body of Sergeant Schirmer might never be known, but there was no shadow of doubt that Madame Vassiotis and her mysterious acquaintance were telling what they knew of the truth.

He nodded and, picking up his glass of wine, raised it politely to the woman before he drank.

"Thank her for me, please, Miss Kolin," he said as he put the glass down, "and tell her that I am well satisfied."

He got out a fifty-dollar bill and put it on the table as he stood up.

He saw an expression of hastily concealed amazement flicker across the fat woman's face. Then she rose to her feet bowing and smiling. She was clearly delighted. If her dignity had permitted it she would have picked up the bill to have a closer look. She pressed them to have more wine.

When, eventually, they were able to bow themselves out of the shop, George turned to Miss Kolin. "You'd better tell her not to mention that fifty dollars to Monsieur Kliris," he said; "I shan't mention it to the Captain. With any luck she may get paid twice."

Miss Kolin was on her sixth after-dinner brandy, and her eyes were glazing rapidly. She was sitting very striaght in her chair. At any moment now she would decide that it was time for her to go to bed. The Captain had long since departed. He had had the air of a man of whose good nature unfair advantage had been taken. However, he had not refused the hundred dollars George had offered him. Presumably he was now celebrating the occasion with his mistress. For George, there was nothing more to be done in Florina.

"We'll leave tomorrow morning, Miss Kolin," he said. "Train to Salonika. Plane to Athens. Plane to Paris. All right?"

"You have definitely decided?"

"Can you think of one reason for going on with the thing?"

"I never had any doubt that the man was dead."

"No, that's right, you didn't. Going to bed now?"

"I think so, yes. Good night, Mr. Carey."

"Good night, Miss Kolin."

Watching her meticulous progress to the door of the café, George wondered gloomily if she kept her rigid self-control until she got into bed or whether, in the privacy of her room, she allowed herself to pass out.

He finished his own drink slowly. He felt depressed and wished to account for the fact. According to the lights of the ambitious young corporation lawyer who, only a few weeks back, had been pleased to watch his name being painted on an office door in Philadelphia, he should have been delighted by the turn of events. He had been given an irksome and unrewarding task and had performed it quickly and efficiently. He could now return with confidence to more serious and useful business. Everything was fine. And yet he was deriving no pleasure from the fact. It was absurd. Could it be that, in his heart, he had hoped, ludicrously, to find the Schneider Johnson claimant and take him back in triumph to that juvenile dotard, Mr. Sistrom? Could it be that what was now troubling him was merely an idiotic feeling of anticlimax? That must be it, of course. For a moment or two he almost succeeded in convincing himself that he had discovered the reason for his state of mind. Then the even less palatable truth of the matter dawned on him. He had been enjoying himself.

Yes, there it was. The talented, ambitious, pretentious Mr. Carey, with his smug, smiling family, his Brooks Brothers suits, and his Princeton and Harvard degrees, *liked* playing detectives, *liked* looking for nonexistent German soldiers, *liked* having dealings with dreary people like Frau Gresser, disagreeable people like Colonel Chrysantos, and undesirables like Phengaros. And why? For the value of such experiences in a corporation law practice? Because he loved his fellow men and was curious about them? Rubbish. More likely that the elaborate defences of his youth, the pompous fantasies of big office chairs and panelled boardrooms, of hidden wealth and power behind the scenes, were beginning to crumble, and that the pimply adolescent was belatedly emerging into the light. Was it not possible that, in finding out something about a dead man, he had at last begun to find out something about himself?

He sighed, paid the bar bill, got his key, and went up to his room.

It was in the front of the hotel on the second floor, and at night the light streaming down from unshuttered windows across the street was almost strong enough to read by.

When he opened the door, therefore, he did not immediately look for the light switch. The first thing he saw as he took the key out of the lock was his briefcase lying open on the bed, with its contents scattered about the covers.

He started forward quickly. He had taken about two steps when the door slammed behind him. He swung round.

A man was standing just beside the door. He was in the shadow, but the pistol in his hand was clearly visible in the light from across the street. It moved forward as the man spoke.

He spoke very softly, but, even for George's scattered senses, the strong Cockney accent in the voice was unmistakable.

"All right, chum," it said. "Gently does it. No, don't move. Just put your hands behind your head, keep absolutely quiet, and hope you won't get hurt. Got it?"

CHAPTER IX

GEORGE'S EXPERIENCE of extreme danger had been gained in the cockpits of heavy bombers and in circumstances for which he had been carefully prepared by long periods of training. Of dangers such as those which lurk behind doors in Macedonian hotels, dangers unrelated to the wearing of a uniform and the organized prosecution of a war, he had had no experience, and neither Princeton nor Harvard Law School had done anything to prepare him for one.

As, therefore, he raised his hands obediently and put them behind his head, he was suddenly aware of an overwhelming, unreasoning, and quite impracticable desire to run away somewhere and hide. He struggled against it for a moment; then the man spoke again and the desire went as suddenly as it had arrived. The blood began to pound unpleasantly in his head.

"That's right, chum," the voice was saying soothingly. "Now just go over to the window there and pull the shutters to. Then we'll have a little light on the scene. Slowly does it. Yes, you'll have to use your hands, but watch what you do with them or we'll have an accident. Don't try calling out or anything, either. All nice and quiet. That's the ticket."

George pulled the shutters to, and at the same moment the light in the room went on. He turned.

The man who stood by the light switch, watching him, was in his middle thirties, short and thickset, with dark, thinning hair. His suit was obviously a local product. Just as obviously he was not. The rawboned, snub-nosed face and the sly, insolent eyes originated, as did the Cockney accent, from somewhere within the Greater London area.

"That's better, eh?" the visitor said. "Now we can see what's what without the neighbours across the street getting nosy."

"What the hell's the idea of all this?" said George. "And who the hell are you?"

"Easy, chum." The visitor grinned. "No names, no pack drill. You can call me Arthur if you like. It's not my name, but it'll do. Lots of people call me Arthur. You're Mr. Carey, aren't you?"

"You should know." George looked at the papers strewn over the bed.

"Ah, yes. Sorry about that, Mr. Carey. I meant to clear it up before you came back. But I didn't have time for more than a glance. I haven't taken anything, naturally."

"Naturally. I don't leave money in hotel rooms."

"Oh, what a *wicked* thing to say!" said the visitor skittishly. "Tongue like a whiplash, haven't we?"

"Well, if you're not here for money, what are you here for?"

"A bit of a chat, Mr. Carey. That's all."

"Do you usually come calling with a gun?"

The visitor looked pained. "Look, chum, how was I to know you'd be reasonable—finding a stranger in your room? Supposing you'd start yelling blue murder and throwing the furniture about. I had to take precautions."

"You could have asked for me downstairs."

The visitor grinned slyly. "Could I? Ah, but maybe you don't know much about these parts, Mr. Carey. All right"—his tone suddenly became businesslike—"I'll tell you what I'll do with you. You promise not to start calling up the management or getting Charlie with me, and I'll put the gun away. O.K.?"

"All right. But I'd still like to know what you're doing here."

"I told you. I want a little private chat. That's all."

"What about?"

"I'll tell you." Arthur put his gun away inside his jacket and produced a packet of Greek cigarettes. He offered them to George. "Smoke, Mr. Carey?"

George produced a packet of his own. "No, thanks. I'll stick to these."

"Chesterfields, eh? Long time no see. Mind if I try one?"

"Help yourself."

"Thanks." He fussed about the business of giving George a light like an over-anxious host. Then he lit his own cigarette and drew on it appreciatively. "Nice tobacco," he said. "Very nice."

George sat down on the edge of the bed. "Look," he said impatiently, "what exactly is this all about? You break into my room, go through my business papers, threaten me with a gun, and then say you only want a private chat. All right, so we're chatting. Now what?"

"Mind if I sit down, Mr. Carey?"

"Do anything you like, but for Pete's sake come to the point."

"All right, all right, give us a chance." Arthur sat down gingerly on a cane-backed chair. "It's a private sort of a matter, Mr. Carey," he said. "Confidential, if you know what I mean."

"I know what you mean."

"I wouldn't like it to go any further," he persisted maddeningly.

"I've got that."

"Well now"—he cleared his throat—"I have been given to understand by certain parties," he said carefully, "that you, Mr. Carey, have been making certain inquiries of a confidential nature in the town."

"Yes."

"This afternoon you had a certain conversation with a certain woman who shall be nameless."

"Madame Vassiotis, you mean?"

"That's right."

"Then why say she shall be nameless?"

"No names, no pack drill."

"Oh, all right. Get on."

"She gave you certain information."

"What about it?"

"Easy does it, Mr. Carey. Your inquiries were *re* a certain German N.C.O. named Schirmer. Correct?"

"Correct."

"Do you mind telling me why you are making the said inquiries, Mr. Carey?"

"If you were to tell me first just why you wanted to know, I might tell you."

Arthur digested this reply for a moment or two in silence.

"And, just to make matters simpler, Arthur," George added, "I'll tell you that, although I'm a lawyer, I'm quite capable of understanding ordinary English. So what about letting your hair down and coming to the point?"

Mr. Arthur's low forehead creased with the effort of thinking. "You see, it's confidential, that's the trouble, Mr. Carey," he said unhappily.

"So you explained. But if it's so confidential that you can't talk about it, you'd better go home and let me get some sleep, hadn't you?"

"Now, don't talk like that, Mr. Carey. I'm doing my best. Look! If you were to tell me what you want to know about this chap for, I could tell certain persons who might be able to help you."

"What persons?"

"Persons with information to give."

"You mean information to *sell*, don't you?"

"I said *give*."

George examined his guest thoughtfully. "You're British, aren't you, Arthur?" he said after a moment. "Or is that confidential?"

Arthur grinned. "Want to hear me speak Greek? I speak it like a native."

"All right, then. You're a citizen of the world, then, eh?"

"Goldsmith!" said Arthur unexpectedly.

"Pardon?"

"Oliver Goldsmith," repeated Arthur; "he wrote a book called *The Citizen of the World*. We had it at school. Lot of crap about a Chinaman who comes to London and sees the sights."

"What part of London do you come from, Arthur?"

Arthur wagged a finger coyly. "Ah, naughty, naughty! That would be telling!"

"Afraid I'll check up on the British War Office lists of troops reported missing in Greece and find out which ones came from where you came from?"

"What do *you* think, chum?"

George smiled. "O.K., Arthur. Here it is. This man Schirmer I've been inquiring about was entitled to some money left by a distant relative of his in America. He was reported missing. I came here really to get confirmation of his death, but I'd also like to know if he ever had any children. That's all. I found out today that he's dead."

"From old Ma Vassiotis?"

"That's right. And now I'm on my way home."

"I get it." Arthur was thinking hard now. "Much money, is there?" he said at last.

"Just enough to make it worth my while coming here."

"And that little bit of homework you've got with you?"

"Miss Kolin, you mean? She's an interpreter."

"I get you." Arthur came to a decision. "Supposing—just supposing, mind—that there was a bit more information you could find out about this German. Would it be worth your while to stay another couple of days?"

"That would depend on the information."

"Well, supposing he'd had a wife and kids. They'd be in line for the cash, wouldn't they?"

"*Did* he have a wife and kids?"

"I'm not saying he did and I'm not saying he didn't. But just supposing—"

"If there was clear, legal proof of that to be had, I'd certainly stay. But I'm not staying just in order to listen to a lot of unconfirmed hearsay, and I'm not paying out another cent to anyone."

"Nobody's asked you to, have they?"

"Not so far."

"Nasty suspicious nature you got, eh?"

"Yes."

Arthur nodded gloomily. "Can't blame you. Tricky lot of sods in this part of the world. Look, if I give you my sacred word of honour that it'll be worth your while to stay a couple of days, will you do it?"

"You're asking rather a lot, aren't you?"

"Listen, chum. *You're* the one that's going to get a favour done. Not me!"

"That's what you say."

"Well, I can't do more. Here's the proposition. Take it or leave it. If you want the information my friends have got, stay here and do what I tell you."

"And what might that be?"

"Well, first of all, you don't say one word to that little bastard of a Captain you were chin-wagging with last night. O.K.?"

"Go on."

"All you do is go to that big café with the yellow blinds next door to the Acropolis Hotel between four and five tomorrow afternoon. Just sit there and have a cup of coffee. That's all. If you get no message from me while you're there, it's all off. If you do get a message, it'll be an appointment. Just say nothing and keep it."

"What about the interpreter?"

"If she keeps her mouth shut she can come too."

"Where would the appointment be?"

"You'd be taken to it by car."

"I see. Just one question. I'm not exactly timid, but I would like to know a bit more about these friends of yours before I do anything about meeting them. Would they be ELAS people, for instance?"

Arthur grinned. "Ask no questions and you'll be told no lies. You don't have to come if you don't want to."

"Maybe not. But I'm not half-witted. You say these friends of yours don't want money for their information. O.K., what do they want? For that matter, what do you want?"

"Sweet Fanny Adams," said Arthur cheerfully.

"Let's quit kidding."

"All right. Maybe they want to see justice done."

"Justice?"

"Yes. Ever heard of it?"

"Sure. I've heard of kidnapping too."

"Oh, blimey!" Arthur laughed. "Look, if you're as nervous as that, chum, forget it." He stood up. "I'll have to be getting along now. If you want to come, be at the café tomorrow like I said. Otherwise—" He shrugged.

"O.K. I'll think about it."

"Yes, you do that. Sorry to mess up all your papers like that, but I expect you'd sooner tidy them up yourself, really. Bye-bye for now."

"Good-bye," said George.

Almost before the word was out of his mouth, Arthur was out of the room and shutting the door noiselessly behind him.

It was not his uncertainty about bedbugs that kept George from sleeping soundly that night.

The café with the yellow blinds was in an exposed position on a busy corner, and everyone sitting in it could be clearly seen from anywhere in the main square. It was, George thought, the very last place he would have associated with the transaction of clandestine business. But then, he was not a practised conspirator. The café's air of having nothing to conceal was probably its greatest asset. In Arthur's world, no doubt, such matters were elaborately calculated.

Miss Kolin had listened blandly to George's account of his interview with Arthur and accepted without comment his decision to postpone their departure. When, however, he had gone on to say that, in view of the possible risks involved, he would leave her to decide for herself whether she would accompany him or not, she had been quite obviously amused.

"Risks, Mr. Carey? But what sort of risks?"

"How should I know?" George was irritated. "The point is that this isn't exactly the most law-abiding part of the world and this guy Arthur's way of introducing himself for a cozy chat wasn't exactly according to Emily Post, was it?"

She had shrugged. "It served its purpose."

"What do you mean?"

"Frankly, Mr. Carey, I think that it was a mistake to give the Vassiotis woman so much money."

"From my point of view, she'd earned it."

"Your point of view, Mr. Carey, is that of an American lawyer. The points of view of the Vassiotis and her friends are different."

"I see. You think that this Arthur proposition is just another shake-down then?"

"I do. You gave that Captain a hundred dollars and the Vassiotis fifty. Now Mr. Arthur and his friends would like some dollars, too."

"He emphasized that there was no question of money involved. I told you."

"You believed him?"

"All right, then, I'm the prize sucker. But, for some reason, I did believe him. For some reason, equally idiotic no doubt, I still do."

She had shrugged again. "Then you are right to keep the appointment. It will be interesting to see what happens."

That had been over breakfast. By lunch-time his confidence in his first estimate of Arthur's intentions had completely evaporated. Sitting in the café with the yellow blinds, glumly sipping coffee, he had only one consoling thought in his head: no matter what happened, no matter what they did, neither Arthur nor any of Arthur's friends was going to get one red cent for his trouble.

It was after five o'clock now. The café was three parts empty. Nobody who looked as if he might conceivably have a message to deliver had been near them.

George finished his coffee. "All right, Miss Kolin," he said, "let's pay and go."

She signalled to the waiter. When his change came, George noticed a fold of grey paper underneath it. He put it in his pocket with the change. When they had left the café, he took out the paper and unfolded it.

The message was written in a careful schoolboy hand and in pencil:

A car with the registration number 19907 will be waiting for you out-side the Cinema at 20.00 hrs. [it said]. If anyone wants to know where you are going you are going for a drive to get some air. The driver is O.K. Ask no questions. Do what he tells you. Wear comfortable shoes. Arthur.

The car was an old open Renault that George remembered having seen once before in the town. On that occasion it had been piled high with furniture. Now it was empty, and the driver stood beside it, cap in hand, gravely holding open the door for them. He was a fierce, sinewy old man with a long white moustache and skin like leather. He wore a patched shirt and a pair of old striped trousers belted in at the waist with lighting flex. The back of the car showed signs of having recently carried vege-tables as well as furniture. The old man scooped up a handful of de-caying stalks and threw them in the road before getting into his seat and driving off.

Soon they had left the town and were on a road with a signpost point-ing to Vevi, a station on the railroad east of Florina.

It was getting dark now and the old man turned on a single head-light. He drove to save gasoline, coasting down the hills with the ignition switched off, and starting up again only just before the car rolled to a standstill. The battery was down, and when the motor was not running, the headlight dimmed until it was useless. With the disappearance of the last of the daylight, every descent became a hair-raising plunge into blackness. Fortunately, they met no other traffic, but after one particu-larly sickening moment George protested.

"Miss Kolin, tell him to go slower down the hills or keep the motor running for the light. He'll kill us if he's not careful."

The driver turned right round in his seat to reply.

"He says the moon will be up presently."

"Tell him to look where he's going, for God's sake!"

"He says that there is no danger. He knows the road well."

"All right, all right. Don't say any more. Let him keep his eyes on the road."

They had been driving for nearly an hour, and the promised moon had begun to rise, when the road joined another coming from the north. Ten minutes later they turned to the left and began a long, steady climb through the hills. They passed one or two isolated stone barns, then the road began to get steadily worse. Soon the car was bouncing and sliding along over a surface littered with loose stones and rocks. After a mile or two of this, the car suddenly slowed down, lurched across the road to avoid an axle-deep pot-hole, and stopped dead.

The lurch and the sudden stop flung George against Miss Kolin. For a moment he thought that the car had broken down; then, as they disentangled themselves, he saw that the driver was standing there with the door open, motioning them to get out.

"What's the idea?" George demanded.

The old man said something.

"He says that this is where we get out," reported Miss Kolin.

George looked round. The road was a narrow ledge of track running across a bleak hillside of thorn scrub. In the bright moonlight it looked utterly desolate. From the scrub there came a steady chorus of cicadas.

"Tell him we're staying right here until he takes us where we're supposed to go."

There was a torrent of speech when this was translated.

"He says that this is as far as he can take us. This is the end of the road. We must get out and walk on. Someone will meet us on the road beyond. He must wait here. Those are his orders."

"I thought he said it was the end of the road."

"If we will come with him he will show us that he speaks the truth."

"Wouldn't you prefer to wait here, Miss Kolin?"

"Thank you, no."

They got out and began to walk on.

For about twenty yards the old man walked ahead of them, explaining something and making large dramatic gestures; then he stopped and pointed.

They had indeed come to the end of the road; or, at least, to the end of that stretch of it. At some time a big stone culvert had carried a mountain stream beneath the roadbed. Now the remains of it lay in a deep boulder-strewn gully that the stream had cut for itself in the hillside.

"He says that it was blown up by the Germans and that the winter rains have made it bigger every year."

"Are we supposed to cross it?"

"Yes. The road continues on the other side and there we will be met. He will stay by the car."

"How far on the other side will we be met?"

"He does not know."

"That advice about comfortable shoes should have warned me. Well, I suppose that now we're here we may as well go through with it."

"As you wish."

The bed of the stream was dry and they were able to pick their way over the stones and between the boulders without much trouble. Clambering up on the far side, however, was less easy, as the gully was deeper there. The night was warm and George's shirt was clinging stickily to his body by the time he had helped Miss Kolin up to the road.

They stood for a moment getting their breath and looking back. The old man waved and went back to his car.

"How long do you think it would take us to walk back to Florina from here, Miss Kolin?" George asked.

"I think he will wait. He has not been paid yet."

"I didn't hire him."

"He will expect you to pay all the same."

"We'll see about that. We'd better do what he says, anyway."

They began to walk.

Except for the chirruping of cicadas and the grating of their own footsteps, there was no sound on the road. Once they heard the faint tinkle of a distant sheep bell, but that was all. They had been walking steadily and in silence for some minutes when Miss Kolin spoke quietly.

"There is someone on the road ahead."

"Where? I can't see anyone."

"By those bushes we are coming to. He moved out of the shadow for a moment and I saw the moonlight on his face."

George felt his calves tightening as they walked on. He kept his eyes fixed on the bushes. Then he saw a movement in the shadows and a man stepped out into the road.

It was Arthur; but a rather different Arthur from the one George had talked to in the hotel. He wore breeches, a bush-shirt open at the neck, and a peaked cap. The thin pointed shoes had been replaced by heavy ankle boots. There was a pistol holster on the broad leather belt round his waist.

"Evening, chum," he said as they came up to him.

"Hullo," said George. "Miss Kolin, this is Arthur."

"Pleased to meet you, miss." The tone was humbly respectful, but George could see the shrewd, insolent eyes summing her up.

Miss Kolin nodded. "Good evening." Her hostility was clearly audible.

Arthur pursed his lips at the sound. "No trouble getting here, I hope, Mr. Carey?" he asked anxiously. He was suddenly like a week-end host apologizing for the inadequacies of the local train service.

"None to speak of. Will that old man wait for us?"

"Oh, you don't want to worry about him. Shall we go?"

"Sure. Where to?"

"It's not far. I've got transport. Just up the road here."

He led the way. They followed in silence. About a quarter of a mile further on, the road ended again. This time the obstruction was due to a landslide from the hill above, which had obliterated a section of about fifty yards. However, a narrow track had been beaten out over the debris, and they stumbled along this cautiously until the road reappeared. That is, George and Miss Kolin stumbled; Arthur went forward as sure-footedly as if he were on a city street. He was waiting for them when they got back to the road.

"Only a little way now," he said.

They walked on for another quarter of a mile. There were tamarisks growing out of the hillside here, and the moonlight cast their distorted shadows across the road. Then the shadows became solid and Arthur slowed down. Parked on a section of road which was wide enough for a vehicle to turn was a small covered truck.

"Here we are, chums. You hop in the back."

He shone a flashlight below the tailboard as he spoke. "You first, miss. Now careful. We don't want to spoil the nylons, do we? See that stirrup there? Well, just put your foot—"

He broke off as Miss Kolin climbed easily into the back of the truck. "I have been in a British army truck before," she said coldly.

"*Have* you now, miss? Well, well! That's nice, isn't it? By the way," he went on as George followed her, "I'm going to have to do the canvas up. It'll be a bit warmish, I'm afraid, but we haven't got far to go."

George groaned. "Do you have to?"

"Afraid so, chum. My pals are a bit touchy about people knowing where they are. You know—security."

"This had better be worth while. All right. Let's get on."

George and Miss Kolin sat on two box-shaped fixtures in the body of the truck, while their escort lashed down the canvas flaps. When he had finished, they heard him get into the driver's seat and start up. The truck lurched off over the stones.

Arthur was a forceful driver and the truck bucked and swayed about fantastically. Inside, it was impossible to remain seated and they stood crouched under the canvas top, clinging to the metal supports. The air inside, which was soon mixed with exhaust fumes, became almost unbreathable. George was dimly aware of the truck turning several hairpin bends and he knew that they were climbing steeply, but he quickly lost all sense of direction. After ten minutes or more of excruciating discomfort, he was beginning to think that he would have to shout to Arthur to pull up, when, after yet another turn, the truck ran on to a comparatively smooth surface and stopped. A moment later the rear canvas was unlashed, moonlight and air streamed in, and Arthur's face appeared at the tailboard.

He grinned. "Bit bumpy, was it?"

"Yes."

They climbed out stiffly and found themselves standing on what had once been the flagged courtyard of a small house. All that remained of the house itself was a ruined wall and a pile of debris.

"ELAS boys did that," Arthur explained; "the other lot were using it as a stronghold. We go this way."

The ruined house was on the summit of a pine-clad hill. They followed Arthur along a track which led from the house down through the trees.

They walked silently over pine needles for about fifty yards, then Arthur halted.

"Wait a tick," he said.

They waited while he went on ahead. It was very dark under the trees and there was a strong smell of pine resin. After the atmosphere in the truck, the soft, cool air was delicious. A faint murmur of voices came from the darkness ahead.

"Did you hear that, Miss Kolin?"

"Yes. They were speaking Greek, but I could not distinguish the words. It sounded like a sentry challenging and receiving a reply."

"What do you make of all this?"

"I think we should have left word with someone where we were going."

"We didn't know where we were going, but I did what I could. If we're not back by the time the *femme de chambre* cleans my room in the morning, she'll find a letter addressed to the manager on my bureau. In it there's the number of that old man's car and a note of explanation for the Captain."

"That was wise, Mr. Carey. I have noticed something—" She broke off. "He's coming back."

Her hearing was very acute. Several seconds went by before George was able to hear the soft rustle of approaching footsteps.

Arthur appeared out of the darkness. "O.K., chums," he said. "Here we go. We'll have a bit of light on the scene in half a tick."

They followed him down the path. It was getting less steep now. Then, as it levelled off, Arthur switched on a flashlight and George saw the sentry leaning against a tree with his rifle under his arm. He was a thin, middle-aged man in khaki drill trousers and a ragged singlet. He watched them intently as they went by.

They were clear of the pine trees now and there was a house in front of them.

"Used to be a village down the hill there," said Arthur. "Wiped out by some of the boys. All flat except our place, and we had to patch that up a good bit. Left to rot, it was. Belonged to some poor bastard of a deviationist who got his throat cut." He had become the week-end host again, proud and fond of his house and wanting his guests to share his enthusiasm.

It was a two-story building with stuccoed walls and broad overhanging eaves. The shutters over the windows were all closed.

There was another sentry by the door. Arthur said something to him and the man shone a light on their faces before nodding to Arthur and motioning them on. Arthur opened the door and they followed him into the house.

There was a long narrow hall with a staircase and several doorways. An oil lamp hung from a hook by the front door. There was no plaster on the ceiling and very little left on the walls. It looked like what it was, a house which had been gutted by bomb blast or shellfire and temporarily repaired.

"Here we are," said Arthur; "H.Q. mess and anteroom."

He had opened the door of what appeared to be a dining-room. There was a bare trestle table with benches on either side. On the table there were bottles, glasses, a pile of knives and forks, and another oil lamp. In a corner of the room, on the floor, there were empty bottles.

"Nobody at home," said Arthur. "I dare say you could do with a snifter, eh? Help yourselves. The you-know-what is just across the hall on the right if anybody's interested. I'll be back in a jiffy."

He went out of the room, shutting the door after him. They heard him clattering up the stairs.

George looked at the bottles. There was Greek wine and plum brandy. He looked at Miss Kolin.

"Drink, Miss Kolin?"

"Yes, please."

He poured out two brandies. She picked hers up, drank it down at a gulp, and held the glass out to be filled again. He filled it.

"Pretty strong stuff this, isn't it?" he said tentatively.

"I hope so."

"Well, I didn't expect to be taken to a place like a military headquarters. What do you think it is?"

"I have an idea." She lit a cigarette. "You remember four days ago in Salonika there was a bank robbery?"

"I remember something about it. Why?"

"Next day, in the train to Florina, I read the newspaper reports of it. It gave an exact description of the truck that was used."

"What about it?"

"We came here in that truck tonight."

"What? You're kidding."

"No." She drank some more brandy.

"You're mistaken then. After all, there must be dozens, hundreds maybe, of these British army trucks still about in Greece."

"Not with slots for false number-plates."

"What do you mean?"

"I noticed the slots when he was shining the flashlight for me to get in. The false plates were on the floor in the back of the truck. When we stopped, I put them where the moonlight would shine as we got out. The part of the number I could see was the same as the one in the newspaper report."

"Are you absolutely sure?"

"I do not like it any more than you, Mr. Carey."

But George was remembering something that Colonel Chrysantos had said: *"They are clever and dangerous and the police do not catch them."*

"If they get half a suspicion we know anything—" he began.

"Yes. It could be most disagreeable." She raised her glass to drink again and then stopped.

There was the sound of footsteps coming down the stairs.

George drank his brandy down quickly and got out a cigarette. The learned judge, whose secretary he had been, had once said that it was impossible to practise law for very many years without learning that no case, however matter-of-fact it might seem, could be considered entirely proof against the regrettable tendency of reality to assume the shape and proportions of melodrama. At the time, George had smiled politely and wondered if he would be given to making such half-baked generalizations when *he* became a judge. Now he remembered.

The door opened.

The man who came into the room was fair and deep-chested, with heavy shoulders and big hands. He might have been any age between thirty and forty. The face was strong, with muscular cheeks, a determined mouth, and cool, watchful eyes. He held himself very erect and the bush-shirt he wore stretched tightly across his chest. With the revolver belt at his waist he looked almost as if he were in uniform.

He glanced swiftly from George to Miss Kolin as Arthur, who had followed him in, shut the door and bustled forward.

"Sorry to keep you waiting," Arthur said. "Mr. Carey, this is my chief. He speaks a bit of English—I taught him—but go easy on the long words. He knows who you are."

The newcomer clicked his heels and gave the slightest of bows.

"Schirmer," he said curtly, "Franz Schirmer. I think you wish to speak with me."

CHAPTER X

THE GERMAN FORCES which withdrew from Greece in October 1944 were very different in both numbers and quality from the field army which had invaded the country just over three years earlier.

If the Twelfth Army of General von List, with its crack panzer divisions and its record of success in the Polish campaign, had epitomized the irresistible strength of the *Wehrmacht*, the occupation forces, setting out to make their way home while there was still a road home left open to them, epitomized no less strikingly the *Wehrmacht's* ultimate exhaustion. The earlier practice of resting troops from the fighting fronts by giving them tours of occupation duty had long been abandoned as a luxury. The Lines of Communication Division which garrisoned the Salonika area in 1944 was, for the most part, made up of men who, for one reason or another, were considered unfit for combatant duty: debilitated survivors from the Russian front, the older men, the weaklings, and those who, because of either wounds or sickness, were of low medical categories.

For Sergeant Schirmer, the war had ended on that day in Italy when he had obeyed the order of an inexperienced officer to make a parachute jump over a wood. The comradeship of fighting men in a *corps d'élite* has meant a great deal to a great many men. To Sergeant Schirmer it had given something that his upbringing had always denied him—his belief in himself as a man. The months in the hospital which had followed the accident, the court of inquiry, the rehabilitation centre, the medical examinations, and the posting to Greece had been a bitter epilogue to the only period of his life in which he felt he had known happiness. Many times he had wished that the tree branch which had merely broken his hip had pierced his breast and killed him.

If the Ninety-fourth Garrison Regiment at Salonika had been the kind of unit in which a soldier like Sergeant Schirmer could have come to take even a grudging pride, many things no doubt would have been very different. But it was not a unit in which any self-respecting man could have taken pride. The officers (with a few exceptions such as Lieutenant Leubner) were the army's unemployables, the kind of officers whom unit commanders hasten to get rid of when they have the chance and who spend most of their service lives held on depot establishments awaiting postings. The N.C.O.'s (again with a few exceptions) were incompetent and corrupt. The rank and file were a disgruntled and decrepit assembly of old soldiers, chronic invalids, dullards, and petty delinquents. Almost the first order which the Sergeant had received from an officer on joining had been an order to remove his paratrooper's badge. That had been his introduction to the regiment, and as time went by, he had learned to fortify and console himself with his contempt for it.

The German withdrawal from Thrace was an ignominious affair. The depot soldiers responsible for the staff work had had little experience of moving troops in the field and still less of supplying them while they were on the move. Units like the Ninety-fourth Garrison Regiment, and there was more than one, could do little to make good the deficiencies. The knowledge that British raiding forces were advancing rapidly from the south in order to harass the retreat, and that *andarte* bands were already hovering aggressively on the flanks, may have lent urgency to the withdrawal, but, in doing so, it had also added to the confusion. It was traffic congestion rather than any brilliant planning by Phengaros that led to the ambushing of Sergeant Schirmer's convoy.

He was one of the last of his regiment to leave the Salonika area. Contempt for his regiment he might have, but that did not prevent his doing his utmost to see that the fraction of it that he controlled carried out its orders properly. As headquarters weapons-instructor, he had no platoon responsibilities and came under the command of an engineer officer in charge of a special rear-guard party. This officer was Lieutenant Leubner, and he had been detailed to carry out a series of important demolitions in the wake of the retreat.

The Sergeant liked Lieutenant Leubner, who had lost a hand in Italy; he felt that the Lieutenant understood him. Between them they organized the party in two detachments, and the Sergeant was given command of one of them.

He drove his men and himself unmercifully and succeeded in completing his part of the work in accordance with the time-table issued with the movement order. During the night of the 23rd of October his detachment loaded the trucks they were to take with them and moved out of Salonika. They were exactly on schedule.

His orders were to go through Vodena, deal with the gasoline dump on the Apsalos road, and then rendezvous with Lieutenant Leubner at the bridge by Vodena. It had been anticipated that the laying of the demolition charges for the bridge would call for the united efforts of the two detachments if it were to be done to schedule. The time of the rendezvous had been fixed for dawn.

At first light that day Sergeant Schirmer was at Yiannitsa, only a little over halfway along the road to Vodena, and trying desperately to force a way for his detachment past a column of tank transporters. The transporters should have been fifty miles further on, but had themselves been held up by a column of horse-drawn wagons which had debouched from the Naoussa road twelve hours behind schedule. The Sergeant was two hours late when he passed through Vodena. Had he been on time, Phengaros's men would have missed him by an hour.

It had rained during the night, and with the rising sun the air became stiflingly humid; moreover, the Sergeant had had no sleep for thirty hours. Yet, as he sat beside the driver of the leading truck, he had little difficulty in staying awake. The machine-pistol lying across his knees reminded him of the need for vigilance, and the dull pain of his overworked hip prevented his settling into too comfortable a position. But his fatigue manifested itself in other ways. His eyes, scouring an area of hillside above the bend in the road towards which they were climbing, kept shifting focus suddenly, so that he had to shake his head before he could see properly; and his thoughts wandered with dreamlike inconsequence from the problems of the task in hand, and the possible plight of Lieutenant Leubner's detachment, to the attack on Eben-Emael, to a girl he had had in Hanover, and then, uneasily, to the moment in Salonika forty-eight hours earlier when Kyra had wept as he had said good-bye to her.

The weeping of women always made the Sergeant feel uneasy. It was not that he was sentimental where women were concerned; it was simply that the sound of weeping always seemed to presage his own misfortunes. There had been the time in Belgium, for instance, when that old woman had stood bleating because they had killed her cow. Two days after that he had been wounded. There had been the time in Crete when it had been necessary for discipline to put some of the married men up against a wall and shoot them. A month later, in Benghazi, he had gone down with dysentery. There had been the time in Italy when some of the lads had fooled about with a young girl. Two days before his jumping accident, *that* had been. He would never admit to such an unreasoning and childish superstition, of course; but if he ever married, it would be to some girl who would not weep even if he beat the living daylights out of her. Let her scream as much as she liked, let her try and kill him if she wanted to, and dared, but let there be no weeping. It meant bad luck.

It was the off-side front wheel of the truck that exploded the mine. The Sergeant felt the lift of it a split second before his head hit the canopy of the driver's cab.

Then, there was something wet on his face and a thin, high singing in his ears. He was lying face-downwards and everything was dark except for one winking disk of light. Something gave him a violent blow in the side, but he was too tired to cry out or even to feel pain. He could hear men's voices and knew that they were speaking Greek. Then the sounds of their voices faded and he began to fall through the air towards the trees below, defending himself against the cruel branches by locking his ankles tightly and pointing his toes, as he had been taught in the parachute jumping school. The trees engulfed him with a sigh that seemed to come from his own lips.

When he regained consciousness for the second time, there seemed to be nothing wet on his face, but something stretching the skin of it. The disk of light was still there, but it no longer winked. He became aware now of his arms stretched out above his head, as if he were going to dive into water. He could feel his heart beating, sending pain from all over his body into his head. His legs felt warm. He moved his fingers and they dug into grit and pebbles. Consciousness began to flood back. There was something the matter with his eyelids and he could not see properly, but he kept looking at the disk of light and moved his head slightly. Suddenly, he realized that the disk was a small white pebble lying in a patch of sunlight. Then he remembered that he was in Greece and had been in a truck that had been hit. With an effort, he rolled on to his side.

The force of the explosion had overturned the truck and smashed the floor of it to matchwood, but the main blast had missed the driver's cab. The Sergeant had been lying in an oil-drenched litter of empty gasoline cans and debris, with his face in the mess of blood which had poured from his head wound. The blood had congealed now on his cheeks and in his eyes. The wreckage of the truck hung over him, shading all but his legs from the sun. There was no sound except the chirping of cicadas and faint dripping noises from the truck.

He began to move his limbs. Though he knew that he had hurt his head, he did not as yet know the extent of his injuries. His great fear was that his hip had been broken again. For several long seconds all he could think of was the X-ray picture the surgeon had shown him of the thick metal pin which had been inserted to strengthen the neck of the damaged bone. If that had been torn away, he was finished. He moved the leg carefully. The hip was very painful, but it had been painful before the mine had exploded. Fatigue always made it painful. He became bolder and, drawing the leg up under him, began to sit up. It was then that he noticed that all his equipment had gone. He remembered the Greek voices and the blow he had felt and began to realize what had happened.

His head was throbbing horribly, but the hip seemed to be all right. He dragged himself to his knees. A moment later he vomited. The effort exhausted him and he lay down again to rest. He knew that the head wound might be serious. It was not the amount of the bleeding that concerned him—he had seen plenty of scalp wounds and knew that they bled profusely—but the possibility of there being internal bleeding from the concussion. However, he would know soon enough if there were, and there was, in any case, nothing he could do about it. His immediate task was to find out what had happened to the rest of the detachment and, if possible, take steps to deal with the situation. He made another effort to get to his feet and, after a bit, succeeded.

He looked about him. His watch had gone, but the position of the sun told him that less than an hour had elapsed since the crash. The wreckage of the truck lay across the road, completely blocking it. The body of the driver was nowhere to be seen. He moved out cautiously into the middle of the road and looked down the hill.

The second truck had stopped slewed across the road a hundred yards away. Three German soldiers lay in the road by it. Beyond he could just see the canopy of the driver's cab belonging to the third truck. He set off slowly down the hill, pausing every now and then to get his strength back. The sun beat down and the flies buzzed round his head. It seemed an enormous distance to the second truck. He began to feel that he was going to vomit again, and lay down in the shade of a bush to recover. Then he went on.

The soldiers in the road were quite dead. One of them, who looked as if he had first been wounded by a grenade burst, had his throat cut. All the arms and equipment had been taken, but the contents of two haversacks were strewn on the ground. The truck had some bullet holes in it and was scarred by grenade bursts, but it seemed all right otherwise. For several wild moments he considered turning it round and driving back to Vodena, but the road was not wide enough to turn in and he knew that even if it had been, he would not have had the strength to do the job.

He could see the third truck plainly now, and with it more dead men. One of them was hanging over the side of it, his arms dangling grotesquely. It seemed probable that the whole of his detachment had become casualties. In any case, there was little point in investigating further. Militarily speaking, it had certainly ceased to exist. It would be in order for him, then, to look to his own safety.

He leaned against the side of the truck to rest again and caught sight of his face in the driving mirror. The blood had congealed all over his hair as well as in his eyes and on his face; his whole head looked as inhuman if it had been smashed to a pulp; it was easy to see why the *andartes* had taken him for dead.

His heart leaped suddenly with fear and sent a shaft of pain to the top of his head. The *andartes* had gone for the moment, but there was more than a possibility that they would return with drivers for the two serviceable trucks. It was even possible that they had left a sentry, and that, somewhere on the hillside above, the sights of a rifle were being steadied on him at that very moment. But at the same moment reason told him that there was very probably no sentry, and that, even if there were, the man had already had more than enough time to shoot if he had intended to do so.

Nevertheless, the place was dangerous. Whether the *andartes* returned or whether they did not, it would not be very long before the local inhabitants ventured on the scene. There were still plenty of pickings for them; the boots of the dead, the gasoline cans, the tires on the trucks, the tool kits. The *andartes* had taken scarcely anything. He would have to get away quickly.

For a moment or two he thought of trying to go ahead on foot in the hope of reaching the fuel dump, but he soon abandoned the idea. Even if he had had enough strength to walk that distance, the chance of his being able to do so in broad daylight unseen by the local inhabitants would be remote. In that area and at that time, a solitary German soldier, wounded and unarmed, would be lucky if he were not tortured before he was stoned to death by the women. The road back to Vodena would be even more dangerous. He must wait for darkness, therefore; and that might give him time to recover his strength too. His immediate course of action, then, was plain enough; he must find water, food, and a place to hide. Later on, if he were still alive, he would decide what to do next.

The water bottles had all been taken. He dragged an empty gasoline can out of the truck and began to drain the radiator into it. When it was half full he realized that he would not have the strength to carry more. There was still plenty left in the radiator, and it was not too hot to drink now. When he had slaked his thirst, he soaked his handkerchief in the water and sponged the blood from his face and eyes. His head he did not touch for fear of starting the bleeding again.

Next he looked for food. The *andartes* had taken the sack with the supplies in it, but he knew the ways of army truck-drivers and went to the tool-box. There were two emergency rations there, some sticks of chocolate, and the driver's greatcoat. He put the rations and the chocolate in the greatcoat pocket and slung it over his shoulder. Then he picked up the can of water and limped back slowly up the road.

He had already decided on his hiding-place. He remembered how innocent the hillside above had looked when he had been coming up the road in the truck, and how well it had concealed the attackers. It would conceal him in the same way. He left the road and started to climb.

It took him half an hour to climb a hundred yards. Once he lay for nearly ten minutes, too exhausted to move, before he could bring himself to crawl painfully on. The hillside was very steep and he had to drag the heavy water can behind him. Several times he thought of leaving it and returning later to pick it up, but some instinct warned him that water was more necessary to him now than food and that he could not risk losing it. He crawled on until at last he could go no farther and lay for a time retching helplessly, unable even to crawl out of the sun. Flies began to settle on his face without his being able to brush them away. After a while, tortured by the flies, he opened his eyes to see where he was.

There was a clump of thorn bushes a yard or so away, with a tamarisk growing among them. With a tremendous effort he dragged the can of water into the shade of the tree and crawled in among the thorn bushes with the greatcoat. The last thing he saw was a column of dense black smoke rising from somewhere beyond the hill in the direction of the fuel dump. Then, realizing that one at least of his decisions had been made for him, he lay face-downwards on the coat and slept.

It was dark when he awoke. The pain in his head was agonizing, and although the night was warm, he was shivering violently. He crawled to the can of water and dragged it nearer to his bed. He knew now that he had a bout of malaria to add to his troubles and to reduce his resistance to a possible infection of the head wound. He might be going to die, but the knowledge did not trouble him. He would fight for life as long as he was able. If he were defeated, it would not matter. He had done the best he could.

He lay among the thorn bushes for nearly four days. For most of the time he was in a sort of half-waking dream state, dimly aware of the changes from darkness to light, but of little else that was outside him. At some moments, he would know with one bit of his mind that he was delirious and talking to people who were not there; at others, he would be lost in the recurrent nightmare of the fall through the trees, which never seemed to end twice in the same way.

On the third day, he awoke from a deep sleep to find that the pain in his head had lessened, that he could think clearly, and that he felt hungry. He ate part of one of the emergency rations and then inspected his water supply. The can was nearly empty, but there was enough to last for that day. For the first time since he had crawled up the hill, he got to his feet. He felt horribly weak, but he forced himself to walk out of his hiding-place and look down at the road.

The two serviceable trucks had disappeared and, to his astonishment, the damaged one had been set on fire and burned out. The charred wreckage of it looked like a black stain on the limestone grit of the road. He had neither seen nor heard anything of this bonfire.

He went back to his hiding-place and slept again. Once, during the night, he awoke to the sound of many planes flying overhead and knew that the final stage of the withdrawal had been reached. The *Luftwaffe* was evacuating the Yidha airfield. He lay awake for a time listening and feeling very much alone, but eventually he went back to sleep. The following morning he felt stronger and was able to go in search of water. He kept away from the road and, about half a mile down the hill, found a stream, in which he washed after replenishing his drinking-water supply.

He had crossed a terraced vineyard to get to the stream, and on his way back he almost ran into a man and a woman working there. However, he saw them just in time and, retracing his steps, made his way round the vineyard. In doing so, he came near the road and found the seven freshly dug graves, with a steel helmet and a cairn on each. There was a stake driven into the ground with a note fastened to it giving the number and names of those buried there and asking that the site should not be disturbed. It was signed by Lieutenant Leubner.

Sergeant Schirmer was strangely moved. It had not once occurred to him that the Lieutenant might find time to interest himself in the fate of the lost detachment. No doubt it had been he who had burned the damaged truck and removed the others. A good officer, the Lieutenant.

He looked at the note again. Seven dead. That meant that three, including the missing driver, had been made prisoner or escaped. The paper was already somewhat tattered and it had probably been there for over two days. It was bitter to know that friendly hands had been so near while he had lain hidden and oblivious among the thorn bushes. For the first time since the mine had exploded he was conscious of a feeling of despair.

He thrust it away angrily. What had he to despair of? His inability to rejoin the Ninety-fourth Garrison Regiment, fumbling its way back to the Fatherland with its tail between its legs? The lack of someone to ask for orders? How the instructors at the parachute training school would have laughed!

He looked down again at the graves. He had no cap or helmet and so could not salute. He drew himself up into the position of attention and clicked his heels respectfully. Then he picked up his water can and made his way back to the hillside and the thorn bushes.

After he had finished the remains of the first emergency ration, he lay down to think things out.

The expedition for water had tired him sufficiently for him to realize that he was still very weak. Another twenty-four hours must elapse before he was fit to move. The food he had left could probably be made to last that long. After that he must forage.

And then what?

The German forces had probably left Vodena two days or more ago. It was idle to suppose that he could catch up with them now. He would have hundreds of miles of difficult country to travel before he could do that. His only chance of getting through unseen would be to avoid the roads; yet if he did that, the long, hard marches would soon lame him. He could try the railroad, of course, but that was almost certainly in the hands of the Greeks again by now. His despair returned, and this time it was not so easily dismissed. The plain fact was that there was nowhere he could reasonably go. He was completely cut off in hostile territory where capture or surrender meant death and the ways of escape were all closed. The only thing he could do, it seemed, was to go on living under the thorn bush like an animal, stealing what food he could from the fields. An escaped prisoner of war would be in a better position; at least he would have had time to prepare for the venture. He, Schirmer, was relatively helpless. He had no civilian clothes, no money, no papers, no food worth speaking of; moreover, he was still suffering from the after-effects of being blown up by a mine and an attack of malaria. He needed time to recover completely and time to plan. Above all, he needed someone to help him get identity papers. Clothes and money he might steal, but to steal papers printed in a language he could not read, and risk using them as his own, would be folly.

And then he thought of Kyra; Kyra, who had wept so bitterly when he had had to say good-bye to her, who had implored him, foolishly, to desert; the one friend he possessed in this hostile, treacherous land.

She had a small photographic processing business in Salonika. He had seen the bold AGFA advertisement sign outside her shop one day and gone in to see if he could buy some film for his camera. She had had no film to sell—it had been hard to come by at the time—but he had been attracted by her and had returned to the shop whenever he had had time off. There was little processing work to be had and to make more money she had set up a small curtained "studio" for the taking of identity-card and passport photographs. When a local military identity card had been issued to the occupation forces, he had been able to suggest to the officer responsible for the issue in his own unit, that she should be commissioned to do all the photographic work. He had also brought her army food. She lived with her brother in two rooms over the shop. However, the brother was a night duty clerk in a hotel which had been commandeered by the occupation headquarters, and was only at home in the daytime. Quite soon the Sergeant had been able to apply for a sleeping-out pass. Kyra was a full-blooded young woman with simple and readily fulfillable demands to make. The Sergeant was both lusty and skillful. The relationship had proved most satisfactory.

Now it could be made to serve another purpose.

Salonika was seventy-four kilometres away by road. That meant that he would have to cover at least a hundred kilometres in order to keep away from the towns and villages. If he marched in daylight it would probably take him about four days to get there. If he played for safety and moved only at night, it would take much longer. He must not work his hip too hard. He must allow, too, for the time he would have to spend getting food. The sooner he started, the better. His spirits rose. The following night, having eaten the last of the army rations and with only the chocolate in his pocket for emergencies, he set off.

It took him eight days to reach his destination. Travelling at night, without map and compass to guide him, had proved too difficult. He had lost himself repeatedly. After the third night he had decided that he must accept the greater risk and travel by day. He had found it easier than he expected. Even in the plain, there was plenty of cover to move in, and it had been possible, except in the vicinity of Yiannitsa, to keep fairly close to the road. Food was the greatest difficulty. From an isolated farm he was able to steal some eggs, and on another day he milked a straying goat; but mostly he lived on the wild fruit he could pick. It was not until the end of the seventh day that he decided that the situation had become desperate enough for him to eat his chocolate.

It was about ten o'clock in the morning when he reached the outskirts of Salonika. He was near the railroad and in an area that offered reasonable opportunities for concealment. He decided to stop there and wait until nightfall before entering the city.

Now that his journey was nearly done, the thing that most concerned him was his appearance. The wound on his scalp was healing well and would not excite much curiosity. He disliked the stubble of beard he had grown, but only because it was unsoldierly; he did not think that it would make him too conspicuous. The trouble was his uniform. It seemed to him that to walk through the streets of Salonika in a German uniform now would be to invite arrest or assassination. Something would have to be done.

He moved nearer to the railroad and began to reconnoitre along it. Eventually he came upon what he was looking for—a trackwalker's hut. It was padlocked, but there were some heavy iron rail-chairs on the ground near by and he used one to smash the hasp through which the padlock was fastened.

He had hoped to find a pair of overalls or a workman's blouse of some sort in the hut, but there was no clothing there of any kind. There was, however, a workman's dinner wrapped in a sheet of newspaper: a piece of bread, some olives, and half a bottle of wine.

He took it back to his hiding-place and swallowed it greedily. The wine made him drowsy and he slept for a while afterwards. When he awoke, he felt much refreshed and began to reconsider the problem of his clothing.

He had on a grey cotton singlet under his tunic. If he discarded the tunic and belted his uniform trousers, the top part of him would look like a dock labourer. At night, when the colour and material of the trousers could not be seen clearly, the only things that would give him away would be his jackboots. He tried to conceal them by wearing the trousers over the boots instead of tucked inside them. The result was not altogether satisfactory, but he decided that it was sufficiently so. The risks he would have to run to steal clothing were probably greater than the risk of having his boots identified in the darkness. So far, good fortune had been with him. It would be foolish to try it too hard within sight of his objective.

By eight o'clock that night it was quite dark and he set off for the city.

He had a disagreeable surprise when he reached it. The quarters through which he had to pass were ablaze with lights. The citizens of Salonika were celebrating their liberation from the occupation forces and the arrival of the "Macedonian Group of Divisions" of ELAS.

It was a fantastic scene. Along the waterfront, long chains of screaming, singing people swayed and capered to music blaring from cafés and bars. The restaurants were jammed. Shrieking mobs danced on the chairs and tables. Everywhere there were groups of drunken *andartes*, many of them Bulgars, staggering about, shouting wildly, firing rifles into the air, and fetching women out of the brothels to dance with them in the streets. To the Sergeant, hurrying along discreetly in what shadows he could find, the city seemed like some vast orgiastic fairground.

Kyra's shop was in a narrow street near the Eski Juma. There were no bars or cafés in it and it was relatively quiet. The shopkeepers with shutters had taken the precaution of putting them up; others had nailed boards across their windows. Kyra's windows were protected in this way and the shop was in darkness; but there was a light in the window above it.

He was relieved at this. He had feared that she might be out taking part in the carnival in the streets, and that he would have to wait for her return. The fact that she was in also meant that she did not share in the popular rejoicing at the turn of events. That was all to the good.

He looked round carefully to see that his arrival had not been witnessed by anyone who might know him by sight; then, satisfied on this point, he rang the bell.

After a moment or two he heard her come down the stairs and cross the shop to the door. The boards prevented his seeing her. He heard her stop, but the door did not open.

"Who is it?" she said in Greek.

"Franz."

"God in heaven!"

"Let me in."

He heard her fumbling with the bolts and then the door opened. He stepped inside, shut the door quickly behind him, and took her in his arms. He could feel her trembling as he kissed her, and then she pressed away from him with a gasp of fear.

"What are you doing here?"

He told her what had happened to him and what he planned.

"But you cannot stay."

"I have to."

"No, you cannot."

"Why not, my beloved? There is no risk."

"I am already suspect because I have loved a German."

"What can they do?"

"I may be arrested."

"Absurd. If they arrested every woman in this place who has loved a German, they would need an army to guard them."

"It is different with me. The *andartes* have arrested Niki."

"What for?" Niki was her brother.

"He is accused of spying for the Germans and informing. When he has confessed and accused others, they will kill him."

"The swine! Nevertheless, I must stay, beloved."

"You must surrender. You would be a prisoner of war."

"Don't you believe it. They would cut my throat."

"No. There are many German soldiers here. Deserters. No harm comes to them if they say they are sympathizers."

"If they say they are Communists, you mean?"

"What does it matter?"

"You class me with these deserter swine?"

"Of course not, beloved. I wish only to save you."

"Good. First I need food. Then a bed. I will use Niki's room tonight. I am fit for nothing but sleep."

"But you cannot stay here, Franz. You cannot." She began to sob.

He gripped her arms. "No tears, my beloved, and no arguments. You understand? I give the orders. When I have eaten and rested, then we can talk. Now, you can show me what there is to eat."

He had driven his fingers deep into her arm muscles, and when she stopped weeping he knew that he had frightened as well as hurt her. That was as it should be. There would be no more disobedience for the present.

They went up to the apartment. When she saw him in the light, she gave a cry of dismay, but he cut short her further lamentations impatiently.

"I am hungry," he said.

She put together a meal for him and watched him while he ate it. She was silent now and thoughtful, but he scarcely noticed her. He was planning. First he would sleep, and then he would see about getting a civilian suit. It was a pity that her brother Niki was so undersized; his clothes would be far too small. She would have to buy a second-hand suit somewhere. Then she could find out exactly what papers he would need in order to move about freely. There was the language difficulty, of course; but perhaps he could overcome that by pretending to be a Bulgar or an Albanian; there would be plenty of that sort of scum about now. After that, he would have to decide where to go. It would be an awkward problem. There were not many countries left in which a German soldier would be welcomed and assisted to repatriate himself. There was Spain, of course—he might get there by sea—or Turkey. . . .

But his head was drooping on his chest, and his eyes would no longer stay open. He roused himself sufficiently to go into the bedroom. At the bed he turned and looked back. Kyra was standing in the door watching him. She smiled reassuringly. He sank down on the bed and went to sleep.

It was still dark, and he could not have been asleep for much more than two hours, when he awoke in response to a violent shaking of his arm and a blow in the back.

He rolled over and opened his eyes.

Two men with pistols in their hands were standing looking down at him. They wore the elementary kind of uniform which he had seen on the *andartes* rioting about in the streets a few hours earlier. Those, however, had all been very drunk; these were very sober and businesslike. They were lean, sour-looking young men with smart belts and brassards on their arms. He guessed that they were *andarte* officers. One of them spoke sharply in German.

"Get up."

He obeyed slowly, overcoming a longing for sleep more desperate than any sensation of fear. He hoped that they would kill him quickly so that he could rest.

"Your name?"

"Schirmer."

"Rank?"

"Sergeant. Who are you?"

"You'll find out. She says you were a paratrooper and an instructor. Is that correct?"

"Yes."

"Where did you win your Iron Cross?"

The Sergeant was sufficiently awake now to appreciate the necessity of lying. "In Belgium," he said.

"Do you want to live?"

"Who doesn't?"

"Fascists don't. They are death-lovers, so we kill them. True democrats want to live. They prove their desire by fighting with their class comrades against the Fascists and the capitalist-imperialist aggressors."

"Who are these aggressors?"

"Reactionaries and their Anglo-American bosses."

"I don't know anything about politics."

"Naturally. You have had no chance of learning about them. They are simple enough, however. Fascists die, true democrats live. You can, of course, choose freely which you are to be, but as time is short and there is much work to be done, you can have only twenty seconds to make up your mind. The usual time allowed is ten seconds, but you are an N.C.O., a skilled soldier, and a valuable instructor. Also you are not a deserter. You are entitled to think carefully before you accept the sacred responsibility which is offered to you."

"If I claim the rights of a prisoner of war?"

"You are no prisoner, Schirmer. You have not surrendered. You are still in the thick of the fight. At present you are an enemy of Greece, and" —the *andarte* raised his pistol—"we have much to avenge."

"And if I accept?"

"You will be given an early opportunity of demonstrating your political reliability, your loyalty, and your skill. The twenty seconds have long ago departed. What do you wish to say?"

The Sergeant shrugged. "I accept."

"Then salute," the *andarte* said sharply.

For an instant the Sergeant's right arm started to move, and in that instant he saw the *andarte's* finger tighten on the trigger. He clenched the fist of his left hand and raised it above his head.

The *andarte* smiled thinly. "Very good. You may come with us in a moment." He went to the bedroom door and opened it. "But first there is another matter to attend to."

He beckoned Kyra into the room. She walked stiffly, her face a tear-stained mask of fear. She did not look at the Sergeant.

"This woman," the *andarte* said with a smile, "was good enough to inform us that you were here. Her brother was a Fascist-collaborationist spy. Her object in betraying you was to convince us that she has a true democratic spirit. What do you think about that, Comrade Schirmer?"

"I think she is a Fascist bitch," said the Sergeant shortly.

"Excellent. That was my own thought. You will learn fast."

The *andarte* glanced at his companion and nodded.

The companion's gun jerked up. Before Kyra could scream or the Sergeant could even think of protesting, three shots had crashed out. The shock waves brought down a small piece of plaster from the ceiling. The Sergeant felt it tap his shoulder as he saw the girl, her mouth still open, slammed against the wall by the force of the heavy bullets. Then she sank to the floor without a sound.

The *andarte* officer looked at her intently for a moment, then nodded again and walked out of the room.

The Sergeant followed. He knew that sometime when he was not so tired and confused he would feel horror at what had just happened. He had liked Kyra.

Sergeant Schirmer served in the Democratic Army of General Markos for just over four years.

After the December rebellion of '44 and the promotion of Markos to the command of the army, he had been sent to Albania. There, he had been an instructor in a training camp set up to discipline the guerrilla bands then being organized in larger formations, in preparation for the campaign of '46. It was in this camp that he met Arthur.

Arthur had been in a British Commando force which had raided a German headquarters in North Africa. He had been wounded and captured. The German officer in charge had chosen to ignore the standing order about shooting captured Commando men and had put Arthur in with a batch of other British prisoners who were being sent to Germany via Greece and Yugoslavia. In Yugoslavia, Arthur had escaped and spent the rest of the war fighting with the Tito Partisans. He had not troubled to return to England when the war ended, and had been one of the instructors provided by Tito to assist Markos.

In Arthur the Sergeant found a kindred spirit. They were both professional soldiers and had both served in *corps d'élite* as N.C.O.'s. Neither had any emotional ties with his native land. Both loved soldiering for its own sake. Above all, they shared the same outlook on matters of politics.

During his service with the Partisans, Arthur had listened to so much Marxist patter that he knew a great deal of it by heart. At moments of stress or boredom he would recite it at length and at lightning speed. It had disconcerted the Sergeant when he had heard it for the first time, and he had approached Arthur privately on the subject.

"I was not aware, Corporal," he had said in the clumsy mixture of Greek, English, and German they used in order to converse; "I did not think that you were a Red."

Arthur had grinned. "No? I'm one of the most politically reliable men in the outfit."

"So?"

"So. Don't I prove it? Look how many slogans I know. I can talk like the book."

"I see."

"Of course, I don't know what this dialectical-materialism stuff means, but then I could never understand what the Bible was all about either. At school we had to say bits of the Bible. I always used to get top marks for Scripture. Here I'm politically reliable."

"You do not believe in the cause for which we fight?"

"No more than you do, Sergeant. I leave that to the amateurs. Soldiering's my job. What do I want with causes?"

The Sergeant had nodded thoughtfully and glanced at the medal ribbons on Arthur's shirt. "Do you think, Corporal, that there is any possibility of our General's plans succeeding?" he had asked. Although they both held commissions in the Markos forces, they had chosen to ignore the fact in private. They had been N.C.O.'s in proper armies.

"Could be," Arthur said. "Depends on how many mistakes the other lot make, same as always. Why? What are you thinking about, Sarge? Promotion?"

The Sergeant had nodded. "Yes, promotion. If this revolution were to succeed, there might be big opportunities for men able to take them. I think that I, too, must take steps to become politically reliable."

The steps he had taken had proved effective, and his qualities as a natural leader had soon been recognized. By 1947 he was commanding a brigade, with Arthur as his second-in-command. When, in 1949, the Markos forces began to disintegrate, their brigade was one of the last to hold out in the Grammos area.

But they knew by then that the rebellion was over, and they were bitter. Neither of them had ever believed in the cause for which they had fought so long and hard and skillfully; but its betrayal by Tito and the Moscow Politburo had seemed an infamous thing.

" 'Put not your trust in princes,' " Arthur had quoted gloomily.

"Who said this?" the Sergeant had asked.

"The Bible. Only these aren't princes, they're politicians."

"It is the same." A faraway look had come into the Sergeant's eyes. "I think, Corporal, that in future we must trust only ourselves," he had said.

CHAPTER XI

It WAS JUST AFTER DAWN and the mountains above Florina were outlined against a pink glow in the sky when the old Renault deposited George and Miss Kolin outside the cinema where it had picked them up ten hours earlier. On George's instructions, Miss Kolin paid the driver and arranged with him to pick them up again that evening to make the same journey. They went to their hotel in silence.

When he got to his room, George destroyed the precautionary letter he had left there for the manager and sat down to draft a cable to Mr. Sistrom.

"CLAIMANT LOCATED IN STRANGE CIRCUMSTANCES," he wrote. "IDENTITY BEYOND REASONABLE DOUBT STOP COMPLEX SITUATION PREVENTS STRAIGHT-FORWARD ACTION TO DELIVER HIM YOUR OFFICE STOP MAILING FULL EX-PLANATORY REPORT TODAY STOP MEANWHILE CABLE IMMEDIATELY TERMS OF EXTRADITION TREATY IF ANY BETWEEN U.S. AND GREECE WITH SPECIAL REFERENCE ARMED BANK ROBBERY. CAREY."

That, he thought grimly, should give Mr. Sistrom something to gnaw on. He read it through again, striking out the unnecessary prepositions and conjunctions, and then translated it into the code they had agreed on for highly confidential messages. When he had finished he looked at the time. The post office would not be open for another hour. He would write to Mr. Sistrom and mail the letter at the same time as he sent the cable. He sighed. It had been an exhausting night—exhausting in some unexpected ways. When the coffee and buttered rolls he had ordered from the restaurant arrived, he sat down to compose his report.

"In my last report," he began, "I told you of the evidence I had been given by Madame Vassiotis and of my consequent decision to return home as soon as possible. Since then, as you will have gathered from my cable, the picture has completely changed. I knew, of course, that the inquiries instituted by Madame Vassiotis would reach the ears of all sorts of persons who, for one reason or another, were regarded as criminals by the authorities. I scarcely expected them to come to the attention of the man we have been looking for. Nevertheless, that is what happened. Twenty-four hours ago I was approached by a man who stated that he had friends who had information to give about Schirmer. Subsequently Miss Kolin and I took a very uncomfortable trip to a secret destination somewhere up in the mountains near the Yugoslav frontier. At the end of the journey we were taken to a house and confronted by a man who said he was Franz Schirmer. When I had explained the purpose of our visit, I asked him various pertinent questions, all of which he answered correctly. I asked him then about the ambush at Vodena and his sub-sequent movements. He told a fantastic story."

George hesitated; then he erased the word "fantastic"—Mr. Sistrom would not like that sort of adjective—and typed the word "curious" in its place.

And yet it *had* been fantastic, to sit there in the light of the oil lamp listening to the great-great-grandson of the hero of Preussisch-Eylau tell-ing, in his broken English, the story of his adventures in Greece. He had spoken slowly, sometimes with a faint smile at the corners of his mouth, always with his watchful grey eyes on his visitors, reading and assessing them. The Dragoon of Ansbach, George thought, must have been very much the same kind of man. Where other men would succumb to physical disaster, men like these two Schirmers would always endure and survive. One had been wounded, had put his trust in God, had deserted, and lived to become a prosperous tradesman. The other had been left for dead, had put his trust in himself, had kept his wits about him, and lived to fight another day.

What the second Sergeant Schirmer had become, however, was a question that the Sergeant himself had made no attempt to answer.

His own account of himself had ended inconclusively at the time of the closing of the Yugoslav frontier by Tito, and with a bitter complaint against the manœuvrings of the Communist politicians which had defeated the Markos forces. But George had very little doubt now about the nature of the Sergeant's subsequent activities. They had conformed to an ancient pattern. When defeated revolutionary armies disintegrated, those soldiers who feared for political reasons to go back home, or who had no homes to go back to, turned to brigandage. And since, quite clearly, neither the Sergeant nor Arthur was, to use Colonel Chrysantos's words, a "simple, deluded fanatic of the type that always gets caught," their gleanings in Salonika had almost certainly gone into their own pockets, and those of their men-at-arms. It was a delicate situation. Moreover, if he were not to seem suspiciously incurious, he would have to invite them somehow to explain their set-up in their own way.

It had been Arthur who had provided the opening.

"Didn't I tell you it'd be worth your while to come, Mr. Carey?" he said triumphantly when the Sergeant had finished.

"You did indeed, Arthur, and I'm very grateful. And of course I understand now the reason for all the secrecy." He looked at the Sergeant. "I had no idea that fighting was still going on in this area."

"No?" The Sergeant drained his glass and set it down with a bang. "It is the censorship," he said. "The government hide the truth from the world."

Arthur nodded gravely. "Proper Fascist-imperialist lackeys they are," he said.

"But we do not talk politics, eh?" The Sergeant smiled as he filled Miss Kolin's glass. "It is not interesting for the beautiful lady."

She said something coldly in German and his smile faded. For a moment he seemed to be reconsidering Miss Kolin; then he turned to George cheerfully.

"Let us all fill our glasses and come to business," he said.

"Yes, let's do that," said George. He had given them the reassuring impression that he was content with his picture of them as simple revolutionaries still fighting for a lost cause. That was enough. "I expect you'd

like to know a bit more about the whole affair, wouldn't you, Sergeant?"
he added.

"That is what I wish."

George told him the history of the case from the beginning.

For a time the Sergeant listened politely, interrupting only to ask for
the explanation of a legal word or phrase he did not understand. When
Miss Kolin translated it into German he acknowledged the service each
time with a nod. He seemed almost indifferent, as if he were listening to
something that was really no concern of his. It was when George came
to the part played in the case by the account of the first Sergeant Schirmer's exploits at Eylau that his attitude changed. Suddenly he leaned
forward across the table and began interrupting with abrupt, sharp-
voiced questions.

"You say Franz Schirmer. He had the same name and rank as me, this
old man?"

"Yes. And he was roughly the same age as you were when you dropped
into Crete."

"So! Go on, please."

George went on, but not for long.

"Where was he wounded?"

"In the arm."

"As I was at Eben-Emael."

"No, he had a sabre cut."

"It does not matter. It is the same. Go on, please."

George went on again. The Sergeant's eyes were fixed on him intently.
He interrupted again.

"Food? What food had he?"

"Some frozen potatoes he'd taken from a barn." George smiled. "You
know, Sergeant, I've got the complete account of all this written out by
Franz Schirmer's second son, Hans. That's the one who emigrated to
America. He wrote it out for his children, to show them what a fine
man their grandfather had been."

"You have this here?"

"I have a copy at the hotel in Florina."

"I may see it?" He was eager now.

"Sure. You can have it. You'll probably have the original eventually.
I guess all the family papers are rightfully yours."

"Ah yes. The family papers." He nodded thoughtfully.

"But what Hans wrote isn't the whole story by any means. There were
some things Franz Schirmer didn't tell his children."

"So? What things?"

George went on to tell him then about the meeting with Maria, about
Mr. Moreton's investigation, and about his discovery of the truth in the
army records at Potsdam.

The Sergeant listened without interruption now; and when George finished he remained silent for a moment or two staring down at the table in front of him. At last he looked up and there was a quiet smile of satisfaction on his face.

"That was a man," he said to Arthur.

"One of the boys, all right," Arthur agreed, nodding; "same name and rank, too. Let's see—Dragoons were . . ."

But the Sergeant had turned to George again. "And this Maria. She was my great *Urgrossmutter?*"

"That's right. Her first son, Karl, was your *Urgrossvater*. But you see the strong case we have through knowing about the change of name. Amelia Schneider's first cousin was your grandfather, Friedrich, and he survived her. You remember him?"

The Sergeant nodded vaguely. "Yes. I remember."

"Legally, he inherited the money. You will inherit from him through your father. Of course your claim may have to be advanced through the German or maybe the Swiss courts. You may have to apply for Swiss papers first. I don't know. It depends on the attitude of the Pennsylvania court. Certainly we can expect the Commonwealth of Pennsylvania to fight. What the attitude of the Alien Property Custodian will be we don't yet know. It'll be tough, but I guess you won't mind that, eh?"

"No." But he did not appear either to understand or to be paying much attention to what George was saying. "I have never been to Ansbach," he said slowly.

"Well, you'll have plenty of time later on, I guess. Now, about the business side of it all. The law firm I represent are the attorneys for the administrator of the estate, so we couldn't act for you ourselves. You'd have to retain someone else. I don't know whether or not you can afford to put up money for the costs of fighting the case. They'd be pretty heavy. If you didn't want to do that we could recommend a good firm. They would act for you on a contingency basis. Explain it all, Miss Kolin, will you please?"

She explained. He listened absently and then nodded.

"You understand?" George asked.

"Yes. I understand. You do all."

"Very well. Now, how soon can you leave for America?"

George saw Arthur look at him sharply. Now the trouble was going to start.

The Sergeant frowned. "America?"

"Yes. We could travel together if you like."

"But I do not wish to go to America."

"Well, Sergeant, if you're going to claim your estate, I'm afraid you'll have to go." George smiled. "The case can't be fought without you."

"You said that you would do all."

"I said we would recommend a firm of attorneys to represent you. But they can't fight the case without producing the claimant. They'll have to prove your identity and so on. The state and the Alien Property Custodian's lawyer will want to ask you a lot of questions."

"What questions?"

"Every sort of question. We'd better be quite clear about that. You're liable to have to account for every moment of your life, especially the bit since you were reported missing."

"That's torn it," said Arthur.

George misunderstood the remark with great care.

"Oh, I don't think the Sergeant has any cause to worry on that score," he said. "This is purely a domestic legal matter. The fact that he's been fighting in a civil war here is of no interest to Pennsylvania. We might run into some trouble getting a visa, but I think we could get over that in view of the special circumstances. Of course, the Greeks could make it tough for him if he wanted to return here afterwards, but beyond that there's nothing they can do. After all, it's not as if he'd committed some felony for which he could be extradited by the Greek government, is it?" He paused. "You'd better translate that, Miss Kolin," he added.

Miss Kolin translated. When she had finished, there was a tense silence. The Sergeant and Arthur stared at one another grimly. At last the Sergeant turned to George again.

"How much you say, this money?"

"Well, I'm going to be frank with you, Sergeant. Until I was quite sure who you were, I didn't want to make it sound too attractive. Now, you'd better know the facts. After various tax deductions, you stand to get about half a million dollars."

"Crikey!" said Arthur, and the Sergeant swore violently in German.

"Of course, that is only if you win the case. The Commonwealth is after the money too. Obviously, they'll try to prove that you're an impostor and you'll have to be able to prove that you're not."

The Sergeant had risen impatiently and was pouring himself another glass of wine. George went on talking without a pause.

"It shouldn't be difficult, I think, if it's gone about in the right way. There are all sorts of possibilities. For instance, supposing for some reason you'd had your fingerprints taken—while you were in the German army, say—why then you wouldn't have any more to worry about. On the other hand . . ."

"Please!" The Sergeant held up his hand. "Please, Mr. Carey, I must think."

"Sure," said George. "I was being stupid. It must be quite a shock to realize that you're a rich man. It'll take time for you to get adjusted."

There was silence again. The Sergeant looked at Arthur and then they both looked at Miss Kolin sitting there impassively with her notebook. They could not say what was on their minds in front of her in Greek or German. Arthur shrugged. The Sergeant sighed and sat down by George again.

"Mr. Carey," he said, "I cannot so immediately decide what I must do. I must have time. There are so many things."

George nodded sagely as if he had suddenly understood the true nature of the Sergeant's dilemma. "Ah yes. I should have realized that, other difficulties apart, this situation presents you with quite a problem in revolutionary ethics."

"Please?"

Miss Kolin translated rapidly and with a faint sneer that did not please George in the least. But the Sergeant seemed not to notice it.

He nodded absently. "Yes, yes. That is so. I must have time to think about many things."

George thought that it was time for slightly plainer speaking. "There's one point I'd like to be clear about," he said. "That is, if you don't mind taking me into your confidence."

"Yes? A point?"

"Are you known to the Greek authorities under your own name?"

"Now, chum—" Arthur began warningly.

But George interrupted him. "Save it, Arthur. The Sergeant's going to have to tell me eventually anyway if I'm to be any use to him. You see that, don't you, Sergeant?"

The Sergeant thought for a moment, then nodded. "Yes. It is a good question, Corporal. I see his reason. Mr. Carey, I am known by another name to the police."

"Very well, then. I'm not interested in helping the Greek police. I'm concerned with the disposal of a big estate. Supposing that alias of yours could be kept out of the proceedings altogether—and I don't see why it shouldn't—would that make your decision easier?"

The Sergeant's shrewd eyes watched him steadily. "Would there be no photographs in the newspapers of such a lucky man, Mr. Carey?"

"Sure, there'd be pictures all over the front pages. Oh, I see. You mean that, names or no names, the fact that you'd been in Greece would be bound to attract attention here and the pictures would identify you anyway."

"So many persons know my face," said the Sergeant apologetically. "So you see, I must think."

"Yes, I see that," said George. He knew now that the Sergeant understood the position as clearly as he did. If the robbery or robberies in which he had been concerned were extraditable offences, then any kind of publicity would be fatal to him. Among those who would know his face, for instance, would be the clerks in the Salonika branch of the Eurasian Credit Bank. The only thing the Sergeant did not understand was that George was aware of the true position. No doubt a day would come when it would be safe to enlighten him; in Mr. Sistrom's office perhaps. For the present, discretion was advisable.

"How long do you want to think, Sergeant?" he said.

"Until tomorrow. If you will tomorrow night come back we will speak again."

"O.K."

"And you will bring also my family papers?"

"I'll do that."

"Then *auf Wiedersehen*."

"*Auf Wiedersehen*."

"You will not forget the papers?"

"No, I won't forget, Sergeant."

Arthur took them back to the truck. He was silent on the way. It was evident that he, too, had plenty to think about. But when they were in the truck again and he was about to do up the canvas, he paused, and leaned on the tailboard.

"Do you like the Sarge?" he said.

"He's quite a guy, you must be very fond of him."

"Best pal in the world," said Arthur curtly. "I was just asking. I wouldn't like anything to happen to him, if you take my meaning."

George chuckled. "How would you like to be the most unpopular man in Philadelphia, Arthur?"

"Eh?"

"That's what I shall be if anything happens to Franz Schirmer."

"Oh-la-la! Sorry I spoke."

"Forget it. Say, what about taking it easy this time on some of those bends going down?"

"O.K., pal. You're the doctor. Easy it is."

The opening between the driver's seat and the rear of the truck had a flap over it, and during the drive down to the culvert George struck a match so that Miss Kolin could examine the false number-plates again. She looked at them carefully and nodded. George extinguished the match impatiently. Any real hopes he might have had that the Sergeant would, after all, turn out to be only another simple-minded zealot of the Phengaros type had long since been abandoned. It was absurd to go on clutching at straws.

Promising to meet them again the following night at the same place, Arthur left them at the culvert. They stumbled back to the car, roused the old man from his sleep, and set out on the road back to Florina.

Although it was the first opportunity they had had of talking privately since they had met the Sergeant, neither of them spoke for several minutes. Then it was Miss Kolin who at last broke the silence.

"What do you intend to do?" she asked.

"Cable the office for instructions."

"You will not inform the police?"

"Not unless the office tells me to. In any case, I'm by no means certain that we have anything more than vague suspicions to tell them."

"Is that your honest opinion?"

"Miss Kolin, I wasn't sent to Europe to act as a Greek police informer. I was sent to find the rightful claimant to the Schneider Johnson estate and produce him in Philadelphia. Well, that's what I'm doing. It's no concern of mine *what* he is here. He can be a brigand, a bandit, an outlaw, a travelling salesman, or the Metropolitan Archbishop of Salonika, for all I care. In Philadelphia, he's the rightful claimant to the Schneider Johnson estate, and what he is here doesn't affect his claim in the least."

"I should think it would considerably affect his value in court."

"That'll be his attorney's headache, not mine, and he can deal with it how he pleases. Anyway, why should you worry?"

"I thought that you believed in justice."

"I do. That's why Franz Schirmer is going to Philadelphia if I can get him there."

"Justice!" She laughed unpleasantly.

George was already tired; now he began to get annoyed.

"Look, Miss Kolin. You are engaged as an interpreter, not as a legal adviser or my professional conscience. Let's both stick to our jobs. At the moment, the only thing that matters is that, incredible as it may seem, this man is Franz Schirmer."

"He is also a German of the worst type," she said sullenly.

"I'm not interested in what type he is. All I'm concerned with is the fact that he exists."

There was silence for a moment and he thought that the argument was ended. Then she began to laugh again.

"Quite a guy, the Sarge!" she said derisively.

"Now look, Miss Kolin," he began, "I've been very . . ."

But she was not listening any more. "The swine!" she exclaimed bitterly. "The filthy swine!"

George stared at her. She began pounding her knees with her fists and repeating the word "filthy."

"Miss Kolin. Don't you think . . ."

She rounded on him. "That girl in Salonika! You heard what he did?"

"I also heard what she did."

"Only for revenge after he had seduced her. And how many more has he treated that way?"

"Aren't you being a bit silly?"

She did not hear him. "How many more victims?" Her voice rose. "They are always the same, these beasts—killing, and torturing, and raping wherever they go. What do the Americans and British know of them? Your armies do not fight in your own lands. Ask the French about the Germans in their streets and in their houses. Ask the Poles and Russians, the Czechs, the Yugoslavs. These men are filthy slime on the land that suffers them. Filth! Beating and torturing, beating and torturing, bearing down with their strength, until they—until they—"

She broke off, staring blankly ahead as if she had forgotten what she had been going to say. Then, suddenly, she crumpled into a passionate storm of weeping.

George sat there as stolidly as his embarrassment and the lurching of the car would allow, trying to remember how many drinks he had seen her have since they had left Florina. It seemed to him that her glass had never once been empty while they had been at the Sergeant's headquarters, but he could not quite remember. Probably she had kept refilling it. If that were so, she must have had the best part of a bottle of plum brandy, as well as her after-dinner cognacs. He had been too preoccupied to pay much attention to her.

She was sobbing quietly now. The old man driving had merely glanced round once and then taken no further interest. Presumably he was accustomed to distracted women. George was not. He was feeling sorry for her; but he was also remembering her pleasure in the anecdotes of Colonel Chrysantos, the man who knew "how to deal with Germans."

After a while, she went to sleep, her head cushioned in her arms against the back of the seat. The sky was beginning to lighten when she awoke. For a time she stared at the road, taking no notice of the wind blowing her hair about; then she took out a cigarette and tried to work her lighter. The breeze in the car was too strong for it and George, who was already smoking, passed his cigarette to her to light hers from. She thanked him quite normally. She made no reference to her outburst. No doubt she had forgotten about it. With Miss Kolin, he had decided now, anything was possible.

He finished his report to Mr. Sistrom and sealed it in an envelope. The post office might be open now he thought. He took the report and the cable and went downstairs.

He had left Miss Kolin over an hour before, when she had gone to her room. To his surprise, he saw her sitting in the café with the remains of a breakfast on the table in front of her. She had changed her clothes and was looking as if she had had a good night's sleep.

"I thought you were going to bed," he said.

"You said you were going to send a cable to your office. I was waiting to take it to the post office. They make so much chi-chi about cables there. They have so few. I did not think you would like to deal with them yourself."

"That's very good of you, Miss Kolin. Here it is. I've done my report, too. Air-mail that, will you?"

"Of course."

She left some money on the table for the breakfast and was going through the lobby to the street when the desk clerk came after her and said something in French. George caught the word "téléphone."

She nodded to the clerk and glanced at George—in an almost embarrassed way, he thought.

"My call to Paris," she said. "I had cabled my friends that I was on my way home. I wished to tell them that I would be delayed. How long do you think we will be?"

"Two or three days, I'd say." He turned to go. "Pretty good work that, to get through to Paris from here in an hour," he added.

"Yes."

He saw her enter the telephone booth and begin speaking as he went upstairs, back to his room to sleep.

At eight o'clock that evening they met the old man with the Renault again, and began their second journey to the Sergeant's headquarters.

George had slept fitfully for most of the day and felt a great deal wearier for having done so. In the faint hope that there might be a reply cable in from Mr. Sistrom, he had risen in the late afternoon and gone down to check. There had been nothing in. He had been disappointed but not surprised. Mr. Sistrom would have some thinking to do and some inquiries to make before he could send a useful reply. Miss Kolin had been out and, sitting beside her in the car, he noted that the leather satchel which she carried slung by a strap from her shoulder looked bulkier than usual. He decided that she had bought a bottle of brandy with which to fortify herself on the journey. He hoped, uneasily, that she would not hit it too hard.

Arthur was waiting for them at the same place and took the same precautions about shutting them in the back of the truck. The night was even warmer than the previous one and George protested.

"Is all that still necessary?"

"Sorry, chum. Got to be done."

"It is a wise precaution," said Miss Kolin unexpectedly.

"Yes, that's right, miss." Arthur sounded as surprised as George felt. "Did you bring the Sarge's papers, Mr. Carey?"

"I did."

"Good. He's been worrying in case you'd forget. Can't wait to know about his namesake."

"I brought along a copy of an old photograph of him as well."

"You'll get a medal."

"What's been decided?"

"I don't know. We had a chat last night after you'd gone but—anyway, you talk to him about it. There we are! All tucked up now. I'll take it quiet."

They set off up the twisting, rock-strewn road to the ruined house and went through the same routine as before when they reached it. This time, however, as they stood waiting among the pine trees while Arthur warned the sentry of their approach, George and Miss Kolin had nothing to say to one another. Arthur returned and led them to the house.

The Sergeant greeted them in the hall, shaking hands with George and clicking heels to Miss Kolin. He smiled, but seemed secretly ill at ease as though doubtful of their goodwill. Miss Kolin, George was relieved to note, was her usual impassive self.

The Sergeant led them into the dining-room, poured out drinks, and eyed George's briefcase.

"You have brought the papers?"

"Sure." George opened the case.

"Ah!"

"And a photo of the Dragoon," George added.

"This is true?"

"It's all here." George took out a folder which he had brought from Philadelphia. Inside it there was a photostat or photograph of every important document in the case. "The Corporal didn't have time to read the interesting part when he searched my room," he added with a grin.

"*Touché,*" said Arthur, unmoved.

The Sergeant sat down at the table, glass in hand, his eyes gleaming as if he were about to be served with some ambrosial meal. George began to lay the documents one by one in front of him, explaining as he did so the origin and importance of each. The Sergeant nodded understandingly at each explanation or turned to Miss Kolin for guidance; but George soon saw that there were only certain documents in which he was genuinely interested—those which directly concerned the first Franz Schirmer. Even a photograph of Martin Schneider, the soft-drinks potentate who had amassed the fortune which the Sergeant might inherit, produced no more than a polite exclamation. The photostats of Hans Schneider's Account, on the other hand, the church-register entries relating to the marriage of Franz, and the record of the baptism of Karl, he studied minutely, reading the German aloud to himself. The copy photograph of old Franz he handled as if it were a holy relic. For a long time he stared at it without speaking; then he turned to Arthur.

"You see, Corporal?" he said quietly. "Am I not like him?"

"Take away the beard and he's your spitting image," Arthur agreed.

And, indeed, for one who knew of the relationship, there was a strong resemblance between the two Schirmers. There was the same heavy strength in the two faces, the same determination in the two mouths, the same erectness; while the big hands grasping the arms of the chair in the daguerreotype and those grasping the photographic copy of it might, George thought, have belonged to the selfsame man.

There was a rap on the door and the sentry put his head in. He beckoned to Arthur.

Arthur sighed impatiently. "I'd better see what he wants," he said, and went out, shutting the door behind him.

The Sergeant took no notice. He was smiling now over Hans Schneider's account of Eylau and the photostat of a page of the Dragoon's war diary, the one recording Franz Schirmer's desertion, which George had placed beside it. That old act of desertion seemed to give him special pleasure. From time to time he would glance at the old man's photograph again. George supposed that the Sergeant's own failure to return to Germany when an opportunity presented itself (he could have taken advantage of one of the amnesties) had been a kind of desertion. Perhaps, what the Sergeant was enjoying now was the reassuring intimation from the past that, contrary to the beliefs of his childhood, sinners were not obliged to dwell with devils always, and that outlaws and deserters, no less than fairy princes, might live happily ever after.

"Have you decided yet what you're going to do?" George asked.

The Sergeant looked up and nodded. "Yes. I think so, Mr. Carey. But first I would like to ask you some questions."

"I'll do my best to . . ." he began.

But he never learned what the Sergeant's questions were. At that moment the door was flung open and Arthur came back into the room.

He slammed the door behind him, walked over to the table, and looked grimly at George and Miss Kolin. His face was pinched and grey with anger. Suddenly he threw two small, bright yellow tubes down on the table in front of them.

"All right," he said. "Which of you is it? Or is it both of you?"

The tubes were about an inch and a half long and half an inch thick. They looked as if they had been cut from bamboo and then coloured. The three round the table stared at them, then up at Arthur again.

"What is this?" snapped the Sergeant.

Arthur burst into an angry torrent of Greek. George glanced at Miss Kolin. Her face was still impassive, but she had gone very pale. Then Arthur stopped speaking and there was silence.

The Sergeant picked up one of the tubes, then looked from it to George and Miss Kolin. The muscles of his face set. He nodded to Arthur.

"Explain to Mr. Carey."

"As if he didn't know!" Arthur's lips tightened. "All right. Someone left a trail of these things from the culvert up here. One every fifty metres or so for someone else to follow. One of the lads coming up with a light spotted them."

The Sergeant said something in German.

Arthur nodded. "I put the rest out collecting them all before I came to report." He looked at George. "Any idea who might have dropped them, Mr. Carey? I found one of these two wedged between the canvas and the body of the truck, so don't start trying to play dumb."

"Dumb or not," George said steadily, "I don't know anything about them. What are they?"

The Sergeant got slowly to his feet. George could see a pulse going in his throat as he drew George's open briefcase towards him and looked inside. Then he shut it.

"Perhaps one should ask the lady," he said.

Miss Kolin sat absolutely rigid, looking straight in front of her.

Suddenly, he reached down and picked up her satchel from the floor by her chair.

"You permit?" he said, and, thrusting his hand into it, drew out a tangle of thin cord.

He pulled on the cord slowly. A yellow tube came into view and then another, then a handful of the things, red and blue as well as yellow. They were strings of wooden beads of the kind used for making bead curtains. George knew now that it was not a bottle of brandy that had made the satchel so bulky. He began to feel sick.

"So!" The Sergeant dropped the beads on the table. "Did you know of this, Mr. Carey?"

"No."

"That's right, too," Arthur put in suddenly. "It was Little Miss Muffet here who wanted the canvas over the truck. Didn't want him to see what she was up to."

"For God's sake, Miss Kolin!" George said angrily. "What do you think you're playing at?"

She stood up resolutely, as if she were about to propose a vote of no-confidence at a public meeting, and turned to George. She did not even glance at Arthur or the Sergeant. "I should explain, Mr. Carey," she said coldly, "that, in the interests of justice and in view of your refusal to take any steps yourself in the matter, I considered it my duty to telephone Colonel Chrysantos in Salonika and inform him, on your behalf, that the men who robbed the Eurasian Credit Bank were here. On his instructions, I marked the route from the culvert, so that his troops could . . ."

The Sergeant's fist hit her full in the mouth and she crashed into the corner of the room where the empty bottles stood.

George leaped to his feet. As he did so the barrel of Arthur's gun jabbed painfully into his side.

"Stand still, chum, or you'll get hurt," Arthur said. "She's been asking for this and now she's going to get it."

Miss Kolin was on her knees, the blood trickling from her cut lip. They all stood watching her as she climbed slowly to her feet. Suddenly she picked up a bottle and flung it at the Sergeant. He did not move. It missed him by a few inches and smashed against the opposite wall. He stepped forward and hit her hard across the face with the back of his hand. She went down again. She had made no sound. She still made no sound. After a moment she began to get to her feet again.

"I'm stopping this," said George angrily, and started to move.

The gun dug into his side. "You try, chum, and you'll get a bullet in the kidneys. It's nothing to do with you, so shut up!"

Miss Kolin picked up another bottle. There was blood running from her nose now. She faced the Sergeant again.

"*Du Schuft!*" she said venomously, and hurled herself at him.

He brushed the bottle aside and hit her again in the face with his fist. When she fell this time she did not try to get up, but lay there gasping.

The Sergeant went to the door and opened it. The sentry who had summoned Arthur was waiting there. The Sergeant beckoned him in, pointed to Miss Kolin, and gave an order in Greek. The sentry grinned and slung his rifle across his back. Then he went over to Miss Kolin and hauled her to her feet. She stood there swaying and wiping the blood from her face with her hand. He gripped her arm and said something to her. Without a word, and without looking at any of them, she began to walk towards the door.

"Miss Kolin—" George started forward.

She took no notice. The sentry pushed him aside and followed her out of the room. The door closed.

Sickened and trembling, George turned to face the Sergeant.

"Easy, chum," said Arthur. "None of the hero-to-the-rescue stuff. It won't wash here."

"Where's she being taken?" George demanded.

The Sergeant was licking the blood off one of his knuckles. He glanced at George and then, sitting down at the table, took the passport from Miss Kolin's satchel.

"Maria Kolin," he remarked. "French."

"I asked where she's being taken."

Arthur was standing behind him still. "I wouldn't try getting tough, Mr. Carey," he advised. "Don't forget, you brought her here."

The Sergeant was examining the passport. "Born in Belgrade," he said. "Slav." He shut the passport with a snap. "And now we will talk a little."

George waited. The Sergeant's eyes rested on his.

"How did you find out, Mr. Carey?"

George hesitated.

"Talk fast, chum."

"The truck the Corporal brought us up in—it had slots for false number-plates and the plates were lying inside on the floor of the truck. They were the same numbers as those mentioned in the Salonika papers."

Arthur swore.

The Sergeant nodded curtly. "So! You knew this last night?"

"Yes."

"But *you* did not go to the police today?"

"What I did was to cable in code to my office to find out what the extradition treaty between America and Greece says about armed bank robbery."

"Please?"

Arthur explained in Greek.

The Sergeant nodded. "That was good. Did she know you do this?"

"Yes."

"Then why does she tell Chrysantos?"

"She doesn't like Germans."

"Ah, so?"

George looked down pointedly at the Sergeant's hands. "I understand her feelings."

"Easy, chum."

The Sergeant smiled enigmatically. "You understand her feelings? I do not think so."

The sentry came in, gave the Sergeant a key with a word of explanation, and went out again.

The Sergeant put the key in his pocket and poured himself a glass of plum brandy. "And now," he said, "we must think what is to be done. Your little friend is safely in a room upstairs. I think we must ask you also to stay, Mr. Carey. It is not that I do not trust you but that, at the moment, because you do not understand, you are feeling that you would like to destroy the Corporal and me. In two days, perhaps, when the Corporal and I have finished arranging our business, you may go."

"Do you intend to keep me here by force?"

"Only if you are not wise and do not wish to stay."

"Aren't you forgetting why I came here?"

"No. I will give you my decision in two days, Mr. Carey. Until then, you stay."

"Supposing I told you that unless Miss Kolin and I are released immediately you'll have as much chance of inheriting that estate as that sentry outside."

"Your office in America will be very sad. Arthur explained to me."

George felt himself reddening. "Does it occur to you that, trail or no trail, Colonel Chrysantos won't take very long to find this place now? In two or three hours he may have you surrounded by Greek troops."

Arthur laughed. The Sergeant smiled grimly.

"If that is so, Mr. Carey, Chrysantos will be in trouble with his government. But you need not worry. If this bad Colonel comes, we will protect you. A glass of wine? No? Brandy? No? Then, since you are tired, the Corporal will show you where you can sleep. Good night." He nodded dismissal and began to go through the photostats again, putting those that interested him specially into a separate pile.

"This way, chum."

"Just a moment. What about Miss Kolin, Sergeant?"

The Sergeant did not look up. "You do not have to worry about her, Mr. Carey. Good night."

Arthur led the way; George followed him; the sentry brought up the rear. They went upstairs to a derelict room with a straw mattress on the floorboards. There was also a bucket. The sentry brought in an oil lamp.

"It's only for a couple of nights, Mr. Carey," said Arthur—the hotel receptionist apologizing to a valued client who has arrived unexpectedly. "You'll find the palliasse fairly clean. The Sarge is very keen on hygiene."

"Where's Miss Kolin?"

"Next room." He jerked his thumb. "But don't you worry about her. It's a better room than this."

"What did the Sergeant mean about Chrysantos getting into trouble with the government?"

"If he tried to surround us? Well, the Greek frontier's nearly a kilometre away. We're on Yugoslav territory. I'd have thought you'd have guessed."

George digested this disconcerting news while Arthur adjusted the lamp wick.

"What about the frontier patrols?"

Arthur hung the lamp on a hook jutting out from the wall. "You want to know too much, chum." He went to the door. "No lock on this door, but, just in case you're thinking of sleepwalking, there's a wide-awake sentry here on the landing, and he's trigger-happy. Get the idea?"

"I get it."

"I'll give you a call when it's time for breakfast. Pleasant dreams."

About an hour had gone by when George heard the Sergeant come upstairs and say something to the sentry.

The sentry replied briefly. A moment or two later George heard the sound of a key being inserted in the door of the next room—the room Arthur had said was Miss Kolin's.

With some idea of protecting her, George got up quickly from the mattress on which he had been lying and went to the door. He did not open it immediately. He heard Miss Kolin's voice and the Sergeant's. There was a pause, then the sound of the door being shut. The key turned in the lock once more.

For a while, he thought the Sergeant had gone, and went back to the corner where his mattress was. Then he heard the Sergeant's voice again, and hers. They were talking in German. He went to the wall and listened. The tone of their voices was curiously conversational. He was aware of a strange uneasiness and his heart began to beat too fast.

The voices had ceased now, but soon they began once more, and softly, as if the speakers did not wish to be overheard. Then there was silence for a long time. He lay down again on the mattress. Minutes went by; then, in the silence, he heard her utter a fierce, shuddering cry of passion.

He did not move. After a while there were low voices again. Then nothing. He became aware for the first time of the sound of the cicadas in the night outside. He was at last beginning to understand Miss Kolin.

CHAPTER XII

GEORGE WAS KEPT for two days and three nights at the Sergeant's headquarters.

On the first day, the Sergeant left the house soon after dawn, and returned when it was dark. George spent the day in the room downstairs, and had his meals there with Arthur. He did not see either the Sergeant or Miss Kolin. After that first night, she was moved to another room in an annex to the house and food was taken to her by one of the sentries. When George asked if he could see her, Arthur shook his head.

"Sorry, chum. No can do."

"What's happened to her?"

"I'll give you three guesses."

"I want to see her."

Arthur shrugged. "I don't mind whether you see her or not. It's just that *she* doesn't want to see *you*."

"Why not?"

"The Sarge is the only one she wants to see."

"Is she all right?"

"Fit as a fiddle." He grinned. "Cut lip, of course, and a bruise or two, but radiant as a bride. You wouldn't know her."

"How much longer is this going on?"

"Search me. I'd say it had only just started."

"After what happened, it doesn't make sense."

Arthur looked at him with some amusement. "I expect you've been nicely brought up. I told you she'd been asking for it, didn't I? Well, she got it, and very nice too. I've never seen the Sarge take such a fancy to a girl before."

"A fancy!" George was getting angry.

"I wouldn't mind betting she was a virgin," Arthur mused; "or as good as."

"Oh, for God's sake!"

"What's the matter, chum? Sour grapes?"

"I don't think there's much point in discussing it. Did Colonel Chrysantos turn up?"

"The sheriff's posse, you mean? Sure. They're sitting on their backsides, like twerps, just on the other side of the frontier. Waiting for something to happen."

"Or maybe waiting for Miss Kolin and me to turn up. Supposing the

American Legation's brought into this and they start complaining to Belgrade. Going to be a bit awkward for you, isn't it?"

"You'll be back before they finish even *talking* about doing anything. And when you do get back, you'll begin to think again about all the fuss your office is going to make over the Sarge, and say it was all a mistake."

"Got it all worked out, haven't you? I don't see what you had to get so upset about."

"No? For one thing they've arrested that poor old sod who drove you. That's not so funny, is it?"

"How do you know?"

"We had word from Florina this morning."

"How?"

"Ask no questions, you'll be told no lies. I'll tell you this, though. The *comitadjis* have been using these hills for fifty years or more. There's not much you can't get away with in these parts if you know the ropes. Don't forget that they're Macedonians on both sides of the frontier. When it comes to small-scale work like this, the Chrysantos boys haven't got an earthly."

"What'll happen to the driver?"

"That depends. He's an old *comitadji*, so he won't say where he got his orders from, no matter what they do to him. But it's awkward. He isn't the only one in Florina. There's old Ma Vassiotis, for instance. They might have a go at her. You know, if the Sarge hadn't changed things round a bit, I'd be inclined to go up and give your Miss What's-her-name another bashing myself."

"Supposing I were to tell Chrysantos that I hired the car and told the old man where to go."

"He might believe you. But how did *you* know where to go?"

"I'd say you told me."

Arthur laughed. "Proper lawyer, aren't you?"

"Would it matter to you?"

"Not a tuppenny damn."

"O.K., then."

Arthur was cleaning a pistol. George watched him for a while in silence. At last he said: "Supposing there had been no question of the Sergeant's going to America. Would you have gone on with this racket of yours?"

Arthur looked up, then shook his head. "No. I reckon we've just about had it now."

"Having pulled off the big job?"

"Maybe. Time to move on anyway." He bent over the pistol again.

"Got plenty of dough put away?" George said after a moment or two.

Arthur looked up, startled. "I've never met anyone with such terrible manners," he said.

"Come off it, Arthur."

But Arthur was genuinely shocked. "How would you like it if I was to ask you how much money you had in the bank?" he said indignantly.

"All right. Tell me something else, then. How did it start? The Sergeant kept very quiet about that. What happened in the end to that Markos brigade you both commanded?"

Arthur shook his head sadly. "Always asking questions. I suppose it's being a lawyer."

"I have an inquiring mind."

"Just plain nosy-parkering, my mother would have called it."

"You forget that, at present, I'm the Sergeant's legal adviser. Between a man and his legal adviser there should be no secrets."

Arthur uttered an obscene four-letter word and went back to his cleaning.

But the following evening he came back to the subject of his own accord. George had still seen nothing of either the Sergeant or Miss Kolin and a suspicion had been forming in his mind. He began to ask questions again.

"What time's the Sergeant coming back today?"

"Don't know, chum. When we see him, I expect." Arthur was reading a Belgrade newspaper that had arrived mysteriously during the day. Now he threw it down in disgust. "Lot of nonsense in that paper," he said. "Ever read *The News of the World?* London paper that is."

"No, I've never seen it. Is the Sergeant in Greece or Albania today?"

"Albania?" Arthur laughed, but, as George opened his mouth to ask another question, he went on. "You were asking what happened to us when we packed up fighting. We were up near the Albanian frontier then."

"Oh, yes?"

Arthur nodded reminiscently. "You ought to have a look at Mount Grammos if you ever get the chance," he said. "Wonderful scenery up that way."

The Grammos massif had been one of the first strongholds of the Markos forces; it came to be one of the last.

For weeks the brigade's position in the area had been deteriorating steadily. The trickle of deserters had become a stream. There came a day in October when important decisions had to be taken.

The Sergeant had been on his feet for fourteen hours or more, and his hip was paining him, when at last he gave orders to bivouac for the night. Later, the officer in charge of an outlying picket caught two deserters from another battalion and sent them to brigade headquarters to be dealt with.

The Sergeant looked at the men thoughtfully and then gave orders for them to be executed. When they had been led away, he poured himself a glass of wine and nodded to Arthur to do the same. They drank their wine in silence. Then, the Sergeant refilled the glasses.

"Does it occur to you, Corporal," he said, "that those two men may have been setting their brigade commander and his second-in-command a good example?"

Arthur nodded. "It's been occurring to me for days, Sarge. We haven't a hope in hell."

"No. The best we can hope for is that they will starve us to death."

"They're beginning to do that already."

"I have no wish to be a martyr of the revolution."

"Neither have I. We've done our jobs, Sarge, as well as we knew how and a bit over. *And* we've kept faith. That's more than those bastards at the top can say."

" 'Put not your trust in princes.' I have remembered that, you see. I think the time has come to seek our independence."

"When do we go?"

"Tomorrow night would not be too soon."

"When they find out us two have gone, you won't see the rest of them for dust. I wonder how many'll get through."

"The ones who always get through, the *comitadji* types. They will hide away in their hills as they have done before. They will be there when we want them."

Arthur was startled. "When we want them? I thought you said something about independence."

The Sergeant filled his glass again before he replied. "I have been thinking, Corporal," he said at last, "and I have a plan. The politicians have used us. Now we will use them."

He stood up and limped over to his kit bag for the tin box in which he kept his cigars.

Arthur watched him with something that he knew was very like love. He had a profound respect for his friend's planning ability. Surprising things sometimes emerged from that hard, heavy head.

"How use them?" he said.

"The idea came to me several weeks ago," said the Sergeant. "I was thinking of that history of the Party which we were once compelled to read. You remember?"

"Sure. I read mine without cutting the pages open."

The Sergeant smiled grimly. "You missed some important things, Corporal. I will give you my copy to read." He lighted a cigar luxuriously. "I think that it is quite possible that from being mere soldiers we may soon become soldiers of fortune."

"It was dead easy," Arthur said. "The Sarge had got hold of a list of all the secret Party members and sympathizers in the Salonika area, and we sorted out those that worked in banks and in the offices of businesses with big payrolls. Then we approached them and gave them their big chance to serve the Party in its hour of need, just as the book said the old Bolshies had done. We could always say we'd denounce them if they got suspicious, but we haven't had any trouble of that kind. I tell you, every single job we've done, we've had a man or woman on the inside, helping us for the honour and glory of the Party." He laughed contemptuously. "Flies in the Ointment, Unite! They couldn't wait to ditch the people they were working for. Some of them would torture their own mothers if the Party wanted them to, and be glad to do it. 'Yes, Comrade. Certainly, Comrade. Glad to be of service, Comrade!' It's made me sick sometimes to hear them," he added self-righteously.

"Still, you did pretty well out of it, didn't you?"

"Maybe we did, but I still don't like people who bite the hand that feeds them."

"Surely, it must have taken quite a bit of courage for some of these people to act on their convictions to the extent of helping you."

"I'm not so sure," said Arthur sourly. "If you ask me, these political convictions that make it O.K. to play someone else a dirty trick behind their backs have something pretty phony about them."

"You're quite a moralist, Arthur. What about the trick *you* were playing?"

"I'm not pretending to be better than I am. It's these phonies I can't stand. You should talk to some of them. Clever. Know all the answers. Prove anything you like. The sort you *don't* want with you if you're going out on a patrol, because, if things get sticky, *they're* the ones who'll start looking round for a reason for everybody to chuck in their hands and go home."

"Does the Sergeant feel the same way about these things?"

"Him?" Arthur laughed. "No. He doesn't bother. You see, *I* think there are all kinds of people. He doesn't. He thinks there are only two kinds—those you'd want with you when things are bad, and those you wouldn't have at any price." He smiled slyly and added: "And he makes up his mind real quick."

George lit his last cigarette and stared thoughtfully at Arthur for a moment. The suspicion suddenly became a certainty. He screwed up the empty pack and tossed it on the table.

"Where are they, Arthur?" he said.

"Where are who?" Arthur's face was all innocence.

"Come on, Arthur! Let's stop playing games. They were here last night, I know, because I heard the Sergeant come in around midnight and start talking to you. But this morning neither he nor Miss Kolin was here. At least, I didn't see him, and no food's been taken up to her. So where are they?"

"I don't know."

"Think again."

"I don't know, Mr. Carey, and that's a fact."

"Has he gone for good?"

Arthur hesitated and then shrugged. "Yes, he has."

George nodded. He had suspected, but, now that he knew for certain, the news came as a blow. "What am I being kept here for?" he asked.

"He's got to have time to get clear."

"Clear of me?"

"No, clear of this country." Arthur leaned forward earnestly. "You see, supposing you went back and Chrysantos started on you, and you blew the gaff about his being on the way out. I don't say you'd mean to, but he's a cunning bastard, that one. You can see it might be awkward."

"Yes, I see. He'd already decided what he was going to do. I think he might have told me."

"He asked me to, Mr. Carey. I was going to wait until after supper, just to be on the safe side, but you may as well know now. You see, there wasn't much time. We've been all fixed up to go for days. He made the final arrangements yesterday and just came back to ask her if she wanted to go too."

"And she did?"

"Like a shot. Can't keep her hands off him. Proper case it is."

"Isn't he afraid she'll try and turn him in again?"

Arthur laughed. "Don't be silly, chum. She's been waiting for a man like that all her life."

"I still don't get it."

"I expect you're like me," Arthur said consolingly. "I like it a little more on the quiet side myself. But about the money—"

"Yes, about the money."

"We talked it over, him and me, Mr. Carey, and we came to a conclusion. He couldn't have claimed it. You see that, don't you? You talked about extradition and all that, but that's not the point. Extradition or not, everything would have had to come out. That'd be no good. He's going to start a new life under a new name, with all this behind him. He hasn't got half a million dollars or anything like, but he's got enough to go on with. If he claimed that money he'd be a marked man. You know that as well as I do."

"He could have told me this the first time."

"He only wanted his family papers, Mr. Carey. You can't blame him for that."

"And he just had me stringing along so that I wouldn't make trouble. I get it." George sighed. "All right. What's his new name going to be? Schneider?"

"Now, you don't want to be bitter, chum. He liked you and he's very grateful."

After a moment or two George looked up. "What about you?"

"Me? Oh, I'll be getting along, too, by and by. It's easier for me, being British. There are all sorts of places I can go. I might even join the Sarge if I feel like it."

"Then, you do know where he's going?"

"Yes, but I don't know *how* he's going. He might be on a ship in Salonika at this very moment for all I know. But I couldn't say for certain. What I don't know, nobody can make me tell."

"So you're just here to look after me. Is that it?"

"Well, I've got to pay off the boys, too, and clear up generally. I'm the adjutant, you might say."

There was a silence. He looked round the room moodily. His eyes met George's. Unsuccessfully, for once, he tried to grin.

"I tell you what, chum," he said. "Now that the Sarge's gone and everything, I reckon we're both a bit down in the mouth today. We got hold of some German wine once. Kept it for special occasions, like last night. What about you and me having a bottle between us now?"

The sun was shining when George awoke the following morning. He looked at his watch and saw that it was eight o'clock. On the two previous mornings, Arthur had roused him, with a good deal of military noise, at seven.

He listened. The house was quite silent and the cicadas outside seemed very loud. He went and opened the door of his room.

There was no sentry on duty there. The "boys" had evidently been paid off. He went downstairs.

In the room where they had eaten their meals, Arthur had left a note and a letter for him.

George looked at the note first.

> *Well chum* [it said], *I hope you have not got too much of a hangover. There's a letter here that Sergeant Schirmer left for you before he went. Sorry I can't lend you my razor today as it's the only one I've got. When you want to go back to dear old Civilization just walk up through the trees past the place we parked the truck and then take the right fork. You can't miss it. It's less than a mile away. Nobody on this side will interfere with you. You will soon meet a patrol on the other side. Don't forget to do your best for that old driver. It's been nice knowing you. All the best. Arthur.*

The letter from the Sergeant was in Miss Kolin's angular handwriting.

DEAR MR. CAREY [he read],

> I have asked Maria to write this for me so that the meaning of what I feel and have to say will be clear and properly expressed in your language.
>
> First, allow me to apologize for having left you so suddenly and discourteously, without taking my leave of you. No doubt, by the time you read this, the Corporal will have explained to you the situation and also the reasons for my decision not to attempt to go with you to America. I trust that you will understand. I was naturally disappointed,

as I have always wished to see something of your country. Perhaps some day it will be possible.

And now, permit me to express my gratitude to you and to those of your office who sent you. Maria has told me of your persistence and determination to find a man you had so much reason to believe dead. It is a good thing to be able to go on a little further when those with less spirit are ready to turn back. I am sorry that you will have no more valuable a reward than my gratitude. Yet that I offer you sincerely, my friend. I would have been glad to receive so much money if it had been possible, but not more glad than I am now to possess the documents you brought me.

The money I cannot think of with great emotion. It is a large sum, but I do not think it has to do with me. It was earned in America by an American. I think it is just that, if there is no other heir but me, the American State of Pennsylvania should have it. My true inheritance is the knowledge you have brought me of my blood and of myself. So much has changed and Eylau is long ago, but hand clasps hand across the years and we are one. A man's immortality is in his children. I hope I shall have many. Perhaps Maria will bear them. She says that she will wish to.

The Corporal tells me that you will be so kind as to speak discreetly for the driver who was arrested. Maria asks that, if possible, you will give him her typewriter and the other things she left in Florina so that he may sell them and have the money. His name is Douchko. She sends you also her apologies and her thanks. So now, my friend, there is only left for me to thank you again and to wish you happiness in your life. I hope we may meet again.

Yours very sincerely,
FRANZ SCHIRMER

The signature was in his own writing, very neat and clear.

George put the letters in his pocket, got his briefcase from his room, and walked up through the pine trees. It was a fine, fresh morning and the air was good. He began to think out what he would have to say to Colonel Chrysantos. The Colonel was not going to be pleased; neither was Mr. Sistrom. The whole situation, in fact, was most unfortunate.

George wondered why it was, then, that he kept laughing to himself as he walked on towards the frontier.

JUDGMENT ON
DELTCHEV

to F with thanks

"Many things in your good people cause me disgust, and, verily, not their evil. I would that they had a madness by which they succumbed, like this pale criminal!"

NIETZSCHE: *Thus Spake Zarathustra*

JUDGMENT ON DELTCHEV

CHAPTER I

WHERE TREASON TO THE STATE is defined simply as opposition to the government in power, the political leader convicted of it will not necessarily lose credit with the people. Indeed, if he is respected or loved by them, his death at the hands of a tyrannical government may serve to give his life a dignity it did not before possess. In that event his enemies may in the end be faced not by the memory of a fallible human being but by a myth, more formidable than the real man could ever have been, and much less vulnerable. His trial, therefore, is no formality, but a ceremony of preparation and precaution. He must be discredited and destroyed as a man so that he may safely be dealt with as a criminal. Sometimes he is induced to confess abjectly to the crimes of which he is accused; but unless he has himself been a member of the party that now seeks to destroy him, such confessions are not always believed by the people; and when, for example, he is the leader of an unliquidated opposition party, it is better to observe outwardly the old legal forms, to bring witnesses, produce evidence, and let him try to defend himself.

So it was with Nikolai Petkov in Bulgaria, with Julius Maniu and Ion Mihalache in Rumania, and with many other liberals in eastern Europe. Petkov they hanged. Maniu and Mihalache were condemned to solitary confinement for life. When Yordan Deltchev's trial took place, the pattern for such occasions had been already set.

The charges against him were of "treason and the preparation of a terrorist plot to assassinate the head of the state." The trial began before a People's Court on the 11th of June. He was described in the indictment as "president of the Agrarian Socialist Party and formerly a member of the Provisional Government of National Unity." In fact, he had been head of that Government and also its Foreign Minister. He was still the leader of the only effective opposition to the People's Party regime that remained.

I had been asked to attend the trial and write a series of articles about it by an American newspaper publisher whom I had met once or twice when he had been visiting London. The request had surprised me. I had never written anything of that kind before and had thought at first that my name had been mistaken for someone else's. There had been no mistake, however, and I had decided to accept.

At some time or other, I suppose, most writers who have never done newspaper work indulge in the belief that, should the occasion arise, they would make brilliant reporters. Some of them, of course, are right. My case is different. With a solemnity that in retrospect seems pathetic, I looked up an old *Times* article on Deltchev, bought some of the likely books, and lunched with an economist who had once read a paper before the Royal Institute of International Affairs. I felt that I ought to learn something about the country I was going to visit, its people, and its problems.

The odd part is that I did learn one thing. It was over that luncheon that I first heard about the Officer Corps Brotherhood. It was referred to as a kind of joke.

Originally, it seemed, this Brotherhood had been a welfare association formed to protect and to help financially the families of a number of army officers who had been shot after the Macedonian *Putsch* of 1925. The founders were brother officers of the victims and sympathetic to their cause; but they were not wealthy men and it was not long before some of them became convinced that the most honorable way of helping and protecting the bereaved families would be to kill those who had condemned their men to death.

By the early thirties the Brotherhood had become a secret society of reactionary extremists and been responsible for at least twenty-eight political murders. Moreover, it was concerned no longer with simple acts of vengeance, but rather with eliminating potential sources of injustice that would later call for vengeance. As in the Brotherhood's dogma any politician or highly placed official with even remotely liberal ideas was a potential source of injustice, the problem of the Brotherhood became a matter of interest to all parties.

Attempts made by successive prewar governments to bring actual murderers to justice and to suppress the organization had been only partly successful because never quite wholehearted. It was easy enough to disapprove of the Brotherhood, but courage was required to become actively concerned with an attack upon it. The Brotherhood had survived and although its earlier "officers only" membership qualification had been relaxed and psychotics from many other sections of the community had found it congenial, it had retained much of its traditional military background. The symbolic revolver and dagger of other Balkan terrorist organizations had become for the Officer Corps Brotherhood the symbolic rifle and bayonet; and during the occupation the Brotherhood had snobbishly preferred to collaborate with the German Army authorities rather than with the Gestapo.

This latter piece of discrimination, however, had not deterred the Provisional Government, set up after the liberation, from making the first serious effort to stamp out the Brotherhood once and for all. Emergency powers had been used to the full. Membership in the organization had been made a capital offense, and arrests, summary trials, and executions had continued over months. So effective, indeed, had been the Government's campaign that there was little doubt in most minds that the Brotherhood had been betrayed from within. Interest in this aspect of the affair, however, had soon faded. When, during the elections, there had been none of the usual Brotherhood murders, it had been assumed with general relief that the organization was at last dead and buried. Now, astonishingly, the corpse had been exhumed and was being declared alive. For part of the case against Deltchev contained the incredible allegation that he, who as head of the Provisional Government had set out to destroy the Brotherhood, was in fact a member of it and the organizer of a plot to assassinate the head of the People's Party Government.

I left London at the end of May and arrived in the capital the day before the trial began.

CHAPTER II

OVER MUCH OF SOUTH EASTERN EUROPE the heaviest summer rains have fallen by early June, and the hardening mud of the roads is being grated into dust. The tinted walls of the villages glow in the strong sun, and the shadows on them are black and sharply defined. Only the higher Balkan peaks still have snow upon them. The corn is becoming tall and rich, and in the river valleys east of the Yugoslav frontier the fields of roses and white poppies that you see from the train are alive with blossom. But in the cities the air is humid, and the insects that swirl in the sunshine over the refuse in the streets or crawl from the dark recesses of hotel beds are in their lush heyday. At that time the human animal has a strange feeling of lassitude; strange because, although the body is sluggish, the mind is uneasily alert, as if it fears that something is being prepared for its discomfort.

I was met at the Central Station by my employer's local representative. His name was Georghi Pashik.

I saw him standing on the platform as my train drew in: a short, dark, flabby man in rimless glasses and a tight seersucker suit with an array of fountain pens in the handkerchief pocket. Under his arm he carried a thin, black dispatch case with a silver medallion hanging from the zipper tag. He stood by a pillar gazing about him with the imperious anxiety of a wealthy traveler who sees no porter and knows that he cannot carry his own baggage. I think it was the fountain pens that identified him for me. He wore them like a badge.

I know a lot about Pashik now. I know, for instance, that the black dispatch case that he carried so importantly rarely contained anything but a stale meat sandwich and a revolver, that the seersucker suit was given to him when he was working in a Displaced Persons camp, that one of the fountain pens came from Passaic, New Jersey, and that those facts can be related directly to his death. I know now some of the ways in which his mind worked and of the strange fantasies that possessed it. Then he was merely a name in conversation—"our man there, Pashik, will fix you up with all the permits you need"—a figure waiting on a station platform. I was not expecting a man of destiny to meet me.

He shook my hand and smiled in a friendly way.

"I'm delighted to know you, Mr. Foster. Have you had breakfast?"

"Not yet. It's very kind of you to meet me."

He gestured a denial. "I have my car outside. We'll have to carry your luggage, Mr. Foster. There are no porters at this hour."

He spoke English well with an accent both foreign and American. He was not a prepossessing person. He had a plump, sallow face with several chins and a two days' growth of beard, and his eyes, as brown and limpid as a spaniel's, squinted slightly through the rimless glasses. He was businesslike and very courteous.

"Good journey, Mr. Foster?" he asked as we walked out to his car.

"Not bad."

"Any trouble at the frontier?"

"No more than usual, I imagine."

"I'm very glad of that."

In the station yard he put my suitcase in a battered Opel with no cushions on the back seats. He took my typewriter from me to put it with the suitcase and then paused, looking at it thoughtfully.

"You know, Mr. Foster," he said, "sometimes the authorities make a great deal of trouble for visitors who they think may not be favorable to the regime."

"Yes?"

"Oh yes." He put the typewriter in the car and then, with his hand still on the carrying handle of it, turned his head. For a moment he seemed about to say something very important. It was on the tip of his tongue. Then he changed his mind. He shrugged. "Things are difficult right now, Mr. Foster," he said. "I'm glad they made no trouble for you."

He had an office in a building just off the Boulevard Marshal Sokolovsky. He called himself the Pan-European Press Service and represented a number of American and a few British newspapers whose proprietors had not found it necessary after the war to re-establish their own offices in the capital. He was energetic and gave an impression of efficiency. I had to be registered as a foreigner with the police and as a newspaper correspondent with the Ministries of the Interior and Propaganda; I also had to have a special permit for the trial. It was early evening before we had finished.

Although there was a good deal of waiting about in the various offices we visited, as well as the ordinary opportunities for conversation, our relationship did not progress during the day. For the most part he remained courteous but reserved, avoiding all discussion of Deltchev or the trial on the grounds, plainly insufficient at times, that we might be overheard, and introducing me to officials with a measured politeness that took no responsibility at all for my subsequent behavior. He had very much the air of the man on the spot who, while giving the specialist from the head office all reasonable assistance, feels entitled to suspect that the results may not justify the trouble taken. This I could well understand; indeed, I would have shared the suspicion. What puzzled me as the day wore on was the growing realization that, understandable and appropriate though his attitude might be, it was only partly a disguise for professional jealousy and that he had some quite different anxiety about me to conceal. It manifested itself in curious ways: sudden bursts of cordiality followed by strained silences, moments when I looked up to find his brown myopic eyes contemplating me furtively, as if to assess my bank balance, and other moments, like that at the station, when he changed his mind about what he was going to say as he opened his mouth to say it. Evidently some bad news had arrived for me while I had been traveling, or he had a request to make that I would be likely to receive badly. The thought bothered me. Unfortunately, I already had a bad conscience about Pashik. I disliked him because of his smell.

I had become aware of it when we entered his car at the station. It was sour and musty and at first I was not sure whether it came from the car or its owner. I don't think that I have an unduly fastidious nose or that the stinks of urban humanity specially distress me. I have known other people afflicted with what is daintily called body odor without disliking them. Yet Pashik I did dislike. Perhaps it was that the personality expressed by his appearance and manner—the suit, the American glasses, the dispatch case, the touch of complaisance—did not in some peculiar way allow for a bad smell. I remember that when I found that he was the source and not his car, I took note of those with whom we came in contact in case what I was finding offensive was the body smell of a city rather than that of one particular inhabitant. But no; it was Pashik. And then, unreasonably, I had begun to dislike him and so was at a disadvantage for what followed.

The sun had not yet set, but the shadows of a church spire and the dome of a mosque stretched like a finger and thumb across the St. Mihail Square when we left the Propaganda Ministry for the last time that day and walked back to Pashik's car; but I had my permit for the trial.

He waved my thanks aside mock-modestly.

"We do what we can, Mr. Foster." He had one of his moments of cordiality. "If you do not mind coming with me and waiting while I clear up at my office, I will then take you to dinner. There is a special restaurant I use."

I should have liked to refuse; instead, I thanked him again.

There was a minute anteroom to his office, with a frosted glass door on which were painted the names of all the newspapers he represented. The list was long and imposing, and after it the office was an anticlimax. It contained a desk, a table, two chairs, and several filing cabinets. The window looked out on a tall fire-escape well. It admitted warm stagnant air and a gray twilight that left the corners of the room in darkness. Standing on one of the filing cabinets and framed as importantly as if it were a picture of his wife was a publicity photograph of Myrna Loy, with a reproduction of her signature on it.

He turned on the desk lamp and began to go through a pile of message flimsies. Most of them he crumpled and tossed aside; two or three he scribbled on and handed to a youth with a glazed peak cap who had been awaiting his return; others he clipped together in a folder. When he reached the last of the messages, he gave the youth some money and sent him off. Then he picked up the telephone and had a conversation, to me quite unintelligible, with a woman whose voice I could hear vibrating tinnily in the receiver. It ended with a brief crescendo of negatives. He stood up and began to tidy the desk. He was frowning and ill at ease.

I watched him from the darkness outside the ring of light shed by the desk lamp. His small hands no longer moved surely. He was making up his mind to a difficult task. He stopped tidying to look out at me. Then he sat down again, leaned back, and, taking out a packet of American cigarettes, began to open it.

"Mr. Foster," he said very carefully, "there is a matter about which I have not yet spoken to you."

Here it was.

"Yes?"

He kept his eyes on the cigarette packet. "The matter of censorship. You know there is a strict censorship here, of course?"

"I was told so."

"In the ordinary way the procedure is that I submit the matter to the censorship office and then file it as a cable or airmail it."

"I see."

"That is in the ordinary way." He laid peculiar emphasis on the words.

"You mean that you would like me to give my stuff to you for submission to the censorship and onward transmission. Is that it?"

He did not reply for a moment or two and began to rock slowly on the back legs of his chair. "Mr. Foster, these are not ordinary times here in this country," he said.

I waited. His glasses, reflecting the light of the desk lamp, winked steadily as he rocked. He went on: "As I understand it, your articles may contain satirical matter hostile and derogatory to this regime."

"They might do so, yes."

He shook his head solemnly. "I can tell you now, Mr. Foster. That's out. Right out."

"Well, we'll see."

"Didn't they warn you at head office that things might be difficult here?"

I smiled amiably. "They said that you might be, Mr. Pashik."

He stopped rocking. "Oh now, Mr. Foster, please. You don't at all understand. The censorship is very powerful here. For writing matter antagonistic to the People's Party regime you would be liable under the February decrees to imprisonment and a heavy fine."

"Yes, but only liable."

"I agree. In your case there would naturally be no question of enforcing the decree, but your permit for the trial would certainly be canceled and you would have a very disagreeable interview with the police."

"I could make an article out of that, too."

His lips tightened. "Obviously your papers would be confiscated, Mr. Foster. If it amuses you to write articles so that they may be confiscated, that is your affair. I am concerned with practical newspaper work."

He had me there; I was not. But I felt that at the moment he was not either. I thought he was trying to show me how helpless I should be without him. I said as calmly as I could: "Very well, you're the paper's representative here and you tell me it's all very difficult. I understand. Now, how do we get over the difficulty?"

I had to wait while he lit a cigarette and blew smoke at the end of it like a bad actor pretending to think. "You could try going down into Greece over Saturday night and Sunday and sending your work from there." He blew some more smoke. "Of course, the police would guess what you were attempting. An American on a Chicago paper tried it."

"Yes?"

Now he looked directly at me. "He just wasted a lot of time, Mr. Foster. Of course he had no written matter when they searched him at the frontier; it was memorized; but they made difficulties about his visa, took his passport away to get it fixed, and kept him at the frontier station for a week. He had a very uncomfortable time."

"I see. Well, now you've told me how it can't be done, what's the answer?"

He was rocking again. "There is no answer, Mr. Foster. Other ways have been tried. The crews of foreign air liners were used as couriers for a while, but no longer. It is too dangerous for them. I have tried to make all this clear to the head office, but what is real here does not seem so in New York and London."

"In fact, you think it's a great waste of time my being here at all."

"No, I do not say that."

"In effect you say it."

"You misunderstand me. I am in favor of these articles. This trial is *dramatisch*—er—" He broke off, feeling for the word.

"Theatrical?"

"Yes, theatrical. Thank you. The trial of a political leader on ideological grounds is most theatrical to Western ways of thinking. So I say that to have a distinguished playwright, such as you, Mr. Foster, write matter about the Deltchev trial is a very cute editorial idea. I am myself looking forward to reading the series. But—" he leaned forward impressively— "you cannot write it here and send or take it out of the country; that is, not unless you paraphrase the Propaganda Ministry's official matter and get every page stamped by the censorship. You must resign yourself to that."

"But—"

"See the trial, Mr. Foster, memorize"—he stabbed his forehead with a finger to show me where—"and then go home and write your articles. That is what you must do."

For a moment or two I did not answer.

I had been in a train for four days and had had very little sleep on the journey. I had arrived at seven o'clock that morning in a strange city under a hot sun and in a sticky, enervating atmosphere. I had left my luggage in a hotel that might, for all I could remember of the geography of the streets, be a hundred yards away or three miles from where I was now; and even if I found the hotel and remembered the room number, I would not know how to ask for the key. I had trailed round cafés and Government offices, listening to conversations that concerned me conducted in a language I did not begin to understand, at the heels of an aggrieved, self-important eastern European with fat hips and a bad smell. I had a blister on the sole of my right foot and a grimy face. I was also hungry and well on the way to wishing I had not come. Now I was being told that the fact that I had come at all was a pity, but that if I behaved myself and cared to waste my time, I might stay and see the fun. Or so it seemed to me then. I felt myself losing my temper and then managed to wait until the moment had passed before replying. I tried to keep my voice level.

"Mr. Pashik, you know as well as I do that these articles are meant for publication during the trial as a commentary on it. They'd be useless afterwards."

"Do you think so?" He looked knowing. "Deltchev will be condemned to death. Your articles will be part of the campaign against the sentence."

"That's not what I was told. I was asked to send the stuff in as I did it."

"And why?" He threw up his hands, smiling with teeth like salted almonds. "In case you, Mr. Foster, the distinguished playwright, should find time to enjoy yourself on the expense account, or get an idea for a new play about life behind that sinister Iron Curtain and forget your commission. Editors treat us all like children."

"Nevertheless, the articles are expected."

"No, Mr. Foster, they are not. I sent a cable to head office saying that they will not be available until you return."

"I think you should have consulted me before you did that."

"I am responsible, Mr. Foster."

There was a thin-lipped silence. Then I said: "Mr. Pashik, are you a member of the People's Party? I didn't think to ask you before."

He smiled again, but the American accent became more pronounced. "Ah, Mr. Foster, you are mad at me. I don't blame you. I will be frank with you."

"Good."

"If there is any trouble with the censorship over anything that goes out of this office, it will be closed up. That means that I will be closed up, finished. I am responsible."

"Then you'll still be responsible if the articles are published after the trial."

"Ah no. If the Propaganda Ministry admits you to the country, it is their affair if you produce hostile matter when you leave. While you are here the responsibility rests with this office that you should not prejudge the trial by sending hostile matter." He shrugged. "It is no doubt for them an expedient. For myself, I am hostile to the regime; but I have been expelled for my opinions before, and Pan-European, representing twenty-seven foreign newspapers, has a responsibility to others besides your editor. So you see I must play ball with the regime, Mr. Foster."

I did not know quite what to say. My impulse was to take the trial permit from my pocket, put it on his desk, and say that I would leave in the morning. Certainly that is what he hoped I would do. It was only my awareness of disliking him for a poor reason that made me hesitate. He pushed the cigarettes toward me.

I shook my head. "When did you send that cable?"

"Four days ago, Mr. Foster."

"Why not before?"

"It was not certain that you were coming."

"It was settled three weeks ago that I was coming."

"I did not know that."

"Have you had a reply?"

"Yes, Mr. Foster."

"May I see it, please?"

"Certainly." He opened a drawer in the desk and brought out a cable and put it in front of me. I read:

> *Your 109 of 6 June understood advise Foster and arrange air passage London soonest close trial.*

"You could have shown me this before," I said.

"I did not realize that you did not trust me, Mr. Foster," he replied gently. "The cable only says to advise you of something and secure an air passage for you. It does not explain what I have been telling you. You still have to believe that I am telling you the truth."

His smile said that this was the moment when I should feel silly and apologize. Perhaps it was the smile that prevented my doing so. Instead I said: "I take it that the other foreign correspondents will be under the same restriction?"

"If they are hostile to the regime they will have to be equally discreet."

"That story about the American who tried to go to Greece for the weekend—I suppose you made that up in case I thought of the idea myself and didn't tell you."

"It was a way of warning you that the method was known."

"You go at things in rather a roundabout way, don't you?"

He looked at me thoughtfully. "One gets in the habit of it, Mr. Foster," he said, and then paused. "Roundabout ways are sometimes safer. However"—his expression changed and he stood up expansively, his smell billowing around him—"it is good to meet a person who cares for frankness. We can understand one another." He smiled cheerfully. "We shall get on well, Mr. Foster. We can help each other, and that is as it should be. I will show you."

He went over to a filing cabinet in the outer darkness, opened one of the drawers, and began to search through it.

"You know, Mr. Foster," he murmured as he picked through the files, "being expelled from a country is not dignified and not at all rewarding. For a few hours you are the brave man who dared to tell the truth. But the next day, when the handclasp of friends is forgotten, you are just another reporter without a job."

He came back to the desk with an untidy bundle of papers and a large envelope.

"When did it happen to you?" I asked.

"Italy, 1930. I was a married man then, too," he said. He hesitated for an instant, then stuffed the papers into the envelope and handed it to me with the rueful smile of a rich uncle for the rascally nephew whom he likes.

"The office file on Yordan Deltchev, Mr. Foster. It will help you."

"Thank you."

"Please." He put up a protesting hand. "I want to help you, Mr. Foster. And I want you to know that I want to. And that is frank. *Avanti!* Now we go to dinner, eh?"

That night I was too tired to sleep. For a while I tried to do so; then I gave up, switched on the light, and began to read the file Pashik had given to me.

At that point I still had the illusion that I could report the Deltchev trial.

CHAPTER III

THIS IS WHAT I LEARNED from the file.

Until the spring of 1940, when his country had joined two of its Balkan neighbors in coming to terms with the Axis, Yordan Deltchev, although an important figure in the councils of the Agrarian Socialist Party, had had no popular following. Originally a lawyer by profession, he had been deputy for a provincial manufacturing area and then, having served the monarchy and later the Republic in various subordinate capacities, had become Minister of Posts and Telegraphs.

At that time he had been regarded by the knowledgeable as a very able man and as either honest or so far insufficiently tempted. That he was not then even considered as potentially a great popular leader is understandable. His special talent was for organization; and while as a speaker he was not without force, the cool logic, dryly delivered, that made him effective in debate seemed unlikely ever to capture the hearts of audiences of peasants. That it did ultimately do so was a phenomenon produced by a peculiar combination of circumstances. Deltchev himself had very little to do with it.

He had been one of the few deputies, and the only Minister, who had opposed the alliance with the Axis at all vigorously; and during the summer of 1940, at the request of the German authorities, he had been interned. Toward the end of the year he was released, but kept under police surveillance. Two years passed before the surveillance became sufficiently negligent for him to embark on the underground political activity with which his name was to become associated.

Before that time, opposition to the pro-German Government and its allies had been expressed chiefly by acts of sabotage against war-supply installations and by propaganda against the recruitment of divisions for the Russian front. This work had been done by groups led by militant People's Party men, but containing a good proportion of Agrarian Socialists. Yet, although it was sometimes spectacular and always dangerous, the amount of inconvenience it caused the enemy was small and its effect on popular morale disappointing. To Deltchev's way of thinking, the policy of the underground opposition should be to leave the winning of the war to those who could fight effectively and to concentrate on planning for the future of the country during the period immediately following the inevitable German collapse. He saw that her fate at the hands of the victorious powers would depend very much on the speed with which she could herself establish a provisional government sufficiently uncompromised to negotiate without cringing and strong enough to prevent civil war.

The resultant Committee of National Unity was not created by Deltchev alone, but it was he who made it effective. Clandestine organizations are mostly recruited from among the dedicated, the romantic, and the mentally ill-adjusted men and women of a community; and in them courage and devotion are more easily found than high-level planning ability and political skill. Because he was the clearest thinker the Committee had and the only member of it with any practical experience of government, Deltchev became in effect (though in fact he never held any specific appointment) its president, its secretary-general, and, eventually, its spokesman. Hundreds of thousands of people who had never heard of Deltchev the Minister of Posts and Telegraphs now came to know of and exult in Yordan Deltchev the patriot. And when the time came for him to speak to them, the dry steady voice and the cool logic seemed, after the hysterical oratory of the war years, to derive from a special kind of sanity and goodness. They felt that he possessed the truth.

If the Provisional Government of National Unity set up by the Committee in the spring of 1944 had done no more than sue for peace so promptly, it would have justified its existence; for by this action it saved all but one of the northern frontier provinces from devastation and kept the minute army intact and available for police duties. Yet it did do more. It was able to secure recognition, qualified but sufficient, by the United Nations, and contrived, in those days of hasty negotiation and shifting authority, to confuse and postpone discussions of such matters as territorial claims and the dismantling of industrial installations. It ensured, at a minimum cost both to the national economy and to the national pride, that most of the vital decisions affecting the country's future were made not in the heat of the newly won battle, but in the milder atmosphere of delayed peace conferences. The credit for these benefits was given to Deltchev. He began to be nicknamed, affectionately, "Papa" Deltchev.

Perhaps but for that nickname there would have been no People's Party regime, and no Deltchev trial.

When the Provisional Government came into power, it was said by neglected members of his own party that the motives behind Deltchev's actions had all along been those of a shrewd, ambitious politician and that, while he could not be blamed for having had greatness thrust upon him, he should not now behave toward his old friends as if he had achieved it. They were soon to wish that they had been entirely right.

One of the main articles of the Committee's original program had been that of insisting on the need for free elections at the earliest possible moment. Its inclusion and the sanctimonious style of its wording were concessions to Anglo-American susceptibilities, which, it had been felt, could hurt nobody. Not that the men of the Committee were cynically indifferent to elections; it was simply that, faced with the task of planning for a great emergency of which nothing was then known and only the worst could be expected, they found such talk unrealistic. A cultivated sense of emergency is not easy to discard, and, later on, the early state of mind about elections tended to persist. When, therefore, the People's Party members of the Provisional Government began to press for redemption of the election promise, their action was interpreted, and correctly interpreted, as a demand for more power; that is, a larger share of the important posts. Only to Deltchev, apparently, did it mean anything different.

The People's Party had lately grown enormously in numbers and influence. The participation of the Agrarian Socialists in the formation and work of the Committee had achieved its object of enlisting wide popular support; but it had also had the secondary effect of making the Committee a powerful recruiting agency for the People's Party. This mishap had long been a subject of complaints and bitter exchanges within the Government, and on one occasion Petra Vukashin, the leader of the People's Party men, had been too frank. "If," he had said, "you are fool enough to introduce your wife to a handsome young man with a bad reputation, you must not complain when you find them in bed together."

When, to the manifest discomfort of Vukashin and the rest of the People's Party faction, Deltchev took the election proposal seriously and began to argue in favor of it, it was assumed at first by his pathetically gleeful colleagues that "Papa" Deltchev was merely calling the enemy's bluff. They knew, had known for some time, that the Provisional Government had the approval and support of the Western powers, who would not press for the promised elections while the country was in Soviet occupation. They had evidence that the Russians, not unimpressed by Deltchev's efficiency, were content to let things stay as they were for the present. Some of its members had even wondered if the word "provisional" might not be dropped from the title of a government with so rich an expectation of life. They could not know that their leader, Deltchev, had already numbered its days.

Many attempts were made later to offer more reasonable explanations of Deltchev's actions at that time than the one accepted by the simpler members of the public—namely, that he was a self-sacrificing patriot who had been directly inspired by God. Since, however, most of their other explanations relied on the assumption that he was monumentally corrupt, none of them was much more convincing.

The material facts were simple.

After the meeting at which the election promise was discussed Deltchev seemed preoccupied and unwilling to pursue the matter in private conversation. To one persistent man, however, he said: "If we have clean hands they cannot accuse us." The man took this to be a comment on the strength of the Government's position and the absurdity of the People's Party maneuver.

That was on a Thursday. For the next few days Deltchev was at home in bed with a severe chill. On the following Tuesday he was due to make a radio speech about a national campaign then in progress for conserving winter foodstuffs for livestock.

He came to the radio station straight from his bed, looking, according to the director of the station, "like a man who has been fighting with devils." In his speech he talked briefly about the conservation campaign and then, after a momentary hesitation, produced a handwritten manuscript from his pocket and began to read a statement from it.

Five minutes later the people knew that, in the considered opinion of "Papa" Deltchev, the time had now come for the Government to redeem the Committee's solemn pledge to hold free elections at the earliest possible moment.

At the beginning of the statement he had declared that he was speaking only for himself and not for the Provisional Government of National Unity. This declaration was both seized upon as evidence of his cynical contempt for his audience and pointed to as marking his absolute integrity. For the former view it was said that no one but a fool would suppose that, whether he wanted to do so or not, Deltchev could in fact dissociate his private opinions on such a question from those of the Government he led; for the latter it was argued that if you accepted the fact of his honesty (and who could deny it?) you would see that his disclaimer was a simple statement of the truth, which he had been bound to make if he were not to deceive the public. As equally divergent constructions could be placed on every other sentence in the statement, neither side could score points. Deltchev himself had returned from the radio station to his bed and, having issued through his secretary the statement that the broadcast speech was "self-explanatory," remained there, silent and inaccessible. But by the time two days had passed, it was clear that the storm over the speech, which raged with mounting fury among the politicians, was no longer of interest to the people. In their eyes the Provisional Government was now committed quite irrevocably to holding elections in the near future and anyone who attacked Deltchev was attempting to deny the fact. Yet it was the People's Party that profited most from the situation.

Those of the unfortunate Agrarian Socialists who had the wit to see that, whatever they might now say in private about Deltchev, they could not hope to win without him as a figurehead were in the majority; but they were terribly hampered by a considerable and vindictive minority whose only concern now seemed to be to oppose and revile him in public. The People's Party, while taking full advantage of this mistake, took care not to make it themselves. By referring to Deltchev patronizingly but respectfully as a kind of elder statesman (he was in fact only sixty then) they managed to convey the impression that he was in a state of derelict senility, which could excuse his continued association with the Agrarian Socialists. Also, by securing the postponement of the elections until the early summer, they gave themselves time to prepare a *coup d'état* that anticipated publication of the election results by a few hours. In the event, it was almost unnecessary. Thanks to Deltchev, they very nearly came into power by constitutional means.

His response to these events was at first curiously passive. True, he protested against the *coup d'état*, but rather formally, as if expressing an appropriate but not heartfelt sentiment; and in the Chamber his attacks upon the new Government had about them the studied moderation of a fencing master with a new pupil. For a long time he seemed unaware or unwilling to be aware of the Government's quick, wary moves to make themselves secure. Soon the anti-Deltchev faction within his own party began to find people ready at last to listen to their tale of a great fortune deposited abroad in Deltchev's name the day after his election statement. Even among the general public he seemed to be losing popularity. It was understandable that the Government's supporters should have come to think of Deltchev almost as one of themselves.

Then came the incident of "Deltchev's football match."

The occasion was the official opening of a sports stadium. It had been completed in 1940 and immediately requisitioned for use by the German Army as a transit camp. Later the Red Army had used it as a garrison headquarters. Its return was a gesture of Soviet goodwill, which the new Government had dutifully decided to celebrate with as much publicity as possible. It was probably the presence of Western diplomatic representatives at the ceremony that determined that Deltchev as leader of the "opposition" should be asked to speak.

He began, deceptively, with a tribute to the Red Army and expressions of his party's recognition of the generous motives that had prompted the early return of the stadium. He hoped that in the near future it would be the scene of a memorable football match with the local Red Army team.

Then, during the mild applause that greeted this suggestion, he moved nearer to the microphones. But this time he took no manuscript from his pocket. He knew exactly what he wanted to say.

"But meanwhile, my countrymen, there is another, more deadly battle for us to fight—the battle for freedom within the state."

He paused. There was a silence, in which the long banners could be heard flapping in the wind. He went on.

"Two days ago I was invited by the leader of the People's Party, Petra Vukashin, to take the office of Minister of Justice in the Government that now has power. My answer was promised for tonight. I take this opportunity of giving him the answer now. I answer that if he thinks that by so betraying my brothers in the Agrarian Socialist Party I should change in any way their determination to fight until this new tyranny is utterly destroyed—if he thinks that, then he is stupid. If our opposition to his party's criminal plans is such that he must try to buy us off with a share of the loot, then he is also frightened. My countrymen, there is no time to lose. These stupid, frightened men are dangerous, not for what they are now, but for what they mean to become—your masters. They are not . . ."

At this point the booming public-address system in the stadium was cut off. In the deathly pause that followed, Deltchev's voice, high and thin in the wind, could only be heard by those near him as he completed the sentence.

Then the cheering began. It came across the packed stadium as a rolling, sighing wave of sound that surged up and broke with a roar that shook the air like an explosion. It lasted nearly a minute and subsided only when another sound came to replace it: the steady, massive chanting of Deltchev's name. Suddenly on the far side of the stadium there was a wide swirling movement in the crowd as a fight developed, and from closer at hand there was angry shouting. Deltchev, who during the cheering had stood motionless in front of the dead microphones, now waved his hand and turned away. There was another tremendous cheer and more shouting. At that moment the officer in command of a Russian military band, which had been waiting to lead into the arena the squads who were giving the gymnastics display, decided not to wait for an order to do so. It was a sensible decision and probably averted serious trouble. As the band began to play and march in, the cheering became ragged and in places gave way to laughter and clapping. In less than a minute the incident of "Deltchev's football match" was over; over, that is, except for the breathless excitement of discussing it and of reporting it to those who had merely heard it on the radio. But nothing about it was forgotten and much that had not happened was remembered. "Papa" Deltchev had come back to them. He had spoken his mind and they had shown that they were with him in his fight against the "masters."

Four nights later an attempt was made to assassinate him.

His house was of the old kind with a walled courtyard. As he got out of his car to enter the house, a grenade was thrown. It hit the wall by the entrance and bounced back into the road before exploding, so that Deltchev, who had gained the doorway, was partly shielded from the blast. There were few people about at the time and the man who had thrown the grenade escaped.

The driver of the car was badly cut about the head and neck, but Deltchev, although he had been flung against the half-open door and much shaken, was not seriously hurt. In the ensuing confusion, however, his protests that the pain in his shoulder was caused only by a bruise were ignored and he was taken to a hospital with the driver. Within an hour rumors that he was dead or dying were circulating in the cafés, and a large crowd gathered outside the hospital. By this time Deltchev had returned to his home, where the police were collecting fragments of the grenade in the presence of an even larger crowd. There was a great deal of hostility toward the police.

It is said that when the Chief of Police reported to Vukashin later that night that the attempt on Deltchev was being described openly as the Government's reply to the stadium speech, the Minister exclaimed: "Did they think we would reply in the Chamber?" The story may be untrue, but, in the light of what followed, it is not incredible. Certainly from that moment on there was an ominous change in the Propaganda Ministry's public attitude toward Deltchev, and it is likely that the decision to try him was made at this time. The Ministry's official statement on the affair had a sort of angry jocularity about it that did nothing to change the general belief that the Government had known of the attempt in advance. It asserted that the grenade was of American manufacture, and went on to suggest that the obvious place to seek the criminal was in the ranks of Deltchev's own party, where there were many criminals with Anglo-American imperialist connections.

The editor of a newspaper that described this statement as "unsatisfactory, but significantly so," was immediately imprisoned. A series of savage attacks on the Agrarian Socialist Party now began. Their violent tone and the barely concealed threats that accompanied every allusion to Deltchev conveyed unmistakable warnings. The opposition had become intolerable and was going to be liquidated; but first Deltchev must be disposed of. He had a choice. He could escape abroad and be condemned or stay at home and be condemned. In any event he would be condemned.

Deltchev chose to stay. A month later he was arrested.

That was all. For a while I looked out of my hotel window across the flat roofs and Byzantine spires of the city, as still in the moonlight as the landscape of a dead world; and at last I became sleepy.

As I collected up the mass of news cuttings, notes, and manuscript that composed Pashik's file and began to put them back in the envelope, I noticed a paper that I had not seen before. It had been clipped to the back of a wad of sheets with cuttings pasted on them and therefore easily overlooked.

It was a page from a memo pad I had seen on Pashik's desk. On it was typed: *"Case of K. Fischer, Vienna '46—Aleko's hand?"*

For me, then, it was not the most interesting thing about the file. I went to sleep.

CHAPTER IV

PASHIK HAD PROMISED to drive me to the trial, and we met for breakfast. He nodded at the envelope I was carrying with the approving smile of a friendly schoolmaster.

"Ah, Mr. Foster, you have been reading."

"Yes. There's a lot of material there. Did you collect it?"

He fingered his chin self-consciously for a moment; he had shaved. "Why do you ask, Mr. Foster?"

"Because a lot of the unpublished stuff was obviously done by someone who knew Deltchev very well and liked him. You?"

"Ah, the memoir"; he looked embarrassed; "that was commissioned by one of my papers from Petlarov."

"Who's he?"

"He was Deltchev's secretary and friend—until the elections. Then they quarreled. He was paid for the memoir, but it was not used. It was not the moment."

"Where is Petlarov now? Is he here?"

"He may be."

"I should like to talk to him."

"He will know nothing about the trial, Mr. Foster."

"I'd still like to talk to him."

"He may not wish to see you."

"Then he will say so. You said you wanted to be helpful, Pashik. Here's your opportunity."

He wriggled unhappily. "Please, Mr. Foster. I see I must explain to you." He lowered his voice. "You do not understand. After the arrest of Deltchev, Petlarov was naturally arrested too. He is released now, but he is still suspect. It would be most indiscreet to have relations with him. I cannot take the risk."

"You don't have to. Just get a message to him from me. I suppose he can speak German?"

"I do not know. Perhaps not."

"Send a message as if from me asking him to telephone me at my hotel this evening."

He sighed. "Very well, Mr. Foster. But I think it will be useless."

I held up the envelope with the file in it. "We don't want to take this with us do we? We could leave it at your office on the way and write a note to Petlarov at the same time. Your office boy can deliver it."

He pursed his lips together at this. "I see you still do not trust me, Mr. Foster," he said.

"What do you mean?"

He saw the danger of explaining just in time. "It is not important," he said with dignity.

He took the envelope from me. Then I remembered. "Oh, by the way," I said, "what does this refer to?" I showed him the paper with the *Aleko* note on it.

He looked at it blankly for a moment. "Oh, that, Mr. Foster," he said, and taking it from me put it in his pocket; "that is nothing. Something from another file."

When once you know how a person lies, it is difficult for him to deceive you again. With Pashik it was a special tone of voice he used for direct lies that gave him away—a cold, too matter-of-fact tone. He had used it before in telling me the untrue story of the American journalist who had tried to go to Greece for the week-end. I supposed the fact that he had lied about this piece of paper to be equally unimportant.

The large courtroom at the Ministry of Justice had been thought too small for a political trial of such moment. It was being staged, therefore, in the main lecture hall of the Army School of Aeronautics, a modern building on the outskirts of the city.

The walls, ordinarily decorated with engineering charts and war trophies, had been hung with flags—those of the Republic and of the Soviet Union, and, at greater intervals, those of the other sympathetic nations of eastern Europe. Just above and on either side of the judges' dais two draped Soviet flags bulged over (but, tactlessly, did not quite conceal) one of the trophies, the tail plane of a Russian aircraft presented by a German flak unit during the war. Pinned to some of the flags were notices printed in four languages saying that smoking was prohibited. In the balcony a row of soundproof booths had been erected for the interpreters relaying translations of the proceedings to the earphones of the foreign diplomatic and press representatives below. In the balcony, too, on heavy stands or clamped to the balcony rail, were big floodlights pointing down into the court to illuminate it for the Propaganda Ministry's film cameras. Besides the judges' dais, on both sides of the prisoner's rostrum, at the corners of the hall, in the balcony, by the doors, and below every flag on the walls guards were posted. They were all officers or N.C.O.'s and armed with machine pistols, which they did not sling, but held ready in their hands. It had been explained by the Propaganda Ministry that when the evidence against the criminal Deltchev was publicly known, attempts might be made by the people he had deceived to kill him before justice could be done.

The courtroom was crowded. My place and Pashik's were in the foreign-press section, below the edge of the balcony and to one side. In the center was the diplomatic section. On the ledge in front of each seat in these two sections were a pair of earphones and four plug sockets marked with letters distinguishing the Russian, French, English, and German interpretation channels. Also on the ledge was a duplicated copy of the indictment in French. There seemed to be no seats for members of the public without tickets, but several rows behind us were prominently labeled with notice cards bearing initials, which Pashik said were those of prominent trade-union organizations. The occupants of these seats were obviously in their best clothes and on their best behavior. They all wore badges, and in one row there was a group of peasants in national costume. They looked as if they were attending a prize-giving. The front rows, however, had a different look about them. These seats were reserved for the important party members and functionaries. Their occupants wore dark neat clothes and either sat with self-conscious, preoccupied frowns or conversed in *affairé* undertones with their neighbors. Aware of being in the public eye, they were concerned to show that they had business there and were not merely favored spectators. It was warm, and most of the women and many of the men had highly colored paper fans.

At about ten o'clock the floodlights in the balcony were turned on and the fluttering sound of film cameras began. A buzz of anticipation went round the courtroom; then, as the three black-robed judges came slowly in, all stood up. The judges went to their places on the dais but did not sit down until the national anthem had been played through a loud-speaker. It was all curiously reminiscent of a royal visit to the opera. Even the low murmur of conversation that began as we sat down again was familiar. All that was different was that instead of the lowering of lights and the rise of a curtain somebody stood up and called out the name of Yordan Deltchev, and all eyes turned toward a pair of glazed doors beside the dais. Then there was silence except for the sound of the cameras and the distant throbbing of the generator set that supplied the power for the floodlights.

After a moment or two the glazed doors were flung open and three men entered the court. Inside the door they paused for a moment, blinking in the lights that poured down on them. Two of them were uniformed guards, tall, smart young fellows. Between them was an elderly man with a thin gray face, deep-set eyes, and white hair. He was short and had been stocky, but now his shoulders were rounded and he was inclined to stoop. He stood with his hands thrust deep into his jacket pockets, looking about him uncertainly. One of the guards touched his arm and he walked over to the rostrum and stepped onto it. A chair had been placed for him, but for a moment he stood there looking round at the flags upon the walls. He smiled faintly. He still had his hands in his pockets. Then, with a curt nod to each of the judges, he sat down and closed his eyes. This was Yordan Deltchev.

There were twenty-three counts listed in the published indictment against him. They charged (principally in count number eight, though the same charge was paraphrased in two other counts) that he had "prepared terrorist plots against the state and conspired with reactionary organizations, including the criminal Officer Corps Brotherhood, to secure, for financial and other personal advantages, the occupation of the motherland by troops of a foreign power." There were other charges concerned with terrorist activity, the smuggling of arms, and plots to assassinate members of the People's Party Government, "in particular P. I. Vukashin." Sprinkled throughout were dark references to "various confedserates," "notorious foreign agents," "hired saboteurs and murderers," "reactionary gangsters," and so on, while the name of the Officer Corps Brotherhood recurred with the persistence of a typewriter bell. It was soon evident that the indictment was a propaganda document intended for foreign consumption. It said, in effect, or hoped to say: "He is the kind of man against whom such charges may seriously be brought"; and: "He is accused of so much that of some he must be guilty."

The public prosecutor conducted his case in person. His name was Dr. Prochaska and he was one of the few members of the legal profession who had joined the People's Party before it had come into power. He was an authority on questions of land tenure, and most of his practice had been concerned with cases involving them. He had had little experience of court advocacy of any kind and none at all in criminal proceedings. A stout, pugnacious-looking man with quick, jerky movements and a habit of licking his lips every few seconds, he seemed more concerned to defend himself against accusations of weakness than to present his case effectively. He made scarcely any reference to the official indictment and dealt with only two of the charges in it. If he could prove, or seem to prove, those, then Deltchev would stand convicted on the whole indictment. That, at least, was the impression I had of it. From the commencement of his long opening address he adopted a tone of ranting denunciation that carried little conviction and confused even the more reasoned pas-

sages. In spite of the earphones on my head, and the voice of the interpreter quietly translating the speech, I was constantly distracted by the
sight and half-heard sounds of its originator.

His case, however, was dangerously simple.

It was generally known that at the time of the German retreat in 1944
Deltchev, who had been secretly in touch with both the Russians and the
Western powers, had gone to great lengths to secure Anglo-American
rather than Soviet occupation of the country. Against the wishes of a
majority of the Committee of National Unity, he had at one point gone
as far as to propose to the Western powers that the national army should
continue to resist the Russians in the north so as to give the Americans
and British time to prepare an airborne invasion from Middle East bases.

It was now suggested by the prosecution that this proposal had come
in fact from the Western powers themselves and that Deltchev's support
of it had been bought with the promise that he would have control of the
reallocation of the German oil concessions. In other words, he had tried
to sell his countrymen's lives for money and power.

The other favored charge was the one that had so amused my economist friend. It was that Deltchev had planned to assassinate Vukashin,
the head of the People's Party Government, and that he was, in fact, a
member of the Officer Corps Brotherhood. If this could seem to be
proved, he could quite legally and with full popular approval be sen-
tenced to death. The case against Deltchev was designed to destroy both
him and the Agrarian Socialist Party, which had produced him, forever.

I left the court that day in a peculiar frame of mind. I felt as if I had
been to the first night of what had seemed to me a very bad play only to
find that everyone else had enjoyed it immensely. A Propaganda Ministry bureau had been set up in a room adjoining the court. On the way
out Pashik stopped to get the official bulletin on the day's proceedings.
The room was crowded and I waited in the doorway. There were a number of tables, each signposted with the name of one of the official languages. As I stood there, I saw a bald young man whom I thought I knew
coming away from the English table. I had noticed him earlier in the day
and been unable to place him. Now as he pushed his way out we came
face to face. He nodded.

"You're Foster, aren't you?"

"Yes. We've met before."

"Sibley, Consolidated Press."

"Oh yes." I remembered, too, that I had not liked him.

"What are you doing here?" he asked. "Getting local color for a new
play?"

I explained. He raised his eyebrows. "Very nice too. Still, I expect you'll
make a play out of it sometime, won't you?"

"I don't know."

"I should have thought that there were masses of material for you. It'd make quite a nice little paragraph, your being here. Do you mind if I use it?"

"Yes, I do." I smiled as I said it, but not very cordially.

He laughed. "All right, I'll spare you. But it'd be nice to send something even a *little* more interesting than these hand-outs." He waved the sheets in his hand. "I'm at our Paris office really. I've been lent for the trial. Why I can't think. An office boy could file this junk for all of us." He turned his head as Pashik came up. "Hullo, Georghi, we were just talking about you."

"Good evening, Mr. Sibley. We must be going, Mr. Foster. I have to get to the office."

"That's our Georghi. Always on the job." Sibley grinned. "Where are you staying, Foster?"

I told him.

"We must have a drink together," he said.

In the car Pashik gave me the bulletin. I glanced through it. Most of it was composed of extracts from Dr. Prochaska's address. They were even more idiotic to read than to listen to. I put the bulletin down. The streets leading back to the center of the city were narrow and crowded and Pashik was a driver who twitched at the wheel instead of steering with it. He squeezed his way none too skillfully between two carts.

"Mr. Foster," he said then, "there is a suggestion which I think I must make to you." He looked round at me soulfully. "You will not, I hope, be offended."

"Not at all. Look out."

He twitched away from a cyclist just in time. The cyclist shouted. Pashik sounded the horn unnecessarily and put on speed.

"It is a small thing," he said—the car swayed unpleasantly across some protruding tram lines—"but I would not, if I were in your place, be too friendly here with Mr. Sibley."

"Oh? What's the matter with him?"

"It is nothing personal, you understand."

"But what?"

"He drinks too much and becomes indiscreet."

"I don't see that that has anything to do with me."

"His associates will be suspect."

I thought for a moment. "Mr. Pashik," I said then, "as a newspaperman don't you think that you're a bit too anxious about the censorship and the Propaganda Ministry and the police and all the rest of it?"

A woman missed death by an inch. He sounded the horn absently and shook his head. "I do not think so. It is difficult to explain."

"What's so difficult about it?"

"You are a stranger here, Mr. Foster. You look on our life from the outside. You are interested in the trial of a man whose name you scarcely know because his situation seems to you to contain the elements of a spiritual conflict. Naturally so. You are a writer of fiction and you make the world in your own image. But be careful. Do not walk upon the stage yourself. You may find that the actors are not what they have seemed."

"Is Sibley one of the actors?"

"I was speaking generally, Mr. Foster."

"Then I'm sorry, but I don't understand what we're talking about."

He sighed. "I was afraid not. But perhaps it does not matter."

I let that one go. A few moments later he pulled up outside my hotel. I got out of the car.

"Shall we meet for dinner, Mr. Foster?"

I hesitated. The air outside the car smelt good. I shook my head. "I think I'll get to bed early tonight," I said.

CHAPTER V

THE HOTEL BORIS had been built by a German company in 1914 and was one of those hotels in which footsteps echo and only the sound of a toilet flushing in the distance reminds you that you are not alone there. The foyer was a cavernous place with a tessellated floor and a hydraulic lift in a wrought-iron cage. The reception clerk was a slow-moving, mentally deficient youth with a charming smile. He spoke a little English.

"There is a message for you, sir," he said. He glanced at a scrap of paper that he had taken out of the key rack. "Mr. Stanoiev called to see you and will call again."

"Stanoiev? I don't know anyone of that name. Are you sure it was for me?"

He looked stupid. "I don't know, sir. He went away."

"I see."

The lift was deserted. I walked up the wide shallow stairs to the sixth floor.

My room was at the end of a long corridor with upholstered benches set against the wall at intervals along it. As I started down the corridor, I noticed that at the far end there was a man sitting on one of the benches. He was reading a newspaper.

It made an odd picture; one never expects corridor furniture to be used except as shelves for trays and chambermaids' dusters. As I approached he looked up casually, then went back to his newspaper. I glanced at him as I passed by.

He was a thin, dried-up man with pale, haggard eyes and gray hair cropped so that the bone of his skull was visible. He had a peculiarly blotchy complexion like that of someone just cured of a skin disease. The hands holding up the newspaper were long and yellow. There was a black soft hat beside him on the bench.

I went on past him to my room. I put the key in the lock and turned it. Then someone spoke from just behind me.

"Herr Foster?"

It made me jump. I turned round. The man who had been on the bench was standing there with his hat under his arm.

I nodded.

"Petlarov," he said, and then added in German: "I can speak French or German, whichever you prefer."

"German will be all right. I'm glad to see you." I finished opening the door. "Will you come in?"

He bowed slightly. "Thank you." He walked in and then turned and faced me. "I must apologize," he said in a clipped, businesslike way, "for answering your note in this fashion. A native of this country would not find it strange, but as you are a foreigner I must make an explanation."

"Please sit down."

"Thank you." In the light of the room his clothes were shabby and he looked ill. His precise, formal manner, however, seemed to ignore both facts. He chose a hard chair as if he did not intend to stay long.

"First," he said, "I think you should know that I am under surveillance; that is to say, I have to report to the police every day. Second, I am officially listed as an 'untrustworthy person.' That means that if you were to be seen entering my house or talking to me in a public place, you would attract the attention of the police, and yourself become suspect. That is why I have used this unconventional means of seeing you. I discovered your room number by leaving a note for you in the name of Stanoiev and noticing which box it was put into. Then I came discreetly up here and waited for you to return. You need therefore have no fear that my name is in any way connected with yours or my presence here known about." He bowed curtly.

"I am most grateful to you for coming."

"Thank you. May I ask how you obtained my address?"

"From a man named Pashik."

"Ah, yes. I thought it must be him." He looked thoughtfully into space.

"Do you know him well, Herr Petlarov?"

"You mean what is my opinion of him?"

"Yes."

He considered for a moment. "Let us say that I do not subscribe to the common belief that he is merely a disagreeable person whose political views change with the person he talks to. But now that I am here, what do you want of me?"

I had held out my cigarettes. His hand had gone out to them as he was speaking, but now he hesitated. He looked up from the cigarettes, and his eyes met mine.

"I have some more," I said.

He smiled in a deprecatory way. "If you had perhaps a bar of chocolate or a biscuit, Herr Foster, it would, I think, be better for my stomach than tobacco."

"Of course." I went to my suitcase. "I have no chocolate, but here are some biscuits."

I had a box, bought in Paris for the train journey and then forgotten. I opened it. The biscuits were the kind with pink icing sugar on them.

"Not very good for a bad stomach," I remarked.

He took one with a polite smile. "Oh yes. Excellent." He nibbled at it with very white false teeth.

"Pashik gave me your piece on Deltchev to read," I said.

"Oh, yes? It was considered unsuitable for publication."

"By Pashik?"

"Yes, but I was not surprised or upset. I knew that it had been commissioned in the belief that because I had had a difference of opinion with Yordan I would therefore write about him in an unfavorable way. If Pashik had asked me, I would have told him what to expect. Fortunately he did not ask."

"Fortunately?"

"If he had known he would not have commissioned the article, and I needed the money."

"Oh, I see. I have a bottle of whisky here. Would it be safe to ask the floor waiter for some glasses?"

"I think not. Perhaps I may have another biscuit."

"Of course, please help yourself. You know, Herr Petlarov, I came here to write a series of articles about the trial of Deltchev. But Pashik seems afraid that I shall offend the censor if I do them here."

"He is probably right," he said calmly. "He is usually right about these things. Yes, I can see. If you offend he will be blamed."

I must have looked disbelieving. He took another biscuit. "I will tell you a little story about the regime. A member of the People's Party wrote a novel about the fight of a group of workmen with the capitalists who wish to close a factory. It was a naïve story in which the capitalists were all monsters of evil and the workmen's leader a People's Party man. The Propaganda Minister, whose name is Brankovitch, would not, however, allow its publication. He said that the hero was not positive."

"I don't understand."

"The author had not demonstrated that the hero member of the party was a *good* man."

"But surely that was inferred."

"Brankovitch would say that you were in intellectual error, Herr Foster.

Inference is not positive. The public must be *instructed* that the man is good, as they must be instructed in all things."

"You must be exaggerating."

"In London or New York I would be exaggerating. Here, no. The sequel to this is that the writer was angry and made a little propaganda of his own. He has now been sent to forced labor. Pashik does not see that fate for himself. You see, Herr Foster, those who must be persuaded to obey are no longer important, for shortly we shall cease to exist. Our liquidation has begun." He smiled significantly.

"What do you mean?"

He took another biscuit and held it up. "This is the third biscuit I have taken," he said. "There are twenty-one left in the box. I can eat nine more."

"You can have the box."

He inclined his head. "Thank you. I had hoped that you would give it to me. I had based my calculations on your doing so. If I eat nine more I shall have eaten twelve. That will leave twelve for my wife. Luckily we have no children to share with us."

I was silent.

"I will explain. It is quite simple. Persons who are listed as untrustworthy are not allowed to work at anything but manual labor. I tried that, but I am not strong enough. So, as I cannot work, my wife and I may not have ration cards. We are, of course, very often hungry, and that can make a good argument for obedience."

I got up and went to the wardrobe for the whisky. Out of the corner of my eye I saw him reaching for another biscuit. He glanced over his shoulder at me.

"Please do not distress yourself, Herr Foster. A bad conscience can, I know, be as unpleasant in some ways as an empty stomach, and the person with the biscuits so often has a bad conscience. The trouble is that most of us with empty stomachs also have bad consciences. That combination will prove deadly."

"I have a metal cup," I said, "and also a tooth glass. If you like whisky—"

"I tasted it once," he said courteously. "I thought it better than schnapps and more interesting than our plum brandy. You need not fear, however, that I shall insist on taking it away with the biscuits."

I gave him the tooth glass. He took a small sip and looked at me. "I know that you will forgive my telling you that before I came to see you this evening I looked up your name in an English reference book I have."

"You'd like to know what a playwright is doing writing articles about a political trial?"

"Oh no, I see the connection. I was putting myself in your place for a moment. You have been in this city for two or three days perhaps. You do not know the country or the people. You are present at a trial that is like a game played for counters of which you do not know the value. Yet you have to interpret it for Western eyes."

"Something of the kind has already been said to me once today."

He nodded calmly. "As a guide you have Pashik, a man so preoccupied with a problem of his own—self-preservation possibly, but we cannot be sure—that he can lead you only to the counter of the Propaganda Ministry." He took another biscuit. "Have you seen the official bulletin of the trial today?"

"This?" I took it out of my pocket. "They gave out copies as we left the courtroom."

"They will do so every day. Tell me, Herr Foster, what will there be in your articles that a clever, malicious journalist sitting in London could not contrive for himself from a set of these reports?"

"I'm sure you have your own answer ready."

"Ah, I have offended you." He smiled. "But not seriously, I think, if you reflect. What I am suggesting to you, Herr Foster, is that you might find it useful to employ my services."

"Yes, that's what I thought you meant. How?"

"As a guide. I make this suggestion without embarrassment. You were kind enough to invite me to tell you some things about Yordan and of course I will do so." He touched the biscuit box. "I should have been well paid for that. But I think that I could be of further use to you." His haggard eyes looked up at me with a cold little smile in them. He licked a crumb off his lower lip.

"I'm sure you could," I said, and waited.

"For instance," he went on, "I wonder if you have considered that some of the evidence against Yordan Deltchev might not be as stupid as the prosecution makes it." He looked into the tooth glass.

An unpleasant suspicion crossed my mind. "Your difference of opinion with him," I said, "was over his radio speech approving the election, wasn't it?"

He was very quick. He said calmly: "If I were an enemy of his I would not need to beg a gift of biscuits, Herr Foster. I should be a witness at his trial. And if, as your caution may suggest, I am here as an emissary of the Propaganda Ministry to try to corrupt your judgment, then you cannot yet have identified the man whose task it will be to do so."

"I'm sorry. I don't know what you're talking about. What man?"

"Our friend Brankovitch has been forced to admit a number of hostile foreign journalists for the purpose of reporting this trial. Do you suppose that while they are here he will make no attempt to neutralize their hostility? Of course he must try. I can even tell you the procedure he will adopt. Tomorrow perhaps, or the next day, after Vukashin's evidence has been heard, Brankovitch will call a foreign-press conference and answer questions. Then, perhaps the next day, someone will approach you privately with a great secret. This person will tell you that he has discovered a way of getting uncensored messages out of the country. He will let you persuade him to share the discovery. Of course, your messages will not be sent, but they will serve as a guide to your intentions, which can then be anticipated in the official propaganda. Brankovitch likes, for some reason, to use *agents provocateurs*." He looked at me sardonically. "I know his sense of humor. It was I who recommended him to Yordan for a place on the Committee."

I offered him a cigarette again. He hesitated. "If I might take two?" he said.

"One for your wife?"

"Yes."

"Please take the packet."

"Thank you."

It was not quite full. He counted the cigarettes in it carefully.

"How did you meet Deltchev?" I asked.

He looked up. "He was my partner," he said. He seemed surprised that I did not know.

I gave him a box of matches and he lit a cigarette.

"Thank you." He blew smoke. "When Yordan first practiced as a lawyer, I was his clerk. Later I became his partner. When he was appointed Minister of Posts and Telegraphs, I became his assistant and secretary. I was also his friend."

"What sort of man is he? Superficially, I mean."

"Quiet, deliberate, very patient. A sound lawyer. If you were a journalist interviewing him in his office, you would probably be irritated by a habit he has of looking past you when he is talking. He keeps his desk very tidy and empties the ashtray as soon as you have put your cigarette out. Yet polite. He would tend to put words into your mouth—criticisms of himself—and then answer them. A bad habit for a lawyer, that. A man with a family—wife, son, daughter—of whom he is very fond, but not a family man. A good man, but not at ease with himself."

"The sort of man who would betray a principle for a bribe?"

"Yordan has never valued money enough to be corrupt in that way. Power might have tempted him once. You speak, of course, of his actions over the election promise."

"Yes."

"If he was paid to make that radio speech, he gave up what he might value—power—to gain what he did not value—money." He shrugged. "I have had plenty of time for thinking, and much bitterness has gone. At one time I thought of killing Yordan for what he did then, but even in hate I never supposed that he had been bribed."

"What is your explanation?"

"I have none. Yordan was often accused of being merely a shrewd politician. In retrospect that seems as ridiculous as the accusation now that he is a murderer. By unnecessarily bringing about the November elections he committed political suicide and betrayed all the people who were loyal to him. You ask for an explanation." He threw up his hands. "It is as easy to say that he was insane as to deny that he was bribed. When I faced him in his room that night he did not look insane. He looked strangely at peace with himself. That made me more angry, and, you know, in anger many things seem clear. 'Why?' I shouted at him; 'why?' 'It is better so,' was all he replied. Then, when I had finished abusing him, I said: 'Papa Deltchev has gone and the Minister of Posts and Telegraphs has returned. Papa Deltchev was not strong enough to bear a people's love!'" Petlarov looked across at me and smiled slightly. "But now I cannot remember what I meant," he added.

After a moment I asked: "Will the election matter be raised at the trial?"

He shook his head. "Not by the prosecutor. For the regime, the less said about the election the better. But they might tolerate the defense's making play with it to suggest Yordan's fundamental sympathy with the regime."

"Who is defending?"

"His name is Stanoiev. It amused me to use it here. He is the party member appointed to defend. His arguments in mitigation will be given prominence. They will serve as the final condemnation." He frowned. "What I do not understand is this affair of the Officer Corps Brotherhood. Yordan's attitude toward Soviet occupation—yes, that is something to argue and misinterpret, to deal with speciously. But the Officer Corps Brotherhood is another matter. They make so much of it that they must have something. Yet the idea is absurd."

"Surely it's easy enough to manufacture evidence?"

"Yes, but that is not their way. Consider the case of Cardinal Mindszenty. He was accused of an offense against the currency regulations. We know that it was only technically an offense and not committed for his own gain, but he was guilty of it and that was the reason it was used. If he had been charged as a corrupter of youth it would have made better propaganda, and no doubt the evidence could have been manufactured. But no—the currency offense could be proved. The lie stands most securely on a pinpoint of truth." He took the last of his twelve biscuits and shut the box. "What do you want of me, Herr Foster?"

"You have already given me a great deal."

"I have a suggestion. Why do you not talk to Madame Deltchev?"

"Is it possible?"

"Yes, for you. She and her household are under protection—that is, they are not permitted to leave the house, which is guarded—but your permits will allow you to pass. I will give you a letter to her. She will see no other journalist, I assure you. You will make a coup."

"Yes, I see that. What kind of woman is she?"

"She was a schoolteacher in the town where we practiced years ago. She came of a Greek family. If she had married me instead of Yordan, perhaps I should have become a minister. But better that you should form your own opinion. If you wish, I will come here every evening at this time to give you what information and comment I can." He leaned forward and touched my knee with his forefinger. "Is it agreed?"

"Agreed. But what is my part of the agreement?"

He hesitated. "Money—a little, what you consider fair—and your ration card. Not the restaurant tickets—those you will need and I could not use —but the ration card for bread, meat, butter, milk, eggs, and green vegetables. As a foreigner, you have one on the highest scale, I think."

"Yes."

"You still have it? You have not already disposed of it?"

"No. It's yours. I'll get it now."

He sighed. "It is as well that my wife is not here," he said. "She would weep."

Later, when he had gone, I sat by the window and had a whisky and water in the tooth glass. I was beginning to feel perceptive and understanding.

That was the point at which I should have packed my bag and gone home.

CHAPTER VI

In the afternoon of the second day of the trial the prosecutor completed his opening address to the court and began to call witnesses.

The first was Vukashin, the head of the Government. There was a stir as he went into the witness box.

He was one of those politicians who in their dealings with the public are like small-part actors who specialize in playing such things as shrewd lawyers, family doctors, and wise fathers; their mannerisms of speech and gesture have been cultivated to fit the stock characters their physical peculiarities suggest. He was square and solid, with a short neck, and he stood awkwardly in the witness box, his big hands clasping the ledge in front of him, the shoulders of his ill-fitting jacket hunched about his ears. He had blunt features, with a muscular jaw and full, determined lips. His forehead was low and permanently knitted in a frown of concentration. In the popular edition of his biography published by the Propaganda Ministry he was referred to as a "veteran front fighter in the class struggle," and from the illustrations you received the impression that he had spent most of his life marching up steep hills at the head of fist-brandishing processions of angry revolutionaries. The role he affected was that of "simple workman."

In fact he was not simple nor, strictly speaking, had he ever been a workman. His father had been a small but fairly prosperous tradesman, and Vukashin himself had been a bookkeeper in a timber warehouse during the early part of his political career. It had been a natural talent for accountancy and office organization rather than revolutionary ardor that had raised him first to the secretaryship of a trade union and later to leadership of the party. He had a reputation for the kind of wit that makes a political statement in terms of some excretory or sexual function. He was a powerful man physically and was said to have once made a brutal assault on a colleague who had opposed him. But it was also said that the victim had been alone in his opposition and unpopular and that the assault had been calculated quite coolly for its disturbing effect on the morale of other intransigent colleagues. He was a brusque, direct speaker and very effective with big audiences. "What are the *real* facts behind this problem?" he would shout; and although he never answered such questions, the sturdy conviction with which he pretended to do so, and his way of enumerating his sentences so emphatically that they sounded like hammer strokes of logic, usually concealed the deception.

The prosecutor's self-effacing deference to him was so abject that it was not even amusing. From a ranting bully who at least existed, Dr. Prochaska became suddenly no more than a disembodied, impersonal voice, a prompter who fed the witness with a short question and then waited until the speech in reply was over and another question was wanted from him.

"Minister Vukashin, in March of 1944 when the armistice negotiations began, what was the attitude of the prisoner, Deltchev?"

"Our policy was peace, immediate peace to save the country from devastation by reactionary-led forces seeking to continue their losing battle with our Soviet ally. Every hour of it meant another cottage, another farm destroyed, every day a fresh horror for our peasant workers in the frontier areas. Who could have said 'Go on'? Not a man with heart and bowels! Only a blood-maddened beast. But there was such a creature. His name was Deltchev!"

"Minister Vukashin, in what ways did the prisoner Deltchev work against the peace?"

"It would be easier, Public Prosecutor, to tell the court in what ways he did *not* work against the peace, for then I could answer shortly: 'in *no* way.' From the beginning of the negotiations he used his position on the Committee to hinder their conclusion. You may ask why this was tolerated, why he was not immediately removed from his post. The answer to that is simple. We believed at that time that he was in misguided but honest doubt about the terms of the negotiations that were under discussion. We were a responsible group acting not for a defeated country —we were never defeated—but for a resurgent nation. The terms offered us by Russia, however, contained, as was natural in the circumstances, military clauses that involved our surrendering certain rights of government. The interpretation put upon them depended upon one thing and one thing only—whether or not Russia could be trusted. We of the People's Party did trust Russia, and in the event we have been justified. All the rights surrendered by us then have now been restored. The prisoner took a contrary view—or said that he did, for we know better now—and it was this view that he urged upon us as a justification for delay and for continuing his negotiations with the Anglo-Americans."

"Did he contend that better terms would be obtained from them than from our Soviet ally?"

"No. The terms were no different in essence. They had been agreed to by the Foreign Ministers at the Moscow Conference of '43. According to the prisoner, what would be different was the way in which they would be enforced. Or so he said."

"Minister Vukashin, did the prisoner take part in the discussions with Soviet representatives?"

"Very little. He was too busy licking the backsides of the Anglo-Americans."

Laughter.

"Minister Vukashin, in presenting his arguments for negotiations with them, what advantages did the prisoner claim would follow?"

"He claimed so many advantages that you would have supposed us conquerors about to impose our will upon the defeated. But what were the facts at that time? First . . ."

The earphones softly droned out the translation, but above this sound his own voice persisted. It was loud and, in the harsh, penetrating quality of its lower notes, disquietingly aggressive. He claimed hostility as urgently as another might claim love, and to hate him was to submit to a seduction. In a way he was impressive.

The voice went on and the grotesque rubbish it talked was passively received in evidence. I watched the judges' faces as they listened.

The floodlights for the cameras were on all the time now. The day was warm, and soon, as the afternoon sun poured in through the high steel-framed windows, those in the lights began to sweat. Most of them wiped their heads frequently and fanned themselves; but the judges, sweltering in their black gowns and biretta-like caps, seemed unwilling to acknowledge their discomfort before the eyes of the cameras. They had been judges before the People's Party had come into power and it was known that all such appointments were under review by the Government. Later, perhaps, in a cool cinema at the Propaganda Ministry, the film would be examined by subtle, hostile men able to construe the wiping of hands or forehead as gestures of disrespect to the Minister and his evidence. No momentary relief from discomfort was worth that risk to the judges. Two of their older colleagues had already been dismissed for showing reluctance to preside at this trial. Now, behind the sweating impassivity of those who had not shown reluctance, there was the terrible anxiety of men who, having sacrificed their principles, fear that the sacrifice may after all go unrewarded.

Only the prisoner did not sweat. He sat with his hands in his jacket pockets and his eyes closed, the back of his white head resting against the wooden rail that separated the lawyers' tables from the body of the courtroom. His face was livid in the glare of the lights and he looked as if he might faint; but, incredibly, he did not sweat. But for the pricking of your own skin you might have fancied that the heat of the place was an illusion and that all the perspiration you could see was simply a visible manifestation of collective guilt.

The afternoon crept on and the shadows moved slowly across the courtroom until there were only narrow strips of sunlight on the walls. There were no more than ten minutes to go before the day's adjournment when the "incident" occurred.

Vukashin had almost completed his evidence and the prosecutor was asking him a series of questions about the meeting of the Committee at which it had been finally decided to accept the armistice terms.

"Minister Vukashin, what was the attitude of the prisoner when it was clear that the majority of the Committee favored acceptance?"

"As always, he attempted to obstruct the wish of the majority. He repeated all his former arguments, and when these were rejected again by the rest of the Committee, he said that he had had further discussions with the Anglo-American representatives and that something might yet be done with them."

"He gave the impression that he was making these proposals to them?"

"He had always given that impression. But now in the heat of the moment he made a slip that revealed his true intention. He said that the Anglo-Americans were only waiting for the word and at the snap of his fingers they would come."

At that moment a strange voice in the court said something loudly and sharply, and, in the dead silence that followed, the interpreter automatically translated:

"That is a lie."

Deltchev had risen to his feet and was facing the witness box. His hands were still in his jacket pockets, but he was standing very straight.

Vukashin looked startled for a moment, then turned his head to the judges.

"The prisoner objects to the truth."

The center judge leaned forward. "The prisoner will be silent."

Deltchev took no notice. "I do not object to the truth," he said. "Nor do I object to the fantastic perversions of the truth that the court has been listening to today, for no person in his senses will accept them. I do, however, object to lies that attribute to me statements which I have never made."

The judge shouted angrily: "Be silent. You will have an opportunity of speaking later."

"Will the Minister Vukashin be available to me for cross-examination?"

"Your counsel may examine the witness if he wishes to do so."

"He does not propose to do so. He values his own skin too much."

There was a commotion at this, and the thin, dark man whom I took to be Stanoiev began to make some sort of appeal to the judges. As several other people, including Dr. Prochaska, were speaking at the same time, the interpreter became tongue-tied. One of the judges began to shout.

"The presiding judges call for silence," said the interpreter.

Vukashin had been standing in the witness box looking on with a grim smile. Now he raised a hand and, as the noise subsided, spoke: "I have given my evidence. Let him say what he wants."

Deltchev faced him again. There was complete silence now. The prisoner's voice was light but very clear and precise.

"Minister Vukashin," he said, "was it with the Committee's knowledge that I made the proposal to the Anglo-American representatives in 1944 that we should fight a delaying action in the north?"

Vukashin hesitated a fraction of a second. "Be careful how you answer," Deltchev put in quickly. "The facts can be checked. The minutes of the Committee still exist."

Vukashin made an impatient gesture. "I am aware of that."

"Then you see the need for caution. Will you answer the question, please?"

"The reply is not as simple as you try to suggest. The Committee was aware that a proposal was made, but it was not aware that you had instructions from your Anglo-American friends to make it appear that the proposal came from the Committee."

"Your answer is that I *was* authorized by the Committee to make the proposal."

"Yes, but . . ."

"Let me continue, Minister. If the Committee authorized the proposal and if, as you say, the Anglo-American representatives wished it to be made, will you explain then why they did not immediately accept it?"

"Do not please ask me to explain the actions of the Anglo-Americans." Laughter.

"It is not the actions of the Anglo-Americans I am asking you to explain, but your own account of them."

Vukashin turned angrily to the judges. "I am here to give evidence, not to answer political riddles. That is enough."

"You have been very patient. The court thanks you, Minister. The prisoner will be silent."

Vukashin left the witness box and sat down. As he did so, Deltchev turned with a pale smile to face the courtroom. "The minister is afraid to answer," he said.

It was at that point that Dr. Prochaska made a foolish mistake. He had been standing there impotent and forgotten during this exchange. He was irritated. He was the prosecutor and yet matters had been taken out of his, the responsible, hands, and an important battle of words had taken place without him. More serious still, the Minister, whom he should have protected, had had the worst of the battle. Now he saw his chance of retrieving not only his own dignity but that of the Minister as well. Never once since the trial opened had Deltchev taken his hands from his pockets, and Dr. Prochaska had found the fact irritating. He suddenly thought he saw just how he might humiliate the prisoner.

"Afraid?" he exclaimed derisively. "The Minister is *afraid* to answer?" He gave a short laugh. "It is not the Minister who is afraid. It is you, Deltchev! No wonder you seek to accuse and discredit the witnesses against you. You are in fear of your life. No wonder you tremble. No wonder you keep your hands in your pockets. Do you think we do not notice? Ah, but the people have eyes, Deltchev. You cannot deceive them forever. You may disguise your fear in other ways, but your trembling hands you dare not let us see. Come, show us your hands, Deltchev. Or else be silent while justice is done."

In the breathless hush that descended, there was one single quickly suppressed giggle and then no sound but the fluttering of the cameras. The prosecutor had a hard, ugly little smile on his lips. At that moment he was not absurd. Vukashin looked down at his own hands, frowning. Deltchev stood quite still, his face expressionless. He was making up his mind.

Then he took his hands out of his pockets and held them out, palms downward, in front of him. They shook with a coarse tremor that must have been visible at the back of the court.

"The prisoner's hands are more truthful than his tongue," said the prosecutor.

Without a glance in his direction Deltchev put his hands back in his pockets and raised his head.

"I speak," he said loudly, "to the members of the diplomatic corps present here and to the representatives of the foreign press."

There was another commotion in the front of the court, and the prosecutor began to protest to the judges. The interpreter began to translate the protest and I took my earphones off. Others beside me were doing the same. Deltchev had spoken in German.

"You may have formed your own conclusions," he went on, "about the quality of the evidence that will be given by the prosecution in this court. In case you are in doubt, this demonstration will convince you. The evidence of my own hands has now been offered against me. I will explain what it is worth."

With an elaborately satirical bow in the direction of the diplomatic and foreign-press sections, the prosecutor abandoned his protest and stood, his arms akimbo and an unsuccessful attempt at a smile on his face, looking up at the ceiling.

"I make no defense of myself in offering this explanation," Deltchev was saying; "my defense is in the safe hands of the prosecution." He smiled faintly. "But perhaps you will be interested in this fact. I give it to you merely as a point of interest."

He paused and then went on very deliberately: "Gentlemen, I am a diabetic and have been so for several years now. That has meant, of course, a careful diet balanced with injections of insulin. The amount of insulin I need is not great—twenty units in the morning and twenty at night. I can, of course, call medical witnesses to prove this. When I was first arrested, the prison doctor was authorized to supply me with insulin. He even increased the injections slightly to compensate for the change in diet. Five weeks ago I was moved to another part of the prison and was not allowed to see the prison doctor. For just over four weeks I have been without insulin. The symptoms of diabetes have therefore returned—thirst, fatigue and other disagreeable manifestations, which I shall not trouble you with. The trembling of my hands is part of my general weakness and debility. If the prosecutor had asked me to show you my knees, you would have seen that they also tremble." He looked round at the prosecutor for a moment and then turned back to us. "I think that if he had known of this illness he would not have drawn your attention to it in this way. It is no part of his task to create sympathy for me. I merely ask you to note that he makes wrong deductions even from facts. The fantasies that he will create from the falsehoods his case rests upon I leave to your imagination."

Then he sat down.

The prosecutor said something quickly to the judges. The center judge said something in reply. I put the earphones on again and caught the translation.

"The presiding judges rule that the remarks of the prisoner shall not be entered in the record, as they were made in a foreign language not intelligible to the court. The case is adjourned until tomorrow."

The court rose.

When the judges had gone, Deltchev stepped down from the rostrum and with his two guards walked slowly toward the glazed doors. Nobody else in court moved. They watched him. At the door he paused and looked back. Then with a small, friendly nod he turned away again and went on through the doors.

I looked at Pashik. He was standing stiffly and awkwardly as if caught in the act of rising. He did not seem to notice his discomfort. He looked at me rather strangely. "A good man, Mr. Foster," he said softly; "in his way a great man."

But I did not pay much attention to him. Even now I can remember everything I thought during that next half-hour. I was very shocked by what I had seen and heard and full of hatred for the People's Party regime. I think that if I had met Dr. Prochaska in the corridor outside the courtroom I should have hit him. But soon I began to think more reasonably.

Nobody, I thought, could share the experience I had just had without also sharing my passionate indignation at what was being done in that sunny courtroom. If I could convey the scene with even a tenth of the impact it had in reality, I would arouse a storm of anger that might damage the regime appreciably. And then an idea began to form in my mind of how I might write about the Deltchev trial.

This, I thought suddenly, was more than just the crooked trial of a politician by his more powerful opponents. Here, epitomized, was the eternal conflict between the dignity of mankind and the brutish stupidity of the swamp. Deltchev, sick and alone, knowing that nothing could save him from a verdict and a sentence already decided upon, was yet prepared to go on fighting for the truth he believed in. Dimitrov at the Reichstag fire trial had fought for his life and won. Deltchev's life was already forfeit, but he was fighting none the less and might win a greater victory. And the fight was of his own choosing. Months back he could have escaped abroad and made the Government's task easy. He had not done so. Long-forgotten sentences began to run through my mind. *"Will you then flee from well-ordered cities and virtuous men? and is existence worth having on these terms? Or will you go to them without shame, and talk to them, Socrates? And what will you say to them? What you say here about virtue and justice and institutions and laws being the best things among men? Would that be decent of you? Surely not? . . . Will there be no one to remind you that in your old age you were not ashamed to violate the most sacred laws from a miserable desire of a little more life?" . . . This, dear Crito, is the voice I seem to hear murmuring in my ears, like the sound of a flute in the ears of a mystic. . . .*

I was deeply moved. I was also beginning to enjoy myself.

And then I got back to my hotel, and Petlarov was waiting in the corridor.

We went into my room and I told him what had happened.

He nodded coolly when I had finished. "Oh yes. Poor Yordan. He is certainly not strong. But how foolish of them not to tell Prochaska how the victim was being prepared! But we may expect foolishness. You see, they have always been able to rely before upon the folly of others. Now that they have to rely on themselves, their deficiencies are revealed. Of course an incident like that will make no difference to the outcome of the trial."

"No, but it will make a great difference to the comments on the trial in the Atlantic countries."

"The comments of the West did not save Petkov or Mindszenty. I think it is interesting, however, in quite a different way." He smiled thinly. "Why do you think Yordan made this demonstration? What did he hope to gain by it?"

"He saw an opportunity of hitting back and he took it. Surely, that's obvious. It was splendid."

"He saw an opportunity and took it, certainly. What exactly did he say finally—the last two sentences?"

I had scribbled down Deltchev's words as he had said them. I read the last two sentences again. " 'I merely ask you to note that he makes wrong deductions even from facts. The fantasies that he will make from the falsehoods his case rests upon I leave to your imagination.' "

Petlarov showed his white teeth. "What a clever lawyer Yordan is!" he said. "Do you not see what he has done, Herr Foster? Oh, certainly he has won the sympathy of the foreign diplomatists and press representatives, and that is very nice; but what else?"

"He made the prosecutor look a fool."

"He did more. Consider. He makes the speech in German. Why?"

"Obviously so that he would be allowed to speak. The interpreters didn't relay what he said, of course. As far as the public was concerned, he was unintelligible. Obviously it was the American and British representatives who mattered to him, and Vukashin and the judges and Prochaska didn't want to antagonize them unnecessarily by shutting him up. If they don't care much anyway about Western opinion, they could afford to let him talk."

"If it was the American and British who mattered, why did he not speak in English? Yordan speaks very good English."

"Oh."

"The educated persons of most small nations need a second language to their own. With us it is mostly German. Many of the party members in that courtroom speak German, and some of them are not unfriendly to Yordan. Those were the persons who interested him. What he wanted to do—and what he has done, perhaps—is to discredit the prosecution's evidence in advance."

"That's not difficult. It discredits itself."

"So far, yes. But perhaps Yordan was wiser than we yet know."

"I don't understand you."

"It is quite simple." He leaned forward with a chilling smile. "You see, Herr Foster," he said, "some of the evidence against him may not discredit itself. Some of it may be true."

CHAPTER VII

DELTCHEV'S HOUSE was on the edge of the city in an old residential quarter behind the Presidential Park. Petlarov had drawn a sketch map for me of the way there, and after an early dinner I walked to it from the hotel. There was a slight breeze and the air seemed cooler. The main streets and cafés were full of people, the women in their shapeless dresses and cheap wedge shoes, the men in their cloth caps, with their jackets over their arms, and their shirts undone at the neck; but beyond the park, where there were few shops and scarcely any cafés, the streets were almost deserted and the only sounds came from the radios in apartment houses.

I found the quarter without difficulty. It was off the Boulevard Dragutin; six quiet streets, paved for a short distance from the boulevard and then ending casually in a hillside wasteland of scrub and tamarisks. The streets were lined with plane trees and with square, solid old houses, each isolated within its own courtyard by a high wall with a heavy wooden door in it. The spaces between the walls of adjacent houses formed narrow lanes, some of which connected parallel streets, but mostly were shut off by tall iron gates and choked with wild vines.

The numbers on the houses were on blue enamel plates over the wall doors, and when I came to the right street I saw that Deltchev's house must be the last in it. But the setting sun was in my eyes and I did not see the guards outside the house until I was nearly upon them.

They were standing in the shadow of the plane tree just by the door. The trunk of this tree was scarred and the lower branches were leafless; the grenade of American manufacture must have exploded just by it. The guards' faces turned toward me as I approached.

They were in the uniform of what I referred to in my own mind as the "military police," though perhaps "gardes mobiles" would have contained a more accurate comparison. They wore the same gray-green uniform as the courtroom guards; but these had rifles instead of machine pistols, and instead of tunics they had blouses bunched in at the waist by greasy leather belts with ammunition pouches. From a difference in their badges I guessed that they were a corporal and a private. They were young, bronzed, and rather stupid-looking. Our eyes met as I came up, and I nodded, but they did not reply in any way or make any movement to intercept me. I stopped by the door, looked up at the plate to confirm that I was at the right house, and then reached up to pull a bell handle bracketed to the wall.

The next moment I received a violent blow on the shoulder. The shock of it made me gasp. I lurched against the door and twisted round. The private had his rifle raised to prod me again. The corporal had his rifle pointed at my stomach, and his finger was on the trigger. I raised my hands.

The corporal shouted something and took a pace backwards. I moved away from the door. I started to say in German that I did not understand what he was saying, but he shouted again, and this time I caught the word for "papers." With the heel of my hand I indicated my breast pocket and said: *"Papieren."* The private jabbed the muzzle of his rifle into my ribs. Then the corporal, stepping forward, tore open my jacket, snatched out my wallet, and stepped smartly away from me.

It all happened in a few seconds. I was absurdly shaken. I must have looked it, for the private grinned at me then in quite a friendly way as if my discomfort were a tribute to his efficiency. The corporal was frowning over my press permit. He looked at the photograph on it and he looked at me. Then he folded the permit, put it back in the wallet, and, coming up to me, began to speak very slowly and distinctly, waving the wallet under my nose to emphasize what he was saying. It was clearly an admonishment. I nodded. Then he gave me back the wallet, saluted negligently, and moved away. Behind me the private stretched up and pulled the bell handle. A bell clanged inside the courtyard. Then he, too, went back to his post under the tree.

They watched me as I waited, the private still grinning, the corporal frowning coldly. My shoulder hurt abominably and I badly wanted to rub it; but a curious shame and perhaps, too, a fear of pleasing them prevented my doing so. I was disconcerted by these unfamiliar and, I could not help thinking, rather childish emotions. I had behaved stupidly and had been roughly treated and humiliated in consequence; but it was no use; my hatred of them welled up like a sickness.

Then I heard footsteps crossing the courtyard inside: the clacking, slithering footsteps of wooden-soled sandals without heel straps. There was a pause and a rattling of bolts. Then the door opened a few inches and an old woman looked out. She had a face like a walnut shell, with woolly gray hair and bright little eyes very deep in their sockets.

She looked past me to the guards.

"I should like to see Madame Deltchev," I said in German.

She snapped out a reply I did not understand.

From behind me the corporal shouted something. I looked round in time to see him raise his rifle threateningly. She snapped again, then very slowly she opened the door. I heard the private laugh as I went inside.

The wall of the courtyard was about fourteen feet high and decorated all the way round with big frescoes of pastoral scenes: peasants dancing, a young man wooing a dairymaid, a village wedding. They were crude and conventional like the decorations on Russian toys. The predominant colors were cobalt blue, terracotta, and ochre, but in some places the paint had flaked so badly that only a faint discoloration of the stones showed where it had been. The floor of the courtyard was paved with square flags, on which stood potted plants of various kinds, some of them in brilliant flower. Out of a square space in the flagstones grew a big cherry tree. Beyond it, in a corner, there was a neat woodpile, with vine poles leaning against the wall by it.

The old woman had stopped to bolt the door again, but now she straightened up and faced me grimly, her arms folded, her eyes bright and full of malice. She said something that must have been: "Well, now you're in, what do you want?" In German I replied that I did not understand. She did not understand that. I got out Petlarov's letter addressed to Madame Deltchev and gave it to her. She took it in her clawed, arthritic hands and looked without comprehension at the writing. I guessed that she could not read. She looked up at me suspiciously for a moment, then held up a hand for me to wait and clacked away round the side of the house.

I rubbed my shoulder and looked at the front of the house. It was about twenty feet from the wall, a blank symmetrical façade in gray stone with white painted metal shutters fastened over all the windows. Double steps curved up to the front door, which was flanked by potted azaleas and looked as if it were rarely opened. I heard the old woman's footsteps on a bare floor inside and a distant murmur of voices. Then for a bit there was silence. I was a small boy again, calling for a friend with rich parents.

The breeze stirred the leaves of the cherry tree and there were other footsteps inside the house. A moment or two later the front door opened and a girl came out. At the top of the steps she paused.

"Herr Foster?"

"Yes."

She came down the steps with the preoccupied frown of a busy person whose time is being wasted. She was in the early twenties, dark and very pale, with high Slavic cheekbones. It was an intelligent face, too, but had an expression of bland self-assurance too determined to be real.

"I am Katerina Deltchev," she said.

"I'm glad to meet you." She had only a remote facial resemblance to her father.

"What is it you wish, Herr Foster?"

"To see your mother. Perhaps Petlarov's letter did not explain that." I knew that it did.

"At the moment I am afraid that is quite impossible. She is very upset, you understand."

"Naturally. Is she specially upset today?"

"Please?"

"I am sure that these are all terrible days for her. I merely wondered if the proceedings today had specially affected her."

"I don't think so."

"Then perhaps you would ask her when I may see her, Fräulein."

"I can tell you anything you wish to know, Herr Foster." She smiled, but not very warmly. "Would you like a drink?"

"No, thank you. Are you quite sure that your mother wishes to be protected from someone who may be of help to her?"

"I don't understand."

"If you will take Petlarov's letter to her, I'm sure she will explain to you."

She stopped smiling. "My mother does not see journalists."

"So I believe. That is why Petlarov gave me the letter to her."

She hesitated, then pressed her lips together. "Very well. Please wait."

She turned on her heel and went into the house again. She was wearing neat white shorts, a *maillot*, and sandals. I felt a little sorry for her. It is difficult, even for an attractive young woman, to make a dignified exit in shorts.

I waited a few more minutes. The light was going. Then the front door opened again and this time the old woman came out. She beckoned to me and I followed her.

Inside, there was a large hallway, with curtained doorways on either side and a slippery hardwood floor. There was a radiator against the wall between two of the doors. It was all very clean and smelt of polish. Motioning me to follow her, the old woman climbed up the stairs. On the landing there was a shuttered window, and by the half-light filtering through the slits in the metal I could see a passage running along the width of the house. The old woman turned to the right along it and, going to a door at the end, scratched on the panel. There was a voice from within. She opened the door.

Red light from the setting sun streamed into the passage through tall unshuttered windows in the room beyond, and as I came to the doorway I could see the bare khaki hills outside the city.

The windows gave onto a wooden terrace with an awning and vines growing over trellises at the sides. There was an iron table there with books on it and some cane chairs.

The room was large and filled with massive red plush drawing-room furniture of the kind made for the wealthy tradesmen of pre-Sarajevo Vienna. On the walls there were heavy gilt mirrors and girandoles, and colored prints in polished wood and ormolu frames. Overhead there was a large gilt electric chandelier. The upholstery was red cut velvet. In winter the room could be quite cheerless, but now with the windows opened on the terrace and with the gilt touched by the glow of the sunset it had a certain richness and warmth.

As I came into the room, a woman sitting just out of the sun by the far window put a book down and rose to her feet.

I had a slight shock.

She was someone who had once been a provincial schoolteacher. Petlarov had said: "Perhaps if she had married me instead of Yordan, I should have become a minister." There was the diabetic husband under sentence of death. There were my pilgrimage to this old house to see her and my interview with the attractive young woman whose mother did not see journalists. There was the quiet shuttered house, the smell of furniture polish. Out of all these things an image of the Madame Deltchev I would find had been composed in my mind's eye. She had been an old woman with white hair, in a wheel chair perhaps or even bedridden; a wiry matriarch with the evidence of her youthful beauty still discernible in her face, and the vitality, which had served the young lawyer and then driven the ambitious politician, still there in the brightness of her glance and the impatient directness of her speech. How this irascible crone had borne a daughter twenty years ago or what disease now immobilized her my untidy imagination had not troubled to inquire. What I was prepared for in Madame Deltchev was the female counterpart of the gray, shaking man I had seen in court that day and with whose mystery and fate I was preoccupied; and I had visualized no other.

What I saw was a slim, erect woman of about fifty in a striped silk blouse and well-cut skirt, and with sleek, black hair only slightly touched with gray. Her forehead was broad and high and she had gentle, very intelligent eyes. The bold regular features, which her daughter had inherited, were in her more masculine, but her complexion was perfect.

She smiled politely as she greeted me. "Herr Foster, I'm so sorry that you were kept waiting outside."

"It's very kind of you to see me."

"Please sit down." She sat down again herself. She had a small lace fan that she fluttered unobtrusively by the side of her face farthest from me. "My daughter had the best of intentions, but she did not understand Petlarov's motives."

The girl stood behind the chair. She did not look at me.

"With Petlarov," she said angrily, "there is only one motive. He does only what he is paid for."

Her mother said quietly: "Please get us some tea, Katerina."

Katerina laughed shortly. "English journalists drink only whisky and soda, Mother. It is traditional." She went over to the samovar. "Isn't that right, Herr Foster?"

Madame Deltchev frowned and said something quickly in their own language. The girl made a sharp retort. Madame Deltchev smoothed her hair.

"I think that Herr Foster will excuse you, Katerina, if you wish to leave us to talk," she said calmly.

The girl stood still looking at her for a moment, her face dark with anger. Then with a bang she put down the tea glass she had been holding and walked out of the room.

Her mother rose and, going over to the samovar, began to pour the tea herself.

"All nerves in this house," she said, "are greatly strained, Herr Foster."

"Yes, I can imagine."

"For my daughter it is perhaps most difficult," she went on; "unfortunately she is in political disagreement with my husband. She sympathizes with that section of the Agrarian Socialists which blames Yordan for the present situation. So her love for her father is in conflict with her feelings toward the man who betrayed his party. It is difficult for her and I cannot help much." She handed me some tea. "You see, Herr Foster, it is not without reason that I avoid speaking to journalists. I do not guard my tongue. The regime would be glad to use the fact that Yordan's own children oppose him politically. But Petlarov says that you are friendly and to be trusted."

"I was wondering, madame, what there was about Petlarov's motives to be understood."

She took her tea back to her chair. "Petlarov is a good friend," she said. "Even after his disagreement with Yordan he remained a friend. When he was released from prison I was able to see him for a short while and I asked his advice about the press. We were already an object of interest, you see. He told me that I should see no one until he sent somebody that could be trusted."

"That is very flattering, but, frankly, I do not see the reason for his choice."

"Did you not read his letter?" She held it up.

"I'm afraid I couldn't."

"Oh yes, the language." She looked at the letter. "He says that you are going to write a series of articles about the trial and sentence which will be published in America and England. He says that your articles will be well written and acceptable and that although they will be politically naïve—" She broke off and looked at me apologetically. "He means, of course, that he does not regard you as primarily a political person."

"He's right."

She smiled. "So many of our circle would be offended." She returned to the letter. ". . . although they will be politically naïve, their simplification of obvious issues and the evident sincerity of their indignation will be admirably suited to the campaign against the outcome of the trial." She folded the letter. "Petlarov is interesting, is he not?"

"Very."

"So very wise, and yet not a whole man." She picked up her tea reflectively. "His nerves were never strong enough for power."

"Unlike your husband's."

She looked up, a little sharply, as if I had interrupted a train of thought. "Yes, let us talk about Yordan," she said; "and about the trial. That is why you are here."

"I don't wish to distress you, but I should like you to know about something that happened today."

She nodded. "Yordan made one of his demonstrations. I already know about it."

"It wasn't in the official bulletin."

"No. Every evening since we have been under house arrest an old friend of our family has come to see us. Every evening he is searched by the sentries and every evening the sentries find some money in his handkerchief. They let him pass."

"I see. The demonstration was very moving."

"Yes, I was told that. It is a great relief. After this they will not dare to withhold his insulin injections."

There was a curious lack of emotion in the way she said it. We might have been discussing a common acquaintance.

"Do you think that was all he hoped to gain from it?"

"What else is there, Herr Foster? Please do not think that you must spare my feelings. Yordan will be condemned."

"Petlarov had another explanation. He said that your husband seized the chance of discrediting the evidence of the prosecution."

"Yordan is a good lawyer."

"From the way your husband used his opportunity Petlarov deduced that there might be some evidence against him that can only be dealt with by discrediting it."

She looked slightly puzzled. "Evidence that can only be dealt with by discrediting it?" she repeated.

"Yes."

She shrugged. "There will no doubt be many things too absurd even for denial."

"There is no true evidence that can be brought to support any of the charges?"

She looked surprised. "Of course not."

"No facts at all that could be twisted into evidence of corrupt negotiations in 1944?"

"Most facts can be twisted, Herr Foster."

"But in this case not credibly?"

"No."

"That would be true also of the alleged association with the Officer Corps Brotherhood?"

"Doubly so. The idea is absurd. My husband was the man primarily responsible for the destruction of the Brotherhood."

"You think that false evidence will be brought?"

"They have no alternative," she said with a touch of impatience.

"Then it will be easy for your husband to disprove the evidence?"

"If he is allowed to do so, yes. But I do not follow the trend of your questions, Herr Foster. The charges are obviously absurd."

"That is what troubles me, madame. If there is no vestige of a case to support them, they are too absurd. As Petlarov points out, if they had to fake evidence, there were less fantastic charges available."

"Petlarov is sometimes too clever. It is perfectly simple. Association with the Brotherhood is a capital offense and today also a disgrace."

"You do not expect to be surprised by any of the evidence?"

"Nothing that the People's Party can contrive would surprise me."

For a moment or two I sipped my tea. There was something difficult I wanted to say. She was sitting attentively waiting for me to go on. The sun was dying and in the faint after-light her face was astonishingly youthful. I might have been looking at the young schoolteacher whom the lawyer Deltchev had married, the young woman of Greek family whose lips may have had even then the same gentle, inflexible determination that I saw now.

"Madame Deltchev," I said, "when you were speaking of your daughter you referred to your husband as the man who betrayed his party."

"I was representing him as my daughter sees him."

"But you do not see him that way?"

"I understand him better than that, Herr Foster."

"That might not be a reply to the question, madame."

"Is the question important for your understanding of the trial?"

"I do not know your husband. It seems to me important that I should."

She sat back in her chair. She had just put her tea down on the table beside her, and her hands rested lightly on the chair arms. There they could reveal nothing.

"You saw my husband in court today. You could see the evidence of most of the qualities you wish to know about—his courage, his cleverness, his sense of timing, his determination. One thing the circumstances would not let you see—his absolute integrity, and I, who know his heart, will vouch for that."

The light was very dim now, and in the shadow of the chair her face was difficult to see. Then she leaned forward and I saw her smile.

"And in case you wish to ask me about his weaknesses, Herr Foster, I will tell you. He cannot accept people as they are, but only as his reason dictates they should be. Feeling he suspects, reason never, and the idea that in him the two may be connected he rejects completely. Therefore he is often mistaken about people and just as often about himself."

I was silent for a moment. Then I got up to go.

"May I come and see you again, madame?"

"Of course, Herr Foster, please do." Then she paused. "I shall in any case be here," she added.

"Afterwards, if you are allowed to do so, will you leave the country?"

"When Yordan is dead, do you mean?"

"When there is no more to be done here."

"Then I shall go on living behind our wall," she said. "Did you not notice our wall?"

"It's very fine."

"You will see such walls round most of our old houses. In Bulgaria and in Greece, in Yugoslavia, in all the countries of Europe that have lived under Turkish rule it is the same. To put a wall round your house then was not only to put up a barrier against the casual violence of foreign soldiers, it was in a way to deny their existence. Then our people lived behind their walls in small worlds of illusion that did not include an Ottoman Empire. Sometimes, as if to make the illusion more complete, they painted the walls with scenes of national life; but only on the inside, for that was where life was lived. Now that we are again inside our walls, the habits of our parents and our childhood return quietly like long-lost pets. I surprise them in myself. This room, for instance. Since Yordan's arrest it has been the only room on this floor of the house that has had the shutters open in the daytime. My feelings tell me it is better so. But why? No reason except that from all the other windows on this floor one can see the street."

"Isn't it dangerous to deny the street?"

"For my children, yes. For me, no, for I shall not try to impose my private world upon the real. My son Philip is a student in Geneva. He will be a lawyer like his father. Already he promises to be brilliant, and Switzerland is a better place for study than here. I hope to make it possible for Katerina to join him there." She paused. "Yes, by all means come again, Herr Foster. When you wish." She pressed a bell-push. "Rana will unbolt the doors and show you out. I will tell her also to admit you if you come again."

"Thank you."

We shook hands and said good night. As I went to the door I heard the old woman's sandals flapping along the passage outside.

"Herr Foster."

"Yes, madame?"

"It might be misleading to pay too much attention to Petlarov's views."

"I will remember what you say. Good night."

"Good night."

The door opened and a shaft of electric light from the passage struck across the darkened room. I glanced back; I wanted to see her face again in the light; but she had turned away.

I went past the old woman into the passage and waited while she was given her instructions. Then she shut the door of the room and led the way downstairs.

The girl was standing in the hall. She was waiting for me. She had changed into a blouse and skirt.

"Herr Foster, may I speak to you a moment?"

"Of course." I stopped.

She said something to the old woman, who shrugged and went away.

"I will show you out myself," the girl said; "but I wanted to speak to you first. I wanted to apologize to you for my behavior."

"That's all right."

"It was unforgivable."

She looked so solemn that I smiled.

Her pale cheeks colored slightly. "I have something to ask of you, Herr Foster."

"Yes, Fräulein?"

She dropped her voice. "Tell me, please. Were you searched by the guards when you came in?"

"No. One of them pushed me in the back with his rifle and they looked at my press permit, but that's all."

"A foreign press permit. Ah, yes." Her eyes became intent. "Herr Foster, I have a favor to ask of you." She paused, watching to see how I took it.

"What is it you want me to do?"

"To deliver a letter for me."

"What letter?"

She took a letter from her blouse pocket.

"Can't you post it?"

"I am not permitted. Besides—" She hesitated.

"You just want me to post it for you?"

"To deliver it, Herr Foster."

"Why can't I post it?"

"There is internal censorship."

"Where is it to be delivered?"

"Inside the city, Herr Foster," she said eagerly. "Near the station."

"Who is it to?"

She hesitated again. "A young man," she said.

"Supposing I'm caught with it?"

"You will not be, Herr Foster. Rana said that when she opened the door the guards were friendly to you. Please, Herr Foster."

I thought for a moment of the guards and of their friendliness. The muscles in my shoulder had stiffened slightly.

"All right, Fräulein. A pleasure."

"Thank you, Herr Foster."

I took the letter and glanced at the envelope. The address was in block letters and quite clear. I put it in my pocket.

Her smile was replaced suddenly by a look of anxiety. "When will you deliver it?"

"Tomorrow sometime. When I can."

She would have liked to ask me to deliver it that night, but I was not going to do that. I made as if to go.

"Thank you," she said again. "I will show you out now if you wish."

She had a small hand-lamp. We went out and across the dark courtyard to the door in the wall. She undid the bolts.

"Good night, Herr Foster," she whispered, and then, standing behind the door so that she could not be seen from outside, she opened it.

The beam of a powerful flash shone in my face, blinding me. I stepped through the wall, and the door closed behind my back. I stood still.

"*Papieren,*" said a remembered voice.

I got out my wallet and opened it with the press permit showing. The private was holding the flashlight. The corporal came into the beam of it. He glanced at the permit without touching it and then, smiling at me grimly, he nodded and with his thumb motioned me on my way. He said something and the private laughed. They were pleased that I had so quickly learned my lesson.

It was only as I walked away up the street and the beating of my heart began to return to normal that I realized that, for a moment or two, while the light had been shining on my face and while I had wondered if they might be going to search me after all, I had been very frightened. I fingered the pocket with the letter. It crackled faintly. I smiled to myself. I was childishly pleased. I did not know that I had just performed one of the most foolish actions of my life.

CHAPTER VIII

As USUAL NOW, I had breakfast with Pashik.

"Last night, Mr. Foster," he said, "I telephoned your hotel."

"I was out."

"Yes. It does not matter." In his brown eyes was the faint hostility of the lover determined not to be possessive. "It was to tell you that Monsieur Brankovitch, the Minister of Propaganda, has called a foreign-press conference for this evening. We, of course, have been invited."

"Oh?" What Petlarov had said about the tactics of the Propaganda Ministry came into my mind.

"Monsieur Brankovitch will speak and also answer questions," said Pashik solemnly. "It will be very interesting. The food and drink will be excellent."

"And there will be a collection taken for the poor of the parish."

"I beg pardon."

"Nothing. A bad joke."

"The conference will be in the state rooms of the Ministry at six o'clock."

"Good."

He dabbled his bread in his coffee. "Have you seen Petlarov again, Mr. Foster?"

"Yes. I thought you'd rather not know about it." For a moment I wondered if I should also tell him that I had been to see Madame Deltchev, and then decided not to.

"As long as there is no indiscretion, Mr. Foster."

"He comes privately to my hotel room. The reception clerk does not know him."

He sighed unhappily. "No doubt he will be discreet for his own sake. Is he still of interest to you?"

"Yes. He is an intelligent man, don't you think?"

"If he had used his intelligence, Mr. Foster, I should be more sympathetic towards him."

"You mean if he had played ball with the regime?"

"Of course. That is the realistic attitude."

We went off to the trial.

That day, the third, six witnesses were heard. All of them had been members of the Committee of National Unity, and all, except one, were members of the People's Party. The exception was a man named Lipka, and he was a member of the anti-Deltchev section of the Agrarian Socialists.

For the most part, the evidence consisted of repetitions of the assertions made by Vukashin the day before. A mass of documents, including the minutes of the Committee meetings for the critical period, was produced, and there was a great deal of pseudo-legal fuss about which documents could and which could not be admitted as exhibits. The minutes were naturally well to the fore. As minutes they were quite often worse than useless, but as ammunition for the prosecutor they were just the thing. I remember one typical item: "After some discussion the Committee agreed that Y. Deltchev should meet again with the Anglo-American representatives and urge them to delay the final decision on the proposals previously made." The prosecutor's witnesses declared that the "discussion" in question had been an effort by Deltchev and his henchmen to stampede the Committee into accepting a set of Anglo-American proposals it had not even seen and that the Committee's decision had made Deltchev "grind his teeth with rage." The judges had a word or two to say and even the defendant's counsel, Stanoiev, felt it safe to join in this sort of argument. At one point, indeed, there was a fair simulation of a legal battle between the two advocates—a battle between two clowns with rubber swords—and, in the approved fashion, high words were exchanged.

The only effective witness was Lipka. He was one of those angry, embittered men who bear the news of their defeat in their faces; prepared always for hostility, they succeed in provoking no more than wary impatience. A talentless but ambitious man, he had been an Agrarian Socialist deputy for many years without achieving office, and his membership on the Committee had seemed to him the long-awaited recognition of his worth and the beginning of his period of fulfillment. In fact, his value to the unconstitutional Committee had resided simply in his status as an elected deputy, and when posts in the Provisional Government were being allotted he had been passed over without a thought. From that moment he had nursed an almost pathological hatred of Deltchev. At one time that hatred had been something over which people smiled and shrugged. Now, at last, the People's Party had turned it to account. His mode of attack was stupid but damaging.

Most of those whose work is directly related to the moods and behavior of the public are inclined to refer to it on occasion in disparaging, even insulting terms. But, while a gibe at popular stupidity from a harassed bus conductor may be amusing, the same gibe from the mouth of a leading politician has, for many, an uglier sound. What Lipka did was to quote Deltchev's private comments on various matters and contrast them with public utterances made by him at the same time.

"Papa" Deltchev had made a speech officially regretting an incident in which some peasants, misunderstanding or ignoring a Red Army order to keep out of a certain area, had been shot down by Russian sentries. In private he had said: "It might not be a bad thing if a few more of the damn fools were shot." After a speech congratulating the farmers on their public-spirited efforts to send more food to the towns "Papa" Deltchev had said privately: "Thank God, they've had sense enough at last to find the black market." On his own proposals for dealing with the fuel shortage "Papa" Deltchev had remarked: "And if they're still cold we can always print a few more copies of the regulations for them to burn."

There were altogether about a dozen examples given of the prisoner's "contemptuous disregard of the welfare of the people whose interests he pretended to have at heart." No doubt there were, as Lipka claimed, many others that could have been quoted. The muttered asides of an overworked minister of state grappling with administrative chaos are unlikely to be distinguished for their sweetness or reason, and if he is an impatient man with crude notions of humor, they may be better forgotten. Certainly they cannot fairly be used as evidence of his true mind and intentions.

JUDGMENT ON DELTCHEV   [489

In his only interruption of the day Deltchev made this point himself. He said: "The doctor called out in the middle of a cold night may privately curse all mankind, but that curse does not prevent his doing his best for the patient."

This remark was immediately excluded from the record as irrelevant. It had its effect in court, but I was beginning to see that it was not in the court that Deltchev was being tried.

Petlarov's comments were not reassuring.

"After sitting for three days in that courtroom," he said, "you may realize that not one single piece of evidence that could be called evidence in a civilized court of law has been offered in support of the charges and that the only piece of sense uttered has been supplied by the prisoner in his own defense. And yet already much damage has been done. The grocer I now visit again—thanks to you, my friend—is an intelligent man and a supporter of Deltchev. He detests the People's Party and suspects what he reads in the controlled press. Yet the trial is important to him, and as he cannot attend in person, he must read the official reports in the newspapers. He reads with great suspicion, of course, and he discounts much of what he reads. But where is his standard of measurement? How can he discriminate? He reads that Minister Vukashin's evidence proves conclusively certain accusations against Deltchev. Can he ask by what rules of evidence Vukashin's statements are held to constitute a proof of anything except their own dishonesty? Of course not. He is a cautious man and hard to convince, but when I ask him today what he thinks, he is uneasy and does not like to meet my eye. 'Evidently,' he says to me, 'there was much evil that we did not know about. Even if these pigs must find it out, it is best that we know. We are in a mess all right.' And you know, Herr Foster, for the Vukashins and the Brankovitches, that is success. The disillusioned do not fight."

"I thought that it was the possible truth of some of the allegations that was worrying you."

"The foreign press is not so easily disturbed by official bulletins as my grocer. What did Madame have to say about the Brotherhood?"

"She said quite confidently that the charges were absurd."

"Did you believe her?"

"I believe she sincerely thinks they are absurd."

"You were impressed, eh?"

"Yes. She said she thought you were being over-clever."

"It is possible. I hope so. But remember that the only parts of his indictment which make statements that can be proved or disproved are those referring to the Brotherhood. You may create a haze of misrepresentation to prove that a man had evil intentions and cast doubts on his denials; but if you claim that on a certain date he went to a certain place and saw a certain person and he can prove that he did not, you are lost.

Because the court invites your contempt, do not suppose that Prochaska and Brankovitch are fools."

"What does Katerina Deltchev do?"

"She was an art student."

"Was?"

"Is, for all I know. But of course she cannot attend classes at present." He looked at my wrist watch. "It is time for you to go. You must not miss Brankovitch."

I went to the press conference in a gloomy frame of mind.

The Ministry of Propaganda occupied one of the wings of what had once been the royal palace. It had been built, during a period of national prosperity toward the end of the eighteenth century, to the design of an Italian architect who had seen Versailles. Only a quarter of the building planned had been completed, but the resultant structure was imposing and quite large enough to contain three ministries and the national bank. The Propaganda Minister's press conference took place in a large state room with a painted ceiling and two vast chandeliers. Chairs had been ranged in a semicircle round the marquetry desk at which the Minister was to stand. To one side there was a long table arranged as a buffet, with napkins covering the food on it.

Among the American and British correspondents Brankovitch was known as Creeping Jesus; he had a peculiar way of walking with his head and shoulders slightly in front of the rest of his body while his arms remained at a position of attention at his sides. By the French correspondents it was said that the posture was imposed upon him, as, in his imagination, Brankovitch carried two portfolios under his arms: that of his own Ministry on one side and that of the head of the Government on the other. He was a pale, dark man with a massive head and supercilious eyes. A graduate of Warsaw University, he had once been a mining engineer and his connection with politics had begun with pamphleteering. He had made a name for himself before the war as the arch-opponent of the foreign oil companies. He was a clever, ambitious man who never missed a chance of referring most emphatically to his loyalty to and admiration of Vukashin. There were many jokes made about these fulsome references to his leader; but it was said that, while he did not laugh at the jokes when they were reported to him, neither did he frown. It was believed that Vukashin disliked him personally but respected his judgment.

There were about sixty persons in the room; about half of us were foreigners. Brankovitch came in briskly, followed by two male secretaries bearing files and notebooks, and those who had been standing about, talking, took their seats. Brankovitch waited, looking round, until the movements had ceased. Then he began.

"Gentlemen of the press," he said in German, "I have invited you to meet me here with three objects in mind. First, I wish to help you as far as possible in your work by giving you certain information necessary to your understanding of the evidence soon to be given in the criminal trial you are reporting. Next, I wish to give you an opportunity of asking me questions on matters of fact, and also"—he smiled slightly—"on matters of opinion to which you may feel you already know the answers. Thirdly, I wished for the pleasure of renewing acquaintance with those of you I already know and of meeting those I don't know. But business before pleasure, as the English say. I will speak briefly and then there will be time for questions."

He glanced at his watch. He had a sort of brusque amiability that was not displeasing; he did not much care what we thought of him or mind if his amiability were not reciprocated. He was the busy man prepared to waste a little time on fools and so, logically, indifferent to foolishness.

"Let me tell you," he said, "about the Officer Corps Brotherhood; not about its origins—I feel sure you know about those—but about its later activities and its methods. Terrorist societies are not recent institutions. Most countries have suffered from them. Many countries, including the United States of America, still do suffer from them occasionally. It is the duty of all civilized governments, when these occasions arise, to seek out and destroy the criminals. It is the duty, I say; yet, of course, the duty is not always performed. Sometimes the government is itself terrorized. In other cases the government may sympathize with the terrorists' aims and secretly wish them well. I need hardly tell you that the Government of the People's Party is neither intimidated by nor in any degree sympathetic to the Officer Corps Brotherhood. We will not tolerate crime of any sort. The workman who kills his mate in a moment of rage and the fanatic who kills his ideological enemy in cold blood shall have the same justice."

"From a People's Court?" somebody in the row behind me murmured; but if Brankovitch heard, he took no notice. He went on:

"Under the reactionary governments of the prewar years the Brotherhood became a great and terrible burden to our people. It is not known for certain how many murders it was responsible for. Without doubt the number must be reckoned in hundreds. I can tell you with more precision that the number of violent attacks on the person committed by the Brotherhood in the ten years between 1930 and 1940 was about one thousand four hundred. This figure includes only those cases serious enough to need hospital treatment. The reason for the greater precision is, of course, that those persons lived to explain what had happened. The injuries included bullet wounds—approximately six hundred cases; stabbings—approximately two hundred cases; acid-throwing—approximately thirty cases; flogging—approximately two hundred cases; and severe bruising and beating with truncheons, rods, and other weapons made up the remainder."

He had been referring to notes in front of him. Now he pushed them aside.

"But statistics can give little idea of the emotional consequences of this state of affairs, of the hatreds and fears aroused and of the effect on the social life of the community. I will tell you, therefore, of one typical case among the known cases and leave the rest to your imaginations. It is the case of Kyril Shatev, who was prefect of this city in 1940. A man named Brodno, a criminal pervert and a member of the Brotherhood, had been arrested on suspicion of murder. There was plenty of evidence on this occasion and Shatev determined to bring this man to trial. Immediately he began to receive the usual threats from the Brotherhood. He ignored them. I will be quite honest with you; past experience told him that when the case came for trial the attentions of the Brotherhood would turn from him to the judge trying the case. The judge might yield, but that was not Shatev's business. However, he miscalculated. The probability is that the evidence against Brodno incriminated senior members of the Brotherhood and was for them too dangerous to be heard. The Sunday before the date of the trial was to be set, Shatev, with his wife, his two young children, and two female servants, was at his house about ten kilometers out of the city. They were about to sit down to the midday meal when a car drove up and three men got out. They said they wanted water for the car. A servant unthinkingly opened the outer door and the men pushed past her, knocking her senseless with a pistol butt. Then they went into the house. Shatev tried to defend his family and was immediately shot. Unfortunately for him, he did not die at once. The men had a bayonet, and the two children were killed with it. Shatev's wife was then forced to witness her husband's sexual mutilation, also with the bayonet. She was then killed herself. The other servant was not harmed. She was to serve as a witness, they said, that the sentence of the Brotherhood had been carried out. She was threatened, however, that if she attempted to identify the murderers she too would be killed. The murderers were never identified and Brodno was never tried."

He paused for a moment and looked round. "One typical case," he said, and sighed. "No doubt," he went on, "much could be said about a government that allowed itself to be intimidated by such means, but it is easy to miss the point. There were, in fact, many members of the Brotherhood in Government circles. This we have found out later, for, of course, membership was always secret. Who were these men? We know of two who were ministers and twenty-seven in posts of high authority in the civil service, the police, and the army. There were certainly others in these high places. The plain truth is that membership in the Brotherhood ran through every class of our society except that of the ordinary workman. This Brotherhood is a bourgeois disease. It is difficult to conceive, I grant you, that a man, presumably of more than average intelligence and ability, who has made his way to a position of authority and responsibility, could have any direct relationship with, for example, the murderous perverts who entered the Shatevs' house that Sunday or with others equally vile. But we found it so. When, during the life of the Provisional Government, we began the attack upon this evil, we had many terrible surprises. Yes, I say, *terrible*. To despise a man politically is one thing. To discover that he is a criminal lunatic is another. It is difficult to believe the most incontrovertible evidence in such cases. Yet we must."

He paused again and there was dead silence. We knew that now he was talking about Deltchev. He clasped his hands in front of him.

"Let me give you an example from history, gentlemen," he said; "not the history of our own country, but that of Italy and France. In 1830 there was in Italy a young exile named Louis Bonaparte, a nephew of the first Napoleon and once his adopted grandson. In Italy also at that time there was a secret terrorist society called the Carbonari—the Charcoal-Burners. Among the members were nobles, officers, landlords, Government officials, peasants, and priests. The members called each other 'cousin' and the only form of resignation ever accepted from a member was his death. This young Bonaparte became a member of the Carbonari and a year after was imprisoned by the Austrian police for his part in a murderous affair. He was not then a very important or responsible person. But twenty-eight years later, when that same man was Napoleon III, Emperor of France, the Carbonari had need of him and sent a reminder by an assassin named Orsini. The reminder was a gift of three bombs, and they exploded one evening in the January of 1858 as the Emperor was arriving at the Opéra in Paris. Eight innocent bystanders were killed and a hundred and fifty wounded, but Cousin Bonaparte was quite safe. What the Carbonari wanted from him was help to make a bourgeois revolution in Italy. He did not hesitate. The responsibilities of Napoleon III, Emperor of France, toward the people he ruled were as nothing beside those of Cousin Bonaparte toward the Carbonari terrorists. And so the Italian Risorgimento was paid for with the blood of the French soldiers that soaked the fields of Montebello and Turbigo and Solferino. It is not a pretty story—no prettier than that of Shatev and his family."

There was silence for a moment.

He added quietly: "Gentlemen, our people will fertilize no more fields for the 'cousins' or 'brethren' of this century. We intend to seek out all the murderers whether they sit on café chairs or on the thrones they have made for themselves above the heads of the people. The People's Party and its great leader Vukashin are pledged to that." He looked round at us again and then sat down. "I will answer questions," he said.

It was quite well done and for a space nobody moved; then an American in front of me got up.

"In December of last year, Minister," he said, "the People's Party Government announced that the Officer Corps Brotherhood had been completely—*eliminated*. I think that was the word used. Are we to understand now that that announcement was incorrect?"

Brankovitch nodded. "Unfortunately, yes. At the time, of course, we believed it to be true. Later developments have shown that we were mistaken."

"What later developments, Minister?"

"I would prefer not to anticipate the court proceedings."

A small dark man got up.

"Minister, was not Deltchev himself responsible for the very vigorous proceedings taken to eliminate the Brotherhood?"

"He was certainly responsible for the action against the Brotherhood that we now know to have been ineffective, but the decision that there *should* be action was taken by the Provisional Government as a whole. In other words, the People's Party participated in the decision but not in the carrying-out of it."

Others began to rise and now the questions came quickly.

"Minister, can your allusion to Napoleon III be taken to mean that the Government links the allegations about Deltchev's peace negotiations with the allegations about his membership in the Brotherhood?"

"You may draw that conclusion if you wish."

"The charge is that Deltchev was to be paid for his efforts. Aren't the two suggestions inconsistent?"

"Possibly. But remember that Napoleon III also had his reward—Nice, the Riviera, Savoy."

"Minister, do you consider that the evidence heard so far in court has gone any way toward proving any of the charges against Monsieur Deltchev?"

"The evidence must be considered as a whole."

"By whom was defending counsel appointed, Minister?"

"By the Government. In all cases when a prisoner fails to appoint counsel to defend him that is done."

"Did this prisoner fail to appoint counsel? Did he not, as an advocate, wish to defend himself?"

"On a criminal charge a prisoner is not by law permitted to conduct his own defense. The law was made for the benefit of poor persons certain of conviction who feared to burden their families with legal costs."

"Minister, could not the law, clearly not intended for persons in Monsieur Deltchev's position, be waived in this case?"

"Are laws waived in England for the benefit of persons in high position?"

"Then you agree, Minister, that it would be to Monsieur Deltchev's benefit if he could defend himself?"

"It would be to the benefit of you gentlemen, I have no doubt. I apologize for our reluctance to have the court turned into a circus entertainment."

"Will the Minister say if, as a result of the prosecutor's unhappy efforts yesterday to provide the court with entertainment, the prisoner will now be allowed proper medical attention in the prison?"

Brankovitch rose to his feet with a smile. "The prisoner is receiving ample medical attention," he said, "and as much insulin as he wishes. It was nothing more sinister than a stupid administrative blunder that prevented his having attention for a few days. Disciplinary action has been taken against those responsible. Naturally the prisoner took the utmost advantage of his plight to gain sympathy—"

"When driven to do so by the prosecutor?"

"Or when a favorable opportunity presented itself." Brankovitch smiled again. "We interpret motives from the standpoint of our own prejudices. But please note that the prisoner was not prevented from addressing you."

"What he said was not reported in the official press, Minister."

"Quite properly. The fact that a man is diabetic surely does not affect his responsibility to the community for criminal acts. Gentlemen, perhaps you would care to continue our discussion over the refreshments. I hope you will not think I am attempting to corrupt you if I say that there is champagne and caviar for you to sample. I am merely performing another of my functions as a Minister in introducing to you two products of our agricultural and fishing industries which we are anxious to export. The champagne is not French, of course, but it is a dry, sparkling wine of pleasing character and I think you will like it."

There were one or two murmurs of amused assent and a scraping of chairs. Waiters entered, obviously in response to a signal, and whisked away the napkins from the buffet.

"He is clever, the Minister," said Pashik seriously.

"Yes, he is. Shall we go?"

He looked shocked. "Do you not wish to ask questions, Mr. Foster?"

"What about? Napoleon III?"

"I think it would be impolite to go," said Pashik earnestly. "The Minister will surely wish to meet you. There is protocol to be observed."

"There are others going." Though most of those present had moved over to the buffet and stood in groups talking, I noticed several making unobtrusive exits.

"Those are local agency men, Mr. Foster. They have met the Minister before."

"All right. Shall we go over?" Brankovitch was talking to a group that included Sibley, the man who drank too much and was indiscreet.

"No, Mr. Foster. Let us quietly have some refreshments. Presently matters will arrange themselves."

We were joined after a moment or two by an American I had chatted with once or twice at the courthouse. A waiter brought us wine and caviar sandwiches. One of the secretaries delivered copies of a long blood-curdling piece on the Officer Corps Brotherhood.

"Did you know that Byron was a member of the Carbonari?" the American was saying. "I think we ought to rechristen our friend Brankovitch. When Ferdinand of Italy tried to liquidate the Carbonari he had his Minister of Police set up another secret society called 'the Braziers of the counterpoise,' *Calderai del Contrappeso.* The Minister recruited all the worst characters in the country for it and what they did to the Italian liberals makes Little Bopeep of that Shatev story. The Minister was a man called Prince Canosa. What about Creeping Canosa for our friend?"

Pashik had left us. I talked to the American and ate sandwiches. After a few minutes Pashik came back rather breathlessly with one of the secretaries, a stony-eyed young man with over-neat clothes.

"This is Monsieur Kovitch," he said; "he is of the Minister's bureau." The secretary bowed and we shook hands. "The Minister is most anxious to meet you, Herr Foster," he said stiffly.

"I shall be honored." I caught the American's eye and he put his tongue very obviously in his cheek.

The secretary stared hard at me. "Have you yet had time, Herr Foster," he said, "to visit any of the well-known beauty spots that abound in the vicinity of our city?"

"I'm afraid I haven't."

"At this time of year," the secretary continued steadily, "there are many varieties of the most remarkable rose blooms in the world to be seen and savored. Our country is very beautiful. However, it is to be hoped that you will wish to be present on Saturday at the official parade and celebration in honor of the twenty-seventh anniversary of the founding of the People's Party."

"I don't—"

"Herr Foster's special pass has already been applied for," Pashik put in smartly.

"Ah, then he will see some of the beauties of the country brought to the city," pursued the secretary steadily. "This year the parade will be a symbolic integration of peaceful husbandry and armed might—the plow and the sword in harmony together."

"Very interesting."

"Yes. It is of the utmost importance that all our visitors leave us with a correct impression. I will myself see that you have an advantageous place, Herr Foster. Here, now, is the Minister."

He stepped aside nimbly, like a *compère* effacing himself for the entry of the star. Brankovitch, with the other secretary in attendance, had stopped to say a word to a Scandinavian group. Now he turned in my direction. The secretary beside me said something in his own language with my name in it. Brankovitch held out his hand and turned on a watery smile.

"How do you do?" he said in English. His warm hand released mine almost as soon as it touched it. He nodded to Pashik as I answered him. "You have not been to our country before, Mr. Foster?"

"No, Minister. But I'm finding my first visit most interesting."

He nodded. "Much fiction has already been written about it, but mostly by strangers. Now that cultural activities are being widely encouraged, however, perhaps a native school of writers will emerge. There is the language difficulty, of course. A knowledge of our language is rare. Yet Ibsen, also writing in a narrowly spoken language, achieved world fame."

"Ibsen's heroes and heroines were not obliged to be positive, Minister."

"Ah, I see you have heard of our special problems. Yes, we are compelled to consider the standard of education of the public here. We must pay still for past injustices. The percentage of illiteracy is high and those who are literate are for the most part still uneducated in the Western sense of the word. But in other cultural fields—the visual arts and music, for example—greater freedom is already possible."

"Ideas do not have to be expressed in words to be dangerous, Minister."

"We do not hinder truth, Mr. Foster—only the facile repetition of lies. But we must have a long undisturbed conversation about such things, for I would be glad to hear your opinions. Tell me, how did you find Madame Deltchev last night? In good health?"

I sensed rather than heard Pashik's sharply indrawn breath. Brankovitch's gaze rested on me with unwavering affability.

"She seemed very well."

He smiled again. "She is not being persecuted?"

"Not that I'm aware of."

"We have tried to spare her as much as possible. Naturally her position is difficult and we have to protect her against possible demonstrations. But I am glad to hear that she is well. You are the only journalist who has interviewed her, I think."

"I think so."

He nodded vaguely. "I am so glad to have had this opportunity of meeting you, Mr. Foster," he said. "We must have another talk. Most interesting."

He nodded again and turned away. The secretary slid past me after him. The interview was at an end.

I looked at Pashik. His face was quite expressionless. He stepped up to me.

"Do you wish to go now, Mr. Foster?"

"Yes, I think so."

"You did not tell me that you had seen Madame Deltchev," he said as we walked away.

"No. I thought you'd prefer not to know."

"We must hope no harm is done."

"What harm can be done?"

He shrugged. "Such things attract attention."

"Does that matter?"

"We must hope not. But I would have preferred that you had told me. I could at least have prevented the embarrassment."

"What embarrassment? The sentries on the house looked at my permit. They reported. What of it?"

"You do not understand."

"I'm afraid I don't. I think you're over-anxious, as I've said before."

"I think my opinion about that may be better informed, Mr. Foster."

"I'm sorry, Pashik. I certainly have no wish to compromise you, but I have a job to do."

"I have the responsibility, Mr. Foster."

"You must try to shoulder it."

Before he could answer, there were quick footsteps behind us. Pashik turned round as if he expected to be attacked. It was Sibley.

"Hullo there," he said breezily; "how are you, Foster? And you, Georghi my friend? What a dreadful party! When are we going to have that drink? Now? I feel the need."

"Please excuse me," said Pashik hastily, "I must go to my office. Mr. Foster, you have messages to send."

"I'll see you tomorrow."

He hesitated. We had reached the door. He gave up. "Very well. Good night, Mr. Foster. Good night, Mr. Sibley."

"Good night."

He went, leaving a slip-stream of malodorous disapproval.

Sibley chuckled. "Poor little man," he said.

CHAPTER IX

WE WENT to a near-by café and ordered drinks. Then Sibley disappeared to make a telephone call. When he came back the drinks had arrived. He picked his up, peered into it as if it were a crystal ball, then downed it at a gulp.

"Well, what do you think?" he said grimly.

"About this evening's performance?"

"Performance! Exactly." He snapped his fingers at the waiter for another drink. "Incredible, isn't it?"

"In what way do you mean?"

"Oh, all of it. That old, old routine! Prejudice, friends? Not a bit of it! Anyway, judge for yourselves, friends. Here are the simple facts given as simply as we know how—the facts about the Brotherhood. What has that to do with Deltchev? Who said it had anything to do with him? You're drawing the conclusions, friends, not us. We're only giving you the nasty facts. And to show you that the facts are really nasty we'll pull an old atrocity story out of the bag. Castration and rape, friends! Yes, we thought that'd get you where it hurts. What has that to do with Deltchev? Well, we don't say definitely that it *has* anything to do with him but—well, you're drawing the conclusions and we can't stop you, can we? In fact, although we're not exactly saying so, the same ugly thought is beginning to cross our minds now. How clever of you to think of it first, friends! But it does seem fantastic, doesn't it? Though, wait! Isn't there a historical precedent that fits the situation like a glove? Of course there is. And doesn't history repeat itself? Of course it does. In fact, there is one point of coincidence we didn't mention. When Murat decided to destroy the Carbonari he gave the job to his police chief. The police chief destroyed a lot of people, and Murat thought the job was done until he found out that the police chief had always been a Carbonaro himself and that the cousins were stronger than ever. Strange, isn't it, friends? How clever of you to remember without our telling you! Any more questions? Yes? Well, let's not get into tiresome arguments. Let's have some caviar and a nice glass of aerated cat water. They make me tired." He swallowed another large plum brandy and sat back.

"Another drink?"

"For God's sake, yes." He leaned forward, his face slightly flushed, his lips still wet with brandy. "How does one deal with it, Foster?"

"Brankovitch's press conference?" I signaled to the waiter.

"All of it. The whole phony business. Perhaps it's all right for you. You've got plenty of time. A series of articles, weeks hence. But I'm supposed to be sending news. All I've got through so far are those damned official bulletins. I suppose Pashik sends those to your people?"

"Yes."

"Do you know what I'd like to do?" His dull, hot eyes brooded on mine. "No, what?"

"I'd like to put it across them. I'd like to split the whole damn business wide open." He frowned suddenly as if with irritation at himself. "Take no notice. I had drinks before the party." He smiled slyly and lowered his voice. "Can you keep a secret, Foster?"

"Yes."

"The funny thing is I can do it."

"Do what?"

"What I said—break it open." He looked round cautiously and leaned farther forward. "I've found a way round this bloody censorship."

"Oh, yes?" My heart began to beat rather unpleasantly.

"I can't tell you the details because I swore not to, but there's a little man in the Propaganda Ministry who doesn't like the regime any more than we do and he'll play. Of course, if he was found out he'd be lucky if they hanged him quickly, but he's prepared to take the risk. There's only one snag." He paused. I waited. "He can't do it more than once and the deadline's tomorrow."

"That should give you time."

"It's a risk." He frowned at the table as the waiter put fresh drinks down. "A big risk. If I'm caught, I'm out. Of course, that wouldn't matter to you. It's not your living. But, by God, it's a risk I'd like to take."

"The little man in the Propaganda Ministry must think it worth while."

He laughed shortly. "You're right. It's funny, isn't it? One minute I'm breathing fire and murder, and the next I'm worrying about a little risk." He laughed again. His performance was deteriorating rapidly. I was not helping him and he would have to come to the point himself. I waited, fascinated.

"Would *you* take the risk?" he asked suddenly.

"I don't know. The question would have to arise."

"All right, supposing"—I thought I detected a note of genuine exasperation in his voice—"just supposing you had a chance to file a short message with mine. Would you take it?"

"Is that an offer?"

"Don't be silly. Why should I give you a beat?"

"I don't know. Why should you?"

"You'd have to make it worth my while."

"What's that mean?"

He did not answer. He was pretending to debate with himself. "Look, Foster," he said then, "let's be serious for a moment. If I'd thought you were going to fasten onto the thing like this, I tell you frankly I wouldn't have mentioned it." He paused. "But since I have, I tell you what I'll do. If you'll undertake to confine your message to pure comment on the trial as a whole, I'll get it through with mine."

"If you do send one, of course."

"Oh, I'm going to send it all right. Don't you worry. And now you can buy me another drink." He sat back with a tremendous air of having sold his birthright. "I make only one stipulation. I'll have to read your stuff before I pass it on. Honestly, I wouldn't trust my own brother in a thing like this. Right?"

"I understand." To give myself time to think I looked round for the waiter. I had had it all now: the confidence-promoting diatribe against the regime, the brandy-laden indiscretion, the indignant denial, the burst of generosity, the second thoughts, the grudging commitment. Petlarov would be amused. Pashik would purse his lips. I looked at my watch. I did not want to have to talk to Sibley any more. The waiter had disappeared. I put some money on the table.

"I have to go," I said.

It took me five minutes and another hastily swallowed drink to do so, but at last I stood up and put on my hat.

"About you-know-what," he said; "you'd better give me the stuff tomorrow morning. Two hundred words maximum."

"Oh, that." I smiled and shook my head. "I don't think I'll bother."

"Are you mad?"

"No. It's different for you. For me it's not worth the risk."

He looked at me coldly for a moment. Then very elaborately he shrugged. "As you will, *mon brave*," he said.

"Good night."

Still seated at the table, he gave me a heavily ironic bow. "Don't change your mind tomorrow, Foster *mio*," he answered, "it'll be too late."

"I won't change my mind." I nodded to him and walked out of the café. Outside I hesitated. Now that the disagreeable part of the encounter was over, I was curious. Sibley the *agent provocateur* and employee of Brankovitch interested me as Sibley the breezy newspaperman never could. I had an impulse to go back into the café, sit down, and try to lure him into explaining himself. I did look back. He was sitting looking down at his drink, his elbows on the table, the thin, fair down on his sunburnt scalp glistening faintly in the evening sun. As I looked, he put his hands up to his head and there was something so hopeless about the gesture that it was quite moving. Then one hand dropped to the stem of his glass and twirled it between a finger and thumb. The other came down too. The money I had put on the table was still there, and now a finger of this other hand crept out rather stealthily toward it and gently sorted it over to see how much was there. Then he looked round for the waiter. I turned away. For the moment there was not much more I wanted to know about Sibley.

I went back to my hotel. I did not eat much dinner. I remembered that in one dim corner of the hotel foyer I had seen a framed map of the city on the wall. After dinner I went to it and got out Katerina Deltchev's letter. The address on the envelope was short: "*Valmo, Patriarch Dimo 9.*"

With some difficulty I located the street on the map and set out. The girl had said that the street was near the station. It was, but it was also on the other side of the main line, and to get there I had to make a wide detour through a crowded street market to a bridge and walk back along the far side of a freight yard. By the time I had found the church that I had noted as a reference point on the map, it was almost too dark to read the lettering of the street names.

It was not an inviting locality. On one side of the main road there were tall warehouses and a power station interspersed with ugly apartment blocks; on the other side were small shops and steep lanes of wooden houses, the roofs of which were patched here and there with sheets of rusty corrugated iron; the old slum. There was a tram terminus a short distance down the road and I considered riding straight back into the city without troubling further about the letter. Then I decided to give the search for the street five minutes. If, as I hoped, I had not found it by then, I would go back. I found it almost immediately.

The street of the Patriarch Dimo was one of the steeper and shabbier lanes. There was a dimly lit wine shop at the corner, and behind it a decrepit wooden building that seemed to be used as a stable for oxen. I walked up the hill slowly. The girl had said hesitantly that her letter was to "a young man." I had, I think, imagined Valmo to be a fellow art student of hers, a handsome lad with other girl friends who would have no scruples about taking advantage of Katerina's enforced absence. Now my ideas had to change.

Number 9 was a house much like the rest, but with the ground-floor shutters crossed with planks and nailed up. There were no lights in any of the upper rooms and the greasy-walled entrance passage at the side was littered with pebbles and marked with chalk lines as if children had been playing a game in it. The house looked empty. I walked along the passage to the door and struck a match.

At some time recently the building had been a lodging-house, for there was a board with names painted on it. The match went out and I struck another. None of the painted names was Valmo. Then, as the second match was going out, I saw it. The top name had been scratched over with the point of a knife and under it the word "Valmo" was crudely written in pencil. I dropped the burnt-out match and stood in the darkness for a moment. I was becoming curious about this Valmo. By the light of another match I looked for a bell and, seeing none, tried the door. It was open.

I went in.

There was a small lobby with a flight of stairs in it. The place was quite still and seemed deserted. I looked round for a light. On the ceiling there was a hook and a smoke shield, but no lantern beneath it. I went up the stairs striking matches. There were two doors on the first landing, both open. I looked in. The rooms were empty. In one of them some floorboards were missing. I went on up. I did not stop on the next landing; obviously the house was abandoned. Only one thing delayed my turning back. The rooms I had seen had been deserted for many months. But Katerina had not been confined to her house that long. It was possible, therefore, that Valmo had only recently moved away and had left a notice of his new address.

As I went up the last flight of stairs I noticed a peculiar smell. It was ammoniac and very sickly. It became stronger as I reached the landing under the roof. I struck another match. There was only one door here, and it was shut. There was no notice on it. I knocked and waited. The match burned out. I struck another and turned the handle of the door and pushed. The door opened. Then I had a shock; the room inside was furnished.

I raised the match above my head and moved forward into the doorway. As I did so, I became aware of a sound; there were flies buzzing in the room.

In the small light of the match I saw an unmade bed, a deal table, and a chair with some newspapers piled on it. There was also a packing-case.

The match burned down and I dropped it. Then, by the pale arc of light it made as it fell, I saw on the floor a dark mass like a crumpled curtain.

As I struck the next match I took a pace forward into the room. The light from the match flared up.

The next instant my heart jolted violently. It was not a curtain on the floor. It was a man; and his face was black.

I stepped back quickly and with some sort of shout, I think. The movement blew the match out or I should have run. I fumbled desperately with the box and managed to get another match alight. I forced myself to look again.

His hair was close-cropped and white except where the blackness spread. The blackness was congealed blood, and it lay on and about him like spilled wax. His mouth was open and there was a gaping wound by his ear. There was no telling what he had looked like. He was lying on his right side, his knees drawn up to his chest and his elbows nearly touching them. He had on a dark serge suit and leather sandals, but no socks. He had been small and thin. The flies buzzed round him. He had been dead for more than a few hours.

I began to retch and went out on the landing.

A minute passed and I was beginning to get my breath again when I thought I heard a sound from below.

The blood was thudding in my head so loudly and my breathing was so quick and shallow that it was difficult to be certain. Then I managed to hold my breath for just over a second and heard the sound again. Very slowly and quietly somebody was coming up the stairs.

I don't know who I thought it was; the murderer, I suppose; at that moment I would have panicked if a fly had settled on my hand. In the darkness I stumbled back into the room, shut the door, lighted a match, and looked feverishly for the bolt. There was a bolt, but the socket of it was missing. I looked round desperately for something to jam the door with. I tried to use the chair, but the door handle was too low. The match I was holding went out. I fumbled with the box again, opened it upside down, and the matches spilled on the floor. I was shaking with fear now.

I went down on my knees and started to pick the matches up. At that moment I heard the footsteps on the landing just outside the door. I remained motionless. Under the door I saw a light flicker. The person outside had a flashlight.

Then the light went out and the door opened.

There was silence for a moment. Suddenly the flashlight went on and swept quickly round the room. It stopped on the body. Then it moved again quickly and stopped on me.

The end of a revolver barrel gleamed just in front of the flashlight. I did not move.

A voice said: "What are you doing here, Mr. Foster?"

It was Pashik.

CHAPTER X

I GOT to my feet.

"Why are you here, Mr. Foster?" he repeated.

"I don't know," I said. "Do you mind taking that light off my face?"

He turned the light down to my feet. I could see him now and the revolver in his hand was still pointing at me. He had his dispatch case under his arm and the medallion on it winked faintly.

"Well, Mr. Foster?"

"I might ask you the same question."

"I followed you, Mr. Foster."

"With a gun?"

"It was possible that we might not be alone."

"We're not." I looked at the dead man on the floor, but he did not move the light from my feet.

"I want to know why you are here, Mr. Foster, and who told you of this place. And I want to know right now." There was a very sharp edge to his voice.

"Katerina Deltchev asked me to deliver a letter for her. This was the address on it."

"Show me the letter."

"Pashik, do we have to stay in this room? Can't we go outside? Anyway, shouldn't we be calling the police? This man's been murdered."

"No, Mr. Foster, we should not be calling the police. Show me that letter."

I got it out. He came forward, took it from me, and turned the light on it.

"She told me that it was to a young man," I said.

Without replying he put the letter in his pocket and swept the light round the room.

"Have you touched anything here, Mr. Foster?"

"This chair. Why?"

"What did you touch it for?"

"When I heard you coming up the stairs I tried to jam it under the door handle."

"Wipe the chair where you touched it and also both sides of the door with your handkerchief. Then pick up all the matches you dropped, including the burnt-out ones, please."

I obeyed him. Just then the wish to get out of the room was stronger than my disposition to argue. He held the light down while I picked up the matches.

"Did anyone know you were coming here?"

"Only Katerina Deltchev."

"You told nobody?"

"No."

"Not Petlarov?"

"No."

"Mr. Sibley?"

"Nobody."

"Did anyone see you come in here?"

"I shouldn't think so. There weren't many people about."

"Your clothes are noticeably foreign. Did anyone turn to look at you?"

"You should know if you were following me."

"I was not close enough to see. Was there anybody in the passage below when you arrived?"

"No." I had collected all the matches. I straightened up. "I can't stay in this room any longer," I said, and went out on the landing.

"Wipe the door, Mr. Foster."

I did so. He ran the light round the room again and came out. "Shut the door with your handkerchief in your hand, please. Yes, that will do. Now, Mr. Foster, my car is at the end of the street by the wine shop. You have your matches. Go down as you came up, walk to my car, get in it, and wait for me."

"What are you going to do?"

"We must not be seen leaving together."

"Why not?"

"Get going, Mr. Foster."

He still had the revolver in his hand and he handled the thing as if he were used to it. Oddly, there was nothing incongruous about the look of Pashik with a gun.

He held the light for me as I went down the top flight of stairs. After that I struck matches again. It was a relief to get into the street. By the time I reached his car I had done a good deal of thinking.

I smoked the greater part of a cigarette before he joined me. Without a word he climbed into the driver's seat, took his gun and flashlight from the dispatch case and, putting them in the door pocket, stuffed a greasy rag over them. He started the car. "And now," he said, "we'll go see a friend of mine."

"What friend?"

"He will advise us what we must do. He is of a special kind of police."

"What special kind?"

"You will see, Mr. Foster. Perhaps the ordinary police should be told. I do not know."

He twitched the wheel suddenly, swerved across the road, and swung round uncertainly into a turning on the left.

I threw away the cigarette I had been smoking and lit another.

"Why did you follow me, Pashik?"

"I had a hunch that you might be about to do something foolish, Mr. Foster."

"But you did follow me?"

"You will agree that I was justified."

I looked at him. "I came through a street market that was difficult to get through on foot. How did you follow me in a car?"

"I cannot answer questions while I am driving, Mr. Foster."

"Then let's stop for a few minutes. I have lots of questions and they won't keep."

He drove on in silence.

"You've been to that house before, haven't you?" I said after a moment or two.

"Why should you think that, Mr. Foster?"

"You knew that that man's body was there before you came in. That is, unless you're quite used to finding corpses with shotgun wounds lying about. You paid no attention to this one."

He had been driving toward the center of the city. Now we lurched into a quiet boulevard with trees along it.

"Another thing," I said: "if you'd followed me and expected to find me there, you wouldn't have shown your gun. As you came up the stairs you heard me move about. If you'd known it was me you'd have called my name. You didn't follow me. You went there on your own account and for your own reasons. What were they?"

"You are making things very difficult, Mr. Foster," he said gloomily.

"Yes. Who was the dead man? Valmo? Who killed him? You?"

He did not answer. Behind the trees that lined the road there were houses with portes-cochères. He slowed down, then turned suddenly into a space between the trees and drove through into one of the courtyards.

He stopped and immediately turned off the lights. We were in pitch-darkness.

"Mr. Foster," he said, "you are arrogant and very dumb. If I were truly a murderer you would be already dead. I have been very patient with you. Now we will see my friend."

He switched on the flashlight and I saw that he had his revolver again. He put it in his dispatch case and we both got out. I looked up. The bulk of quite a large house was visible against the sky.

"Where is this?" I asked.

"My friend has an apartment here. This way."

I could see very little. We went through a side door down some tiled steps to a small hydraulic lift with a rope control. The cage bounced as we got into it. Pashik hauled on the rope and we shot upwards with a faint hissing sound.

At the top floor the lift stopped automatically and we got out on a bare stone landing with a small doorway in it and a steel ladder up to a skylight. Pashik knocked on the door.

After a moment or two a woman in an apron opened the door. She had gray hair scragged back into a bun, and a bitter mouth. She obviously knew Pashik. He made some explanation to her. She nodded and looked at me curiously as we went in; then she led the way along a narrow passage and showed us into a drawing-room. She switched on the lights and left us, shutting the door behind us. If there had been a faint smell of disinfectant in the air, it would have seemed like an appointment with a dentist. The room we were in, indeed, had very much the look of a waiting-room. The chairs stood round the walls and there was a large table in the middle with one small ashtray on it. All that was wanting was a selection of magazines.

"What's your friend's name?" I asked.

Pashik sat on the edge of one of the chairs. "I will introduce you to him, Mr. Foster."

"What did you go to that house for?"

"You do not believe me when I answer your questions, Mr. Foster." His brown eyes looked at me mournfully. He took off his glasses and began polishing them.

"You never do answer them. Why didn't you tell me that Sibley was working for the Propaganda Ministry? You must have known."

"How do you know that, Mr. Foster?"

"Petlarov warned me to expect an approach from someone pretending to have a way round the censorship. It came from Sibley. If you knew, why didn't you warn me?"

"Would you have believed me if I had, Mr. Foster? No. You would have thought that I was trying to stop you sending news out."

"Yes, I'm afraid you're right. I'm sorry."

"It is unimportant, Mr. Foster. It is simply that you do not like me."

He put his glasses on and stared at me. "I am used to being disliked," he added; "I no longer mind."

But I was spared the deathly embarrassment of replying to this. The gray woman appeared at the door, nodded to Pashik, and said something. He got up and turned to me.

"My friend wishes to see me privately for a moment, Mr. Foster," he said. "Perhaps you will wait."

He picked up his dispatch case and went out of the room.

I sat down.

Until that moment I had been feeling all right. Now, suddenly, the smell of the dead man was in my nostrils again. I felt sick and giddy. I put my head between my knees and tried to think of other things. I suppose that if Pashik had not arrived on the scene I should have hurried back to my hotel, had several large brandies and a sleeping-pill, and gone to bed. Instead I was sitting in a strange room in a strange house with a desperate feeling of having lost all contact with reality. At that moment I would have given anything to be back in London, quietly doing in my own way the work I understood. I had realized that the delayed reaction to the horror of finding a decomposing corpse in a dark room was only the surface of my discomfort. Beneath, there were fears of another kind. I had thought to write about the trial and condemnation of an innocent man. Now, in spite of the obvious injustice of the trial itself, I was having to accept the disagreeable possibility that really the man might not be innocent, that the rubbish Prochaska was talking might have a basis in fact, that the trembling hands of the diabetic Deltchev might have clasped in brotherhood those of the murderers of the Shatev family; and the foolish trouble was that if those things were true, I feared to know about them. Petlarov's grocer, I reflected bitterly, was not alone in his ill-informed uneasiness; Mr. Valiant-for-Truth, the great journalist, had also caught a whiff of the odor of corruption and was wishing his delicate nose elsewhere. It was curious how preoccupied I had become with smells; they seemed easier to deal with at that time than other ideas; the smell of the dead man, the smell of Pashik, the smell of furniture polish in Deltchev's house; those three things were related. And if I looked for reassurance to the other senses, I could recall the taste of the plum brandy I had had with Sibley, the feeling of the sentry's rifle on my shoulder, the image of Petlarov's white false teeth, and the sound of his voice saying: "Some of the evidence may not discredit itself. Some of it may be true."

I got up and began to wander round the room. I knew now that the train of thought I had been avoiding could be avoided no longer.

If you accepted the seemingly incredible proposition that Deltchev was, and for years had been, a member of the Officer Corps Brotherhood, it was possible to explain some things about him that had hitherto defied explanation. To begin with, you could explain the inexplicable election affair; Deltchev had done what he did, not because he had thought it right or necessary, or because he was a saint, or because he had been bought; he had done it in obedience to the orders of the Brotherhood. And having said that, you could also explain why he himself had been able to give no explanation for his action. You could explain, though with difficulty, how a prosaic, undistinguished Minister of Posts and Telegraphs had been able to become the leader of a secret nationalistic revolutionary movement and ultimately seize power. You could even explain the "football match" incident in that context; the fanatically nationalistic Brotherhood, having through fear of the growing People's Party misjudged the election timing, had commanded their puppet Deltchev to retrieve the position. Napoleon III had done more for the Carbonari. Besides, had not Petlarov himself admitted that power was a bribe that might be used with Deltchev? In a fantastic way it all fitted. It might be objected that, as a lawyer, Deltchev would not have qualified for membership in the early days of the Brotherhood; but the class distinction between professional men and army officers was not great. His membership was not impossible. It was certainly not improbable. Idealistic young men very often joined societies supposedly dedicated to the human struggles for freedom and justice; and very often, too, they later regretted having done so. When, I wondered, had Deltchev begun to regret the association? Then another objection occurred to me. Why, if the Brotherhood had supported Deltchev, had it also collaborated with the German occupation forces? But this I disposed of easily. What better cover could there have been for the subversive activities of the Brotherhood than half-hearted collaboration with the German Army? Not with the sharp and skeptical Gestapo, mark you, but with the army. It would be interesting to know about the men who had made the Brotherhood's policy. Perhaps the trial would reveal them.

But meanwhile Deltchev's daughter had sent a letter to a cheap lodging where there was a murdered man. I thought about that. Who was Valmo? Katerina's middle-aged lover? I doubted it. This rather too knowing young woman had offered me a drink because she had thought that the engaging way with an irritable reporter; she had said that the letter was to "a young man" because she had thought, perhaps less incorrectly, that that was the engaging way with a reluctant letter-smuggler. If I had had the presence of mind to do so, I might have looked more closely at the room for signs of a relationship with Katerina; her photograph perhaps, or a letter in her handwriting. A letter. And that brought me back to Pashik.

I had made a mistake about Pashik. I had thought of him as one of those hapless, over-anxious persons who cannot help entangling themselves in systems of small, unnecessary lies. It had not occurred to me that he might have anything of more than private importance to conceal. Now I had to reckon with the news not only that could he be concerned quite calmly with the body of a murdered man but also that his tiresome preoccupation with "discretion" had its origins in something very unlike the old-maidish timidity to which I had attributed it.

At that moment, with a jolt, I came out of the haze of cowlike rumination in which I had been lost and began to think clearly. If Pashik had known that the body was there before he came to the house, why was it now necessary to consult his "friend in the special police" so urgently? Answer: because I had been there, because I had seen the body, because I had seen Pashik, because I had drawn certain conclusions, because I might be indiscreet.

I had been pacing up and down the room. I stopped, then went to the door. From another part of the apartment there came very faintly a murmur of voices. I glanced at my watch. Pashik had been gone five minutes. I was suddenly convinced that it would be wise to leave without waiting to be introduced to Pashik's friend—to leave now, quietly. I hesitated momentarily, then I made up my mind. I put my hand on the doorknob and turned it gently. Then I began to pull. But the door did not move. I had been locked in.

CHAPTER XI

FOR A MOMENT OR TWO I stood there looking stupidly at the door as if I expected it to open itself. To find oneself locked in a room and know that the locking cannot be accidental or a practical joke is an extraordinary sensation. My feelings were confused and are not easily described; I was angry and frightened and depressed all at once. Then I broke out into a sweat. I tried the door again, then turned away from it. The room suddenly looked different, very large and empty, and I could see every detail in it. There was something familiar and yet not quite right about it.

When I had been walking about I had noticed an inch or two of string looped round one corner of the carpet. Now I saw it again; I was standing on the hardwood surround just by it. At that moment I was wondering if I should hammer on the door and demand to be let out, or sit there quietly and pretend not to have noticed that I had been locked in. Absently I reached down to pick up the string. I wanted something to fidget with. I got the string, but the corner of the carpet came up with it. The string was threaded through the edge of the carpet and tied to a label. The label had some figures written on it and a printed name, obviously that of the dealer who had sold it. It was an expensive carpet, a Sparta, yet the owner had not troubled to remove the price tag. It had simply been tucked away out of sight. I was puzzled. I let the carpet fall back into place and walked round the room again. At one end by the windows there was a buhl cabinet. I opened one of the drawers. There was a small brass screw in it and some dust. I tried the other drawers. All were empty except one, which contained a price tag from the same dealer who had supplied the carpet. I went round quickly looking at the wood of the chairs. They had been used a lot and yet there was a certain *un*used look about them. And then I knew what was familiar about the room: it was like a stage set when all the furniture has just been brought in and placed in position.

At that moment I heard voices and footsteps in the passage outside. I sat down. They came to the door and there was a slight pause. I knew why. The person who was about to open the door was preparing to turn the knob and the key simultaneously so that the sound of the latch would conceal that of the unlocking. If I did not know that I had been locked in, they did not want to tell me of the fact. My heart beat faster.

The door opened and after a momentary pause Pashik came in. He was followed slowly by a small man in a loose tussah suit and a black tie. I stood up.

Pashik put his hand on my shoulder and enveloped me in a broad smile. "Herr Foster," he said in German, "let me introduce you to Herr Valmo."

I had no time to digest this surprise. The other man came forward with a polite smile and held his hand out tentatively.

"So pleased, Herr Foster," he said.

He was about fifty, short and very slight, with wispy and receding gray hair brushed back from a sunburnt forehead. It was a thin, pointed face with large, pale blue eyes and an expression that might have been cruel or amused or both. He looked like a retired ballet dancer who has taken successfully to management. In his hand was Katerina Deltchev's letter. It had been opened.

"Herr *Valmo*?" I said.

He smiled. "I am afraid a little explanation is due to you, *mein Herr*." He had a quiet, monotonous voice.

"It was not possible for *me* to explain, Herr Foster," said Pashik. "I could not break a confidence."

"Please sit down, Herr Foster, and you, my dear Pashik. A cigarette? Ah, you are already smoking. As our friend Pashik explained to you, I am, you might say, some sort of a policeman, a very"—he made a belittling gesture with his hand—"a very confidential sort of policeman." The woman appeared at the door with a tray and he glanced round. "Yes, come in, Mentcha. Put it down." He turned again, pulled round a chair, and sat facing me. "Coffee and a little brandy, Herr Foster. You have had a very upsetting experience, our friend tells me. Thank you, Mentcha. Shut the door. And now," he went on as she went out, "we must set your mind at rest. In the coffee, the brandy?"

"Thank you."

Pashik was sitting deferentially by as if at a conference between his superiors. The hand holding his cigarette was trembling slightly.

Valmo handed me a cup and went on talking as he filled the other two. "There is one thing," he said, "that I must ask of you, Herr Foster. That is that you respect the confidence of what I am about to tell you." He held a cup out to Pashik but he looked at me. "Pashik tells me that you are not friendly to the regime here. I understand. But I am not a politician. I am a civil servant. Our country is a center for many conspiracies against the law and it is my task to destroy them. Can I be certain that you will respect my confidence, Herr Foster?"

"Yes." I tasted the coffee.

"Very well." He put his cup behind him on the table and then leaned forward toward me with his elbows on his knees and his hands together. "In my role of policeman, Herr Foster, it was my duty to seek out the perpetrators of the bomb outrage against Herr Deltchev that took place shortly before his arrest. I made certain secret inquiries and investigations. It was believed that the criminals had had the Deltchev family under surveillance, and members of the family co-operated with me in identifying them. I have said that my function is not political. Herr Deltchev's trial does not relieve me of the responsibility of tracing these criminals. You understand?"

I nodded.

"For reasons with which I will not trouble you," he continued, "it became necessary for me to install an agent in the Patriarch Dimo. For convenience and identification, the agent employed my name. Very well. Three days ago my agent reported to me that he had news of the men we were after. That night he was killed." He paused impressively.

"Who found him dead?" I asked.

He stared at me for a moment. Then he turned round and picked up his coffee cup again. "I did, Herr Foster," he said blandly. "However, let me continue. The agent had collected certain documentary evidence against the conspirators, which he kept hidden in the room. I discovered that this had not been stolen. Therefore, I argued, they did not know of its existence. Therefore, if they were made aware of its existence they would return for it. Therefore I replaced the true documents with some false ones that I prepared and sat down to wait for results."

"You mean you put a secret watch on the house to catch the murderer when he returned?"

He smiled gently and shook his head. "I am afraid you do not know the street of the Patriarch Dimo, Herr Foster," he said. "That sort of secret could not be kept there. No. I set a different kind of trap. All I wanted was to get the false documents into the conspirators' hands. I had reason to believe that in fact that had happened. Tonight I asked Herr Pashik, who is a friend of mine and also sometimes a helper, to go to the house and make sure." He spread his hands out like a conjuror. "He finds you there."

"With a letter addressed to you."

"Exactly. Katerina Deltchev had recalled an important piece of evidence. She wrote to tell me of it."

"Through your agent."

"Naturally. This address is most confidential, Herr Foster. So you see how it has happened and the need for your discretion." He sat back with a smile, clicked his lighter, and held the letter in the flame of it. As it caught fire, he smiled at me again. "I'm sure you do," he added.

I thought quickly. It was just not quite good enough. The man who called himself Valmo and said that he was of the secret police had had a certain initial advantage; he did not look like the conventional secret policemen of fiction. If he had been vaguer and more mysterious about his story, it might even have been convincing. There would have been nothing unlikely about a secret policeman who was secretive. But this man had seen the holes in his story as he was telling it and instead of leaving them had tried to cover them up. For instance, having indicated an official connection between the Deltchev household and Patriarch Dimo Street he had decided that it did not satisfactorily cover Katerina's letter, so he had added another detail: that weak one about her recalling an important piece of evidence. It would have been better to let me see the hole and question it. He could then have replied with a knowing shake of the head that he was afraid he could not permit himself to give me that information. And that, in turn, would have prevented my asking the awkward question I did in fact ask.

"Herr Valmo," I said, "what I don't understand is why Fräulein Deltchev, who is under house arrest, has to get me to smuggle out a letter to the head of the secret police. Why didn't she just give it to one of the sentries?"

He crushed the ashes of the letter onto the tray. "She is a girl. No doubt she was afraid I would not get it."

"She seemed more concerned about the censorship than anything else. She made me promise to deliver it by hand."

"Confinement affects some people strangely."

"Shall you go to see her?"

"It may be necessary. I do not know." He was getting confused now. He pulled himself together a trifle impatiently. "Those, however, are not matters of immediate concern, Herr Foster. It is your position that we must make clear."

"Yes?"

"I have given you a great deal of confidential information. It must, please, remain confidential." His pale eyes stared at me coldly. "I may add, Herr Foster, that if you were not a distinguished journalist, it would have been considered advisable to put you in prison for a short while to make sure of your behavior. That, however, we need not discuss. You have already assured me that you will be discreet. I require now three further undertakings from you. First"—he held up a finger—"that you will not return to the house in the Patriarch Dimo or tell anyone of it. Secondly, that you will not again visit the Deltchev house. Thirdly, that you will make no attempt to identify this house and that you forget its existence, and mine."

I did not reply immediately. I knew now the kind of conversation that must have taken place between Valmo and Pashik while I was safely locked up and waiting. My one desire was to get out of the place as quickly as possible. But I had the sense to realize that if I showed my anxiety and agreed to the terms too hastily, they would not feel quite safe. They were both watching me narrowly. I frowned, then looked up and nodded.

"All right," I said curtly. "I agree. And now, if you don't mind, I'd like another brandy."

Valmo stood up. "Yes, of course," he said perfunctorily. He poured a small one. He could not wait to get rid of me now. "Herr Pashik?"

"Thank you, no."

They stood looking at me impatiently while I sipped the brandy. It was the only moment of enjoyment I had had in the whole evening and it lasted about ten seconds. As I swallowed the first sip, I heard the front door of the apartment open and close and footsteps in the passage outside.

"It is my brother," said Valmo quickly.

Then the door opened and a young man came into the room. He saw me and stopped.

"Good evening, Jika," Valmo said. "We are talking a little business. I shall be with you in a minute."

He was about twenty-five, dark and very tired-looking. He had a raincoat on and his hair was blown about as if he had been in an open car. He looked at us suspiciously. For a moment he did not move; then he turned away slowly and went to the door.

"Don't be too long, Aleko," he said. "I have something for you."

I raised the brandy to my mouth again. I was not looking directly at Pashik, but I could see his face and it had gone the color of mud. He knew that I had seen the "Aleko" note in the Deltchev file and for some reason was terrified lest I had remembered it. Aleko himself was waiting for me to finish my drink. The use of his Christian name had not visibly upset him. But the situation was delicate. I had seen something I should not have seen, but Pashik did not know if I realized it. The main thing then was to get out of the apartment before he could make up his mind what to do. I drank the brandy at a gulp and held out my hand to Aleko.

"Thank you, Herr Valmo, and good-by."

He smiled agreeably. "I hope your stay is pleasant here, Herr Foster," he said.

I turned to Pashik. "Are you going to drive me back to my hotel, Pashik?"

"Yes, Mr. Foster, yes," he said heavily.

We went along the passage to the front door. Aleko came out to the lift with us. Aleko shook my hand again.

"I have liked you, Herr Foster," he said; "and with a journalist that is a new experience for me. I have faith in you. Good-by."

He might have been sending a promising young dancer on a first international tour.

Pashik was already in the lift. I got in after him. We went down in silence.

It was not until we were in his car and out on the road again that I broke the silence.

"Aleko Valmo," I said. "A curious name."

"In these parts it is quite common, Mr. Foster," he said calmly.

He had made up his mind that I had forgotten the other name.

I was not feeling very friendly toward Pashik, and for a moment or two I toyed with the idea of asking him suddenly: "What was the case of K. Fischer, Vienna '46, about, Pashik, and what had Aleko to do with it?"

Then I decided not to. We did not speak again until he drew up outside my hotel. As I went to get out, he put his hand on my arm, and his brown eyes sought mine.

"Mr. Foster," he said, "it has been a lousy experience for you this evening and no doubt you will wish to forget all about it. That is, if you are wise."

I did not answer. His voice took on its cautious roundabout tone.

"I wish only to tell you," he said, "that I understand your feelings and share them. But you have your own profession and need not trouble about what happens to deadbeats and bums far away from your home. Men are dying all over the world for the causes they believe in. You cannot fight their battles."

"Are you telling me that I should mind my own business?" I asked.

"Ah, please, Mr. Foster!" He spread his hands out. "You are mad at me."

I was exasperated. "I'm not mad at you, Pashik. I'm merely trying to get you to say straight out what you mean without all this double talk. I don't mind being advised to mind my own business. That's all right. I don't have to take the advice if I don't want to. I'm still capable of deciding what is my own business and what isn't. I'm not fighting any battles. I'm trying to find out what goes on here."

"That is what I mean, Mr. Foster. It does no good to try."

"You mean I won't be able to find out?"

He looked away from me and picked at the steering-wheel. "You force me to be frank, Mr. Foster."

"What's the matter with frankness? Why has it to be forced?"

"You say you fight no battles, Mr. Foster," he said quietly; "but I tell you, you are wandering like a fool between the opposing forces of those who are. That is a crazy thing to do. Once, years ago in Vienna, I saw street fighting between troops and revolutionaries. The fighting went on for many days. But there was one street that was swept equally by the fire of both sides, and neither could advance. Then one afternoon something very silly happened, as so often it happens in war. Into this empty, silent street there came a man. We heard his footsteps first. Then we saw him. He staggered from a side turning right into the middle of the street and stood there swaying. He belonged to neither side. He was drunk and did not know where he was or what he was doing. He began to sing and wave and call out for a woman. At first the soldiers laughed and shouted jokes at him. But after a while their officer noticed that the enemy was taking advantage of the distraction to run across the far end of the street in ones and twos so as to outflank the troops. He shouted a warning and they opened fire. The enemy replied with covering fire and the street was swept from end to end with machine-gun bullets. The drunk was killed immediately. You see, Mr. Foster?"

"Which side were you on?"

"I was a soldier then. I have been many things, Mr. Foster."

"Yes. Tell me. The reason that your friend Valmo doesn't want me to go to the Deltchev house again is that he doesn't want me to ask Katerina Deltchev to confirm his story, isn't it?"

"I don't know, Mr. Foster. As long as you keep faith with Mr. Valmo it does not matter. One thing I have to ask of you myself, however. I thought it discreet not to mention your connection with Petlarov; it would have complicated the affair. None of these things must on any account be mentioned to Petlarov. Or Mr. Sibley. That is most important."

"All right." I was tired of the whole business now. I wanted to get to bed. I opened the car door. Pashik put out his hand again.

"You will think over what I said, Mr. Foster," he said anxiously. "It is for your own good I ask."

I got out of the car. "I'll be very sober," I said. "That I promise you. Good night."

I was about to slam the door. He leaned across and held it open. His glasses flickered in the light from the hotel entrance as he looked up at me.

"I hope so," he said slowly. "But if you do not intend to take my advice, Mr. Foster, it might be less painful to be drunk. Good night."

Then he shut the door and drove off.

I did not sleep well that night.

CHAPTER XII

IT WAS ON THE FOURTH DAY of the trial that the evidence connecting Deltchev with the Brotherhood was given.

When the court opened, a man named Kroum was called into the witness box. He was about fifty, with a bald head and glasses and an erect military appearance. He looked shrewd and brutal. He described himself as a brigadier of police in the detective department of the Ministry of the Interior. He was carefully washed and brushed and his manner was irritatingly complacent.

Prochaska began his examination in what was for him an unexpected way.

"Brigadier Kroum, how long have you been a member of the police?"

"Thirty years, sir."

"How long have you held your present appointment?"

"Twelve years, sir."

"Are you a member of any political party?"

"No, sir."

"Have you any political affiliations?"

"No, sir."

"None at all?"

"I do not interest myself in politics, sir. I have my work to do."

"An excellent citizen! Have you ever arrested a man or ordered his arrest for political reasons?"

"The only reason for any arrest, sir, is that a man breaks or is suspected of breaking the law. I do not make the law. It is my duty simply to enforce the law under the constitution. That is the duty of every police officer," he added.

Someone near me sniggered at this; but my impression was that Brigadier Kroum meant what he said.

Prochaska glanced at a paper. "In March," he said, "were you concerned with the arrest of eight persons on the charge of trading illicitly in prepared opium?"

"I was responsible for the arrests, sir."

"Did you also examine the prisoners?"

Kroum hesitated. "Unofficially, sir, and solely for the purpose of obtaining information about other members of the gang. The examining magistrate was responsible, of course, for the official interrogation."

"You were not usurping the magistrate's function, but merely doing your duty as a police officer. Is that correct?"

"Yes, sir. That is correct."

"But you gave the prisoners the impression that they were making official depositions?"

"It is sometimes necessary, sir."

He had a blubbery mouth with bad-tempered creases round it. Interrogation by Brigadier Kroum would not be an agreeable experience.

"Was one of those arrested a man named Rila?"

"Yes, sir."

"Did you interrogate him?"

"I did, sir."

"Tell the court about this interrogation."

"Yes, sir. This Rila is a criminal well known to the police. He is an old man who has served many prison sentences. I knew that his eldest granddaughter was pregnant for the first time. I told him that this time he would surely die in prison and never see his great-grandchild, but that if he assisted the police by telling all he knew, a permit might be obtained for the child to be brought for him to see." He looked doubtfully at the prosecutor. "It is customary to offer such inducements to prisoners. No regulations would be broken, sir."

"No, no. Continue please."

"At first he refused to talk. Said he knew nothing. The usual." Kroum was gaining courage. "But the following day, when I saw him again, he was in a better mood. He had thought over my offer and he was worried. After a while he asked if I would protect him from any consequences there might be of his talking. That, too, is usual with criminals informing," he added confidentially.

"Yes. Continue please."

"I asked him for the names of the other members of the gang. He said there were no other members and that we had them all and that there was no information he could give about that case. But he wanted to see his great-grandchild and there was other important information he could give in return for the concession. I said that if the information was valuable it might be possible."

"Continue."

"He then told me that there was in existence a conspiracy to assassinate Minister Vukashin and that the conspirators were members of the Officer Corps Brotherhood." He paused.

"And did you believe him—this criminal who wished to purchase a concession with information?"

"No, sir. At first I thought it was merely an impudent lie and sent him back to his cell. But on thinking it over I decided to question him again. Even though I thought that what he had said must be fantastic, the suggestion was so serious that I felt it necessary to make quite sure. I felt it my duty," he added virtuously.

"Yes, yes. So you questioned him again."

"Yes, sir, and again he began by asking for protection. Again I reassured him. Then he told me a strange story. He lodged in a house in the Maria Louisa quarter. One of his fellow lodgers was a man named Pazar." He paused. He was at his ease now, talking more as an experienced policeman and less as an applause-hungry functionary. "We know that house," he went on; "it is a place for crooks; and because we do know it we let it be; but anyone living there is automatically suspect. Pazar, however, was new there. Rila was curious about him. For Rila there was always the possibility that a stranger might be a police spy. So he took note of this man's movements and was watchful. All he discovered to begin with was that on certain evenings Pazar would be visited by three or four men unknown in the Maria Louisa quarter. They did not look poor, and Rila wondered what they were up to. It is probable, I think, that all along he had an idea of joining in what he thought might be a profitable racket, but this, of course, he denied when I suggested it. He gave another explanation. However—"

"Just a moment, brigadier. What was the explanation he gave?"

Kroum looked embarrassed. "He said, sir, that he was only interested in human nature."

There was some laughter. Prochaska frowned. "Go on," he said shortly.

"Yes, sir. Rila said that Pazar had been living there for about a month when one day he stopped Rila on the stairs and asked to speak to him privately. Rila agreed and they went to his room. After a lot of talk Pazar came out with what he wanted. Someone had told him that Rila dealt in illicit drugs and Pazar wanted some heroin for a friend. Rila's first thought was that Pazar was a police spy after all and he pretended to be shocked. But after a little more talk Rila became convinced that Pazar himself was a heroin addict and needed the stuff badly. Now Rila is quite frank about what followed. Pazar had little money and asked for credit. Rila refused. With heroin addicts one might as well give the stuff away as give credit. Instead he referred to Pazar's well-dressed visitors and said that if he, Rila, could afford smart clothes like that he would be very grateful to the person who had helped him. In other words, he asked for a share in the profitable business he thought was being done by Pazar's friends. Pazar refused angrily and went away. Rila shrugged and waited. Pazar would have to have his stuff, and if he had been driven to asking Rila for it, that meant that his old source of supply had for some reason been stopped. Two days later Pazar came again to Rila, who repeated his price. Pazar again refused, but this time he did not get angry; he pleaded with Rila. His friends, he said, had nothing to do with any trade. They were political. He went on pleading and Rila went on refusing until Pazar became desperate. He begged on his knees, and when Rila told him to go away he broke down and wept. Then it came out. Pazar and the friends who visited him were members of the Brotherhood."

Kroum paused. He had his audience now. There was dead silence. He went on:

"At first Rila did not believe him. When he did believe, he was worried. Our criminals have never liked the Brotherhood. They have been resentful of the extra vigilance it has caused, but also they have been afraid. It is curious," Kroum went on thoughtfully; "a man who kills for money they understand, but the Brotherhood killer troubles them. This old criminal Rila talked about the Brotherhood as a boy might talk about ghosts and demons."

"Yes, yes. Continue."

"Pazar worried him very much, for he knew the ways of heroin drug addicts, as I have said, and he knew that they were treacherous and spiteful. If he refused Pazar and Pazar told his mysterious friends of the Brotherhood that their secret was known to Rila, then Rila would be in danger. So to keep Pazar quiet he gave him some heroin. After a few days Pazar came back for more, and soon Rila was supplying him regularly. Pazar would come into his room and stay and talk and gradually he became more indiscreet."

That word! I glanced at Pashik next to me. His face was quite impassive, but his hands were tense.

Kroum had paused again. Now he went on very slowly:

"One day—Rila cannot remember which day—Pazar began to tell him of something he called the secret of power. He was very mysterious about this secret, but Rila let him talk and after a while Pazar took a round of machine-pistol ammunition from his pocket. 'This is the secret of power, my friend,' he said, 'for this beautiful little thing can make a revolution.' Rila was afraid to ask him what he meant, but Pazar told him eventually. The Brotherhood were planning to assassinate Minister Vukashin."

The prosecutor nodded and looked up at the judges. "The man Rila made a deposition to the effect of what the witness has told the court," he said. "The deposition is signed by him and properly witnessed." He picked up a bundle of papers. "I submit it to the court in evidence, together with three certified copies."

The copies were passed to the clerk of the court, who handed them up to the dais. The center judge glanced at the top paper, nodded gravely, and said something.

"The presiding judges accept the documents in evidence," said the interpreter's voice, "and call upon the prosecutor to continue."

Prochaska turned to the witness box again. "Brigadier Kroum, what action did you take as a result of what you had heard?"

Kroum had prepared this answer: "I considered it my duty, sir, to inform the Minister of the Interior at once so that those responsible for the protection of Minister Vukashin might be warned."

"And then?"

"Then, sir, I set about investigating the truth of the story."

"You doubted it?"

Kroum very nearly permitted himself a tolerant grin. "The police, sir, are obliged to think suspiciously of persons who wish to help them," he said, "especially if they may gain an advantage by doing so."

"Very well. You investigated. What did you discover?"

"That there was a man named Pazar at the house in Maria Louisa, that he did occasionally receive the kind of visitors described, and that he had a reputation for drug-taking. He was not known as a criminal. He was believed to have been at one time a schoolmaster. He had also made a living as a language tutor."

"And then what did you do?"

"There were three possible explanations, sir: that Rila had made up the rest of the story or that Pazar had invented it to impress Rila and get drugs from him; second, that Pazar was mentally unstable as a result of drug-taking and not only invented the story but also believed it to be true; thirdly, that it was in fact true. Although we believed this last possibility unlikely, we decided that no harm would be done by acting upon it. We therefore set a watch on the house with the idea of identifying Pazar's visitors and possibly confronting them in Pazar's room. On the evening of the third day Pazar did not return to the house at the customary time. That same evening a man arrived at the house and was identified by the woman who kept it as one of the regular visitors. He went straight to Pazar's room, which was on the second floor. He received, of course, no reply to his knock and waited for a time. Then he decided to go. When he was stopped by one of my men, he immediately drew a revolver and began to shoot, wounding two policemen. He then attempted to escape, but was shot down. He was identified as a man named Eftib, a university student with a reputation for fanatical views of the kind associated with the Officer Corps Brotherhood."

"He was killed?"

"Unfortunately he died before we could question him, sir."

"Continue."

"The fact that Pazar had not returned and that only Eftib had arrived for a meeting suggested to us that Pazar had been warned of our activity and had passed the warning to the other conspirators. This view was confirmed by the fact that Eftib had been visiting his parents in the country and had only that evening returned. He, therefore, had not received the warning. In any case, our interest in the house was now exposed. We therefore entered Pazar's room and made a search of his belongings."

"And you found?"

"The complete dossier of a conspiracy to assassinate Minister Vukashin on the occasion of the anniversary celebration, including a plan of the operation and detailed orders for the five men participating in it."

A stir ran round the court. Prochaska looked up at the judges. "I ask the court for discretion in this matter," he said. "I have the dossier here and will with permission proceed to offer it in evidence. I ask leave, however, to withhold that part of it concerned with the actual plan of the attempt. It is of great ingenuity and, for reasons that will appear in a moment, unsafe for publication at present. It is in any case not essential to the prosecution's case."

"The permission asked for is granted by the presiding judges."

A bulky file was handed to the clerk of the court. Prochaska continued: "The witness is, of course, not quite accurate in describing what he found as a dossier. He found the operation plan concealed under the floorboards of the room and in other hiding-places a number of documents. These things were later collected into dossier form."

The center judge nodded.

Prochaska turned to Kroum again. "I will ask you now to identify the various items. Item one." He nodded to the clerk, who handed Kroum a clipped wad of papers.

Kroum looked at it.

"Do you recognize those papers?" asked Prochaska.

"I do, sir. I identify them as those I found concealed beneath the tiles of the stove in Pazar's room."

"Have you ever seen papers like that before?"

"Yes, sir. These are pledge forms used as part of the initiation ceremony of the Officer Corps Brotherhood. I recognized them at once. They were secretly printed by a member of the Brotherhood now dead. His name was Markoff. He was arrested, tried, and hanged in January '45. But these were his work."

"Read the pledge to the court."

Kroum cleared his throat. He said: "The form is headed: *Brotherhood of the Officer Corps for the Holy Protection of all Kindred Families and of the Sacred Motherland which gave them Birth and Honor.* Then follows the pledge: *I, Brother X, having, from the dictates of my own heart and conscience and for no other reason, submitted myself to the judgment of my Brethren in honor, and having, through the mingling of my blood with theirs, received absolution before the Mother of God*

*for all acts committed in their name, do hereby dedicate my soul and
body to the service of the Brotherhood until and unto death. Recognizing
that between Brothers thus specially united by ties of blood there may
be no contention or preference or inequality, I swear unconditional and
immediate obedience to all orders given to me by Brothers to whom
authority has been delegated by the Brethren assembled, and should
authority be so delegated to me I swear to accept it and use it faithfully
in the knowledge that the responsibility is shared by all equally and that
my loyalty to the Brotherhood is superior to all other loyalties and avow-
als, private or public. My reward for faithful service shall be the honor
and love of my Brothers and their protection of me and of my family.
But should I betray or in any other way fail the Brotherhood, my own
death will be only part of the price to be paid for the offense, for by
this oath now taken I bind my whole being, and in betrayal of it all that
I hold dear is forfeit. All this I understand and accept. All this I believe
just. All this I freely swear to on my blood, my honor, and my life and
by this act become of you my Brothers.*" Kroum looked up. "That is all,
sir."

"A license to commit treason and murder," commented Prochaska, "as
the acknowledged crimes of this fraternity have long since proved." He
nodded to the clerk, who handed up another document to Kroum.

Kroum looked at it.

"Do you recognize that document?"

"I do, sir. It was hidden in Pazar's room with the papers I have just
read from."

"What is it?"

"A list of names under the word 'Active.'"

"Is the name of Pazar there?"

"It is."

"And Eftib?"

"Yes, sir."

"Is there any other name there familiar to the police?"

"Yes." He hesitated. "The name of Deltchev."

There was dead silence in the court now. Deltchev was sitting in his
usual position with his eyes closed. He did not move.

"Is there any other peculiarity about the list?"

"Yes, sir. Certain names on it are underlined."

"Which names?"

"Those of Pazar, Eftib, Vlahov, Pechanatz, Radiuje, and Deltchev."

There was a faint murmur in the court. Deltchev opened his eyes and
looked at Kroum thoughtfully.

"Did you say that the plan to assassinate Minister Vukashin required
five persons to operate it?"

"Yes, sir."

"Then the sixth person might be the leader?"

"It seemed likely, sir."

"What action did you take?"

"I informed the Minister of the Interior, and warrants for the arrest of Pazar, Vlahov, Pechanatz, and Radiuje were issued."

"Did you execute the warrants?"

"Pechanatz and Radiuje were found to have already left the country. Vlahov was arrested while attempting to do so. It was at the airport and he was placed in the waiting-room to await an escort. The arresting officer had neglected to search him and while in the waiting-room he shot himself. Pazar has not yet been traced."

"What action has been taken about the other names on the list?"

"I ask permission not to answer that question, sir."

"I understand, brigadier." He turned to the judges. "I would point out to the court that at least one man connected with the conspiracy is still in the country and free and that he may attempt to find other confederates even now. It is for that reason that all information cannot yet be made public."

"The presiding judges acknowledge the point."

Prochaska bowed and nodded to the clerk. More papers were handed to Kroum.

"Do you recognize those documents?"

"Yes, sir. I identify them as from Pazar's room."

"Describe them."

"They are messages, mostly typewritten or inked in block letters on plain paper."

"Read from them."

"The first reads: '*Meeting for Thursday to take place Friday. Notified V. and P.*'"

"No signature?"

"None is signed, sir."

"Continue."

"The second reads: '*Await advice as arranged.*' The third: '*P. remains incomplete. Progress others.*' The next: '*V. unsuccessful. Will expedite.*' Next—"

Prochaska interrupted him. "One moment, brigadier. I do not think we need trouble you to read all the messages. I wished only to show their character. They continue like that?"

"Yes, sir. There are over thirty of them."

"Do you understand their meaning?"

"I think so."

"They have a direct bearing on the assassination plan?"

"Yes, sir."

"Then we will be discreet. I come to another point. Do these messages constitute a correspondence or are they only messages received?"

"Messages received, sir."

"What initials appear in the messages?"

"V., P., E., R., and D."

"Referring to?"

"Vlahov, Pechanatz, Eftib, Radiuje, and Deltchev, I believe."

"It seems likely. What is the general character of these messages? Are they, for example, instructions?"

"I would say they are reports."

"To the leader of the conspirators?"

"I think not, sir. It is difficult to say, but in my opinion Pazar, who received the reports, was responsible for co-ordinating the information. We learned that he received no messages at the house. My belief is that the others used a café or a shop as a post office and that he collected the messages from there, copied them, and redistributed them for information to those concerned. The nature of the plan would call for constant communications of that sort during the period of preparation. No doubt each conspirator had an accommodation address."

"Very well. The messages have been numbered for convenience. Please find message number twenty-seven."

"I have it here."

"Read it please."

"It reads: 'V. in difficulty. Advise D. urgent.'"

"Is that written or typewritten?"

"Typewritten."

"Is there anything else on the paper?"

"Yes, sir, some pencil writing."

"Read it please."

"It reads: 'Strumitza, twelve.'"

The courtroom stirred.

"Is that an address?"

"Yes, sir. It is the prisoner's address."

"What explanation have you for its being there?"

"It is in Pazar's handwriting. I suggest that as the message was urgent he did not deliver it to the usual accommodation address for the prisoner, but took it direct to his home. The pencil note was a memorandum of an address that Pazar would not normally use."

I looked at Deltchev. His eyes were closed again. He had not moved. It was impossible to believe. And yet—

Stanoiev did not cross-examine. Kroum left the witness box reluctantly, like an aging prima donna on a farewell tour, and one of his colleagues took his place. The questioning was resumed. What Kroum had said was now elaborately confirmed. I no longer paid much attention. I was trying to digest what I had already heard.

CHAPTER XIII

IT WAS TRUE; of that I had little doubt. Prochaska had an air of confidence that was not of the kind he could assume. Perhaps clever cross-examination could have made much of Kroum's evidence look weak; Deltchev was not an uncommon name, and when you pointed out that the prisoner's identification with the D. of the messages rested solely on a penciled note of an address alleged to be in the handwriting of a man who could not be produced, you might have shaken a jury's belief in the whole story. But here there was no jury to be shaken and, after the massive certainties of Vukashin and the rest, the very flimsiness of the thing gave it probability. Someone named Deltchev who lived in Deltchev's house had been in close touch with persons desperate enough, as Eftib and Vlahov had been, to shoot when confronted by the police or to commit suicide when arrested. Madame Deltchev? Absurd. Katerina Deltchev? By the time the luncheon break came, I thought I was ready for Pashik.

"Well," I said, "what do you think?"

"It is very interesting."

"Yes. Where do you think Pazar is now?"

He shrugged elaborately. "It is a mystery."

"So they say. When do you think they'll find that man in Patriarch Dimo?"

The brown eyes looked at me steadily. He did not reply.

I stared back at him. "I would guess that it's Pazar's body in that room, wouldn't you?" I said.

"What makes you think that, Mr. Foster?"

"Just an association of ideas. Someone in Deltchev's house sent messages to a man named Pazar. That man is now missing. Someone in Deltchev's house sends a message by me to a man who lived in Patriarch Dimo. That man is now dead."

"That is bad logic, Mr. Foster."

"It might be good guessing. Do you believe that Deltchev was in a conspiracy to assassinate Vukashin?"

"It could be so."

"Yes, it could be, but do you think yourself that it was so?"

"Who else could there be, Mr. Foster?"

"Katerina Deltchev could be the D. of those messages."

He showed his brown teeth in a smile. "A nice young lady of twenty in a Brotherhood conspiracy? That is a very funny idea, but it is no more than funny. The Officer Corps Sisterhood! Ah, please, Mr. Foster!"

"Yes, it's silly. I'm trying to find a reasonable explanation, that's all."

"The reasonable explanation is the one already given. Mr. Foster, we are newspapermen, not attorneys for the defense. We need only observe and report. We are lucky."

He had a bland, noncommittal look on his face. At breakfast I had not mentioned the events of the night before. In the morning light they had assumed the proportions of a bad dream, and until I could talk to Petlarov I was content to leave them so. Besides, I was tired of Pashik's denials and warnings and had made up my mind to discover something about the case of "K. Fischer, Vienna '46" before I tackled him again. It looked now as if he thought I had taken his advice. I put aside a temptation to correct the impression.

"What was the Brotherhood plan they're being so secretive about?" I asked.

"I know no more than you, Mr. Foster."

"Doesn't Valmo know? Surely a man in his position would know such things?"

"I am not in his confidence to that extent."

"Did you know Pazar or Eftib?"

To my surprise, he nodded. "Eftib I knew. He was a young man with a great dislike of dogs. A dog he found tied up one day he beat to death with a piece of chain. The other students disliked and feared him. He was not sane, I think."

"How did you know him?"

"The dog he killed belonged to one of the professors at the university. There was a scandal. I reported it for a newspaper, but his family paid to avoid the publicity. By now," he added thoughtfully, "they may wish he had been safely put in prison."

The waiter came up with our food. This particular section of the restaurant was reserved for the pressmen attending the trial and across the room I could see Sibley talking earnestly and confidentially to one of the Americans. Then out of the corner of my eye I saw Pashik looking at me. He looked away almost as I saw him, but not quite fast enough. He had to cover up.

"Yes," he said, "Mr. Sibley is busy still. He may succeed with someone who has no reason to suspect him. It is very strange."

I smiled. "There's something I find even stranger, Pashik."

"Yes, Mr. Foster?" He was on his guard again.

"I find it strange that although you are quite ready to serve someone you say is of the Government secret police, you put obstacles in the way of Sibley, who is trying to serve the Propaganda Ministry."

He stared at me for a moment and I thought that he was about to reply. Then he changed his mind, cleared his throat, and picked up his knife and fork. "Mr. Foster," he said heavily, "I think we should get on with our eating."

I could get nothing more out of him. After the luncheon break the conspiracy evidence was resumed. Now that he had something like real evidence to deal with, Prochaska spread himself. Every detail of Kroum's evidence was sworn to by three or four different persons, every document certified and proved. Had you not heard the earlier days of the trial, you might from Prochaska's attitude have supposed the judges to be pettifogging martinets hostile to his case. When you remembered the rubbish that had already been admitted as evidence by that pathetic trio, the present solemnity was funny. But not for long. Presently it became boring. Only one thing kept me there: the possibility of Deltchev's speaking in his own defense. But he seemed as bored as I was. As witness after witness was brought in to swear to the authenticity of the message with his address on it, I expected a protest from him. It would have been easy enough:

"These conscientious policemen swear to the presence of my address on this piece of paper. Nobody disputes that it is there. Why waste the time they might be devoting to more useful duties? Produce a really serious witness: the man who wrote it or who saw it written or, even better, the man who can tell us *why* and in what circumstances it was written down there. Those questions are important, gentlemen, for I, too, have been plotted against by assassins. They threw a bomb and badly wounded my chauffeur. That was outside my house, and to find my house you need the address, and to remember it you have to write it down. I have no wish to deprive Minister Vukashin of his martyr's laurels, but if I am to be convicted of plotting against his life, at least make sure that the evidence you use is not part of an old plot against *my* life. For a new plot new evidence should be manufactured. Economy in such matters is discourteous."

But Deltchev said nothing at all and the afternoon drowsed on. Curiously, it was only the diplomatic and press sections who seemed bored. For most of the spectators it was an exciting afternoon. As each witness appeared, there would be a buzz of interest, then dead silence while he gave his evidence, then breathless whispering as he stepped down. It was the factual nature of the evidence that did it. There must have been many in that courtroom who had been unwilling to believe in Deltchev's guilt and privately uneasy about the trial. Now they were enjoying the illusion that the legal forms were being properly observed and that they were free of the responsibility of condoning an injustice. I was glad when the afternoon was over.

Pashik had nothing to say as he drove me back to my hotel. He knew that I was going to see Petlarov and he was saving himself for a farewell admonishment on the subject of discretion; so I thought, at least; and I was tired of him; I was tired of his smell, of his admonishments, of his evasions and mystery-making, of his long-suffering brown eyes, of his dirty seersucker suit, and of his bad driving.

He stopped jerkily outside the hotel and turned to me. "Mr. Foster—" he began.

I interrupted irritably. "Look, do you have to go on calling me 'Mr. Foster' all the time? Can't you make it 'Foster' or 'you'? It would be easier for you and I shouldn't feel so stiff-necked."

He began again picking at the vulcanite covering of the steering-wheel. He already had most of it off and the metal beneath looked bare and squalid.

"I am sorry, Mr. Foster," he said, "I wished only to be polite."

"Yes, of course. It's not important."

But he was upset. "I am afraid you are not a good-tempered man, Mr. Foster," he said.

"No, I'm not. I apologize. You wanted to tell me to be discreet again, didn't you?"

He picked for a moment or two in silence. He was working on a big piece and it peeled away like a strip of sunburnt skin.

"I don't know what more I can say to you, Mr. Foster," he said. "I have tried to warn you, not because I like you or even because I have a responsibility to the New York office, but in the spirit of any man who sees another by accident going into a danger he does not realize. I can do no more. There are things more important than the safety of a stranger. You will not take advice; then you must take your chance. I will not discuss the case with you further. The services I am paid for are yours, however. Tomorrow I will be getting your press ticket for the anniversary celebration. When the end date of the trial is known, your return passage by air will be available. If there is any other service you wish performed, you must tell me. Meanwhile, when we meet we can talk of other things." He turned and looked at me. "Good night, Mr. Foster."

"Good night."

I got out and went into the hotel. I was both impressed and depressed. As I walked up the stairs I decided that I would take his advice. I told myself that it was only my personal dislike of the man that had prevented my taking it before. That was really stupid. My task was to write articles about the trial, not to play policeman. I had stumbled on a political murder in a country where political murder was a commonplace. The fact that for me it was a novelty did not give me a license to inquire into it. I should remember that I was a foreigner, there on sufferance, that I had a very lucrative profession to return to, and that in my temporary role of newspaper reporter I had done very well to get an exclusive interview with Madame Deltchev. That was enough. I would now mind my own business. And it might be a good idea to apologize to Pashik. He had been very patient with me and I had behaved with the bumptiousness of an amateur. And, by the way, since when had Mr. Foster been entitled to object to being called Mr. Foster by someone who wished to be courteous? Mr. Foster was making a very tiresome fool of himself. He'd better stop.

Petlarov was sitting stiff and straight on his usual seat in the corridor. Without speaking he followed me into my room and sat down. I went to the wardrobe and got out the whisky. He took the tooth glass with his usual polite bow and then glanced up at me.

"You look tired, Herr Foster."

"I've had a tiring twenty-four hours."

He nodded politely. He did not even look a question.

"What about today's evidence? What do you think?" I asked. "It's more or less what you feared, isn't it?"

He considered for a moment, then he shook his head. "No. I don't think it is. You see, I expected something possible. I thought that Yordan might have committed some indiscretion capable of being shown badly. But not this. It is really very funny. I know Yordan and I know that he is incapable of this kind of association. And with men of the type of Eftib and Pazar it is grotesque."

"He associated with Vukashin and Brankovitch?"

"He did not like them, but he recognized their importance. Both are considerable men, leaders. But conspiracy with this delinquent riffraff? It is impossible! Yordan is too much of a snob."

"What sort of indiscretion did you expect?"

He shrugged. "Many things are possible. For example, it would not have greatly surprised me to learn that some of the exiles were planning a *coup d'état* and had nominated Yordan their leader. If they appealed to him he would be flattered. He might temporize, but he would treat with them. In transactions of that kind many foolish things are written. Now with this, all is different. We have circumstantial evidence of the kind that is used to convict ordinary criminals—the piece of paper with the note on it, the scribbled address, the conspirators who escape and those who do not, the mysterious Pazar, who is missing but really dead—it is all of a different pattern." He shrugged again. "But that is only what I feel."

"What did you mean by saying that Pazar is really dead?"

"If he were alive they would certainly have found him before the trial. They could not risk his being found unexpectedly. He might be an inconvenient witness and it would look bad if he, too, were killed resisting arrest."

So then of course I told him. Whatever else was not my business, the problem of the evidence against Deltchev certainly was, and I had come to rely upon Petlarov's opinions. I told him about the letter I had carried, of the dead man in Patriarch Dimo 9, of Pashik's arrival, of the visit to Aleko, and of the Aleko note. He listened in silence and was silent for a time when I had finished. I noticed that he had gone very pale. Then he put down his drink and stood up.

"Herr Foster," he said slowly, "I too have something to tell you. Every two days I have to report to the police to get my papers stamped. It is part of the control to which, as an untrustworthy person, I am subject. Today when I reported, I was warned. I was told that I had recently made an undesirable association and that if I did not wish to be removed with my wife to a labor camp, the association must cease. That was all. Your name was not mentioned." He hesitated. "When I came here this evening, Herr Foster, I had almost made up my mind to ignore the warning. I thought that if it had been a serious matter I should not have been warned but arrested. I see now that I was wrong."

"What do you mean?"

But he did not reply. He was fumbling agitatedly in his pocket. He got out the ration card I had given him and held it out to me.

"I am sorry, Herr Foster," he said; "I cannot keep our bargain."

"That's all right. I understand." I didn't, but he was so obviously upset that I wanted to soothe him. "Keep the ration card anyway. I don't want it."

He shook his head. His face looked pinched and there was sweat on his forehead. I had a curious sense of shock. I had come to think of Petlarov as some kind of genie who inhabited the corridor outside my hotel room, ready to explain, to enlighten, to serve when I needed him. Because his own account of himself had been quite calm and impersonal, because he had not exuded the self-pity I should have been so quick to condemn, I had not found it necessary to think of him as a human being. Now suddenly he was very much a human being; he was frightened. The realization gave me a curious feeling of discomfort.

"Herr Foster," he said, "please take the card. I cannot use it any more, and if I am arrested I do not wish to have it found in my pocket."

I took it. He picked up his hat and went to the door.

"Just a moment," I said.

He stopped. The effort he made to control his agitation was almost painful to watch. He just wanted to be gone.

"Can't you give me any idea what this is all about?" I asked.

For a moment I thought he was going without answering. Then he swallowed and licked his lips. He looked at his hat as he spoke. "I will tell you one thing, Herr Foster. K. Fischer, Karl Fischer, you mentioned him." He hesitated before he went on with a rush. "He was a Left-wing politician, very popular in the working-class quarters of Vienna. A good man and a fearless speaker. He was in principle for the Soviets, but still in '46 he protested against the Soviet kidnappings of Austrians from the American sector. An honest man. He did what he thought right. He was murdered." He hesitated and swallowed again.

"Yes?"

"In September it was," he said. "He went out one evening to see his married daughter in Favoriten. Next day the railway police found his body behind a shed in the marshaling yard outside the Ostbahnhof." He paused and looked up at me. "You said that the man you saw at Patriarch Dimo had been killed by a bullet wound in the back of the head, by the ear."

"Yes."

He nodded. "That was how Karl Fischer died," he said. "That was the hand of Aleko."

Then he went.

CHAPTER XIV

THAT WAS ON FRIDAY, the 14th of June. The assassination took place on the Saturday.

I have since been described in the People's Party press as "a well-known agent of the English secret service," "the leader of a foreign murder gang," "Anglo-American spy and pervert," and in other less reproducible ways. In one article the fact that I am a writer was acknowledged by a reference to "the notorious pornographer and English murder-propaganda lackey Foster."

That part of it has been less amusing than I would have thought. Some of the stuff was reproduced in London papers, and among my friends the "notices of Foster's Balkan tour" were quoted hilariously for a day or two. But when the news of the Deltchev verdict came and the mass executions of Agrarian Socialists began, the attacks on me became related to events that were anything but funny. I began to be asked questions that the Foreign Office had suggested I should not answer.

With the newspapers it was not difficult; I did as I had been asked and referred them to the Foreign Office. With friends and acquaintances it was less simple. It is, I find, extraordinarily embarrassing to be described in print as a member of the British secret service. The trouble is that you cannot afterwards convince people that you are not. They reason that if you are a member you will still presumably have to say that you are not. You are suspect. If you say nothing, of course, you admit all. Your denials become peevish. It is very tiresome. Probably the only really effective denial would be a solemn, knowing acknowledgment that there *might* be some truth in the rumor. But I can never bring myself to it. Foreign Office or no Foreign Office, I have to explain what really happened.

To begin with, I think I should make it clear that I am not one of those persons who enjoy danger. I take pains to avoid it. Moreover, my timidity is speculative and elaborate. For instance, in Paris at the time of the Stavisky riots I was living in a hotel room overlooking a street in which the police fought a revolver battle with rioters. My first impulse was to lean out of the window and watch. The firing was several hundred yards away and I knew perfectly well that at that distance a revolver is about as dangerous as a water pistol. What I remembered, however, was that Wilfred Ewart, the author of *Way of Revelation*, had had a similar impulse of curiosity in Mexico City and died of it, absurdly with a stray bullet through his head. Instead of leaning out of the window, therefore, I had knelt on the floor by it and tried to use my shaving-mirror as a periscope; but by the time I had arranged all this, the battle was over and I saw nothing but an indignant woman with an upset shopping-bag.

The war did nothing to make my attitude to danger bolder or more philosophic. I do not have heroic impulses. The news that a bomb had killed my wife in our London flat had many other effects on me, but it did not send me out in a murderous rage to exact retribution of the enemy, nor did it make me volunteer for some suicidal duty. For a long time my life felt less worth living than before, but I did not for that reason become careless of it. Accounts of great bravery sometimes move me deeply, but they arouse in me no desire to emulate them. The spirit of romantic derring-do runs somewhat thinly in my veins.

The truth about my part in the Deltchev affair is untidy. I did not even blunder into the danger; I strayed into it as if it were an interesting-looking tangle of streets in an old town. Certainly I had been warned that they were dangerous; but only to those who warned, I thought, not to me. When I found out that I was mistaken and tried to get out, I found also that I was lost. That was how it felt. The last moment at which I could have turned back was when Petlarov went out of my room that evening. If at that point I had shrugged my shoulders, had another drink, gone out to dinner, and spent the evening at a cinema, I should have been fairly safe. And I very nearly did do that. I had the drink—it was the last of the whisky—and I looked at a cinema I could see from my window. It was called LUX and was playing a dubbed version of a German film called *La Paloma* that I did not want to see. I considered opening a bottle of plum brandy I had bought, decided against it, and then caught sight of the typewriter I had brought with me but not yet used. I thought of the solemnity of my departure with it from London ten days or so before and felt absurd. Images came into my mind of those groups of toys you see mounted on highly colored boards in the shops at Christmas time; the Boys' Conductor Set (complete with ticket punch), the Boys' Detective Set (complete with three disguises), the Boys' Tank Commander Set (complete with binoculars). I spent a self-abasing minute or two thinking of a new one: the Boys' Foreign Correspondent Set, complete with type-writer, whisky bottle, invisible ink, and a copy of John Gunther's *Inside Europe*. Then I did a foolish thing: I decided to pull myself together and be sensible.

What, I asked myself over dinner, were the facts? Quite simple. I was supposed to be reporting the trial of a man named Deltchev who was accused of planning an assassination. Probably he was innocent. Yet some of the evidence against him had a ring of truth about it. Moreover, his daughter had been in touch with someone concerned in the assassination plan. I had found that person dead, killed in the same way as an Austrian politician and most likely by the same man, Aleko. Aleko had pretended to be of the secret police but was probably an agent of another kind. Who had employed him? Deltchev? Or the People's Party to implicate Del-tchev? But why should either employ Aleko when they had dangerous psychotics like Eftib and Pazar ready to hand? It didn't make sense. And where did Deltchev come in? That was the important thing. I was prepar-ing to defend him before a very large public. It might be just as well (might it not?) to make sure that I had the facts right. *Might* be! A fine fool I should look if the noble Deltchev I had postulated turned out to be in reality as murderous as his persecutors but rather cleverer at concealing the fact. "Mr. Foster, what steps did you take to check the validity of your impressions?" "Well, none really. I thought it better not to be inquisitive. Too risky." Oh dear, oh dear! By the time the wine arrived I no longer had any doubts. Nothing I already knew about the case seemed either logical or in any other way satisfactory. Far too much was hidden. Well, it must be revealed; and if the intimidated Petlarov did not want to help me, I would find it out for myself. The first thing for me to do any-way was to see Madame Deltchev at once—that evening—and hear what she had to say about the day's evidence. Then I would give myself the pleasure of an interview with little Miss Katerina, tell her the news about her friend Valmo, and ask her the questions that Aleko did not want me to ask. After that I would decide what to do next.

I finished my dinner and walked out to the Deltchev house. As I turned into the street where it was, the mood of hearty resolution in which I had started out suddenly weakened. The guards I had passed before might not be on duty. A different set might have taken over. Then, as I approached, I saw that the same guards were there. It made no difference; my anxiety deepened. I realized that the real source of it had nothing to do with the guards but with the undertaking I had given to Aleko and my too ready disposal of it. If, I had reasoned, Aleko had really had any police powers he would not have asked for an undertaking not to visit the Deltchev home again; he would simply have issued an order to the guards not to admit me. Therefore, I had concluded, he had no police powers and I might call his bluff. But it was one thing to have arrived at a theoretical conclusion and quite another to act upon it in this way. All sorts of un-considered possibilities occurred to me as I walked toward the house. Sup-posing, for instance, he really did have police powers and had planned to test my good faith by including this prohibition in the undertaking. For a moment I hesitated and was about to turn back; then I realized that the corporal had seen and recognized me. Retreat was impossible now. I walked on up to him and took out my press permit. He nodded curtly, but examined the permit carefully again while the doltish private stood grin-ning at me. At last the corporal handed back the permit with a faint shrug (ominous?) and nodded to the private. The latter hitched his rifle sling more snugly on his shoulder and, crossing to the door in the wall, pulled the bell.

It was as before. I waited. They watched me. There was the clacking of old Rana's sandals on the paving of the courtyard. The door opened cautiously. But then she recognized me and held the door for me to go in. Inside she said something and signed to me to wait. She was not long. Soon I heard her sandals flapping down the stairs inside the house. She opened the front door and beckoned me in.

I went upstairs. The same slippery floor, the same smell of furniture polish, but this time no Katerina. She, I thought, would be standing with her man-of-the-world air behind her mother's chair. I hoped, uncharitably, that my arrival would alarm her.

But Madame Deltchev was alone. She was standing facing me by the window as I came in. The light was behind her, but there was tension in the way she stood. On the table by her were two empty tea glasses. The old friend had delivered his report for the day.

She turned quickly. "Good evening, Herr Foster. It is good of you to call again."

"You are very kind, madame. I am afraid I have more questions."

"Naturally. Please sit down."

"Thank you."

There was a *grande dame* artificiality about her manner that accentu-ated the feeling of strain she meant it to conceal. "Although," she went on, "I think it unlikely that I shall be able to give you the information you need. Tea?"

"No, thank you."

"Of course. You have dined, and the English do not drink tea after dinner." She smiled mechanically and, picking up one of the glasses, went over to the samovar. "With us it is a habit," she said; "Russian, of course. Most of our habits are Russian or Turkish or German or Greek. We have few of our own." Boiling water spluttered from the tap into the glass. "You see now why our patriots mean so much to us here. Their unquestioning belief that we are indeed a nation with our own cultural and political identities, and not merely a marginal tribe with some curious ethnological affinities, is a great comfort. The truth about many of our great traditional patriots is ugly or ludicrous; but it makes no difference. They are defended angrily. National feeling in small states is always angry; it must be so, for its roots are in fear and self-doubt, and for those things reason is no protection."

She spoke as glibly as a journalist quoting without acknowledgment from an article he has just written. I was not sure whether she was talking for concealment or whether I was being offered an elaborately wrapped hint. Was there perhaps an ugly truth to be known about patriot Deltchev?

"Your husband has meant a great deal to his people," I said carefully.

"Yes, yes, he has." She had carried her tea over to her chair. Now she sat down facing me. "They will not give him up easily, no matter what lies are told about him. A cigarette, Herr Foster?"

"Thank you; I'm sure you are right. Have you heard about today's court proceedings, madame?"

"Yes, I have heard about them."

I lit the cigarette she had given me. "Do you consider that the evidence was false in itself or that it was false only in relation to your husband?"

"Some of his witnesses may be truthful, but their testimonies compose a lie."

"May I put a hypothetical question? Supposing that the evidence were all true, that your husband had in fact been involved in this plot, would you have known about it, madame? Would he have confided in you?"

She did not answer immediately. Then: "He always confided in me. I should have known."

"It would be a dangerous secret to confide to anyone."

"If it had existed; yes, very dangerous."

"For comparison's sake, madame, can you tell me if your husband confided in you his intention to make that radio speech about the elections before he made it?"

She sat quite still for several moments, staring out through the window at the bare hills. I almost wondered if she had heard what I had said. She had heard, I knew, and understood too, but her air of preoccupation was very nearly convincing. Then, with a slight puzzled shake of the head as if to banish other thoughts and face the immediate reality, she turned her gentle, intelligent eyes toward me.

"I am very sorry, Herr Foster," she said with a faint, confused smile, "I am afraid I was not paying attention. I had other thoughts." She put her hand to her forehead as if she had a headache. "It was inexcusable."

It was not badly done; I have known actresses make a worse job of it; but if I wanted to parody a particular style of drawing-room comedy I would have that speech, and the performance that goes with it, well in mind. She must have seen it in dozens of bad plays. Probably she was expecting from me one of the two conventional reactions to it; the guilty ("Forgive me, you're tired") or the aggrieved ("I'm a busy man and my time is valuable"). However, I felt neither guilty nor aggrieved. I did feel intensely curious.

I repeated the question.

Her lips twitched with annoyance. "Herr Foster, what is the point of this question? Please be honest with me."

"Certainly. You deny that there is a word of real truth in the evidence put before the court today. I wish to know what value I may put upon that denial. Is it based on knowledge or an emotional conviction? You must see that that is important."

"What I see, Herr Foster," she said coldly, "is that this trial is beginning to have the effect intended by the Propaganda Ministry."

I felt myself flush with anger. By the light of the setting sun she did not see that, but I did not reply and after a moment she began to apologize. I must forgive her; she was tired and overwrought; she had not slept for many nights; she was distracted with worry. I listened carefully. What she was saying was all quite reasonable and genuine, but it was also a protective screen. Something had happened to her since our first meeting; some inner certainty had gone. Before, she had been facing with calm courage the prospect of her husband's conviction and death. Perhaps that courage had rested upon a belief in his innocence which no longer went unquestioned. Perhaps the unworthy doubts of which she now accused me were merely the projections of her own misgivings.

I tried a different way.

"In the theater," I said, "a little fact will sustain a lot of illusion. As Petlarov says, 'the lie rests most securely on a pinpoint of truth.' Brankovitch is not a fool. He knows that although he can impose any nonsense he likes upon the people of his own country, abroad it will not be so easy. With that trumped-up case he cannot hope to deceive the outside world. But what he can do is to confuse it by mixing with his lies a little truth. This plot against Vukashin. Why is it there? To prove that your husband is a member of the Brotherhood? Nonsense! Better evidence could be invented. Besides, even a stable government will regard an assassination plot as bad propaganda and try to conceal it if they can. No, this evidence is there because it is specially valuable. It is valuable because it is true. And those in court today recognized that it is true. It was not much—a few statements confirming a small set of facts—but it was true, and already in their minds this truth had grown and obscured the great mass of falsehood that surrounds it. You say, madame, that there may be truthful witnesses, but that they compose a lie. But how much of a lie? Where does the truth end and the lie begin? You cannot defeat the prosecution's case with blank denials. It is not as simple as that. You have to give the whole truth, and that is what I want."

There was a long silence. She looked stonily out of the window, and when she spoke she did not turn her head.

"Herr Foster, there is not a court of law in the civilized world that would accept the case against my husband. I have been well advised of that."

"No civilized court of law is going to be asked to accept it," I retorted. "If the truth is not told, the final judgment will be delivered here. A few persons may doubt and speculate, but they must all come to the same conclusion."

"What conclusion?"

"That there must have been something in the accusations against Deltchev, that the conspiracy evidence was never seriously disputed, that if he wasn't the criminal they tried to make him out, he was something very nearly as bad—a fool. Forgive me, madame, but what you do not seem to realize is that any protest against your husband's trial is a political act. No foreign office and no responsible newspaper is going to make that protest unless it is absolutely certain that he is innocent. They must know the truth."

"It isn't true. The case against him is a lie. What else can I say?"

"To what extent did your husband confide in you?"

"What does it matter? If I tell you that he always confided in me you will say that this particular matter might have been too dangerous to confide. If I say that he did not confide it, it is no different."

"If he were in any way involved in this conspiracy would you have known?"

"Yes. He was not involved."

"Did you know that he was going to make that election broadcast before he made it?"

"Yes, I did."

"Did you know why he was going to make it?"

"Yes."

"Why was it?"

She shook her head hopelessly. I knew she was lying.

"Was it because at one time, long ago, your husband had been a member of the Officer Corps Brotherhood?"

For a moment she was quite still. Then, slowly, she raised her head and stared at me. "Is that a serious question, Herr Foster?" she asked coolly.

I knew suddenly that it was not a serious question, but part of a fantasy in a locked room. I began to mumble: "It was a faint possibility, madame." She still stared at me. "It could have been a youthful indiscretion, a mistake. . . ." I petered out.

She smiled in a twisted sort of way. "Yordan does not make that kind of indiscretion. He is always an intelligent man. Are there any other questions, Herr Foster?" she added.

If I had had any advantage it was suddenly quite gone. "Have you ever heard the name of Pazar before?"

"It is a Turkish name. I know no one who has it."

"Or Eftib?"

"No. Nor any of the other persons mentioned today."

"Aleko?"

"Was that name mentioned?"

"No. Do you know it?"

"It is a short name for Alexander. That is all I know."

"Valmo?"

"It is a fairly common surname, but it means nothing in particular to me. Should it do so?"

"I don't know." I stood up. "Thank you for receiving me, madame."

"It is nothing." She stood up too and switched on a reading-lamp.

"Before I go, I should like, if I may, to speak to your daughter," I said. She stiffened. "Why?"

"I should like to ask her some questions."

"Perhaps I can answer them for you."

"Perhaps." I hesitated. "When I left here two nights ago, madame, your daughter asked me to take out a letter for her and deliver it to a man named Valmo." I paused.

She tried unsuccessfully to smile. "My daughter is an attractive young woman. She has her affairs of the heart."

"Yes, that was the impression of the letter she succeeded in giving to me. I agreed to take it."

"That was chivalrous of you."

"The address on the letter was Patriarch Dimo, nine. I found the place. It is a disused house in a slum."

"And did you find the young man?"

I shook my head. She relaxed perceptibly.

"If you will give me the letter, Herr Foster, I will see that it is returned to my daughter. It was good of you to take so much trouble." She held out her hand.

I said: "I did not find a young man, madame. I found a dead one. He had been shot."

Very slowly she sat down. "Had he shot himself?" she asked softly.

"No. The wound was in the back of the head."

She did not move. "A young man?"

"No. Gray-haired, about fifty I should think. Why do you ask?"

She straightened up a little. "I thought perhaps some poor young student—" She broke off and drew a deep breath. "There are so many tragedies. You must have gone to the wrong house, Herr Foster."

"No. It was the right house. But if the dead man was the person who had called himself Valmo, then your daughter knew Pazar. For that was the dead man's real name."

There was a silence. She did not look at me.

"Did the police tell you that?" she said at last.

"I did not go to the police. It would have been difficult to explain how

I came to be visiting the Brotherhood assassin they are supposed to be searching for. Difficult and embarrassing for us all."

"We are in your debt, Herr Foster."

"Perhaps you would prefer your daughter to explain," I said.

She looked at her handkerchief. "My daughter is not here."

I was silent.

She looked at me. "I am speaking the truth, Herr Foster."

"I understood that everyone here was under house arrest."

"My daughter is not here. She has gone."

"Do you mean that the police took her away?"

"No. She escaped."

"How? What about the guards?"

"Katerina has lived in this house all her life, Herr Foster. There are other ways of leaving it than by the gates."

I hesitated. "A few minutes ago, madame, I asked you if you had heard of Pazar before. You said that you had not. Do you still say that?"

"Yes. It is the truth."

"But others in this house do know him?"

"I do not."

"Do you know where your daughter has gone?"

"No."

"When did she go?"

"This evening."

"Can you think of any reason why she should go?"

"Herr Foster, I am very tired."

I waited a moment or two, but she did not look up again. "I'm sorry," I said; "I think I might have been of help to you."

"I have told you all I can."

"You have told me all you think it advisable for me to know, madame."

"Good night, Herr Foster." She pressed the bell-push.

I said good night and picked up my hat, but as I got to the door she spoke again.

"Herr Foster."

I stopped.

"My daughter's letter. Will you give it to me, please?"

"It is burned."

"Are you sure?"

"Quite sure."

She hesitated. "Forgive me, but do you know what was in it?"

"I did not open it. In any case I cannot read your language."

She came a little way across the room toward me. "Herr Foster," she said, "I have not been helpful to you, but I would not like you to think that I am ungrateful for your kindness and patience. I do most sincerely thank you."

I bowed. I could not think of anything coherent to say that would not have deepened my embarrassment. The sound of Rana's sandals flapping along the passage outside came like the answer to a prayer.

"Good night, madame," I said, and got out of the room as quickly as I could. It did not occur to me until I was walking down the stairs that my twinges of guilt were unnecessary. Beside the monumental evasions to which I had been listening for the past half-hour my own reticences were trivial.

CHAPTER XV

IT WAS VERY DARK outside the house. The old woman had no lamp to guide us and I blundered rather than walked after her across the courtyard. The fact contributed somehow to the feelings of inadequacy, futility, and blank exasperation which were beginning to grow in me.

I stubbed my foot against the edge of a flagstone and said: "Damn!" violently. The old woman opened the door in the wall and the flashlight from outside shone in my face. I scowled at it and hauled out my wallet as the door closed behind me. The light left my face and I saw the corporal.

"*Passieren, vorwärts!*" he snapped, and waved me on peremptorily.

"Don't you want to see my permit, you fool?" I inquired in English.

"*Passieren, passieren!*" he repeated, and waved me on again.

"Grinning lout," I said with a smile to the private.

He nodded, grinning, and saluted.

I walked away. The corporal was not troubling to examine my permit any more. The corporal had decided that I was harmless. The corporal was absolutely right. Tomorrow, I decided, I would send a cable to the man who was paying me, tell him that he was wasting his money and my time, then take the first plane I could get out of the place. It was high time I stopped this foolishness and got back to work again. Not, I thought savagely, that the trip had been a complete loss. I had increased my knowledge of Napoleon III. I had also had two interesting experiences: that of finding a dead body in a strange house, and that of being locked in a room in another strange house. In the unlikely event of my ever wanting to write the kind of play in which incidents like that occurred, the knowledge would be useful. Meanwhile, to hell with it!

I turned into the Boulevard Dragutin.

It ran in a gentle curve round the high boundary wall of the Presidential Park. It was a wide road, lined with big plane trees and cobbled. Most of the buildings in it were apartment houses; there were no shops or cafés. The lights were on tall standards set among the trees on the building side of the road. I walked on the other side. Beneath the dense foliage of the trees it was very dark.

I walked slowly. The air was pleasant and after a while something happened to make me forget my immediate troubles. Before I had left London I had been trying to write the third act of a new play and had got into difficulties with it. Indeed, I had practically made up my mind to scrap the whole thing. The commission to report the Deltchev trial had come at an opportune moment; it had given me a reason for suspending work on the play that left the real reasons for doing so in abeyance. But now, quite suddenly, I found myself thinking about the play again and seeing quite clearly the point of the problem that I had missed before. The shape of a third act began to emerge. Of course! The wife's lover wasn't her own choice, but her husband's, and it was her realization of this fact that made it possible for her to leave him. Of course! It was the key to her whole attitude toward her lover. He was not *her* choice. Of course! How curious it was! I had practically sign-posted the thing all the way through without realizing the fact. Why? My mind nosed round the discovery suspiciously like a terrier at a strange lamppost. There must be a mistake. But no, it was all right. I had been too close to it before and too anxious. Now all was well. I drew a deep breath. Forgotten were the Deltchevs and the enigma they represented. I had just finished a play. I felt light-hearted and alive. I quickened my pace.

Then I heard it. It was only a slight sound and it went almost immediately; a sort of ringing of my footsteps on the paving stones. But I was very much aware of everything at that moment; of the soft, warm breeze that was beginning to stir the air, of the smell of the trees, and of the slow movement of a distant point of light. At this moment of heightened sensibility the ringing of my footsteps was a matter for appreciation and curiosity. The pavement was solid enough. Where did the rest of the sound come from? I slowed down a little and heard it again, a kind of echo. From the wall? I stepped out again, but in a more emphatic way this time. Then I understood. It was not an echo I was hearing. Someone was walking behind me.

It is easy to separate sounds once you know they are there. As I walked on, I could hear the other set of footsteps quite plainly. I slowed down again. The sounds separated and then again they coincided. Even then it took me a moment or two to grasp what was happening. The person behind me was varying his pace with mine. He did not want to change the distance between us. I was being followed.

My heart suddenly beat faster. I looked round. I could just see him, a faint thickening of the shadows under the trees about thirty yards behind me. I walked on, fighting down a desire to run. Perhaps I was imagining it all, like a neurotic spinster with fantasies of being raped. But no; the footsteps kept pace with mine. Wild ideas of turning quickly and challenging the follower went through my mind, but I kept on walking for a bit. The calves of my legs began to ache. Then, suddenly, I turned and crossed the road to the lighted side. Out of the corner of my left eye I tried to see if he was crossing too. I could hear his footsteps. They had slowed down. He wasn't going to cross. He was going to stay among the shadows. For a moment or two a feeling of relief flooded over me. It was not until I was nearly to the pavement that I realized why he had not crossed. A hundred yards or so ahead there was a stretch of road with no buildings and no lights. I remembered walking along it earlier. He was going to cross there.

I reached the pavement and hesitated. Then I bent down and pretended to tie my shoelace. I wanted time to think. If I went back the way I had come, I could stay in the lights. I remembered also that I had seen two policemen yawning and spitting on a corner. But what was I to do then? Explain to them? But there was nothing to explain. The only thing was to wait about like a frightened child until someone else came along with whom I could walk in company through the dark. Ridiculous! What was there to be afraid of? Someone was following me. Very well. Let him follow. What did it matter? There was nothing to be afraid of in that. Nothing at all.

I stood up again and walked on stiffly toward the darkness.

It lay at the end of the lighted strip of pavement like the black mouth of a tunnel. The building I had to pass before I reached it was a huge baroque mansion that, judging from the lighted windows, had been converted into flats. I looked across the road. I could see him moving along under the trees now, a little behind me but at the same speed. The darkness came nearer and I began to see a short way into it. The footpaths ran on between a stone wall and the trees, but the surface of it changed from stone pavement to dust. At the end of the pavement I paused. The leaves above stirred faintly; there was a radio playing somewhere and the breathing sounds of distant traffic, but that was in the background; the darkness before me was quiet and still. The gritty dust crunched beneath my feet, and the branches seemed to close in as I walked on again. I had gone about thirty paces when I heard the sound of an approaching car. It passed, going in the opposite direction. Then, as the sound died away, I heard footsteps on the road; the man from the shadows was crossing it behind me. I went on faster, stumbling slightly over the swellings in the path made by tree roots. My heart was beating sickeningly now and I could feel the cold sweat stealing down my body. I fought against the desire to run. It was absurd, I told myself. I had been in situations fifty times more dangerous. Here there were no mines or alarm wires to tread on, no machine guns or mortars waiting to open fire. All I had to do was to walk along a path beneath some trees in a badly lighted city street, followed by someone who might or might not be ill-intentioned. He might be a detective, one of Brankovitch's men instructed to report on my movements. Petlarov had been warned off me by the police. They might now be checking to see if I had any other contacts. Indeed, the man could have been following me about for days without my having noticed the fact. Yes, that must be it. I almost chuckled with relief and slowed down, listening for the footsteps behind me. But there were none. Perhaps they were muffled by the dust. Perhaps—

I stopped dead. Something had moved in front of me.

I stood quite still for a moment, trying to control the thudding of the blood in my head so that I could hear. Something had moved—a shadow, something. I took a step forward and my foot grated on a pebble. The next instant there was a blinding flash of light.

It came from a powerful hand-lamp a few yards in front of me and lasted for less than a second. And that, too, was the time I took to react. As the light went out I fell sideways, sprawling at the foot of a tree.

I only heard the first shot, a thudding crack that made my ears sing; but the next two I saw—yellow blots of flame that seemed to be exploding in my face as I rolled over and clawed for cover behind the tree. Then there was a silence.

I was gasping for breath as if I had been held under water, but my brain was working all right. He had missed me three times and then lost track of me. He would have to risk another flash from the lamp to locate me again, and it would be a risk; he could not be sure that I was unarmed. In any case, I was prepared now, and unless he was a first-rate shot or very lucky he had not much of a chance. For the moment I had forgotten the man behind me.

Five seconds went by. I was slowly straightening up and easing round away from the tree when the light flashed on again. It was not directly on me, and in the fraction of a second it took him to realize that, I had begun to move. I was halfway toward the next tree when he fired. The bullet whipped past my head. I reached the tree and swung round it as if to take cover again, but immediately scrambled on to the next one. The shot he fired at that moment was yards wide. But he had learned one thing; I was not going to fire back. The lamp shone out again, and this time it stayed on. He did not fire. He moved forward. He was going to make sure of it this time. Bent double, I scuttled on again. I saw my shadow twist among the long casts of the trees as the light swung round. Then, as I pulled up against the next tree, a different pistol fired.

The bullet tore through the bark an inch or two from my right eye, and a splinter of wood stung my cheek. I dived for the ground again. The other gun, I thought, had been a .38, but this had a heavier sound. I could see how it was. If I had not crossed the road, the man behind me would have shot me in the back. The second man had been there to make sure I did not get away. Probably he had crossed ahead of me while I was still in the lighted section.

I was out of the light for a moment now, but both pistols fired again and the bullet from one of them ricocheted off the road. They were getting worried. Nearly half a minute had gone by since the first shot, and I could hear shouting in the distance. The lighted stretch was only a hundred yards away now, but if I broke cover and made a dash for it, I would have to pass the heavy pistol with the other man's light behind me. It would not do.

At that moment the man with the light began to run forward, yelling hoarsely. The heavy pistol fired again as I rolled sideways and found myself on the edge of the road. I hesitated for only a split second. Then I scrambled to my feet and ran, swerving like a rabbit, for the trees on the other side of the road. They both fired, but by then I was a hopeless target for a pistol. I dived through the trees, came up against the boundary wall, and ran along it toward the lighted section.

I was safe now. I stopped to get my breath. There were people from the houses standing on the pavement opposite, talking and pointing toward the trees where the sound of the firing had come from. The two policemen I had passed farther back were approaching at a run. I was out of sight. My breath was beginning to come back, and with it my wits. I had not seen either of the attackers. I had no information about them to give. But even that would take a lot of explaining to the police, and they would certainly detain me while an interpreter was found and my story checked. If I could avoid the police altogether, I should do so. If, while they searched among the trees for the dead and wounded that were not there, I could make myself scarce, I would be saving them trouble. If, in fact, I now did what I should have done five minutes earlier—kept my head, walked back to a café, and there telephoned to the hotel for a car to fetch me—everyone would be much better off. I had begun to tremble violently. My ears were singing and felt deaf. I leaned against the Presidential wall fighting down a desire to vomit. Through the singing in my ears I could hear shouts from farther up the road. Then my head began to clear. Reaction or no reaction, if I was going to get away unobtrusively I would have to be quick about it. Keeping close to the wall, I started to walk.

It was an hour before the car arrived at the café, and by that time I had had several plum brandies. I was not drunk but I felt sleepy. It was silly of Aleko, I thought, to want to kill me. Very silly. I was perfectly harmless. However, I had now acquired another useless piece of information: I knew what it felt like to be shot at in civilian clothes; it was exactly the same as it felt when you wore a uniform. That was interesting. In the car I went to sleep and had to be wakened by the driver when we got to the hotel.

The reception clerk was asleep. I took my room key from the rack myself. The lift was not working. I walked upstairs slowly, yawning. I was really very tired. I was also beginning to feel stiff and bruised. If the water was hot (and late at night when nobody wanted it, it usually was hot) I would have a bath and attend to the knee I had cut on a stone. My suit was a mess too, but that could wait until the morning. A bath, then sleep; that was it. I felt curiously relaxed and happy. The odd thing was that this feeling had almost nothing to do with the plum brandy. It was because I had survived an ordeal.

I opened the door of my room. There was a small foyer with a cupboard and a hat rack between the door and the bedroom itself. I switched on the foyer light, remembered with a twinge of irritation that I had lost my hat and would have to buy one of the local Homburgs next day, and went into the bedroom.

My hand was on the bedroom light-switch when I saw what was there. I stood quite still.

A woman was lying face-downwards across the bed. By the foyer light I could see that she had a loose raincoat of some kind spread about her as if it had been thrown there to cover her up.

I pressed the light-switch, and the room was flooded with the bright hard light from the naked lamps in the gilt chandelier.

Her hair was dark and one of her tightly clenched hands concealed her face. I walked over to the bed, and a loose board cracked loudly. I looked down.

She stirred. Her hands moved and she rolled onto her side. The light poured down on her face and she raised a hand to shield her eyes.

It was Katerina Deltchev.

CHAPTER XVI

I shook the bed, not gently, and she sighed. Then, with a start and a gasp, she was awake. She sat up quickly and the thin raincoat she had thrown over her slipped to the floor.

"Good evening," I said.

For a moment she stared at me, then she scrambled off the bed and looked round defiantly.

"There's no one else here," I added.

She drew herself up as if she were about to deliver an oath of allegiance. "Herr Foster," she said formally, "I must apologize for this in-trusion, but it was unavoidable. I will explain. I—" She broke off and looked down as she realized that she was in her stockinged feet.

"They're down there," I said. Her shoes had slipped off while she had been asleep and were lying beside the bed.

She opened her mouth to say something, then shut it again, went over to the bed, and put her shoes on thoughtfully. She was a young woman who was used to being in charge of a situation; now she was casting about for a way of taking charge of this one.

"I am sorry—" she began.

"Quite all right," I said. "You wanted to see me, so you came here. I was out. You waited. You fell asleep. I am afraid I can't offer you any-thing but a cigarette. Will you smoke?"

For a fraction of a second she weighed the possible moral advantage of a refusal; then she shrugged her shoulders. "Yes. Thank you."

She took a cigarette and I lit it for her. She sat down again on the bed and looked at me calmly.

"Herr Foster," she said, "it is not really quite as simple as that for you, is it?"

"No, not quite."

I went into the bathroom, dipped a towel in water, and wrung it out. Then I went back into the bedroom, sat down in the armchair, rolled the trouser leg up, and went to work with the towel on my cut knee. She watched uncertainly.

"Who told you I was staying here?" I asked.

"There were three hotels where you might have been staying. This was the second one I telephoned."

"How did you know the room number?"

"By asking for another room number when I telephoned. Of course I got the wrong number. The operator corrected me."

"Who let you in here?"

"The floor waiter. I said I was your lover and gave him some money. Does it matter?"

"Not a bit. It's just that at the moment I am in a suspicious mood. Now, then. How do you get out of the house without being seen? What do you do?"

"Our neighbors are friendly. Between our wall and theirs there is a tree. With two vine poles one can crawl from the top of our wall to the tree. From the tree one uses the branches to reach their wall. For a child it is easy. For a heavier person there is some danger, but it can be done."

"Then why did you ask me to deliver that letter for you, Fräulein? If it was so important you could have delivered it yourself."

"I did not wish to risk my life if there was another way."

"Are you risking your life now?"

"Yes, Herr Foster. I am also risking yours."

"That I guessed."

"But only if I am found here."

"Splendid."

"If I get back tonight without being seen, I shall be safe too. The guards inspect us only in the morning."

"Good."

"I would not have come, Herr Foster," she said severely, "if it had not been absolutely necessary to see you."

"You didn't have to leave the house to do that. I was there myself an hour ago."

She shrugged. "I did not know. I wished to see you because—"

I interrupted her. "Do you know a man named Aleko?"

"Aleko? It is common."

"Who was the Valmo you sent that letter to?"

"I don't know."

"I see."

"It is true. Valmo was only a name I was given to send letters to. The letter was for someone else."

"Who?"

"My brother, Philip."

I sighed. "The one who's studying law in Geneva?"

"He is not in Geneva."

"Your mother said he was."

"My mother was lying."

"I didn't think so."

"She did not intend you to think so. Will you please listen to me without interruption for a moment?"

"All right, I'm listening."

"My brother has been in hiding here since before Papa was arrested. My brother, Herr Foster, had five friends. Their names were Pazar, Eftib, Vlahov, Pechanatz, and Radiuje."

I dropped the towel. "Do you know what you're saying?"

"Perfectly. That is what I came to tell you. This evidence that they have brought against my father is quite true. Only it is not he who is guilty. It is my brother, Philip."

I sat back and stared at her. She was telling the truth. A lot of things were suddenly and appallingly clear.

"When did your mother find out?"

"She did not tell me."

"Does your father know?"

"He must have known from the beginning of the trial, or guessed. But what can he do? He cannot accuse his own son, and Brankovitch would certainly not let Philip give evidence."

"Nobody would believe it anyway. They'd laugh. Dutiful son takes blame for father's crimes? I'd laugh myself." I thought about it for a mo-

ment. It explained quite a lot of things, but not everything by any means.
I looked up at her again. "What's the idea of telling this to me, Fräulein?"

"I want you to publish my brother's evidence."

"Does he want to give it?"

She set her lips firmly. "He must."

"Does your mother know of this idea?"

"I would not tell her. She would say that it would not help Papa, only condemn Philip."

"She'd be right."

"But abroad they must know the truth."

"Would your mother agree with that?"

"I do not know. She is too clever to be simple. She would discuss the idea and think of possibilities nobody else had dreamed of. Then she would say she was tired. You would not know her real thoughts."

"What was your brother up to? Is he crazy?"

She shook her head slowly. "When Papa betrayed the party," she said, "he and Philip quarreled. They were always in conflict, but this time my mother could do nothing." Tears came to her eyes. "We were all against him, even I was; and when the People's Party came to power, Philip joined a student political club that had for secretary this man Pazar. Pazar always needed money, but the students liked him. He talked very amusingly and they used to pay him for coaching. When they formed a club they would sometimes make him secretary and give him a commission on the subscriptions. Philip soon felt that the club was not serious, but he became very friendly with Pazar. Then, one day, Pazar told him that he was a member of the Brotherhood."

"There must have been pleasure in telling that to the son of the man who had done so much to destroy it," I remarked. It was all too easy to catch the flavor of those dangerous exchanges of confidences between the middle-aged drug addict and the fanatical youth.

She shrugged. "Perhaps. I know that when Philip joined the Brotherhood it was only to revenge himself on Papa. He did not mean then to do more than join."

"But once he had joined, he found that they expected more than a gesture. Was that it?"

She nodded. "There were six of them elected, and Philip was named the leader. Their task was to kill Vukashin at the anniversary-celebration parade. But—"

"Just a moment. Who was the man who gave them the job?"

"It was not one man, but a group of men. They called themselves the Survivors."

"When did Philip tell you all this?"

"Before he went to Switzerland. Mamma had become worried about him. He looked so ill and tired. She persuaded Papa to send him there to study. Naturally, he refused to go at first, but after a day or two he said no more. That was at Christmas. He had arranged to return in secret when Pazar sent for him." She paused before she added: "I knew then that he was not the real leader, but had been given the role of leader because of his name."

"Did you say that to him?"

"He already knew it, I think. But if I had said it he would have made some other foolishness to prove to me that I was wrong. Besides, I thought that in Geneva he might change his mind and forget about it."

"But he didn't."

"No. We had arranged a code for our letters, and when the attempt on Papa was made, I heard from him that he was returning. I only saw him once. We met secretly at a place near the station."

"Patriarch Dimo 9?"

"No, another. But he gave me two addresses which I might send letters to. Valmo, Patriarch Dimo 9, was one of them. The other he told me I must use only in case of an extreme emergency if I had to find him."

"What was in the letter you gave me?"

"I begged him to escape to Greece and publish the truth about the conspiracy against Vukashin from there."

"What made you decide to come to me?"

She frowned impatiently. "Today's evidence, Herr Foster. Surely you see. The police know everything. Philip and Pazar are the only two left. They must be in hiding somewhere, helpless. Philip can do nothing now even if he wished. It must be done for him."

I thought hard for a moment or two, then I shook my head. "I don't think that it's as simple as you believe, Fräulein."

"What do you mean?"

"Well, to begin with, Valmo was the name Pazar was hiding under. When I tried to deliver your letter, I found him dead. He'd been shot through the back of the head and had been there some days."

"What happened to my letter?"

"That was burnt by a man named Aleko who said that he was of the secret police and that *his* name was Valmo. He also said that your letter was addressed to him and was something to do with the attempt on your father." I described Aleko. "Does that mean anything to you?" I added.

She looked utterly bewildered. "No, Herr Foster."

"What does your brother look like?"

She gave me a description.

I nodded. "A young man who looks like that came into Aleko's apartment while I was there. I only saw him for a moment. Aleko called him Jika."

She stood up quickly. "That is Philip. He likes his friends to call him that. Herr Foster, where is this place?"

"I don't know for certain, but I should think that it may be the other address your brother gave you. Have you got it?"

"Philip made me remember it. He said it was too dangerous to write down."

"What is it?"

"Pashik, Pan-Eurasian Press Service, Serdika Prospek 15," she said.

I went to the wardrobe, got out the bottle of plum brandy, and poured myself a big drink.

"Do you like this stuff?" I asked.

She shook her head.

"All right, Fräulein. You'd better go back now. I think I know how to reach your brother."

CHAPTER XVII

PASHIK LIVED in a modern apartment house near his office. He had pointed out the place to me on the day I had arrived. I thought now that I could find it without much difficulty. There were no taxis. I walked.

The way there lay through the business quarter, and by that time the streets were mostly empty and still. Earlier that day they had been decorated in preparation for the anniversary parade, and the bright moonlight striking obliquely through the flags overhead cast a multiplicity of shadows that stirred and twisted in the warm breeze. It was like walking through the dark forest of a dream. But I had gone some distance before I became frightened.

It was a very unpleasant sensation. The brandy-engendered resolution with which I had set out seemed to drain suddenly away. I began to shiver uncontrollably and an icy, numbing kind of logic invaded the small corner of my conscious mind not whimpering with the effort required to keep on walking. What I was doing was incredibly foolish. Not three hours ago two men had tried to kill me in the street. I had been very lucky to escape. Now here I was in the streets again, giving them another chance. For obviously they must be waiting for me. Ruthless determination of the kind they possessed would be intensified by failure. They would not fail a second time.

Soon every shadow had become a man with a gun, every doorway the place of an ambush. I kept on simply because I was afraid to go back.

I walked now simply because I was afraid to break into a run that might precipitate action. My legs ached with the strain. My shirt clung to my back. I had so completely lost my head that I went on fifty yards past my destination without seeing it. There was a frantic ten seconds on the corner of the Boulevard Sokolovsky while I got my bearings. Then I saw the apartment house from a familiar angle. I ran the fifty yards back.

It was a tall, narrow building with massive ferroconcrete balconies, from the sides of which rusty weather stains drooled down the walls. In the daylight these stains gave the place a tired, unhappy air—you wanted someone to wipe its face for it—but in the moonlight they were hard shadows that made the balconies seem to project like freakish upper lips. The main entrance doors, ornate affairs of wrought iron and rolled glass, were still open, and the lobby beyond was dimly illuminated by a light from the concierge's room.

As I stood for a moment or two recovering my breath, I looked back along the street. There were two or three empty cars parked in it, but they had been there already. Nobody had followed me. I went in and pressed the concierge's bell. Nothing happened. After a minute or so I went over to the lift. Beside it was a list of the tenants. Pashik was on the fourth floor. The lift did not work, of course. I found the stairs and walked up.

At the moment of deciding to see Pashik that night I had had a clear image of the sort of interview it would be. I had seen him already in bed and asleep when I arrived. In response to my insistent ringing he had at last appeared, a bleary, nightshirted figure (I had been sure he wore nightshirts), fetid and protesting. I had cut through his protests decisively. I had given him no time to build up his defenses. I had pelted him with the facts I had discovered and watched his features grow pinched as he realized how much I knew. Then, at last, wearily he had shrugged. "Very well. Since you already know so much, Mr. Foster, you had better hear the rest." And I had sat down to listen.

The reality was somewhat different.

The door to his apartment was at the end of a short passage near the main staircase landing. As I turned into the passage, I saw that the door was ajar and that there were lights in the apartment. I went along the passage and up to the door. Then, with my hand on the bell, I paused. Inside, someone was speaking on the telephone. Or listening rather; there was a series of grunts, then two or three words I did not understand. The voice, however, was not Pashik's. I hesitated, then rang the bell.

The voice ceased abruptly. There was a movement from within. Then silence. Suddenly the door swung open and clattered gently against a picture on the wall behind it. For a moment the small lobby beyond looked empty. Then I saw. Between the doors of the two rooms facing me was a narrow strip of wall. On that wall was a mirror and, reflected

in it, the face of the man who had pushed the door open with his foot.
It was Sibley.

He moved slowly out from the wall just inside the entrance and looked
at me. There was a heavy bottle-glass ashtray in his hand. He put it down
on the hall table and grinned.

"Well, Foster dear," he said archly, "this *is* a nice surprise! A small
world, I always say. Do *you* always say that? Of course you don't! Come
to see our smelly friend?"

"Naturally. What are you doing here?"

He looked at me oddly. "I've come to see him too, and also naturally.
Doesn't seem to be about, though, does he? I've looked high and low."

"Who were you expecting to have to beat over the head with that ashtray?"

"Somebody else who shouldn't be here. Like me. You're quite a logical
visitor, of course. Been here before, I shouldn't wonder."

"No."

He grinned again. "I thought not. Come on in and make yourself at
home. I was telephoning."

"Yes, I heard."

"Don't speak the language though, do you?"

"No."

"I thought not. This way."

He went through the left-hand door. I hesitated and then followed.

It was a sitting-room that had obviously been furnished by the owners
of the building. There were built-in cupboards and bookcases and a
built-in sofa. There were cube-like easy chairs, glass-topped circular tables,
and an oatmeal-colored rug. You could have seen the same sort of things
in any other furnished apartment building in any other European city.
The extraordinary thing about this room was the decoration of the walls.

They were covered, every square foot of them, with pages cut from
American magazines and stuck on with scotch tape. There were pictures
of film stars (all women), there were near-nude "studies" of women who
were not film stars and there were artlessly erotic color drawings of re-
clining seductresses in lace step-ins. All would have looked quite at home
in the room of an adolescent youth. Yet that was the comprehensible
part of the display; it was not remarkable that Pashik should have the
emotional development of a sixteen-year-old boy. The startling thing was
that for every Ann Sheridan, for every sandal-tying beach beauty, for
every long-legged houri, there was a precisely arranged frame of advertisement pages. The nearest Betty Grable was surrounded by Buick,
Frigidaire, Lux, and American Airlines, all in color. A sun-tanned blonde
glistening with sea water had Coca-Cola, U.S. Steel, Dictaphone, and
Lord Calvert whisky. A gauze-veiled brunette with a man's bedroom slipper in her hand and a speculative eye was framed by Bell Telephone,
Metropolitan Life Insurance, General Electric, and Jello. The baffling

thing was that the selection and grouping of advertisements seemed quite unrelated to the pictures. There was no wit, no hint of social criticism, in the arrangements. Many of the advertisements were not particularly distinguished as such. It was fantastic.

Sibley had gone back to the telephone. He had said something into it, listened again, and then, with a last word, hung up. He flicked his fingers at the wall as if he were launching a paper pellet.

"Lots of fun, isn't it?"

"Lots. How did you get in?"

"The concierge has a pass key and is corrupt. Would you like a drink? There must be some about." He opened one of the cupboards and peered inside.

"Do you know Pashik well?" I said.

"Would you believe me if I said yes?"

"No."

"Then let's say that I think I know a bit more about him than you do. Cigars but no drinks," he added, producing a box. "Cigar?"

"No, thanks."

"No, it's a drink you need. You're not looking your usual cheerful self, Foster dear. A bit pinched round the gills and upset. Let's try this one." He went to another cupboard.

"I take it you're not afraid of Pashik's suddenly turning up and finding you here searching his room. That wouldn't embarrass you?"

"Not a bit."

"Was that why you came? Because you knew he wouldn't be here?"

He looked up from the cupboard he was searching and shook his head. "No, Foster *mio*," he said softly, "that wasn't why. I just wanted a little chat with him. When there was no answer, I had another thought and fetched the concierge. Silly of me, wasn't it?—but I actually thought our Georghi might be dead."

"Why should you think that?"

"It was just a thought I had." He straightened up suddenly with a bottle in his hand. "There now! Our old friend plum brandy!" And then he looked directly at me. "You know about Pazar, of course?"

"What about him?"

"Tonight's police statement that they've found him shot in a derelict house."

"Oh yes, that." I tried to make it casual.

He reached down and brought out two glasses. "A house in some street with a funny name," he said slowly. "What was it?"

"Patriarch Dimo." My voice sounded unnatural to me.

"That's it. Who told you? Georghi?"

"Yes. He had the statement."

He brought the bottle and glasses over and put them on the table. "When did you see him?"

"Oh, earlier on."

He shook his head. "It won't do, Foster dear," he said. "No, don't get cross. I set a little trap and you fell into it, that's all. That statement was only issued half an hour ago. I was on the phone to the office when you came in. That's how I know." He thrust his head forward. "How did *you* know?"

I was feeling sick again. I sat down.

"*Did* Georghi tell you?"

I shook my head. "I found him by accident."

He whistled softly. "My, my! You *do* get around! What sort of an accident was it that took you to Patriarch Dimo? The same sort that got you into the Deltchev house?"

"Not quite."

"Doing a little private investigating perhaps?"

"That's the idea."

He shook his head regretfully. "Someone must be very cross with you."

Another wave of sickness came. I drew a deep breath. "Then that's probably why someone's just tried to kill me," I said.

He stared at me expressionlessly for a moment. "A joke, Foster dear?" he said gently. "A joke in bad taste?"

"No joke."

"Where was it?"

"In that road that runs round the park."

"When?"

"An hour or two ago."

"One man or two?"

"Two."

"One of them couldn't have been Georghi by any chance?"

"No."

He seemed to relax again. "Well, well! Poor Foster! No wonder you look peaky. And here I am chattering away instead of pouring the much-needed drink. There."

I swallowed the drink and sat back for a moment with my eyes closed. I hoped he would believe that I was feeling faint. I had to think and it was difficult. Sibley was Brankovitch's paid man and already I had given myself away appallingly. Pashik was involved with Aleko and Philip Deltchev in a Brotherhood plot to assassinate Vukashin. The wreckage of that plot was being used to convict the elder Deltchev. Now the dead Pazar, probably murdered by Aleko, had been officially discovered on the eve of the anniversary parade at which Vukashin was to have been assassinated. There was a contrived, bad-third-act feeling about the whole thing; as if . . .

"Feeling better?" said Sibley.

"Yes, thanks." I opened my eyes. He was looking down at me coldly. I had not deceived him. He smiled.

"What a busy week you've had! Have you any idea, I wonder, what you know that makes you worth killing?"

"None at all."

He sat down opposite me. "Maybe if you were to tell me what you do know, I could make a suggestion about that."

"Or perhaps find a way through the censorship with it? By the way, how is your little man at the Propaganda Ministry?"

He drank his drink down and looked at the empty glass as if waiting for someone to fill it. "Do I detect a note of bitchiness and distrust, Foster dear?"

"Yes, you probably do."

He looked at the bottle and poured himself another. "Drink will be the death of me," he said. "I was tiddly, of course, but it seemed such a good joke at the time. Although, Foster *amigo*, I won't deny that I should also have been interested to see what your angle on the affair was going to be."

"My angle was and is that your little man in the Propaganda Ministry was Brankovitch."

He giggled. "Who told you they played that trick? Georghi?"

"Not Georghi."

He giggled again. "Oh dear! Not Georghi, you mean, but someone else whose name you don't want to mention in case I'm a Ministry spy who might get him into trouble. Oh dear, oh dear! I do see. I played right into your hands, didn't I? No wonder you were so maddening. The thing was that they'd tried it on me days before. I could send anything I wanted if I knew how. That was the line. It would cost a bit, of course, but that was to make it sound right." He sighed. "I don't like being taken for a fool, do you? I was a bit vexed, so I decided to amuse myself. I thought at first of pretending I'd fallen for it and sending a really dreadful story I'd heard about Vukashin's sex life. Then I sobered up and thought again. In the end all I did was to lift their dialogue and try it on someone else. Georghi was my first customer and I frightened him out of his wits— or he pretended I did. And that was the crazy part of it; because it wasn't until I saw him looking at me with those big brown eyes of his and got a breath of that subtle perfume that I remembered where I'd seen him before. Do I convince you?"

"By no means."

He gazed upwards soulfully. "It's so sad. I can never make the truth sound convincing. Of course, I *look* so shifty. I should stick to lying, shouldn't I?"

"Where was it you saw Pashik before?"

"Ah, I have your interest. If only I can keep it until the knock-out drops that I slipped into your drink begin to work, all will be well."

Involuntarily I looked down at my glass.

He grinned. "You're really very tiresome, aren't you, Foster dear? If

I didn't want badly to know what makes you worth killing, I wouldn't say another word."

"It's late. I'm very tired. And—"

"And it's always so upsetting to be shot at," he said quickly. "How inconsiderate of me not to remember that!"

"I wasn't apologizing."

"Of course you weren't. You were just hoping that I'd cut the cackle. I do understand. These affectations of mine are such a bore. All right. Let's talk about Georghi Pashik—why he exists and in whose image he is made. What has he told you about himself?"

"He was expelled from Italy for writing something Mussolini didn't agree with. He did his military service in Austria. He admires Myrna Loy. The last item I deduced for myself from a picture in his office."

"She must be his spiritual Mum, don't you think? All right, here it is. Technically, a stateless person. Born in the Trentino, of Macedonian Greek parents who were themselves of doubtful national status. He takes Hungarian nationality. Treaty of Trianon muddle. He does his military service in Austria. He goes eventually to Paris and works for Havas as a messenger. Intelligent, ambitious, a worker. He writes odd pieces. He gets on. Eventually they give him a job in the Rome office. He gets important. Then he's expelled, which is all very difficult because he's married an Italian girl and the *squadristi* make it hot for her family. He has a lot of trouble squaring things. After a bit his wife dies and he returns here to the home of his forefathers with very peculiar ideas about the way the world ought to be run."

"What sort of ideas?"

"I'm coming to that. Well, the war breaks out and in 1940 Georghi skips to Cairo. For a time he's on a newspaper there, then he decides that it's time to do a little war work and gets taken on as an interpreter by the British. Later on, when the United States Middle East contingent arrives, he is transferred to them. In 1945 he turns up in an American Civil Affairs unit in Germany."

"Still as an interpreter?"

"Still as an interpreter. Only by now he has a bastard sort of uniform and is working in a D.P. camp near Munich. He worked under an American major named Macready. I had business there, and that's where I first saw Georghi and got to know about him."

"What was your business?"

"Intelligence—the British lot." He caught a glance I gave him. "Oh dear me, no! Not any more. I was just the wartime variety, uniform and everything. I was liaising with an American who was on the same job as me—checking up on the bad boys who'd gone to earth in the D.P. camps and then digging them out—and it was this man who told me about Georghi. Another drink?"

"I think I will."

"That's good. There's another bottle in there if we run short or if
Georghi comes home. All right, then. We go back to the time Georghi
went over to the Americans in Cairo. Almost the first thing that happened
was that he was sent up to a small hill town in the Lebanon with a lieutenant, a tech sergeant, and an enlisted man. The job was to operate a radio station monitoring an intelligence network operating in the Balkans. I
believe there was some short-wave oddity that determined their position,
but that's not important. The thing was that our Georghi was stuck out
in the wilderness for nearly a year with three Americans who didn't like
it either and talked about home. I don't know anything about the sergeant
and the enlisted man, but the lieutenant was a radio engineer named
Kromak and he came from Passaic, New Jersey. Do you know the
Lebanon?"

I shook my head.

"In the evenings the sky is like wine and the shadows falling across the
terraces have purple edges to them. Overhead, vines—grape and other
things with big flowers and a wonderful smell. Everything is very still and
warm and soft. It's the kind of atmosphere in which myths are born and
the pictures in your mind's eye seem more real than the chair you're sitting on. I wax lyrical, you see. However, the point is that Lieutenant
Kromak talked about Passaic, New Jersey, and read aloud his wife's letters while Georghi listened. He heard about Molly's graduation and
Michael's camp counselor, about Sue's new baby and the seeding of the
front lawn. He heard about the new refrigerator and the shortage of gasoline, about his friend Pete Staal, the dentist, and the Rotary Anns. He
heard about the mouse in the cedar closet and the new screens that had
been bought for the porch. And when the weekly letter was exhausted,
the reminiscences would begin. 'Pete Staal, Pete Staal,' Kromak would
say dreamily, 'a good dentist and a lovable son-of-a-bitch, but what a
crazy guy! I remember the night Kitty and me, the Deckers, and the Staals
went to Rossi's—that's an Italian restaurant at the far end of Franklin
Street—and had ravioli. Ever had ravioli? At Rossi's they make the best
ravioli in the world. Well, we didn't want to take two cars, so we rode
down in mine. A Dodge I had then. Well, right after we'd eaten, Helen
said she wanted to go over to the Nutley Field Club. That made Pete
mad and he said that if she was going to Nutley he was going to fly down
to Wilmington to see his mother. Of course, he knew what Helen really
wanted—to see Marie and Dane Schaeffer—I told you about them, remember? Well . . .' And on he went while Georghi listened and drank
it in. Do you know Passaic, New Jersey?"

"No."

"Chemical plants and some light industry and the homes of the people who have to work there. But to Georghi Pashik, looking through the
eyes of Lieutenant Kromak, who wanted so much to be back with the
wife and kids, it must have represented a paradise of domestic security

and gracious living. You know how it is? Lots of quite intelligent Europeans have fantastic notions about the way most Americans live. Sitting on that terrace in a Lebanon hill town, poor, unhappy, exiled Georghi must have been a push-over for the American way of life. Just to put it in terms of food—reason might tell him that the ravioli he'd get in Rossi's on Franklin Street, Passaic, would not be as good as he'd eaten already in Rome and Florence, but Rossi's ravioli had become the desirable ones. They had the approval of those legendary figures the Staals, the Deckers, and the Schaeffers, and that was what mattered. He began to understand why the Americans didn't like the Lebanese they came in contact with. Lebanese standards of sanitation and behavior are not those of Passaic, New Jersey. Georghi heard local ways that he had accepted or failed even to notice condemned quite angrily. He was troubled and began to question himself. You see what was happening, of course? Along with his dream of Passaic, New Jersey, he was beginning to acquire an American conscience."

He paused for a moment to swallow another drink and fill my glass.

"How much are you embroidering this story?" I asked.

He shrugged. "Not much. But the man who told me was an American and he could reproduce that Kromak stuff so you'd think you were really listening to him. I just give you the bits I remember and fill in the rest. The effect's the same, though. Anyway, after nearly a year of the American Way and Purpose according to Lieutenant Kromak, Georghi was shifted back to Cairo. Americans again, only this time the high priest was a dairy chemist from Minnesota and the dream was in a slightly higher income bracket. Georghi read the Declaration of Independence, the Constitution of the United States and the Gettysburg address. After that there was a filling-station proprietor from Oakland, California. He was followed by an insurance man from Hagerstown, Maryland. Then came 1944 and the surrender negotiations between Deltchev and the Anglo-American representatives. There was a British military mission operating with the partisans in Macedonia at that time. They controlled quite a large area and had a landing strip, so it wasn't too difficult to arrange the meetings. The Anglo-Americans flew in from Foggia. Deltchev traveled overland somehow. They met in a village schoolroom. Georghi was one of the interpreters. It was after the second meeting that Georghi's little cap went over the windmill."

"Wait a minute. Had he known Deltchev before?"

"Known of him, that's all. Well now, we get to the second meeting. They had their meeting all right, but storms delayed their return and they had to wait for twenty-four hours in the village. The atmosphere of the negotiations had been quite friendly and the wait produced a lot of general conversation about conditions inside the country, the problems, what was to be done about them, and so on. The man who told me this was on that trip. Anyway, one of the subjects discussed was the Officer

Corps Brotherhood. Deltchev was very frank about the problem and the difficulties of dealing with it. Some of his revelations, in fact, were deeply shocking to the Anglo-American brass and they didn't hesitate to tell him so. Deltchev must have wished he hadn't mentioned the thing. But that night Georghi went to see him privately. It must have been a curious meeting. After extracting from Deltchev a lot of secrecy and immunity pledges, Georghi revealed that he was a member of the Officer Corps Brotherhood, had been one since he had returned to the land of his fathers from Italy in '37. I told you he'd had peculiar ideas then about the way things ought to be. He'd expressed them by joining the Brotherhood. But now, he told Deltchev, all that was changed. He'd seen the light of Western democracy—all the way from Passaic, New Jersey, to Hagerstown, Maryland, he might have added—and wanted to make reparation. The long and short of it was that the Provisional Government's big clean-up of the Brotherhood was made possible because Georghi turned stool pigeon."

"How do you know?"

"Because the man who told me was the officer Deltchev went to for a check-up on Georghi. The old man's first idea, of course, had been that Georghi was either an *agent provocateur* or crazy. So he was very careful. But after the next meeting he had another talk with Georghi and a plan was made." Sibley grinned. "You know, Georghi did a very brave thing really, when you come to think of it. He could have stayed safely with the Americans. Instead he asked them to lend him to Deltchev and came back here. The risk was really appalling, when you think. For all he knew, the Brotherhood might have already condemned him as a traitor. He'd not stayed to collaborate. He'd been in the service of a foreign army. And now he'd turned up again, safe and sound at a time when for a civilian the journey from Athens was all but impossible. However, he took the risk and got away with it. I suppose that outside this place the Brotherhood's intelligence system didn't operate, and in all the confusion nobody bothered to ask many questions. Georghi rejoined his cell and the game began. There were ten Brothers to a cell. Georghi would turn in the names of seven of them to Deltchev. Then the three survivors, Georghi among them, would attach themselves to another cell and in the next cell-purge the survivors of the first one would go with the rest. All except Georghi. He was the permanent survivor. But because of the secret way the Brotherhood was organized, nobody could know how many purges our man had survived. He always arrived with the credentials and code words of the cell just betrayed and he'd always see that those who came with him were at the top of his next list. So there was never anyone to say that where he went disaster followed. It was always the first time with him. But still risky. After a time the word got round that there was treachery, and the remainder of the Brotherhood disintegrated. As a safety measure, Georghi had himself arrested on suspicion and then re-

leased. He'd done all he could. Deltchev had him quietly shipped back
to the Americans. That's when I met him."

"But why didn't you recognize him at once?"

"He had a mustache then and, as I told you, a uniform. As a matter
of fact, he was so American it was difficult to believe that he'd never been
out of Europe. His boss in Germany, Colonel Macready, was the last
of the prophets as far as Georghi was concerned. He came from Texas.
You know that seersucker suit Georghi wears? Macready gave it to Georghi
as a going-away present. It came from a department store in Houston. It
was also a kind of consolation prize. Georghi had tried every way he
could to get a quota number for America, but it was no good. So he came
back here and claimed his reward." He paused.

"What do you mean?"

"Well, just think. Four or five years ago he came back here without a
penny to his name. Now he's got this place, which I can tell you is quite
expensive by local standards, and an established press agency with a dollar
income. How did he do it?"

"He's quite efficient."

"But no genius. Besides, the Pan-Eurasian was a going concern long
before the war."

"You know the answer?"

"Yes. I did a bit of checking up. The Pan-Eurasian was originally a
French company incorporated in Monaco. It took a bit of doing, but I
managed to find out all about it through our Paris office. I got word today from them. Like a little surprise?"

"Yes."

"All right, then. All the shares in the Pan-Eurasian Press Service were
purchased in 1946 from the French syndicate that owned them. Forty-
nine per cent of them are in the name of Georghi Pashik. All of them
were bought with a draft signed by the person who owns the other fifty-
one per cent." He stopped and grinned again.

"Well, who is it?"

"Madame Deltchev."

My mind turned a somersault. "Are you sure?"

"Sure? Of course I'm sure."

"She'd be a nominee, of course."

He laughed. "Nominee? That woman? Don't be silly. She ran Papa
Deltchev as if he were a family business. And if you've fallen for that
holier-than-thou line of hers, you'd better think again. I'm a newspaper
reporter, Foster, dear, and I've met some very tough ladies and gentlemen,
but that one is up near the top of the list. When I was here two years
ago, she was running the country. If there were any nominees around they
were her husband and that secretary of his, Petlarov. She did the thinking.
She wrote the speeches. She made the policy. Do you think that dried-up

little lawyer could have got to power on his own? Not on your life! The only thing he ever did without consulting her was to make a damn-fool radio speech that virtually handed over the whole country to the People's Party. Papa Deltchev? Don't make me laugh! They're not trying a man in that courtroom. It's a legend they're after and I bet she's still fighting like a steer to preserve it. Why shouldn't she? It's her work. She's the only Deltchev they're sitting in judgment on."

I shook my head. "Oh no, she isn't."

He stared. "No?"

"No. You may be right about her husband, but she didn't control all the Deltchevs."

"What are you talking about?"

"Her son, Philip. He's a member of the Brotherhood. He was recruited by Pazar. And he's the Deltchev who was the leader of the conspiracy against Vukashin. You see, they're using the evidence against the son to convict the father and they know it."

Sibley stared at me, his face sagging.

"What's more," I went on dully, "the conspiracy is still in existence. And Philip Deltchev is still alive. I carried a letter from his sister, Katerina, to him. The address was Patriarch Dimo 9 and instead of Philip I found Pazar shot through the back of the head. Then Pashik turned up. Where he is in this I don't know. But he turned up and took me to see a man named Aleko, who says he is of the secret police, but isn't. In fact he's a professional assassin who makes a habit of shooting people through the back of the head. He seemed to be in charge of the whole affair. Philip Deltchev was there under the name of Jika. The Patriarch Dimo thing was explained to me as part of a cunning police trap to catch the man who tried to kill Deltchev before he was arrested. I pretended to accept that and agreed not to make any further visits to the Deltchev house. Of course, they didn't want me to ask Katerina any questions. Pashik warned me privately too."

"But, all the same, you went?" Sibley's face was the color of dirty chalk.

"Yes."

"And you wonder why they tried to kill you?"

"Not any more. Of course, if the fact that Philip Deltchev was the Deltchev of the evidence were known it would make the trial look rather silly."

He jumped up.

"Rather silly!" His voice rose. "You poor bloody fool! Don't you know anything about this country? Don't you see what's happened? The People's Party has taken over the whole conspiracy. Aleko's *their* man, not the Brotherhood's, and he's going to do the shooting. Young Deltchev's only the scapegoat."

"Scapegoat for what?"

"For tomorrow's assassination, you nitwit! Don't you see? It's Judgment Day! The People's Party are going to liquidate their boss, Vukashin!"

CHAPTER XVIII

SIBLEY HAD HIS OFFICE CAR and he drove me back to my hotel or nearly to it. He was so frightened that I thought at first that he was going to refuse to do even this. But in my own panic I had made up my mind to kill him if he tried to leave me to walk, and he must have known it. From the moment we left Pashik's apartment until we arrived we did not exchange a word. He stopped at the corner of the street by the hotel. I looked at him.

"I'm not driving up to the entrance," he said curtly; "you can get out here."

"All right."

The moment I was out of the car he slammed the door and drove off. I could see his point. If Aleko's men were waiting at the hotel for me, it would not be a good place to stop at. I turned the corner and paused. There was a police van outside the hotel entrance. I walked slowly toward it. The revolving doors were set back slightly, and as I approached I saw the sleeve of a uniform in the recess. I walked on more boldly. If the police were there, there would at least be no gunmen in ambush.

I reached the entrance and went in, stared at by the policeman. Inside the foyer there was a group of military police and the night clerk in his shirt sleeves. They seemed to be questioning him. Then, as I came through the revolving doors, they all looked at me. The night clerk pointed.

"Herr Foster," he said.

An officer stepped forward and two of his men moved round behind me.

"Your papers please?" He spoke in German.

I fumbled them out somehow. My hands were trembling. He glanced at them, pulled my jacket open to see if I had a gun, then nodded to the men behind me. "You are under arrest," he said to me as the escort closed in. "You will come with us."

I turned round and walked toward the revolving door again. I just managed to get through it before, very violently and painfully, I vomited.

I sat with the escort on benches in the van. The officer locked us in and got up beside the driver. I did not see where we went. It was not far. I managed to recover sufficiently to ask what I was charged with, and found that the escort spoke no German. The van turned onto cobbles and stopped. I heard the officer get out. Then there was silence. We stayed there for about ten minutes. When the van was stationary, the roof ventilators did not revolve and soon the air inside became warm and stagnant. I could smell the uniforms and greased-leather equipment of the escort and their sour, wine-laden breaths. At last there were footsteps on the cobbles, and the door of the van opened. The officer shone a flashlight.

"Get out."

The escort clambered down and I followed. We were in a quadrangle with a high entrance arch. On the three other sides the space was enclosed by a building with barred windows. A prison, I thought. The only light came from a narrow doorway near the van.

"Forward!"

Going toward the doorway I stumbled on the cobbles and one of the escort held me by the arm. I shook his hand away and went inside. There was a long stone passage with the smell of a barracks about it. Led by the officer, we marched along the passage and up some stone stairs. Then there was another passage and more stairs. The place was certainly not a prison. At the end of the second passage there was a wooden door with a guard on it. As we approached he unbolted the door. The officer went through ahead of us, and the ring of his footsteps was suddenly muted. The corridor we now entered was carpeted. We walked on between heavily ornamented walls reaching up to a vaulted ceiling. At intervals there were marble pedestals with busts standing on them and gilt wall brackets with electric candle lamps. There were no doors. Before we reached the end of the corridor, however, we turned off into a narrow passage like the alleyway of a liner. Then there were several doors. The officer peered at each in turn, then opened one of them and motioned me in.

It was evidently a committee room. There was a long table with a dozen or so chairs placed round it, a table with a telephone, and a bookcase. Over the rich marble fireplace there was a portrait of Vukashin in a gilt frame draped with the national flag. There were green linen blinds over the windows, and beside the fireplace a curtained door. The room smelt of stale cigarette smoke.

The door by which I had entered shut behind me and I heard the key turn in the lock. I turned round and found that I was alone. I looked at the time. It was two o'clock. I sat down at the table. My head was aching and there was a horrible taste in my mouth. There was a water carafe and glass on the table in front of me. I drank some of the water. It was strongly chlorinated and made me want to be sick again. I lit a cigarette. Minutes went by. Every now and then I would hear a movement or a cough from the passage outside. The escort was still there. When I had finished one cigarette, I lit another. If I were going to be put into a jail, my cigarettes would certainly be taken away. I might as well smoke while I could. However, this feeble effort at a philosophical approach to the situation was not successful. Whether or not I had cigarettes to smoke would probably not seem of much importance in the near future. If Sibley was right —and I knew that he was—my arrest could mean only one thing: that Aleko, having failed to kill me himself, had left me to be dealt with by his employers. It was not a pleasant thought. On the other hand, the party might have decided that to murder a foreign journalist would not be a wise move at a time when they would be busy denying their guilt of a more serious crime. But supposing their wisdom was of a different kind. Supposing they decided that the inconvenience of killing somebody who knew too much was as nothing compared with the inconvenience of being revealed as the accomplices of their leader's murder. Death seemed very near at that moment. I hoped it would come mercifully. Perhaps if the hand were that of Aleko—

I turned sharply, my heart pounding, my skin crawling. The curtain over the door on the far side of the room had moved.

I stood up. The fantastic thought went through my mind that if I were going to be shot from behind the curtain, I must stand up so as to present an easy target.

The curtain moved again. A draft from somewhere had caught it. There was the sound of a door closing in the adjoining room, footsteps; then the door behind the curtain opened and a hand brushed the folds aside.

Brankovitch came into the room.

He glanced at me casually before turning to shut the door behind him; then he came round the table toward me.

"Sit down, Mr. Foster." He nodded to a chair and sat down himself facing me. His face was haggard and he needed a shave, but he did not look as if he had been roused from his bed. Probably he had been attending a meeting. The hours before a *coup d'état* that was to begin with an assassination would be busy ones for a propaganda minister. I must be one of the inevitable hitches.

He sighed. "A cigarette?" He brought out a case.

"I have one, thank you." This was idiotic. "I'm glad to find that you allow prisoners under arrest to smoke," I added.

He pursed his lips. "I think it will be better, Mr. Foster, if you avoid facetious comment. You are being treated with great consideration, as I think my presence here indicates. It would be polite of you to recognize the fact. You realize, I hope, that you are in a very serious position."

"It's difficult for me to realize anything, Minister. All I know is that I have been arrested and brought here. I should like to know what the charge against me is and I should like the British Legation informed."

His dark, supercilious eyes stared at me coldly. "It would be convenient if you would abandon your pretense of innocence, Mr. Foster. It wastes time. If you prefer to be treated as a common criminal, that can be arranged. If you will recognize the fact of my sitting here talking to you as evidence of consideration toward a distinguished foreign writer, we may make progress."

I was silent.

He lit a cigarette. "Very well, then. Early tonight on the avenue that runs round the Presidential Park, shots were fired by two men at a third. Police pursued the men who had fired the shots. They escaped. So did the other man. But something was found by the police. A hat. It had your name in it, Mr. Foster. Was it your hat?"

I hesitated. "Yes, it was my hat."

"Why do you hesitate? Were you thinking of lying, Mr. Foster?"

His eyes were on mine and at that moment I understood the nature of the interview. Brankovitch knew what Aleko knew. He knew about the letter to Philip Deltchev and my finding of Pazar. He knew that Aleko had forbidden me the Deltchev house and that I had that night ignored the prohibition. He knew that Aleko had tried to kill me and failed. He might know that Katerina had talked to me. What he was trying to find out now was how much I knew, how dangerous I was. If I did not know the truth about the conspiracy against Vukashin, I was unimportant. If I did know or if I had an inkling of the truth, I must be eliminated.

I leaned forward and put my cigarette out in the ashtray by him. Then I smiled ruefully. "Surely you understand my position, Minister. The last thing I want to do is get involved in police proceedings. Two armed men attempted to hold me up. Luckily, I managed to get away from them. It happened on a very dark stretch of road. I didn't see either of their faces. What use would I have been to the police?"

"It was your duty to report the occurrence to them. By running away in that fashion you have raised a grave question in the minds of the police."

"What question?"

"It might be that you were one of the men who fired shots."

"Do you believe that, Minister?"

"What I believe is not important. This is a police affair. It is referred to me initially as a matter of policy because of your status here as a newspaper representative. But I cannot prevent their dealing with you as a criminal. I can merely advise them of my opinion."

"If I were a criminal, Minister, would I have been so careless as to leave behind a hat with my name in it?"

"The police argue from the stupidity of the criminal, not from his cleverness. But assuming, Mr. Foster, that your version of the affair is true, what do you think was the motive for this attack on you?"

Here it was. I look puzzled. "Motive? Robbery, I imagine. What else could it be?"

He pretended to think this over. Then: "You have not, for instance, made any enemies here?"

I felt relieved. If this was the best he could do, I had nothing to worry about.

"Enemies? I don't think so."

"You have been involved, for instance, in no unusual circumstances that might give a clue to the police?"

I hesitated again.

"I should advise you to be frank, Mr. Foster. You see, armed robbery of that kind is a most unusual crime here. I do not imply that we have no violent criminals, but that it is unusual for them to be armed with revolvers. The reason is that to carry a revolver here is in itself an offense punishable by death. The law was made to deal with the Brotherhood criminals, but of course it applies to all. Robbers would try to kill you with knives. These men did not. If they were not robbers, then who were they? That is what the police ask."

I still hesitated. I was in a terrifying quandary. Obviously, the "unusual circumstances" he was inviting me to tell him about were my finding of Pazar and my meeting with Aleko. But to which would it be better to pretend—frankness or cunning? Which would conceal from him more effectively my actual knowledge? Frankness had its dangers. He would be able to cross-examine and perhaps catch me out. Or he might decide from my manner that I was less artless than I seemed and unlikely to have been genuinely taken in by Aleko's explanation of the affair. Perhaps an obstinate silence would be better. The silence itself would have a useful meaning. It would say to him: "This man does not know that I know what he is concealing. His pretense of ignorance shows, therefore, that he is truly ignorant of the important facts." But it might also add: "And that is just what he hoped I would think. Clearly he is bluffing."

"Yes, Mr. Foster?" He was watching every movement of my face.

Suddenly, hopelessly, I decided. I drew a deep breath. "Very well, Minister. I will be frank. I have a confession to make."

"A confession, Mr. Foster?"

"Yes." And then I had a desperate inspiration. I looked at him angrily. "That was what you were expecting, wasn't it?"

"Expecting?"

"Minister, with all due respect, I've had enough of this cat-and-mouse game. I've been silly. I stuck my nose into something that was none of my business and found out some things that I wasn't supposed to know. All right, I admit it. I didn't think Herr Valmo would bother you with it. I was hoping he wouldn't. But since he has, I'm sorry. One thing I can promise you is that no reference to it will be made in any of my articles. I can't say more than that."

He stared at me. The skin of his face was stretched tightly. It was for a moment a most extraordinary and horrible mask. The lips moved.

"Can't you, Mr. Foster?"

"What is there to say? I found a dead body that your secret-police people had baited a trap with. Naturally Herr Valmo was annoyed. But he didn't blame me. I acted in all innocence. I don't see what all the fuss is about."

"Did you make certain very solemn promises to Herr Valmo?"

I looked embarrassed. "Yes, I did."

"And yet you again went to the Deltchev house."

"Unfortunately, I did."

"Why did you go?"

"I felt I had to have Madame Deltchev's comments on the trial evidence. To be quite frank, I thought it more important to have those comments than to obey an instruction I couldn't really see the point of."

"Did you speak to Katerina Deltchev?"

I looked puzzled. "No, it was the old servant who let me in."

"Who do you think were the two men who tried to kill you tonight?"

"I've no idea. I told you. I didn't see their faces."

"I think you are pretending to be more stupid than you really are, Mr. Foster. How on reflection do you explain those men? If they weren't robbers, what were they?"

For an instant I thought that I had failed after all. It was the phrase "on reflection" that did it. If he was thinking ahead to a moment when, with Vukashin assassinated, I was beginning to put two and two together, I was really done for. If he thought that there was the remotest chance of my getting at the truth, he would decide against me. I made a last attempt.

I stared at him with sudden horrified comprehension. "You mean that they were Brotherhood men?"

For about ten long seconds he did not answer. Then, slowly, he nodded. "You see, Mr. Foster, this prohibition of Valmo's that you so irresponsibly ignored was not without reason. Naturally, Valmo did not tell you all the facts, but there was reason to believe that the Brotherhood was interested in reaching Madame Deltchev. You were mistaken tonight for one of Valmo's men. You are lucky to be still alive."

He had swallowed the suggestion whole. And he had given himself away. I sat back with a sigh which could have meant anything but which came actually from a feeling of relief that was almost painful. Fortunately, I still had my wits about me. There was one thing he had not mentioned. If he did not bring it up I would have to and I did not know how. I took another risk.

I frowned suddenly. "There's only one thing I don't understand," I said. "Your office issued a statement this evening saying that Pazar had been found shot. The details sounded as if he was the man I found. Why didn't Valmo tell me who he was? Why the secrecy?"

"Would you have respected the confidence, Mr. Foster?"

"Of course."

"As you did your undertaking to Herr Valmo?" He was quite sure of me now.

I tried to look embarrassed.

He smiled unpleasantly. "I will speak plainly, Mr. Foster. I think your behavior here has been, to say the least of it, unethical. If you were a professional newspaperman I should make a very strong complaint both to your employers and to the British Legation here. As it is, I shall recommend to the police that you are released in the morning. However, I shall withdraw from you all facilities for attending the Deltchev trial. I also advise you unofficially to leave the country immediately—let us say by tonight's train at the latest. In case you decide to ignore that advice, I propose to have your visa and *permis de séjour* canceled forthwith. Do I make myself clear?"

I protested as convincingly as I could, demanded that an official expulsion order be issued, became angry, and finally pleaded. He was obviously and satisfactorily bored with me. It has occurred to me since that he must have been nearly as relieved as I was that the problem I represented had been disposed of. He may even have disliked the idea of having to have me killed. It is possible. The last thing he said to me could be taken that way. To stop me talking he rapped on the door to summon the escort. When they came in he gave them an instruction and turned to go. Then he paused and looked back.

"Mr. Foster," he said, "I once saw a performance of a play of yours and I enjoyed it. Why not stay in the theater? I think, for you, it would be much safer."

I was taken out of the building by the way I had come in. It must have been a wing of the Propaganda Ministry. There was another ride in the van, another oppressive wait, then a cell in a police station. The cell had a bug-infested plank bed, but I was too exhausted and shaken to care much about bugs. As the patch of sky I could see got lighter, I fell into a headache-ridden doze. I even slept a little. At nine o'clock the cell door opened and I was taken to a sort of waiting-room near the entrance.

There, dirty and unshaven, in his seersucker suit with the three fountain pens in the pocket and his briefcase resting on his knees, sat Pashik.

He rose to his feet as he saw me, and nodded.

"Good morning, Mr. Foster."

"How did you get here?" I said.

His eyes flickered warningly in the direction of my escort. He spoke in German. "I have just been informed that you were arrested by mistake and were here. I understand that an apology has already been given and accepted."

"Yes. Am I free to go?"

"I am told so."

I shook hands with the escort and followed Pashik down the steps into his car. He drove off and turned a corner before he spoke. His tone was bleak and noncommittal.

"What happened, Mr. Foster?"

"I was interrogated by Brankovitch."

"Yes?"

"He wanted to find out how much I knew and how much I suspected."

He turned to look at me. The car wandered in the direction of an obelisk.

"If we're going to talk hadn't you better stop?" I added quickly.

He straightened up but did not stop. "And what did you know and suspect, Mr. Foster?"

"That the Brotherhood plot to assassinate Vukashin has been taken over by the anti-Vukashin movement in the People's Party. That Aleko has been brought in to organize the job efficiently. That Philip Deltchev was involved in the original plot and is still involved. That when Vukashin is assassinated at the anniversary parade today, Philip Deltchev will be executed for the crime. That the story will be that when his father was arrested Philip took over the conspiracy and with the knowledge and approval of the Agrarian Socialist executive carried it through. That the Agrarian Socialist Party will be made illegal and liquidated. That Brankovitch will take over the Government."

He kept his eyes on the road. "And what did you tell him you knew?"

"Only what he must have been already told by Aleko—that I found the body of Pazar and believed Herr Valmo's explanations."

"And you convinced him?"

"Do you think I'd still be alive if I hadn't?"

"No, Mr. Foster, I don't. May I say that I have always had the greatest respect for your intelligence?"

"Thank you."

"You must have talked with Mr. Sibley, of course."

"Yes."

"I was sure he had recognized me and that someone had been indiscreet. How much does he know, do you think?"

"He's got the general idea. And he's very frightened."

"I see. We have much to tell each other, Mr. Foster."

"Yes. By the way, my permit for the trial has been withdrawn and I've got to be out of the country tonight."

He nodded. "That was to be expected. There is a train for Athens at five, which I strongly recommend."

"Athens? Why Athens?"

"Because that is where Philip Deltchev is."

I stared at him. He had a curious smirk on his face. He even began a wheezy kind of chuckle.

"What on earth are you talking about?" I demanded.

He swung exuberantly into the street that had the Hotel Boris in it.

Already crowds were beginning to line the roads in preparation for the parade. He looked at his watch and nearly mowed down a family group in national costume.

"It is now twenty of nine," he said. "In an hour Philip Deltchev will be at the Hotel Splendid Palace in Athens. Apart from Madame Deltchev and myself, you are the only person who knows this. You can be the first newspaperman to interview him, the first to expose the People's Party's political murder conspiracy."

"But how did you know?"

"I think you could have guessed, Mr. Foster. I saw him across the frontier myself last night."

CHAPTER XIX

WHEN PASHIK was secretly rewarded for his services to the Provisional Government with shares in and management of the Pan-Eurasian Press Service he was not unduly grateful. He had risked his life to serve a political ideal; but it was an ideal that in his mind belonged exclusively to the United States of America; elsewhere it was not valid. He had performed his service somewhat in the spirit of the prosperous immigrant to that country who endows a public library or a childbirth clinic in his native land. The act is charitable, but it is also a reparation, a propitiatory rite that makes the separation final and complete. For Pashik there was little satisfaction in the knowledge that his contribution had been so frankly and practically recognized. His pleasure in the gift resided in the fact that the agency's clients were nearly all American and that he could feel, not preposterously, that as their representative he was in a sense an outpost of the American way of life. One day, perhaps, he would go on a visitor's visa to America; and, perhaps one day, before he was old, he would get an immigration quota number. Meanwhile he was in touch. For Pashik, who had learned not to expect too much of life, that was a singular blessing and he enjoyed it. After a while he could almost forget that the Brotherhood had existed.

The reminder that it had indeed existed and the news that in an attenuated way it still did exist came as a blow. The messenger was Pazar. He told of cautious overtures being made, of small, tentative meetings, of wary soundings, and of half-formed plans. It was as if the Brotherhood had been decimated by a plague and as if the survivors had now begun to raise their heads and look about them, uncertain whether or not the infection still persisted. Gradually, in an atmosphere of intense suspicion and extravagant fears, contacts were being re-established. The security precautions were formidable. All surviving members were invited to re-apply for membership and submit to the most searching investigation. Refusal to reapply when asked was to be deemed evidence of guilt. There had been no refusals so far, Pazar told Pashik grimly. The Brothers awaited him.

Pashik nodded and went to see his principal shareholder, Madame Del-tchev. This was just about the election time and Madame Deltchev ad-vised Pashik to reapply. Apart from the fact that it would be dangerous for him not to do so—Pashik did not think that this alone would have weighed heavily with Madame Deltchev—she felt that it would be ad-visable to be informed of the new Brotherhood's activities. She had al-ways had in mind the possibility of the People's Party's manipulating the Brotherhood for its own ends. This resurgence might not be merely what it appeared.

So began again a double life for Pashik. He was reinitiated into the Brotherhood and sat in judgment on the applications of others. The purges had proved fatal for nearly all the senior members and soon he found himself being admitted into the higher councils of the organiza-tion. Some two months before the arrest of Yordan Deltchev he heard of the membership of Philip and of the plot against Vukashin.

For once Madame Deltchev was at a loss. She had already planned the football-match incident and was maneuvering as best she could to bring about an Agrarian-Socialist coup before the People's Party was quite se-cure. Her son's activities imperiled everything. Whether he succeeded or failed, it made no difference. As far as the people were concerned, Philip Deltchev was an extension of Papa Deltchev. The murder of Vukashin by Brother Philip would serve to unite the People's Party as never before and shatter the Agrarian Socialists irretrievably. She could not betray the boy, for to do so would bring the same evil consequences. It was useless, she knew, to attempt to persuade him, for he was too deeply committed. She could not even discuss it with him lest he should identify Pashik as her informant. Not that she would have minded sacrificing Pashik; it was simply that she saw no point in sacrificing him to no purpose. All she could do was to instruct Pashik to work within the Brotherhood to keep in touch with Philip and perhaps undermine his belief in the project. It was a feeble plan, but for the moment she could think of nothing better. Then events began in the most curious way to play into her hands.

In the days before the purges Pazar had been a comparatively unim-portant member of the Brotherhood whose weaknesses had been clearly perceived and carefully reckoned with. He would certainly not have been allowed so much as to know about a plan as important as that he now administered. That he should tell someone of it was inevitable. That it should be the petty crook Rila whom he told was very nearly lucky. If Rila had not happened at that time to get into the hands of the police, things might have turned out very differently.

The casualties in the assassination group put the Brotherhood in a panic. The survivors had raised their heads only to find that the plague was still with them. It was another betrayal, another purge. Within a few hours the great majority of the readmitted Brothers were dispersed and in hiding. The rest—those who had no means of hiding—sat in their rooms rehearsing denials. Only Pashik was in a position to know that the plague had not returned and that there must be a more banal explanation of this disaster. He made his report to Madame Deltchev and waited.

A week later, things began to move. One night Philip Deltchev came to see him. He brought news. He and Pazar had escaped and were for the moment safe. Meanwhile the Brotherhood had reorganized. Pazar had been superseded as administrator—his nerves were bad—and a new man had taken over. His name was Aleko and he was a dynamo of a man with great determination and drive. But others were needed. Several Brothers had refused, cravenly. Would he, Pashik, come in with them? The plan would now go on to success, in which all would share.

Pashik accepted and reported to Madame Deltchev. She agreed with him that the whole affair felt peculiar. Their suspicions were aroused in the first place because of the failure of the police to arrest Pazar and Philip. Pashik knew that there was documentary evidence against them and that in such a dangerous case—a Brotherhood plot against Vukashin —the price of concealment was beyond the fugitives' capacity to pay. And there was Philip's name. Why was the People's Party not publicizing the affair? By way of reply to this question Madame Deltchev produced her theory that the People's Party would ultimately take over the Brotherhood. Pashik listened respectfully. But he had an unworthy thought: that Madame Deltchev's preoccupation with the idea was dictated by her annoyance at having failed to take over the Brotherhood herself. She was, to Pashik's way of thinking, a remarkable woman, but inclined to underrate the cleverness of others.

A day or two later he was summoned to meet Aleko. The meeting took place in the apartment I had been in, and it was soon evident to Pashik that Aleko was not what he pretended to be. For one thing, he noticed— as I had noticed—that the furnishings had been assembled from second-hand stores and arranged hurriedly in an unlikely way. But there might have been reasonable explanations for that. What decided him was Aleko's way of talking. Pashik had met many members of the Brotherhood and he had learned to recognize the habits of thought and speech that were the private currency of their relationships. For instance, the Brethren scarcely ever talked of killing anybody without at some point using the phrase "removing an obstacle." Aleko used the word "eliminate." It was a small difference, but it was one of many. And there was a mannerism he had that was peculiar. When he spoke of firing a gun he would point with his forefinger at the back of his head and make a clicking noise with his tongue. For the Brethren a gun was a serious matter; you did not click facetiously with your tongue to convey its moment of power. The whole gesture reminded Pashik of something he knew he would remember later. By the end of that meeting he was sure that Aleko was not a bona-fide member of the Brotherhood. Yet he was dispensing money and making sound plans to assassinate Vukashin. In the early hours of the morning Pashik came to the conclusion that Madame Deltchev had been very nearly right. Someone had employed Aleko; someone who could hamstring police action and also pay well; someone in the People's Party. But not necessarily the People's Party as a whole. A faction within the party, then? It was probable. Somebody was going to get killed and somebody else was paying for the event. Pashik decided to learn more before deciding upon the identity of the principal.

The attempt to assassinate Deltchev was organized, Pashik thought, by Vukashin himself and without Brankovitch's knowledge or approval. The press releases that came from the Propaganda Ministry bore marks of haste, improvisation, and uncertainty of line which suggested that Brankovitch had been caught unprepared. Moreover, Aleko was disconcerted and talked vaguely about "bungling." The term could have referred to the failure of the attempt, but Pashik's impression was that it was more in the nature of a comment on a situation that permitted the attempt to take place at all. That was interesting because if the impression was correct, it meant that Brankovitch and Aleko had one thing at least in common—ignorance of Vukashin's intentions. And that in turn might mean that they had other things in common too.

The arrest of Deltchev created a new problem for Pashik. Hitherto he had had no difficulty in arranging for private meetings with Madame Deltchev. Now that she was under house arrest, it was impossible for him to see her personally. He knew that all visitors would be reported and he could not afford to have his name on the list. His whole position was, indeed, highly equivocal. He was certainly known to Aleko's employers as a member of the Brotherhood. The faintest breath of suspicion as to his motives would result in his being informed upon and promptly hanged. He had Philip Deltchev on his hands and an obligation to extricate the young man if he could. He did not know exactly what was afoot. He was without allies. All he could do for the present was to remain as inconspicuous as possible, cultivate Philip Deltchev, and check up on Aleko. But for a while he did not make much progress with either intention. Philip Deltchev did not like him. The best he had been able to do about Aleko was to remember what the gun-pointing gesture had reminded him of. The "K. Fischer" note that I had found was the result. It was Pazar who finally supplied the essential information.

When Aleko had taken over the conspiracy, Pazar had been in a pitiable state of exhaustion and terror. The arrest of Rila had cut off his drug supplies. He was without money or lodging and was hunted by the police. Philip, who then had (in the name Valmo) the room in the Patriarch Dimo, had taken him in, and for nearly a week the two had remained there, hungry, because they feared to go out to buy food, and in constant fear of discovery. The night Aleko arrived on the scene, Pazar had collapsed and was in a state almost of coma. It took him several days of ready access to the supplies of heroin that Aleko had miraculously procured to bring him back to anything like normality; and when he did come back, it was to find that he had been superseded.

Pazar was not unintelligent. Quite soon he perceived what Pashik already knew—that Aleko was not of the Brotherhood—but, unlike Pashik, he drew a wrong conclusion. His drug-twisted mind linked his discovery with his own fall from power and also with the memory of the traitor who had never been unmasked. All the paranoid projections of his mind focused suddenly upon a single object—Aleko. From that moment he began to plot against Aleko and to spy on him. Philip had moved into Aleko's apartment, and Pazar had the Patriarch Dimo room to himself. It was easy, therefore, for him to keep track of Aleko's movements outside the apartment. One night he followed Aleko to a house in the suburbs. It was a big house and there was a car outside of the kind that usually has a chauffeur. Aleko was there an hour. When he came out Pazar did not follow him, but stayed to watch the house and the car. Ten minutes after Aleko had gone, a man came out, got into the car, and drove off. As he passed by, Pazar recognized him. It was Brankovitch. Two days later, seething with malice and excitement, he told Pashik of his discovery.

It took Pashik ten seconds to make up his mind what he had to do. The first thing was to control Pazar and urge discretion. The second thing was to make him tell the story to Philip Deltchev in Pashik's presence so that while the boy would at last realize what was really happening, his desire for revenge could be usefully canalized. Obviously, Brankovitch's idea was to destroy his rival within the party and to put the guilt for the crime on the Deltchev family. In other words, he could manipulate the original conspiracy so as to convict the father and use the second conspiracy, his own, to dispose of Vukashin and have in his hands the perfect scapegoat, Philip. Pashik's idea was to remove the scapegoat when it was too late to change the assassination plan and let the whole affair recoil on Brankovitch. What was more, Pashik knew just how the idea could be put into practice. But everything depended on Philip.

It was a ticklish business. When Philip's first neurotic outbursts were spent he lapsed into a hopeless depression, which persisted for some days and which was noticed by Aleko. Fortunately, Pashik had managed to make his proposals understood, and Philip Deltchev had presence of mind enough to play the part he had been given. It was not too difficult. All he had to do was to continue to appear fanatically devoted to the task of killing Vukashin; and fanatics do not have to make much sense. The problem was Pazar. His hatred of Aleko soon wore so thin a disguise that an outburst of some sort was inevitable. All Pashik could do was to remind him constantly of the need for absolute secrecy, and hope that when the explosion came, Pazar the drug addict would be more in evidence than Pazar the conspirator. And so it turned out. The occasion was one of the biweekly meetings at which Aleko insisted on going over the entire plan of campaign afresh and rejustifying each part of it. The plan itself was simple enough, and clearly the object of the meetings was to keep the conspirators in hand; but that night Pazar chose to put a different interpretation on the meeting. Quite suddenly and fantastically he accused Aleko of having police hidden in an adjoining room to listen to the conversation. Without a word Aleko rose and showed the next room to be empty. Pazar replied that there were microphones hidden and began to tear up the carpet to prove it. Philip Deltchev sat as if he had not heard. Pashik sat sweating for what was to come. Aleko watched with a smile, but listened attentively to Pazar's babbling. There was just enough sense in it for him to guess what Pazar had discovered. When, in the end, Pazar collapsed, sobbing, Aleko gave him a big injection of heroin. When Pazar was quiet, Aleko looked at the others and shook his head. "We cannot rely upon him," he said. "He will compromise us all."

The other two nodded quickly. They were in heartfelt agreement.

Aleko smiled. "Leave everything to me," he said.

At the next meeting Pazar did not appear and Aleko announced briefly that he had committed suicide in his room, that the body would be left for the police to find, and that, as his services had never really been necessary, no Brother would be sought to replace him.

It was on the day after that meeting that I arrived.

I presented a serious problem to the harassed Pashik. To have someone in and about his office, poking and prying, hampering his movements, possibly endangering his neutral relations with the Propaganda Ministry —that was bad enough. To have someone directly concerned with him in contact with Petlarov was alarming, for who knew what that might not suggest to Brankovitch? He had already recognized and been recognized by Sibley, whom he remembered as one of the intelligence officers who could know his story.

Sibley knew me. Another potential danger. Especially as I was inquisitive. My interview with Madame Deltchev threw him into a panic. The night he learned of it, he faced Aleko with his gun in his pocket instead of in his briefcase. But nothing unusual happened at that meeting. It was after it that Aleko took him aside, gave him a wad of papers, and asked him to put them in Pazar's room to "mislead" the police who found them.

Pashik guessed that Brankovitch wished to take the opportunity afforded by Pazar's death of planting further incriminating evidence against Deltchev. When he got to Pazar's room, he found me there.

His dilemma was awful. I could be explained in several ways. I was telling him the truth or I was lying. But even if I was telling the truth I might still be an unwitting agent of Brankovitch's and this might be a trap to catch him out. On the other hand, I was doing work for one of the American clients and was therefore under the protection of the Pan-Eurasian Press Service. If this was a trap, then the only safe thing to do was to take me to Aleko for questioning. If it was not a trap, however, he might be taking the representative of an American client to his death.

"What made you decide to take me?" I asked.

Pashik blinked at me sheepishly. "I did not quite decide, Mr. Foster," he said; "I compromised. I left part of the decision to you."

"What do you mean?"

"While I hid the papers Aleko had given me in the room, you were walking to my car at the end of the street. I thought you might take the opportunity to escape. If you did not—" He shrugged.

"Do you know why I didn't run?"

"Because you were not alarmed?"

"No. Because I wanted to ask you questions."

He sighed. "You have been very lucky, Mr. Foster," he said. "It was difficult to persuade Aleko that you were harmless, and very embarrassing when he found that you were not. I certainly did not expect to find you alive this morning. And when you tell me of Katerina's foolishness I marvel."

"I suppose she got back all right."

"If she had not done so you would not be here. The check on the Deltchev house is carried out at eight every morning."

"Does Madame Deltchev know what's happened?"

"I have been able to send her brief messages."

"By that old friend of the family who drops in for tea?"

"You are too well informed, Mr. Foster."

I finished my fourth cup of coffee. "When you begin to make flattering remarks, I am suspicious," I said. "You really mean that I still don't know at all what's going on."

His brown eyes contemplated me through his rimless glasses. He was smelling strongly that morning. The seersucker suit was horribly dirty. He shrugged. "As for instance, Mr. Foster?"

"As for instance—why are you here at all at this moment? Why aren't you in Athens with Philip?"

We were in my hotel room. He opened his briefcase, took out a battered meat sandwich, and began eating it. He had his mouth full before he answered. "You forget, Mr. Foster, that there is to be an assassination here today."

"I hadn't forgotten it. What I was wondering was why you've been so cagey about it. What exactly is going to happen? What's the plan? When did Philip come into it? What happens now he isn't here?"

"They do not know he is not here. He did not leave until after the final meeting last night."

"But what's going to happen?"

"I will tell you. Pazar's original plan was simple and stupid. The cele-bration march takes place in the St. Mihail Square. The parade marches in along the boulevard and out along the prospect. The saluting base is the stone platform halfway down the great steps that lead up to the por-tico in front of the Ministry of the Interior. It was the main state entrance to the old palace. From the bronze statues at the bottom up to the plat-form there are forty steps. On these occasions the steps are flanked with troops, forty each side. They are a bodyguard and they are armed with machine pistols. It was Pazar's idea to kidnap four of these men and re-place them with his men. They would shoot Vukashin as he stood on the platform and hope to escape in the confusion, because it would seem to be the real troops who had fired. This, I may tell you, was the plan that the prosecutor at the trial did not wish to explain."

"Why not?"

"Because the absurdity of it would make people laugh. Does it not make you laugh, Mr. Foster?"

"It might have worked."

He shook his head mournfully. "I can see, Mr. Foster, that you would not be a good conspirator. One has only to think for a moment of the kidnapping—"

"What were all those messages about?"

"The uniforms, naturally. They could not buy them. Instead they stole them from the soldiers' brothels. It was all very childish. When Aleko took over he made a new plan. Uniforms were wanted, but those of ordi-nary line troops, not those of the bodyguard. Three men only would be needed. It was a good plan. You know, when there is a parade great care is taken to guard against assassins. The occupants of rooms overlooking the square are carefully checked by the police, and the flat roofs of the buildings round it are guarded by troops from outside the city. The first part of the plan was to conceal a machine gun and ammunition on one of the flat roofs. Then just before the parade men in uniform would go up to the roof and tell the troops already there that the guards were being doubled as trouble was expected. As the real troops were from outside, these would not expect to recognize men who said they were from a city battalion. The false men would have bottles of brandy and things to eat in their haversacks. After a while they would offer to share it. The brandy would be heavily dosed with morphine. The soldiers would go to sleep; the gun would be produced and set up and trained on the platform. All would be in readiness for the appearance of Vukashin. And when the thing was done, escape would be possible. It would be difficult in the surprise and confusion to say exactly where the shots had come from. The troops on near-by roofs might think they were from a window below. But there would be doubt. And while there was doubt, there would be time for us to descend to the street and mingle with the crowd. Who is going to suspect three soldiers? Until the real ones wake up, hours later, nobody will know how it was done, and by then it will be too late."

"Philip Deltchev will have escaped?"

"Exactly, Mr. Foster. That was why the plan seemed so good at first to Philip and Pazar and so strange to me. Until I knew that Brankovitch was deeply involved and saw that it would be quite easy for him to arrange for the police to be warned that, say, thieves disguised as soldiers would be raiding such-and-such a building during the parade and that a patrol waiting at the exits could catch them redhanded."

"So as there will be no Philip, there will be no assassination. Is that it?"

"No, Mr. Foster; that is not it. There were to be three on the gun— Philip, myself, and one of Aleko's men."

"One of those who tried to kill me?"

"That is so. But there is another man and Aleko himself. What, I asked myself, would they be doing while Vukashin was being assassinated?"

"Leaving the country, I should think."

"Yes, I thought that. But three days ago there was a serious complication. Aleko told us that there would be a second gun on another roof and that he and the other man would man it. Philip would have the honor of firing first, but Aleko would be there in case of an emergency. What would that suggest to you, Mr. Foster?"

"That he was suspicious? That he didn't trust Philip?"

"Yes, I considered those possibilities. But then another thought occurred to me, a very interesting idea. Luckily I was able to check it. The following night the guns were hidden on the roofs we had selected—"

"Which are they?"

He smiled. "That I think I will not tell you, Mr. Foster. You will discover."

There was something very disturbing about that smile. I suddenly became uneasy.

"Go on," I said.

"The guns were wrapped in sacking and hung by wires inside the brick chimneys. Very early in the morning I returned by myself and examined them." He paused, smiling again.

"And—?"

"The gun on Philip's roof had no firing pin. It had been taken out."

I looked blank. "I'm sorry. I don't see—"

"Don't you, Mr. Foster?" His eyes gleaming through the spectacles were no longer sad. "Power is a great thing, you know. To be able to move and control great affairs—not the characters and situations on a stage, Mr. Foster, but the real—that is the greatest of all pleasures. You feel it in the stomach." He patted his own. "Here. I feel it now."

"Yes?" I wondered suddenly if he were mad.

"Consider." He stood up and strode over to the window. "A man in Aleko's profession is always in a difficult position. He must always be sure that his master has the power to protect him. He must always be sure that the master wishes to protect him. And he must consider the future. It is dangerous for him to serve one powerful person at the expense of another who may later do him harm. Aleko is clever. He would not have survived if he had not been. He is used to weighing advantages. And so I ask myself questions. Why are there two guns? Why is there no firing pin in a gun that Aleko expects to pour bullets into Vukashin. I answer, because it is Vukashin who is Aleko's best master and has been so perhaps from the first. What ultimate chance has Brankovitch in a struggle for power over Vukashin's dead body? None! He would go down in the end. His own intelligence would trip him. The sort of brutal cunning that lets him dig his own grave will always win. That is Vukashin's strength and Aleko knows it. Philip would have pressed the trigger of a gun aimed at Vukashin and nothing would have happened. Aleko would have pressed the trigger of the second gun, aimed at Brankovitch, and the gun would have fired. Philip and I and Aleko's man would have been arrested and hanged. The gun that would be used in evidence would be the one Aleko left on the other roof. The two murderous Deltchevs would hang together. The murderous Agrarian Socialists would be punished. Vukashin would be secure both from the opposition and from the plots and ambitions of Brankovitch. Aleko, who loves skiing, would be waiting, rich and happy, for the snow at St. Moritz. A pretty picture, Mr. Foster!"

"Yes." There seemed nothing else to say.

"But a picture that will not be seen."

"Because Philip is in Athens."

He held up a finger. "And because I am here."

"I don't understand."

"You will see now why I wish you to understand. The one obstacle is Aleko's man—one of those who tried to kill you—the one who was to have been with Philip and me. In one hour's time he will go to a rendez-vous to meet us. If we do not arrive he will go to Aleko to warn him, and when Aleko knows that Philip is not there he will not fire. Brankovitch's life will be saved."

"I see."

"But if I stop this man, Aleko will fire. Brankovitch will die, and because there is no Philip to arrest, Vukashin will have to take Aleko. And when Philip has told his story to you and it is ringing round the world, Vukashin's day will begin to end. That is, if I stop this man."

I said nothing.

For a moment he continued to stare out of the window; then he turned to face me, his self-assurance gone, his face working grotesquely. "Do I stop him, Mr. Foster?" he demanded. "*You* tell me!"

I stared at him, and he read my thoughts.

He shook his head. "No, Mr. Foster, it is not in your hands. There is nobody here for you to tell this story to. That is if you yourself wish to live. Warn Brankovitch, and you will be rewarded by him with a bullet. Warn Vukashin and it will be the same. You know too much for either's safety."

"There's our Legation. They could warn Brankovitch."

"Then you would be killing me instead. I do not think you will choose that alternative. You have no moral dilemma, Mr. Foster. It is my own I put to you."

I was silent.

He sat down and gazed sullenly into space for a moment. "Do you know America well?" he asked suddenly.

"Not very well."

"No," he said slowly, "neither do I."

He was silent again. I did not speak. I knew, as if he were thinking aloud, that he was submitting his problem to the judgment of Passaic, New Jersey, Oakland, California, and Hagerstown, Maryland. It was perhaps as good a way of resolving it as any other.

When at last he stood up he was as calm and businesslike as the day we had met. He took an envelope out of his pocket and handed it to me.

"Your ticket for the press box at the anniversary parade, Mr. Foster. I should have given it to you before. Even after what has happened, I do not see that there can be any objection to your using it. Your train, I would remind you, is at five. Have you money?"

"Yes, thanks."

He held out his hand. "I will try to get to the station to look after you, but there will be the cables and so on to attend to. You will forgive me if I cannot make it."

I shook hands with him. "Yes, of course. Thank you very much for all your help."

He put up a protesting hand. "A pleasure, Mr. Foster."

He turned away briskly, picked up his briefcase, and walked to the door. Then he paused.

"You're welcome," he added, and went.

CHAPTER XX

THE PARADE BEGAN at two o'clock.

It was only a quarter of a mile or so from the hotel to the square, but the crowds along the route of the parade and in the streets approaching the square were dense. It took me a long time to get through. The day was very warm and I felt tired and ill and frightened. I had not eaten any lunch. My legs were like paper and I kept thinking that I had lost something valuable. The sensation was curiously familiar. I had felt like that once before. And then I remembered: it had been when I was walking back to a hotel in Seville after seeing my first and only bullfight.

The press box was in a wooden stand built over the cathedral steps and at right angles to the front of the palace. The parade would pass below it, then bear left to march past the saluting base halfway up the palace steps. There a waist-high balustrade had been erected. It was draped with flags, and on the step below, flowers were banked to give an appearance of depth to the structure. Behind and above it were the crowded boxes of the lesser dignitaries. The whole square was a mass of flags and brilliantly colored flowers. The façades of the buildings that formed the square were mostly of a honey-colored stone, but the paving had been spread with white sand, and in the bright hot sunshine the effect was dazzling.

It was five minutes to the hour when I got there, and all but a few seats in the box were already filled. I could see the back of Sibley's head near the front. Nearly everyone had sunglasses, but I had forgotten mine, and the glare from the sand was painful. Somewhere a military band was playing, and every now and then a section of the crowd would raise a cheer. Heads would turn at the sound, but the cheer would die away. I looked at the rooftops. There was a canopy over the stand I was in and I could see only a small section of them. From there to the saluting base was a little over two hundred yards. At that range even a recruit could hit a man with one burst from an automatic gun. Perhaps even now an eye was peering through sights at the palace steps.

I wiped my face and neck with my handkerchief and looked at the official program. A duplicated translation had been slipped into it for the benefit of us foreigners. The parade would symbolize the plow and the sword in harmony together. First would come the floats carrying the tableaux of the various industries and crafts. Then the massed representatives of sport and culture. Finally the parade of military and air power.

The whole parade would be led by a special tableau depicting the victory of the People's Party. This tableau would halt before the Ministry of the Interior to summon the party leaders to witness the parade, the visible demonstration of the triumph of their work for the motherland.

I had seen this float lurking in a side street just off the square. It was a huge affair mounted on a platform carried by an aircraft transportation truck. Art, Science, Industry, Agriculture, and Armed Might, each with its subsidiary tableau, were grouped round a white flag-decked plinth supporting a huge Winged Victory in wood and plaster. The subsidiary tableaux had the usual props: for Industry there was an anvil, for Science a retort on a bench, for Agriculture a plow, and so on. There were brackets and ledges jutting out from the sides of the plinth obviously for the use of the girls in voluminous white robes who would presently drape themselves round the feet of the Victory.

At eight minutes past two another band entered into the square and formed up round the statue in the center. Then the bodyguards marched in with machine pistols at the ready and to the accompaniment of excited cheers took up their positions on the steps below the saluting base. The stage was being set. At two eleven a squadron of cavalry clattered round from the far side and halted in line beneath the stand I was in. An order was shouted. The cavalry drew their sabers, and a single note on a bugle sounded. With a crash the bands began to play the national anthem. All those who had seats rose to their feet. Then with a roar of cheering, a waving of flags and hats, and another crash of music the Winged Victory float began to move into the square.

My heart was beating so quickly and the blood was thudding so violently in my head that the din of brass bands and cheering was like a continuous rushing sound. I sat down, but it was no better. I stood up again. A man's voice came through the loudspeakers. He was talking very quickly—giving a description of the tableaux, I suppose. The Victory, preceded by a small detachment of troops on foot, turned jerkily and passed our stand. The statue was wobbling as it moved along and the girls posing on the plinth wobbled with it; but I had no desire to laugh. I found myself staring at the tableau of Industry on one corner of the platform. A man in a leather apron had a sledge hammer raised above the anvil as if to strike. His arms were already feeling the strain and I watched the head of the hammer gradually getting lower. Then the float began to turn again and he was out of sight. On the far side of the square, troops presented arms as the Victory came into view. It crawled on until it was nearly level with the center statue, then swung across to the foot of the steps exactly facing the saluting base and stopped. The girls on the plinth took up a new pose so that they all faced the palace.

Suddenly there was a tremendous roll of drums, and over the entire square the crowd fell silent. The drums ceased abruptly. Then the bands began to play the People's Party marching song. All heads were turned toward the palace portico and the aisle of steps that ran down between the upper boxes to the saluting base. Through the loudspeakers came the sound of a choir singing the song. The crowd joined in. The air seemed to quiver with the sound. Then, as the song reached its climax—the great shout of affirmation that came on the final note—Vukashin appeared at the top of the steps and the cheering began.

He was wearing a black suit and had a cloth cap in his hand. For a moment he stood there motionless. Then he raised a hand in salute and began to walk down the steps toward the saluting base, while the cheering swelled up. When he was about two steps down, a man in the uniform of a marshal stepped from the group behind him and began to follow. The Minister of the Interior came next. And then Brankovitch started down.

He, too, was dressed in black, but very neatly, and he wore a gray Homburg. He walked down slowly and deliberately as if he were unaware of what was going on in the square below. As he passed the upper boxes, the occupants of which were clapping, he nodded casually to someone he knew there.

Vukashin had reached the base. Now he walked forward to the balustrade and looked down. A fresh storm of cheering greeted him. The marshal and the Minister of the Interior moved to left and right of him. Brankovitch moved to the balustrade beside the Minister of the Interior and said something to him. The latter smiled and pointed to the Victory. By this time the whole length of the balustrade was occupied. There were two or three uniforms, but most wore dark suits with gray Homburgs. There was only one cloth cap—Vukashin's. On the other side of Brankovitch was a stout man who held himself as if he had a boil on his neck. They were about a foot apart. Brankovitch turned sideways to say something to him.

Vukashin raised his hand in acknowledgment to the Victory tableau, and with a jerk it set off again. At the same moment the bands struck up and the main procession began to move in.

It was headed by a detachment of men in white dungarees marching eight abreast. But I barely noticed them. My eyes were on Brankovitch. He was still talking to the man at his side.

As clapping and cheering broke out again, I began desperately to try to reassure myself. It just could not be! I had been listening to the babblings of a lunatic. Or—better, far better!—the verdict of Passaic and Oakland and Hagerstown had been that those things which were God's should be rendered unto God, that—Article something-or-other-of-the-Constitution-of-the-United-States-of-America—nobody can do anything that affects the life, liberty, or person of anybody, without the aforesaid democratic procedure is properly and faithfully observed, and that the best thing Georghi Pashik could do would be to get his fat arse the hell out of it and send that suit to the cleaner's.

I was suddenly sure that it was going to be all right. At any moment now Pashik would appear beside me, businesslike, courteous, and all for playing ball with the regime. I almost laughed with relief. The time was two nineteen.

And then it happened.

The head of the parade had curved into the straight in front of the saluting base, and Brankovitch turned to look at them. For a second or two he stopped talking and was absolutely still. The next moment the toneless, tearing rattle of a burst of Spandau fire echoed round the square. And almost, it seemed, before the echo of the first had done one leg of its journey, a second burst came.

I had my eyes on Brankovitch. There must have been some sort of stool or bench behind each of them to rest against during the parade, for he lurched back as if he were falling and then stopped for a moment. I saw the second burst hit him in the neck. Then he turned slightly sideways as if he were going to talk to the Minister of the Interior again and crumpled out of sight behind the balustrade.

The man with the boil was the quickest-witted. He took cover behind the balustrade a second after Brankovitch fell. There might, after all, have been other bullets on the way. The Minister of the Interior just stood staring. Vukashin gave one quick look round, then went as if to help Brankovitch. I think that for about ten seconds only a very few of the spectators realized that there was anything amiss at the saluting base. Most of them had just shifted their attention to the parade. But someone screamed. At the same moment men began shouting above the noise of the bands, and the bodyguard closed in defensively round the saluting base with their guns pointed at the crowd. Then a wave of panic came.

All at once everyone seemed to be shouting or screaming. The bands stopped and the parade slowed uncertainly. The Winged Victory, now on the far side of the square, jerked to a standstill. I saw one of the girls fall off the plinth as a great mass of people trying to get out of the square surged forward round the thing. A man near me in the press box was shouting like a maniac. I was very near the exit. I stumbled to it and got down the steps. An official coming up shouted something and tried to stop me, but I pushed past him and made for the narrow street that ran between the cathedral and the adjoining building in the square. This street had been closed by the police and made to serve as a main entrance for box-ticket-holders and I thought that if I could get behind the cathedral before the crowds in the square were completely out of control and the surrounding streets impassable, I might reach the hotel in time to finish what I had to do.

Others in the boxes had had the same idea. The street was filling rapidly and most of the people were running. I began to run too. By the time I reached it, the police barrier at the end had been swept away and people were clambering over the remains of it to join the frantic stream pouring out of the square. It would have been difficult to walk then even if I had wished to, for to the shouting and screaming in the square behind us was now added the sound of shooting as the bodyguard fired over the heads of the panic-stricken crowd. Everybody ran. I must have run about a quarter of a mile before it seemed safe to walk. People had begun to sink down exhausted on the pavements. Many of them were crying. I walked on and found myself in a street of small shops. I had no idea whereabouts I was. The shopkeepers had put their shutters up for the day and I did not want to try asking directions of anyone who knew what had happened. It was not a good moment to reveal oneself as a foreigner.

I walked on aimlessly, looking for a familiar landmark. What I felt I had to do was to see Madame Deltchev and tell her about Pashik before I went. In the confusion I had had the absurd idea that I might get my bag and typewriter from the hotel, be driven to the Deltchev house in a hotel car, and go straight on to the station from there. I knew now that that was out of the question. Even if I managed to find my way to the hotel and hire a car, the chance of getting anyone that day who was willing to drive to Yordan Deltchev's house was small. And that made me realize something else. Unless I could get to the house before news of the assassination reached the sentries on the door, the chances were that I would not be allowed in. It was twenty to three now. Almost certainly the radio had shut down the moment the thing had happened. It would be at least an hour before any official statement was issued; but meanwhile the news and wild distortions of it would be spreading all over the city by word of mouth. I would have to be quick.

I hurried on. The sun was in my eyes. If I kept on walking west I must eventually come to the wall of the Presidential Park. Then, if I followed the wall round, I must come eventually to the quarter in which the house was.

I got there, but it took me well over half an hour and toward the end I began to think that I must be too late. The atmosphere of the city was extraordinary. Just by looking along a street you could see that something serious had happened. People stood about in small groups on the pavements outside their houses, talking very quietly. I had guessed right about the radio being off. Not a sound came from the open windows of the apartment houses. There were armored cars about, too, parked at road junctions or slowly cruising. Vukashin must have been ready to put a standard emergency control plan into operation the instant he got back into the Ministry. As I walked along in the hot sun, I began to see that I might have difficulty in leaving the city that night.

To my dismay, there were several groups of people standing about outside the Deltchev house, and as I drew nearer, I saw that there were extra guards on the door. I wondered if Vukashin yet knew that there was no Philip Deltchev to be arrested. The chances were that, with Vukashin unable to admit to any precise understanding of the situation, things at the palace were still confused. The people waiting here in the street must have heard fantastic rumors and gravitated to the Deltchev house simply because it was the nearest place with important political associations. I could even reflect brutally that, with Brankovitch dead, the worst thing that could happen to me here now was that I would be refused admittance. The same corporal was there. He was looking more sullen than usual and anxious. That probably meant that he knew nothing. I went up to him and he recognized me with a nod. I produced my papers. He glanced at them doubtfully and handed them back, but made no signal to let me through.

"I don't know, *mein Herr*," he said in German. "I must await orders."

"What orders?"

"Something has happened."

"What?"

He shook his head uneasily. "There are many rumors."

"You mean the riot?"

He looked at me keenly. "You know what it is?"

"There was a riot in the square during the parade. The troops had to fire."

"A riot? You are sure it is nothing more?"

"It was very serious, I heard. Many were killed."

"But a riot?" he insisted.

"But of course. I was told by an officer ten minutes ago."

"An officer told you?"

"Yes. I have said—"

He sighed impatiently. "These sheep!" he exclaimed, nodding toward the waiting people. "These silly sheep, with their gossip! They tell me the Agrarian Socialists have attempted a coup and that a revolution has broken out. Sheep!" He spat and then grinned. "A riot, you say. I know a way with rioters."

I grinned back. He nodded to one of the sentries. The bell pealed and after a bit came the familiar sound of Rana's sandals in the courtyard. I felt the eyes of the street upon me as I went in.

There was the same smell of furniture polish and the same slippery floors. There was the same room, and she rose from the same chair to greet me. There were the same gentle, intelligent eyes below the same broad forehead and there was the same polite smile. And yet for me nothing was the same; I saw her now in a different context.

The smile went out. "Herr Foster," she said quickly, "I am so glad you have come. What has happened? Something has. Rana says that there are people waiting outside in front of the house and additional guards. I don't understand it."

I did not answer for a moment. Then I said: "If you are asking me whether Aleko has succeeded, the answer is yes."

"Aleko?"

"I have a train to catch, madame. Perhaps it will save time if I tell you that Pashik and I have talked very frankly to each other and that at this moment, and because it has been difficult for Pashik to keep you fully informed, I know a great deal more about the affair than you do. I came to tell you what you don't already know."

She stared at me and then very calmly sat down. "I see. You are a messenger from Pashik."

"No. Pashik doesn't know I'm here."

"Where is he? With my son?"

"Your son is in Athens. Pashik is in the city somewhere."

"You tell me Vukashin is dead. You saw it happen?"

"I did not say Vukashin was dead, madame. I said that Aleko had succeeded. Brankovitch was assassinated just about an hour ago."

"Brankovitch?" Her hands came down on the wooden arms of the chair with a violence that would have been painful if she had been able to feel pain at that moment.

"Yes, Brankovitch."

"You saw it yourself?"

"Yes."

"Well? Go on."

I went on. It was difficult, for she kept interrupting with questions to not all of which I knew the answers. I said nothing of Katerina's visit. There was no reason to do so. She probably knew of it anyway. When I had finished, she sat back slowly and shut her eyes. Her face was very smooth and beautiful.

"I am leaving for Athens on the five-o'clock train. That's if they'll let me out, of course. I'll see Philip tomorrow. His signed statement and mine will be in New York, Paris, and London by Tuesday at the latest. That will give Vukashin two days to make a fool of himself. After that he hasn't got a chance."

Slowly she opened her eyes. "My dear Herr Foster," she said wearily, "do you suppose that you can defeat men like Vukashin with external propaganda? The conception is naïve."

"I rather thought it was yours."

"Mine?" She stood up angrily. "Pashik's, perhaps. Not mine. Don't you understand? They have defeated us."

"Then you were defeated anyway."

She shook her head. "No. You see, Herr Foster, we could have come to terms with Brankovitch. He would have needed the Agrarian Socialists. He would have thought he was using them."

"And your husband?"

She looked vague. "Agreement could have been reached about that. An acquittal and then temporary retirement."

In a very short space of time a lot of things went through my mind.

Above them all, however, was the memory of my own voice asking if it were not dangerous to deny the street, and of the reply, the beautiful, saintly reply: *"For my children, yes. For me, no, for I shall not try to impose my private world upon the real."*

I was aware then of a profound dislike of her and did not trouble to keep it out of my voice.

"Do you really believe that?" I answered.

She turned away to the window. "Herr Foster," she said thoughtfully, "do you think you are safe here?"

It was very unexpected. My wretched stomach jerked unpleasantly. "Safe?" I said.

"Aleko must realize by now what has been done by Pashik. You say he has already tried to kill you once. He might guess you were here."

I saw then. I was being punished. I laughed. "If Aleko realizes what has been done, he will be far too busy getting out of the country to trouble about me. I can't hurt him. If he doesn't know what's happened, then he is most probably under arrest by now. In that case I don't think he would talk until he knew whether Vukashin was going to save him or not."

"You are very confident," she said coldly. "I think you are unwise to stay here."

"Then I shall go. I should like to say good-by to your daughter if I may."

"I will give her your message."

"Is there any message you would like me to give your son?"

"Yes, Herr Foster. You may tell him if you will that he did well and that it is not our fault, his and mine, that we are defeated. If it is possible Katerina and I will join him soon in Athens."

"I'll tell him. There's one thing I should like to know."

"Yes?"

"What induced your husband to make that election speech? What had gone wrong?"

"Nothing that would make a newspaper story, Herr Foster."

"It is for my own information that I ask."

She shrugged. "As you please. It is no longer important, I suppose, what sort of man my husband was."

When she had told me, I left.

I did not go back to the hotel. I reached the station with half an hour to spare. My passport got me on the train. The delay was at the frontier. It took me thirty-six hours to get to Athens, and by that time the Vukashin account of the Brankovitch assassination was out. The assassin was a man named Alexander Gatin and he, together with an accomplice named Pashik, had been shot and killed while resisting arrest.

Philip Deltchev was a pompous but amiable young man and very grateful for his mother's message. He said that it made him feel much better about everything. He was quite sure that she would contrive to join him. He did not mention his father.

CHAPTER XXI

I saw the end of the Deltchev trial in the projection room of a newsreel company in London.

In the hard blacks and whites of the Propaganda Ministry's cameramen the scene looked more real than the one I remembered. Perhaps the film gave it an authority the original had lacked. Or it may have been the sound-track that produced the effect; there was no interpreter to divide one's attention. With the six reels of film that Brankovitch's successor had selected for foreign consumption a translation of the proceedings had been sent; but for the moment I wanted just to look at it, and to look at Deltchev.

There was not a great deal of footage that included him. Only one of the three cameras had covered the dock, and the film had been received in an edited form that favored the judges and Dr. Prochaska; but during one evident denunciation of the prisoner there was a shot that showed him frowning anxiously and shifting his position in a way that made him look guilty. Most likely the shot had some other true explanation—boredom or some physical discomfort—but for me, as for the Propaganda Ministry, it had another significance. The Propaganda Ministry saw a scheming villain brought to book. I saw a prewar Minister of Posts and Telegraphs struggling to be a statesman. But then, I had listened to his wife.

It was the word "Papa" that defeated him.

The first time Deltchev saw the word printed in front of his name it pleased him; for, knowing his countrymen, he recognized the note of wry affection in it. It meant that they trusted him and that, although they might grumble, they would accept hardship at his hands and would not hate him too intensely. With amused pride he showed the newspaper to his wife and son. The small pang of anxiety he experienced he found unaccountable and ignored.

The nickname soon gained currency, and its use was no longer an occasion for comment; but he did not, for some reason, get used to it. On the contrary; as time went by, he began to experience discomfort whenever he saw it or heard it used. It had begun to feel to him like an accusation.

"Yordan always invites criticism," his wife had said, "and always fears it."

Deltchev was aware of the jokes about his motives and had hitherto thought himself a better and not more prejudiced judge of them. Shrewd he might be; yet in 1940 he had opposed the Nazis, not for any personal advantage—unless internment and oblivion were advantages—but because he had thought it right to do so. Ambitious he might be; yet he had organized the Committee of National Unity, not for the risk of dying a martyr's death at the hands of the Gestapo, but because he thought it right to do so. But now, with his power increasing daily and that word "Papa" fastened to his name, he was no longer sure of himself. The whole climate of his thought and feeling seemed to be changing. If he were held in affection, trusted, he must be worthy. His conscience told him that he was not.

"Yordan is a self-torturer," his wife had said.

A terrible conflict now began within him; and the battleground chosen was the question of the election promise.

Reason and experience told him that the Provisional Government was the best that could be devised for the country in the present situation and that elections might well mean the accession of the People's Party to power. He believed that would be a disaster for the country. Reasoning, a lawyer's reasoning, told him, too, that the promise had been one of *free* elections and that the essential condition of freedom was not at present obtainable.

Yet the other voice, the cruel, accusing, contemptuous, punishing voice that haunted him, offered arguments of a different kind. "Why are you so anxious?" it inquired. "Why do you hesitate? Is it because you know in your heart that you have become corrupt and that these reasons you invent for keeping the power in your hands are mere devices to conceal the fact? Is it? You dictators are all the same! You whine that what you do is for the people's good and that they love and trust you. But when there is a chance that you may have to put that love and trust to the test, you find reasons—oh, excellent reasons!—why you should not do so. And the reasons are always to the same tune. It is for the people's good, you cry. That, my friend, is the spiral of corruption you are ascending. Government by consent of the governed! You know the phrase? Who are you to determine what government they shall consent to? Your power and their trust in you give you a responsibility above your party interests. You see now the distinction between a statesman and a politician. The statesman has courage. Did you speak? Ah no! Not the courage of his convictions. (How you twist and turn, my friend, to avoid the truth!) The statesman has the courage to be impartial—even at the risk of his own destruction."

He told no one until after it was over, and then he told his wife.

"My hands are clean," he said. It was as though by violating all his own beliefs and interests, as well as those of other honest men, he had performed an act of absolution for some unnamable sin.

"Last reel," said the cutter who was supervising the running. "Judges' summing up and sentence."

I looked at the screen again. I looked at the tired shell of a man who had been Yordan Deltchev and at the presiding judge delivering the sentence of death by hanging, which had since been carried out.

There was silence in the courtroom after the sentence. Probably the spectators were expecting him to say something. But there was nothing. He nodded his head slightly and turned to go. The guards stepped forward. Then he climbed down from the dock and walked slowly away between them.

I recalled another departure he had made from the courtroom and the parallel I had attempted to draw from the trial of Socrates. My memory of it was better now. There were words more apt than the others I had chosen.

"But, sirs, it may be that the difficulty is not to flee from death, but from guilt. Guilt is swifter than death."

"That's the lot," said the cutter. "Would you like to see the assassination of Brankovitch? I've got it here."

"No, thanks," I said. "I've seen it."

A NOTE ON THE TYPE

THIS BOOK is set in *Electra*, a Linotype face designed by W. A. Dwiggins. This face cannot be classified as either modern or old-style. It is not based on any historical model, nor does it echo any particular period or style. It avoids the extreme contrasts between thick and thin elements that mark most modern faces, and attempts to give a feeling of fluidity, power, and speed.

Typography based on original by
VINCENT TORRE

ERIC AMBLER was born in London in 1909. His career has been almost as unusual as his stories. After his graduation from London University, he served a three-year apprenticeship in engineering, followed by short periods as a vaudeville comedian and song writer and several years in an advertising company. His first finished novel was immediately accepted by a London publisher, and his famous four—*Background to Danger* (1937), *Cause for Alarm* (1939), *A Coffin for Dimitrios* (1939), and *Journey into Fear* (1940)—followed in quick succession. He joined the British Army in 1940 as a private, was soon commissioned, and was transferred to an army film unit in 1942. Ambler finished the war as a lieutenant colonel in charge of the production of all military-training, morale, and education films for the British Army. Since the war he has written and produced a number of motion pictures for the J. Arthur Rank Organisation, and was nominated for an Academy Award for his screenplay of *The Cruel Sea*. The novel-writing habit, seemingly lost when he joined the Army, returned to him with *Judgment on Deltchev* (1951), followed by *The Schirmer Inheritance* (1953), *State of Siege* (1956), *Passage of Arms* (1960), and *The Light of Day* (1963). He now lives in California.

September 1964